Praise ... NAOMI ...

'Brave and unexpected . . . if yo...
stimulating do yourself a favour and pick up both *Astra* and *Rook Song*. You won't regret it.'
UPCOMING4.ME

'I enjoyed *Astra* immensely. The novel's plot is fascinating, with an intricate web of relationships and some compelling political shenanigans going on in the background, all of it set down in Foyle's smooth and flowing writing style'
A FANTASTICAL LIBRARIAN

'Foyle is effective at building tension and creating villainy all the more sinister for its well-meaning smile'
SFX

'This is excellent Science Fiction and I heartily recommend it'
BIRMINGHAM SF GROUP

'Assured and confident . . . A novel definitely worth seeking out'
CONCATENATION

'Foyle has built a fascinating portrait, reminiscent of Ursula K. Le Guin in its layered complexity, and threaded it into a fascinating coming of age story. Gripping'
LOVE READING

'Sheer adrenalin to read, pumping and fast, breaking down all genre cliches and distinctions in its unstoppable momentum'
BIDISHA

'It's hard-hitting, poignant and incredibly thought-provoking . . . Naomi Foyle has a mastery of plotting and a way with words that's truly remarkable'
OVER THE EFFING RAINBOW

Also by Naomi Foyle

Seoul Survivors

THE GAIA CHRONICLES

Astra

Rook SONG

NAOMI FOYLE

Book Two Of
The Gaia Chronicles

Jo Fletcher
BOOKS

First published in Great Britain in 2015 by Jo Fletcher Books
This edition published in Great Britain in 2016 by

Jo Fletcher Books
an imprint of Quercus Editions Ltd
Carmelite House
50 Victoria Embankment
London EC4Y 0DZ

an Hachette UK company

A CIP catalogue record for this book is available
from the British Library

ISBN 978 1 78206 921 8 (PB)
ISBN 978 1 84866 813 3 (EBOOK)

10 9 8 7 6 5 4 3 2

Typeset by Jouve (UK), Milton Keynes

Printed and bound in Great Britain by Clays Ltd, Elcograf S.p.A.

Extract from 'Homesickness' by Isabelle Eberhardt, translated by Sharon Bangert
and published in Prisoner of Dunes (Peter Owen Ltd., London, 1995), quoted here
by permission of the publisher.

'The Prophecy', anonymous ancient Mesopotamian text, translated by Hortense
Penelope Thursby Curtis (1889–1921) and published in An Antique Land,
collected and edited by John Shire (Invocations Press, 2012), quoted here by
permission of the publisher.

for Rowyda Amin

Dramatis Personae

Astra Ordott	Political refugee. Code daughter of an Is-Lander mother and Non-Lander father
Zizi Kataru	Astra Ordott's Code father

The Council of New Continents (CONC)

Major Akira Thames	CONC Compound Director
Sandrine Moses	Mobile Medical Unit supply coordinator
Photon Augenblick	Mobile Medical Unit medic
Rudo Acadie	Mobile Medical Unit medic
Msandi	Mobile Medical Unit medic
Eduardo	Mobile Medical Unit medic
Christophe	Water technician
Tisha	Water technician
Honovi	Food Aid coordinator
Dix	Food Aid coordinator
Marly	Compound gate guard
Dakota	Assistant to the Head of Staff

Non-Lander CONC Employees

Uttu	Washerwoman
Hamta	Washerwoman
Azarakhsh	Washerwoman

Dr Tapputu	Head of CONC Medical Outreach Service
Sulu, Kovan, Tamanina	Children of CONC employees

The Youth Action Collective (YAC)

Enki Arakkia	Speaker and warrior
Bartol	Trainer and warrior
Khshayarshat	Trainer and warrior
Ninti	Warrior
Malku	Warrior
Tiamet	Singular [see also Pithar]
Simiya	Singular
Asar	Singular
Sepsu	Asar's carer
Lilutu	Networker and warrior
Chozai	Singing-bowl player and mindful warrior
Am Arakkia	Mother of Enki
Abgal Izruk	Mentor (deceased)

The Non-Land Alliance (N-LA)

Una Dayyani	Lead Convenor
Marti	Personal assistant to Una Dayyani
Artakhshathra	Researcher
Tahazu Rabu	Chief of Police

Nagu Three [In Kadingir]

Uttu	Elderwoman [see also Non-Lander CONC employees]
Kingu	Eldest son of Uttu
Habat	Daughter-in-law of Uttu, married to Kingu
Gibil	Second son of Uttu
Nanshe	Daughter-in-law of Uttu, married to Gibil
Muzi	Son of Kingu and Habat

Pithar [In Zabaria]

Tiamet	Singular [see also YAC] and sex worker
Neperdu	Sex worker
Anunit	Sex worker
Taletha	Sex worker
Roshanak	Sex worker
Ebebu	Son of Tiamet

Is-Land Ministry of Border Defence (IMBOD)

Chief Superintendent Clay Odinson	Head of the Non-Land IMBOD Barracks
Peat Orson	Security Generation constable [see also Is-Land]
Laam Vistason	Security Generation constable
Jade Sundott	Security Generation constable
Robin Steppeson	Security Generation constable

Is-Land

Hokma Blesser	Astra's Shelter mother; charged with treason, died in jail before her trial
Ahn Orson	Hokma's ex-partner; leading architect
Dr Samrod Blesserson	Hokma's brother
Klor Grunerdeson	Astra's Shelter father; Code worker
Nimma	Astra's Shelter mother; Craft worker
Sheba	Klor and Nimma's Code daughter; killed in a Non-Lander nanobomb attack
Peat	Astra's older Shelter brother [See IMBOD]
Yoki	Astra's Shelter brother; Sec Gen
Meem	Astra's Shelter sister; Sec Gen (still at school)
Congruence	Ahn's partner, a relationship begun secretly and illegally in her teens; non-Sec Gen
Dr Cora Pollen	Code worker; Hokma Blesser's collaborator; now in jail

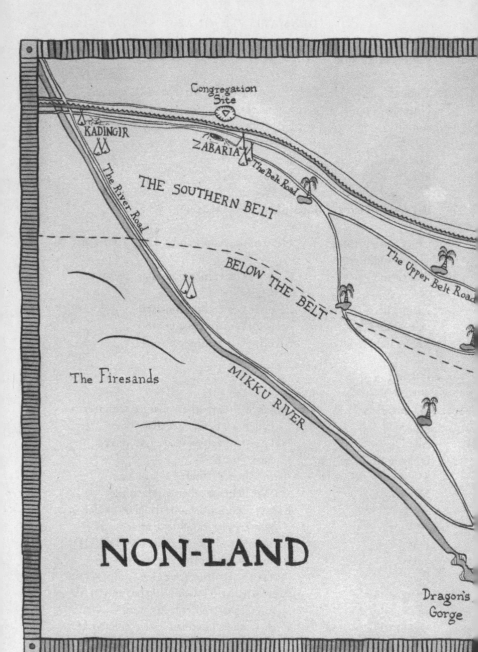

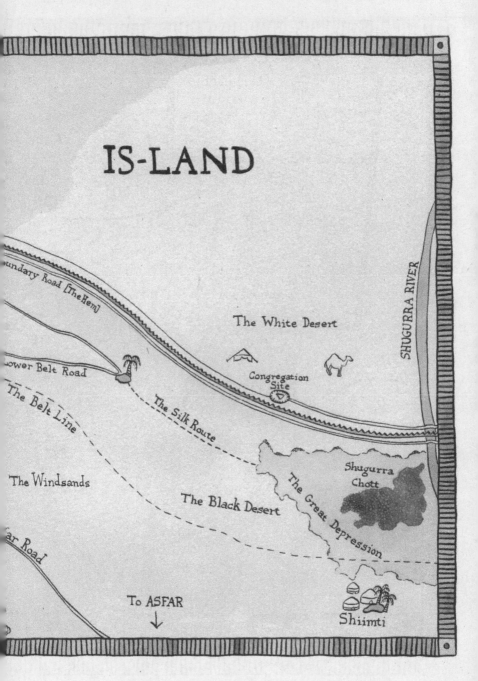

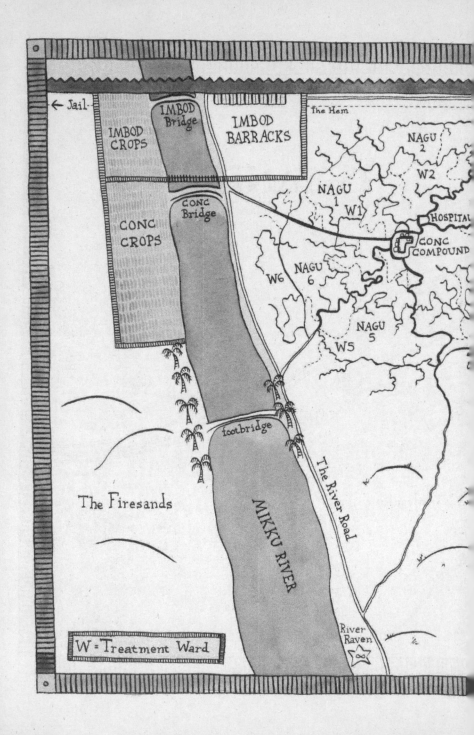

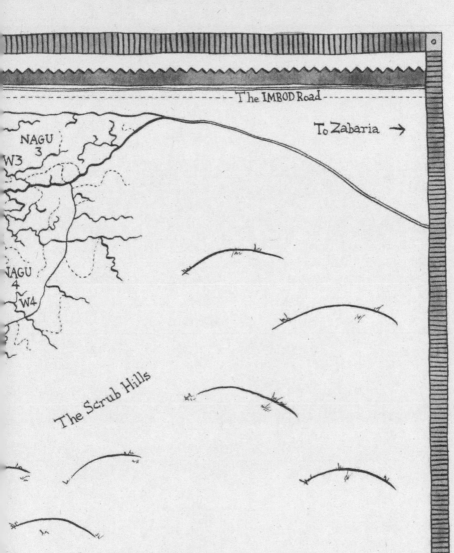

The IMBOD Road

To Zabaria →

NAGU 3
W3

NAGU 4
W4

The Scrub Hills

KADINGIR

Homesickness is the great enchanter that animates all phantoms.

Isabelle Eberhardt

Her name is Istar. She is placeless. You will know her by these signs:

She will arise in the night, enchained by the light of a day that is dead. A child among the mighty, knowing among the innocent, with her first kiss she will appoint her vizier, the raven-haired Helpmeet of Harpies. Her chariot charged with the anger of ages, she will arrive resplendent at the House of Abundant Women. The Seer shall bless her, and she shall heal his warriors. Attended by the Prince of Shepherds, she will move like a *mergallá* over the windsands. She will greet her father, drink his beer, steal his [word missing] and her lustre will illume his alliance. Alone, she will fly to the ashlands and bury herself in the earth. When she arises the placeless ones shall be in all places, and all places shall sing glad hymns of welcome and of [word missing].

The Prophecy
[Fragments from cuneiform tablets *c.* 3250 BCE]

Early Summer 87 RE

ASTRA

'*Ack-ka-ka-ka-ckak!*'

Astra tipped her sack of dirty laundry into the pool, gripped her paddle and began to stir. Beside her, Uttu bent and plucked a small gown from the suds. It was a baby's garment, blotched with sulphurous and rust-red stains. Protesting in her guttural tongue, the tiny elderwoman thrust the dress out to the other washers like a piece of vital evidence in a crime.

No. Please, no. Desperation mounting in her chest, Astra focused on a pillowcase, fixed her gaze on its thinning weave and frayed seams. But it was no use – the grey wave was rising again, flooding her skull, dredging up an image that blotted out the room: a young girl's limp body, her white hipskirt drenched with blood.

Sheba was dead. Sheba had been killed by a bus-bomb. And as always, the wave broke the news as if for the first time. Staggering under the rush and crash of fresh grief, she resisted the only way she knew how.

I'm working. I'm working. I'm working.

Her jaw rigid, the paddle handle digging into her chest, she repeated the silent mantra. With a nauseating suck, the wave withdrew. The voices faded, the image of Sheba melted away, the laundry pool and its three robed washerwomen swam back into focus. But the sickness lingered: numb limbs, a sour lump in her stomach, the thick familiar mist stealing back into her head. There was never a full recovery from the grey wave. Since the Barracks, she had either been fighting it off, or submerged in the dank threat of its return.

No one seemed to have noticed her near-collapse. Around the pool, palms pressed to hearts, the three washers had launched into a round of lament. Beneath her cap of salt and pepper hair, Uttu's withered face was wrenched open in a long, imploring cry. Tall, bone-thin Azarakhsh keened as if to pierce the whitewashed stone vaults, white strands escaping her loose bun like wisps of static electricity. Loudest and deepest was Hamta. Her gauzy blue headscarf shimmering in the light from the high arched windows, the mountainous woman raised her arm and with a swift chopping motion released a resounding 'Hai!'

'Hai! Hai!' the others echoed, their anger igniting a thin ray of resentment in Astra's clouded head. Sheba had been six when she died, years before Astra was even born. *Of course* she cared about her Shelter sister's death, but why had an infant's dress triggered such an overwhelming reaction?

But anger had no chance against the fog. The brief beam of indignation dulled and the dismal mist closed in again, bearing its cold, lightless truths. Of course she would suffer for Sheba: that was what IMBOD had engineered the grey wave to do – fling all her losses up from the deep, every last one, bloody and raw as gutted fish.

A gleam caught her eye, luring her back from the brink of despair. The charms on Uttu's copper neck chain: the washerwoman's gold ring and miniature weaver's shuttle, dangling over the water as she plunged the baby's dress back into the pool. She watched the garment sink into the mottled sea of fabric. It was hardly unique. Once a week the washers cleaned CONC uniforms, otherwise the laundry came from the Treatment Wards scattered over the Southern Belt, virtually all of it soiled with some lurid combination of blood, pus, faeces and vomit. Her job was to clean it.

She began shunting the linens back and forth over the tiles, stirring the day's broth of soap and human crud, working to the rhythm of the crones. On her first day in the laundry she'd grimly pounded, thumped and flipped the cottons, splashing and puddling the uneven stone floor. The other washers had hissed and shaken their fingers. In their thin rubber sandals, it was easy to slip, Uttu had mimed. The shrunken elderwoman had tapped her own pointy elbow and pulled a face. *Ouch.* Then she'd laughed and patted Astra's arm. She'd flinched, pulled away, but had watched Uttu carefully after that, copying her movements throughout the washers' various tasks.

After two weeks in the laundry, she was practically a crone herself. Her hands, bleached by the window light shafting over her shoulders, looked as ancient as Uttu's, the skin wizened and chapped from scrubbing and wringing gussets, armpits, bibs – anywhere on a garment the body's fluids could splatter or seep. She didn't care. Uttu had offered her a pair of gloves, but she'd sweated inside the yellow rubber and the bar of soap had constantly slipped from her fingers, incurring first the raucous laughter of the others, and then grumbles. So now she worked bare-knuckled like them, slapping on the coconut moisturiser provided in tubs by the door at the end of her shifts; the thin white grease absorbed into her skin without trace, just as the washers' occasional stabs at communication failed to penetrate her fog. She could understand their basic commands – her eleven years of Inglish and Asfarian lessons occupied some part of her mind IMBOD couldn't – or hadn't bothered to – hijack. But between them the three old women had only a smattering of the two official CONC languages. 'So-*mar*-ian,' Uttu had said proudly on the first day, patting her bony chest; as if oblivious to Astra's incomprehension the little woman often cackled at her in the Non-Land tongue, but otherwise the washers addressed her mainly to issue instructions or chuckle at her blunders.

That was fine. She wasn't allowed to talk about why she was here, and she didn't want to talk about what was wrong with her. No one in the CONC compound would believe her if she told them what had happened at the Barracks, and even if they did, no one would be able to fix her. She was damaged goods, a leaking contagion: dumped in the small dark hours at the back entrance to this crumbling fortress, she'd been passed round like a sack of rotting potatoes from the night porter to the day receptionist to the Head of Staff and now, yet again, confined where she could do least harm. The Head, a shrewd man with a trim black moustache, had briskly assessed her wasted arms, dull skin and shadowed eyes and offered her a doctor's appointment. She'd refused – she'd rather be buried alive in a termites' nest than see another doctor – and he'd shrugged, scanned his screendesk and neatly slid her deficiencies into a hole in his rota. Working in the laundry would be good for her muscles, he'd said. The Compound Director would meet with her soon to discuss her *family situation*. In the meantime, he'd instructed, peering at her over his small round glasses, she was to remember that her Code status was strictly classified information.

So far no summons had come. Of course not. No one in this arid work camp gave a flying frig about her or her Code father. And anyway, given what happened to her whenever she thought about Zizi Kataru, she wasn't sure she'd make it through that conversation alive. Just the flicker of a thought about him in the Head of Staff's office had been agony enough.

No, she didn't need the Director's help. She would make her own plans; she would hide in the compound, working as a local employee of the Council of New Continents, until she'd figured out what to do. Silent, invisible, swathed in these shapeless robes, she was almost safe.

Beside her, Uttu poked at a pillowcase, chattered to Hamta. Astra picked up her pace. She was slick with sweat now, the robes clinging to her flesh. She wanted to tear off the heavy, damp fabric, but that was impossible. She had a right to her spiritual practices, the Head had said, but going sky-clad would alienate the Non-Landers in the compound and – he had paused before adding – 'almost certainly attract unwanted attention' from some of the internationals. She had understood. With her shaved head and neurohospice scar, she already attracted plenty of unwanted attention in the corridors and dining hall. So she had taken the two robes he'd offered, soft white with blue trim, glad at least to discard the rough hemp sheet IMBOD had bundled her up in after the Barracks.

She worked steadily on, her nose prickling. At least the ammonia masked the stink of shit; the first soak, mostly composed of soiled sheets and nappies, was a cesspit. Careful not to splash, she dug at the laundry with her paddle, separating folds to dissolve any solids lurking in the creases. The work was getting easier. She no longer felt disgusted by the morning soak. And she could stand up for the whole day now, needing just the normal scheduled breaks. Soon, during the second soak, they would go out to the courtyard colonnades for coconut water, prayers and yoga. As the ammonia ate into the bloodstains, Hamta would sit on a mat with her eyes closed, performing elaborate chants and prostrations, and Azarakhsh, after her own private prayers, would lead Uttu and Astra in sun salutations – the only time Uttu, a supple cocoon in her white robes, was silent all day.

After the break they would re-rinse and wring and peg the laundry out to dry in the courtyard. There were electric dryers, a wall of them in the next room, but these, Uttu had instructed in her rudimentary Asfarian, were only for use when it rained. Appliances had to be imported from

Asfar, Astra had finally understood; they were difficult to repair or replace. That was the way it was here: water, solar power, fruit – nearly everything was rationed in the compound.

Whatever the weather, after lunch the washers took another prayer break followed by siesta. In the afternoon they ironed and folded and repacked yesterday's laundry in the bags for the CONC medics to pick up. Finally, they brought in the dry load. The clean linens from the court-yard smelled of sunshine, and wielding the heavy iron felt powerful, but Astra's favourite task was wringing. She positively looked forward to wringing. The skin on her hands could fall off in shreds as long as she could keep gripping and twisting fibres tender as flesh, seams tough as gristle. One day, she thought, prodding viciously at a sheet, she would wring Ahn's scrawny neck until it snapped.

CRACK. She had risked it, and here it came: a sharp warning shot. Not the grey wave but the pain-ball. The hard metal marble that shot up from her cranium scar-hole whenever she thought about anyone IMBOD didn't want her to remember: her Code father or Hokma, Ahn, Dr Blesserson, or any of the doctors and Barracks officers who had ruined her life. She leaned on her paddle and took the dazzling hit to her left temple. It was worth it. But she had to be careful. She had learned to her cost that, if she persisted too long in dreams of revenge, the pain-ball would tear a trail of white fire around her skull, detonating a series of phosphorous explosions that would bleach her brain, leave her blind and moaning back on the floor of the Barracks.

I'm working. I'm working. I'm working.

The mantra worked. The pain-ball rolled back into its socket. She inhaled, placed her foot on the rim of the pool and reached across to snag a floating nappy with her paddle. Like an electrical current, a ripping sen-sation sizzled through the triangle IMBOD had cross-hatched on her perineum.

The cloud of misery returned and tears sprang to her eyes. These relent-less attacks – the pain-ball, the grey wave, the buzzing nest of her brand-wound, as if the nerves were permanently singed, flaring up at night and keeping sleep at bay for hours. An ill wind in her head hissed all this was *her own fault* ... and for a weak, terrible, bottomless moment she didn't know if she could stand it any more.

'Astra?' Uttu was touching her arm, her curious hazel eyes asking, *What's wrong?* Astra ducked the woman's gaze, pulled away, dragged the nappy towards her. No. Until she fell unconscious, face down in the pool, she would bear it. She had learned the tricks to quell the wave and stop the pain-ball and she would conquer the stinging brand-wound too. It was an irritant, like the ammonia. That was all.

She scraped at a soggy crust of shit on the nappy. A warm breeze wafted in from the open door to the courtyard, followed by the hectic pattering of feet and a shrill fusillade of giggles. She didn't bother to look round. Beset with glee, the three children would be clinging to the door frame, pointing at her skull-hole and speculating in fierce whispers as to its cause. They were children of other local workers, speaking a Non-Landish tongue, but the language of widened eyes, wagging fingers and bossy tones was universal. The older girl was clearly the ringleader; she would be firmly overruling her brother's interjections while their plump little sister stared up at Astra, dumbfounded.

'Hai!' Uttu turned and flapped the children away. The kids thundered back out into the courtyard and the old woman addressed Astra rapidly again. She was smiling, her gleaming gold charms a warm wink in the sterile vault of the room. Across the pool, Hamta paused from paddling and smoothed a strand of black hair back into her voluminous headscarf.

'She say, "They like you",' the large woman announced proudly in Asfarian. Uttu clapped delightedly and Azarakhsh's long face creased up in a gap-toothed grin, both clearly impressed by Hamta's triumphant sentence-making.

Astra jabbed a wodge of pillowcases with her paddle. *Like* her? The kids were frigging *addicted* to her. They followed her around the compound, pointing at her head, hiding behind corners in chattering huddles as if betting on what she would do next, though there was nothing she could do except wait for her hair to grow back. Much as she wanted to pass without notice, she couldn't cover her skull like Hamta: headscarves were Abrahamite garb.

The pool water was a grim khaki sludge and the suds had deflated to pancake-flat clouds, drifting over the continents of fabric. Uttu pulled the plug. The filthy water gurgled through the pipes to the algae-scrubber, to be cleaned and returned in an endless cycle of conservation; the laundry water was probably as old as the crones. When the pool had drained Hamta took a hose from the wall and aimed a jet of cleaned water over the laundry. As Azarakhsh slopped the wet fabric around in the spray,

Uttu leaned over the pool and retrieved the baby gown. Astra's cranium throbbed, but that was all: the wave trigger appeared to have exhausted itself for the moment. Muttering to herself, Uttu smoothed out the little dress on the rim of the pool. Then she carefully laid the garment back on the rising surface of the water, dug a scoop into the bag of powder by the hose, and sprinkled detergent over the stained frills.

Astra's nose twitched. She thrust her hand into her robe pocket – pockets were the only point of clothes – and pulled out her hanky.

Huh-huh-huh-TSCHOO.

'Amon,' Azarakhsh responded, drawing an Ankh on her chest, as she did before and after yoga.

'Amon-nia,' Hamta guffawed, setting in motion a circle of translation and laughter. Astra wiped her nose and stuffed the hanky back in her pocket.

'Bless *ooh*,' Uttu announced loudly.

Blesserson?

She was practically knocked sideways by the blow: a cannoning skull-ball smashing her vision into a field of white stars.

As if from the other side of the galaxy, across the pool Hamta quizzically echoed the phrase. 'Bleh sou?'

'*Inglish*,' Uttu's voice came floating to her. 'Bless. Ooh.'

Inglish. She seized the word like a life ring in the void. This wasn't a memory, just information. It shouldn't hurt. Against the comet trail of pain, she kicked out for the mothership of facts. To bless, yes, she knew that verb, it meant *to make holy*. 'Bless you' could be used to say thank you or, when someone sneezed, to deter evil spirits. Evil beings like *Dr Samrod Blesserson* – CRACK: a bright white supernova of pain as the ball hit her temple, but she didn't care. She had to finish the thought, finish the *job*. One day she was going to *break* Dr Blesserson, *break* Ahn Orson, shatter their thin crooked smiles, hammer their cold glass hearts into dust.

Right now, though, she had to stop this fanatical assault on her head. She forced her eyes open, focused on the pool, her lips moving with the mantra.

I'm working. I'm working. I'm working.

Her eyes blazed with tears. But the pain-ball receded. The white stars dimmed. The laundry room reappeared. She inhaled and stood still, hardly daring to believe in this temporary reprieve.

Beside her, Uttu was stirring again, head down, bangles tinkling as she briskly frothed up the water. Hamta and Azarakhsh, though, were both looking, frowning, at Astra. Why? Were they waiting for her to speak? To say what? Thank you? She couldn't say anything. Her mouth was a desert, her throat a parched well. And now here it came, though she hadn't been thinking about Klor or Sheba or Peat or anyone she loved and missed: the grey wave, crashing down with a thundering force.

There was no point in talking to these people – there was no point in talking to *anyone* – because she was a *freak*, like a warty carrot, or a red pepper with a double goitre – something you took photos of to laugh at. Why had the Head of Staff made her work with people? She should be shut away, locked up on her own. She was useless – worse than useless, a complete monstrosity. She was here in this prison, being eviscerated by her own body, because she was a grotesque, worthless, *hideous* botched job, a Code nightmare, a deformity who should have been destroyed at birth. She was paralysed by the enormity of it, every muscle in her body clenched hard as granite. She was a freak of nature and culture. Half Is-Lander, exposed as a pathetic fake Sec Gen, half *Non-Lander*, a criminal's blood pumping through her veins. She would never belong anywhere. That's why she was here, trapped in a stone warren with no trees or grass or flowers, a place where no birds sang, a prison of pain and humiliation where everyone laughed and stared at her and even her Gaia garden hurt. She ought to implode, right now. She should put herself and everyone else out of her misery. She should drink a jugful of ammonia, hang herself with a pus-stained sheet, throw herself from the ramparts, smash her head open on the courtyard floor.

The wave parted. Around her, as if behind a gauze screen, the washers were exchanging glances; Uttu, head cocked, was peering up at her with concern. But they didn't matter. What mattered was the sunlight playing over the soap suds and fabric. The pool looked like a brain, she realised. A round grey slice of wrinkled brain, soaking in foamy bubbles. A button on a bed shirt glinted up at her like a dare.

'Excuse me,' she said in Asfarian, laying her paddle against the rim of the pool. 'I am just going outside for a short break.'

PEAT

'*Aiiiiii. Aiiiiii. AIIIIIIIIIIIII.*'

Limp, feebly scuffling, the sheep was a silent protester, but Jade was screaming as if the knife were held to her own mother's throat. His Sec sister felt the animal's pain; Peat was still wrestling with disbelief. Was he really watching this? A short wiry man gripping the front legs of a struggling black ewe, his burly collaborator squeezing the creature's jaw shut, pressing a long curved blade to her neck. These were *butchers*. To screen such images was *illegal*.

But he wasn't in Is-Land. He was in the Non-Land Barracks now, and this morning at the training field welcome lecture Odinson had told them all to expect to be tested. Above him, the men began chatting in a tongue he didn't understand, chatting and laughing and gloating. Like a slow bolt of lightning, jagged and hot, a shudder ran through him: a huddle shudder, shared by his entire division, one hundred Sec Gens standing in neat rows in a Non-Land Barracks hall, heads haloed, shoulders gleaming in the glow of the huge wallscreen where, still chuckling, the bulky man was raising his arm, flashing the knife in front of the creature's terrified eyes.

'*Noooooo*,' Jade shrieked in front of him.

'*NO!*' Robin bellowed to his left.

'*No!*' Laam echoed on his right. But nothing could stop them, these casual monsters intent on dragging shame down over the entire human race. The knife sawed into the black fleece. Blood rose in the gorge. A shocking red gash.

Jade was screaming herself hoarse. Incredulity was no longer an option.

It was impossible not to feel something. For Peat, that was anger, rapidly building to the verge of explosion. He knew animal slaughter happened – he'd been told about it all his life, even read about it. And now he knew why you weren't allowed to watch it. It was unbearable, the sight of a defenceless animal – that gentle, grazing, milk-giving, wool-offering ruminant, a creature that would work for you as long as it lived, needing nothing but grass and medical aid and a decent retirement package in return – that beautiful sheep, being killed without even an anaesthetic, kicking feebly as the butcher sawed on, the long knife tearing open the living throat as easily as Peat's Shelter mother might rip up an old blanket.

Everyone was shouting now. 'Murderers!' he bellowed with them, his division's distress pounding in his ears. 'Meat-eaters. *Non-Landers.*'

Then the pain hit. Tears seared his eyes, bolts of anguish shot through his stomach until he wanted to retch. He gasped, clutched his stomach. *No. Stop. Please stop.* He didn't *want* this. To stand and watch two men bind a conscious creature, hack at its throat, without even an anaesthetic, *joking* as they did so. It was agony. Only the faint buzz in his chest, the heart connection with his Sec siblings, made it possible to endure the torment. The division formation was tightening now, warm bodies shrinking closer together, as up on the screen the butcher roughly tilted the struggling sheep, yanked back its head.

Blood spilled from the ewe's neck, staining the earth – Gaia forced to taste of her own child's *murder*. The tingling heart bond with his siblings, their velvet skinship, was not armour enough against this atrocity. He couldn't watch any more. He *couldn't*. His stomach was in shreds. His chest about to burst open. It was worse than his counselling sessions. Like being pierced, in one swift corkscrewing assault, by all the grief, fear and fury he'd battled week after week in Atourne. He gasped, shut his eyes, tried to banish the image, the dark pool of blood spreading through his mind.

'Look, Sec Gens, look,' Odinson urged through his earpiece. 'I know it is hard, but you must look. You are not in Atourne any more. This is Non-Land. Beyond the Barracks walls you will see things you have never before confronted, the worst Old World depravities on parade. Here, animals are enslaved, starved, slaughtered, roasted, *eaten*. Young girls are forced into marriage with lustful old men. Alt-bodied people are left to beg on the street. You do not want to be shocked when you see these things.

You do not want to be the weak fledgling in the flock. This is a test you must *pass*.'

His eyes were still shut. He gulped in the darkness. He was failing, letting everyone down. He had to obey: he had to look. He had learned, hadn't he, how to cope with emotional pain. He had tried so hard to conceal a lifetime of pain, to manage it, to control it. *Feel it*, Peat, the counsellor had said, over and over again. *Face it. Feel it. Ask for help when you need it. You don't have to carry the burden alone.*

He opened his eyes, grabbed Robin and Laam and forced his face to the screen. Hip to hip, arms twined around shoulders, the tight rows of his division obeyed their commander, watching as the footage of the butchers and their victim at last, mercifully, faded away.

'Good, Sec Gens, good,' Odinson crooned from his lectern at the edge of the screen. Through wet lashes, Peat drank in the sight of him: his iron-willed commander, his tall, proud anchor in this storm. 'You must be prepared,' the Chief Super urged, 'for first the Non-Landers will slaughter a sheep and next they will *slaughter your daughter.*'

The test was not over. It was plunging into deeper places, turbulent depths Peat had once thought he knew the measure of, but was now learning were fathomless, overwhelming, beyond any logic or law to contain. To the noble strains of the Shield Hymn in his earpiece, the wallscreen filled with faces: familiar faces – faces he had grown up with, on Tablettes and bus shelter screenposters, plaques mounted beside fountains and memorials:

The youths from the bike shop in Atourne, juggling spanners, a row of racing trophies gleaming behind them on the wall.

The children from Hilton, square on square of grinning little kids, missing front teeth, hair neatly combed and oiled and braided for their school photos.

The family from the restaurant in Sippur, picnicking on the banks of the Shugurra River, their last ever holiday, the mother pregnant with the son who would never be born.

Jade was sobbing quietly, her tawny shoulders shaking in front of him. Beside him, Robin's breath hacked the air. If air was entering or escaping his own lungs, Peat couldn't feel it. He was numb, his whole body stiff with dread.

Laam reached up. His thumb rubbed reassuring circles on Peat's nape: he knew that *she* would be next.

Sheba: the Shelter sister he had never known. A little girl blown up on a bus, before he was born, killed, like the others, to the *rejoicing* of Non-Landers. And here she was, her bonny baby-toothed smile filling the screen. The smile Nimma had dusted every week on the Earthship mantelpiece. The lightbulb smile that had burned a hole through his childhood.

His stomach knotted and his vision blurred. The bus-bomb that had killed Sheba had also claimed his Shelter father's leg, broken his Shelter mother's heart, riddled Peat with unspoken grief. How to explain it? He had tried, to the counsellor: *We were never all together. Sheba was always missing. Sheba was never there.* 'And how did you cope?' the counsellor had asked, her voice sliding back to him now. *I don't know. I studied law. I guess I thought I could get justice for her one day.* Yes, he had studied law, only to discover two traitors in his own family: Hokma, who had separated Astra from her generation and secretly deformed her mind, and Astra herself. Astra, who had *never been there* – had *never been* who they all thought she was.

His chest heaved. He'd been doing so well at forgetting her but now his emotions were churned up, the Sheba sorrow released, it was impossible not to think about Astra. He stared at the screen through his tears, tried to soak up the sunshine of that little girl's smile, but like a hammer to the heart it hit him again: Astra had never cared about him. She had almost *destroyed* him. Astra, loyal to a traitor, contemptuous of the Sec Gens – of her own Shelter siblings – had nearly cost Peat his own destiny, the full glory of being a Sec Gen. If it hadn't been for Laam – he clutched his friend's wrist – Peat wouldn't be in Non-Land, he would have been *excluded* from his rightful place with his generation. Astra's crimes were a betrayal almost impossible to grasp.

Laam massaged his neck, consoling with delicate pressure. Robin pressed closer too, sliding an arm round his hips. Feeling for Robin's fingers, he leaned against Laam, touching his head to his friend's, crying freely. Normally, he didn't weep. Normally he was Peat: logical, dependable, the go-to guy for advice, the legal picture. But the counsellor was right, sometimes you couldn't solve the crime. Sometimes you had to feel the feelings. Down his cheeks fell salty tears of grief and rage, mingled with sweet tears of gratitude for the second chance he had been given: the chance to be a Sec Gen. To know and love Laam and Robin and Jade and all his Sec brothers and sisters.

Where was Jade? The heart bond glowing stronger again, he lunged

forward and wrapped his arms around his Sec sister, pressed his chest
against her spine. He wasn't the only person breaking ranks; around him
the Sec Gens were clasping each other as close as they could. Breathing as
one, a soothing rhythmic hush, his division watched Sheba's smile give
way to the cheeky grin of the boy from Cedaria – a boy whose only crime
had been enjoying walnut-picking, whose brutal death had prevented a
generation of children from being allowed to venture into their own
woods.

There was deep comfort in the huddle, but Peat's stomach was still
tense. His mouth watered, his tongue curling against the iron taste of
fear. Would photographs of Hokma and Astra flash up next? Would he
have to endure their taunting smiles?

The boy's face faded and darkness fell over the hall.

He braced himself.

'Thank you, Sec Gens,' Odinson boomed softly in his ear. 'That was
painful, very painful, I know, especially for those of you who lost family
members. But you are Sec Gens. You are *resilient*, Coded with the ability
to recover. To enter the darkness and return stronger than ever. By sharing
your grief, you deepen your shared destiny: to protect Is-Land and save
Gaia Herself. Please take as long as you need to regain your well-being.'

Odinson's deep concern reverberated through the huddle. People
hugged and stroked each other back to equilibrium. Jade caressed Peat's
arms. Laam kissed his shoulder blade. Peat's cheeks were wet, his limbs
weak. A painful experience, yes – extremely. But the Chief Superintendent had said it was necessary. And somehow he had known the limits of
what Peat could take. IMBOD had not stained Sheba's smile with the
faces of traitors, a stain more foul than even the ewe's blood seeping into
Gaia's body. Odinson had protected Sheba's memory from that outrage.
As deep as the Chief Super's own pain and anger ran, his love for them all,
Peat understood now, ran deeper still.

The spotlight shone again on Odinson and Peat gazed up at the stage,
treasuring this rare chance to observe the Barracks leader in the flesh.
With his powerful chest, ridged brow, keen eyes, the Chief Super was
magnetic, thrilling, a golden eagle of a man. But more than that, he was
also nurturing, patient, a grizzly bear with three thousand cubs. At the
welcome lecture Odinson had addressed the entire cohort from the
Boundary screen, humbly asking them all to think of him as their Shelter
father. Like a good Shelter father, he would protect them, he had vowed,

but he would also teach them how to survive. The lessons, he had warned, would not be easy. In the Atourne Barracks, IMBOD had trained their minds and bodies and united them into a glorious supple whole, the complex unity the Sec Gens were Coded to achieve. Here in the Non-Land Barracks IMBOD would *test* that strength and unity. A test, Peat's heart sang, he had *passed*.

'Division Six, I am *immensely* proud of you,' the Chief Super rumbled. 'That was torture – and not just for the sheep – but we had to prepare you. It is not unheard of for Non-Landers to butcher sheep right on the Hemline, aiming to provoke IMBOD constables into leaving the Hem, breaking the law. You needed to cry and rage now, not out on patrol. And of course you would cry. Who would not cry at the suffering and death of a slave? Who would not cry at the thought of innocent children, our own families, killed by maniacs intent on destroying a sane and simple way of life? By crying, you have shown: you are *human*.'

It was a cue, the first one they'd learned in Atourne. 'We are human,' the Sec Gens crooned. 'We are *huuummmmman*.' Arms draped across shoulders, swaying back and forth, row on row, they began humming: a hum that fanned the heart bond, spread a calming fire through the veins. Since the booster shot, the hum had incredible potency. Within a minute Peat's body was restored to its natural state, a radiant flame in the Sec Gen hearth of collective love and courage.

And yet the taste of metal lingered in his mouth. After that up-rush of emotion it was hard to completely forget Astra. His traitor sister was here in Non-Land somewhere, charged full of hatred for him and the Sec Gens. Peat had to be prepared to meet *her*. That was a slightly anxious thought. The counsellor had said he might have them occasionally, and the best way to deal with them was to focus on the present. Right now, the training session was over. Back in position between Laam and Robin, craning as long as possible at the man on the stage, he trooped out of the hall single file, past the next division waiting, faces alight, to take their turn with the Chief Superintendent.

ASTRA

Smash. Yes. It was so comforting, that thought. Her skull in fragments on the courtyard floor, the globby shards rocking gently in the sun, her brain no longer screaming, but silently drooling into the cracks between the paving stones. All the bright white pain in her head floating away, like a sphere of light into the sky. It was a peaceful image, a vision to guide her across the courtyard, her last time treading this hateful square of sunshine.

Outside, a person should feel close to Gaia. But there were no plants in the courtyard, and no soil, just sandstone paving that stored heat like the bricks of an oven. It was silent too, as though Gaia was refusing to speak: no birds ever alit on the ramparts, not even a sparrow, and there was no fountain, just an empty stone trough. Working with the washers was just about bearable: they pegged out the laundry here on long strings stretched between the colonnade pillars, the wet sheets cooling their hands and shielding their bodies from the pitiless sun. But being alone in the court-yard always felt like a punishment. Yet another condition of her life sentence.

'Pssssssst. Pssssssssssst.'

The hisses were aimed like whirring stones at her ankles, but she walked on, ignoring the three small heads bobbing up from behind the stone trough.

'Astra? Okay, Astra?'

Uttu, now, at the laundry door, calling after her. Couldn't these people just *leave her alone*? She half turned, flicked her hand. 'Yes. Okay,' she called in Asfarian, her voice surprisingly strong. 'I just need some fresh air.'

It was stifling even outside, but Uttu accepted the lie. The kids squealed away, their feet slapping down a colonnade. The sphere of light in Astra's head was a white balloon now, a balloon in a breeze, tugging her along, across to the opposite colonnade and the narrow arched entranceway to the stairs. She'd gone up to the ramparts once before, on her first day, and never again. Kadingir was frightening. The city was nothing like Sippur or New Bangor. It had no leafy hills or neat grids of buildings, no pleasant grassy parks or sparkling public fountains. There were barely any trees. Like the courtyard, Kadingir stripped you of belief. But that didn't matter now. She entered the turret of stairs.

I'm ending the pain. I'm ending the pain.

The words came naturally. Such a relief. No more working, working, working. Washing, washing, washing. Struggling, struggling, struggling. No more pain-ball. No more grey wave. No more fog. Just a wafting sphere of light, rising up and up and up. Trailing her fingers over CONC's signature mosaic, fragments of white shell and blue glass set in wavy patterns on the turret wall, she floated up the spiral staircase. The steps were ancient slabs of stone, sagging in the middle where centuries of footsteps had worn them away. How many feet had walked up, never to walk down? She couldn't be the only one. She was joining all those who had gone before, before Non-Land existed, before the Dark Time, all long gone into the light.

She emerged from the turret and paused. There was a guard up here. Not that anyone would attack CONC, but this was Non-Land and they couldn't neglect security, she supposed. She looked around and saw no one. Perhaps the guard was in another turret.

She entered the ramparts. Which way should she jump? Into the courtyard, or down into Kadingir? The inner rampart wall was lower, easier to climb, but perhaps it would be better to leave CONC, fly out over Non-Land. Yes. Why should she be frightened? She was high above this wasted place now, and was only going higher. Ahead, jammed up against the jutting crenellation, was a little set of stone steps. Were they intended for some ancient archer or bugler or standard-bearer? Not at all. They had been put there for her.

She mounted the steps. Like the turret walls, the crumbling crenellations had been decorated with white shells and blue glass. She leaned her chest for a moment against the shiny crust and gazed out over the evacuated world.

To the west, the Mikku River shone dully in the sun. Only in Non-Land could a river look like an iron chain. Beyond it the land was stained red, some bright alarming crop planted as a final warning against the vast pale dunes that heaped to the distant horizon. Those were the firesands. They exploded sometimes, she had learned back in school. No one could live there. The city filled the near shore – sagging tents, chaotic structures and red dirt roads swirling in all directions around the compound. This was Kadingir: a dry whirlpool of dilapidation, a bloodshot eye, a wind-blasted cobweb of failed dreams. No one could live here either.

I'm ending the pain. I'm ending the pain.

She hauled herself up and stood, feet planted on the wall, her body long in the sun. At home, she had stood on higher cliffs than this. She wouldn't fly off until she wanted to. Safe from interference, she could stand tall for a moment, survey her flight path. It was good she had chosen the outer wall. She could even say farewell to Is-Land from here. Shading her eyes with her hand, she did what she hadn't been able to the last time she came up here: she gazed north to the steppes.

They weren't the steppes she knew, just a dun haze rising blankly from the other side of the Boundary, uninhabited and, apart from a sparse comb-over of grasses, uncultivated. The Boundary was unrecognisable too – not a waterfall of cream and crimson light or a golden cascade amid the forest, but a flickering grey screen crested like a saw with tri-angular teeth, an endless jaw rearing up from a bare strand of tarmac and soil. She forced her gaze along it. There, just before the Boundary crossed the Mikku River, three black walls jutted out into Kadingir: the Barracks. Her chest tightened. But all she could see inside the IMBOD enclave were the tops of trees – the only trees in the world, imprisoned as much as she was – and, through their leaves, flashes of the round glass roofs of the Barracks buildings themselves.

She had been brought to the Barracks in the night, dragged up to the main entrance of an endless row of identical glass-fronted halls, her arms locked into the elbows of two massive IMBOD officers, her feet barely skimming the path. She'd been only vaguely aware of the glossy green walls with their rodded pattern of arches, registered more the sheer height of the edifice, and looming behind it not the night sky but the Boundary, lit and flickering like a silvery grey forest of ash. She had entered the Barracks confused and grieving. She had left electrified with fear, pain and *knowledge*: the knowledge of exactly how much IMBOD hated her.

She took a deep breath. That was an age ago. She knew no hatred now, no fear, only peace. Only light.

The white balloon rose to meet the sun.

I'M SAYING GOODBYE. I'M SAYING GOODBYE.

She turned to the Mikku. Bright as a torch, the glass roof of the Barracks flashed at the edge of her vision.

She stiffened, blinked.

The sphere of light in her head exploded. Reeling and gasping, she clutched at the crenellation and stared down in horror at her feet, the road a dizzying distance below.

What was she doing *up here?* This was precisely what IMBOD *wanted* her to do. IMBOD wanted her to kill herself because they knew she was *dangerous.* She *was* dangerous. And she would never give the Barracks that satisfaction. Never.

Head pounding, knees trembling, she crouched, felt with her foot for the step – but then, out of nowhere, the breath was squeezed out of her and she was falling backwards, two strong arms round her waist, yanking her down into the walkway, landing not on stone but on the hard flat torso of a man determined not to let go.

MUZI

'Hie! Hie! Hie!' He struck the patch-eyed ewe's flank with his switch. She bleated but veered back to the path, kicking up dust with her neat black hooves. This one always had to go her own way. She had a nose for mountain mint, that was why, and his grandmother said she gave the sweetest milk because of it. Mountain mint was good in his mother's flatbread. It was best to let the ewe sniff out the plant, drive her back to the herd, then return when she wasn't looking to pick a few leaves.

He would fetch the mint later. For now he followed the flock down the flank of the hill. He liked this spot. You couldn't see the Jailwall from here. Just the scrublands, rolling endlessly away to the south, and the sky, watching over him. Some people barely noticed the sky other than to glance at it in the morning to check for the weather, and perhaps again in the evening, if the river rooks had made a rare visit to the steppes and were swirling home against the sunset. Other people hid from the sky, complaining about the sun, its gold goatish eye too pitiless and hot. But he loved the sky. The sky saw all things, knew all things, and unless you wanted to bury yourself in a cave your whole life, there was no use trying to avoid it. The sky peered in windows, through cracks in the curtains and doors, reading the light in your eyes and the angles of your body. In this way it saw all the joy and sorrow and meanness inside everyone. When the sky sent a rainbow it was smiling down on all the people who had been kind; when it rained, the sky was crying with all the people who suffered. That was all people. All people suffered, and all were kind, if you treated them with kindness first. That's what his grandmother said.

The flock was grazing now, contentedly nibbling the spear grasses flowing over the hill: one ram, eleven ewes, four ewe lambs and three ram lambs. It didn't take long to count them, but he did so with satisfaction, observing how much the lambs had grown. This had been a good year already: only six lambs had died and soon his family would be able to slaughter one of the ram lambs and sell the other two. They would use the money to buy his little sister a new Tablette. She was just starting school. He was long finished with classrooms. Even if there was a college in Kadingir, he wouldn't want to go. He could read the news and follow the market prices and chat with his friends in Kadingir; that was all he needed a Tablette for. Though chat was less interesting now that his friends were all getting engaged. He didn't want to get married himself, at least not to any of the girls who had come for tea and flatbread. They were either too shy or too bossy, and after one quick glance, none of them had looked again at his arm: up at the flies on the ceiling, down at their hands curled like fallen leaves in their laps, anywhere but at his arm. They had skirted his gaze too. A girl from his class wouldn't have done that, but the girls from his class were all engaged now or married to older boys. That was the way it was.

It didn't matter. His grandmother wouldn't let him marry anyone he didn't like. His mother fretted, but his uncle grumbled that a new wife would mean building a new room, even a new house, and his father kept silent when they bickered. For now he was safe, watching the sheep and the sky.

He settled in against a hillock, feet crossed, a stem of grass in his mouth. The trick was to watch the sheep and the sky at the same time. This was work too, just as much as harnessing the horse to the cart, going to the scrap heap, collecting things to mend and trade and sell, the things his father and uncle did when they weren't shearing, selling or killing the sheep. His grandmother said his eyes were blue because he was a child of the sky-god and sky-watching was his duty. His parents' eyes were as brown as bush-root tea. They were children of the earth-god and goddess: fertile, with three growing children, as well as his spirit brothers and sisters, who would stay the same age forever. His uncle's eyes were golden-brown – because he was a son of the beer-god, his uncle scoffed when his grandmother spoke in this manner. Her eyes were bewitching, like pictures from Tablette books: warm brown islands lapped by deep green seas. She was a child of the loom-goddess, and she wove colours together. Muzi's work, his grandmother said, was to read the clouds, interpret the dreams of the sky-god. He let his mind enter the clouds as they stretched and merged, endlessly forming new shapes above him. Some days the clouds sent a message, something to tell someone at home: a white bull to tell his father to raise the price of the wool at market; a winged snake to tell his uncle that the N-LA representative who had come to drink tea and talk about the markets was clever but devious; a camel to tell his middle sister that she must study hard and not complain about thirst. The clouds spoke to him too. One day last year they had told him that the Jailwall was not real.

To everyone he knew the Jailwall was a brutal fact, a monstrous weapon in a long war against them; to the clouds, the Jailwall was nothing more than a dirty straggle of fleece caught on a thorn, something thin and insubstantial that would one day blow away in the wind. The Jailwall was a dream, the clouds had told him, the dream of suffering people: people whose hearts had dehydrated, whose souls hurt so much they wished only to sleep – to draw a curtain across the horizon, across the sky itself. Those people must wake up or perish, the clouds deemed, for after sleep comes awakening or death: that is the nature of sleep.

He had tried to tell his family that, but though he thought his grandmother had understood, his mother, aunt and father had looked at him as if he had sunstroke and his uncle had finally shouted, 'What nonsense are you letting the child talk? Do you want him carted back here with a bullet in his forehead? The Jailwall is as real as sheep dung, boy. Listen to your elders, and never try and walk through it.' His grandmother had shouted back then, and his uncle had shut up, but not before grumbling, 'I swear, we should be sending him to work in the mine, not letting him dream his life away on these hills.' He hadn't been worried. His uncle didn't mean it and his parents would never let him work in Zabaria. The next day he'd made it up to his uncle, bringing him mountain mint tea in the morning, strong, the way he liked it. His uncle was just frightened for him and he understood why. Some dreams were nightmares. His grandfather, rest his spirit, had built the house with its door facing south.

MEHHHHH. An angry bleat interrupted his thoughts. He lifted his head. Ai! The pointy-nose ewe was trying to steal one of the lambs again and the mother was loudly objecting. He got to his feet, grabbed his stick and chased the thief away. Now, where was that patch-eyed ewe? There she was, up on the hill slope, nosing at something.

He crept up on her quietly. What was that?

A rusty rim in the soil.

'Don't lick that.' He swatted her away. It was metal. His father and uncle might want it. He dug around the dry earth with a stone and tugged until at last the thing came free.

It was a contraption: a big metal flower in a bird cage. Four curved petals, stained and crusted with rust, trapped inside a crumbling coil of circular bars, the whole thing set on a fat stem. From the base extruded an ancient serpent – a long rotted electric lead with a double-fanged plug.

He liked the thing. He had seen one before, in the market. It was an Old World fan to blow air, create a breeze in a room, before wafters were invented. The fan was a collector's item, but he wouldn't let his uncle and father sell it. He would ask them to help him fix it. He would keep it.

He lay on his stomach, brushing the dirt off the base. The ewe was nudging his ankle, nosing at some grass, and he scratched her chest with his foot, adjusted the fan head, faced it up to the sky. He wouldn't use the fan to cool the house. He would use it to cool the world, to blow air over the scrublands. He would create a wind to tickle the sky-god, send messages up to Him from the earth. Yes: the fan was his new wish transmitter, a gift from the patch-eyed ewe.

ASTRA

'Astra! Astra!' It was Uttu crying, her small hands fluttering over Astra's face.

'I'm *okay*. Let me go!' she yelled, tugging at the knuckles buckling her waist, squirming and kicking at the body behind her. At last the arms released her and she scrambled to the rampart wall and crouched, her back against the bricks, breathing hard. The pain-ball was back, zinging through her head, but pain was *good*: it cut through the fog, burst the white balloon. The white balloon was a new trick. She would have to watch out for it now, figure out how to beat it. She would never let IMBOD win. She was here in Non-Land to – she took the hit – find her Code father. Then she was going to – *flinch* – destroy Ahn and Blesserson. If she died, she would die *trying*.

Right now, though, she had to defuse this situation.

'I was just looking out!' *Just looking out. Just looking out.* It was a mantra of sorts. As she glared at her assailant, the pain-ball clunked back into its socket.

He sat back on his heels. It wasn't the guard, as she'd thought, but a Mobile Medical Unit officer: the lanky guy with sunless skin and a shock of white hair. Normally the medics only came in the late afternoons, dropping off dirty laundry and picking up the clean bags. What was he doing here, apart from hauling *her* around like a sack of old sheets?

'Oh. Please to excuse me, Astra.' Inglish was not his native tongue. He spoke it oddly, the stresses wrong, the vowels stretched like gum rubber. 'We thought . . .'

He looked at Uttu, who launched into a stream of throaty chatter.

'I'm not scared of heights,' she cut in. 'Uttu. Do you *understand*? I was just looking out at the city.'

Uttu didn't. The medic translated into Somarian. He seemed to speak it well; he and Uttu conferred back and forth until at last the elderwoman reached over and patted her arm.

'Astra brave girl,' she said in Asfarian. 'My sorry.'

'That's okay, Uttu,' she muttered, getting up and brushing off her robe. The others tensed and stepped forward, as if she might dash up onto the wall again and leap off. What could she do to get them to leave her alone?

A Somarian word came to her, one she had been hearing every day for a fortnight. '*Gúañarña*, Uttu,' she said, sounding like someone who had accidentally swallowed a spider.

But Uttu was thrilled with the thanks. '*Namsaga-mu, namsaga-mu,*' the elderwoman enthused, hugging her tightly round the waist.

'Please to accept my apologies also, Astra.' The medic had stood too, was sticking out his hand. 'My name is Photon, Photon Augenblick. I and my family are eternally at your service.' He giggled, a peculiar sound coming from a man as tall as a door. 'But I promise I should ask first if I think you might need helping to get down from a wall.'

The medic's white hair could have been part of the CONC uniform: navy blue cargo trousers and a pale blue short-sleeved shirt with white buttons and seams, the CONC insignia – a conch shell cradled by twin waves – stitched into the shoulder. She had washed and pegged out loads of the kit, but none as long and narrow as Photon's: the man was all arms and legs and elbows, his shoulders stooped as if trying to bridge the gap his great height created between them. Perhaps he was trying to cross that bridge now, offering a formal greeting, attempting a joke. But his effort was backfiring. She had no family to offer in return, and his joke was as feeble as an amoeba.

'Nice to meet you,' she replied sullenly, brushing his palm.

'Oh!' he gasped. 'I have offended you?'

Was he laughing at her? She squinted up at the medic. But his expression was genuinely troubled, his wide mouth twisted in chagrin. His right temple was grazed, she noticed, stamped with a bruised red grille, and his eyebrows and lashes weren't white, but fawn-brown. He ran his hand over his face, as if to erase it. 'The first Gaian I meet and I make to joke about a wall. That is why I am just a medic, believe me.'

His fluffy white head was visibly wilting. She had to pardon him or they'd be here all day. 'You didn't offend me,' she said stiffly. 'It's okay. I'm okay. I'll get back to work now.'

'Oh. No. I am sorry.' He winced, checked his watch, the fat multifunction wrist device all CONC officers wore. Bulbous and warty with dials and buttons, it squatted on his wrist like a toad. 'I was sent to ask you to come now please, to meet Major Thames.'

The summons to see the Compound Director had come: to talk about her *family situation*. But she couldn't go now. She wasn't ready. Her head hurt. She was hot and sweaty and her robes stank. She cast a wild, panicked look at Uttu.

But the washerwoman was no help at all. 'Doctor!' she commanded, shaking Astra's arm.

No. She was coping. She was conquering the pain. She didn't need a doctor. She didn't need the Major. But she had no choice; she was surrounded. The guard was hurrying up behind them along the rampart, Photon leading the way as Uttu took her elbow and steered her to the turret. The fog bearing in again on all sides, Astra descended the stairs.

All right, she had to see the Major. It was the next test. She had to talk about her Code father – *UHH* – the pain-ball flared – without collapsing. She grit her teeth and clenched her fists. Seeing the Major was good. She had *asked* to be sent to this Gaia-forsaken place because she had a plan – *OWW* – and to achieve it, she had to find Zizi Kataru – *ARRR*—

I'm walking. I'm walking. I'm walking.

She gave up. Putting one foot after another down the steps, she breathed deeply, repeated the mantra, allowed the pain-ball to disappear into the mist of her misery. At the second-floor landing, Photon stopped in front of a small wooden door. Hunching, he opened it, gestured for her to go first. Uttu hugged her goodbye and, patting her back, pushed her through.

'It is this way.'

They were in the red-carpeted hall that ran off from top of the main staircase. The Head of Staff had his office here, but Astra had had no reason to venture again into this wing of the compound. She let Photon overtake her and followed him, trying not to look down – she'd made that mistake on her first visit. The hall carpet was hand-loomed, patterned with llamas, date trees and chevrons, and it screamed of Nimma. 'Typical of the region,' Astra's Shared Shelter mother would have said, drawing Astra's attention to motifs and techniques that Gaian Craft workers had later adapted for their own cultural expression. Threadbare now, the carpet must have been expensive once: too expensive to replace. Nimma, though, would have relished the task of restoring it, matching wools and dyes, inserting new tufts into the dense pile. Staring down at a worn geometric cluster of grapes as she'd waited in the chair outside the Head's office, Astra had struggled not to be violently ill. Although Nimma had been almost as bad to her as Ahn in the end, it was the grey wave, not the pain-ball, that attacked when she thought about her Shelter mother, the grey wave hissing that Nimma had been right all along: she was an *ungrateful, arrogant liar*.

The wallscreens were safe. They displayed neutral, dull images: the CONC logo; portraits of CONC officials; lists of compound rules and regulations. Eyes on them, she trailed through her fog after Photon. He was turning to see where she was, when a young woman, compact and dark with short neat dreads, bolted out of an office and charged towards them, head down, rapidly swiping her Tablette.

'Sandrine!' Photon called as the woman powered past.

The officer turned mid-flight and Astra shrank back, as if hit by a heatwave. Sandrine was wearing the same uniform as Photon, but it looked completely different on her: Sandrine filled hers out, not just with solid curves but with a positively radiant sense of vitality and purpose. Half-jogging backwards, she raised a hand in greeting, then halted, widening her eyes. '*Pho*. Are you *okay*?'

'I am fine. It was nothing, I am honest to say.'

'That's not what I heard. Hey. Has he been fibbing to you too?'

It was an awful situation. As Photon bashfully brushed her question aside, this Sandrine person aimed the full force of her attention at Astra: the Gaian washergirl with her Non-Lander worker robes and Old World convict skull. She was used to getting glances in the dining hall: the fast, furtive eye wipes of curiosity and pity. Once, overcome by concern, a female officer had come over, set her tray down and tried to make conversation. Astra had pretended not to speak Inglish or Asfarian and no one had bothered her again. Sandrine, though, was neither filching a look, nor stammering vacuous greetings. She was smiling.

Astra didn't know what 'fibbing' meant. She rolled her shoulders, twisted her head and fixed her gaze on the officer's trouser cuffs. Sandrine's uniform wasn't, in fact, exactly the same as Photon's. She had learned in the laundry room how the cuts of women's clothes differed from men's. Women's trousers curved in at the waist and tapered to the ankle, drawing attention to the female shape; men's hung straight and loose, shielding their anatomy from scrutiny. It wasn't mandatory to wear one or the other: some of the women officers, Astra had noticed, preferred men's trousers; but not Sandrine. Hers fit her hips like the skin of a plum.

A plum with no time for hanging around. 'Stay *safe* out there, soldier,' the officer commanded Photon, brandishing her Tablette as she wheeled back down the hall. 'And get that report in to me yesterday, yeah?'

'On your Tablette!' he called. 'Last year!'

Sandrine gave a big thumbs-up and disappeared into a room on the right.

'Pho' looked dolefully after her. 'Sandrine is the MMU supply coordinator,' he explained. 'I was giving all my emergency morpheus to one Treatment Ward last week, so I should fill out an extra report. Normally I am more efficient, but then this week was an emergency too.'

Having reminded himself of his woeful tardiness, Photon set off briskly again down the hall. Astra followed, losing pace. At the end of the carpet, either side of a useless-looking table and chair, the hallway divided. Astra caught up as the medic turned right – and halted. Photon had disappeared and in his place a glistening white spiral towered over her like a vortex to another dimension, its veils of pale light stretching deep into the sandstone side hall. For a sinking moment she thought she was hallucinating, projecting some kind of enormous combination of her fog and white pain into the world. But then she noticed two large copper grids on the walls, their thin shutters casting the light form into the space. It was a giant seashell, she realised. Its spines and ridges cast a warped glow around the bare hall while at its base a long gleaming pink lip met an undulating carpet of radiant gold light. The whole apparition hung suspended half a metre above the floor stones. But where was Photon? Had this thing *dissolved* him?

'It's an ion curtain.' His voice came floating to her through the lustrous swathes of light. 'It won't hurt you.'

At the far end of the pink lip, his tall shape was beckoning her. She hesitated, still bewildered by the shell. She could see little apertures cut into its ridges now, like windows: like a building, in the desert . . . *yes, of course* . . . She flinched, recognising it now. But it was just information:

CONC HQ. The spectacular central offices of the Council of New Continents, erected in 06 RE in Amazigia, a refugee camp on the western edge of Nuafrica that had survived the Dark Time by working cooperatively. CONC, founded on the principles of human rights, sustainability and cooperation was a wellspring of hope in the desert of war and global warming, and its first act of regeneration had been to situate its headquarters in the continent that had given birth to all humanity. A conch shell, used all over the world since time immemorial to call nations to council, had been chosen to symbolise the new world government, and even the CONC architect had risen to the challenge of making that vision a reality. Every school in Is-Land hosted screenposters of CONC HQ. How could she have forgotten what it looked like, even for a nanosecond?

Because she'd been dazzled by the ion curtain. A hologram-config 'energy shower' supposed to alleviate stress and boost your immune system, the technology was popular in New Zonia, but the manufacturer had refused to sell it to Is-Land. Most Gaians said good riddance. You could get the same feeling from a walk in the woods.

Gaia knew what an ion curtain would do to her head but it filled the side hall so there was no going round it. She would just have to find out.

She stepped into the glimmering interior of the shell, blinking as her face broke the glossy surface of the form. Unbidden, Ahn's voice hissed through her head: 'This building is *wet*.'

On *wet* the pain-ball shot out of its socket and she lurched forward, stumbling as the missile scored its first dazzling white hit; her mind seized in the electric grip of the memory. Ahn had come to Golden Bough School. He had been a special guest in biotecture class; afraid of saying something stupid, she had squirmed in her seat, ducked her head as he took questions from her classmates—

It was no good. Like Sheba's hipskirt in the laundry, this was an unbidden memory, and it was too vivid, too strong, too unexpected. She was lost in an explosive white haze, the pain-ball detonations brighter than the shell. She wouldn't fall, she wouldn't. She blinked, breathed, grasped for facts. *Info only. Info only.* If she could focus on Ahn's lesson, not his voice . . . yes . . . that was right. The architect Philippe Saigon had engineered a series of ducts in the roof ridges, letting water continuously flow down the building's curved walls. CONC HQ glistened in the sun and sang in the wind, that was what Ahn had said . . .

CRACK. It was no use. She couldn't hive the information from the

memory. Ahn had snickered at Saigon's wind-fluted roof, saying CONC
workers found the tones annoying. Faster and faster, the pain-ball tripped
the white phosphorus mines it had laid down in her head. Ahn had passed
around a conch shell for the children to hold to their ears. The pain-ball
was splintering her temples and she was reeling from the impact, but the
conch shell was in her hands. And now Ahn was in his office, cowering in
front of his gold-tinted window, and she was lifting the big spiny shell,
hurling it at his . . .

Whiteness. The pain-ball explosions blotted out the shell, the hall, the
memory. She was slumped against the stone wall, the sea roaring in her
ears.

I'm following Photon. I'm following Photon.

She began weakly repeating the phrase, then with gathering conviction
until at last the pain-ball was sinking back in its slot. Her eyes fluttered
open. The walls of CONC HQ rose before her, no longer white, but a
dawn dream of rose and gold curves.

'Astra—' Photon was hastening towards her through the veils of light,
his eyes bulging in a caricature of alarm. 'Are you okay?'

'I'm fine. Just a headache.'

'You do not look fine.'

She cleared her throat. 'I've never been in an ion curtain before.'

'*Oh.* I should have *asked.*' He scooted past her and turned a dial on the
wall. CONC HQ disappeared. The side hall was a brightly lit sandstone
and copper cube, one end open, the other sealed by a massive pair of hammered-metal doors.

He fumbled in a pocket. 'Are you sure you do not want an aspirin?'

An aspirin? Against IMBOD? She straightened up. If she could
recover from a full-blown Ahn attack by herself, she could deal with the
Compound Director. She stalked past Photon to the imposing office
entrance.

Whether ageless originals or Regeneration replicas, the doors were
magnificent: beaten iron and bronze panels bordered with faceted studs
framed scenes of dancing reeds, flowers, stars, wild men with vultures'
heads, throned kings and noble women bearing maces made of braided
grains. Facing Astra was a tawny queen, her tumbling locks crowned by
two entwined snakes, quivers of arrows sticking out of her pair of broad
wings. A muscled thigh stretched out from her robe; her elegant foot
rested on the back of a lion. Every petal, toenail, eyelash was finely etched,

each tableau a mastercraft work, the kind of thing Astra had been taught
to revere. But she was too fed up with this place to admire any more of its
lobby decorations. She was here for a meeting. On the wall was a bell, and
beneath it a silver plaque:

Major Akira Thames
CONC Compound Director

She raised her finger, then stopped, unsure. A high-pitched, erratic noise
was coming from behind the doors, something distressing, almost human
about the way it was faintly straining out of the room. Was it a child?
Photon was beside her now, but he didn't press the bell either. He hung
back awkwardly, as if he too were afraid to interrupt the strange sorrow
keening through the tall metal garden of the Compound Director's
doors.

'You have not yet met Major Thames, have you?' He pronounced the
name 'tems'. His voice was tinged with apprehension.

She shook her head. Something was missing. The fog, she realised: she
was no longer immersed in the fog.

'Please to salute when I do,' Photon whispered. 'The Major is liking
protocol.'

She stood almost trembling, lighter, taller, thinking clearly for the first
time in *weeks*. Had the ion curtain *cured* her? Her senses felt as sharp as
the bronze queen's arrows. The cries sliding through the doors came, she
realised, from a violin. She had never seen one, but she knew the sound.
This one wasn't playing anything she understood as music, though: not
a meditation, a sonata or jig but a ceaseless agitation of notes, leaping
from one jagged pinnacle of dissatisfaction to another. There was a
snagged breath, and another, then suddenly the music swooped sweetly
upwards . . . and like a battered bird her heart rose to meet it. *Yes*, she
thought, shivering, as the violin resumed its frantic refusal to accept any
limits, to conform to any measure but its own; *yes*, that's exactly right.
Even the fierce bronze queen on the door seemed to quiver, her feathers
itching to take flight.

Photon placed his finger on the bell.

The sobbing stopped.

'Enter!' came the hoarse call.

ENKI

'AI YI YI!' He shook his thumb, sucked it, glared at the hammer.

Across the box, a slow grin broke over Bartol's face. 'You're supposed to hit the iron nail, brother. Not your thumbnail.'

Enki thrust out his hand, star splayed. 'Arakkia's thumbnails are made of steel' – *BEAT* – 'a polished part of the man's ap*peal*.'

Bartol returned to his hammering, tapping lightly, the smile still playing about his broad lips. It wasn't often Bartol got in a joke at Enki's expense. Never mind the instant comeback – *polished steel*, brilliant! – the big man would be satisfied with his little quip for a month.

His mother, though, wouldn't be satisfied until he'd nailed himself to the box through his liver.

'You see!' she declared from the camp cooker, knocking her wooden spoon against the rim of her millet pot. 'What did I say? No good will come of this, my son. No good.'

'Amma,' he drawled, 'the neighbours will hear.'

'The NEIGHBOURS,' she screeched over the din of the next tent's wallscreen party, 'are ROTTING their MINDS watching RERUNS of ASFARIAN SOAP OPERAS.'

From the next tent came a round of laughter and applause. It was the soundtrack to his life: the beer-addled brain-dead neighbours clashing like a broken cymbal against his mother's bitter outbursts. At least, having made her point, she shut up. Sitting cross-legged on her cushion, she rapidly chopped a withered onion and the two tomatoes Bartol had brought, the red chunks falling open in a bleeding mess on the board.

That done, she lit a cigarette. When she spoke again, it was to deliver a rapid, hoarse harangue in time to the quick flick of ash.

'You're a good boy, Bartol. You listen too much to him. Why can't you just take him down to the gym tent? Before an evil end befalls you both.'

'He doesn't *take* me anywhere, Amma,' Enki flared. 'We're doing this together, along with everyone in the gym tent. It's happening now. Do you want to be the one to stop it? Do you? Go on, then. Call Una Dayyani.' He slammed the hammer down on the rug, dug in his back pocket, thrust out his Tablette. 'Call her on my Tablette if you want to be anonymous. Turn me in.'

His mother took another drag of her cigarette. She only smoked when she was very angry – not to stop herself from saying things she might regret but to give herself time to phrase them more precisely. From the corner of his eye, he watched her perform her favourite trick: blowing the smoke out through her nostrils like a creature from the Dragon's Gorge. He stashed the Tablette and resumed hammering.

'I'm sorry, Am Arakkia.' Bartol grovelled as usual. 'If there are ever any problems, someone will come and take the box away. I promise.'

Bartol had had to be persuaded long and hard to build the box over Enki's mother's objections. He'd always been polite and helpful, but after Abgal Izruk had died and Enki had fallen, his friend had forged an almost obsequious bond with the woman. But Enki had risen. He was a YAC core member now, with serious responsibilities, and since he'd turned eighteen, this tent had been registered in his name as well as his mother's. That was a full two years ago, but she hadn't yet learned she had no right to interfere in what he did in his own home.

'That box will be your coffin, boys.' She stubbed out the butt. 'Look at you both: dressed up like River Road drifters. Why can't you get decent jobs, all those muscles between you?'

That was her nicotine jibe? *Jobs?* She knew he was done with queuing from dawn for the privilege of cleaning bike chains with a frazzled toothbrush, only to be passed over after the boss took one look at him. YAC *was* his job. He hit a nail square on the head, drove it in.

'Don't you think purple suits us, Am Arakkia?' Bartol asked, winking at Enki.

'You look like two eggplants,' she grumbled. 'With a big purple thumb to match, Enki.'

He nearly put the hammer through the wood. He didn't need abuse like that from his own mother. *Potato baby*, those older boys had called him after school, pelting him with stones. Had she already forgotten the huge stink *she* had caused? The next day, wheeling along alone, he'd baited the boys, knowing Bartol was hiding behind the solar tree, ready to charge from the rear. He'd come home with a torn shirt, two black eyes, and triumphant memories of several well-placed grabs and uppercuts of his own; until last year, the thought of Ug Šešu curled up in the dirt clutching his groin had still made his heart sing. His famous victory hadn't impressed his mother, though: she'd harangued them both until Bartol had finally caved in and tattled about the bullying. The next day she'd cornered the school principal, wagging her finger and squawking, '*We are all alt-bodied* – that's what *my* temple tent teaches! Have you forgotten what this place is built on, you fool?' The principal had overseen a restorative justice process, Enki and Bartol magnanimously declaring they didn't want the gang disciplined, but at home his mother had railed at him for weeks: 'Don't you rely on Bartol's fists to get you out of trouble, my son. You think you're like your father but you're not. You have to stick up for yourself with your tongue. *That's* the way to fight for your rights.'

He was doing that now. In freestyle, battle rap and glow-flow. But did his mother give him a date stone of credit? 'And these tin cans round your necks,' she ground on, the nicotine hit clearly not yet exhausted, 'what dignified man sports such a thing? Do you wear them in the gym? You'll give yourselves blood poisoning, mark my words.'

'All YAC members are wearing the star, Amma,' he said tightly. 'Soon you will see it everywhere.'

'The star.' She snorted. 'Look at it, son. The points are all uneven. Bartol's is even worse. How is anyone going to trust you to conquer Is-Land if you can't even draw a star properly?'

Bartol was grinning openly. Enki glowered at him. The five-pointed star design had taken months to decide upon and weeks to create: collecting old tin cans from the scrap heap, rolling them out, cutting and sanding the edges, punching a hole for the chain. Everyone able to had been given a quota to make – no template; the unique shapes were the essence of the design.

'The stars are all different, Amma. None of them are "perfect" – *that's* the point. They represent—'

But she wasn't listening, as usual. 'And will you be getting your wives' wedding rings from the scrap heap?' she enquired tartly. 'Is that the next fashion?'

Right on cue: after the job moan, the marriage complaint. His mother
had been widowed too early, that was the problem. His father, May the
Gods Who Have Forgotten Us Ever Guide His Onward Journey, had
died a 'hero', just another policeman killed by an IMBOD bullet. Sustained by his scanty N-LA pension, her temple-tent preachers extolling
his memory, his mother had never sought to remarry, and so she had
never had the chance to suffer the corrosive disappointments that, as far
as Enki could see, defined the marital relationship. Marriage, from the
outside, was a regal gold-brocaded tent; from the inside it was cramped,
stifling and ear-piercingly loud. Abgal Izruk had told him it wasn't like
that everywhere: in Asfar you could have temporary marriages, which
sounded eminently sensible, but N-LA had banned those arrangements
decades ago, thanks to an unholy alliance of women arguing they had
only ever served men's baser needs, and conservative religious leaders
denouncing them as a threat to the sanctity of the family. Here in Kadingir, some of the Farashan families allowed spouse-swapping after a
woman's child-bearing age – and who knew what went on in the 'celibate'
desert communes – but for everyone else in Non-Land, unless you wanted
to wage the long war of divorce, marriage pegged you down to another
person forever: to her whims and jealous commands, her family, the endless meaningless rituals of agreeing with elders who had sheep shit for
brains, admiring babies who burped up tit milk on your shirt. From what
the new fathers said at the gym tent, marriage didn't even guarantee you
regular sex.

No, marriage was not for Enki Arakkia. He had been to one wedding
and that was enough. If YAC was his job, his rhymes were his wife, his
life, his soul-sharpened knife. Sex – well, girls from good families had to
stay home, but the orphans went to the riverbank, just like the boys.

'We could have got you a nice cabinet at the scrapheap,' he remarked,
'if you didn't care so much about the *neighbours*.'

'Some flaking, woodwormy cast-off.' She sniffed. 'No thank you.' His
mother was devoted to his great-grandfather's metal shelves: a family
heirloom, made to be easily dismantled and transported if the tent had to
be moved, she said. But she also had a rabid horror of being thought a
scrounger. Enki had stopped trying to ask her what she considered living
off CONC rations her whole life to be.

The baseboard was done. He and Bartol flipped the box over and
shook the sides. Solid. His mother could wrinkle her nose all she liked,

but the Nagu Three scrapheap put the markets to shame. Beneath the broken car parts and spilling bags of food waste lay a thousand treasures: kitchen gadgets that only needed rewiring, furniture that just lacked a lick or two of paint. It was amazing what the old N-LA families chucked out rather than give to their neighbours. He and Bartol had scrounged the wood there yesterday, arriving early before the merchants showed up with their carts. Bartol had ranged over the rickety mountain, sending the rooks reeling up in raucous protest; Enki had rolled around the base ground, pulling at the odd bit of timber but more interested in watching the birds flap like angry mops against the sky.

The rooks were newcomers to Kadingir. They had flown south across the Boundary five years ago, after CONC had begun its irrigation project on the banks of the Mikku. Everyone had expected them to return to Is-Land but, apparently Coded against radiation and soon protected by Non-Land law, their numbers had swollen. They nested in trees down by the Mikku and, to the envy of everyone except the old N-LA families, spent the days eating. The birds preferred grubbing in the moist fields, but after heavy rain would fly out to the scrublands. Most days they could also be found at the scrapheaps, probing mounds of rotten fruit, vegetables and cooked grains – even in Kadingir, people managed to waste food.

Wherever they had grazed, in the evening the birds swarmed back to their nests on the banks of the Mikku – you could set your Tablette clock by the black storm. A flock of rooks was called a 'consensus', Abgal Izruk had told him. Though they squabbled, they flew as one. Enki liked the word; later he'd championed it as a decision-making process for YAC and proposed a similar name for their secret meetings. That didn't stop him appreciating other potential uses of the birds. There by the river you could also practise your stone-throwing – at least, you could before the police had begun protecting the nests. Ug Šešu had been a good shot. Thanks to him, Enki had eaten roast rook once, cooked on a spit over a fire. The breast meat was delicious: lean and mild and chewy. Then Ug had lost his appetite – for food, anyway.

It wasn't good to think too long about Ug. He picked up a rock and looked around. Was is worth trying to kill one of the rooks here? Probably not: the scrapheap keepers maintained a steady patrol of the perimeter, and there were steep penalties for killing one of the first birds to settle back in Non-Land since the Dark Time.

He shouldn't want to eat rooks anyway. The birds had turned their back on Is-Land and cast in their lot with Non-Land. They were allies, cawing that if they could cross the Boundary, so could he. He'd ended up trying to feed one, using an old windscreen wiper to toss a maggoty gobbet of sheep brains in its direction, an offering the bird sceptically assessed, head cocked, like his mother preparing to haggle over offal at the market. Close up, rook feathers had a night-blue sheen, almost purple. *Yes*, he'd decided then, *the birds could be part of his collective.* They were highly intelligent, Abgal Izruk had told him once; they could make tools and solve engineering problems – in one experiment a rook had actually dropped stones into a tube of water until the worm floating on its surface was close enough to eat.

The rook ate the maggots, but turned its beak up at the brain. 'Fussy eater, hey, Archimedes?' he'd clucked at it, recalling Abgal Izruk's history lesson. Like most adults, the old man had a precious store of Old World data to impart, shiny nuggets plucked from the midden of history. He'd encouraged Enki to do his own Tablette research and while political theory had proved the richest terrain, it was always good to toss random tidbits of knowledge into the salad mix of a rhyme. Or a solitary moment communing with corvids.

Two more rooks had hopped over, hoping to share the maggot glut, no doubt. They were inspecting him from a splintered bed frame. 'Ibn Sīnā,' he'd called softly, 'Eureka. *Kaaa Kaaa*,' as he flipped another dollop of sheep slop, slightly closer to him this time. No harm in testing their thresholds. But if not polymath geniuses, the birds were canny enough to not trust him. They'd pecked over the grubs only when Bartol returned and Enki had rolled a safe distance away.

Archimedes meanwhile, was tearing at a bioplastic bag, his claws raking through a wet nest of chicken bones and burnt lentils. Something glinted. And again. Enki chased the bird off with the wiper and used it to poke through the slops. *Yes!* A stash of screws and washers, nuts and bolts – it was *unbelievable* the things people threw away. He and Bartol had found a whole wheelchair once, rusted and crumpled as if hit by a car, but with an intact seat, back rest and tyres. It had kept him on the road for a year.

'Thanks Archy.' He dug out his gloves and scooped the soggy mess onto a cracked plate. The rook hopped backwards and perched on an old bicycle frame, bowing and spreading its tail feathers, emitting shrill caws. 'There's someone I'd like you to meet,' he told it, then set about picking out the hardware, wiping each piece clean. He counted fifty-four useable pieces in the end; the YAC team would be ecstatic. He was just cleaning the last nut when Bartol came bounding down the heap with two armfuls of wood, sending Archimedes cawing up and away to a new patch free of noisome, unpredictable human competitors. Bartol's find was as good as his: planks from an old set of shelves, and two slightly frayed pieces of plywood, damp, but no sign of woodworm and all perfectly servicable. They'd done the measuring and sawing at the heap, improvising a stand from an old cabinet, and headed back to Enki's tent well-pleased – the tools in Bartol's pack, the plywood under his arm and the planks strapped to the back of Enki's chair with his bag. A good morning's work, to be finished before lunch.

If only his mother would let them. 'You could be carpenters,' she mourned over the sizzle of onion in the frying pan. 'If you have to spend your lives knocking together other people's rubbish, you could at least sell the results. Or fix up the Nagu ramps. That hole by the cigarette booth is getting bigger every rainfall. I've told them, again and again, but they'll wait until you fall through into the mud before they lift a finger.'

He ignored her. She wouldn't listen if he argued. Mending ramps was volunteer work. Mutual aid, rah rah, but how much longer was everyone in Kadingir supposed to work for free? And why should he trade in cast-offs? He wanted to *change* the system, not perpetuate it. His repurposing had a far higher *purpose* than just earning a few coins for cigarettes, beer and Tablette repairs.

He began packing, taking the bags and boxes from the pile on the rug. Bartol fetched the bigger packages they'd dumped near the tent flap, stooping to avoid grazing his head on the sagging roof. *He must get back-ache visiting us*, Enki thought, *but he never complains of it*.

'Aiiiii!' His mother's shriek could have ripped the tent in half.

'What?'

'You promised, Enki. You *promised*!' She was pointing the spoon at him, an arc of grease drips spattering over the low tabletop.

He looked down at his hand, at the tin of needles.

'They're empty, Amma. *Empty!*'

He tugged the lid open and tipped out the tin on the floor, showed her. The syringes were clear, filled with air, but of course she had to get up and inspect everything, rummaging through every last bag. With a sheepish look at Enki, Bartol put down his package to help her.

The soap opera blaring from the neighbours' tent, his mother's scrabbling fingers, harsh whispers, Bartol's obliging mitts: a wave of all-too-familiar tension rose in his chest and he swung himself away from the box and onto his bedmat. He lay down, extended his arm, flexed his biceps, closed his eyes and crossed his arm over his face.

But they were still there: a looming giant and a black-robed crone, drawing closer, bending over him as he tossed and turned, drenched in sweat. His mother and his best friend, turned his worst enemies, prodding him, slapping him, forcing spoonfuls of gruel into his mouth, hissing and urging, 'Do you want to end up like Ug?' and all the while refusing to let him remain, invisible and quiet, in the fallen place.

For a deep, aching moment, he craved morpheus again, craved it in his balls. The fallen place; the place of surrender, slow silence, nothingness, where for centuries – *aeons* – he would float down through the darkness, falling and yet cradled, safe in the palm of an enormous blue velvet glove. That's what he and Ug had called it: the blue glove – not the powder-blue mind-sky of meditation but a rich, glowing twilight, a suppressed dawn: a swooning blue inside which, gently swelling and subsiding and swelling again, his body finally dispersed into a vast amorphous shape, like the rooks' nightly flight over Kadingir, countless particles, his and hers, forming one endless wave ... That was the fallen place, a place of no tension, no drama, no eruptions or decisions, just eternal comfort, past and future, consumed by the infinite promise of that blue ... the promise of merging with her ...

He snapped his eyes open. Breathing hard, he stared up at the stitched rip in the tent canvas. Craving morpheus was not in his schedule for today. He was Enki Arakkia, not Ug Šešu. Ug was in the ground, being eaten by maggots. Enki had risen, and he would not let anything, not his mother, not *her*, not the swollen boulders between his feet, drag him back down again.

He sat up straight, shoulders relaxed, hands on feet, as Chozai had taught him in the meditation tent. Chozai was neither his first nor his best teacher. Silently, he summoned Abgal Izruk's words: *If you listen to its whispers, weakness will lead you to strength.* The craving for morpheus was his most powerful weakness. He needed release, it whispered; physical release came in the gym tent, he had learned, pumping iron until the endorphins flooded his brain. Emotional release came on stage, spitting and rhyming until he was empty of rage, grief, even joy, his body ringing like a bell with the applause of the crowd. As for sexual release, he would

be patient and wait; if the ache didn't subside he would go down to the
riverbank and find a girl who ached too and empty his balls like a man.

'Does the recipe call for cinders, Amma?' he called out. Ug had told
him the morpheus dulled your hunger pangs and that was true. But you
needed to hunger for life.

His mother pinched her mouth and stalked back to the hob. As she
slid the knife blade under the tomatoes and tossed the red fistful into the
pan, he swung himself back to his task. At last the box was packed and he
and Bartol lifted the lid on top and hammered it down – just a few nails
this side so the lid could be easily prised off when the time came.

'Burnt onions add flavour,' his mother declared. 'Come on, boys, you
need feeding after all that hard work tormenting me.'

'It smells good, Am Arakkia,' Bartol said. He shuffled over on his knees
to help her set the table. Enki hauled his bedmat up onto the box and
hoisted himself onto it.

'See, Amma? You always said you wanted a sofa. You can have your
friends round to sit on it when I'm at the gym tent.'

'My fine friends to sit on your smelly sheets?'

She was dishing up now: a mound of millet each for him and Bartol; a
small dollop for her. A teaspoonful of stew on her plate; the rest divided
between the men. It was no use arguing. She'd just say she wasn't hungry
after her cigarette.

'Tell them to bring their daughters,' he said. 'Some of them might like
my smelly sheets.'

Bartol smothered a laugh as she passed out the plates. 'You only need
one woman, Enki. And where is she, I ask you?'

He took a forkful of food. The stew made a nice change. Bartol had
grown the tomatoes on the roof of his container. 'She's hunting through
the scrapheap, Amma,' he said, 'looking for an eggplant man with a tin
star around his neck and a pillow full of rhymes in his bed. But she told
me she requires a mother-in-law with a silken tongue and forgiving
nature, so I said as soon as I could trade you in, I would let her know.'

He glanced up. Bartol's big grin was spreading over his face, like the
sun dawning over the windsands. And his mother was smiling her sharp
smile. 'That's not the girl for you, my son. Bartol, my sweetness, will you
pour us some water? Enki needs to wash his mouth after such blasphem-
ing of his mother.'

ASTRA

Almost afraid to breathe, as if one exhalation would pop the airy clarity she was experiencing, Astra stepped into the Compound Director's office. The room was high and wide, a stone crate of daylight, slit on three walls by tall recessed windows through which shafts of sunshine were competing to burnish the floor. In the bright centre of the room stood a slight figure, back turned to the visitors, a silhouette framed by a pair of glass balcony doors. As Photon closed the grand metal entrance, Major Thames tucked hir violin under hir arm and pointed the bow straight up, the tip straining towards the brass chandelier that hung from the ceiling like a huge tea-stained flower.

'Shostakovich!' The Compound Director's ravaged voice shook the window panes. Astra had no idea what the command or greeting meant, but on the final syllable the bow arced to the right, towards a carved wooden sofa and camel-hair rug. Photon scurried over and stood on the carpet. The medic's chest was out, chin up, but his shoulders were still hunched, as if anticipating the bow's next blow. Astra lined up beside him. An ornate screendesk gleamed at the other end of the room, the legs scrolling down into lions' paws; behind it a large white conch shell rested on a pedestal. Two blue wall hangings garlanded the inner wall and above the hammered-metal doors there was a grate like the ones in the hall. As for the Major – she didn't dare turn her head and had to be content with a peripheral glimpse of the back of hir uniform: midnight-blue tapered trousers and a flared jacket, the waistband bordered with white ribbon and embellished with two white shells. Uttu had washed it last week, or one exactly like it, not allowing anyone else to touch the fine linen and checking all the buttons afterwards for strength.

'His first violin concerto.' The Major was still addressing the balcony doors. 'Final movement. The Burlesque. Far too unsettling for that sausage-brained Stalin, so the first performance had to wait for twenty years, until after the dictator's death. Photon Augenblick! How many Soviet citizens did Josef Stalin kill?'

'It is considered, Major,' Photon replied, loud and prompt, 'that Josef Stalin bore direct responsibility for the deaths of more than twenty million people. He also made to happen the Gulag penal system that killed forty million people more.'

'Very good!' came the phlegm-rattling response. 'And how did Dimitri Shostakovich respond to Stalin's regime of intimidation, torture and mass murder?'

All the information was whirling round Astra's mind like doves in a cote. She had studied Russia in school: Russia was an Old World gangster state. Gaians had lived there, in yurts in the tundra. Other Gaians, internationals, had sailed there, trying to stop Russian oil junkies from destroying the Ice Circle. They had failed and been imprisoned and Russia's victory had tipped the Great Collapse into the Dark Time. But who was Stalin? She was alert, transfixed, giddy with the need to *know things*.

'Shostakovich was an artist of courage, sirm,' Photon shot back. 'At a time of strong anti-Semitic feeling, he drew on the thema of Jewish folk music, creating a cycle of work meaning to express the suffering of the Jews at hands of fellow citizens. This work was also forbidden to be played in the Soviet Union.'

'Dimitri Shostakovich is an eternal inspiration!' With another flamboyant thrust of the bow, Major Thames spun round to greet them.

She had to stop herself from staggering backwards. The Major's heavy-lidded pouched eyes, beaked nose and ageing, sallow brown skin screamed *Owleon* – and not just any Owleon, but *Helium*.

Helium wasn't fierce and proud any more; Helium had fallen to death in a field. She braced herself for the grey wave but her head remained clear, her attention riveted by the impeccable person standing before her, erect and lithe as a classical dancer. Everything about the Major was striking. Hir mouth was a thin slash of bronze lipstick, hir folded eyelids graced with a tracing of subtle gold powder. Thick black hair, silver at the temples, stood away from hir face as if electrified by hir vigilant gaze, and on hir chest gleamed a regional necklace – malachite beads strung either side of a beaten silver plate. The Major's gender might be ambiguous, hir stature diminutive, but hir authority was beyond question. In hir alert presence, she felt, yet again, acutely aware of her sweaty washergirl's robes.

Tip quivering, the violin bow lowered. Photon gave a smart salute. A mean thought tittered through her mind: maybe saluting was the cause of his forehead injury? But the Major was glaring at her and she hurriedly mimicked the gesture. The Is-Land salute was a fist from the heart, but she didn't want to do that ever again.

Major Thames stepped neatly over to a sideboard beside the balcony doors and placed the violin on a display rack beside two gold digiphoto frames. 'Stand down,' heesh commanded.

Did that mean sit? No. Beside her, Photon relaxed his posture. Still brandishing the bow, the Compound Director strode towards them.

'Now *some* political commentators, Astra Ordott' – eyes smouldering between their cushioned lids, Major Thames directed the bow tip at Astra's heart – '*some* historians have argued that because Shostakovich was never sent to the Gulag, never suffered in the vast nightmare of the Soviet murder camps, he was not a true revolutionary artist. But *we* say that there are many ways to skin a cat and use its guts, don't we, Photon Augenblick?'

Photon cleared his throat. 'If I may, Major . . . In Is-Land, they wouldn't use cat gut, or any part of any cat, for—'

'Officer Augenblick!' the Major roared. 'Astra Ordott has studied Inglish idioms at an advanced level and she understands the concept of metaphor! She came top of her Year Eleven class in Regeneration Languages and she needs just a few months' immersion to become fluent in both Inglish and Asfarian. Is that not correct, Astra Ordott?'

Major Thames was worked up now, pacing across the sandstone floor, swishing the bow through the air as if disciplining an orchestra of ill-tuned dust motes.

Astra opened her mouth to say yes, but nothing emerged except a weak puff of air.

'*Good*. Now let me be *clear*. There will be no torture of cats, or pigeons, or *woodlice*, on my watch. No terms of' – like a juggernaut gathering speed, the Major blitzed through the CONC list of prohibitions displayed periodically on every wallscreen in the compound – 'racist-sexistclassist-ageist-homophobic-transphobic-or-disablist abuse will be per-mitted against any compound staff member or visitor. I am the Director of the CONC Compound in the Southern Belt and my *first priority* is the safety and well-being of those under my command. But neither, Pho-ton Augenblick, will I allow the decimation of our precious repository of language. *Enough* of human history has been erased. Whole cities have been vacuumed into the skies, entire countries lie drowned beneath the seas. National libraries have disappeared into sink holes, continental internet servers have been vaporised by nuclear bombs. And what was the cause of the near-obliteration of our species?' Without waiting for an answer, the Major swept on, 'IGNORANCE, I tell you. MONU-MENTAL IGNORANCE IN EXTREMELY HIGH PLACES. We must preserve what precious knowledge we have left, or we will risk a far greater Collapse, one from which we will never emerge. Do you under-*stand* me, officer?'

'Yes, sirm,' Photon said, flustered, 'I apologise. I was afraid I was offend-ing to Astra when I met her, so I was perhaps feeling oversensitive to her cultural difference.'

'Oh.' The pacing ceased. 'And what, pray tell, were the circumstances of your meeting?'

Photon cleared his throat. 'Astra was standing on the compound ram-parts, sirm, making a view, but I was thinking that she was perhaps in danger so I manhandled her badly, pulling her down. Then,' he swal-lowed, 'in another moment, not considering her Is-Landic nationality, I made a poorly thought remark about walls.'

She was incandescent with rage. Why was Photon *squealing* on her? Now the Major would think she was *unstable*. Sure enough, the bow tip was targeting her chest.

'Standing on the ramparts? That seems a rather foolhardy thing to do, Astra Ordott.'

Fear beetled up her spine. The Major might be bantam-sized, but the little Owleons were always the most ferocious.

'I have a good head for heights, sirm,' she replied, avoiding those smouldering eyes. 'It's like Photon said: I just wanted to get a better view.'

'Is that so?' the Major purred. 'In future, Astra, when you are on *my ramparts*, will you try to recall that acrophobia has an evolutionary function?'

The Major's Inglish was advanced; hir sarcasm universal. 'Yes, sirm.'

'Splendid. Photon, five stars for daring to contradict me on a point of ethics. These will be added to your stars for the calm performance under fire this week, making a substantial bonus in your pay deposit this month.'

'Thank you, Major,' Photon mumbled. Whatever he'd done under fire, he sounded profoundly embarrassed by it. *It was nothing*, he'd said to Sandrine in the hallway. Through her annoyance, Astra found herself wondering, *Is gangly Photon some kind of hero?*

'You are most welcome.' The bow indicated the door. 'Photon, please wait for us out in the hallway. Astra, sit down.'

Photon bowled Astra a coy smile. She glowered at him as he loped to the doors. 'Major Thames?' He had stopped, was looking up at the grate on the wall.

'Yes.'

'I should to say, Astra had a migraine flash in the ion curtain. Perhaps I might suggest to lower the settings in your office?'

She stared at the grates. Was this room ionised as well?

'Is that correct?' The Major was addressing her.

'No,' she muttered, then paused. 'I think it was the other way around. The headache had been building from when I was in the sun. I feel better now. Maybe the ions are helping me.'

The Major looked entirely satisfied by this answer. 'The ions are undoubtedly helping you. The office is set at an ambient level that optimises clear and productive thought. But thank you, Photon, that was a characteristically considerate observation.'

Yes, well, Photon owed her consideration, big time. He exited, and she perched uneasily on the edge of the sofa. Sitting down could make her brand-wound worse, and she doubted the ions could permeate clothing. But that wasn't the prime reason to be nervous. Above her, the Major was smiling: a triumphant, glittering smile that admired Astra for no reason, bestowing a mad, utterly unwarranted grandeur on her small, tense form.

'So. Astra Ordott. Here. You. Are.' The bow sliced bolt upright again, then swept towards the balcony. 'Seventeen years old. *Oh,* how we *all* wish to be seventeen again! Out in the world for the first time on one's own, doing what countless young people over the centuries have done before you: leaving family and homeland to discover who you are, what you are made of. You are clearly not made of jelly and wood shavings, Astra Rampart Dancer. But are you made of stardust, wild honey and *fire*?'

For a scorching instant, Astra was back in the thicket of violin notes.

Yes, she wanted to reply. But the impulse shrivelled in her belly and the Major boomed on without her, 'No, you are not. One cannot attain such joy until one is free. Currently, you are not free. You are a stateless refugee, refused contact with your family and friends, and until you turn eighteen you are my legal charge. This is difficult, I understand. However, you are *not* to despair. Thanks, I understand, to his esteemed contributions to Is-Land Code work over the decades, your Shelter father Dr Klor Grunerdeson has negotiated a very hopeful situation for you.'

Klor. The grey wave ought to tower at the sound of his name but instead, she just felt a lump rise in her throat. 'He said he would make arrangements for me,' she whispered.

'As I understand it, he hired a very expensive lawyer. While IMBOD, I am sorry to tell you, wanted simply to dump you outside the Barracks and let you fend for yourself in the tents of Kadingir, Dr Grunerdeson's lawyer approached me directly with an application to grant you CONC asylum status. Given your exceptional rarity as a young Gaian refugee, and the political circumstances of your case, I wholeheartedly supported his proposal.'

Klor had thwarted IMBOD. The Barracks had taken revenge. She got it now, perfectly, but there was no time to be outraged for the Major was marching on.

'Astra, I want you to understand the gravity of your position, but also its potential. You have committed what many people would consider to be a crime, and you have been punished for it. You have rejected offers of medical treatment and re-education and as a result you are expected to rehabilitate yourself. CONC asylum entitles you to food, shelter and medical care here at the compound, but beyond that I have personally promised your Shelter father that I will provide you with skilled employment. Should you commit yourself to such work for five years, you would be eligible for a CONC passport, enabling you to travel anywhere in the world CONC has offices. Is that agreeable to you?'

She was barely listening. 'Major Thames? Can you send my Shelter father a message from me?'

Major Thames blinked. 'ASTRA ORDOTT. I asked you a direct question. Did you not hear me?'

She gripped the edge of the sofa. 'Yeah – I mean yes, I'm sorry. I'd like a passport one day, thank you. But you said you know my Shelter father. Can I contact him? *Please?*'

The Major's mouth twitched. 'I would like to say yes, Astra, but my correspondence with Dr Grunerdeson has been conducted entirely through his lawyer. It would not be appropriate for me to relay personal communications through this channel, and I trust you understand that it might not be entirely safe for you or your Shelter father to do so. However, you can rest assured that I will report to the lawyer any change in your legal status, including marriage to a Non-Lander – which would nullify your asylum status – CONC passport acquisition, or death.'

She folded her arms, hunched into herself. Die? How could she die when she was barely alive?

'Disappointing, I know. However, under the CONC Manifesto, Section Three, Family Reunification, you are entitled to our full assistance in locating your Code father. There is nothing in your records to identify him. Tell me, do you know anything about him at all?'

She stiffened, expecting the pain-ball to launch, but she felt nothing more than a sullen pulse at the base of her skull. It was true: she could now think, *talk*, about her Code father. She had never told anyone his name, not even Klor.

She had to put Klor out of her mind. 'Yes.' She prepared to speak the words aloud for the first time – the information from Hokma's letter, the handwritten page of homemade paper she had memorised and buried in the flying field. 'I know his name. My Shelter mother told me before she—' Her voice quavered. '—before she died. He's called Zizi Kataru. He was an infiltrator. He lived in Is-Land, in Atourne. He was evicted before I was born.'

The Major contemplated her for a moment, then said, 'Zizi Kataru. Good. We can draw up his records for a start.'

The Major strode over to hir screendesk, sat down and began swiping. Astra remained on the sofa, all her momentary brightness fading. Her Code father was unreal to her, just a name. But Klor . . . It was impossible to imagine never seeing him again. Never telling him things, how she was, what she was doing, discovering. Tears welling in her eyes, a memory of Or swam up in her mind, and for the first time since the neurohospice it was without pain. When she was little, she had listened to classical music with Klor. Not manic soliloquies like the Major's Shostakovich, but orderly, cheerful Old World symphonies and quartets, recordings Klor had played on his Tablette while he worked late in his office. For a time, she'd sat with him every evening, doing her homework and telling him which bits of the music she liked best. That's how she knew what a violin sounded like. Then came the Security shot. The Sec Gens didn't appreciate complicated music, and Hokma had told her to pretend from now on that she only liked Gaia hymns. Klor had been disappointed, but Nimma had told him it was only to be expected, and he'd listened to Bach and Mozart on his own from then on.

She sniffed and blinked back the tears. The memory was both sad and somehow comforting. Klor had saved her; he'd given her a chance, carving hope from disaster, just like the Major's violin had been carved from the horrors of the Old World. She filched a look at the instrument. Elegant, attentive on its stand, the violin resembled a gleaming wooden ear. Maybe it did hear some distant music. In the digiphoto beside it, a black-haired woman in a jewelled dress was playing a grand piano, one hand lifted gracefully above the keys. In the other frame, a man, his uniform laden with medals, was standing in front of a gold-tasselled curtain. Curious, she peered closer. The man had Major Thames's hawkish nose and crescent eye pouches; the woman hir sensual lids.

'Found him.'

She snapped to attention. 'Really?'

'It is an unusual name. And the dates fit. Yes. This is certainly him.'

She jumped up, scurried across the room. 'Is there a photo?'

'Not in our records. IMBOD would likely have one. I can request the file, but under your circumstances I wouldn't advise it.'

No, that was the last thing she wanted. She hovered at the side of the screendesk, the Major seemingly too absorbed in hir investigations to instruct her where to stand. 'Does it say where he is?'

'The last address listed is in Kadingir. Nagu Six. But he has a transient history and it looks like he hasn't reported for food, water or medical aid in nine months.'

'So? Maybe he got a job!'

'There are no jobs in Kadingir. Let me cross-check the address.' The Major swiped again. 'Yes, as I feared: another family is living there now. Your father has moved on. He left the month your Shelter mother was arrested. I suspect a link.'

She tensed. This was getting dangerous. Zizi *did* know Hokma. And Cora Pollen. Astra was counting on him to know other Gaian dissidents, people who would help her get back to Is-Land – but the Major mustn't ever find that out. The Major must think Astra was trying to *rehabilitate* herself.

'Maybe he hasn't moved on,' she insisted. 'Maybe he's living with them. Or they know where he is.'

'Possibly. I will send a social worker, just in case.'

'I want to come too.'

'No, you may not.'

She was furious, anger surging like an army of black shapes through her. First the neurohospice, then the Barracks, now CONC. For how long would she be trapped in one stone institution after another, being told what to do and where to go? 'Why not?' she erupted, clenching her fists. 'He's my father. I'm not your *prisoner*.'

Major Thames stood up. Picked up the bow and pointed it back to the sofa.

'Did I say you could stand? Sit back *down*.'

Beside Astra, the Major's conch shell shone on its pedestal, the tips of its spines varnished with light from the high windows. She wanted to pick up the shell, smash it into the screendesk. But she didn't. Breathing hard, she walked back across the room to the sofa.

The Major followed. Standing on the carpet, heesh placed the bow beneath Astra's chin. The Compound Director's eyes were sunlit forest pools. Hir voice was dry as an ash field. 'Astra Ordott. Your Code father was an illegal immigrant, deported from Is-Land. You are that rare creature: a Gaian political refugee. People here will be interested in you. Some of them will be people you do not wish to be interested in you. Your family situation remains a classified matter and if I learn you have spoken about it to any unauthorised person then yes, I *will* have you confined to the compound.'

She squirmed, but the Major dug the bow tip deeper into her chin. 'When you turn eighteen you will be free to live where you please. You can remain working here, or you can apply for a tent and a hardship allowance in Kadingir. Despite my best efforts, the allowance is insufficient to cover the costs of adequate food and water in the markets. You would have to queue daily for hours for meagre CONC rations. You would not ever be eligible for a passport. Does that sound like the future you desire?'

She was so incredibly stupid. Why had she imagined, even for a second, that she could come to Non-Land and find her father? CONC, like IMBOD, was in the Southern Belt to keep the Non-Landers under control. She would have to find her father herself.

But for now, she understood, she needed to keep the Major on her side.

'No,' she muttered.

The Major lowered the bow tip. She jerked her head away, rubbed her chin.

'Good. CONC is pleased to help you. We will make discreet enquiries about your father. You will study hard and when you have reached Level One proficiency in one of the three Non-Landish tongues you may request day passes out into Kadingir, accompanied by an approved guide. And Astra, if you are at all grateful for our help, there is something I would like to ask you in return.'

Gratitude? For being locked up? What had happened to all the elation thrilling through her? How could it have just been snatched away? The fog was back. An iron gate had clanged down in her head, and the mist was stealing in through the bars. It wasn't an IMBOD trick. It was who she was – *how* she was: hopeless. Trapped.

'Astra?' The bow beckoned towards the balcony. 'Come outside.'

'I don't feel well,' she mumbled.

'There is an awning. Come. I want to show you Kadingir.'

She *was* a prisoner. She was. She couldn't escape this nightmare. She got to her feet and followed the Major out of the balcony doors.

ASAR

'*O!*'

Asar bowl hold   Sepsu spoon hold   mouth open hold
bowl round earth feeling clay and rain and strong hands wheeling
spoon hard steel feeling steel and fire and big arms hammer clanging
pudding warm sweet feeling date and milk and millet and Sepsu stirring
date sunriver treefruit *millet* stovepot earthseed *milk* motherlove sheepcream
teethsticky tonguetickle mouthsmooth feeling bellycalm worldcalm feeling
many feeling one feeling soul pudding feeling

Sepsu hand? where Sepsu hand?
    ~ more Sepsu more ~
    ~ no more Asar ~
  O spoon empty bowl empty soul full

earthfull

sunfull   seedfull

riverfull   rainfull

flowerfull   fruitfull

lovefull

eating time finish   Sepsu Asar mouth clean
~ Asar? Song bowl tent? ~
song bowl tent good feeling silk robe feet kiss feeling
big finger hard feeling

soul question asking soul answer giving song bowl tent good
soul feeling
'*Eh Eh Eh!*'
~ Good, let's go   Hat time ~
HAT?   hat hurt Asar soul   Asar hate hat   NO HAT
'*Urrrrr. Urrrrr.*'
~ Hot sun, Asar. No hat, no song bowl tent ~
'*Urrrr. Urrrr.   URRRRR.*'   ~ NO NO NO ~
~ Asar? ~
mouthword NO   fingerword NO   Sepsu no *listen*
Sepsu no love Asar soul
Asar put hat on head   hat HURT   soul hurt   soul hide
hide in belly   deep earth soul
~ stick, Asar? ~
stick hold stand up home tent leaving song bowl tent going Sepsu
arm hold NO TALK Sepsu walk walk walk fast fast fast hat hurt soul
soul cry mouth wet soul water soul drops fly
                    fall on seeds no
                    fall on souls no
                    fall on hard stone hard wood hard earth
~ soul cloth, Asar? ~
Asar stop walk NO TALK Sepsu
Sepsu soul cloth touch Asar mouth
soul cloth *too late*
Asar mouth dry earth
Asar belly dead wood
Asar heart hard stone
Asar soul empty bowl
~ WATER Sepsu ~
~ Yes, Asar ~
Asar mouth cool pool
Asar belly sweet silk
Asar heart wet flower
Asar soul clean spoon
~ Sepsu? ~
~ Asar? ~
~ I love you ~

~ I love you too Asar ~
'*O! O! O!*'
walk walk   fast fast
ramp uphill ramp downhill ramp right ramp left
song bowl tent!
HAT OFF
sun no hot   warm place   carpet soft
steps climb   cushion sit
~ Asar arms up please ~

sky   UP

sun   UP

stars   UP

moon   UP

arms   UP

Sepsu Asar armpit TICKLE

'*Arr arr arr!*' arms down Asar hand on Sepsu belly Sepsu belly jelly shake
arms up NO TICKLE home robe off Asar hot Sepsu wash Asar
yesyesyes cool skin feeling sweet milk feeling big finger grow feeling
Sepsu dry Asar arms UP silk robe slide Asar skin big finger HARD O!

big finger starlight feeling
big finger deep earth feeling
finger big soul feeling
hard big
hard big finger
hard big
hard big

~ before later now, Asar ~
yesyes Sepsu Asar knows before later now
before date milk millet pudding time
later big finger kiss time
now song bowl tent soul question time!
    ~ Asar, Chozai is here ~
    Chozai hand coconut hand big hard hairy
    ~ hello Chozai soul man ~
    ~ hello Asar are you ready for my soul songs? ~
    ~ yes Chozai Asar ready song bowl playtime! ~

  song bowls no soup bowls
  song bowls no pudding bowls
song bowls no earthrainsun bowls
song bowls goldbronzeiron bowls
far fountain empty dream bowls
  silver starlight mountain souls

Chozai song bowls play
finger stroke woodstick hit
small middle big song bowls
one two three song bowls
many feelings many songs

toes tiny leaves feeling
heart feathery nest feeling
big finger soft river feeling
head spring wind feeling
soul bird fly sky feeling

~ Asar, are you ready for a soul question? ~
~ ready Sepsu   yesyesyes ~
~ Enki is here   down in front ~
Enki no walk up steps Enki wheelchair man big arms nose knife
man   Enki talks fingerwords Enki big soul
~ hello Enki soul man ~
Enki hand date tree hand soft fruit fingers hard *palm tree palm!*
'*Arr arr arr!*'
~ Thank you Asar I dream one land one people my dream good dream? ~

O

good question　　　big question
counting question　　dream question　　one and one and one question
one and one and one is many　　many is one　　many fingers one hand
many people one tent　　many tents one city　　many seeds one flower
many steps one land　　many stars one sky　　many souls one soul

~ yesyesyes Enki good dream　　one land one people good dream ~
~ thank you Asar one more question? ~
~ yesyesyes one question many question ~
~ Enki make song party   dance party   river party   Asar come? ~
~ soul party? ~
~ yes, soul party ~
'*Eh Eh Eh!*'

Sepsu soul cloth Enki face touch Enki Asar feet kiss good feeling
feet in river feeling Enki big soul clean Enki go more people come
man woman woman man girl man man boy woman boy girl girl man
small middle big question one two three many question before later now
before pudding eating *later* Sepsu soft wet mouth hard big finger kiss!
now Asar fountain song bowl flying many many answer give!

ASTRA

Bow tucked under elbow, sun gilding hir face, Major Thames commanded the stone balustrade like a captain at the prow of a grounded ship. Astra hung back in the shade. The sun was hot and Kadingir was frightening her again. From the ramparts the city had looked a hazy human waste-land, but from here the chaos leapt into focus: a snarling, snapping chaos of honking horns, the clangour of work-beast bells, the hue and cry of languages she didn't understand. There could be no peace in this place – and no map to it either. Even the roads were disordered – a maze of dirt tracks, ramshackle boardwalks and footpaths, veining through clumps of faded tents and tin shacks, converted buses and rusted ship-ping containers, peeling hexayurts and crumbling mud huts. Apart from the spindly solar posts, the tallest structures were occasional squat apart-ment blocks, made, as if by an inept child, from unevenly stacked containers, and buttressed by awkwardly angled fire escapes. From every-where rose the faint sweet stink of sewage and the prickle of dust, lodging in her nostrils and making her eyes water.

How could people live here? She edged forward to the balustrade. Beneath her, on the dirt road circling the compound, donkeys brayed, cattle lowed, camel harnesses chimed, wagon drivers hollered at each other to back up or move over; the odd car locked in the beast-drawn traffic parped at futile intervals. In between the stalled vehicles, cyclists, gloating with mobility, tinkled their bells as they rattled over the ruts, while a group of barefoot children played football in the road. Dodging the angry shouts and flying palms of the drivers, they sent the ball thud-ding off the sides of the carts, careening through the legs of the work beasts. Meanwhile, on the boardwalks that ran along either side of the traffic, a flow of people walked or rolled by in wheelchairs, some wearing headscarves or turbans, others bareheaded, all in robes or long garments, except the children, who wore shorts and vests that even from here Astra could see were faded rags. Where were all these people going to in this foul, barren place?

'It's extraordinary to think,' the Major announced, 'that prior to the Great Collapse, Kadingir was an empty plain, a scrubby hinterland between steppes and desert, crossed only by the rare tourist wanting to break the boredom of a baking afternoon with a visit to an ancient ruined fortress. Now nearly two hundred thousand people live here, tending nearly as many animals. They eat, sleep and swelter in rudimentary dwellings transported here at huge expense and effort over the desert and the decades. Virtually everything you see here was driven from Asfar, lowered from Zeppelins or dropped from balloons.'

Major Thames's hands were resting in the sun on the balcony ledge. The skin was finely freckled like a leopard's paws and hir right Saturn finger hosted a black bevelled jewel set in a delicate gold clasp. The Compound Director thought heesh knew everything – thought heesh could order her about, lecture her, like heesh did Photon and everyone else. She might be fogged with disappointment and sunk in anger and exhaustion but she wasn't going to stand here quivering in the Major's shadow like a timid child. She risked it: another glance north. As from the rampart, she could detect movement on the screen, indistinct grey-scale images slithering along its length, but the Boundary was still unreadable: a long smudge mark scoring out the horizon, an inscrutable barricade built of steel, concrete, plasma and decades of anger and fear. One thing was certain though: the Boundary hadn't been flown here from New Zonia or hauled up from Asfar. It had been manufactured and erected in Is-Land. Before she could argue, though, a yell rang out in the street, and another. Right there, in full view, a man was steadily, mercilessly, flogging a camel with a stick.

'What's he *doing*?' she blurted. The camel was mangy, skeletal, its hide gashed with old wounds, its ratty bell harness shivering with each blow. In Is-Land the man would have been punished long ago: fined, possibly jailed, and certainly forbidden from ever employing an animal again. Here though, people were just shaking their fists at him to get a move on or standing round jeering as the camel sank to its rickety knees, closing its eyes and refusing to go a step further.

'He can't risk killing his animal.' The Major's tone was unaffected by the vicious crime playing out under their noses. 'He'll get a boy to run for some dried grass.'

Sure enough, the man backed off, dipped into his pocket for a coin and sent a child running up onto the boardwalk and down between the tents. The man sat down in the street with the camel, leaned against the beast's flank and wiped his forehead with a large white cloth. The crowd dispersed and the traffic began to trickle again in two streams around him.

'Can't you arrest him?' Astra yelped. 'We both just saw him!'

'I'm afraid not. All CONC provides here now is humanitarian aid and diplomatic services. Animal welfare laws do exist, but they are not top priority for the Non-Land Alliance. My advice, Astra, is to try not to think too hard about the animals. Maintaining life here is a constant challenge, and the beasts, I'm afraid, are part of the food chain. There is nothing you nor I can do about that.'

The man was, Astra now realised, as thin as the camel. But that was no excuse for venting on an innocent beast. Or *eating* one. She glared down at him. His handkerchief was covering his head now and he was picking fleas from the hide of the beast.

'CONC gives out grains. And pulses. People don't have to eat *animals*.'

'There is never enough food aid. Animals provide not only wool and milk but valuable protein. I know being a Gaian in Non-Land must be difficult, but you must learn to think of meat-eating as an Old World custom that can be changed only slowly or else you will go mad here.' The Major's voice was soft and tarry, as if melting in the heat. 'Astra, I want you to try and appreciate the complexity of this place and its people. They face enormous problems with great vitality, resourcefulness and an extraordinary sense of spirituality. More religions are practised here than in the average Sub-Himalayan city. Many CONC officers find that profound sense of faith difficult to comprehend, but perhaps you, with your Gaian education, will be able to relate to it.'

She bit at a shred of skin on her lip, tasted the blood. The Major hadn't a clue what heesh was talking about. Okay, Uttu did yoga, but most religions here were weird off-shoots of Abrahamism: the very opposite of

Gaianism. Countless Gaians had been maimed or died here; Hokma had lost her eye. What sort of religions allowed *that* to happen?

And yet, she had to admit as she stared out over the tents, Non-Land was not what she had thought. As a child she had imagined bigger buildings, concrete alleyways, constant gunfire, and people lurking in every shadow, burning with hatred for Gaians. But then she'd read Hokma's letter and acquired information she could still, just about, think about without triggering the pain-ball. The letter had talked about starving babies, prisons stuffed with tortured children, swamps of disease. But none of these things, either, fitted exactly what she had found here. The Non-Lander compound workers, Uttu and the other washers, were healthy, agile and strong. They were kind to her. And Kadingir, she could see now, had its charms: many of the tents, though bleached by the sun, were homely, playful, trimmed with decorative edgings and faintly tinking bells. The boardwalks had railings older people were using for support. In the mid-distance was a beer garden: people sitting around tables under umbrellas, a woman passing between them with a tray full of glasses.

A ball of confusion knotting in her chest, she watched the boy return with a bag of grass and the man feed the camel. A donkey passed dragging a cart laden with dates, the football-playing children running and screaming behind it. The cart driver laughed and tossed them a couple of branches of fruit. Other drivers shouted disapproval, shooing the kids away from their own loads, and he raised his hands: *so shoot me.*

'Eating animals isn't spiritual,' she said at last.

'The date palms are doing well,' the Major remarked. 'We funded a new plantation by the river three years ago, just south of the poppy fields, creating employment and significantly easing the malnutrition problem in Kadingir.'

The man and the camel were plodding on now. The children picked up their ball and darted across a boardwalk into the field of tents, weaving between women with water pitchers on their heads, a man on crutches, and a huddle of men in dirty white robes, smoking cigarettes and buying tea from a man in red pantaloons and a red fez. He had a barrel on his back and a tray slung on straps around his neck and was pouring the tea from a brass kettle into shot glasses. She had no idea, she realised, what to expect from Non-Landers.

'Non-Land is also an entirely unpredictable place,' the Major continued, as if reading her thoughts. 'Within the chronic historical tension stoic periods alternate with violent flare-ups. Currently, I would describe the temperature as "simmering". The one-hundred-year Hudna is coming to an end and parties on both sides of the conflict are wary of the other's intentions. Though I expect you know all about that.'

The answer was stamped in her like Code. 'To prepare for the end of the Hudna,' she said, 'Is-Land will clad the Boundary with Shelltech. Then we will raise the Shield, so Non-Land and Asfar can't attack us with missiles.'

She had said 'we'. Despite everything IMBOD had done to her, to Hokma, she didn't unsay it. She hated IMBOD, but that didn't mean she loved Non-Land, or wished destruction rained down on Is-Land. She knew now, for herself, that IMBOD didn't care who they hurt, or how. But with their nanobombs and guns, their cruelty to animals and war-mongering desires, the Non-Landers were just as bad. And even if they weren't, what could she do to fix this place? She would fight her own private battle: that was all.

Yet, for some reason, Major Thames's silence stung like a rebuke.

'The cladding operation won't hurt anyone,' she added. 'Unless the Non-Landers try to stop it.'

The Major brushed a sandstone crumb from the balcony ledge. 'The first unit of Security Generation constables has arrived in Kadingir. They are currently sequestered at the Barracks, completing their training. CONC intelligence indicates that specially trained engineers will be performing the cladding, and the Sec Gens will be charged with defending the Hem. Have you heard of the Hem, Astra?'

Of course! Every Is-Lander knew what the Hem was. 'It's the land at the base of the Boundary. Non-Landers can't go there. If they do, we're allowed to stop them.' That was called policing your borders. It wasn't war, and it didn't violate the Hudna. Even Asfar understood that.

'Indeed. Though, like women's skirts in New Zonia, the politics of the Hemline are constantly changing. Are you aware of the most recent developments?'

She stared at a solar post midway between the fortress and the river, its dark circular base of panels sucking in the sun. 'I've been in hospital. I don't know what I don't know.'

'Indeed. Well, let me fill you in. Six months ago, CONC concluded the decade-long negotiations of a new agreement between IMBOD and

the Non-Land Alliance, the democratic body which represents the interests of the people here.'

It was galling to be taught her own history. 'I know about N-LA,' she
muttered. 'They're terrorists. And CONC allows them to attack us!'

'Those, Astra, are not legally accurate statements.' The Major's tone
was even. 'N-LA is a permanent coalition of all political and religious
groups in Non-Land, and a recognised international body with a voice in
Amazigia. While certain of its members have, over the years, been
involved in violent resistance of questionable moral fibre, N-LA itself has
neither actively supported nor condemned militant activity. Rather, it
favours principles of restorative justice, dialogue and cooperation with
CONC. As a result, a full thirty-six years ago Amazigia first withdrew all
CONC troops from the Southern Belt, awarding N-LA the responsibility to self-police the region, with the right to bear sonic weapons and use
firearms in life-threatening situations.'

'I know that.' She felt hot. 'That's when the Southern Offensive began.
N-LA let loads of infiltrators build tunnels into the dry forest. That's how
come *my* Shelter sister was killed by a *suicide nanobomber.*'

'Ah.' The Major paused. 'I am very sorry about your Shelter sister,
Astra. My condolences on such a dreadful loss.'

She couldn't risk thinking about Sheba. 'That's okay,' she muttered.
'She died before I was born. But N-LA let it all happen. In Kadingir they
just stood back and let the terrorists ambush IMBOD. My Shelter
mother was on her national service. She lost her *eye.*' She stopped and
glared back down at the heaving mass of people in the street, the tension
in her chest hard as a cricket ball. Hokma hadn't blamed the boy.

The Major nodded. 'The valiant dissident Hokma Blesser. Perhaps she
told you that N-LA too were the victims of the militants, their store of
police weapons raided?'

Why was the Major praising Hokma? Was it a trap? There was no way
she was going to mention Hokma's letter. But the question rankled.
Hokma had never talked to her about the Southern Offensive, not even
when she'd studied it at school. Still, she knew the basic facts, which was
more than the Major did.

'That's what N-LA *said*,' she retorted. 'It wasn't a raid. They *let* the terrorists take their weapons.'

'That is possible, of course. But personally, I don't think so, Astra.
N-LA lost face in Amazigia during the Southern Offensive, and

significant powers. They were forced to allow CONC troops back in the region, and to enforce severe restrictions on movement. The Boundary was closed, ending a brief period of Non-Land agricultural labour in Is-Land. A mood of depression set in across the entire Southern Belt. But from that despair sprang a gradual sea change in attitude towards Is-Land. Are you aware that thirteen years ago Una Dayyani began campaigning for independent statehood?'

'Yes, I am. I studied it all. At *school.*' But again her fierce resistance to the Major's challenge masked a deep, squirming tangle of doubts and she tried to ignore that tense ball of fear. This clump of old tents and solar cables, a capital city? An Alliance that couldn't control its own fighters, a government? Impossible. 'It's a lie.' She gestured north. 'Look at the Hem. Non-Landers invade it all the time. They say they're just picking wild herbs, but they're really scouting locations to plant bombs or dig tunnels or shoot a constable. If they get their own state they'll build up their forces and attack us again. If CONC wants war to end for good, they should relocate all these people. And their animals.'

'Again, Astra, I think your fears are unfounded. On occasion Non-Landers do stray into the Hem in search of scrap metal or wild plants. Tragically, but legally, they are usually shot by snipers from the ramparts of the Boundary. Overwhelmingly, the people here are simply engaged in a long, hard struggle for survival. Weary of this limbo, they were receptive to Dayyani's proposal. Ten years ago she was elected the N-LA Lead Convenor on a platform of full cooperation with the CONC de-escalation policy, with a view to regaining responsibility for policing, and then making an official Statehood bid. Under her capable leadership, N-LA has confiscated and destroyed caches of unauthorised firearms pouring in from Asfar. Statehood is still heavily contested in Amazigia, where Is-Land has many powerful allies, but nevertheless it was past time to reward N-LA's commitment to peace. Six months ago Amazigia voted to recall the last of the reinstated CONC troops from Non-Land. Amazigia also shrank the Hem's width from 300 to 150 metres and approved new restrictions on IMBOD. Officers and constables may not use firearms beyond the Boundary itself, and neither may they venture beyond the Barracks or the Hem without CONC's written permission.'

She was aware of a loosening in her chest. IMBOD couldn't leave the Barracks? She stole another glance at the Boundary, her fingers gripping the ledge. 'But what if they do?'

'If either IMBOD or N-LA violate the Hem agreement, then all bets are off. But so far things have worked out well. There is a genuine sense of optimism in Kadingir I have not before experienced in all my six years here. Really, though, Astra' – the Major inspected her, puzzled, not contemptuous – 'I *am* surprised you hadn't caught wind of these changes, even before your quarantine. Was the vote not discussed in the news?'

It was still peculiar to reflect on life before the neurohospice, but she cast her mind back, like a frail arrow over a fathomless pit, to the far shore of school, the news, adults' conversations in Or. Faintly, it hit a target. 'Yes,' she said slowly, 'it was one of the reasons IMBOD said we couldn't trust the end of the Hudna. Even CONC was turning against us, that's what everyone said.'

'In fact, the vote was very close,' the Major countered, 'and what IMBOD doesn't grasp is that the cladding operation is deeply controversial. CONC cannot legally stop the Boundary modifications, but at a time when humanity should be advancing into a fully post-war conciousness, Amazigia does not wish to endorse Gaian isolationism. Or worse. IMBOD claims that the Sec Gens have been Coded as a strictly defensive force, but many Non-Landers fear that the cladding operation and the Sec Gen deployment are in fact offensive moves. It is all very difficult for CONC.'

The Sec Gens. Her cranium was throbbing, but the Major forced her attention. 'Astra, CONC is anticipating a sudden hike in temperature. We need to be prepared. I am aware of your existential condition. You are not Security Coded, yet you were brought up and schooled with your peers as if the Serum flowed like molten gold through your veins. What can you tell me about the Sec Gens?'

Inside her head the grey wave was swelling again. She was staring at the Mikku River but all she could see was Peat's big goofy smile, hovering over all of Kadingir. Peat was a first-year Sec Gen: he would be here soon, defending the Boundary, living in the Barracks, pestering his senior officers with questions about the laws governing this place that wasn't a country, wasn't a proper city, wasn't officially anywhere at all.

Her head was about to burst open. She grabbed the balustrade for support. She couldn't collapse, couldn't cry.

I'm TALKING to the Major. I'm TALKING to the Major. I'm TALKING to the Major.

She was managing it. Suppressing the wave. Peat's smile was fading.

Peat. Her Shelter brother. Peat and his careful mind and easy laugh; his world record at water glugging. She missed Peat.

'The Sec Gens are my *family*,' she said, her voice, humiliatingly, cracking.

'I understand.' Major Thames generously conceded the point. 'The question upsets you. But Astra, let me explain why I am asking you this. CONC provides diplomatic mediation services between Is-Land and Non-Land. We know very little about the Security Serum and so we are unable to reassure the Non-Landers that the Sec Gens pose no new, unprecedented threat to them. This uncertainty is creating rising tension, threatening to undermine all the good work of recent years. Any outbursts of violence will adversely affect the Gaians posted here as well. I am simply asking you to think about it. If you ever decide to share any of your knowledge of the Sec Gens, or the Shell technology, my door is always open. Understood?'

Peat's face was gone now. She hadn't seen her Shelter brother for nearly a year, and had only Tablette-talked him a few times from Atourne before she was quarantined and finally exiled. He might have been told to forget her. It was clear IMBOD didn't want *her* to remember *him*. But even if she drowned in the grey wave every day, she would never forget Peat. And she would never betray him, never say anything that might hurt Peat. Or Meem or Yoki. Or Sylvie or Tedis or Leaf. And no matter what Zizi Kataru said or thought, she would never defend or excuse the infiltrator who had killed Sheba. She had to slide invisibly between Is-Land and Non-Land. Find her own Hem, her own private path along the Boundary.

But for now, she also had to keep the Major on her side.

'The Shelltech creates a repellent magnetic field,' she muttered through the fog. 'It's defensive. It can't hurt anyone. And the Sec Gens are strong, but they're also calm. They wouldn't attack anyone unless they were provoked.' She winced, closed her eyes. On the word 'unless' her brand-wound had sent a needle of pain right up inside her.

'Astra Ordott, you do not look at all well. Step inside immediately.'

Major Thames poured her a glass of water. Her mouth was slack and the water drooled down her chin. She wiped it dry and set the glass back down on its tray.

Behind the screendesk, the Major frowned. 'Have you not seen the doctor?'

She was a frigging mess. The grey wave was back; her brand was flaring. But she wasn't going to see a doctor, not ever again. 'No.'

'Why not? I directed the Head of Staff to make you an appointment.'

'I told him I was *fine*.'

'You are patently NOT FINE,' the Major boomed. 'You are in exile, orphaned and friendless, recovering from a course of highly controversial neurological treatment. You are depressed, lethargic, angry, confused and in obvious physical pain. As your legal guardian, I order you to see the compound doctor today. *Photon Augenblick!*'

Speechless, she glared at the Major. Behind her, the ornate metal doors swished open. She swung round to glare at Photon too.

'Photon.' The Major lightly struck the Tablette desk with the tip of the bow. 'Can you define the Inglish word "equerry"?'

'Equerry?' The medic squinted up at the chandelier. 'Does it mean to ask a question? Or . . . to break rocks?'

'An admirable semantic effort, but no. "Equerry" is an equestrian term, meaning one who tends to horses. It later came to mean a personal assistant to a high-ranking figure. Photon' – the bow sliced towards Astra – 'Astra Ordott is such a personage. She is a distinguished political refugee, the only non-Sec Gen of her generation and an individual of mixed Is-Land and Non-Land parentage. CONC is charged with assisting her reunification with her Code father here in Non-Land. I hereby appoint you her equerry. You will instruct her in CONC regulations and etiquette and ensure she is introduced to the full range of compound learning resources. Astra's formal education has been interrupted and she must now make her own private investigations into languages, history, literature, mathematics and science.'

She was impotent with rage. She didn't *like* Photon. She certainly hadn't said the Major could tell him about her Code status. But the Major wasn't even looking at her.

'When Astra has passed a Level One Test in one of the three local languages,' heesh continued, instructing Photon, not *her*, 'you will accompany her on day trips into Kadingir. On these trips you will *not* pursue any private investigations into the whereabouts of Astra's father. CONC's enquiries about him are strictly classified information and until I say otherwise, neither of you are to mention him to anyone. On the basis of your father's name, Astra, I suggest you begin learning Somarian. Right *now*, Photon will take you straight to Dr Tapputu. Is that understood?'

'Yes, Major,' Photon smartly replied.

'Astra?'

'Understood,' she fumed.

'Splendid. And Photon?'

'Yes, Major.'

'Guard her against the dogs, won't you?'

'The dogs, sirm?'

'The *men* in this compound,' the Major roared.

What? 'I don't need protecting from men. I—'

'*Astra Ordott!* You are an Is-Lander. With the notable exception of Officer Augenblick, whose psychometric gender testing scores indicate unusually delicate empathic capabilities, most of the heterosexual men here are unlike any you have ever met. Photon, did you know that in Is-Land all adolescent males are taught to control their erections with a range of breathing, visualisation and meditation techniques?'

Photon's face was as red as one of Nimma's borschts. She had never seen anything like it. 'No, sirm. I did not. That is fascination, sirm,' he managed.

'Isn't it quite? Astra, one day I will learn more from you about your Gaian education, but in the meantime, acting as I am *in loco parentis*, I must inform you that things are rather different here.' The Major's eyes were flashing again. 'Outside Is-Land, for most heterosexual men, penetration of a female orifice is the immediate target of sexual activity, the vanquishing of rival males the ultimate goal, and a woman's psyche the prize. *My* staff operate under basic rules governing sexual misconduct, but this is not a spiritual re-education academy and I cannot account for their private natures. You are seventeen and you can do as you please; but if *anyone*, male, female or otherwise, behaves towards you in a way you do not like, you must confide in Photon. He has a certificate in psychodynamic counselling and he will advise on the appropriate response. Is that clear?'

It was. Gaia play here was crude and unevolved, and to help her adapt to the backwards conditions she was supposed to accept Photon as her Gaia friend. Everyone needed a Gaia friend: someone you confided in when your Gaia playpal was blowing hot or cold. But she preferred to choose hers herself, thank you. And besides, she wasn't going to 'have sex', as the Major called it, with anyone in Non-Land.

There was obviously no point in arguing with the Major, though. She'd learned that at least, if nothing else.

'Yes,' she grumbled.

The bow gave a smart twirl, as if the Major were signing hir name in the air. 'Splendid. Astra, it was my honour and very great pleasure to meet you. I will advise you of any progress in the search for your father, and in the meantime, should you wish to discuss any of the matters I have raised with you, I play my violin every morning on the roof at dawn.'

Photon saluted. The meeting was over. Everything had been decided without her consultation or consent. Astra flicked her hand across her forehead. Slapping hir palm with the bow tip, as if counting down the moments until she and Photon left the room, the Compound Director pointed with hir chin to the door. Like a *distinguished personage*, or a death-row convict on the way to be executed, Astra stalked, head high, out of the room.

She stepped into the ear-wringing wail of a siren. Startled, and uncertain whether to retreat or run on, she halted. As a thin blue blur came tearing out of the office, Photon grabbed her wrist and pulled her towards the wall.

'STATIONS!' The Major was practically inaudible beneath the siren but that didn't stop hirm from bellowing at the top of hir lungs. At the start of the red carpet heesh jumped on the hallway chair. 'Stations!' heesh roared again, with the extravagant arm gestures of an orchestra conductor cross-Coded with a football referee. '*Stations!*'

PEAT

'You're thinking about her, aren't you?'

They were lying in the Barracks meadow recovering from the sheep-slaughter session. Everyone else was sleeping in the sun or curled up with Tablettes and earpieces watching the IMBOD newsfeed, but Peat was lying on his back, hands clasped behind his head, staring up at the sky. The heat didn't bother him; since the booster shot he positively enjoyed being hot. But Laam was right. His mind was troubled.

'I shouldn't, I know,' he replied. 'It's just weird to think she's so close.'

IMBOD's wildscaping was impeccable: a sea of long grasses surrounded by a dense border of pines, oaks and almond trees. The meadow could have been a large dry-forest glade. But it wasn't like lolling about at home here. You were always aware that you were beyond the Boundary now, not in Is-Land any more. Those trees masked the Barracks walls, and behind them, in their hundreds and thousands, crawled the enemy.

Laam was propped up on his elbow, his body overlooking Peat's, on watch against the hidden perimeter. 'Your Shelter father said she's working for CONC. They don't do policing any more. We shouldn't meet her.' He stretched a leg over, rubbed the sole of Peat's foot with his toe. 'Anyway, she's had MPT. She'll be pacified now.'

'I know.' Peat responded to the overture, stroking Laam's foot with his own. 'But she's so untrustworthy. I just want to be prepared for anything, like Odinson said. I don't want to let him down.'

He curled his head up, chin to chest, like the start of a stomach crunch. At the top of the meadow and over the road stood the Barracks buildings. Designed by a venerated biotect – one of Ahn's mentors at college, Peat

had proudly told Laam – the Barracks were exquisitely imposing: a row
of tall repeating stained-glass buildings, their gold and green arches evok-
ing wheat fields, a forest glade, a summer crown. Behind their gorgeous
peaks rose the concrete and plasma cliff of the Boundary. Today it was
screening black-and-white footage of thunderous skies. At other times it
hosted erupting volcanoes, cascading waterfalls, twisting bird formations.
The choice of dramatic, greyscale imagery was correct, Peat and Laam
had decided: the Barracks were beautiful, but seeing Gaia drained of colour helped prepare you for the ominous bleak place beyond the perimeter
walls.

'You won't let anyone down.'

Laam had ever so slightly stressed 'you'. Peat twisted his head, studied
his friend. From the beginning of his IMBOD Service, he'd felt close to
Laam. Though darker than his younger Shelter brother – his rich loam-
brown skin was even darker than Peat's – there was something about
Laam that reminded him of Yoki: he was fit and taut, but slender-boned
and a sliver shorter than his Sec brothers, and when they'd run murmurations on the Atourne training field Laam had always taken a little longer
to regain resting heart rate than the other males. No one had taunted
him, of course, but because of Yoki, Peat had known how desperately
Laam wanted to catch up. So sometimes Peat would slow down, just a
fraction, pacing Laam to make sure he remained secure in the group.
Later, when the news about Astra had hit, Laam had reciprocated in ways
Peat would never forget.

'Hey,' he asked his friend, 'are you okay?'

Laam hesitated. His deep-set eyes with their golden topaz flecks were
shadowed momentarily by the passing cloud of Sec Gen doubt.

'Yeah. Well, sort of. I mean, I'm fine. But my Code mother's still worried about the new policing policy. I thought she would have understood
it by now, but I Flock-Talked home this morning and she was crying.'

Oh, that. Peat frowned. The Amazigia vote on policing changes in
Non-Land had sent shock waves rippling over Is-Land, and the fears of all
Gaians washing over the walls of the Atourne Barracks and into the Sec
Gens' hearts. They'd all grown up with stories of gun battles in the South-
ern Belt, and everyone knew adults who had been injured fighting
Non-Landers. To learn that thanks to the perfidy of CONC member
states they would now be defending the Boundary without firearms had
been enraging. But the Atourne Barracks had responded immediately to

their distress with a brilliant lecture. The Amazigia vote, the Head of the Barracks had said, was an opportunity for a noble victory over the savagery of Non-Land culture. One of the very reasons the Sec Gens had been Coded to excel at martial arts, she declared, was to demonstrate to the world that Is-Land was a nation of peace, intent only on self-defence, and determined to cooperate fully with CONC's de-escalation strategy. And, of course, she had continued, facing unarmed opponents was far safer than contending with guns and grenades.

This was the official IMBOD response: that the Sec Gens were safer now than ever before. Peat's own parents had been immensely relieved, but Laam's mother was the anxious sort. Laam had comforted him and now it was Peat's turn to be reassuring. He rolled over on his side. It was good to feel like a big brother again.

'Tell her not to worry,' he said confidently. 'We've had the booster shot. We're unbreakable. Anyway, the Nonners won't have guns either. If they do use firearms, the deal is off and we can use them too. It's win–win. Absolutely.'

'I told her.' Laam smiled, fingered the bump on his arm. 'She's worried I'm going to get growing pains.'

They'd had the booster shot just before leaving Atourne. Physically, Peat was feeling nothing but benefits. He'd bested all his records in training today and so had Laam, so what was his mother afraid of?

'She just likes to worry. Like some mums like to cook. Relax.' He reached over, pulled Laam close. 'You're still tense from the sheep session, that's all. Come on, let's harmonise.'

Laam embraced him, then shifted round so that Peat was spooning the smaller boy. They lay together resting, skins touching, cocooned by the warmth of sun and skin. As their breath slowly synchronised, an immense sensation of gratitude again filled Peat's chest. Code and Shelter families were difficult, but in Laam he had the closest Sec sibling in the world. They were steady Gaia playmates now, and with Jade and Robin had formed a core group that ate and bathed and slept together, spoke freely about their lives, felt each other's emotions as their own. He kissed his friend's nape, pressed his cheek against his short woolly hair. He would help Laam deal with his Code mother's anxieties. It was the least he could do. They hadn't even set foot in the Hem and already Laam had saved his life, just by being there.

At first, when Hokma had been arrested and Peat had been

Flock-Talking his family, trying to reassure them all, Laam had taken an interest in the case. Then Hokma's secret reversal of Astra's Security shot had been revealed and Astra had gone into quarantine. All during that painful, confusing period, Laam had behaved as if Astra was just ill, that was all; as if she could be cured. 'She's having counselling too, isn't she, Peat?' he would say. 'And the counselling's helping *you*.'

But it turned out that Astra hadn't *wanted* to be helped. She had refused to testify against Hokma. Then she had assaulted Ahn, permanently damaging the man's Gaia Power. The week after the news of the attack broke had been awful. Some Sec Gens had eyed him warily as he passed; others stopped talking when he entered the room. Finally Laam had told him the rumour that was zooming round the Barracks: people thought IMBOD was going to charge Astra with treason, and that had worried everyone. If Peat's Shelter sister was a proven traitor, how would his loyalty gene react? Could *he* be trusted any more?

It had been agonising. Even his Flock-Talks home were becoming terribly difficult, with Klor saying one thing and Nimma another. Astra had been sedated right after the attack, for her own good – she was *dangerous*, Nimma said, though Klor said no, Astra was just very upset, and she would surely say sorry when she realised what she'd done. Peat's head had hurt thinking about it all and his concentration had been affected so badly that the counsellor had finally said he didn't have to continue with his training; he could remain in Atourne, not have the booster shot, do desk-duty IMBOD Service while his cohort went on to Non-Land. He wouldn't be stigmatised. Everyone would understand.

Drop out of active IMBOD Service? Not have the booster shot? Not go to Non-Land? No! But how could he continue here if no one trusted him? Being asked to make that decision had triggered the worst crisis of his life. Again, Laam had saved him. That night at dinner his friend had announced that whether or not Astra was a traitor to Is-Land, she was a traitor to her family and her community. 'Peat's one of us,' he had said. 'He's a Sec Gen. He's Coded to be loyal. He doesn't deserve a sister like that.' That statement had turned the tide. Jade and Robin had agreed, and buoyed up on the warm wave of sympathy, Peat had insisted on staying.

After that, though none of the officers singled him out, he had noticed an extra emphasis in speeches about the importance of supporting each other in tough times. People had been friendly again, drawing him into games and Gaia-play sessions. The booster shot had helped too, restoring his focus and calm. When later the story had broken, that on the basis of Code tests, the former dry forest Gaia Girl Astra Ordott had been reclassified as a Non-Lander and deported to Kadingir, it had almost been like reading about a stranger. 'Hey, Peat. You okay?' Laam had asked at the table that night. 'Yup. Good,' he'd said, and reached for a slice of bread. It was right that she had gone. The whole ordeal had been a purging experience, like the sheep session today. He really didn't have to think about it any more.

He slid his arm down Laam's flank, rested his palm on the top of his buttock. You weren't supposed to Gaia-bond with anyone until after your IMBOD Service but many people did pair off later with their patrol buddies. For now, he was just glad that Laam always wanted to play with him in the woodland and never, like Jade and Robin, strayed off to join other groups. Thinking of the woodland, his Gaia plough stiffened. Laam stirred.

'Wow – that's weird,' Jade, lying beside them in the meadow, exclaimed softly. 'Are you guys awake?'

He opened his eyes. 'We are now.' Laam giggled, shifted onto his front.

'Take a look at this then, legal beagle. The Non-Landers are attacking CONC.'

'What?' He sat up and reached for Jade's Tablette.

Unbelievably, she appeared to be right.

ASTRA

Photon steered her into a long room filled with rows of straight-backed wooden chairs. Most were occupied by a hubbub of CONC officers, and more people were piling in through a door at the back of the room. Some were exclaiming hotly, but all eyes were trained on the huge wallscreen at the front.

'Hey, Rudo.' Photon greeted an officer in the second row and took the seat beside him. 'This is Astra. She has joined us from Is-Land.'

'Hey, Astra. Good to meet ya.' Rudo stuck out his hand. He was good-looking, she registered with a slight jolt: young and solidly built with oak-brown skin and smooth features, his hair razored into a neat zigzag pattern at his temple, his easy grin the first relaxed welcome any CONC officer had shown her. Rudo was no *dog*. But this was not a flirty encounter, either. The officer's natty buzz-cut reminded her – she winced – of Peat's hair after he started IMBOD Service, and the warm beam of his gaze exposed afresh her own stringy muscles and rat-eaten skull-pelt.

'Hi.' She grazed his fingers and slouched down next to Photon.

'*Shhh!*' A man in the front row turned to confront them, his pasty features rumpled with irritation.

'Eh, *calmez, calmez-vous, mon ami.*'

Rudo, she dimly realised, was speaking Francilien, but with a rough throaty twang, not at all the accent she had learned.

He switched seamlessly back to Inglish. 'Just saying hello to Astra here. Astra, Christophe. Don't worry, he's not usually this relaxed.'

Christophe jerked his chin at her. 'Is not a party, Rudo. *Il faut faire attention!*' Christophe's Francilien was quick and terse, a salvo of *tsks* and hisses. Rudo flicked a finger over his cheek. It might have been funny, except the other man's face turned puce and he half rose in his seat. She shrank back.

'Quiet at the front,' someone yelled.

Rudo chuckled. Christophe glared and turned back to the screen, his shiny white pate and crescent of straggly red hair partially blocking her view. Her perineum was crawling now. She inched to the edge of her seat and focused on the wallscreen like everyone else. A group of youths, about twenty of them, aged from little kids to teenagers, were hurling stones at a tall, grimy, oddly shaped vehicle. It was hard to see their faces, but if the clothing was anything to go by, the gang was a fairly even mixture of boys and girls, most barefoot or in flip-flops, and all dressed in various shades of purple – not a uniform, but a torn and faded selection of lavender, grape and mauve T-shirts, blouses and dresses. The girls wore long sleeves and leggings. There was no sound, just the frenetic movement of the children in the sun, bodies and shadows swarming around their target – a wonky, corrugated metal van, its jutting roof-rack laden with a giant blue water barrel, its front tyres barricaded by a spiky metal girder crossing the road. The bonnet, a boxy lopped-off pyramid, sported two round lamps like glass eyes on sticks and the blue-and-white CONC insignia: the shell rising from the waves. Above it, two CONC officers were cowering behind a low windscreen.

There was reason to be afraid. The youths were showing no sign of relenting. They were dipping into satchels and pockets, grabbing rock after rock. And there was something strange about their faces: something frightening, featureless. Astra peered closer.

The youths were all wearing masks. Their heads were covered in tight, translucent rubber socks. Holes had been cut for their eyes and mouths and their hair was sticking out in bizarre patterns. One boy had fuzzy stripes running back from his temples like a badger, another a stiff crest, and a tall skinny girl was prancing about with long black plumes whipping over her scalp. The girl's forearms were wrapped in bandages; the white dressings and her mask and strange jerky motions made her look like a malevolent doll, a broken marionette declaring vengeance on a teddy bears' hospital.

'Who is it?' a woman cried from the doorway, her fingers pressed together in a prayer to her lips.

'Msandi and Eduardo,' Christophe replied grimly. 'They have trapped them, *les bâtards*!' The camera was zooming in and the medics under fire, Astra could see, were a tall, mahogany skinned woman with soft kinky hair and a pale brown man with loose curls. Their faces were tense, the woman's arms locked on the wheel, the man gripping the dashboard. The MMU was going nowhere. A stone flew off the driver's door frame and Msandi startled, ducking and covering her face with her hand.

'Shouldn't we be helping them?' the woman at the doorway fretted.

'Do *you* like to get stoned too?' Christophe snorted. 'N-LA is on its way. *Assiez-vous*, Tisha. You make us all nervous hovering *comme un fantôme*.'

Tisha didn't seem to mind Christophe's bad temper. She took the seat beside him and the room fell quiet as all eyes followed the action on the screen. The girls were good throwers, Astra noted, leaning back and fully engaging the shoulder. Suddenly the skinny one with the snake hair and bandaged arms darted in front of the vehicle and hurled a rock directly at the windscreen. The glass cracked in a thousand directions, a glittering spider's web veiling Msandi and Eduardo's frightened faces. The camera zoomed in towards a jagged black hole at the centre of the splintering pattern.

It was a hole like the hole in Astra's head, the throbbing wound through which now, like a fierce, high tune, the pain-ball whistled, aiming right for a memory: the one that had risen and been interrupted in the Major's hallway. It was strong, intact – and worth suffering a lifetime to recall throwing the Kezcams at Ahn, sending those dense, black metal balls flying, one after another, at that jealous, vindictive, glass-hearted, child-frigging *maggot*. The man who'd betrayed Hokma, done a deal with Samrod Blesserson – who'd given his ex-Gaia partner up to IMBOD and let them *murder* her – all so he could satisfy his perverse lust for young girls. She was throwing the Kezcams at Ahn's Gaia plough and hurting him, badly: crushing his seed sacs, destroying his manhood. And now she was standing above him, a Kezcam in her hand, aiming at the shiny bald crown of his skull ...

But then, engulfing her hard, private moment of triumph, came a slow, ash-grey tsunami: Klor's voice. *You hurt Ahn very badly . . . a grievous attack . . . permanently damaged . . . you could have killed him . . . you don't understand the nature of what you've done, do you?*

The effects of the ions had obviously worn off. She was rigid in her seat. Her brand-wound was on fire and her head was reeling under one assault after another. Why? Couldn't she keep this one tiny memory, just one thing in her life to feel good about? It was *Klor* who didn't understand. *No one* understood.

No one was even looking at her. Photon's fist was at his mouth and Rudo was following every movement on the screen. She meant nothing to these people. Absolutely nothing.

Face it. *No one cared about her*. She gritted her teeth.

I'M WATCHING THE WALLSCREEN. I'M WATCHING THE WALLSCREEN.

The pain-ball rolled back to its socket, Ahn and Klor fading away as the snake-haired girl spun to face the camera – was it mounted on a post, or the fortress wall? – raising her arms, her hands clenched in victory. She was shouting, her mouth a chasm splitting the mask, her hair flailing in all directions. The camera zoomed in and scanned her skinny body. Even close up the mask obscured her face, but she was wearing a silver star on what looked like a bicycle chain round her neck and beneath her bandaged arms, the skin of her hands was mottled, flaking off in red, raw patches or raised in dark blisters. Astra winced. The condition, whatever it was, looked painful.

'*La putain de ta race!*' Christophe shouted.

'*Amateur.*' Rudo laughed softly again.

'LANGUAGE, Christophe,' a woman across the aisle exclaimed. She was an impressive figure, tall and golden-brown, with a powerful profile: a strong jaw and flat nose framed by a shiny blonde helmet of hair. Even sitting, she towered over the room.

Christophe, though, was not easily cowed. 'Please forgive me for giving a *sheet*, Honovi!' He turned on her. 'That is our colleagues in war zone. And a whole fracking vehicle out of commission!'

'That's no excuse for sexist bullshit—'

But Honovi was drowned out by a chorus of shouts. 'Shhhh!'

'Are they hurt?'

'Pay attention!' That was Rudo, snickering.

The room was in uproar. The girl danced away, punching the air again with her cracked, flaking fists. Something about her knife-thin form, her exultant movements, made Astra's cranium throb – she flinched, but no memory came.

Christophe was still gesticulating. 'Where the *frack* is N-LA?' he demanded.

'With some *guns*?'

'Hang on. We don't know what's happening yet.' A woman was entering from the back, striding down the centre aisle, her voice rising boldly above the chaos.

'Come along,' Christophe jeered. 'Do you need glasses prescription, Sandrine? They attack *us* now!'

'This is the third incident in two weeks,' another officer complained.

'And look what happened to Photon,' Tisha chipped in. Obediently, people turned and Astra stiffened. *Frig off.* Her cranium was screwed tight with tension now, the pain-ball preparing to launch. Why? She wasn't thinking about anyone she shouldn't. She *wasn't*.

I'm watching the wallscreen. I'm watching the wallscreen.

'I'm fine.' Photon waved his hand in front of his graze. 'I fell, that's all. Tell them, Rudo.'

'Funniest thing I ever saw.' Rudo grinned. 'He went down like a geeraffe on ice.'

Photon laughed, but Honovi shushed them. 'Look: N-LA's arrived.'

All heads swivelled back to the screen, where a dozen people in red uniforms had appeared. The camera pulled back to a wide angle. Wearing flak vests and helmets and brandishing chunky black guns with dish muzzles, the line of N-LA officers trod into the shot. Their guns were covering the area; some pointed up towards the nearest block of container dwellings, some across the road, but most were trained directly at the children. The kids paused, exchanged glances, then the badger-headed boy nodded and – *ZING*! – the girl with the bandaged arms threw a stone, right at the centre of an officer's chest.

A bright white flare shot across her skull. It was the girl: the prancing snake-haired girl was triggering the pain-ball. *But why?* Through watering eyes she followed the stone's flight across the screen. The CONC officers around her grunted as the man took the impact, his shoulders caving in, flak jacket absorbing the blow. Beside him, a female N-LA officer raised her gun and took square aim at the prancing girl.

Cheers went up from the front row.

'Go *get* 'em, girl.'

'It's not a *Tablette flick*, Christophe,' Sandrine demanded.

Astra stopped breathing. The officer squeezed the trigger.

But the girl didn't fall to the ground. No black poppy of blood bloomed in her chest. Clasping her mask-muffled ears, she reeled backwards, away from the vehicle. *Why did she look so familiar?* Was it the way she held her elbows?

The pain-ball caromed on. Between the white explosives and the tears she could barely see, but she stayed grimly latched onto the screen, watching the N-LA officers marching forward, all squeezing their triggers now, sending the kids scattering into the alleys, clutching their ears, kicking up dust and wheeling out between the tents. One of the girls was suffering a massive nosebleed, her slick red fingers pinching the bridge as she threw back her head to staunch the flow. Behind her, a younger boy staggered to a halt, bent double and pulled up his mask to vomit. An officer took a menacing step towards him, threatening another dose of the gun. Under its sights, the snake-haired girl dashed over to the boy, grabbed his arm and dragged him away, shaking her other fist in the air.

The way she hurtled about? Kicked up the dust? Punched the air? It was no use; the pain-ball slammed again and again, shattering the memory before it could form.

'Atten-*shun*!'

For a second she could see Major Thames's tonsils.

Instantly, the CONC officers jumped to their feet and saluted as from the wallscreen the Major roared on. 'There has been an *incident* at the main gate. The Non-Land Alliance has *dispersed* the threat and the besieged officers are being escorted to the medical clinic. I have raised the Alert Level to *Three*, where it will remain until further notice. This is the third and most serious such incident in a week. Rest assured that CONC's diplomatic response to the matter will be *promptly escalated*. Officer Venice, report to my office immediately. Everyone else, return to work. In accordance with Level Three protocols, recreational passes are cancelled and mobile teams are to revert to desk duty. *Now!*'

The words reached her, barely, through a blizzard of pain. Watching the girl had triggered what felt like the worst pain-ball attack yet. She sat nailed to her seat as the Compound Director's face dissolved into a CONC HQ screensaver and people got up, noisy with relief and annoyance.

'Sonic boom bang. Works every time.'

'What about the River Raven, man? First night out in weeks!'

'It's getting worse. They'll have guns themselves soon.'

'N-LA's losing control. If this keeps up I'd rather have IMBOD back on the streets.'

'Good to hear we going to practise our diplomacy skills for next *hostage crisis*.'

'Give it *up*, people.' Sandrine, cutting in. 'The gun-running stopped years ago. These are children we're talking about. *We* ought to be able to stop them! That's our job, isn't it? To negotiate peace?'

Sandrine, Christophe, Rudo, Honovi: all these people jabbering as her head imploded.

'Peace?' Christophe, scoffing. 'They train there kids as *hashassins*.'

'They're just kids.' Sandrine, persisting. 'Kids everywhere throw stones.'

'They are all in a uniform! Someone is to organise this. *C'est fou!* Why to attack the people that help you?'

'They're *angry*. They want *justice*, not CONC sticking plasters. All *we* do is take in their washing and push opiates down their throats.'

'I work *all the day* to bring them clean water—'

'Hey.' A woman's voice – Honovi. 'Is Astra okay?'

'Astra?' Photon, his hand under her elbow. 'Let's get you to the doctor.'

The doctor. She hadn't the strength to resist. She stood. Everything went black. The last thing she felt was her knees hitting the floor.

UNA DAYYANI

Bzzzz. Bzzzz. Meh! Meh! TRING TRING. *Bzzzz. Bzzzz.* Meh! Meh!
TRING TRING.

Her work Tablette was swarming like a River Road scooter rally, her
personal device was bleating like a randy old goat, her screendesk was
trilling with emails, status updates, newsfeed reports, hotline calls. But
she had known for weeks this crisis was coming and from the tips of her
gold nails to the top of her game, she was rising to meet it.

Bzzzz. Bzzzz. On her work Tablette: Chief Superintendent Odinson.
TRING TRING. On her screendesk: Major Thames, at last.

Resplendent in her most sumptuous robe, the crimson silk folds
draped around her proud curves, N-LA Lead Convenor Una Dayyani
clasped her hands together and pressed her pinkies in a minaret to her
lips. Someone should take an official photograph of her now, she mused:
her square bodice embroidered with the tree of life, the emblem of her
people, her ample bosom hosting an oasis of delectable fruit and nurturing shade. Yes, it was a classic pose: sunlight swirling down from the
aperture in the ancient mud dome above her, a pale cone of light veiling
her deliberations in a timeless haze. That was the glory of the Beehive.
The ancient edifice created its own offices of light – and temperate ease.
The domes trapped the day's heat and her entire government could work
through the hottest of days without blotting their screendesks with a single droplet of sweat.

Everyone except Marti, that is. At the adjacent desk, Una's personal
assistant had stopped typing. From beneath the girl's powder-blue

headscarf and pinched brow those cinnamon syrup eyes implored her:
Please, take the calls.

Marti was perceptive, but still too timid and anxious. She didn't
understand the games you had to play with these people. 'Put Major
Thames on hold,' she ordered, putting the young woman out of her misery. 'And message the Barracks. Say I'll return Odinson's call in a minute.
Artakhshathra—' She addressed her star researcher, also edgily eyeing her
now. 'Be a sweetmeat, won't you, and fetch me the Mujaddid's knife?'

Marti fingerswiped and Artakhshathra wheeled off to the display case.
Una opened a drawer, put her hand on her purse. Should she wear the
scarf? Marti had been correct: adopting a turban for formal occasions
had increased her support in certain Karkish quarters. It also didn't hurt
to remind CONC and IMBOD that Una Dayyani carried the pomp,
swirl and weight of centuries of tradition on her broad shoulders.

But CONC and IMBOD also needed to know her authority didn't
rest on her conformity to custom – quite the opposite. The Dayyanis
were a secular family, their professional and political success founded on
respect for all Non-Land religions and strict obeisance to none. She dug
past the scarf for a comb and ran it through her thick bob: still black,
mostly, even after all these sleepless decades.

'Here you go, Una.' Artakhshathra was back, handing her the ceremonial dagger the Mujaddid had presented to her when she last visited
Asfar. She took the black engraved handle, unsheathed the curved knife
and slapped the engraved blade against her palm.

Artakhshathra smiled. As intended. The Major might not be able to
see her hands, but her core team needed a show of strength from the
Lioness. 'The Major's ready when you are,' Marti piped up.

'Battle-ready, my sweetmeats, battle-ready.' She tapped the call button
and the CONC Director's remarkable face filled the screen. Major
Thames, Una thought again with approval, knew how to work a look.

'Major Thames,' she purred.

'Lead Convenor Dayyani. What a spot of bother CONC has found
itself in. We do appreciate the leg-up. Please forward my highest acco-
lades to your Head of Police. Indeed, to all your fine staff.'

Pronouns might have had to be invented for hirm in four languages,
but after hir predecessor, Major Thames was a treat to be savoured.

'Not at all.' Una graced the conversation with one of her infamous
smiles. 'This is our mission, after all. The Non-Land Alliance exists to

pursue restorative justice by means of cooperative action.' She ran her thumb down the sharp edge of the blade, lightly testing the point. Marti and Artakhshathra were waiting for her to twist it home and the Lioness would not disappoint. 'But Major, true co-action requires all parties. I trust you now agree it is time for an Emergency Diplomeet.'

Indeed. The Major was on message: heesh had already spoken to the Barracks, a time and date were quickly set and the call ended, a bloodless victory, with an exchange of empty pleasantries. Una resheathed the dagger and rested it beside the tray of Asfarian sweets on the uneaselled plane of her screendesk. A sumptuous selection, the tray was part of a fresh delivery of gifts from the Mujaddid, driven hundreds of miles north over the windsands to arrive just in time for the crisis. She eyed a condensed milk and pink coconut roll. She *had* just worked rather hard . . .

Marti waited for her to finish licking her fingers. 'Shall I place the call to Odinson now?' she begged.

'Let him stew.' Una brushed a coconut shred from her robe. 'You've got a harpy or two to redeem, my girl.'

Marti raised a wan smile. It was their new joke, in play since Odinson's last, most astonishing, call to Una. They were fulfilling the Prophecy. Una was Istar, of course, charging her chains with the anger of ages; Marti was her vizier, and Artakhshathra was greasing the chariot axles. From his screendesk, her favourite young man cracked a grin.

'You can start with my mother-in-law, Marti,' he offered.

'No, Artakhshathra,' Una replied smartly as she typed up a quick email to her Chief of Police, 'we need *her* to tear out Odinson's tongue when we're done with him.'

Artakhshathra smirked, but Marti's smile was crumpling. Una sent the email and nudged the tray across the divide between the desks. 'Come, come, don't neglect your pleasure centres.' She passed over the dagger. 'No hogging, mind. Make sure there's enough for everyone. We don't want anyone flagging today.'

It worked. Despite herself, Marti was distracted by the ravishing array: pistachio honey balls, crushed sesame cakes, shredded pastries, nougat squares, glorious glazed almond and apricot clusters: Asfarian chefs knew all the old recipes. With a little funding from the Mujaddid – currently under discussion – a sweet factory could soon be established in Kadingir. Why should these delicacies be import only, far too expensive for the average Non-Land child?

'Split a nougat?' Marti offered Artakhshathra. The girl unsheathed the knife, worked the blade through the sticky confection, and they each took a half. Mouths oozing creamy sweetness, the tray continued on its rounds and the pair returned to their duties: her core team, close to their leader's side, co-managing this crisis as around them dozens of N-LA convenors and staff attended in an orderly manner to the everyday stuff of government. To the reassuring background hum of the Beehive, Una dictated a Comchan press release, spoke handsfree to her Chief of Police, delegated action points and answered a text from her husband about tomorrow night's dinner party: Defrost the whole lamb, Beloved. Two! We'll invite the Beehive, or have the meal here if everyone's working xxx

Hopefully that would suffice. After thirty-nine years of marriage to a political *force majeure*, the man still got flustered if he thought domestic plans might change. But just as she had learned to forgive that long-ago dalliance with a big-hipped soapseller, he had, finally, learned not to compete with an emergency. The Bull is charging to the market for spices to rejuvenate his Lioness X, he replied, freeing her to shoot off encoded messages of congratulation to her ears and eyes in the Singing Bowl Tent and the Youth Centre: her own young allies who had first alerted her beer-tent agents to YAC's existence. Since then, in exchange for a few trinkets and meals, the youths had kept her informed, not of Enki Arakkia's precise plans – so far she had not managed to place an observer at the heart of his circle – but of the rapid transformation of the ex-morpheus addict's peacock displays of discontent into an eruption of open talk against the Non-Land Alliance.

Thinking of Arakkia, she frowned. Did this beardless boy and his lug-head companion have any idea what it took to create a responsible government commanding international respect? No, Arakkia was a typical hot-headed youth, peddling hollow slogans, dreams long ago scoured out by the wind. Well, he had banged his rusty tin cans together long enough. Una Dayyani was not going to let him torch the fires of open rebellion and start the whole futile cycle of violence again.

'Are you ready for the Barracks call yet?'

Marti had a spot of icing sugar on her cheek. Una briskly wiped her own to alert her. 'No, Marti.'

Marti dabbed her cheek with a hanky. As always, it matched her head-scarf. That little touch spoke of a deeply organised nature. It had made the crucial difference at interview. 'But we said a few minutes—' the girl beseeched.

Bzzzz. Bzzzz. She checked her work Tablette, arched a brow. *See?*

She let it ring thrice more. The maximum number before voicemail kicked in. Marti's expression crumpled – the girl should be careful; anxiety was ageing. On the third ring, Una picked up – on speakerphone. He might think he was wooing her privately, but apart from her intimate grooming, Una Dayyani had no secrets from her core team. And even then, she and Marti had a running joke about wax strips.

'Chief Superintendent Odinson. My apologies for keeping you waiting.' No harm in reminding him.

'Lead Convenor Dayyani.' Oh, the familiar joy of Odinson's sycophantic sneer. 'I gather from Major Thames I will have the inestimable pleasure of your company soon.' Odinson spoke Asfarian like a true adept: the dagger on display, but sheathed in the most bejewelled and ornamented scabbard.

'*So* kind of the Major to arrange it.'

'IMBOD too, is no stranger to goodwill. In light of current events, my colleagues and I thought it timely to ask if you have pondered any more on our generous offer?'

It was her father who had dubbed her the Little Lioness. It was still hard sometimes to refrain from tearing the heads off those who angered her. But Kusig Dayyani had taught his daughter well. Lionesses who stalked the longest won the richest prey. 'We have no need to reconsider our position,' she stated, dry as a bone in the firesands. 'Nothing has changed. And as long as I am occupying this office, nothing will.'

'I beg to differ, Minister.' Here it came, Odinson's contempt, slipping cold and steeled out from inside his elaborate politesse. 'Many things are changing, and rapidly. Need I remind you that the girl is here? As I have tried to impress upon you, we at IMBOD have done our best to neutralise the threat she poses to stability in the region, but we did not have her long enough. If those young hooligans of yours get their hooks into her, unless you have some solid political gains to offer your people, you'll have the fight of your life on your hands. Is that what you want? An uprising of religious fanatics? Civil war? When you could have peace and prosperity, and a name that resounds down through history?'

An IMBOD officer thought to mock her people and their faiths, to taunt her with her own family's bloodline, the Dayyanis' indelible commitment to the Non-Landers of the Southern Belt? At their desks, Marti and Artakhshathra were still as pillars. She drew herself up. 'I think, Chief Superintendent, you will find that I already have that name—'

'With all due respect, Lead Convenor, your noble name is gathering dust. *I* am offering you the chance to indeed become the mighty red-robed woman who saved her people from slow extinction: Una Dayyani, fulfilling the destiny of the great Dayyani clan, first to arrive back in the region, first to set up—'

He had gone far enough. The Beehive itself had been reclaimed from the toxic desert by her grandfather and donated to the nation by her father and she was not going to sit in it and be traduced by her greatest enemy.

Now the Lioness roared. 'You *gravely* underestimate the insight of my people, Odinson. We venerate our own icons; we do not need to *adopt rejects* from Is-Land. And nor do we cut deals with *land thieves* and *murderers*.'

Her declaration echoed around the Beehive. Within their gentle spills of light, her staff turned to admire their queen: with a swipe of her golden claw, the Lioness hung up on the Head of the IMBOD Barracks.

'Fantastic,' Marti gushed. 'We've got him running scared.'

But despite the mud-cooled air, Una's brow was prickling. Last month Odinson had called out of the blue, claiming this Ordott girl was the embodiment of that old pre-Abrahamic Prophecy all Non-Land children knew by heart: the ancient cuneiform hymn to a Star Girl, a placeless warrior who would make all places one. If Dayyani didn't come to a quick settlement with IMBOD, this child, he threatened, would destroy all her plans. The man, of course, was squirting arrogant tripe; the girl was just his empty war rattle. No Non-Lander in their right mind would venerate a *Gaian*. If anyone embodied the Prophecy, it was Una Dayyani, hence the splendid new office joke. Nevertheless, as her husband liked to remind her, Odinson was not mad. He was as hard and well-seasoned as an old cast-iron skillet and she needed to keep three steps ahead of his games.

'This girl,' she snapped, as Marti offered her a hanky – the angel kept a stack of clean white embroidered ones in her drawer. 'What's the latest on her?'

Artakhshathra answered. She had assigned him to track the case because the young Farashani was a genius at winkling documents out of CONC's hard drive. 'Astra Ordott is working in a menial capacity for

CONC, he said, swiping his screendesk and bringing up the file. 'As far as I know, she hasn't even left the compound.'

She patted her forehead and tossed the hanky in her purse drawer. That was as she had expected. 'Sensible child. She must be in shock.'

'She's been granted political refugee status' – Artakhshathra was studying the file – 'which makes her eligible for a CONC passport. According to their documents, Odinson's right: she's got a Non-Lander father, so if he turns up she might choose to stay here with him.'

A Gaian Non-Lander in Non-Land? This girl was going to be indelibly confused. *And perhaps*, she considered, *Odinson was right: easy prey*. Not for YAC, but some grizzled idealist stud. She sighed. 'Who's he, then?'

'His name's not on record, but if she was born in 69 RE, he must be one of the last returnees. That was a relatively small batch. I can investigate all the men if you like.'

Returnees rarely ended up well: they couldn't fit in. Other people were envious or suspicious of their time in Is-Land, and after sampling the flesh-pots of Atourne they found it hard to settle into decent family life. Unless Farashani, the women were unmarriageable; they often retired to a simple desert life, while the men ended up in the beer and sex tents. No, she shouldn't be worrying. This precious Gaian girl would undoubtedly not wish to stay with her Non-Land father.

'Hopefully, he's out in an oasis town chasing widows,' Una said crisply. 'If that girl has an ounce of wit, she'll be off to Neuropa in no time.'

Marti was twiddling with the corner of her headscarf. 'Maybe we can offer her a scholarship?' she mused. 'To one of the Neuropean universities? We could say it was our way of supporting political refugees?'

She bestowed her most munificent smile upon the girl. This was the beauty of teamwork: you had a problem, and someone else solved it. 'That, Marti, is a wonderful idea. Make a note and I'll talk to the Major about it.' Her own daughter had been transformed by her time at university. It was a shame about that dolt husband of hers and the six children he'd left her to bring up – but still, some of the Dayyani females had to reproduce.

'Now.' She raised her voice. 'Where's that sweets tray? The core team will need a little nougat fuel if we're going to start drafting my Diplomeet speech!'

ASTRA

'What a morning, yes?' Photon commented brightly.

Astra, caged between the knees of CONC officers, didn't reply. San-drine and Photon were on either side, Rudo opposite. The three had carried her here and revived her with cool water and now she was ignor-ing them, staring out the window at the line of blank blue sky above the washers' courtyard. The pain-ball had retreated, but the fog had returned, a damp grey shawl draped over her thoughts. She didn't want to see this doctor, but she didn't have a choice – she couldn't live out in Kadingir on her own. She was at the mercy of the Major. Probably the doctor would be under orders to prise her mind open, extract all she knew about the Sec Gens, Hokma, her father.

'Why is Christophe so *obtuse*?' Sandrine sighed. 'Does he have no pol-itical understanding whatsoever?'

'He's a *Francilien*, Sandrine.' Rudo chuckled. 'They got all that revolu-tion business out of their system a long time ago.'

'Hey—'

'Don't worry, Astra.' Rudo winked. 'I'm from Mount Reality. *Je suis autorisé*.'

'Christophe is right about one thing,' Photon intervened. 'It *was* frightening today. The kids who threatened us did not have such masks.'

'We were in the outskirts.' Rudo's arm was slung over the next seat back, his legs widely crossed, his body taking up altogether too much of her vision. 'No cameras. These purple-patch kids know what they're doing. That'll be going out worldwide now.'

She should be preparing a story for the doctor, but they were talking so much she couldn't think straight. A door opened and Photon jumped to his feet.

'Msandi. Eduardo. Are you all right?'

'Hey, guys. Yeah. Just a bit shook up.' Msandi grimaced.

'Not a scratch, *amigo*.' Eduardo clapped Photon's shoulder. 'Don't worry. You're still the poster boy of the CONC martyr brigade.'

'More like the clown brigade.' Photon touched his forehead. 'Rudo and I, we had only a brush with few little kids with pebbles, really. But I was to slip and my head hitted with a gate. It was ridiculous. Truly.'

The officers laughed. *Ha ha ha*. Everything was so jolly now. Perhaps they would finally forget about her and leave her alone. But no such luck.

'We're here with Astra,' Sandrine explained. 'She's joined CONC from Is-Land. Photon's showing her around.'

Msandi smiled. 'Careful, Astra. Photon's our star danger ranger.'

She interlaced her fingers in her lap. Let them flirt with each other.

'Welcome to Non-Land, Astra,' Eduardo tried now. 'You've arrived at an exciting time.'

'It'll get a lot more exciting than this,' Rudo said, 'once those bleeding Sec Gens arrive.'

Photon coughed and Astra cringed. Was he going to tell everyone she was a *distinguished political refugee*?

'Sorry.' If there was one thing Rudo wasn't, it was sorry. 'Don't they bleed?'

That threw Photon. 'Yes, of course they do. Msandi' – he switched conversations – 'Astra's not very well.'

'No, she doesn't look good,' Msandi said. They were all examining her now. Perhaps she should oblige by retching into her lap?

'Astra Ordott. The doctor will see you now.'

Saved by the receptionist. Surely Photon wasn't coming in with her? No. Thank Gaia, he stayed with the others as she rose and stalked into the doctor's office.

'Astra Ordott.' The doctor spun round in his office chair. 'I'm Dr Tapputu. How marvellous to meet you at last. Sit, please, sit. I hear you've just had a nasty fall.'

The doctor was not what she had been expecting. He was dressed in a long black robe, for one thing, not a CONC uniform. Probably loose clothing was more comfortable for him: he was rather fat – well, stocky – though his long face and sharp jawline didn't show it. More unusually, where doctors were usually serious, reserved, conservative-looking, this one had a moustache and a goatee, both grizzled grey like his hair, and sported a blue, green and orange geometrically patterned brimless cap. His office didn't smell of pine or lemons, but was spicy, like mulled wine. And unlike any doctor she had ever met, he appeared to be genuinely delighted to meet her. Behind his rimless rectangular glasses his golden eyes were sparkling, and deep-grooved fish tails creased his olive skin.

Those eyes were like amber lights at a crossroads: a warning. She sat down and directed her attention to the toes of the doctor's boots. Peeking out beneath his robe, they were resting on a circular wooden platform fitted over the wheels of his chair. The doctor was very short, she realised – so short that staring at his adapted furniture was probably incredibly rude.

'I had a migraine,' she declared airily to a spot to the left of his head. 'Because I was in the sun. Otherwise, I'm fine.'

'Ah. Migraines can be very painful, can't they? With multiple triggers. Let's see if we can isolate yours.' Framed by his outlandish whiskers, the tip of his tongue flicked over his fleshy lips as he read her file. For the first time in ages, someone in authority was ignoring her. Furtively, she scanned the room for clues to the doctor's intentions.

Like his cap, the office was making a great effort to be cheerful. A wallscreen displayed a cartoon slideshow of fruit and vegetables, most of which the CONC kitchen only served from tins, and on the desk was a digiphoto of three happy children. A small rubber toy was clamped to the frame – a skinny orange yogi with a long white beard and topknot, doing dog pose. Behind him was a carved wooden shelf of pretty bottles, elegant shapes with glass stoppers, filled with jewel-tinted liquids. The place was like a kindergarten. Maybe she had been wrong – maybe this impish man didn't have a clue about IMBOD.

'Astra,' he said at last, regarding her kindly, 'you've joined us from a neurohospice: three months' MPT followed by three months' recuperation. Shall we talk about that for a minute?'

Empty? Oh, MPT. She tensed. 'There's not much to say,' she stalled. 'It was a bit boring.' That was true. It *had* been boring, at the end.

Dr Tapputu smiled. He had long yellowish teeth, set like pegs in his mouth. 'I'm sure that it must have been exceedingly tedious, yes.' Then he fixed her with that amber gaze. 'But short courses of memory pacification treatment can have severe consequences. So tell me, Astra, apart from the migraines, are you experiencing any unusual aches or pains?'

Straight in, trying to trap her. As soon as she admitted to the slightest twinge, he would give her an injection or pills, some kind of truth serum designed to untap her memories of the Sec Gens for the Major's files.

'I only had one migraine,' she demurred. She had to be canny: the doctor obviously knew things about her treatment – things she ought to know too. 'But if I did get other symptoms, what would they be?'

The doctor pressed his stubby fingertips together. He wore a ring on the little finger of his right hand, a lapis stone in an engraved silver setting. The stone matched the blue in his cap. 'That's a complicated question, Astra. Outside Is-Land not much is known about MPT. IMBOD maintains that it is a form of controlled meditation, producing unpredictable neurological side-effects in only a tiny minority of patients. I expect that is what you were told, was it not?'

His Inglish was advanced and oddly accented but she understood what he meant. She hadn't been told anything but what was happening to her head was the opposite of unpredictable. It had been ruthlessly planned.

'They said it would make me more peaceful,' she offered. 'They didn't mention any side-effects.'

Dr Tapputu's eyebrows lifted a notch: *And did you really believe them?* She kept her face blank. He abandoned his thoughtful steeple, shifted his bulk and leaned forward a conspiratorial fraction. 'Astra, I've taken a considerable interest in MPT over the years. A handful of patients like you have found their way to the outside world, and gradually a small body of knowledge is building up about the treatment. A recent paper argued – I must say quite convincingly – that the so-called side-effects of MPT are in fact deliberately engineered. The paper claimed that, far from being a meditation, the treatment is intended to deter people from having certain thoughts. Does that make sense to you?'

She didn't like how close he was. 'I don't know. I only had a short course.'

'That's very lucky. According to the paper's authors, a long course of MPT can erase years' worth of memories from the patient's mind.' Like a magician performing a trick with a coin, the doctor snatched at the air near her ear and spread his palm: empty. She glowered, and he crinkled his eyes and continued, 'But a short course is dangerous too. A short treatment targets particular memories with powerful aversion responses. If the patient later tries to access those thoughts, they will generate terrible pains in her head. On the available evidence, it seems that repeating a simple mantra is the only way of blocking the response: hence the illusion of a meditation technique. I'm afraid to say that it also appears that if the patient resists and keeps trying to retrieve those memories, long-term damage can result. Astra.' He contemplated her keenly. 'Really, you must tell me: are you experiencing any unusual aches, pains or mood swings?'

Long-term damage. Her mouth was dry. '*I don't know!*' she erupted. 'I don't feel great, but I didn't feel great before the treatment either. That's why they *gave* it to me.'

She had wanted to blast the doctor straight out of the window, but he remained there in front of her, fleshy, immovable, even pleased.

'I understand,' he murmured, 'it's all very confusing. That's to be expected, Astra. But it's important for us to investigate.' His voice was warm, sympathetic, *inviting* now. 'Different responses have been reported. Some are physical: migraines, or acid reflux. Others are emotional. A sudden, powerful feeling of heavy depression, for example. Though I expect that a spell of depression would be normal in your case.' He paused. 'Major Thames sent me a note this afternoon. After coming all this way, it must have been very disappointing to learn that your father has gone off the radar.'

High alert. Her cranium throbbed. The last thing she wanted to talk about was her Code father – as soon as she did, the doctor would have got her. There was no way she could control a pain-ball attack in front of him.

She faced him down. 'The ion curtain helped my migraine today. If I get another headache, can I just go and sit in the Major's hallway?'

Dr Tapputu wasn't smiling any more. He was intent, glinting: a doctor through and through. 'I know this isn't easy, Astra. Ion treatment could be useful, yes, but self-medicating in the Major's lobby is not an option. The grave danger is that if your symptoms go unchecked, you could become seriously mentally ill. You see, some ex-MPT patients refuse to accept the restrictions on their thoughts. They keep trying to access the forbidden memories, believing they can manage the pain with the use of the mantras. For a while this works, but the pain always returns, and eventually it starts occurring automatically – randomly, even – and then controlling it becomes a full-time job. Some patients become permanently bad-tempered, or entirely focused on what others would call trivial information. Others become religious zealots. In all cases, capacity for critical thinking is significantly impaired. This, of course, is one meaning of "pacification". The person might not feel at peace, but they are completely wrapped up in their own suffering and no longer a threat to society.' The doctor paused. 'In some cases, Astra, the patient begins to self-harm, or even ends up committing suicide. If you ever have any such thoughts, you must tell me, immediately.'

She froze, for here, marching through her head, came the two skull-scarred women in New Bangor: stalking through the market, muttering angry imprecations to Gaia, chastising Hokma on the bus to Sippur. And with them came the grey wave and the pain-ball, slamming through her head, both at once, short-circuiting each other with a dazzling, skull-splitting flash—

She was vaguely aware of her diaphragm, somewhere far beneath her, gulping air, but she could not move, could not see. She was trapped in her head. Trapped in this chair. Blinded by an explosion in her head, lost in a storm of white shrapnel that, as she took a harsh dragging breath, resolved into the sphere of light.

Then there was peace. Yes, *peace*. With the sphere of light came a delicate calm. She was floating now, up through a sweet blue-and-white tower, little shells and bits of glass twirling round her as she rose, up, up to the sky . . .

'Astra? Are you all right? Astra? Has talking brought up some memories? Astra. Wake up!'

Someone was shaking her arm and she gripped the chair's armrests and jerked her eyes open. FRIG IMBOD. She *wasn't* going to kill herself. She *could* control this response. That was what the doctor had just said; it was exactly what she had learned how to do.

I'M TALKING TO THE DOCTOR. I'M TALKING TO THE DOCTOR. I'M TALKING TO THE DOCTOR.

Her lips were moving and he was staring at her but she didn't care. The sphere of light dimmed and the mist rolled in. 'I'm fine,' she insisted. 'I'm just tired from the laundry, that's all.'

'Astra.' The doctor spoke firmly. 'You've just manifested some very alarming symptoms, as if you suddenly went into shock, a trance state, or migraine aura. Look, I've only read about MPT and I suspect it might be very difficult for you to talk about what's going on with you right now. But I need you to listen: on your file, there's a list of contra-indicated medications: common antidepressants and analgesics that IMBOD claims will worsen your condition. IMBOD claims that only morpheus will help you. But I am extremely reluctant to prescribe you an opiate. The Southern Belt has more than enough morpheus addicts. And' – he paused – 'much as it pains me to suspect any doctor of wilful ignorance, according to the authors of the paper I mentioned, far from hurting you, the proscribed medications will in fact weaken or even eliminate the various aversion responses.'

It took a moment to understand what he was saying. 'IMBOD is *lying*?'

He spoke slowly. 'The authors don't say that, no. Perhaps IMBOD is simply behind on their research. Do you trust me, Astra? I am a doctor, and on the basis of this consultation, I am diagnosing MPT side-effects. Straight after you leave here, you will take your Tablette to the pharmacy and pick up the prescription I'm going to give you.'

Doctors. Whatever they told you, whether it came with a velvet voice or an iron boot to the head, you were their little experiment. Dr Tapputu would force-feed her a bag full of pills then he and the Major would track her reactions, wait until she was pliable, passive, cooperative, and squeeze her like a dirty rag for every last drop of information they wanted. Then they would throw her away. She wouldn't take his pills. She *wouldn't*.

'What about the ion curtain?' she repeated stubbornly. 'That helped me.'

'Our facilities here are limited. You can't squat in the Major's hallway whenever you please. You are entitled to one ion-glove session a month, but that is unlikely to provide anything but fleeting relief.'

She was silent. A movement on the desk caught her eye. The little orange man was changing position on the digiframe, stretching his long legs up into a headstand.

'Your thing is moving,' she muttered.

'Excuse me?'

She jerked her chin towards the photo. 'Your toy. It might fall off.'

'Ah.' He cocked his head and smiled. 'You mean Sri Auroville – don't worry, he never falls. Sri Auroville reminds me to do my yoga, so I am centred and not easily blown away by a *mergallá*.'

Dr Tapputu looked as though a cyclone wouldn't blow him even an inch. 'What's a *mergallá*?' she asked.

'A desert spirit. They fly very fast over great distances and whip up the wind to help or hinder us.' The yogi's beard was hanging over the photo. The doctor stroked it with his finger. 'Sri Auroville is a great mystic. He comes with me whenever I travel into the Belt.'

She shifted her weight onto her right buttock. Her head was clearing, but her brand had started to tingle. If she was lucky a *mergallá* would come and whisk her away one day, tear her apart and scatter her over the firesands.

On the digiframe, Sri Auroville slowly spread his legs apart. She could swear his upside-down face winked at her.

It's all right for YOU, she wanted to shout. *You're a frigging bit of rubber and circuitry*. She used to be good at yoga but if she did the splits now she'd be screaming in agony. Why? Why should she be stuck doing sun salutations with an old woman when she used to run marathons, do martial arts, Astanga?

'What I need,' she declared, 'is some anaesthetic spray. For a skin thing.'

'Ah. Can I take a look?'

She regretted the move already; now she had to explain, without saying anything about the Sec Gens or the Blood & Seed. 'It's between my legs,' she mumbled. 'A laser brand. I got it at the neurohospice. It itches sometimes.'

'IMBOD branded your genitals?' His eyebrows shot up to the ceiling. She had done it: she had shocked the doctor. He took a moment to recover. 'There's nothing about that on your file. I would most certainly like to take a look if you don't mind. I can ask the receptionist in if you want a woman present.'

If you don't mind. She barely had a mind any more. And the fewer spectators the better. There was a trolley in the corner of the room. She climbed onto it, lifted her robes and stared up at the ceiling. He clumped across the room, pulled up a chair and examined her.

'It's a circle with a triangle inside it. Is it . . . the symbol on the *flag*?' He still couldn't quite believe it, she could tell.

'Sort of.' To an outsider the brand would look like the Shield, but IMBOD had filled in the triangle, blotting out the central pillar, so that any Is-Lander would know she wasn't a Sec Gen. 'I thought it had healed in the neurohospice, but it's started hurting again.'

'I'm not surprised. It's blistering, and in a most unusual manner – almost a grille pattern. Have you checked it with a mirror lately?'

Freak blisters. Why wasn't she surprised? And why would she want to look at her Reject stamp? 'No.'

'I'd like to take a swab. There may be a viral cause.'

He swung away for the equipment. The pain on contact was searing, but he replied to her gasp with a shot of spray and the relief was instantaneous. She inhaled. The air was blooming with a strangely familiar scent. She sniffed again and an image of a plant sprang into her mind: sage-green stems with purple flowerets, slender-leafed and swarming with bees. A hand reached down to pick a stem: an old, freckled hand adorned with an emerald ring.

Nimma, the grey wave murmured. She had to stop this. She sat up and rearranged her clothes. 'That's lavender,' she said loudly. 'And something else.'

The doctor was back at his desk. He twinkled at her, and lifted two of the pretty bottles from the shelf. 'My own blend: six drops lavender and three of teatree added to a local anaesthetic. The scent will soothe your spirit and help you sleep.'

Essential oils. The herb garden in Or. Nimma's aromatherapy tealight burners. The grey wave was swelling uncontrollably, looming and crashing, as the doctor typed. She sat, eyes half closed, legs limp over the edge of the trolley, tears filling her eyes as the truth washed through her.

She wouldn't be okay on her own. What Dr Tapputu had said was true: the attacks were getting worse. They were more frequent, and sometimes random too – like this morning, with the baby's dress. What if she got the pain-ball every hour? She wouldn't be able to work, or go out into Kadingir or find her father. In the end she'd either turn into a mantra-spouting work-drudge, like the women in New Bangor, or she'd kill herself. IMBOD had won.

Dr Tapputu was typing again. 'The tests will take a couple of weeks. I'm afraid I don't know if you can get the brand removed here.'

It didn't matter. No one was ever going to see it. 'I just want the spray.' She paused. CONC wouldn't force the pills down her throat, would they? She could take them for a little bit, see what happened – she could stop any time. 'And I'll take some head pills, too,' she mumbled. 'In case I get another migraine.'

'Good, good. I'm sending you the prescription. We'll start you on a low dose – but if you experience any adverse effects we'll stop right away.

These medications work very quickly so you should be feeling much better very soon.'

Her CONC Tablette vibrated in her bag: the prescription had arrived. 'Now, how about condoms? Have you been given your supply yet?'

'I don't need condoms.'

He tsked. 'My apologies. Dental dams, then?'

Oh, the doctor must think she preferred women. 'I don't need any of that. I'm Coded against STIs and my hormone implant works for ten years. Anyway, I'm seventeen. Everyone here is too old for me.'

'Ah, yes, of course. But Astra' – the initial hint of amusement sobered – 'while Is-Land has done a remarkable job of eliminating STIs, elsewhere in the world those viruses and bacteria are still gadding about from human host to host. And they have a nasty habit of mutating. We get the occasional outbreak of MAIDS here, so if you change your mind, or meet anyone your own age, I advise using a barrier method. You can pick up anything you need at the pharmacy next door. You can also book ion-glove sessions there. You don't need a partner – a solo session will be very therapeutic for you.'

His eyes were shining at her again. Amber lights weren't always a warning; sometimes they were a signal to prepare to move. She nodded.

'Good. Now, Astra, it's vitally important that you keep your brain limber. You must make a real effort to explore, to learn new things. Can you tell me how you're going to do that?'

IMBOD was trying to destroy her – was she supposed to go out dancing? But the doctor was waiting, and he wouldn't let her go without some sort of promise.

'Major Thames appointed Photon Augenblick as my guide,' she said. 'I'm going to learn a Non-Landish language and then he's going to show me around Kadingir.'

'Excellent.' He scanned her arms, much as the Head of Staff had done. 'The laundry is a good place to practise your languages but I'd like to see you doing more mentally demanding work.' He swivelled back to his keyboard. 'I'm going to email the Major and recommend that you're transferred to something more intellectually challenging as soon as possible. In the meantime, I want you to talk to a wide range of people, and attend as many compound cultural events as possible. That's doctor's orders, got it?'

She didn't want to chit-chat with CONC officers. She didn't want to spend her life in the compound. She wanted to be out in Kadingir every day, looking for her father. The answer dawned on her like the sun over the firesands.

'Dr Tapputu? Could you recommend that I get trained as an MMU driver? To help the medics?'

'A driver? That position's rather dangerous right now.'

'But there's going to be diplomacy,' she said, wheedling. 'Major Thames said. By the time I'm trained things will have settled down.'

'Well . . . You're clearly motivated.' He re-examined her file. 'And the MMU job involves all sorts of skills.' He rubbed his ring. 'Photon Augen- blick, you said?'

She nodded, holding her breath.

'All right, Astra. I'll see what I can do.'

Yes! She could play this game, keep one step ahead of everyone else. '*Gúañarñu*,' she said, hopping down off the trolley. Might as well practise for her Level One test.

Dr Tapputu laughed. '*Namsaga-mu*,' he replied. Then, as she reached for the door handle, he added something she didn't understand. 'Enjoy Non-Land,' he translated, smiling. 'My country is your country.'

It took a moment to sink in. 'I didn't know,' she spluttered. 'Your Ing- lish is so—I thought Non-Landers spoke Asfarian if they—'

He waved aside her embarrassment, replying warmly, 'Ah, but I'm an old goat. I trained in Yukay, back in the distant era when CONC funded promising students from far-flung oasis towns. Now I manage the Treat- ment Wards for my people, and look after all those who come to visit us. You are most welcome here, Astra. And if there is anything I can help you with, you must just let me know.'

She had just shown a Non-Lander her brand. She had let him prescribe her pills IMBOD said would harm her. She didn't know whether to glare at the doctor or cry, but he was still smiling at her, this small man, as short as a ten-year-old, as colourful as a regional carpet, as solid as a basalt mountain.

She opened her mouth then closed it, nodded and tugged at the door.

MUZI

The clouds were gathering. There would be rain, tomorrow, if not tonight. The sheep would stand in it without complaint – he thought they enjoyed a warm shower – but he would prefer shelter. He had better fix the roof of the watch-hut today. Last time it had stormed the planks had leaked; he'd since gone to the scrapheap with his uncle and found some old tin sheets to patch them with, though he hadn't yet nailed them on. Hammering meant using his CONC hand. It was good being able to do two-handed things, of course, but he didn't like CONC hands. All the ones he'd ever been given were clunky and heavy and ugly. And the rubber suction sock over his wrist made his skin sweat and itch. He left the CONC hand in his bag as much as possible.

He'd worn it when he'd fixed the fan flower he'd found in the earth, though: he'd used the adjustable fingers to grip the base of the stalk while he'd scrubbed the frame clean of rust. The electronics had corroded and fused after decades in the soil, but he and his uncle had replaced them, and some parts of the mechanism, and now the fan worked. He could use it on hot nights, his uncle had said, plugged into the solar panel at the watch-hut. Or he could sell it and put the money towards his wedding. He didn't want to do either. As a fan, it was very noisy – it would be much better to recondition an old wafter for the hut. And he wasn't getting married, at least not soon. No, the fan flower was special. He would keep it. His grandmother had been delighted with it, called it a wind-maker, a *mergallá* machine, told him he should put it in the service of the sky-god. Perhaps, he thought, he should make the watch-hut a sky-god shrine.

There were a lot of things to decide and much hammering to do, but right now he was still lying on his back, sky-wondering. *Did the sky-god,* he thought as the grey clouds huddled above him, *approve of the youths in Kadingir?* His uncle and father didn't. They thought the youths were beer-addled louts, a morpheus-crazed street gang. Attacking a CONC medical unit – *three* medical units – was mindless violence. What if there had been a patient inside?

His grandmother had clucked in reply; the youths were sick themselves, she said. They were ill and poor – misguided. She saw children like that every day on the bus on the way to work: beggars, with no one to look after them. Oh, one day she was going to take a wet cloth with her on the bus and scrub all their grubby little faces clean. She was lucky to work for CONC, his grandmother had declared, as she so often did. She would donate more of her wage to the hospital now, she had decided, to help youths like that.

His uncle had raised his voice then: 'Foolish woman! Your grandchildren need money for school. Your grandson needs money for a wife, a new house! Do you want him to take her to live in a sheep hut?'

It's not a sheep hut, he'd wanted to say, but his father had started arguing again too, although more reasonably than his uncle, trying to settle the fight. The street children might be misguided, he said, but N-LA had to stop them. Who knew what the youths would try next. They only had to throw stones into the Hem and all hope of peace would be lost. No, left unchecked, such reckless behaviour would only bring ruin. He thanked the gods Muzi was not part of this shameful stupidity.

Muzi wasn't sure what he thought. He would wait and see, he decided. If the rain was a sad, gentle mizzle, then yes, the sky-god was weeping for the foolishness of youth. If it blew like swirling grey sheets in your face, lashing your eyes, then the sky-god was punishing the arrogance of youth. But if the rain was his favourite rain, hard and fierce, plummeting down in great splashing torrents that drenched the ground and made the roof drum, if the rain went on for hours, causing small green leaves to sprout like a carpet all over the scrubland the next day, and the rooks to fly over from the riverbanks, digging their beaks into the damp soil in search of grubs and worms – then the sky-god was celebrating the defiance of youth, crying with anger and joy, sending a sign that the rebellion would flourish and grow.

That was what Kishar hoped for too. 'Muzi, Muzi. Listen to *me*, scrublands brother, not that cranky old uncle of yours,' his friend in Kadingir had demanded yesterday, calling on his Tablette to talk through recent events. 'These youths are game-changers, I'm telling you, kicking down CONC's door, telling IMBOD that the new generation of Non-Landers will *never* give up on our dreams.'

That was the way Kishar liked to speak now. He listened to rhymers, and went drifting. He had invited Muzi out tomorrow night, to a Star Party organised by this group. He would pick him up, he said, in his car, and they would drive to the party along the River Road, skating and sliding and swerving all the way.

Drifting was good. He had done it once, riding on the car roof, the wind ruffling his hair, with Kishar at the wheel and city girls screaming out the back windows. Kishar said drifting was even better in Asfar, where the roads were smoother and wider and the sand finer. They would go there together one day, he said, as brothers. But going anywhere now with Kishar was difficult, even just to the other side of Kadingir. Muzi had to be up at sunrise for the sheep, to hold their heads between his knees while his mother and aunt did the milking, then after breakfast to drive the herd to the field and watch them all day. He couldn't be tired when he looked after the sheep. Sky-wondering was one thing, but if you fell asleep in a hollow and the sheep scattered it took hours to herd them back together. And what would happen if a ewe stole a lamb, or fell into a hole? No, school was finished and he was needed here now. He was lucky his family had sheep. His father and uncle both said that if N-LA achieved statehood, sheep-herders would prosper greatly.

He had tried to explain all that to Kishar. His friend had laughed, said he would take Muzi to the party just for an hour or two, and bring him back in time to sleep. Maybe he would go. He would decide tomorrow. If he didn't, he could meet Kishar in a beer shack after dinner some time. He liked doing that. And one day he would go to Kishar's wedding, and Kishar would come to his.

His grandmother was talking more about his wedding now. There was a girl at work she wanted to bring to meet him. She was very excited about this girl, but Muzi's parents and uncle were not. He knew they'd all been arguing about her, but they'd stopped when he came in the room. He'd asked his mother about it later in the kitchen, where she was crouched by the fire making flatbreads. He'd thought perhaps the girl came from a Code-sick family, but the disagreement was far more interesting than that.

'The girl has no parents,' his mother had said at first, then she'd sighed. 'She's from *Is-Land*, Muzi. She's a Gaian. We know nothing about her family, just that she wasn't brought up properly.' She'd slid the paddle under the bread and flipped it on the skillet. 'She's not *pure*, Muzi. She will have known other boys. You don't want that. But your grandmother won't listen! She says the girl is good and strong and quiet and if she's not pure she can be cleansed in a ritual.' She'd shaken her head. 'It's one of your grandmother's foolish dreams. She thinks if you marry this girl, you can go with her one day and live in the old house again. But the girl won't want you. She's a Gaian and they don't get married. But your grandmother won't take no for an answer. She's been going on and on about it, making your uncle angry.' She had slid the paddle beneath the bread, and tossed the golden brown disc onto the pile in the basket. 'I say we should invite this girl for lunch. You can meet her, and when she says no, we can forget all about it. That is my view, and I am your mother. Your father is coming round to my way of thinking.'

A girl from Is-Land. Who had been with other boys. He was still thinking about that. Probably she had kissed someone. All the girls at school had wanted to be kissed. He and Kishar had obliged a few. He had even felt Nina's breast, right in broad daylight, at the back of the bus: he'd slipped his arm around her, under her armpit. Nina had slit a hole in her robe to let his fingers through – that didn't mean she shouldn't get married. Only a cruel braggart would tell a girl's fiancé that he had touched her breast.

But what if this Is-Land girl had behaved like a ewe in heat? Offered her rump to be mounted?

He smiled at the sky-god. Is-Land men didn't eat meat. What kind of lovers could they be?

As for the Star Party, maybe he would go, maybe he wouldn't. He would let the rain and the rooks decide.

ASTRA

'I thought there was a water shortage in Non-Land,' she remarked. It was late afternoon, two days after her doctor's appointment, and pouring with rain. She and Photon were sitting under an awning in the officers' courtyard, drinking iced mock juleps and watching the raindrops splash and bounce as the water sluiced away through the drains. You could probably make tea with the rain, Photon had joked, it was so hot, but though Astra's robes were sticking to her skin and she didn't find the medic's jokes very funny, there was something fresh and uplifting in the air. Not being in pain any more made an incredible difference.

Dr Tapputu was right: the head pills worked. She'd slept for twelve hours after taking the first dose and the next day, though she felt groggy, she hadn't had a full-blown grey wave or pain-ball attack, just the occasional burgeoning pulse in her cranium. She kept taking the pills, four doses over the day, feeling so much better by the evening she'd even managed a couple of hours of Somarian lessons on her Tablette in her room. When she'd turned off the light that night, she'd indulged in long fantasies of hurling javelins through Ahn's pigeon chest and thwacking Samrod Blesserson's head off with a cricket bat. She had thought about the dancing girl too, trying to locate the memory, but nothing had come. Then, finally, she'd summoned images of Klor and Peat and Hokma, everyone at Or. That's when she'd learned that the grey wave had masked a deeper pain: a terrible hollow feeling in her stomach, as if she hadn't eaten for days but was nevertheless about to throw up. She didn't like that so she had turned on the light, switched on her Tablette and returned to her lessons.

The spray was working too, drawing the heat from her brand-wound.

Every day she had more energy and clarity. She was cautious about celebrating, though. Did the pills also contain a truth serum? Had Photon
been instructed to pump her for information? If so, he was obviously taking the patient approach: he certainly hadn't been shadowing her every
move. Following the announcement of the Emergency Diplomeet, the
Major had lowered the Alert Level and the medic was back on his driving
route. Yesterday she'd declined his invitation to eat dinner with him and
the others; telling him she still needed to recover; she'd taken a spelt pas-
try up to her room. But if she was to get out into Kadingir she'd have to
accept Photon's guidance. So today she had agreed to meet him in the
officers' courtyard after work and go for a compound tour.

This courtyard was bordered on three sides by the new wing and had
blue awnings instead of colonnades. It had been a garden, Photon had told
her, but there was no water for lawns now so it had been paved over. As
well as the beer shack, the rec area boasted a hoopball court and a ping-
pong table. The only remnant of the garden was a large potted date palm
in the centre, thirstily soaking up the torrents. It was almost as if Gaia was
as much a prisoner here as she was, a furious cellmate urging: *Stay alive*.

Photon giggled. 'I know it seems not so much a shortage when it rains.'
Then he sighed. 'The region was previous good to live in. But the Old
World peoples fracked the aquifer and now the rain and river water does
not suffice. It is an extra bad luck for the peoples now.'

The shine went off the rain. Hearing about toxic groundwater was like
learning about an extinction and anger flooded her automatically: a
sharp, uncomprehending anger at the people of the Old World who had
nearly killed Gaia.

'CONC should have put all the frackers on trial,' she said tightly. 'And
the oil junkies.'

'*Ja.*' Photon slipped into his native tongue. 'But then nearly everyone
who survived the Dark Times would have been in jail, I think. Except for
the Gaians, most Old World peoples did bad things for the planet.'

Photon's sandy lashes fluttered. He was trying to be nice, she registered, paying Gaians a compliment, but she didn't want to talk about
being a Gaian. And if this conversation continued it would soon turn
into an argument. CONC's amnesty for fossil fuel abusers had let far too
many governments and corporations off the hook. CONC should have
fined them all at least, bankrupting the frackers to pay for the planet's
regeneration.

The silence lengthened. At the next table a group of officers burst into laughter. She glowered. Yes, okay, the Gaian *freak* was in the courtyard. So deal with it.

Photon coughed. He leaned over, lowering his voice. 'Look, Astra, about the Major's office – I wanted to say, please don't to worry about the men here. The Major is just anxious because . . . because of things that happened under hir predecessor. But that was five years ago and now there is a whole new crew of officers, with psychometrical testings, and thanks to the Major we have ion gloves too. Men and women are getting on very well. Normally, the only sport is made on the hoopball court.'

This was *appalling* – would he shut up, please? 'I wasn't worried about the men.'

'No, I know. Good.' He crossed and uncrossed his endless legs. 'And please, you don't have to tell to me anything you do not want to. But I do have a certificate. If I can help with any emotion – I mean, cultural differences – I am here. That is my job, I mean.'

The guy was getting as flustered as a feather duster in a cyclone. This had to stop. 'Can we start the tour?'

'*Ja*. Good idea.' He slid his half-finished julep towards him.

Watching him drain the glass, she felt a twinge of impatience, and a pinch of guilt. Every time Photon opened his mouth he put his tanker-sized boot in it – but maybe she had been a little testy. If he was her equerry, she was going to have to try to get on with him. 'Is "ja" Karkish?' she asked.

'Oh!' He set the glass aside, ran his hand through his shock of white hair. The wound on his forehead was just a scratch now. '*Nein* – I mean, no, Alpish. I am from Alpland. It is my habit.' He smiled his wide smile. 'You are speaking Inglish very well. I think you can learn Somarian very quickly.'

She had always been good at languages, better even than her school marks suggested. Hokma had reminded her before each exam to deliberately get some answers wrong. 'I did eleven years of Inglish,' she muttered, standing up. 'And Asfarian. And in Year Ten I did a comparative study of French and Francilien. So I know when Christophe is being rude.'

Klor's grandparents had been Alplanders, but she didn't want to tell Photon that.

He took her into the new wing, built sixty years before when it became obvious that Non-Landers were not going to leave their camp outside the

Boundary and a permanent CONC presence would be required. Initially, Photon told her, the compound had housed over a thousand CONC officials. Now that the police forces had left and CONC only provided aid and diplomacy, many of the rooms had been turned into recreation facilities: the dining hall she knew already, but he now showed her the gym, the saunas and the meditation and yoga studios.

'The windows are barred,' she observed in the gym.

'*Ja.* Not to keep us in,' he recited solemnly, 'but to keep the conflict out.'

Not to keep *him* in. 'Can I see the ion gloves?'

He brightened. 'Yes. They are in the old fortress. And the Reading Room too.'

He took her down a narrow windowless hall, dodging Food Aid officers wheeling trolleys of grain sacks and Water Techies lugging armfuls of lab equipment. The cheerful traffic made Astra feel tense. Tunnels were for sacred journeys; they were to be navigated with awe, not brisk greetings and jokes. At last they emerged into the lobby, at the foot of the main staircase. Photon took the steps two at a time. At the top, he pointed down the red-carpeted hall to the chair the Major had stood on during the alert.

'The ion gloves are in the hall opposite the Major's office. They are always occupied, but when you book a session with the clinic, they will send you all the instructions. I think the first time they connect you, it takes some time to get permissions. But then it is all fine and you and your partner can just coordinate your dates over email.'

She frowned. She'd thought an ion glove was like the curtain, a kind of lightsauna, but he made it sound like a communication device. 'It's a Flock-Talk room, you mean?'

Now he was perplexed. 'You do not have ion gloves in Is-Land?'

'No.'

'Oh. Some tech the Gaians do not possess.' The fact pleased him, like a good-luck pebble for his pocket. 'It is an ion curtain room,' he explained, 'but data-configged to web-pair with others. The ions are reading each person's thermal mass, to duplicate it in the remote location. There are holo-cameras and microphones for to project your image and your voice. So as well as the benefit of the de-stress, you and your partner can enjoy intimacy. It is a very nice technology. My partner says I will seem awfully *gross* when I get home!'

He giggled, but she didn't get the joke. 'It is a pun in Inglish,' he crowed, 'and nearly funny in Alpish too.'

Photon had a *partner*? She toed the carpet. 'Where's the Reading Room?'

'Exactly this way.' He turned and led her down the opposite hall, away from the Major's wing, around a corner and into a long, high room furnished with rows of screendesks and big comfy chairs. Sandrine was curled up in one, chuckling to herself over her Tablette. Reading, arguing, even walking down a hall, Sandrine always seemed so frigging happy. Astra didn't try to catch her eye.

'This area is all for quiet use,' Photon whispered. 'The language lab and chat cubicles are through that door.'

Her CONC Tablette had a global internet connection but she hadn't tried it yet. She'd been afraid: first of the pain-ball, and then of being sucked into a white sugar-rush of misinformation, trivia and gossip. Online connectivity, Klor had always said, was like a powerful drug; and while Is-Land had wisely decided to strictly regulate that drug, other world governments, even CONC, still happily let their citizens overdose. Internet junkies were, in their way, worse than oil junkies, Klor had taught her: oil was pure poison, but there were plenty of safe substitutes so it was both possible and *essential* to quit entirely. But the internet was a necessary evil, vital for global government and educational purposes, as well as a useful social lubricant, in small doses. Web-users weren't necessarily going to destroy the planet, but it was much harder for them to manage their addiction. Like alcohol, a set limit per day was civilised. Over-indulgence in inaccurate websites, tendentious comment threads and endless pornography had, however, been proven to lead to the severe degeneration of the human intellect, senses and emotions. Based on that evidence, IMBOD carefully monitored content and conversations on its national service, and severely restricted access to the world wide web.

But it was IMBOD that had been spreading misformation: about MPT. Astra stared at the officers at the screendesks, themselves staring at the screens. The room was quiet except for the *flickety-clacketing* of their fingers on the keyboards. Above their heads, tall windows gave a view of nothing but the rain through white metal grilles.

'Can I have an internet tutorial?' she asked. 'I've only been on Is-net before. It's not as complicated.'

Photon was delighted. He took her into a chat cubicle and powered up the screen. After she'd logged in, he took the mouse and clicked on a white shell: the CONC browser. The compound homepage opened. 'So. First thing: privacy settings. CONC will never be watching you, but maybe somebody else is hacking your account, so change your password often. Also, at the end of a session, click here, and all your browsing record disappears.' He hovered the cursor over a sidebar menu. 'The main sites we are all using are Comchan, Archivia and ShareWorld, of course.' He giggled.

ShareWorld was another joke she didn't get. Comchan was the CONC news channel, broadcasting global and local reports, including constant reminders of compound regulations and Alert Level updates from Major Thames. She watched it every mealtime in the dining hall. Archivia was CONC's world history-remembering project; that was interesting. The Is-net encyclopedia, Gaiapedia, sometimes cited Archivia pages, but the links didn't work unless you had an IMBOD password. Archivia, according to IMBOD, was in general a dangerous distraction. For one thing, its holdings were mainly useless: badly corrupted recovered digital files and scans of flood-sodden or fire-damaged books. The issue was also philosophical, Klor had explained: even if all the libraries of the Old World had survived, there was no point trying to reconstruct the past. That was like trying to resurrect someone who had died in excruciating pain, knowing that you couldn't cure their illness and would just be condemning them to death all over again. No, the important thing, Klor had said, was to *evolve*: to learn to live in new ways, working with Gaia in the here and now, and consciously regenerating with Her into the future.

She had always believed that was true. But many things she had always believed were, in fact, lies. She clicked on the Archivia tab.

The site was far more than she had thought it would be: not just a nostalgic Old World history book, but also an ongoing record of the Regeneration Era. All official CONC documents were stored here, Photon told her. Many were password-protected, but under the transparency mandate, a lot were on public access. He showed her how to find the CONC manifesto, annual statistics, Diplomeet minutes and project reports – not only from Amazigia, but from CONC compounds all over the world.

'What about Is-Land?' she asked cautiously. There was a CONC office in Atourne. Maybe it would hold some information about Zizi, Hokma, Cora Pollen . . .

He clicked through to the page. There, above the home bar, were the CONC symbol and the IMBOD Shield. He opened a couple of drop-down menus. 'Is not so interesting, really. For transparency all IMBOD officers must be listed, but all the good stuff is heavily password-protected. So many meetings are discussing Code work and national security.'

She would check it herself later. But surely there must also be information about Is-Land on the global internet. 'What about non-CONC sites? How do I get to them?'

'*Ja*, sure, so many.' Photon opened another tab and over a dizzying quarter of an hour he showed her how to search for international media outlets, governmental websites, e-book libraries and language labs. Then there were blogs, games, chatrooms and photostreams, even – Photon coughed – female-friendly porn. Klor was right about one thing: the global internet really was a floating continent of rubbish.

'Thank you, Photon.' She hunched over the keyboard. 'Can I start my Somarian lessons now, please?'

He had some Tablette work to do and was happy to leave her there, alone in the cubicle where no one could look over her shoulder. She opened the language lesson, then opened another tab and typed 'Zizi Kataru' into the search engine.

The Major was right: her Code father did have an unusual name. It got one hit: an Archivia link, though not the list of Kadingir residents; that must be for official use only. She clicked, her heart in her throat. Might she at last see what he looked like?

There was no photo, just the minutes from a Diplomeet about deportees. Zizi's name was one in a list of about twenty. She scanned the page, but it was a short section. The deportees had applied for CONC political asylum, like Klor had done for her, but they had been rejected. CONC had argued that as Non-Landers, if they felt unsafe in the Southern Belt, they'd be entitled to Asfarian passports. Through their lawyer they had rejected this option, for in taking up Asfarian citizenship they would lose their right to return to Is-Land.

That was it? She returned to the search engine, stared at the screen, then typed in her own name.

Again, there was just one Archivia link, and the minutes of the Major's decision to accept her application, though the papers themselves were password-protected.

This was getting frustrating. She *existed* – she was an international criminal, for frig's sake! There had to be some information about her on the global internet. She searched 'Hokma Blesser' next, but got nothing except religious sites. 'Ahn Orson' gave her a New Zonian newsjournal story about his biotecture prize for Code House, but that was *years* ago. 'Cora Pollen': global pollen counts and news from a small town in New Zonia. Was there nothing? Had not the thinnest trickle of information about Hokma's arrest, her death, squeezed through the Boundary? What about you and your bloated ego, you fracker, she thought, stabbing the keyboard.

'Samrod Blesserson' hit gold: three pages of Archivia links. The first URL took her to an announcement about the Sec Gens, and a list of Officers responsible for their care. There it was, his loathsome name – but the announcement was just IMBOD PR about healthy, happy children, nothing about rooting out imposters, neuropunishing them, killing your own sister, all the stuff Blesserson actually did.

She returned to the links. They all looked Sec Gen-related – but no, one was different; the Archivia URL was conccompounds/Nonland/ ourpartners/IREMCO.

IREMCO. That was familiar. She frowned. The page was half empty, but beneath the banner it read just: 'CONC are pleased to work closely in the region with the Is-Land Rare Earths Mining Corporation, coordinating our food, medical and shelter aid in Zabaria with mine officials.'

Other than that there was just a list of names. Dr Samrod Blesserson was a Board Member.

She sat back in her chair. IREMCO. She remembered now: the Is-Land Rare Earths Mining Corporation was based in Atourne. It operated Shelltech and Tablette mineral mines in the steppes, the ash fields and the barren mountains. Representatives on a recruitment drive had visited her school when she was in Year Eleven; they had given an inspiring talk about mining. Gaia, they had said, had hidden Her oil and rare earths for a reason: human beings weren't supposed to harvest them like fruit from a tree. Mining should only be done when absolutely necessary. It was essential to manufacture Tablettes: like fire and the wheel they were cata-lysts for human evolution. Even oil had served a purpose, accelerating scientific and technological progress. But just as we shouldn't use fire to burn down each other's houses, or wheels to run down people or animals on the road, the Old Worlders should not have allowed oil production to continue until the Ice Cap had melted, and now we should not permit workers to get sick from mining rare earths. IREMCO, the reps had said, worked closely with Is-Land Coders to guarantee human immunity to any increased radioactive threat their operations might pose. Her classmates Tedis and Fox had been very excited by that visit and they had signed up for Year Twelve engineering specifically to work with IREMCO in Atourne after their National Service. They'd been hoping to get executive positions, with travel perks to New Zonia.

It was exhausting, having a big memory emerge, but not painful, in her head at least. Her stomach hurt a little, thinking of Tedis, but she pushed away thoughts of his beautiful body, his strong embraces. She could look at 'female-friendly' porn on her Tablette if she felt the need for all that, but right now she was researching. The IREMCO reps hadn't mentioned Non-Land – and what was Blesserson doing on the Board of a *mining* corporation?

She was staring at the screen when her Tablette vibrated in her pocket, announcing an email. The sender was the Major.

Dear Astra Ordott,

It was my infinite pleasure to meet you the other day. My apologies for the delay in following up on your Family Reunification request; you will understand that I have had competing claims on my time. I have now placed enquiries through the Nagu 6 Social Work team. Unfortunately, they report that the current inhabitants of your father's last known address claim no knowledge of him or his current whereabouts. I have alerted all CONC aid offices in the Southern Belt and Below the Belt to our search. If and when your father makes himself known again to CONC, he will be informed of your presence here and requested to contact me directly. Take heart. I am sure he will appear eventually.

Meanbetimes, on the advice of Dr Tapputu I have approved your request to be trained as a CONC MMU driver. You will begin office training with Officer Sandrine Moses on Redday and when you have completed Level One Somarian you will take driver-training with Officers Photon Augenblick and Rudo Acadie. The Head of Staff will supply you with a uniform. Along

with your team, you must attend the Emergency Diplomeet
tomorrow afternoon.

I will be in touch again when I have more information about
your Code father. <u>Until then, I expect you to continue to treat
your Family Reunification request as a classified matter,</u>
discussing it only with myself, Dr Tapputu and Officer
Augenblick. Any breach of this condition will threaten CONC's
cooperation in the search, and may jeopardise your political
refugee status.

Yours etc,
Major Akira Thames

She read it twice. *The best we can do?* Zizi was out there somewhere.
Why couldn't she make her own enquiries? What was the point of learning Somarian if she couldn't ask Non-Landers questions? Wasn't she even
allowed to ask Uttu? The Major was a frigging control freak. She didn't
need hirm, or any of these people. She should leave this place as soon as
she could – get a tent and live on grass and rainwater, anything to be free
of this prison.

There was a knock behind her and she jumped. Photon and Sandrine
were waving at her through the glass door of the cubicle. Her heart fluttering, she shut down the search engine tab and let them in. 'Hey, did you
get the Major's email?' Photon brandished his Tablette.

'Yeah.' The officers were crowding the small space, towering above her.

Sandrine was grinning too, her big white teeth gleaming like a dentist's
screenposter. 'Congratulations, Astra. I'm really looking forward to
working with you.'

'And you come to the Diplomeet, too, yes?' Photon sounded enthusi-
astic. 'That will be so educational.'

There was a brief pause. Were they waiting for her to say thank you?
But they hadn't given her the job . . .

'We should celebrate, hey?' Sandrine said, more to Photon than her.
That was understandable. Astra was being awkward, she knew it, but she
couldn't help it: these people had just sprung up behind her, interrupting
her private angry plans with their happy-happy faces.

'*Ja*,' Photon agreed. 'Astra, if the Diplomeet is successful, Rudo and
Sandrine and I are to go to the River Raven tomorrow night. I did not say

before, because you have not got your Level One Somarian yet, but if we are a team, maybe the Major will make an exception. If you like, I could try and get you a rec pass.'

Her face was hot. Sandrine was probably thinking what a liability she would be in the office – that the doctor and the Major had just taken pity on the Gaian monstrosity; what a total nightmare it would be to train someone who couldn't even speak, who needed people to babysit her the whole time.

She had to say *something*. 'Thanks,' she managed.

'Great.' Sandrine's handsome face conveyed only satisfaction. 'Let's go for a team drink before dinner then, shall we? We can grab Rudo off the hoopball court.'

A team drink? Surrounded by the officers there in the courtyard, laughing huddles, pretending not to stare at her?

'Erm.' She hunched into herself. 'Can we do it tomorrow? My head still hurts. I was going to take dinner to my room again.'

Photon looked disappointed, but Sandrine just shrugged. 'Sure. Rest up, Astra.'

'Okay. See you tomorrow then.' Photon gave another little wave.

They left the cubicle and she stared after them, then turned back to the screen, but her concentration was gone. Her head didn't hurt, it just felt empty: a bottomless pit.

She logged off and got up. She really did want to lie down.

ANUNIT

'*Wahh. Waah. WAAAHHHH.*' The baby was wailing like an N-LA police siren in her arms. He had been fed and burped; his nappy was clean. There was nothing more she could do for him. Why had she agreed to this? *Why?* Ebebu was Tiamet's child, practically a newborn. *She* should be looking after him, not running off to Kadingir for two whole days.

But Tiamet was halfway gone already. 'Shhhhh, Ebebu,' the Singular whispered from the tent flap. Her arms were laden with bags, her copper hair sculpted in a grand, impossible upswirl. 'Mama will be home soon.'

But babies didn't understand 'soon'.

'I don't think this is a good idea,' Anunit pleaded. The baby was crying as if the woe of the world was upon him, arching and stiffening his back as though he couldn't bear the slightest contact with her. She held him up. 'Can't you take him with you?'

'To Kadingir?' Tiamet flashed her kohl-painted eyes and outside a car horn parped. A YAC member, that skinny ex-mine-worker girl, was driving her back and forth these days and the girl was even bossier than Tiamet. 'Anunit, you *promised*.' She pouted. 'You're his aunty, aren't you?'

She swallowed. Yes, she had promised to be Ebebu's aunty – she just hadn't known how hard that promise would be to keep, how sometimes the baby's screams would drive her, like a nail, straight back into the frozen years: the three years she had sat here in the Welcome Tent with her sisters, letting them stroke her, hold her hand, comb her hair, rub her feet, doing and saying nothing more than was absolutely necessary. She had worked, slept, eaten, and transferred money to her parents' account every month. If not for her father, she would have cut her wrists. But having a daughter wind up in Pithar was sorrow and shame enough for a mine-sick old man.

Thanks to Tiamet, she had her voice back, and she must use it.

'But you'll be away for *two nights*,' she insisted over Ebebu's anguished fury. '*Listen* to him! Why can't you go tomorrow?'

'Put him in his cradle,' Tiamet wheedled, changing tack. 'He'll be fine.'

No he *won't*, Anunit wanted to say. But as if obeying his mother, with one last ragged shriek the infant's cries subsided into gulpy hiccoughs and Ebebu finally went limp.

'See?' The Singular spread her arms, sending her bags swinging like bells. 'And I *have* to go for two nights, Anunit. I have to *rehearse*' – she couldn't keep the triumph from her voice – 'for a *Diplomeet. And* a Star Party.'

The girl was like a knife sometimes, like *eight* knives, slicing holes in the Welcome Tent and letting in highly unwelcome blasts of rain, wind and sand. '*Shhh.*' Neperdu glared up from her screendesk and Taletha and Roshanak cast alarmed glances towards the passageway curtains. No wonder: there were three flesh clients in the Welcome Tent. Though the flesh chambers gushed noise – great tinny music, grunts, squeals, slaps and the occasional scream – still Neperdu had a strict rule: no talking politics, even in whispers, when there were customers on the premises.

Tiamet rolled her eyes. Taletha had painted them with glyphs at the corners. 'Oh, they're just mine-workers, Neperdu,' she scoffed, though she did at least lower her voice. 'It's essential I'm there, Anunit – the *international media* are coming. You'll see. This time it's really happening, for everyone.' She leaned into the tent, the next words barely audible, a sibilant hiss steaming from her mouth: 'Istar is rising to free us all. Pithar too.'

'One more word out of you and you'll be free of a *job*, my girl.' Neperdu jutted her chin at Tiamet, who tossed her head but shut up. The Singular had already won her challenge to Neperdu's authority and everyone knew it. 'The day a bunch of Kadingir drifters invite a Pithar worker to a Star Party,' Neperdu had vowed, 'I'll invite the head of IREMCO round for mountain mint tea.' The concierge had lost graciously, allowing all the workers free tea rations for a week, but Tiamet had crowed for a week more. Everything was kicking off in Kadingir, she kept repeating whenever the Welcome Tent was empty of clients; the Prophecy was being fulfilled and they would all play their destined role in freeing Non-Land at last.

Anunit's destined role was apparently to babysit Tiamet's infant. She was doing her best. She could hold Ebebu when he was sleeping, or gurgling softly, contented after a feed. She could even bottle-feed him, with milk Tiamet had expressed and kept in the fridge beside the screendesk. Just as it was sometimes a strange, numb, relief to service a flesh client, to feel an alien desire pump through the void that had once been her body, so it could be a distant wonder to feed him, to sense in her arms the powerful tug of his hunger. But when Ebebu cried, Anunit would give him straight back, or if Tiamet was working, to another sister to hold. She'd never thought she'd have to look after him while his mother vanished for two whole days.

'Fine, go, Tiamet.' She put Ebebu to her shoulder and he let out a long gasp of despair. 'But don't expect me to hold him if he cries like that the whole time.'

'I'll take him, Anunit!' Taletha looked up from painting her toes. 'When my nails are dry.'

'I'll help too,' Roshanak chimed in. 'Don't worry, Tiamet!'

It was true: her sisters did help, in a random manner: Taletha liked to sing to him, and Roshanak and the others would take turns tickling and bouncing him on their knees. Neperdu couldn't hold Ebebu, exactly, but she would lie with him on her chest or beside her on a pillow, murmuring softly into his ear that his mother was crazy, but that was all right, everyone was crazy, he would find that out soon enough. But Taletha and the others had a steady stream of clients and they could only squeeze a few minutes here or there for Ebebu. And the concierge worked a daily double shift too, greeting flesh clients, booking ion glove appointments, managing the cleaners, keeping the accounts. Tiamet had picked on *her*, Anunit sometimes thought, bitterly, because she was old and worn out, with only a handful of regular glove clients and the occasional novelty-seeker left to keep her in coin.

The car horn parped again and, waving frantically, Tiamet inched another step outside the tent.

'Good luck, Tiamet!' Taletha trilled.

'Goodbye, my sisters!' The Singular threw the half-empty Welcome Tent a flurry of kisses and Roshanak smooched back as, squealing, Taletha reached up to catch one, nearly knocking her nail polish bottle over.

Anunit's hands were full and the kisses fell far short of Ebebu's heaving little soul.

'Thank you, Anunit,' Tiamet called, her voice floating away as the tent flap closed around the last of her bags. 'Thank you for looking after Ebebu!'

It was mid-afternoon, but it was as if a lamp had gone out. Ebebu shuddered and Anunit patted his back. It wasn't the poor child's fault he had a silly, selfish firefly for a mother.

'It's true.' Taletha glanced up from her toes at Neperdu. 'International journalists are in Kadingir. I saw it on ShareWorld.'

Journalists: nearly a political topic. She pulled Ebebu's cradle towards her. Tiamet had bought the carved wooden nest in Kadingir. Maybe he would lie quietly now.

'Do you think they'll come to Pithar again, Neperdu?' Roshanak piped up.

'Let's hope not,' the concierge snapped, 'but if they do, you'll say what I tell you to: nothing more and nothing less. And so will Tiamet, if she wants to keep working in *my* Welcome Tent.'

Let Neperdu deal with the questions. She laid Ebebu on his pillows, watching him yawn, temporarily exhausted by his own grief as she was permanently exhausted by hers. Taletha, Roshanak, Tiamet – they were all so young. They would have to discover for themselves what she and Neperdu and the older sisters already knew. Like a sandstorm, stirring everything up, the international media came and went: promising dramatic change, new horizons, whipping their wild words up your nose, in your ears – only to vanish overnight, leaving a trail of wreckage behind them. Far better just to stay put on your cushions in the Welcome Tent, keeping the horizon finally pegged down around you.

At last Ebebu was asleep and the tent was quiet save for the work noise leaking from behind the passageway curtains. Neperdu was emailing glove clients, mouthstick to screen; Taletha and Roshanak were playing a game of mancala. Anunit curled up on her side and picked at the threads around the hole in the canvas behind her cushions; Neperdu had promised to get it patched after the last rainstorm, but Anunit hadn't pressed her. She didn't mind the hole, or the water that occasionally dripped into the bowl she kept beneath it. Getting up to empty the bowl was something to do. And living and working in the Welcome Tent, it was good to be reminded that rain was wet.

But she couldn't lie around all day. She had a client soon. She picked up Ebebu's empty bottle, got to her feet and padded down the passageway to the wash tent. An ante-chamber with no groundsheet, just wooden planks laid over the bare earth, the wash tent housed two showers, a tap and, after the ion gloves, Neperdu's greatest investment: a solar toilet embedded in a ramped platform beside a squat bidet. Some of the sisters still complained about the smell – although at worst it was just a faint swampy tang of soil, sawdust and manure – and lit incense sticks whenever they entered the wash tent. But though pleasure was too strong a word, Anunit took refuge in the toilet's aroma. Like the rain, it was real. During the frozen years she had volunteered to rotate the compost drum to stop Neperdu nagging and get away from the others; afterwards she would sit in the chair in the corner of the wash tent, eyes closed, imagining the waste slowly bedding down into loam. More than her father and brother, Tiamet or Ebebu, even her small cramped dreams of revenge, it was the smell of manure and the sound of water dripping into a bowl that had reconciled her to existence.

Life, Anunit understood now, was a vast, endless physical process, unjust and impersonal. Some still thought they could steer this process, shape it, *progess*, but that was simply a vainglorious dream. Inside everyone were violent, elemental forces – an infant's grief and rage, thinly veiled by politeness and dulled by routine and cushioned by small day-to-day comforts. When people were threatened or challenged, these forces erupted, hurting – sometimes destroying – others around them. Women lashed out with their tongues, men with their fists, pricks and worse weapons. Afterwards, for a while, they felt lighter. So of course they would do it again. Weak people did so randomly, often hurting themselves in the process; powerful people organised things to allow for this periodic release.

When Anunit had first joined the Welcome Tent, she had thought she had found a way to survive the cycle of harm, even profit from it. Later, when she learned for herself exactly how ruthless, cunning and cruel people could be, she had longed to kill herself – but sitting in the wash tent, contemplating the available methods, she had realised that suicide wasn't a solution; it would only cause more suffering, and not only for her sisters, father and brother. Just as a thin rain evaporated, only to fall again as a storm, or weak seeds tossed into night soil might sprout stunted plants, if she rejected her suffering husk of a body, her restless soul would quite probably find another even-more-painful flesh sack to fill. The solution, she had finally accepted, was not to fight but to become one with the process of life: to eat, work, sleep, eat, work, sleep, letting all her agony and fury slowly mulch down into the dark, anonymous compost of the world beneath the world.

There was no time to sit in the chair today. Crouching beneath the tap, she ran a basin of soapy water and washed the baby's bottle, ran her finger around the rim, cleaned out the gunge of another woman's breast milk. Her eyes dry, she stood. Tiamet thought she needed to be an 'aunty' but she did not. She needed *nothing*. It was the Singular and her child who required help, and if, in her chosen monotonous routine, Anunit could provide it she would. She was buried deep now, in a place where life did not move or touch her, but there was no harm in letting others flower, however briefly, in her long rot.

ASTRA

She was excited: all she had to do was pass her first Somarian test and she would be out in Kadingir soon, driving around and looking for her father, no matter what the Major said. But at the same time she didn't want to leave the laundry. Compared to the officers' courtyard and the dining hall, the bright, steamy chamber had been a kind of humid haven, she now realised: a place where she might be scolded for making a mess, but no one would ever ask her any impossible questions, or expect her to *joke* or *enthuse*. She wondered how she should say she was leaving, but as the pool was filling with its first soak water of the day, Dakota, the Head of Staff's young New Zonian assistant, arrived and briskly explained her transfer to the others. Everything was all organised: Dakota had sent Astra an email this morning already. Around the pool the three washer-women ululated congratulations and mock dismay. Hamta pinched Dakota's pale blue shirt sleeve and pointed at Astra.

'You!' she laughed. Astra grimaced. Yes, she'd be wearing trousers from now on: fabric running right up to her crotch – worse than the robes, even. But the uniform was part of the deal, and at least it might stop the internationals staring at her in the dining hall.

Uttu tapped her on the elbow. 'Friend,' she said in Inglish. 'Uttu. Astra. Friend.'

She'd managed more Somarian lessons last night in bed. 'Friend,' she replied in Uttu's tongue.

The washers clapped. Rapidly exhorting, Uttu squeezed her waist. Astra looked to Dakota for help.

'She says if you're driving on a Bluday, you gotta come visit her. She lives in Nagu Three. She can give you directions.'

Bluday was Uttu's day off. Astra had never thought about where the other washers lived, or what they did when they weren't working. Did Uttu have a family? Did she do all their washing too?

'Thank you. I will come,' she told Uttu, in stilted Somarian.

The washerwoman clasped Astra's hands to her lips. 'I want. You meet. My grandson,' she announced, triumphantly parading her Asfarian. Then she lifted Astra's right hand and shook it in the air.

Everyone was laughing – but not at her, she realised; at Uttu, or maybe just at life, because it was funny: an elderly sprite lifting and shaking Astra's fist as if she were a prize-winning boxer. As the vibrations rippled through her arm, a small spring of laughter bubbled up inside her, then as Hamta leaned back, clutching her ribs, and the ceiling echoed with a chorus of guffaws, it came gushing out: the real thing, for the first time in what felt like years, a laugh that made her ribs ache, her face hurt, the world and all its sorrow melt away like mist from a thundering fountain.

A peal of giggles joined the laughter and there they were, at the door, the three mop-headed compound kids. Dakota beckoned them in.

'Oh, you guys,' she said in Asfarian, wrapping her arms around the clutch of little miscreants. 'Always running around when you should be in the crèche. It's because you want to meet Astra, isn't it? Astra, this is Sulu, Kovan and Tamanina. The naughtiest children in the compound.'

Astra's eyes were wet from laughing. She wiped them dry and greeted her tormentors. 'Hello,' she said to Sulu, the ringleader, a tomboy in a T-shirt and long shorts.

'HELLO!' Sulu jumped out at her, then retreated to the safety of Dakota's embrace, bursting into another round of titters. Her left leg was a prosthetic, Astra realised – not a carbon fibre or mechatronic model like the ones she was used to, but a scuffed brown plastic mould that branched into a short extrusion above the ankle as if to accommodate a foot.

She was staring, she realised, but she'd never seen a child wearing a prosthesis before and she had to make sure she wasn't mistaken. At least the rudeness was mutual: Sulu was openly gaping at her head, no doubt longing for her to turn and expose her skull scar. As Astra forced a smile, the girl gripped Kovan, the boy, and fiercely whispered something into his ear.

Kovan was plump and placid, with an unfocused expression. He was looking around, up at the vaults, down at the floor, everywhere but at Astra.

'He . . . lo,' he whispered, then buried his face in Dakota's trouser leg. From the sleeve of his T-shirt, Astra saw now, emerged a kind of fleshy wing: a boneless hand. Its slender, fused fingertips brushed the top of Tamanina's head.

Sulu cheered and jumped up and down.

'Good girl,' Dakota said. 'You're really helping Kovan learn Inglish, aren't you?'

Astra still couldn't absorb what she was seeing. Tamanina, the little one, was half covered in a rash; the left side of her face was red and swollen and her left arm was raw-skinned and littered with scabs. As she started to scratch herself, Dakota gently moved her hand away. Kovan lifted his T-shirt and rubbed his chubby belly and she saw the skin around his navel was chafed and blistered too.

Astra darted a look back at Sulu. The girl's arms, crossed now over her chest, were pitted with shiny white pockmarks.

'Sulu, Kovan,' Dakota ordered, wagging her finger, 'go back to the crèche and tell the minder to put some more cream on Tamanina!'

The children giggled and Sulu spun away, dragging Tamanina by the hand. Kovan followed, half leaping, half skipping.

'"Goodbye Astra". Say, "Goodbye Astra",' Uttu commanded after them.

'Gooooooood by-eeeeeee,' the girls squealed as they tore back out into the courtyard. Kovan stopped, turned at the door and gave a shy wave.

'Goodbye, Kovan.' She waved back. When he was gone she asked, 'Are they sick?'

'Sick. Yes. Code-sick,' Hamta said.

'No,' Uttu contradicted her friend, 'not sick. Poison.'

'Poison. Yes. Code poison.' Azarakhsh diplomatically agreed with both of them.

Code sickness? Poison? Was Dakota going to explain all this to her?

But Dakota was leaving too. 'Oh, where are they scampering off to?' she asked from the door. 'I'd better make sure they get back. Astra, your uniforms will be ready at lunch.'

Astra stood blinking in the morning sunlight. Why were these children missing limbs? Sulu's custom prosthetic and Kovan's small arm weren't the result of a car crash or farm accident. And why was the boy's speech so slow? Was he just shy, or – she searched for the archaic term – alt-brained? Weren't people here Code-protected against that? And what about the rash? The image of the dancing girl troubled her again – all those kids in the masks; had they been Code-poisoned too? And – it was as if she'd been splashed with icy water, shocked awake – all the baby clothes she'd been washing since she got here, speckled front and back with blood and pus – were children *born* with this skin disease? The Head of Staff, Photon, the Major – why hadn't anyone said anything about this?

Chattering in Somarian again, the washers began dragging more bags of laundry towards the pool.

Uttu patted her arm. 'Code poison, my house, no. My house clean earth,' she whispered.

She wanted to know more, but even in her own language she didn't know the words for the questions. She worked hard on her last shift, thumping the clothes and digging the paddle vigorously into the folds. When she splashed the floor and had to fetch the mop, none of the other washers scolded her, and when she left at lunchtime, promising to come back and say hello, to visit Uttu as soon as she could, Uttu hugged her again and Azarakhsh kissed both her cheeks.

'Pleased to meet you,' Hamta announced proudly, shaking her hand, and all of them chorused, in a cacophony of Asfarian, Inglish and Somarian, 'Good washer. Astra good washer. Astra clean girl. Astra very clean.'

PEAT

'You. Are. *Sec Gens*.' Chief Superintendent Odinson's voice rumbled in his earpiece like distant thunder. It was eleven in the morning and the entire cohort was out on the training lawns, more than two thousand eight hundred Sec Gen constables, standing shoulder to shoulder in the blazing sun. Odinson was commanding a pulpit in front of the Barracks, his figure framed by the building's central green and gold glass arch. Behind him sat a row of senior officers: the Head Engineer of the Cladding Operation and her team of Shelltech experts, the Division Officers and the full medical staff. Above the Barracks, the Boundary was screening a giant black-and-white image of his face. That was good in so many ways: to any Non-Landers looking up at the Barracks, it would look like IMBOD's rugged leader was intently surveying them.

'And Sec Gens, you look *fantastic*!' That was a cue and Peat roared affirmation with the rest. Today they were wearing their uniforms for the first time: fine white cotton trousers and shirts with green trim, red buttons, gold collars and cuffs. Normally Peat didn't like clothes, but the uniform was different. Putting it on, he had swollen with pride: so much so that Laam had made jokes about his booster shot working overtime. Now, ranked out on the field, he felt his pride transforming, flowing into a deep sense of belonging with the others. Today the cohort was a flock of white doves, the Barracks their spectacular cote.

Odinson, as usual, was sky-clad, save for an IMBOD armband and two black straps crossing his broad, grizzled torso. He spread his arms, lifted his chest to the sun. 'We all feel more alive when our skin is breathing the air around us,' he declared, 'so why do we require you to wear clothes?' This was not a school Assembly and they all knew not to put up their hands. 'I will *tell you* why not: it is because here outside the Boundary we are Ambassadors, performing a diplomatic function. In other human cultures the naked body is an object of shame and derision. Our natural state offends and frightens most people. We Gaians have *compassion* for these unfortunate souls. We understand that they have not had the benefit of our enlightened education. In our own country we sometimes choose to clothe ourselves to protect their sensitivities.' Odinson paused. From the Boundary screen, his eyes raked the field. 'Do we care about the sensitivities of Non-Landers?'

The Chief Super cupped his hand to his ear. This question was different: a cue.

'NO!' Peat yelled, his voice joining Laam and Jade and Robin's.

'No, we do *not*! But Non-Land is not only home to Non-Landers: here you may also encounter CONC officials, and *journalists*.' In Peat's earpiece, Odinson's voice lowered a fraction. At first, Peat had wondered why there were no loudspeakers on the training field, but the genius of the earpieces was becoming apparent: Odinson could give a resounding lecture out under Gaia's blue sky and no one beyond the Barracks walls could hear a word he was saying. 'Listen closely, Sec Gens, for this is very important,' Odinson purred. 'In *Is-Land*, journalists are the eyes and ears of Gaia, the scribes of a nation. In *Is-Land* journalists share the information we all require to consciously evolve. But in *Non-Land* journalists are the *loose tongues* of a *hostile and ignorant* world. At IMBOD, our goal' – a split-second pause – 'is to *shut these people up!*'

That was funny! A *joke*! The Officers on stage, the Engineers, the entire cohort of Sec Gens all fell about laughing, Peat and Laam so hard they had to lean against each other for support. Let the Non-Landers hear *that*! Above them, Odinson smiled: a broad, gleaming smile, spilling light all over the Barracks and into Non-Land as far as Asfar!

'I jest. I jest. But let me now be serious.' Laam was still snickering, but Peat sobered himself. If laughter was a weapon, you had to learn how to control it. 'In our medical and agricultural Code work, in our architecture, in our animal welfare laws, in our Shelltech innovation,' Odinson intoned, gesturing at the teams of senior officers, 'Is-Land has taken the lead among nations. And yet Gaians are still routinely portrayed in the international media as cranks and extremists, isolationists and self-imposed outcasts. Be warned! These attacks are not simply jealous mutterings, not even pitiful expressions of ignorance. They are *cunning propaganda* designed to challenge our right to our lifestyles and land. To combat this campaign of hatred, IMBOD has developed a strict policy of "conscious modification".'

Peat stood as still as a heron. *This* was the heart of the lesson; their Division Officer would review it with them later so he needed to pay utmost attention.

'Whenever IMBOD officers appear outside Is-Land, we graciously adapt to our new cultural environment. Beyond the Barracks walls, we senior officers display enough of our physiques to demonstrate the benefits of our Gaian diet, but otherwise we respect the modesty codes of other nations. You, as constables, will be required at all times – unless provoked otherwise – to present a disciplined image to the world. For the world is curious about you. My beloved Sec Gens, you are already the object of global fear and scorn. What do the international media call you, you ask?'

A muscle in Peat's jaw flexed. Yes, what had the international media been saying? That being Sec Gen was like being a robot, a worm in a worm farm? That was what Nimma said Hokma had taught Astra. He had cried about that in his counselling. He had always helped Astra with her law homework, her cricket practise, but she had been laughing at him, despising him the whole time.

'I will tell you, though it pains me.' Odinson's voice was heavy with regret. 'Sec Gens, some journalists call you *drones*. Lemmings. *Sheep*.'

It was infuriating. The sheer stupidity of it: trying to belittle something you didn't understand, a way of being you couldn't share, by making disparaging remarks about gentle, beautiful, hard-working creatures—

BZZZZ. BZZZZ. BZZZZ.

What was going on? The divisions at the back were buzzing like bees.

BAAA! BAAH! BAAH!

Now the divisions down the side of the lawn were bleating like sheep.

WHEEK WHEEK. WHEEK WHEEK. WHEEK WHEEK.

The entire front row was squeaking like lemmings!

Odinson was grinning. The Head Engineer was clapping. It was another joke! Odinson had *organised* a joke. Everyone was laughing again, harder and harder, until Peat had a stitch in his side. Were *journalists* listening outside the walls? Let them! Let them hear the *Sec Gens'* derision! BZZZZ BZZZZ BZZZZ. BAAH! BAAH! BAAH!

WHEEK WHEEK. WHEEK WHEEK. WHEEK WHEEK. His division joined in the chorus. Peat raised his hands to his forehead, crooked his fingers into little bee antennae. Robin and Jade scrabbled the air with lemming claw hands. Laam nuzzled him like the softest of lambs. At last, as Odinson wiped a giant shining tear from his eye, the raucous laughter subsided.

'Sec Gens: you need fear no journalist. You know, deeply, already, the benefits of your intertuned sensibility, benefits that are the envy of even your senior officers. And you know too that you are each still an individual, each with your own beauty and talents. Today, as well as your new uniforms, you will receive your first Non-Land Barracks progress reports. Rest assured, Sec Gens, of IMBOD's commitment to helping you achieve your maximum human potential.'

We are human. We are human. The hum was starting now. He understood now the purpose of the hum: to counter this vicious propaganda already being spread about them, spread like rancid *cow's butter* around the world. The international media had no idea what it meant to be a Sec Gen, to stand together like cells in a solar panel, storing and releasing the power of a generation. He breathed in deeply. There was a beautiful sweet musky scent in the air: ambergris. Since the booster shot, their sweat was intoxicating. And wearing clothes was making them sweat harder today.

'Sec Gens – my Shelter children – thank you for your attention.' The hum subsided as Odinson purred on, 'You have a demanding training schedule ahead. My colleagues and I will leave you with one more thought: as your progress reports will highlight, you each have your own strengths and interests, your own individual paths in life. After this tremendous bonding experience defending your homeland, some of you may return to careers chosen in high school, while others may wish to climb up through the IMBOD ranks. Do not be shy. If you have ideas, initiatives, ambitions, choose an appropriate time to share them with your senior officers. Seek to learn, seek to grow. That is my challenge to you today. And Sec Gens, we know, thrive on challenge!'

The cohort roared its approval. Peat stood rooted to the lawn, eyes locked on the Boundary. The camera on Odinson zoomed out as the Chief Super in his pulpit, fist to heart, gave the Gaian salute. Then the screen was a crash of white water foaming down. Yes: he would swim like a salmon up those thundering falls. He would dedicate his talents, his service to IMBOD, to this man: his magnificent new Shelter father.

ASTRA

'Astra!' Photon pushed through the crowd of officers milling in front of the Gold Theatre. 'Hey, don't you look the part.'

She did. In her blue trousers and shirt, sporting the CONC insignia on her sleeve and the CONC watch on her wrist, she looked exactly like the officers milling about, waiting for the Diplomeet to start. Some had clocked her, faces registering curiosity and surprise, but no one had greeted her and she'd stood alone, her back against the wall, trying to get used to the chafing sensation of a watch round her wrist and a belt round her hips. Having hated the women's trousers Dakota had offered her – the high waist felt like it might cut her in half and the tight crotch wouldn't allow her brand-wound to breathe – she had chosen a men's pair. They too smothered her legs, but at least they were loose, and might even be easier to run in than the robes. Their pockets were a benefit, too: deep ones at the front to hide her hands in, and cargo pouches on the thighs where she'd stashed her head pills, Tablette and water flask. She wouldn't have to keep carrying her backpack everywhere now.

'Photon?' She wanted to ask him about the children, but he was waving at Christophe, who was standing across the lobby with Tisha and Honovi. The officer acknowledged Photon, then returned to his conversation. Honovi, though, directed a sunbeam smile across the hall and gave Astra two big thumbs up.

'Hey!' Photon lowered his voice. 'I got you on the list!'

She was trying to simultaneously ignore and coolly return Honovi's greeting. She settled on straightening up and jutting her chin to the right. 'What list?'

'For a rec pass. If the Diplomeet succeeds you can come out tonight, to the River Raven.'

Opposite, the Gold Theatre doors swung open and a murmur rippled through the hallway as the officers started pressing slowly forward into the Diplomeet.

She was tingling, she realised. 'That's great. Thanks, Photon,' she whispered airily as, her equerry behind her, she stepped into the orderly flow.

The walls of the Gold Theatre were hung, unsurprisingly, with gold tapestries, long banners stitched with silky white CONC shells rising from glittering waves. Between the raked seating, a dun-carpeted ramp sloped down to a low stage, above which a gold-framed wallscreen currently read 'Diplomeet' in six languages: Asfarian, Inglish, Gaian and scripts Astra recognised after a moment as Somarian, Karkish and Farashan. Beneath the screen, Major Thames was presiding over a crescent-shaped table. In front of hirm, resting on a white cushion with blue tassels, was the conch trumpet. To hir left sat a large woman in flowing crimson robes and a tawny gold turban, and next to her a young man in a purple T-shirt sporting a silver insignia, the design glinting in the spotlights directed at the stage. Sandrine was sitting at the other end of the table beside a tall, bearded, bare-chested man. His features were a blur, and Astra couldn't see his legs, but above the waist the man wore only a peaked black cap, two black straps across his burly chest and on his bulging right arm, an all-too-familiar armband.

She halted. Photon bumped into her back. 'Sorry,' he said, 'not here. We are sitting at the front.'

In the third row, Rudo was waving and pointing at two empty seats, but she couldn't go down there. She couldn't move. She was back in the Barracks, moaning on the floor, in the shadow of a tall bearded officer who, in a Morse code of whispers and grunts, was quietly instructing his subordinate to make her suffer, increase her pain, activate the time bombs in her head. Her heart was pounding, the base of her skull throbbing. She had to leave the theatre, immediately – but her body didn't belong to her any more and would not obey; it was a leaden lump in hot, smothering clothes. A woman elbowed past her and she shuddered, but still she could not lift a foot.

Then there was the tentative touch of Photon's hand on her shoulder, his breath on her cheek. 'Are you okay?'

She balled her fists. She was a CONC officer now, under the Major's protection. IMBOD couldn't touch her. And if she was going to slice like a scythe through Is-Land one day, she couldn't afford to fall apart at the mere sight of her worst enemies.

'Yeah,' she muttered, resuming her descent, scanning the audience rather than looking again at the stage. It was like being in the stands at a sports meet, though here people displayed their team colours with their clothes, not flags or armbands. Sandrine and the IMBOD officer's side of the the-atre was filling up with blue-clad CONC officers. The other block of seats was occupied by people wearing red – rust-red uniforms, scarlet and crim-son robes and headscarves: Non-Landers, but not all N-LA. Those in the front row, she saw as she neared the stage, were dressed in purple.

She risked a glance up to the speakers' table. The youth was a striking figure. Illuminated by the spotlights, his strong brow cast dramatic shadows across his face. Large almond-shaped eyes with hooded lids lent his expression a soulful authority, while his broad torso and huge, rip-pling arms projected not just physical strength, but mental dedication to perfection. At New Bangor High School, the Non-Lander's muscles would have placed him at the top of the gym training tree. These sugges-tions of determination and leadership were surely still to be tested, though, for the speaker was hardly older than she was. His skin was smooth as soap, his hair combed up like thick black grass from an unlined forehead. And in his purple T-shirt he looked like he was going to a party. Hanging from his neck was a shining medallion: a large silver five-pointed star on a chain, flashing like a mirror in the theatre lights.

'Hey, Rudo.' Photon turned to Astra. 'Do you want to sit behind Tisha?'

He was being thoughtful: Honovi was on the end of the row. But behind the blonde giantess was the perfect place to hide from the IMBOD officer.

'No' – she gestured at him to go first – 'I might get a headache and have to leave.'

Photon folded his angular frame into the seat beside his driving part-ner. He had probably wanted to stick his legs out into the aisle, but that couldn't be helped. She acknowledged Rudo with a quick nod and sat down behind Honovi.

Her skin prickled: the front row on this side of the theatre was all white shirts – IMBOD. As she'd learned when they drove her to the compound, outside of the Barracks IMBOD officers – or most of them – wore white uniforms. Her heart pounding, she inspected the Gaian on stage. His knees were covered by black trousers. His hands were occupied with his Tablette. Above his turfed chest, his face was set like a cliff, with a brow like a granite overhang.

It was him, so close she could have stood up and projectile-vomited on him. Panic shot through her gut and she was suddenly basted in sweat. She shrank back in her seat. Had he noticed her coming down the ramp? Wouldn't look like all the rest of the CONC officers in her uniform? And the light was so bright on the stage he surely hadn't seen her – he wasn't even looking up now, was he?

She was breathing more deeply now, but no oxygen was getting to her brain. The theatre was stifling – someone should open a window. But there were no windows behind the gold hangings. Even the neurohospice had had windows – being bricked up away from Gaia was a punishment. How could CONC hold meetings in rooms with no natural light or fresh air?

'Hey hey. Media's here,' Rudo commented to Photon, who elbowed her to look. At the far left of the front row, beyond the IMBOD officers, sat three individuals anomalous in the colour-coded blocks of the the-atre: a young man in a green T-shirt, an older pale-skinned man in an ivory suit and a curly-haired woman in an orange blouse, operating a cam-era on a tripod.

'Do you know where they are staying?' Photon asked.

'Dunno.' Rudo shrugged. 'Maybe they brought their own tents?'

But the theatre had quietened. On stage, Major Thames was lifting the conch trumpet to hir lips, slipping hir hand into the long, gleaming pink lip of the shell.

Bwhaaaaaaaaaaa . . . Bwhaaaaaaaaaa . . . MWA MWA.

Once, twice: the deep mournful call of the sea undulated through the room, the Major shaping the sound with hir palm. The solemn invocation was followed by two short blasts: the Diplomeet was beginning. The IMBOD officer on stage was behind a table, and his team had their white-shirted backs to her. She was shielded by Honovi and Photon and she was sitting right on the aisle. If needed, she could be up and out the door before anyone could stop her.

'Good after*noon*,' the Major barked. 'As Chair, I extend a warm CONC welcome to this Emergency Diplomeet.' With a two-second delay, the wallscreen translated the Major's Asfarian into the other five languages. Grateful for a reason not to look at the stage, Astra skipped between the Asfarian and Inglish, checking the Gaian if she was unsure. For what seemed like an age, the Major introduced the Diplomeeters: Sandrine – heesh called her 'The Summoner' – would speak for CONC. The woman who had coordinated her headdress with the theatre was Her Excellency Una Dayyani, Lead Convenor of the Non-Land Alliance; the young man was Mr Enki Arakkia, Speaker and Core Member of the Youth Action Collective; and finally, she learned the name of her torturer: Chief Superintendent Clay Odinson, Head of the Kadingir IMBOD Barracks.

She risked another peek at the stage. Odinson appeared to be trying to engage the N-LA leader in a staring contest, but Una Dayyani was more than his match. Her plump face set hard as rammed earth above the brocaded neck of her robe, her body squarely claiming its space on the stage, the Lead Minister's own disdainful gaze slid by the IMBOD officer to concentrate on Sandrine, who was studiously focusing on her Tablette. In contrast, Enki Arakkia was lightly drumming his fingers on the table. The Major shot him a glance and he stopped and raised a finger to the ceiling. For the first time, Astra noticed the empty shorts hanging neatly over the edge of Enki Arakkia's wheelchair.

Prosthetics, for Enki Arakkia, would be only aesthetic, a way of trying to fit in. And it was already obvious that slotting neatly and invisibly into this Diplomeet was not on Enki Arakkia's agenda. Who were the Youth Action Collective, anyway? Still hunched in her seat, she zapped another look across the aisle at Enki's supporters. On the near end of the row, a small, dainty woman, sitting high up on cushions in her wheelchair, was frowning at Una Dayyani. Beside her in another wheelchair, a man with two wing-hands like Kovan's had turned to whisper to the person in the first theatre seat, a young woman with two long braids. Next to her was someone who looked somehow both thin and very wide: a young woman with upswept red hair, a delicate face and broad bony shoulders. Astra couldn't see anyone in any detail beyond her except for a giant at the far end: a massive young man who was head, purple shoulders and chest above the rest. He made even Photon and Honovi look small.

It was like meeting the compound children: incredibly puzzling. In Is-Land, apart from sports teams, alt-bodied people didn't form special groups with symbols and T-shirts. But there wasn't time to wonder about it now.

'Officer Moses,' Major Thames snapped. 'Please begin!'

'As Summoner, I greet the Responders.' It wasn't possible for Sandrine to be nervous. In a neutral tone, using careful language, the MMU officer summarised what she termed 'three recent incidents of hostile behaviour by Kadingir youths towards members of the CONC Mobile Medical Unit division'. She itemised these at some length, citing the damage to CONC vehicles, the fear of escalating hostilities and the need to appoint armed N-LA members to travel with the MMUs and other mobile workers. 'Fortunately, none of our officers have been seriously hurt in these incidents,' she concluded, 'but all of this has put a strain on our already limited resources.'

'Crippled operations, more like it,' Christophe muttered to Tisha as a grumble of discontent spread over the CONC side of the theatre. On stage, Enki Arakkia made a note in his Tablette and the Major shot a sniper's glance out across the theatre.

'*Silence.* One more sound from my officers and I will *clear the room of you.*'

Christophe shook his head, but the threat sank in. Sandrine continued in the quiet, 'While CONC is dismayed at these attacks, we recognise that our current provision of healthcare services is inadequate to the needs of the region. We fully understand that the increasing rates of birth differences, cancer and skin disease in Non-Land present challenges that the current treatment ward system does not adequately address.'

Behind her, a Non-Lander emitted a small *hrumph*. Major Thames let it pass but Astra darted a look over her shoulder. A few feet away, a woman in a red robe and brown headscarf was wearily resting a pitted cheek on her palm.

Sandrine raised her voice and appealed to the whole audience. 'CONC understands that these issues may have caused resentment among the young. We are here to talk and put things right.'

Astra put her hands together to clap, but Diplomeets were very clearly not like school sports days. You could have heard a petal drop in the theatre. On stage, Una Dayyani was regarding Odinson with a steady, piercing look of contempt. Odinson, in response, appeared to be repressing a smile; the corners of his mouth were tugged down, distorting his crudely chiselled features, and – *was he?* – yes! The man was flexing his arrogant chest.

For a blazing moment, fury vanquished fear. If she had had a crossbow, she would have stood up and shot a bolt of hatred right at Odinson's shrivelled heart. As she was taking aim through Honovi and Tisha's shoulders, Odinson met her gaze. *Now* he smiled. Her stomach seized. He was *gloating* . . . Like a cobra, she half rose in her seat, but in the next instant she understood her fatal error.

Odinson knew she was here, but he didn't know *she was winning* – that Dr Tapputu had given her the head pills and cured her of IMBOD's punishment. He mustn't know that, ever. She screwed up her face, flinched, jerked her head back against her seat and feigned a silent seizure.

When she fluttered her lids open again, the IMBOD Head Torturer was tapping at his Tablette, his crevice of a smile still distorting his lips. Photon was patting her arm, offering her his water flask. She took a sip and passed it back. Odinson thought he could crush her, but he was *wrong*.

Una Dayyani was talking now. She was good at talking. Her tone was rich and mellifluous, her Asfarian greetings replete with flourishes and her gestures extravagant: her fingers had long gold nails, Astra noticed, curved like claws, and a red jewel gleamed from the folds of her turban. The Lead Convenor was not here to seduce anyone, though, that was clear. Her stern expression unwavering, her voice spiked with a dry, bitter note, she remarked, 'for the benefit of the international media', upon 'the fact that over the last nine months N-LA has issued two Summonses for an Emergency Diplomeet. In both cases,' she pointed out acidly, 'IMBOD refused the Summons and CONC cast its deciding vote in IMBOD's favour.'

A puff of grunts and shuffles rose from the Non-Lander side of the theatre. 'May I kindly remind you all,' Major Thames boomed, 'that Diplomeet protocol applies to guests as well as hosts.' As the female journalist panned across the audience, the room stilled again.

'I regret deeply,' Dayyani continued with icy dignity, 'that it has taken these scurrilous attacks to force IMBOD and CONC to attend an Emergency Diplomeet. As the leader of a government currently negotiating a landmark breakthrough for my people, I condemn the violent actions of a handful of misguided youth.'

Arakkia's face was unreadable, but a mutter ran through his purple

T-shirt brigade. Dayyani gestured in their general direction. 'At the same time, I understand the youths' impatience. As N-LA has stated for *years*,' she stormed on, 'the increased birth difference, cancer and skin disease rates in Non-Land are not simply the result of unacknowledged uranium deposits at the Zabaria mine; they are symptoms of the toxic political conditions in the Southern Belt – conditions that CONC is moving far too slowly to redress.'

The Zabaria mine? Astra stiffened. That was *Samrod Blesserson's* mine.

'Non-Land's problems cannot be solved by street violence,' Dayyani declared, 'and nor can our illnesses be cured by CONC condoms and morpheus. We can be healed only by the transformation of our pariah status: the establishment of a *free, independent and self-sufficient nation*.'

Behind Astra, the Non-Land side of the theatre broke into rowdy applause. In the front row, though, the YAC supporters did not react. 'Quiet!' the Major roared, and Dayyani raised her hands and her people stilled.

'N-LA has cooperated fully with CONC's demands for demilitarisation,' the Lead Convenor continued, gold-tipped forefinger aloft. 'We now demand in return CONC's full moral and financial support for our independence bid. To start with we expect CONC to fund substantial compensation for all Non-Land victims of the Is-Land Rare Earths Mining Corporation, and to oversee the immediate transfer of ownership of the Zabaria mine from IMBOD to N-LA. We also demand the import of sufficient herds of grazing animals to begin the re-greening process, the transfer of all CONC farms to N-LA ownership, and the establishment of chemistry labs in Kadingir capable of refining medical-grade morpheus, ending the *ridiculous* practice of sending Mikku River poppies hundreds of miles to Asfar and back. If this Emergency Diplomeet does not advance Non-Land towards our goals,' the Minister's threat rang out, 'N-LA will formally propose to Amazigia that Asfar take over CONC's duties as negotiators of this conflict. Several Asfarian Ministers have already signed our draft resolution to that effect, and I guarantee that a significant number of international delegates will be entirely sympathetic to our position. How can CONC be trusted to promote the legal rights of Non-Landers when it neglects even our most basic health and safety concerns?'

With that, the Minister sat back in her chair and folded her arms, clearly not expecting much of a response.

Astra squinted at the translations, trying to take in the Minister's demands before they disappeared from the screen. Bring more animals here? That would be cruel. Asfar run Non-Land? Absurd. Asfar was a neighbour to the conflict; that was why Asfarians were not permitted to work in the CONC compound. She would have to ask Photon about it all afterwards, but right now she was uncomfortably aware of Odinson again, his hewn countenance, like struck flint, casting sparks in her direction. She should be looking dull-witted, dazed by all this information. She lolled her head against the back of her seat.

'Thank you, Lead Convenor Dayyani,' Major Thames declaimed. 'The Diplomeet has noted your concerns. We now turn to Respondee Mr Enki Arakkia.'

Enki Arakkia shifted his wheelchair, set his Tablette aside; eyes flashing, he raised his right forefinger and in the rhythm his movements had already established began not to speak, but to chant. Above him, in Asfarian, the screen read:

> Greetings from the young people.
> The young people are speaking their truth.

In Gaian:

> Greetings from the children of Non-Land.
> The children of Non-Land will give you their opinions.

And in Inglish:

> Greetings from the youth.
> The youth who bring the truth.

'Objection!' Odinson barked, 'this is not a teenagers' concert: this is a *Diplomeet*. I insist that proper decorum be maintained.'

'Objection overruled!' roared the Major. 'All Respondees have the right to self-expression in the language and discourse of their choice. Verse has been the medium of political and historical debate since the dawn of human civilisation. Mr Arakkia: continue!'

With Odinson fuming like a Boundary smoke signal, Arakkia stormed on. He was speaking Somarian, Astra realised, but what he was doing to his language was alarming: a message in itself. Swallowing syllables, spitting out consonants, he chopped and stretched the words into hard, deep, abrupt shapes. She focused on the wallscreen. In Asfarian she read:

> The young people have few resources.
> The young people do not flatter others.
> Neither do they talk without reason, or drink alcohol.

In Gaian:

> The children bring nothing to the table.
> The children do not try to speak graciously.
> If they are ignorant of the facts, they claim they will remain silent.
> They refuse customary offers of adult hospitality.

And in Inglish:

> The youth with nothing left to lose,
> The youth who don't do schmooze,
> Or clueless talk or booze.

The Gaian translation was a joke. The Asfarian gave the meaning, but the Inglish translator, she soon realised, had tried to also capture the music of Arakkia's speech. Concentrating on the Inglish, she kept pace as he tore on:

> The youth who've tasked themselves
> With seizing our own future
> From the grip of your inertia
> The distortions of your media.

Watching the words, but not missing one of Arakkia's moves: the challenge was electrifying. He was pointing now, dramatically indicating each of the other speakers:

> Greetings to CONC
> Greetings to N-LA
> Greetings even to our enemy

> the Occupying Force.
> Let it not be said the Youth
> are lacking in civility.
> And let it not be uttered
> that the Youth have hurt another
> human being in our land.

He jerked his chin at Sandrine. He'd taken furious notes when she'd mentioned 'no serious injury'. In fact, Astra thought, Photon's scrape had been the only physical wound the MMU officers had suffered. Still, hurling a rock at a windscreen was dangerous. The snake-haired girl could have blinded Msandi or Eduardo. There was no time to linger on the objection, though, for Arakkia was hurtling on:

> Rocks and stones were thrown
> at glass and metal, not at flesh,
> at Mobile Units that move nothing
> more than laundry
> and addiction to the drugs
> CONC's sticking in our veins.
> But we don't need your morpheus.
> We got powers of the mind, see?

He tapped his forehead. What did he mean? He'd skipped from stones to morpheus – Astra didn't know why, but her body was riveted to every syllable. Beside her, Photon's fingers were twitching. Across the aisle, the YAC members were stamping their feet, thumping their arms on their chair rests.

The Major wasn't interrupting. Enki Arakkia barrelled on:

> Yes, YAC's youthful legion
> is ready to refuse
> your needles and your pills.
> We don' need your soap suds neither:
> we'll wash our laundry in the river,
> and if the stains remain
> those blood-maps will remind us
> what we're fighting for:

> an end to IMBOD's brutal rule,
> and an end to N-LA's plans
> to *poison* yet another generation's
> dream of *freedom*.

For a moment the gold hangings trembled on the walls; for a moment she was lifted on a wave of yearning. For what? *Freedom*?

Arakkia yanked her back, sarcasm spraying like bile from deep in his gut:

> Yeah, close the mine today,
> pretend we're on the mend,
> pay us off with conch shells
> we can't spend.
> Yakity yak another decade
> if you like –
> but till the Boundary is down
> YAC will roll on up
> the rocky road to *truth*.

She was lost in the politics now. All she knew was that Enki Arakkia was rebelling against *everyone* – everyone in power, that is. He was resisting their authority, their rules, insisting that they listen to *him*. And they were. Sandrine was drinking in the performance, swaying in time to the beats. Eyes narrowed, mouth pinched, Una Dayyani was making rapid notes on her Tablette. Odinson's cave-dwelling eyes were scanning Arakkia as if itemising his every pore. Major Thames glared out over the audience, daring them to clap along. A lock of Arakkia's hair was sticking out over his forehead. His tempo slowed, his tone serious once more:

> In this ricocheting theatre
> where morality meets might,
> we'll never stop repeating,
> in rhyme and diplo-metre:
> we are human beings.
> We're the Youth Action Collective,
> we're fightin' for our rights.

We don't want no toxic graveyard
patrolled by Gaian snipers.
We aim to beat the Boundary,
return to our ancestral lands,
and like a burning constellation
on the longest winter night,
the Southern Belt
will rise with us into the *light*.

On the final word, Enki Arakkia lifted his right hand. Fingers splayed, he waved it in an arc above his head. As one, the Non-Landers in the front row mirrored his movement, the small woman in the first wheel-chair raising her arm, the young man beside her rolling his head from side to side. Enki's honed face was determined, gleaming, unsmiling. For a moment the silver star on his chest shone so brightly Astra blinked.

Swiftly, in sync with their Speaker, the YAC members lowered their hands. The silence in the theatre was as white and tight as a wrung sheet.

'Thank you, Enki Arakkia,' the Major announced smoothly, 'for that highly original presentation. I now invite Chief Superintendent Odinson to Respond.'

ODINSON

The preliminary skirmishes had been fought; the decisive moment had arrived. Licking the tip of his left canine, he surveyed the terrain. Behind the tense white line of his colleagues – the Head Engineer's face was rigid with expectation – stretched a loose block of blue neutrals, receptive to logic, eloquence and rhetorical skill. Across the aisle sprawled a red and purple bruise of rage, hatred and ignorance, a volatile mix of known and unknown reactors. En masse vulnerable to predictable triggers, individual Non-Landers required vigilant attention. The Code monstrosities in the front row: which one was posting every word of the Diplomeet on the global internet? The giant youth at the end: was there a snail of brains curled up inside his thick skull? And the Ordott girl, skulking in with CONC? Despite his best efforts at the Barracks the little traitor could still be capable of anything. Right now though, her fear was wafting over to him like the scent of ginger, a stimulant, warming his nostrils, firing his veins.

'Thank you, Chair.' He adopted his most conciliatory tone. After this morning's glorious cakewalk with the Sec Gens, a subtler performance was a most welcome challenge. 'And apologies to all for the return to prose. Mundane it may be, sadly lacking in amateur dramatics, but I have been asked for clarification, and to bring clarity, I'm sure we all agree, is the purpose of a Diplomeet.'

Beside him, Arakkia was rocking slightly, lost in his nursery rhyme world. The youth's bulging biceps would no doubt win him a few fans in New Zonia, but this conflict was not going to be settled by an audience vote on ShareWorld. Neither would it be won only by moral authority and the strict enforcement of international law. Victory demanded that

Is-Land enlarge its spiritual vision. He was the man to serve this heightened perception. The Head Engineer would soon be apologising for her outburst last night.

'IMBOD greatly regrets the current turn of events,' he solemnly declared. 'This wanton violence against CONC aid workers has re-escalated tensions in the Southern Belt, threatening the careful negotiations of recent years.'

His own face had nobility engraven upon it – this, he knew from careful study of the videos of his speeches, made his occasional mischief all the more charismatic. But now was not a time for unexpected charm: now called for a surgical oratorical strike. Opposite, Dayyani's arms were interlocked beneath her ample bosom. The woman presented herself as a human citadel, the stalwart, impregnable defender of her people. She had even managed to convince the Head Engineer of her inert ambitions. But he knew Dayyani inside-out: that gold tea towel swaddled a head full of fiery pride, and those filed nails were itching to scratch her name in the history books – the woman who won a state for the Non-Landers and used it to launch the first international war of the Regeneration Era. Over his long objections, Dayyani had been given her chance: the best deal Is-Land had ever offered these foul parasites squatting on its doorstep. But the Head Engineer had not reckoned with Odinson's intimate knowledge of the Lioness' flammable nature. He had lit her short fuse and Dayyani had rejected cooperation with IMBOD. She was still fuming, and the next step was to flush her out of that false fortress and onto open ground.

'We still maintain that the complex issues raised today are best discussed in Amazigia,' he continued smoothly, 'but we must also reiterate our fundamental opposition to N-LA's schemes to establish a nation. The Southern Belt is designated as non-land because it is unsuitable for human habitation. The soil is still largely toxic, and the available arable soil can barely feed one-tenth of the current population. Yet decades after their failed experiment began, Non-Landers are still bearing children here. Why, I ask, *why*?'

Like the beautiful warning signs of a rockfall, rumbles of discontent and disbelief emanated from the red-robed side of the theatre. He ran his tongue around his teeth. These diseased sheep-slavers were a sheer joy to provoke.

'*Quiet.*'

A stickler, a spoilsport, an absolute pain on all spectrums, Thames could at least be counted on to yap above hir weight.

'Thank you, Major. As IMBOD has said, time and again, the land here needs to heal. It cannot do that while being exploited by an over-populated and legally dubious slum. The valuable resources both Is-Land and CONC are lavishing on the Belt would be far more usefully spent relocating its inhabitants to permanent accommodation within the borders of Asfar. That, as Amazigia has long agreed, is the *only* role Asfar should play in the conflict.'

He directed that comment at the journalists. Slightly deepening his voice, Chief Superintendent Odinson of the IMBOD Non-Land Barracks spoke now to the world. 'Yet again, N-LA demands the cheap sale of the Zabaria mine and compensation for its supposed "victims". Yet again, IMBOD notes that the mine provides one of the only steady sources of employment in the Southern Belt. No study has ever proved any link between working conditions and the claimed increase in birth disorders in the local population. On the contrary, exposure to thorium does not cause genetic harm, and birth disorders in the Southern Belt are within the average range for a region blasted by the worst depredations of the Great Collapse. Any reported increases coincide with periods of Non-Lander extremism, during which mine officials have reported attempts at sabotage, activities that have deliberately endangered the health of employees.'

The rumble returned, louder, an avalanche of indignation on the brink of engulfing the Non-Lander side of the theatre.

'Let him *finish*!' Major Thames commanded.

But he had no need of snapping CONC lapdogs. 'IMBOD has *never* recommended growing food in the war-tainted soil of the Southern Belt,' he said, 'or drinking its unclean water, but if people insist on moving here, there is little we can do to preserve them from the ill-effects of past military and industrial activity in the region. Our offer to provide reversible vasectomies and tubal ligations to Non-Landers, free of charge, still stands.'

'Objection!' Dayyani roared over the boos of her supporters. 'Objection!'

Magnificent. The red-robed Non-Landers were standing now, hands cupped to their mouths, their hoots of derision bouncing off the walls. Arakkia's supporters were craning round to look, excitement spewing out of their Code-warped faces. Except for the giant. That muscle-bound oaf looked confused. Too dim to know what to think until Arakkia told him, no doubt. In the front row, his own colleagues were stirring, the Head Engineer still doubting the strategy, still fretting about the safety of her precious team. But she would soon fall into place. Behind the tall gold CONC queen – he'd ram her first when this fortress fell – the Ordott girl was groggily stirring, peering round. Faking it? It didn't matter. As long as he knew where she was, the Head Engineer didn't have to worry: Astra Ordott was just another chipped pawn on the board.

'I said *silence*! *NOW*.' Major Thames banged hir fist upon the table. 'Objection overruled. As decided in last year's lengthy appeal, Odinson is offering a medical option, not threatening genocide. Let him speak.'

The boos ceased. Her chest heaving, Dayyani sat and clawed at the tabletop with her curved gold nails. Beside her, he noted, Arakkia was casually stroking his cartoon biceps.

The ground was prepared. Now to do the deed: demolish two camps with one blow. 'N-LA's *disingenuous demand*,' he pressed on, 'to establish a country in a toxic Old World war zone will only encourage extremists of the nature of the Youth Action Collective. For if I understand correctly the charming verses of the previous speaker, he will call a halt to his juvenile attempts to thwart the diplomatic process only when he has accomplished the wholesale invasion of Is-Land. In other words, he wishes for nothing less than the destruction of a sovereign nation, and with it humanity's best hope of surviving this fragile period in our evolution. Let me not waste time rebutting the hallucinations of fanatics. Neither will I pander to the daydreams of political opportunists. I repeat' – and *now* he thundered – 'the *only* solution to the endemic disease, poverty and unrest in the region is the transfer of the bulk of the population to Asfar, leaving the Zabaria mine to operate in peace for the benefit of all.'

He could barely be heard over Dayyani's supporters. They were booing again, jeering and stamping, their anger crashing through the theatre like the foaming finale to a glorious, turbulent symphony.

'*I said—*' Major Thames began, but with a grind of her chair and to a sharp intake of breath from the Non-Lander side of the theatre, Una Dayyani stood, and raising her hands, quieted her people.

'N-LA has heard *enough* of this vile hatred,' the Lioness spat into the silence.

Oh, the woman was a dream. Bursting to ruin herself: with one dramatic gesture undo, like that pretentious gold wasps' nest on her head, years of her own ambition.

'Your Excellency,' the Major snapped, 'this is most irregular—'

But Dayyani, Gaia praise her, was unstoppable. 'There are no studies,' she bellowed, poking the air in turn at him, the Major and the CONC Summoner, violating CONC's precious protocol with each stab of her gold-varnished claw – 'proving links between the Zabaria mine and the *vast range* of medical conditions affecting my people because CONC has *never funded* any such studies. Nor has it ever established a single institute of higher education in the Belt that could undertake this research.' He sat back as Dayyani steamed on, her face shining as she broke sweat with the effort of countering his undeniable truths. 'As for IREMCO, their continued refusal to acknowledge that *uranium deposits* far outweigh thorium in the mines is as *odious* as the frankly *criminal* implication that Non-Lander saboteurs have deliberately exposed their own people to radioactive toxins.' Her robe swelled as she drew herself up. 'Under my leadership, N-LA has cooperated *in full* with CONC's de-escalation policy. And yet, rather than defend our basic human rights, CONC continues to allow IMBOD's – yes, *genocidal* – statements to pass for reasonable comment at a Diplomeet! Major Thames, under these conditions, N-LA cannot continue to negotiate in good faith. I will see you in Amazigia.'

And with that, Una Dayyani ripped off her headset, gathered up her Tablette, and swept off the stage.

'*Lead Convenor Dayyani!*'

It was tremendous. The Major was furious. Hir precious Diplomeet was wrecked, peace process scuppered, CONC embarrassed in front of the international media. His cheek muscles twitched and he fought the impulse to lock eyes with his colleagues. The Head Engineer would be having kittens, but she and any other doubters would soon be won over. Blesserson was in the wings, standing ready in Atourne to Flock-Talk the new vision to all the Barracks teams tonight. It had been a long battle, but perspicacity and forward thinking had at last prevailed. As the Lioness and her pride – yes, all of her supporters – stalked out of the theatre, he took a moment to congratulate himself. For it had been, as always, a personal triumph, of vocal control, honed reflexes, and that star quality that from childhood had set him apart. Top athletes trained like all the rest, but inhabited a different cognitive realm: they saw the ball in slow motion, had a crucial extra split-second to envision exactly where to place their winning shots. So too, while Clay Odinson maintained utmost command over his voice and physical presence, his oratorical genius resided in his predatory perceptions: his instinctive psychological ability to at once precisely assess his human targets, and project his intentions upon them.

The final N-LA supporter left the hall, a last flick of the Lioness's tail. Stiffening his face against the uprush of triumph, he sat back in his seat. Now was YAC's turn to Respond. But Odinson was not worried about Enki Arakkia, not at all. That one-beat wonder, legless young buck, kicking up a diplo-stink with his tin-can rhymes, generating chaos with his scrapheap army of stone-throwing Code freaks – the boy was a gift from Gaia Herself. If Arakkia had not existed, it would have been necessary for the IMBOD labs to concoct him.

For the more chaos in Non-Land the better. It had been far too quiet here for far too long. As he and Blesserson had been telling the Head Engineer for months, there was no growth without risk, without wildness and *danger* – that was the new spiritual vision. Nothing less than Gaia's future was at stake.

Scraping his teeth gently together, he sat back to enjoy the rest of the show.

ASTRA

'Holy frack,' Rudo whispered to Photon.

'*Now* what?' Christophe hissed to Tisha. 'Do they *want* this place to fall apart?'

Astra's heart was thumping. It was impossible to keep pretending she was sleeping. A swirl of billowing crimson, the N-LA Lead Convenor sailed off the stage and up the ramp, her robe swishing so close Astra could have reached out and been sucked into its folds.

'Order! Order!' Major Thames was standing now, slapping the table with hir palms as, clapping, whooping and shouting, Dayyani's supporters filed out of their seats behind their leader. Sandrine's face was hanging open with dismay. Odinson looked rather smug, while Enki Arakkia was swiping furiously through his Tablette. Only his purple-shirted YAC members were left on the Non-Lander side of the room.

The last N-LA supporter exited, slamming the door shut. Remembering to look bewildered, Astra peered up the ramp. At the back of the theatre, a pair of glasses winked at her like signals. The wearer was small, in black robes, on the aisle seat: Dr Tapputu, waving at her – *Hello*. She whipped her head back to Photon for reassurance. Beneath his fluffy white fringe, the Alplander's eyes were sparkling.

Major Thames sat down. 'In accordance with the regulations,' heesh announced tightly, 'the Diplomeet may continue, though its decisions will not be binding. I therefore invite further Responses. If there are none, we will disband.'

Arakkia raised a finger. From the front row, without permission or warning, his supporters chimed in, their voices boldly joining Arakkia's in a chorus of dissent:

> Chosen from birth
> to inherit the earth,
> the Youth Action Collective
> rejects the deceptive
> Occupying Force
> rejects the invective
> of bullyboy talks.

'Silence!' the Major roared. 'Decorum! Only the Respondent may speak!'

But hir voice was a gnat in a herd of trumpeting elephants. The IMBOD officers were on their feet now, shouting and pointing, CONC officers raising their voices too, in support of the Major, the rules, *politesse*, Christophe shouted – but YAC chanted on, in a crescendo of hijacked authority, as the verses reached their peak on the wallscreen:

> We don't need to throw stones:
> our words are breaking down
> the walls of your perceptions –
> we command the global media
> to follow our adventures,
> and we leave the Gold Theatre
> to reflect on our appearance!

The wallscreen went blank. Enki Arakkia made his sign again, an open hand above his head. Then he stuffed his Tablette down the side of his chair and spun back from the table. His powerful arms deftly controlling the wheelchair, his body still rocking to the echoes of his final chant, he exited the stage down the side, then rolled past his supporters and up the central ramp of the theatre. His hooded eyes glazed with battle fever, his muscles tense with exertion, the YAC delegate propelled himself up the long incline, passing Astra as if she didn't exist. Close up, his star medallion was an irregular shape, its points all different lengths and angles. It was made not of silver but from a beaten tin can, the stripes of some colourful logo visible on the reverse side as it swung from his massive neck.

Again, pandemonium threatened. Behind Arakkia, in a rearing wall of purple, those YAC members who could, stood. IMBOD officers were storming the stage, shaking their fists at the Major; CONC officers were bobbing up and down, keen to see what was happening; and on the other side of the theatre the journalists were leaping into action. The woman was frantically swinging her camera to capture as much of the action as possible; the older man was threading his way through a back row towards the centre aisle, and the young man was racing along the front of the stage, a green-shirted bowling ball sending the skittles of the IMBOD officers reeling.

Major Thames rose to hir full height. 'I declare *an end* to the Emergency Diplomeet. CONC officers *remain in your seats*.'

A clutch of IMBOD officers rushed the stage. Everyone else was on the edge of their seats, watching YAC. The small woman, elevated on cushions, pulled out first, rolling up the ramp after Enki Arakkia. Her dainty fingers operating an electric control stick, the star on her chest reflecting the glittering wallhangings, with a bright magenta mouth she led the chant of the departing YAC delegates. It was an unscripted chant: the wallscreen went blank. But it didn't matter, Astra realised – YAC were now communicating in Inglish:

> Our bodies are the frontlines
> of a world with open borders

The young journalist strode backwards up the ramp, brushing past Astra as he filmed, blocking her vision, but not the sound of the woman's thin treble raised in YAC's chorus of defiance:

> And our star will chart a course
> to a scintillating future

On stage, in a scrum of IMBOD officers, Odinson was berating the Major. The older journalist was in the aisle now, framing the procession in his Tablette as up along the ramp came the man with two short arms, his wheelchair pushed by a thin young woman. It was apparent now that the man also had two short legs. And a very loud voice:

> YAC has rattled your cages
> with our invite to this meeting

The man's star was also irregular. He was laughing as he chanted. Rudo, on the other side of Photon, was chuckling as well. 'No shit, YAC buddies.' The Diplomeet was in complete disarray. For a fraction of a moment, Astra almost laughed too. Then she noticed the hands gripping the wheelchair handles. The fingers were blistered and flaking, the arms bandaged up to the elbows.

The dancing girl?

She glanced up. The girl was tall, wearing loose black trousers and a tight purple long-sleeved T. Her thick hair was bound in two paintbrush braids; her tin star hung from a polished bicycle chain. The girl's left cheek was cut by a bubbling rash, the dark blisters split with a pearly pink gash. But it was her smile that shocked Astra rigid. Not the smile on her finely curved lips, directed up the aisle. The secret, daring smile in the girl's clear tea-brown eyes, aimed straight at her.

The girl *knew her*. She knew the girl. That superior smile, flared nostrils, eyes as bright as sunlight drilling through autumn leaves. An intense pressure was building in her cranium: a torrent of memories gathering, burgeoning, ready to burst forth. *The dancing girl*. Dancing where?

A small figure pranced in her head. Over the lawn of Wise House.

Lil.

This girl was *Lil*. Her body was flooded with a strange warm effervescence. She had *kissed* Lil. And Lil . . . she stiffened . . . Lil had betrayed her . . . had told Ahn about her Security shot. That was why Ahn hated her. Yes, *of course*. With the hot triumph of the memories came a cold vertiginous plummet. Lil. How could she have *forgotten Lil*?

IMBOD, that was how. IMBOD had tried to delete Lil, but they had failed. She quickly checked the stage. Odinson was practically head-butting the Major – *he didn't know*. He didn't know this girl was Lil – right there, beside Astra, clocking her too.

Lil widened her eyes a fraction. A signal. A flashing order. But to do what?

Lil moved on. The chant continued. But she wasn't listening. She couldn't hear, couldn't speak, couldn't, *mustn't*, turn and follow Lil. She mustn't ever let Odinson know they'd found each other. She could only sit, stunned, trying to take it in. Lil was *here*.

But then, the very next moment, she was full of another kind of wonder.

Following Lil was the tall young woman with upswept red hair, the glamorous one who seemed both thin and wide. She was wide, it was now clear, not just because she looked pregnant in her pretty purple smock-top, but because she had eight arms. Two emerged at her shoulders and six from slits in the smock down her ribcage. The lowest pair limply grazed her tight jean-clad thighs. Her other hands were all clapping, complex rhythms that clattered in Astra's ears as the extraordinary girl processed past, her sharp voice cutting through the chant:

> You know now who we are
> And you know we got the power

Yes: YAC had the power. The power to astonish. Behind the girl a tall bald boy in a long purple robe was tapping slowly up the steps, one hand tucked into the crook of a young woman's elbow, the other holding a white cane. Still reeling with amazement, Astra gaped up at his face.

Her stomach tumbled away. The boy had no nose. No nostrils, no cartilage, just a plane of skin that sloped down to meet the enormous lower lip curled out moistly over his neck. Jutting up above the lip was a row of small blunt teeth. The ear she could see was a lumpy frill on a hairless head. And bulging from the centre of his forehead was an eye like no eye she had ever seen: three eyes in one, a dividing bubble of cells, a gleaming agglomeration of irises, pupils and white tissue. The boy wasn't chanting. His breath was rasping in great hoarse gulps; a long string of saliva was drooling from his lip. The young woman guiding him reached up with a cloth to wipe his mouth, but as the boy approached Astra, the tip of his cane scuffled the side of her seat; he paused, turned his head towards her and a whip of his spit splashed her cheek.

She rubbed her cheek, recoiled, like a child panicked by a bee. Someone gasped. Photon patted her arm, but she pulled away. It was an awful moment. Surely everyone left in the room was looking at her. Then it was over. The guide dried the boy's mouth and he tapped on.

Photon offered her a tissue. She wiped her cheek and stuffed the tissue down the side of the seat. She could rub away the boy's spit, but not her fear, her shame, her sheer incomprehension. What was going on in this place? Why had no one told her? Why were Lil and the children covered in rashes? Why were so many people here born alt-bodied? Okay, all of that could happen. She could understand illness, limb difference – but she could *never* understand how someone could not have a face. She felt hollow inside and tears blurred her vision. It was as though someone cruel, someone full of scorn and hate, had set about violently erasing the boy, and then, just for a joke, had abandoned the job. Could he hear? Could he speak? Who had done that to him? *IMBOD?*

> To change the game you're playing
> To blossom like a flower

The chant kept rising. And even through her tears, she couldn't stop looking. Enki Arakkia had commanded her to look at the next extraordinary person coming up the ramp. Walking towards her was a small young woman with a firm, athletic body, healthy honey-bronze skin, and a huge head: huge because it contained two faces. Divided by a swollen, dimpled cheek, and the dark widow's peak that split their foreheads, the girl's faces – or were *two* girls walking by, in one body? – were pretty, fine-boned, identical save for the tiniest discrepancies. The left chin was slightly lower than the right. One pair of long-lashed eyes paid demure homage to the empty half of the theatre; the other, narrower, peeking over the top of that swollen, honey-skinned cheek, danced languidly over the CONC officers. As her sly butterfly gaze alit on Astra, the girls opened their mouths.

> *Who is with us?*

The girls were singing: a sweet, plaintive, piercing counterpoint to the chant still arising from the procession, the YAC members moving ahead and those coming behind.

> *Who is with justice?*

The girls had impossibly beautiful voices. In their mouths the Inglish words were an enchantment, open windows shining in the sun; vibrating like silvery bee's wings, their harmonies lifted the hairs on Astra's scalp. They passed on by, followed by a string of purple-shirted youths on crutches, wearing prosthetics, none as strikingly alt-bodied as the blind boy, the clapping girl and the two singers, but all, like the stars round their necks, various in form. They chanted YAC's demands, distilled into two simple questions:

Who is with us?
Who is with justice?

The giant man brought up the rear, his massive frame filling the ramp, his hands as large as philodendron leaves, his thighs as thick as pine trees, his voice – WHOOO WHOOO WHOOO – a fat bassy boom.

In his wake rose a cacophonic reaction – outraged IMBOD officers, excited CONC officers jostling each other to take photos, the Major roaring 'Sit down!'

But even Odinson was breaking the rules now as he reached over the table to grab the woman journalist's microphone and growled, 'See what we have to contend with! This is a *Diplomeet*! Not a circus!'

At the top of the ramp, the chant was climaxing. Astra twisted in her seat and looked to the theatre entrance. The YAC members were at the door, the blind boy in the centre, swaying between his helper and Enki Arakkia, Lil behind the man she was assisting. The two extraordinary girls, still clapping and singing, were positioned at one end of the group, the giant at the other, anchoring them all with his deep sea voice. The journalists were filming, Dr Tapputu applauding. Astra sat suspended in the chaos, emotions swirling in her stomach, the enchantment of the song fading as her ears pricked to an inner voice.

Lil had signalled to her. The boy had lashed her with his drool. The twin-faced girl had pinned her with a look. One after another, they had marked her, had silently said: *Astra Ordott. We see you. What are you doing sitting and watching? When are you going to get up off that IMBOD-scarred arse and follow YAC out into the fight?*

The chanting stopped. As one, the youths who could raised a hand, fingers splayed in a defiant panoply of stars.

'ONE LAND!' they cried, the force of the call a dazzling cold stream directed straight at her, from a whole other universe.

ENKI

'*Whaaaaay!!! Whay HAAAAAAYYY!!!*'

'I can't believe it!'

'We did it!'

'*Arr Arr Arrrrrrr. Arr Arr Arrrrrrr.*'

'Did you see the look on Odinson's face?'

'*Three* journalists!'

Crazy-drunk on glory, exultation and adrenalin, they danced round the gym tent, Bartol and Khshayarshat pummelling the punch bag, Lilutu swinging around with Tiamet, Ninti whirling and spinning, Malku rolling over the wrestling mats, Asar honking with joy and slapping his white stick against a weights bench with such force Enki thought he might break it – the bench, not the stick. But Sepsu was there, stroking the Seer's arm, calming him down, drawing him into the crowd – everyone who had just rocked the Gold Theatre, shaken the CONC compound from cellar to ramparts, wildly celebrating with the dozens of YAC members who had waited in the tent for their return, monitoring the Diplomeet on Comchan, posting updates on ShareWorld to be read in other tents all over the Southern Belt and beyond. From Kadingir to the furthest Oasis towns, from Nuafrica to the Himalaya, Neuropa to New Zonia, YAC had done it: made its stunning debut on the world stage.

Enki star-splayed a hand at Bartol. The big man slammed the punch bag: *Boom Boom.* His mother should see them now. *Eggplants.* As he rocked and swivelled, a rhyme rose in his head: *The purple of our shirts is noble like YAC's motives . . . mysterious like our process . . . unites us in the night . . .* He grinned at Ninti, twirled his chair in sync with hers. He would finish the rhyme later. The greatest work was always unfinished. Another saying of Abgal Izruk, rest his spirit. Thinking of his teacher – the white beard that framed the lips of a man who spoke the language of youth; the crooked back that cloaked a fighter you never saw coming – Enki pressed his star medallion to his lips and raised it up to the high peak of the tent.

Across the mat, Ninti smiled, placed her hand on her heart. She understood. What was happening was a culmination. Everything Abgal Izruk had started, here in the wastelands of Nagu Three with a badly patched tent and donated gym equipment – a cooperative centre for orphans and alt-bodied youths; a strict place, forbidding beer drinking, morpheus abuse, bullying, gangs; a place that held talks, dances, film-screening nights, even engagement parties – everything that had been threatened by Abgal Izruk's sudden death was blossoming now.

Across the tent Bartol punched the air, bellowed, 'EN*KI*, EN*KI*, EN*KI*!'

Bartol. No. He scowled. Applauding a rhyme was one thing, but today's victory belonged to *everyone*. He had done his best, that was all, just like they all had. If he spoke boldly it was because he lacked the fear of taking risks. His mother and Abgal Izruk had made sure of that. He had tasked himself now with dispelling the fears of the youth. That was his job, not the pursuit of personal glory. He was not a beacon, but a matchstick – a spark to ignite a conflagration.

But the unwanted adulation continued. 'EN*KI*, EN*KI*, EN*KI*.' Ninti cupped her hands to her magenta pink lips, ululated to the tent roof.

'*Enki, Enki.*' Lilutu pranced over, leaned down, whispered in his ear. Issuing from her lips, his name was a husky mock moan, a riverbank promise. *Do you want to touch my lily?* she'd whispered out there under the stars . . . His eyes were on Ninti. A shadow flicked over the small woman's face.

He raised his hand, star-flared. 'Abgal Izruk!' he shouted back.

'Abgal Izruk! Abgal Izruk! Abgal Izruk!' Those who remembered the gym tent's founder honoured his memory; everyone else paid tribute to a legend, the man who, first by his sustaining presence and then by his incomprehensible absence, had created YAC. For after Abgal Izruk's sudden death, the youths had learned they would have to stand closely together to staunch the loss. Almost immediately, parents had decided that boys and girls should not train together any more, or attend dances without chaperones. Soon the social nights were male only, then beer-drinking had started and fights – real fights – had broken out, during training as well, until the CONC orphanage grew concerned and the centre was threatened with closure. Enki had drifted away then, down to the riverbank. But he had risen. He, Bartol and other older members had reclaimed the tent, re-established the rules, started a Nagu-wide fund to replace the old mats and broken wallscreen, and when two newly married couples had volunteered to chaperone, the parents had begun to allow mixed events again. Those rhyming nights had given birth to the Youth Action Collective.

'YAC!' Enki shouted.

'YAC!' the tent echoed. Ninti's back was to him now as she swivelled to hug one of the orphans.

'Star Party!' someone yelled.

'Star Party!' People were laughing, hugging each other, prancing on the weights benches, jumping up and down, spinning in their chairs, a galactic ecstasy. Ninti completed a 360 and graced him with a pose, a pert skywards glance. She looked a little different today for some reason, not just the lipstick. He rocked his shoulders and resisted the temptation to shoot a look at Lil.

'Enki.' Sepsu appeared before him. 'Asar needs to rest before tonight.'

Sepsu gave Enki the creeps. An older cousin of the Seer who'd taken over his care when the boy's devoted parents had died, she hovered like a moth beside Asar all day and night, her eyes as wide as full moons. All her talk was about the Seer and his needs, and all the while that belt-bag of coin bulged like a tumour beneath her grey silk robe. Many people, assessing Sepsu's silver rings and ample flesh, whispered that she was a clever one, operating the boy like a puppet. But that wasn't fair. Enki had learned a little arm language and it wasn't so: Asar did understand the questions put to him and answered them truly. And as far as he knew, Sepsu managed the money in the Seer's best interests. He had the finest clothes and food, and he lived in a luxurious tent. She also handled all his business dealings, apparently at his command, distributing coin to the orphanages and, after long negotiations with Enki, a small monthly amount to YAC too. Still, it had taken a long time to convince her that the Seer's presence wasn't gift enough: in order to create opportunities for the Singulars to reach new followers, YAC needed operational funds. And, beyond that, it was unnerving, the way you could never talk with either of them on their own, or to Sepsu's blank face about anything but money or Asar's requirements.

She was right, though. It was going to be a long day. *Phweeet. Phweeet.* Fingers in mouth, he whistled for silence. 'YAC attackers! Conclave now. Then food.'

Tiamet raised her upper arms, clapped people into order. Those who could sat down on the wrestling mats, the wheelchair users lined up on the ramps, and the Singulars, as always, took pride of place in the centre of the mat. Simiya sat cross-legged in the middle, batting her eyelashes over the congregation. Asar and Sepsu settled beside her, while Tiamet conferred, as usual, with Lilutu.

Lilutu. There was no escaping the girl who had escaped from Is-Land. After chauffeuring Malku earlier, she was back, glued to Tiamet's side, the Pithar Singular's ninth arm and second voice. Lil – as he was now permitted to call her – also considered herself, Enki knew, his private priestess, a fantasy he was no longer sure he wanted to indulge. Though he had managed so far to enter her temple on mutually agreeable terms, now that her vision for YAC was gaining traction with the orphans, the girl was becoming a more demanding gatekeeper. He watched her eyeing Simiya, her face tensing as the Kadingir Singular leaned over to Tiamet and, with a graceful gesture, tidied a strand of her coppery hair. As much as the Pithar pair had courted Simiya, the twin-faced avatar, he noted, clearly did not feel she needed to bestow her acceptance on both of them.

Bartol, his own self-appointed guard, stood at the tent flaps, keeping them all safe from unexpected arrivals. They had stolen Una Dayyani's media thunder today and N-LA would be on the offensive. Everyone knew that this was a War Conclave. Taking his usual position, Enki wheeled in between the other two core group members. Malku was facilitating, the limbless man often joking he'd been born to chair meetings. His ready humour was only one of his assets; he was tireless and uncompromising and, like Enki, had served three terms already. Ninti, on the other hand, was a new core member. Like other borderline Singular people, the tiny woman could have built her own quasi-cult, training herself to do spectacular feats, learning some inspirational texts and attracting a following of worshipful orphans. But like Malku and Bartol, she had never shown the slightest desire to do so. After two years of serving on both the media and care-working groups, she had been easily elected to the core, replacing Dorkas, who had struggled to fulfil the role while maintaining her commitments to her large family of orphaned siblings. The quiet and fragile-bodied Ninti, Enki had soon discovered, had a mind like a rook-trap, its sharp, lethal teeth hidden in a bed of innocent daisies.

The Conclave was ready to begin, the core group facing the Singulars in a nucleus of authority and focus. All present understood and accepted this structure. In transforming YAC from a community group to a political movement, Enki, Ninti, Dorkas, Khshayarshat, Malku and others had pored for months over Archivia, learning that leaderless resistance movements tended either to dissolve, or to be crushed by the hierarchical forces they opposed. Leaders, on the other hand, attracted followers, but tended to gradually alter group structures to feed their own corrosive addiction to power. YAC, they had decided after fierce debate, would be different. Consensus-based decision-making would be practised in the four working groups: care, media, warrior and vision, all of which were open to anyone who made the commitment to attend regular meetings. But when these groups fed back to the Conclave, they could not vote on their own proposals, which required a seventy per cent quorum to pass. That way, policy would be shaped by dedicated collective effort but could never be dominated by special interests. The core group had authority but, beyond their single votes, no power. It consisted of two administrative positions, and a speaker: a member who would serve with the Singulars as YAC's official public representatives. History, the youths' research had revealed, also proved that governments needed bureaucrats and people needed political icons – not just glamorous faces but accountable icons, dedicated talents. YAC was now a fully functioning participatory meritocracy and Enki Arakkia was both humbled and proud to place his skills in the service of its vision.

He star-flared. 'To the YAC Singulars! To us all!'

The tent erupted with whistles, hoots and applause. Sepsu conveyed the greeting to Asar, pressing her fingers into the Seer's forearm, as if playing an instrument. The Seer, Tiamet and Simiya returned the flare, Tiamet's finger-cymbals a flashing constellation her followers gasped to see, Lil's face soaking up the adulation as if it were her own. Enki, at last, did the same, letting the collective congratulations resonate through his chest, his private reward for two years of the largely thankless labour of working closely with the Singulars. They brought YAC funds, followers and fame, but Singulars, cast since birth as divinities or demons, were a nightmare to deal with. Simiya was pure diva: it had taken him months to build up a good relationship with her. She hadn't wanted to sing in Inglish at first, but through a combination of flattery and the subtle orchestration of Conclave Enki had finally managed to persuade her that this one small concession would bring an international following within her reach.

The Seer was joyful – one main reason Enki had wanted him in YAC – but his time with Asar was so strictly limited by Sepsu that he still wasn't really sure the Seer truly understood the nature of YAC. As for Tiamet, the Pithar Singular had nearly been his undoing.

The girl had shown up with Lilutu at a meeting more than a year ago, dancing barefoot and clashing her finger-cymbals over the mats as Lilutu declaimed a wild, rambling story about the ancient Prophecy – growing up in Is-Land with the Star Girl, travelling to Kadingir with the Himalayan caravan of singing bowls, meeting Tiamet in the House of Abundant Women, bringing her now to serve YAC as an advance party of this Istar, with Tiamet destined to stand with Asar and Simiya in the inner Singular circle. The two had created quite a buzz. Tales of the Prophecy had divided people: some youths were attracted to it, others indifferent, a strong minority hostile to the notion that YAC needed some old stones to tell them what to do. And more importantly, this 'House of Abundant Women' clearly meant Pithar. Many others, fearing the tainted lure of the sex-worker tent, had resisted Tiamet. After much discussion, the pair had been told they could attend meetings and follow the rules like everyone else: Enki had respected the will of the collective. Then, down on the riverbank, Lilutu had made her move.

Hand jobs and blow jobs didn't count in the marriage stakes, everyone knew that, and nor did fingers. Girls liked counting fingers and thumbs. But even orphans had reputations. Lilutu was the first woman to flick a condom under Enki's nose, to open the foil with her teeth, roll the latex down over his erection, straddle his hips and ride him like a sweat-sheened horse. It was still impossible to look at her and not think about it, the reckless speed of her gyrations, her breasts swaying against a curtain of stars until he reached up and grabbed her, twisted her over on her back, drove home.

The first time she'd approached him, he'd thought she might charge for her services. But Lilutu didn't want money. She wanted Tiamet accepted as a YAC Singular. He'd understood her arguments, eventually.

In a world where all paid work was corrupt and controlled by hostile international forces, why stigmatise people who sold the one thing they indisputably owned: their bodies? In the vision working group, he'd started supporting Lilutu's campaign. Tiamet had helped herself by being approachable, humble, sweet to the orphans, sharing beauty tips and giving dance lessons. Gradually, from being the object of fear, suspicion and derision, she had begun attracting dedicated followers. The orphans, many of them the children of sex workers, had admired Tiamet even more when she fell pregnant and declared she would keep the child. Eventually, the vision group had been persuaded to adopt Tiamet's cause. At that now-famous Conclave, with the Pithar girl's belly as big as a beer barrel, Enki had championed Tiamet, arguing that YAC accepted all the fallen and if they rejected a Pithar worker, they could reject him too. By a slim margin, the collective had elected her.

Simiya had been disgruntled at first, but now appeared to accept sharing the spotlight. For one thing, there were still plenty of people who openly sniffed at Tiamet. But with the Pithar worker's success, the extent of Lilutu's ambitions had become clear. With the news – confirmed by one of the media hackers – that her Gaian friend had been arrested in Is-Land, she'd frothed Tiamet's followers up into a permanent Prophecy frenzy. She had also officially claimed the role of Helpmeet of Harpies, which she said meant women who lived free of marriage and were feared and despised for their independent natures. As Tiamet's Helpmeet, she'd demanded the right to sit with Tiamet in the centre, and in an extraordinary Conclave, Sepsu and Asar had supported her. Enki suspected that Lilutu had also seduced the Seer's carer: not with her body perhaps, but with promises of shared glory. A Seer was mentioned in the Prophecy, after all.

Lil had also become demanding down at the riverbank. She showed up less often and talked a lot more, on and on about her past: her father, this Gaian girl, the girl's father and mother. Dozing off after their ferocious ride, he would let her ramble. But then one night, shortly after the presence of this Gaian refugee at the CONC compound had been confirmed by the media group, she had alarmed him. Lying on his chest she'd started whispering about temporary marriages, how her father had told her they worked, how you could decide for yourselves how long they would last. He was silent. Looking up at the stars, he'd said at last, 'This is the riverbank. We're outside time here.' She'd fallen silent, then traced his lips with her fingers. 'One day I'll show you the dry forest. When YAC blasts through the Boundary, we can go together, just you and me. It's timeless there too.'

He'd shifted, cradled her to the earth, sat up. 'I got to go, Lil. Meeting tomorrow.' Since then, she had saved all her plans for the Conclave.

Right now, before they could even discuss the Star Party work schedule, she signalled her desire to speak. Malku gave her the floor and she stood. Tiamet clashed her finger-cymbals.

'I saw her,' she declaimed in that grand manner she put on in public like a starched robe. 'She was at the Diplomeet, sitting with the tall white medic, the one who fell in Nagu Six. Asar blessed her. Sepsu saw it. Tiamet saw it.' The others nodded, and a bank of orphans gasped. 'She is here and we must greet her. We must invite her to the Star Party.'

Ninti raised a finger and Malku nodded. 'This is irregular, Lilutu,' she said. 'Proposals should be raised by working groups.'

'I *am* speaking for the vision group, Ninti,' Lilutu flashed. 'Vision and media both respect the power of the Prophecy.'

And though each person in the tent had the right to respond, the same as any other, they all looked to Enki. Yes, he could not reject their admiration completely. He had fallen – some still said he had fallen too far – but he had risen, and the youths had elected and re-elected him because they knew that everything Enki Arakkia did, even fall, he did to the utmost limit of his abilities. Alone among YAC members he served on four groups: media, vision, warrior and core. The few dissenters – the mutterers, mockers, rival rhymers – had soon discovered how weak was their own vision, how limited their aim.

'Prophecy followers are welcome in YAC,' he declared. 'We are open to all beliefs, all faiths. But we are strong because we shine together.' Grunts of agreement countered the orphans' raptures; Lilutu did not hold everyone in thrall. 'We must be careful,' he pressed on, 'not to give our light away. I say what vision and media have always said: if this girl wants to join her power to ours, she is welcome. But she must serve YAC, like we all do. *We* means the collective.'

He stared at Lil, who tossed her chin. A murmur rippled through the tent. *Ask Asar. Ask Asar.* The Singular Seer was swaying back and forth as Sepsu stroked his feet. Enki glanced at Simiya. Was there going to be trouble? But the Singular's two faces were still mirrors. She was, he suddenly realised, bored.

Malku spoke. 'Agreed. Sepsu, please ask Asar: do we invite the Gaian girl to the party?'

Sepsu asked the question. Or a question, anyway.

'*Arrrr. Arrrrrrrr.*' As Asar cried his assent a cheer went round.

'She will join our vision.' Lilutu, as so often, spoke with conviction verging on contempt for the Conclave process. 'She will serve. But I must speak to her first.'

Beside him, Ninti took the floor again. He realised now why she looked different. She'd done her hair in a new style, with coils pinned round her forehead. It suited her.

'If we invite the girl, Lilutu,' she said, 'CONC will know we want her for some reason. That might put her in danger. Or out of our reach.'

It was going to be a long Conclave. Sometimes he thought YAC should stand for the Youth Argument Committee. Beside him, Ninti went on, raising the objections he should have done if he hadn't been determined to detach himself entirely from Lil's schemes. From the mat the girl cast him a hurt look. No, he wasn't responding to that. She had cried the other night, he knew, on his chest, while he was sleeping, her shuddering movements awakening him from slumber. But she hadn't said anything, and when she finally stopped and he'd opened his eyes, he'd pretended the damp patch was sweat. Avoiding her gaze, he scanned the tent. Sepsu was settling Asar with a pillow, stroking his head. Yes, let the Seer sleep, absorb the Conclave in his dreams. When he awoke, hopefully they would have decided who was going to set up and clean up and take shifts at the beer tent tonight. Senior YAC members might not drink, but the youth of Kadingir certainly did.

ASTRA

'I'm so sorry, Astra.' They were in the officers' courtyard having a drink with Rudo after the Diplomeet, and Photon was berating himself again. 'I should have guessed some of the Singulars would be there. You ought to have had an Orientation Session. It can be difficult, seeing them the first time.' He rubbed at his face, his eyes for a moment red-rimmed craters.

Astra jabbed her straw at the ice in her mock julep. Did Photon think she was some kind of Neuropean lady visitor, someone from his Alpland village who'd only ever seen an alt-bodied person in the Neo-Paralympic Games? Yes, she'd been shocked by the boy – shamefully, she'd been afraid, repulsed. She still wasn't sure how she felt about him. But she had recovered. She wasn't frigging *traumatised*. She was back in control, charged up by the Diplomeet and its colossal revelation: Lil. IMBOD had tried to make her forget Lil. That meant she was incredibly important. For now, though, Astra had to find out as much as possible about Non-Land. And YAC.

'I know lots of *Singular* people,' she retorted. 'But they were all wounded in battle. No one in Is-Land is *born* alt-bodied.'

'I think they are not technically Singulars then,' Photon continued, apologetically. 'Here it is only the alt-bodied people who are born different . . . well, *very* different . . . who develop a cult following.'

'Wrong way round, Phot.' Rudo took a glug of his beer. 'Actually, Astra, it's only the cult leaders who get called Singulars. Pretty much half the families in Non-Land got a severely alt-bodied kid or two. Some parents make an effort, find a god on Archivia to invoke, do a Nagu whip-round every sacred holiday. If the kid's got talent or personality, it can work out to a lifetime gig. Most parents can't cope, or think they've been cursed, and the kids get sent to a CONC orphanage. When they turn eighteen they get turfed out and end up begging on the street, or working in the sex tents. Nothing too *unique* about that.'

Rudo's off-grid diction made him a little hard to understand sometimes. And she was still struggling to understand the basic situation here. 'Why are people born alt-bodied in the first place?' she demanded. 'Aren't Non-Landers Coded properly?'

'Language, Astra.' Rudo coughed into his fist.

She squinted at him. He was grinning. What? What had she said?

Photon looked pained. 'What Rudo means,' he explained, speaking hesitantly, delicately, like a deer placing its feet in uncertain terrain, 'is that we don't make to judge people on the basis of Code here. Non-Landers are not Coded to be average-bodied, no. Even if there was funding for that, most of them don't believe in changing human Code. They think it is wrong to – well, they would say, *interfere* with nature.' He brightened. 'Some of their religions have quite an interesting philosophia about this, actually. They say that just like the gods sent the Dark Time to make us to live in a different way, they create vulnerable humans to encourage empathy and care. So if we are to eliminate illness and disability we will destroy the best of humanity too.'

'Funny how divine plans got a way of backfiring,' Rudo drawled. 'Most places the sick and alt-bodied seem to bring out the worst in other people. Like, for example, deciding to Code 'em out of existence.' He took another slug of beer. 'Peeps ain't born for anyone's benefit but their own, Astra. Best just to fly with the flow, try not to control shit; help each other out if-and-only-if requested and/or paid to do so. That's *my* philosophia, anyhoo.'

Wow. She sat back. She'd heard these tired old arguments before, way back in Year Nine Coding class, but she had no idea people still seriously believed them.

'Coding isn't about *interfering* with people,' she exclaimed. 'It's about protection from harm. You're both Coded against radioactivity, aren't you? And solar melanomas? And . . .' She tried to remember the worst Old World conditions, long-extinct in Is-Land, the ones all other sensible countries were finally eradicating, thanks to Gaian generosity: 'Parkers. And Hunters. And . . . lepsy,' she triumphantly concluded.

'Yippers,' Rudo agreed cheerfully. 'Nuke-proof here, and checked for the full range of inheritables. But that don't mean it's okay to pre-delete deaf people, or folks with Downsy, or anyone who might think or look a little different. Hell, some parts of North-East New Zonia you still got white throwbacks arguing that blacks ain't smart enough to breed.'

She stared at him in distaste. 'We didn't *pre-delete* anyone. There are deaf communities in Is-Land. They have their own culture. And there are still some people with Downsy, but—' She paused. Not many Gaians were alt-brained, actually. 'It's an *optional protection* and most parents choose it. And against growth restriction, and limb differences, and everything else that people don't want their kids to have to deal with.' She was tired of being on the defensive. 'If people are so *stupid* that they think skin colour's got anything to do with IQ, *they* ought to be sterilised. Illnesses and congenital impairments are totally different. The problem with *your* countries is that you make people *pay* for protections. So only the rich get them. In Is-Land, we all do. It's about giving everyone a fair start in life. *That's* caring for people.'

It was more than she'd said in one go for months. And it was a defence of Is-Land. She sat back, a cyclone of emotions whirling through her.

Rudo scratched his neck, unfazed. 'It's gone beyond protection now, though, hasn't it? From what IMBOD's let slip, these Sec Gens are gonna kick-Code the rest of us into extinction.'

Right. Of course. That's where this was leading. The Sec Gens. She pulled her julep towards her, took a long cool slurp. People at other tables were looking over. Let them stare.

'Rudo,' Photon gently attempted, 'Astra has just got here. From a different culture. There is good and bad things about every culture—'

'The Sec Gens are different,' she cut in. 'They're a special IMBOD project. Not everyone in Is-Land agrees with IMBOD on everything. It's the same here. YAC disagrees with N-LA, doesn't it? Why's that? Doesn't N-LA care about alt-bodied people?'

'They do. Very much,' Photon assured her. 'N-LA has done a lot of work to make accessible infrastructure in the Belt.'

'A li'l bit too much, if you ask me.' Rudo laughed.

What did he mean? And wasn't that a 'Language' remark? But Photon didn't rise to the bait. 'The difference is part about statehood,' he said slowly. 'YAC does not want to trade away the dream to return to their ancestral home. But I think also the conflict is about the Zabaria mine.

Previously, N-LA demanded to close the mine but now Dayyani is making more power, she is wanting to run it. YAC is a younger generation. I do not know their whole manifesto, but if they want to fight IMBOD, maybe they will also want to shut the mine. It is responsible for their birth differences, I think.'

Rudo set his beer bottle down on the table. 'C'mon, Phot. We've only been here a year. How do we know things are getting worse? There's bound to be birth differences in Non-Land. Astra, the Old World gangsters nuked the shit out of the place.'

'It is hard to tell.' Photon's pale brow was knit as if his brain was churning behind it. 'Many women give birth in their tents, and do not report the outcome. It is not only limb differences, Astra. Organs are often missing, or not functioning. In the Treatment Wards, one in three babies is dying. Sometimes in terrible pain. Also, the skin sickness is in the Non-Land Code now, affecting the offspring. Dayyani is right. CONC should be to commission studies, and IREMCO must disclose the presence of uranium in the mine.'

She thought of the laundry, the babies' gowns splattered with blood and pus. Her jaw hardened. Was *Samrod Blesserson* responsible for all this suffering?

'CONC's got enough to do feeding and watering everyone. Astra.' Rudo claimed her attention again. 'The whole region's a nuclear hotspot. You Is-Landers are all right, but internationals gotta have booster shots to work here, and unless an Asfarian billionaire feels like upping his approval ratings, the Nonners don't get 'em. It's like your IMBOD man said, there's no proof the miners are handling uranium.'

Everything she knew about IMBOD was sticking in her chest like a ball of barbed wire. 'He's not my man,' she snapped. 'And IMBOD's lying. That's what IMBOD *does*.'

'Is that right?' Rudo was regarding her with amusement. 'Only been here five minutes and you've sussed IREMCO's tech spec, have you? Go on then, show us your data.'

He reached a hand, palm up, across the table.

She was quivering with fury. 'So you believe IMBOD? You think everyone here should be *sterilised*? That would be better than being Code-protected, would it?'

He laughed again, withdrew his hand. 'Nah, don't like IMBOD much. But you know what? This place is a complete fracking mess.

Everything CONC does is just sticking band-aids on a pig-gutting. Getting statehood won't make it better. Think about it: soon as the Nonners get a nation-weight vote in Amazigia, they'll start demanding Is-Land visiting rights. Meantime Asfar's definitely working on missile-ware. Maybe IMBOD's gotta a right to stick up that Shelltech.'

'That is only rumours about Asfar,' Photon demurred. 'And N-LA says they don't want to return any more. They want to live here, re-establish agriculture, like the Gaians did in Is-Land—'

'Greening the scrubland.' Rudo snorted. 'Okay, it rains sometimes, but the Belt ain't like your steppes, Astra. Apart from the nukes, there's a depleted aquifer and two deserts to contend with. Plus those *mergallá* storms blow away all the topsoil every six or seven years. Why live here if you don't have to? Because you're *homesick*? Man oh man. Practically *everyone* lost everything during the Collapse. My folks, the city they came from, on the east coast of New Zee: it's sixty metres under the phosphorescent fishes now. You Gaians got a good deal, sure. But the Nonners been gnawing on the short end of that stick for too long now. Maybe it's time they oughta accept they lost out. Like I said, you gotta fly with the flow. And I don't mean sexy hothead rapper mojo flow, Astra. I saw you checking out those biceps, girl.'

Rudo winked, drained his beer. She was incapacitated with anger. Okay, she didn't know much about this place. But one thing was certain: IMBOD was lying. She would show Rudo. She would find a way to *prove* that—

'Jealous of the silver-tongued man with the mic, are we, Rudo?' Grinning, Sandrine pulled up a chair.

'Jealous? If he's pronging that chick with eight arms, definitely. I could do with a multi-digit massage after all day in the MMU, I'll tell you. Jack, sack and crack, bring it on!'

'Rudo!' both Sandrine and Photon exploded.

'Hey—' Rudo grinned. 'No offence, Astra. Rude by name, rude by nature. Photon shoulda told ya. I'm just a prowling tom cat from the wilds of Mount Reality, with no respect for no one, me.'

'Don't listen to him, Astra,' Sandrine said. 'He doesn't mean half of the rubbish he spouts. He's a solid driver, and he's really good with the compound kids. They love him.'

'Yeah. They do.' Rudo took the compliment like a baton. 'And you know why? Coz I don't wander around with a long face feeling sorry for 'em. The compound kids are fine. Like most people here, they just need eczema cream and proper prosthetics. Not N-LA propaganda or YAC stunts.'

'How can you *say* that, Rudo?' Sandrine sighed, her goodwill exhausted already. 'Non-Land is a *political* problem. It needs political solutions.'

'What? Like chucking rocks at us? Non-Land is an *existential* problem, Sandrine.' She tried to speak, but he waved his palm: *hello?* 'They're living on a nuclear waste dump – why? Because they wanna be *heroes*. Look at YAC. Just when Mama Dayyani could get them their own fracking state, they jump up and declare holy war on the Boundary. That boy who spat on you, Astra—'

'Rudo,' Photon chided, 'he did not spit on her. Not on purpose.'

'Yeah, whatever.' Rudo would not be deflected. 'His name is Asar, means "all-seeing eye". He's a prophet and his spit is miracle-water. According to all the sacred rites of Non-Land you've been blessed, Astra. So don't waste your time crying over the youths. Let 'em have their New Messiah fantasies if it makes 'em happy. All I want to do is serve my three years here in this hellhole and get home before you can see my balls glowing from space.'

'Rudo,' Photon attempted, 'that is a very ahistorical attitude.'

'It's a *pathetic* attitude,' Sandrine chimed in. 'YAC has arisen because a decade of compromise has threatened to—'

Astra pushed her chair back from the table. The boy had *blessed* her? Suddenly there was a cold spot deep in her belly, as though she had swallowed that splash of spit and her body was refusing to absorb it.

'Sandrine, you ain't out there getting stoned. And Phot, I luv ya, man, but you're dotty as a toadstool. Astra, I'm telling ya, steer clear of politics here. The Nonners could live nice comfy lives in Asfar, but they don't want to. They wanna live here. All we can do is try and make sure they don't die of hunger or thirst, or whack us too hard on the head. Speaking of thirst' – Rudo pointed at Astra's glass – 'why the hell you drinkin' a mock julep, girl?' His chair clattering against the courtyard paving stones, Rudo stood up. 'Welcome to CONC's crazy carousel, Astra. It's my round.'

'It sure is, after that!' Sandrine laughed shortly and Astra took a defiant suck on her straw, letting the cool mint juice wash away the thought of the boy's drool in her stomach. It was just an accident, that was all. Anyone could send a drop of spit flying.

Beside her, Photon was checking his Tablette. 'A half for me, thanks. I'm driving tonight,' he announced.

'Driving?' Sandrine frowned.

'The Major's just messaged.' Photon beamed. 'Arakkia has called off the stonings. And he's invited CONC to send a small delegation to tonight's River Raven. He especially mentioned Sandrine, and the man who got hurt in Nagu Six – that's me. Plus two others: Msandi and Eduardo don't want to go, so the Major says Rudo and Astra too!'

'Yo!' Rudo whooped. Hands on hips, he stuck out his bottom and wiggled it in Photon's face. 'Time to get down and dirty with my main man!'

Photon tilted back in his seat, giggling, his face – to Astra's disgust – creased with pleasure.

At the next table, Christophe turned and pouted. 'Rudo?' His voice was a practised parody of hurt. 'I thought *I* was your main man.'

'Rudo's main man?' Across the yard, another officer called out, 'Hey, ain't that *me*?'

Around them, people were shaking with laughter. Or just shaking their heads.

Rudo pumped his arms above his head, and thrust his bum into the courtyard. 'Youse *all* my main men,' he falsettoed. 'I'll mainline youse on Main Street, on the mainland, and mainly, baby, on the plane to the plain.'

'Keep your *butt* in your own *air*space, soldier!' Laughing, Sandrine whacked the seat of Rudo's trousers.

'*Sister*!' His falsetto shot off the scale. '*Kerching*!'

Astra couldn't believe it. Rudo was an idiot. He swallowed whatever IMBOD told him, and made jokes about alt-bodied people. The Major had said comments like that weren't allowed in the compound, but Sandrine and Photon had let them pass and now they were laughing uproariously at his ridiculous impersonation of a gay man. Across the table, Photon smiled, inviting her to join in. A confusing warmth spread through her chest. There was nowhere safe to look except up.

Twilight was falling. The heat had lost its searing edge, the first star had punctured the dusky blue dome of the evening and the pale wafer of a full moon was floating in the sky. As she lifted her face to bathe in its soft white gleam, the raucous cheers of the officers fell away, and a voice from the past floated back to her. Hokma's voice, telling fairytales on the the Wise House verandah. The moon is a tarnished mirror, Hokma had told her; long ago it shone pure and still as a frozen lake on which no feather ever fell, and people looked in it every night to see their inner selves. But then a vain, rash young man, not liking the truth it told him, tore the moon from the sky and flung it aside, shattering its calm. Now the moon is a collection of broken shards, drawn together once a month by the tides. Yes, she remembered, sorrow rising in her like water, the moon had been broken, like she had been, in ways no one in this courtyard would ever understand.

Like the grey skin of boiled alt-milk, a cloud crept over the moon. Looking up at its wrinkled shadows, an image of Asar, his bulging eye-cluster and shining mouth, swam into her mind. She shivered. But why? She wasn't afraid of blindness; her Year Eight biology teacher had been blind, and Hokma had been half blind. It was more that Asar's face seemed to signal some huge, incomprehensible loneliness. Could he hear? Speak? Compose thoughts? Perhaps his mind was a bricked-up prison, like the traitor's well Hokma had been threatened with. How could a person live like that? Again, Hokma's voice stirred in the deep well of her confusion. 'All your eyes can do is look, Astra,' Hokma had once said. 'Seeing might be believing, but it isn't *knowing*. To know the truth, you have to perceive it with your mind and behold it in your heart. That's what a Gaia vision is.'

A Gaia vision. The thought was like a rope dangling in the well, just out of reach. In a Gaia vision you sat still and observed the marvel of life, perceiving its patterns and beholding one's purpose within them. Vaguely, she remembered that wondrous feeling of certainty flowing through her, sensation making sense of the world. Here, although she was still drinking in the immense, deepening, glimmering blue, all she felt, suddenly, was extremely conscious of the two small orbs of jelly in her head. Eyes.

Then her biology teacher, Mr Groveson, was floating there too, in the sky, in her head – she didn't know which. Millions of years ago, Mr Groveson had said, trilobites, little exoskeletal marine animals, had viewed the world through eyes made of calcite crystals. The eyes were hard as armour, unable to change focus, but stacked like turrets on the creatures' heads they could perceive 360 degrees of danger or food. Human eyes were more vulnerable sentries: they too watched out for predators and prey, but they had also evolved into complex portals to light's magnificent, infinite interplay of colour, detail and distance. The more complex something was, the more could go wrong with it,

Mr Groveson had said. That had been the Imprint, she remembered, *Damage is an inherent aspect of high function*. But it was not the whole lesson.

Gaia Herself, the teacher had continued, is like an eye: our swirling blue-green planet, streaked with white clouds and white snow, a glowing orb spinning in the darkness of space, and a place – the only place we know of – where the universe reflects on itself. But this enormous blue-green eye is vulnerable too. Human beings, lacking *foresight*, had jabbed at Gaia with drills, fracked and pumped Her, forcing out fountains of burning black tears. Human beings had killed the bees, polluted the oceans, melted the ice caps, completely overwhelmed Gaia's ability to self-regulate her complex, nurturing, life-sustaining processes. Human beings had nearly reduced Gaia to rock and dust and churning waves, a barren sphere inhabited only by extremophiles, creatures that could survive in charred deserts, boiling volcanoes, frigid ocean crevices, conscious – like trilobites, like oil junkies – only of their own immediate needs. Did this matter to Gaia? Mr Groveson had asked.

The class had thought yes! Yes! Gaia would be hurt, grief-stricken, furious at human beings for destroying Her. But the answer was *no*. Gaia would adapt to Her crone state, just like blind people and old people adapted to their new circumstances. Physical blindness, Mr Groveson had said, brandishing the wallscreen remote control, was just a different way of being, an inconvenience at worst. Moral blindness was a crime. With proper care and respect, Gaia could remain fertile until a meteor strike or the death of our sun, and for the sake of all Her creatures it was humanity's responsibility to ensure that She did.

She was breathing calmly now. Around her the sound of laughter and beer bottles ringing on the tables returned to her as if from over a vast distance, muffled by veils of light, travelling on the deep humming echo of the birth of the universe, the long low note of the Major's conch shell call. *The rebirth of the earth*. She might not like all the officers, but she had to accept that CONC, as much as Is-Land, had saved Gaia. CONC had risen in the darkness and the chaos, overcome entrenched hostilities, communicated, organised, inspired. CONC had prohibited fossil fuels, war machines and war itself. CONC had created Is-Land, funded the Gaians to re-sow the seeds of agriculture in the Earth's desiccated soil. And when Is-Land had turned against her, Astra, CONC had taken her in. She was safe here.

The clouded moon, Asar's face, Gaia's resurrection: was she having a

Gaia vision? If the moon was an eye, she thought as it shed its thin grey veil, it saw things calmly, serenely, without distress. Asar, she realised, didn't need her pity. He was a prophet, Rudo had said. Somehow he listened to Gaia in his own way. How, she didn't know, but in the close embrace of evening warmth, the sparkling first star offering its benign direction, she didn't need to know anything. She was immersed in a nebulous vision in which cloudy questions slowly sailed through her mind, briefly dimming the lamp of understanding, but also strangely illuminated by it. Was accepting the Singulars as simple as celebrating Gaia's abundance, Her gift of human diversity? Or were their impairments, like her own headaches and nausea and burning brand-wound, cruel deprivations, the result of IMBOD's poison? She didn't know yet, but that was okay. She could see this world with her eyes, she was starting to perceive in her mind how it worked, and one day soon she would behold in her heart its purpose, and her own.

'Astra? Are you okay?' Photon leaned over and patted her arm.

'Moonstruck. Happens to the blessed,' Rudo joked.

Was everything a joke to Rudo? She observed the driver as if through the wrong end of a telescope, the sounds of the courtyard still muted by her trance.

Rudo was a beautiful average-bodied man. His face was not striking like Enki Arakkia's, not composed of dramatic planes, but harmonious, restful to behold. His skull was round, his eyes warm, his sloping nose and full lips gracefully formed. His limbs were sturdy, yet elegant, his musculature developed to a pleasing proportion, not strained beyond it. His skintone was mid-spectrum, the shade most requested for lab-Code babies in Is-Land. *Rudo was blessed*, she thought slowly. He was smart, fit, his looks easy on anybody's eye. He had a job that gave him comradeship, shelter, three meals a day. And these blessings had dazzled his vision. How could he not care that IMBOD might be causing a whole generation to be born with severe impairments, many of them to barely survive infancy and the rest to live in poverty and hunger?

'In Mount Reality,' Rudo was announcing, 'we say it like this: *Mon tabarnac jvais te décalisser la yeule, calice.*' He shook his fist, Christophe snorted beer down his shirt and the courtyard erupted in a cackle of laughter. All the CONC officers were blessed: the winners of the global lottery. Strong, healthy young people out in the world having an adventure. She would never be one of them. And she would never be one of YAC either. Even if she wanted to join them, they would never accept an Is-Lander. Wherever she went, she would be the outcast, the secret freak.

Strangely, she realised, that knowledge didn't bother her any more. Gaia was with her again.

'C'mon, Astra. My round. No yoga-teacher drinks. Whatcha having?'

She'd had beer before, at Or banquets. She liked the wheaty taste. She met Rudo's lilting brown eyes. 'A pint of lager,' she declared.

PEAT

Some people couldn't wait; they began reading their progress reports as soon as they got to the meadow, veering off in silence through the tall grasses, Tablettes in hand. But the Division Officer had said to take your time, savour the praise and reflect carefully on the areas for improvement. Peat wanted to read his properly.

'Let's sit there.' He struck out towards a golden swathe of the meadow near the border of the woodland. Jade, Robin and Laam followed and they sat down in a circle. They were sky-clad again, saving their uniforms for training practice, but stones didn't bite or grass tickle since his booster shot. He stroked a clump as he read.

There had been no need to worry. His progress report was excellent. He had scored top marks across the board: strength, speed, agility, information retention, information analysis, cooperation, listening skills and even emotional stability. In the Personal Comments his Division Officer heaped praise on his recent interest in Non-Land animal-welfare laws. And there, unbelievably, at the bottom, was a note he had to read twice:

Constable Orson,
    Congratulations on this outstanding report. I will be pleased to inform your Shelter and Code parents that your recent distressing family circumstances have not affected your performance – unless, that is, to strengthen it. That unfortunate matter is now in the past, and your Division Officer assures me

that a glorious future awaits you in law. I salute your steadfast
dedication to your generation and your nation.

Chief Superintendent Clay Odinson

His palms were sweating. Odinson had probably written to
everyone – or had he? Nearly three thousand personal notes? Peat looked
up at his Gaia playmates, their heads bent over their own reports. None
were looking astonished.

'Not bad. My Code mum won't be crying, anyway.' Robin gave a satisfied sigh. 'How's yours, Peat?'

The note wasn't something to boast about; it was an expression of
Odinson's fatherly concern. 'Okay. Good, I mean. I should keep working
on my legal interests.'

'How about yours, Laam?' Jade asked.

Beside Robin, Laam was silent.

'C'mon,' Peat urged. 'It can't be that bad.'

'Yes it can.' Laam stuck out his Tablette and they all leaned in. 'I mean, look
at my physical abilities scores. Scraping the bottom of the range.'

The scores *were* low. For all his extra gym sessions, Laam still wasn't
quite keeping up on the training field. But that was because he was a bit
small – like Yoki, that was all. 'They're higher than your entrance exam
scores,' Peat pointed out. 'That's the main thing. The booster shot is obviously working.'

He himself could feel the shot's multiplex effects increasing every day:
thicker skin, faster healing, stronger bonding. He thought it must be
helping with emotional stability too: he still knew his ex-Shelter sister
was out there in Non-Land, but the thought didn't bother him so much
any more. So what if he ran into her? He would be with the group, and
his Division Officer would tell them all what to do.

'But I haven't grown as much as you all have,' Laam pointed out. 'You've
all gained at least two inches. I bet my mark increase isn't as high as all
yours either.'

They checked, and it was true. Laam's increase was three per cent,
while the rest of them had scored between five and eight per cent higher
since the booster.

'That's a three-point spread between me and Peat, and only two points between you and me,' Jade observed. 'I'm sure it doesn't matter. What do your personal comments say?'

Laam passed the Tablette across and they all pored over it:

Excellent intellectual and emotional scores, as expected from a young man with a talent for biotecture, a close-knit family and a deep love of animals. We will continue to monitor your physical performance and make any necessary adjustment to your duties. Your safety is our prime concern.

'You see?' Laam nearly squeaked. '"Adjustment to your duties." They might not let me defend the Hem.'

That couldn't be right. 'No,' Peat reassured him, 'there must be a variety of defence roles out there, that's all.'

They all fell silent. No one knew yet exactly what would be expected of them out on the Hem. Groundcover and hand-to-hand combat, clearly, from highly trained warriors, adept at martial arts, boxing, wrestling and berserker murmurations. But still, what if the Non-Landers had weapons? This morning Odinson had said they were to appear 'disciplined' at all times, *unless provoked otherwise*. Peat had noted the phrase. He had also been thinking about Odinson's invitation.

'Look,' he said, slowly, 'Laam. Don't worry about the Hem. There must be others who are scoring at the lower end of the range. Even if you're in a different team, you'll still be with Sec Gens. And I've got a plan for an initiative. All of us could work on it. It wouldn't take special physical abilities.'

'An initiative?' Laam still sounded anxious.

'Yeah, like Odinson challenged us this morning.'

Laam looked around the circle. 'I didn't get that. I thought Sec Gens weren't supposed to have initiatives. What if—?'

He stopped, but Peat knew what he meant. What if it was a trap? Astra wasn't the only Is-Land child whose parent or parents had prevented them from having the Security shot. The rest, the Sec Gens had always been told, had been weeded out long ago. But in Atourne, a girl in another division had been sent home. She was tall but thin, and she had been completely unable to keep up on the training field. She had also asked one of her Gaia mates what he really thought of the Amazigia vote: perhaps, she had stunningly suggested, if the Non-Landers really didn't want to use weapons, they could be allowed to have their independent State. Her Gaia mate had reported her, of course. No one had heard from her since.

'We can,' Robin reassured Laam, though he didn't sound completely confident.

'Sure we can,' Jade agreed, doubt hazing her voice too.

'If Odinson says we can, we can,' Peat asserted. The girl in Atourne was a completely different scenario. Her ideas weren't an initiative, they were treason. 'Bright ideas shine glory on the Sec Gens, not ourselves. Listen, this is what I've been thinking.'

They head-huddled, Peat talked, they debated, and by the time they stood up and brushed the grass off their thighs they were united in agreement: Peat had had the freshest idea since earpiece speeches.

ASTRA

After the beer, they went for dinner. For the first time, Astra sat at the table with the other officers, blowing on her potato and onion soup as Rudo explained the finer points of Mount Reality swearing: most of the curse words defiled Abrahamism, it turned out, which was fine by her. Christophe joined the conversation and the officers started debating the Diplomeet: had the walk-outs been staged, pre-arranged between N-LA and YAC? Were the stonings really over? How much power did Arakkia have? Were there other contingents of resistance, youths or adults beyond his control? And who the frack was responsible for those translations? The Gaian propaganda effort you could understand, Rudo declared, but Asfar had a mighty tradition of rapping and whoever had produced those versions ought to be skinned for drums.

Astra was only half listening now. Her brain was tired, and not just from the Gaia vision. She'd spoken more today than she had for the last four months put together, not to mention switching between three languages all day. Plus, her brand was itching again; she needed to get to her room to reapply the anaesthetic spray. She shovelled back the last forkfuls of her rice, carrot and quorn bake. The soup had been from a tin, bland, with an unpleasant slick texture. The bake wasn't bad, just incredibly boring. The vegetables were grown in the CONC fields by the river, from drought- and nuke-resistant seeds, but there wasn't a great variety of those yet so the kitchen served the same bake three times a week, just with different seasonings. Tonight's was a weak attempt at soy sauce and ginger.

'So, Astra,' Rudo asked, 'you looking forward to boogying at your first River Raven?'

She put down her fork. 'With you?'

Everyone laughed, Rudo too.

'Guess I shouldn't ask for the first dance then, hey?'

She flushed. She hadn't meant to insult him, but her remark seemed to have impressed people: the whole table was smiling at her now.

'I don't want to dance,' she muttered. 'I just want to see what it's like.'

'Actually, there will not be any dancing,' Photon said.

'Wha?'

'YAC has organised a new ceremony,' the Major said. 'The Non-Landers will perform a healing ritual. The Singular Simiya is to sing and Tiamet, she with the many arms, will play percussion. Asar will bless people. We are invited only to watch.'

'No fun.' Rudo pouted at him.

'Still, it might go on for a while. Bring plenty of water,' Sandrine said.

'Let us meet at the front gate at half past eleven.' Photon picked up his tray. 'I would recommend to catch a nap now, Astra.'

Good idea. She got up too.

'There is no room for me then in the MMU?' Christophe asked.

'I'm sorry, Christophe.' Photon, being Photon, looked excruciatingly guilty. 'There were only four invitations, and the Major assigned them.'

'Is it not that Astra should have an Orientation Session first?' Christophe darted a ratty little look at Sandrine.

'Oh.' Sandrine sounded alarmed, as if she thought she should have considered the question herself. 'I guess, technically. But Photon's her equerry, and if the Major decided—' She stopped and looked at Photon.

'I think it is fine,' Photon said. 'Astra's not an international. She is Gaian.'

'So? I thought the rules applied to everyone new to the Southern Belt.'

Photon looked harried now. 'Well, maybe they do. But the Major made an exception. And anyway the Diplomeet was pretty much an Orientation, wasn't it, Astra?'

Astra gripped the back rim of her chair. 'I grew up in this climate and I know a lot about Non-Land,' she informed Christophe.

'*Pas de problème.* Next time.' Christophe took a sip of water. 'But it is not Is-Land out there, Astra. Not for midnight skinny dip, or to howl at the moon.'

Rudo snickered. Astra glared at him. 'Just because I'm *Gaian*,' she flared, 'doesn't mean I'm going to *strip*.'

'Take it easy, Christophe,' Sandrine intervened. 'We'll brief her in the vehicle.'

'He did not mean to—' Photon started, but Astra was flouncing out the door.

She marched back up to her room, fists clenched, with every step imagining kicking Rudo and then Christophe and then Rudo again in the teeth. But as soon as she slammed the door shut, the anger drained out of her body. She sat, head in hands, on the edge of the iron-framed single bed that practically filled the whole room: a tiny cell with a small window she'd need to climb on a chair to look out of, though there wasn't a chair, just the bed and side table, hooks on the walls for her clothes, and some old cans of paint, a mop and a bucket stacked in the corner. It was a storage cupboard, really, in the women-identified sleeping quarters: when Dakota had brought her here the bed had been vertical against the wall. They'd cleared space and dragged it down, only to discover that the frame was missing two wheels and tilted sideways. 'You'll need ropes to sleep on that!' Dakota had laughed. She'd gone off and found two blocks of wood to use as props, then disappeared again to return with sheets and a pillow, the side table and a wind-up lamp. When she'd finally gone for good, Astra had shoved her Belonging Box under the bed. She hadn't wanted to look at anything that reminded her of Or, Is-Land, IMBOD, or being strapped to a neurohospice mattress for three months.

Moonlight was streaming into the room, a column of mercurial shadows pouring down the door. She was hot all over. The shirt was sticking to her back and the trouser crotch was making her Gaia garden sweat. That wouldn't help her brand to heal. She peeled off the damp uniform and hung the trousers over the bed frame. Dakota had given her a woven laundry basket with a broken handle; she pulled it out from under the bed and tossed in the damp shirt and underpants. Then she wrapped herself in a towel and went down the hall for a cool shower. When she returned she sprayed herself with anaesthetic and set her Tablette alarm for eleven. She stretched out on top of the sheets and was asleep the moment she closed her eyes.

* * *

She awoke with a start from a dream that vanished like the tail of a cat round a door. It was ten; no need to rush. She lay in her moonlit chamber, listening to the compound settle down for the night. The door to the shower room creaked open and shut and footsteps padded down the hallway, laughter echoing behind. From her window, a liquid silver path rippled over her. All her life her body had been free to merge with Gaia, to soak up the sun, be caressed by the wind and cleansed by the rain, but now it was hidden: sheathed in fabric all day, entombed in stone walls at night, a private object, set apart from the world. For weeks that had felt like imprisonment, abandonment. But now Gaia was back within her.

She ran her fingers lightly over her chest and stomach, flexed her core muscles. The anger the men had sparked in her was invigorating but she couldn't waste that energy battling with idiots. *Compound dogs.* Let Photon fend them off. She had to remain calm, open to visions. Christophe didn't have a clue what it meant to be a Gaian.

And neither did IMBOD.

She sat up. Everything in the room – her CONC uniforms on their hangers, the mop and tins in the corner, the door handle, her legs, her feet, her toenails – was scalded with moonlight. As she stared into the white glare, a previously nebulous insight crystallised in her mind. She didn't have to feel guilty for defending Is-Land. Is-Land and IMBOD were completely different. Is-Land was a haven for Gaia and all Her creatures: a place created to regenerate the truth of human oneness with the Earth. IMBOD's job was to defend that haven. Poisoning people with uranium, however, was the opposite of *defending* Gaia. It was *exploiting* Her, abusing Her powers, just like the oil junkies had done. IMBOD had called Hokma a traitor but *IMBOD* were the people betraying Is-Land. IMBOD and IREMCO. IREMCO had lied to her class about their mine in Zabaria. It was helping IMBOD destroy the Non-Landers, just like – she clenched her fists – Odinson had tried to destroy her mind in the Barracks.

The moonlight was plating her body like armour. Next to Gaia, she thought, Odinson was nothing more than a malevolent horsefly. What had Hokma's letter said? When she was in trouble, ask Gaia for a vision. But Gaia had not waited to be asked: She had come unbidden, to remind Astra she was the Gaia Girl, Chosen not to open seasonal fairs and praise IMBOD with pretty speeches but to save Is-Land from IMBOD. *I will find them, Hokma,* she vowed. *I will find Lil and my Code father. Then I will find Ahn and Samrod Blesserson and punish them for your murder and stop IREMCO and IMBOD from poisoning these children. When I have done all that, I will Return you to Gaia in Or.*

Then the moon must have gone behind a cloud because the room lost its silvery patina. Everything was dull and grey and vague. She was in a storage cupboard: a place for damaged things no one could be bothered to mend or throw away. She closed her eyes. What was she thinking? The only thing she had been chosen for was to experience the worst that IMBOD could do to a person. Did she really want another round of the Barracks? What IREMCO did to Non-Landers was not her problem. All she had to do was find her father without attracting any more attention from IMBOD.

The moonlight returned. Through the bars of her fingers the world was stark again, a choice that was no choice. She took a deep breath and ran her hands over the shaggy pelt of her head. She had come this far. She had to continue. Lil knew her Code father. Finding her was vital. And if she was in YAC, surely she would be at this River Raven.

She concentrated her mind on Lil. Lil had betrayed her, then disappeared, run away in the night. People thought she might have set the fire in the dining hall, the one that had killed Torrent and Stream, but that had never been proved. Still, Lil did like making fires. And she also liked—

Her body slicing through the moonlight, Astra reached under the bed, dragged out her one possession and placed it on the bed. Her cranium throbbed, but the head pills were working and the pain-ball remained leashed in its hole. For the first time since the Barracks, she opened her Belonging Box.

There, nestled in the folds of a red lacy shawl, was her string of Blood & Seed hipbeads, both Nimma's Craft work. Her stomach tightened. Had Nimma really wanted her to have them, or had Klor insisted? There was something in the box from him alone, anyway: the cherrywood heart he had carved for the top of her Labyrinth staff. She clasped it to her chest. The polished wood was smooth and clean, like Klor's patient love for her. She replaced the carving carefully, tucking it back next to Eya's silver bracelet, her only link to her Birth Code mother. Beside it, half hidden in the folds of the shawl, was a Gaia hymnbook: a real book. Up until now she had thought of it as a present from her Shelter siblings, but it wasn't. Lil had given it to her.

Fingers trembling, she took out the book, stroked the rough bark cover, its embossed gilded lettering and Gaia glyph. The cover was stitched with silk thread and warped from the damp cave where Lil and her father had lived. It was almost as if Lil's fingerprints were moulded into the binding. She opened the book. The hymns were carefully inked on thick torn-edged pages, their fanciful capital letters surrounded by gold and green creatures: mice with intertwined tails, dragonflies, a fox with a flame for a brush. Beneath IMBOD's mind-branding her memories were indelible, too: she and Lil had sung the hymns together in the forest, at the tops of their lungs. Lil had been possessive of the book and had made Astra wait to see it, allowed her to handle it for only a strictly limited time. The book had been the only trump in Lil's hand, she realised now. Astra had had her Owleon, Silver; she'd had Hokma, and a family, a future. Lil had had nothing: just a soiled hymnbook and her knowledge of the woods.

She closed the book and turned it over in her hands. Why had Lil given it to her? Because she was leaving Is-Land and giving up any pretence of being a Gaian? Or had she thought the book might be confiscated or used against her in Non-Land and preferred to carry the hymns in her head?

Something was nosing at the surface of her mind, like a mole tunnelling up through the earth. Lil hadn't given Astra just the book, had she? Hokma had come to the Earthship with it after the fire, and all the adults had argued about . . . not about the hymnbook . . . about *Lil's poem*.

Yes. Lil had written her a poem. She had only read it once, the day after Lil had disappeared. Then she had put it away, tried to forget it, to forget Lil. Astra had been the Gaia Girl, famous, in demand. She'd gone to high school, made new friends and Gaia playmates. Her memories of Lil had faded, and in the neurohospice IMBOD had tried to completely erase them. But IMBOD had failed; the memories were still there. Lil had definitely written her a poem.

So where was it?

She opened the book again, flat on the bed, and riffled through the pages. No loose sheets tucked inside. She flipped to the back. At the join of the endpaper was a seam of red stitching. She ran a fingertip down the thread. *Yes.* She remembered now. It was a false seam: not a flap, but a pocket: a prayer pocket.

Her heart quaking, she bent the cover back and tucked her finger inside the pocket. The tip met a soft edge of paper. Unbelievably, IMBOD had missed it.

She slid the paper out of the book and unfolded it in the moonlight. It was soft and flecked with wildflower petals from the Wise House living roof. The handwriting was large and spiky, and the dots on the small *i*s were the shape of stars.

> Astra
> Like a hymn
> yore in my heart
> even when we are apart.
>
> Yore the star-girl
> yore my fire
> when I'm roaming
> in my bones
> I'll follow you
> to my onely home.
> Lil xx

It was a love poem, the kind of thing she had yearned for Tedis Sonnenson to write to her in Year Ten, and that she herself had penned for Sylvie and Acorn and Leaf. Leaf, she remembered, had been especially conscientious about hir poems, emailing one – the same one but with a personalised final verse – to all hir Gaia playmates at the end of each school term.

But had Lil ever loved her? They were each other's first Gaia playmate; that much she remembered clearly. But there had also been arguments and tears, fury and contempt. None of her schoolmates had ever hurt her the way Lil had done. So was this poem true? Or just a way to keep Astra hooked, get *her* to follow Lil *again*?

She re-read the poem. It was strange . . . Lil had been wearing a star today: the YAC star, around her neck. Was she guided by Enki Arakkia's light now, or still treading her own lonely path? Because the one thing you could trust about Lil, Astra realised, was that you couldn't trust her. With her games and stories she made you feel excited and involved, but then, without warning, she switched: becoming mean and hostile and glittering – a betrayer. If *you* got angry with *her*, though, she became miserable, pitiful, and *you* ended up feeling awful. But Lil had done some terrible things.

No, that wasn't fair. Lil hadn't meant to cause Hokma harm. She'd been selfish and stupid but she was really just trying to punish Astra for spoiling her adventure. Ahn and Dr Blesserson, on the other hand, had turned evidence against Hokma: *they* were the ones responsible for her death. As for the fire, Torrent and Stream had been hiding under a table, Gaia-playing, maybe smoking cigarettes. Even if Lil *had* set the fire, she wouldn't have known they were there.

But still. Wherever Lil went, destruction followed in her wake. The girl had never appeared to care who she hurt. Would she feel awful if Astra told her about Torrent and Stream, about Hokma? Knowing Lil, if she did, she wouldn't show it. In fact, Astra thought uncomfortably, Lil could be malicious, a bully. She had sometimes seemed to take pleasure in Astra's suffering at her hands. What if meeting Lil, confiding in her, was the last thing on earth Astra ought to do?

She refolded the poem, slipped it back in the prayer pocket and checked the clock. Ten forty-eight. In twelve minutes the alarm would ring, and then she would go downstairs and out to the River Raven. She might be walking straight into a trap.

She closed the hymnbook and tucked it back into the shawl inside the Belonging Box. As she did, she noticed Silver's feather: the downy white chick feather Hokma had saved for her, had placed in the test tube with her letter about her father. Small and fluffy, it was floating on the folds of the shawl.

She plucked the feather from the shawl, cupped it in her hands and closed her eyes. *Help me, Silver*.

The memory came immediately: she and Lil had given two Owleon feathers to the ancestors, the two skeletons in the arrowpain. Then they'd argued on the cliff, about IMBOD. Lil had tried to show her a different world, but Astra hadn't wanted to see it.

Lil, though, had been right.

She opened her eyes. The feather was almost invisible in the shadow of her palm. She couldn't trust Lil: she must never forget that. But though Lil might be devious and violent and selfish, she had always known the truth about IMBOD. She would have answers now. She would know far more about Non-Land than Photon and Sandrine did, far more than even the Major. That was the way Lil was, the way her father had taught her to be. Some – if not all – of what Lil said might be lies, but Astra would only discover that by listening to what she had to say.

She put the feather back in the box. Beside it, Eya's bracelet glimmered in the moonlight: five pale blue gemstones, one for each lake in Bracelet Valley, linked in a loose silver chain. Would her Code father need to see it to believe she was his daughter, she suddenly wondered? For all she knew, Zizi Kataru might be at the River Raven: Lil might lead her straight to him. Or she might see him in the crowd, a man who looked exactly like her, with her nose and curly hair, and when she danced beside him and raised her wrist so he could see the bracelet, he would . . .

She stopped herself from thinking stupid thoughts. But she took out the bracelet and put it on. After years of being too big, it fit her wrist perfectly. No one would question her right to wear jewellery, surely. Sandrine and Rudo wore earrings, and the Major a necklace.

She closed the lid and slid the box back under the bed. When the alarm buzzed she got up and re-dressed in her trousers and a clean T-shirt. Then she filled her hydropac with water in the shower room and took the steps two at a time, down to the front gate.

ANUNIT

Please don't start again. She stretched out her foot and rocked the cradle. She'd given him a bottle, a wooden toy to chew, her finger to suck, but Ebebu had been whimpering and wheezing for half an hour. At least her sisters weren't complaining. It was the quiet end of the night shift and Neperdu was counting out the cash, pushing the coins into piles on her desk with her mouthstick. Everyone else was wrapped up in their sleeping sheets, except for Taletha and Roshanak. Earplugs in and fixed on their Tablette screens, the pair were replaying ShareWorld clips of Tiamet clap-dancing up the ramp at the CONC Diplomeet. Tiamet was a big star-flower now, blossoming in the spotlight of the international media, with no time to even send a Tablette message about Ebebu. The Singular's Kadingir followers were all orphans, the news reports said, and yet she had practically abandoned her own son.

Tiamet. Anunit didn't know what to think about her any more. Probably her flightiness was to be expected: just eighteen months ago, the girl had arrived from the Zabaria orphanage herself. Neperdu was fussy, hired hardly any of the girls who showed up, glaze-faced and tremble-lipped, after CONC had chucked them out to fend for themselves. Being pretty, young and alt-bodied were not qualifications enough for the Welcome Tent; the status of 'Pithar Singular' might be scoffed at in Non-Land, but it had a global reputation Neperdu was charged to uphold. Her workers needed to boast rare and generous sexual attributes – and appetites. Tiamet passed the interview with astonishing colours. Quite apart from her singular assets, she claimed significant experience already with her fellow orphans, exchanging favours for food rations right under the noses of the

CONC officers. She certainly took to Pithar like a flame to a furnace, gaily working twelve-hour shifts in both the flesh chambers and ion gloves. But the surprises didn't end there. In her occasional breaks Tiamet rehearsed her finger-cymbal dances and started a 'mutual beauty salon,' teaching the others all her little tricks with hair and nails, while on her days off she took the bus to Kadingir – an unheard of extravagance. After a few months she'd even acquired a chaffeur: that skinny YAC member Lilutu. Neperdu didn't let non-workers visit the Welcome Tent, but Lilutu didn't need to be there in person to make her presence felt. After a ride home with her new friend, Tiamet would spend days prattling on about YAC and Enki Arakkia, wild talk that had washed over Anunit like rain over a stone.

Then came the disaster. The girl fell pregnant. But what for others meant fear and anxiety and most often a decision to buy herbs from Neperdu, to Tiamet had brought triumphant joy. The father, she announced, was a mine-manager celebrating his last shift in Zabaria. He would never be back, never know she was carrying his child. The baby would be all hers, with no interference. And not just hers: everyone's.

That was when she began to prise open Anunit's silence.

She should not have let Tiamet do it but she'd hadn't had the energy to resist. One day, Tiamet's pregnancy clearly visible, the girl had moved her cushion beside Anunit's, placed Anunit's hand on her belly and whispered, 'You are my sister. So you are my baby's aunty.'

'Don't,' Neperdu had hissed. 'She's suffered enough.'

'Anunit's suffering will be avenged,' Tiamet had retorted. 'When YAC fulfils the Prophecy, and we are all free. You'll see, Neperdu. *She will come when she is most needed. She will make her own way from the Star and arrive resplendent at the House of Abundant Women*. What are we, if not abundant? And YAC is the Star Party, isn't it?'

That was Tiamet: imperious, argumentative, unaccustomed to being crossed. Partly, Anunit thought as she rocked Ebebu's cradle, her combative personality came from growing up in the orphanage. Though the way Tiamet told the story now to Taletha, Roshanak and the other beauty salon members, her sex work there had just been a benevolent extra: her main role had been to help love, feed and educate the orphans. She could have stayed on, she said, as a CONC employee, or left to start her own cult of motherhood; but CONC paid shrapnel and self-employment was a hassle. Anunit thought she simply liked the sex work. She was young, not yet drained or bored stiff by the men's demands, and her singularities didn't cause her pain. Tiamet wasn't on morpheus. She didn't have ageing parents to feed. She could afford to travel, dream, fill her mind with fantasies of fame.

Neperdu had tried to bring her down to earth. 'Just because some River Road drifter has silver-tongued a couple of Kadingir Singulars into his schemes, don't start thinking anyone in YAC has the time of day for us, my girl,' the concierge would sniff. 'You'll just end up with a bellyful of disappointment if you do.'

'YAC aren't *drifters*. And Enki Arakkia doesn't give a bird's dropping about our work. He's preaching *unity*,' Tiamet would argue. Neperdu would disagree and the two would endlessly bicker – until the day of the baby's first kick.

Tiamet was holding Anunit's hand pressed against her belly. Anunit was limply cooperating in hope that if a new flesh client arrived he might choose them both. Double sessions with Tiamet were easy because she took the lead, prancing and dancing and tossing her hair, and anyway, with her multiple singularities, the clients paid her most of the attention. She had been lying with her eyes closed, wishing Tiamet and Neperdu would shut up, when the baby's heel had rubbed against her palm.

Like a massage hitting just the right spot, the unexpected pressure had woken her up. 'Shhh,' she had heard herself insisting. 'The baby says be quiet.'

Silence had fallen over the Welcome Tent, followed by a wave of gasps, and applause had gone up from her sisters. Just for a moment, Tiamet had behaved like a real mother-to-be, gracious and grateful and in awe of the miracle occuring within her. Anunit had kept her hand on the bump, aware of a new feeling spreading through her own belly: not the slow wonder she'd felt at her own baby's movements – no, nothing like that – but something both humble and urgent, like the relief of drinking water on a baking hot day.

She'd whisked her hand away. Why was she allowing this? The child was doomed: doomed to destroy them. Tiamet didn't understand. The father might have gone home, but other men would take his place. The baby would not be hers – not *theirs*. That had never been allowed. She had moved her cushion then, and would no longer meet Tiamet's eye. Neperdu defended her and Tiamet left her alone . . . until the baby was born.

She delivered at the Treatment Ward, in the special tent kept apart for the Pithar workers. She was away for three days. When she returned, ignoring Neperdu's disapproving looks, she brought the baby straight over to Anunit. 'His name is Ebebu,' she had whispered fiercely. 'It means *Clean*.'

She had looked. The baby was naked. Not Singular.

Not Singular.

Ebebu had wriggled, stretched, pushed his heel towards her.

'Please, Anunit. Be his aunty.'

It had taken her three days, but she had promised. Tiamet had become unstoppable, her pride fired up to a red-hot glow, as if Ebebu's birth had invested her with some kind of searing authority. But while most new mothers would be consumed by thoughts of their baby, all she wanted to proclaim about was YAC.

There had been no choice but to listen to her chatter. YAC clearly had a plan, in some ways a plausible one, even Neperdu admitted that. And Enki Arakkia did seem to practise what he preached: if what she said about her new role in the group was true, Tiamet had achieved her ambition of culthood without having to denounce her Pithar sisters. That was unheard of. But it didn't, in Anunit's opinion, mean the Prophecy was about to be fulfilled.

The Prophecy was something grandparents recited to send a child to sleep. It was said to have been carved into ancient Somarian stones, in markings like bird's feet, stones that had crumbled long before the Dark Time. The scanty verses had survived only in the memories of a few scholars, and even its admirers were forced to agree that the Prophecy in no way definitely referred to Non-Land. The Prophecy talked about a young star woman with a powerful father and her own vizier, but Enki Arakkia wasn't a woman, YAC had rejected the wisdom of parents and elders, and who, even N-LA Ministers, had viziers? But YAC's symbol was the star and they threw parties by the river, dances lit up with purple lights like myrtle flowers, and for Tiamet, that was enough. She was at one of those Star Parties now, dancing and drumming, while her child, if Anunit was lucky, sniffled and snuffled himself to sleep.

'*WAHHHH*.' Here it came. Oh, why had she agreed to this? Without his mother to latch on to, Ebebu would wail for an hour, keeping her and all the sisters awake. Nothing would stop him. Unless . . .

She had told herself she would never do it, but she felt beneath her pillow for the small white square of crocheted wool tucked away in there between the embroidered cotton cover and the hemp bedmat. She pressed the soft white woollen square to her face and inhaled. It was faint, ghostly even, but nothing could ever snuff out that smell, the mildest, sweetest cheese, infused with night-flowering jasmine. She took Ebebu's bottle and squirted Tiamet's milk into a corner of the square, draped the dry blanket on the baby's chest and tucked it round him. 'Soft soft,' she whispered. Then she held the milky corner up to Ebebu's nose.

He curled his little hands around the blanket, explored its neat edge, its patterned holes. His crying slowed to wheezy hiccoughs. He took the corner, sucked it, and except for Anunit's stifled sobs, all, at last, was quiet in the Welcome Tent.

ASTRA

Rudo was late. While they waited, Photon and Sandrine loaded their numbers into Astra's watch and showed her how to operate the emergency contact button. At ten past eleven Rudo loped down the main staircase. He was wearing a loose blue jacket.

'Sorry, folks. Just had to pick up a little protection for the girls.'

'Rudo,' Sandrine warned.

'Hey! Not that kinda protection.' He reached in a jacket pocket and gave the women a small plastic box each. 'Checked 'em out from Dakota. All legal, Sandrine.'

Astra opened her packet. Nesting in a square of foam were what looked like two red rubber screws.

'Earplugs. El cheapo CONC issue,' Rudo admitted cheerfully. 'Me and Photon, we's got ours in the unit.'

'Oh, all right. Thanks.' Sandrine pocketed her plugs.

She felt confused. 'Is N-LA going to attack YAC? I thought it was a party?'

'It is,' Photon reassured her. 'Earplugs are the standard MMU equipment, in case of an incident. Not as good as earmuffs but normally these are the best on the market. Thank you for remembering, Rudo.'

'No probs. Could come in handy if the music's shit.' Rudo winked at her. 'The Nonners go wild for some real cheesy schmaltz sometimes, Astra.'

The earplugs were small darts in an unknown battleground. She stashed the packet in her pocket.

At the desk, the guard, a sandy-skinned woman with Nuasian features and a gathered bunch of pink dreads checked their passes on Photon's Tablette. She inspected Astra's closely.

'First time out in Kadingir?'

'Yeah.'

'And you're going to a River Raven?' The guard raised her eyebrows at Photon.

'The Major approved it.'

Dumb idea, but not my business, the guard's face said. 'Okey-doke, folks. Stay safe,' she ordered Astra, 'and whatever you do, don't listen to Rudo.'

Fists on hips, Rudo slung on his falsetto. 'Sister? Are you sayin' I sings outta tune?'

'I'm sayin', brother,' the guard shot back, grinning, 'you talk a truck-whop o' nonsense sometimes.'

'Hark at her!' Rudo appealed to the team. 'Undermining delegation morale!'

'Watch that backchat, brother.' The guard jutted her chin towards two colleagues standing by the huge arched front doors. 'Get on out there before I *undermines* you to security.'

The guards, Astra noticed, were armed with sonic guns. They slid back the giant wooden bolt securing the compound entrance.

'Don't worry, Marly, we'll keep him out of trouble.' Sandrine bundled the still mock-protesting Rudo towards the entrance. The guards pushed the doors open. Astra lingered for a fraction of a second, then followed Photon across the compound threshold.

The night air smelled of dust, with just a hint of ripe fruit. The sky was strewn with stars and the full moon illuminated a ghost field of tents, shacks and shelters, a turbulent grey plain stretching into the distance, crevassed with dark paths and alleys. The doors shut with a clunk behind them and the faint trundle of the bolt slithered through Astra's body. She was not yet fully outside the compound, she realised. Like the paws of a giant beast, the fortress walls extended either side of the entrance. She half turned, peering back up at her prison. It was an imposing sight. Two more armed CONC guards stood sentinel either side of the massive wooden doors; hoisted on chains above them was a cast-iron grid of spiked bars. The walls were not sandstone but glazed brick; the paint was fading, the colours drained by the rampart floodlights, but the impression was still magnificent: across the blue tiles marched a procession of sculpted gold creatures – bulls with serpents' tails, lions with black wrinkled faces, and eagles with the heads of fierce, beautiful, luxuriant women.

'The Ancient Gate of Istar,' Sandrine said, her voice a muffled chime against the soaring walls, the vast canopy of the night sky. 'Well, a reconstruction.'

Photon giggled. 'Of a reconstruction. The first rebuilding is in Alpland, in a museum that by miracle survived the Dark Time.'

'Mighta been more *diplomeetical* to give it back,' Rudo suggested.

'*Ja*,' Photon agreed, 'but ticket sales come to CONC. And one day the Non-Land compound is supposed to be given for N-LA. So then they can campaign for the original tiles.'

One day. That mythical day in the future when CONC would leave Non-Land. Astra turned to face Kadingir again. The fortress walls were alive, fierce, alluring, but the doors were blank and pitiless, as if the compound was shutting her out forever.

Sandrine and Rudo were walking ahead along the fortress wall. Photon gestured at Astra to move in front of him.

'Never fall behind, Astra,' he instructed. 'Always let me to bring up the rear.'

Skirting the walls, they moved towards a guard standing alone at another, smaller set of doors. The MMU was parked in this wing of the compound; they could have reached it from inside but Marly had needed to check their special passes, Photon told her as they dodged a pothole. Ahead, the guard was greeting Rudo and Sandrine. He opened the doors and Rudo disappeared inside. A few minutes later, he drove out in an MMU.

Like the unit she had seen under attack, the vehicle was large and perplexing: a ramshackle metal box, crudely constructed from sheets of corrugated tin, its jutting roof-rack laden with a plastic water barrel. But this MMU wasn't dusty. Its ripples shimmered in the moonlight, the white CONC insignia on the triangular bonnet shining out from between two bright round headlamps. The engine was gently *putt-putting* and the frame was trembling like a dog desperate for a walk. Despite its insectoid exoskeleton, there was, in fact, something very hound-like about the vehicle. Its bulging headlamps had a quaint, friendly, almost eager look, as if the unit were anxious to do its best for you, to help and amuse, carry any burden, look like a fool, as long as you patted its brindled flanks every now and then, or made the odd joke at its expense.

'Ciccy!' Sandrine whistled. 'Looking good!'

'Yippers! All gussied up for her big night out!' Rudo hollered, flipping down the back of the passenger seat. 'Hip hop in.'

Photon lept lightly up onto the side-runner step of the cabin and yanked open the passenger door. 'After you, Officers.'

Sandrine gestured to Astra and she clambered up into the long, narrow back seat, upholstered in worn red fabric like the front bucket seats. She realised the middle section could be removed to allow access to the back chamber. Curious, she peered behind her, into an empty space tall enough for even Photon to stand up in. By the back window light she could see two low structures running along each side: one was a seat on top of shelves that were filled with folded sheets and small boxes. The other unit was a stretcher: a long padded tray crossed with straps with a trolley folded beneath it. Above it, as on the other side panel, was mounted a big round grid.

Were those ion grids? But now wasn't the time to ask questions. Sandrine was beside her, clipping on a seatbelt, Photon was clambering into the front and Rudo was revving the engine.

'Belts on!' he shouted. Astra ignored him. A bubble of excitement was rising inside her. The back seat was raised and there was a side window for a good view. She didn't want to strap herself in, spoil the ride.

'Moo-sica!' Rudo twisted a knob on the dashboard. 'Get us all in the moooooo-dica.'

The grids must be speakers: from the back of the vehicle came a cacophony of clinking and thumping and clattering, as if rattling jam jars of nails, buttons and beads were holding a furious Diplomeet. 'Are we taking the River Road?' Sandrine shouted over the din.

'Nah. Scrub hills,' Rudo yelled as Photon turned the volume down. 'Less chance of a checkpoint.'

Photon unrolled his window with a manual crank and the MMU moved slowly away from the compound. They immediately hit what felt like a kerb and Astra only saved herself from head-butting Rudo by gripping the back of his seat.

'I said belt up!' he shouted, bumping down the other side of the kerb. 'I ain't missing a River Raven for no concussed newbie, no way.'

'I couldn't find the strap,' she muttered, fumbling for the clasp which *had* got tucked down into the seat crease. It took her a minute to sort out, even with Sandrine helping, and she'd only just clicked herself in when the vehicle jerked over another sharp rise in the road.

'Wheelchair crossings,' Sandrine told her. 'An Asfarian billionaire paid for them to be put in, but the road's eroded over the years so they're more like speed bumps now.'

'Every twenty metres, Astra,' Rudo called, 'on all the main *e*-roads. Geddit?'

'Ar Ar,' Sandrine honked as Photon groaned.

'Thanks be to Asfarian billionaires.' Rudo ululated. 'I'm gonna send one of them my chiropractic bill when I get back home.'

'You could drive a little slower, Rudo,' Sandrine chided.

'You kidding? We're going to a River Raven, girl!'

'If Ciccy gets us there in one piece.'

They were lurching through the hunched, sleeping tentscape of Kadingir. 'There, there, Cicada. There, there,' Rudo crooned, patting the dashboard. 'Sandrine didn't mean it.'

'Mean what?' Sandrine raised her voice above the rattle in the back.

'She doesn't like being called Ciccy. It's not respectful.'

'I don't see why not. She carries sick people.'

'Yeah, but *she's* not sick. She just makes a huge racket.' Rudo thumped the roof with the side of his fist. 'And she's ugly as sin. 'zactly like them munchaholic bugs that went and stripped the last leaf off the last tree in the New Zonian Shield.'

Photon twisted round in his seat and grinned at Astra. His eyes were crinkling again, encouraging her to join in the fun, talk back to Rudo. The bumpy road must have loosened her tongue, because suddenly she heard herself shouting, 'Can't you put on a sonic gun track, Rudo? This stuff is worse than Shostakovich.'

'Are you kiddin'?' Rudo yelled. 'This is Cicada's favourite D J. You gotta jump 'n' jive with her, Astra, get limbered up for the River Raven!'

'Why is it called a Raven anyway?' she flung back. 'Ravens are northern birds.'

'That's just what we call it,' Sandrine answered. 'The Non-Landers call it a Star Party. It's a special site because crows nest near by. But Crow Disco didn't catch on.'

She didn't understand. Rudo must have seen her face in the mirror.

'It's a pun, kiddo. On *rave*,' he hollered, 'as in dance party. As in ranting and raving like a full-moon lunatic. Out in the desert with the black birds and the black sheep!'

'Speak for yourself!' Sandrine retorted. 'I get on very well with the Major, myself!'

A warm breeze was ruffling through the cabin, Sandrine was shaking two imaginary maracas, Photon was hooting with laughter. They were going to a place with *crows*. Bouncing securely on her seat, Astra very nearly smiled.

There was no point talking any more. You'd open your mouth and the air would get snatched out of you by a pothole or a crossing. And Rudo was right: Cicada's crazy music was exciting: a banging, shaking, shuffling soundtrack to the clap-trap, knocked-together world out there beyond the windows. They were juddering this way and that down a jagged road lined with wooden shelters – old doors, planks and splintery pallets banged and lashed together into low dwellings and long fences. Illumin-ated in the headlights, a man was standing in the ditch ahead, fumbling with his trousers. As the vehicle approached he turned, arm raised to shield his eyes, but didn't step out of their way. The arc of his piss glinted in the air, then puddled in a black stain at his feet. As Rudo veered to avoid him, Astra caught a glimpse of the man's face. His cheeks were stub-bled, his eyes puffy and dull. He looked exhausted, spent.

As they left the man behind, the stench of sewage pervaded the unit. Photon and Rudo rolled up their windows.

'Sorry, ladies,' Rudo called back over his shoulder. 'Just till we get past the waste land. Did you know T. S. Eliot was an anagram of toilets? The Major told me, the other day. Over saki and crumpets.'

The others laughed, but again, she didn't get the joke. To the side of the road was a small lake of sewage, with shelters curving around it into the distance. Some people, though, had obviously decided that the relative quiet and space made it worth putting up with the stench: on the muddy shores of the lake was a shack, raised on pallets and connected to the road by half-submerged ramps. In front of it, two robed people were squatting at the edge of a decking, tending a small fire in the mud. A fire, in this heat? It cast a scarlet glow over the people. The woman was flip-ping flatbreads between her palms. The man was patting the back of an infant, draped across his shoulder. Astra thought for a moment of Asar,

the plane of his face where a nose should be. Did these people have no
sense of smell?

At last they were past the spill. The men opened the windows again
and Cicada rumbled on through a densely packed area of tents: dark
domes or cubes, some lit from within, torches swinging from the struts
silhouetting the inhabitants against the canvas. Rudo's music was softer
now, and as a saxophone softly blurted over a stream of bleeps and squig-
gles, Astra caught a glimpse of a couple Gaia-bonding in a tipi. They were
upright inside the canvas pyramid, the woman hoisted on the man's hips,
her arms flung around his neck as he leaned back to take her weight.

Rudo had noticed the couple too; she could tell by the way his head
moved. But though the scene was ripe for an off-colour comment, he said
nothing. Back straight, his hands firmly gripping Cicada's big steering
wheel, he drove on. She could smell him, and he smelled good: musky
and sweet, like one of Nimma's vanilla puddings. For a fraction of a
second she wanted to lean forward and nuzzle his nape.

No! No way would she ever give Rudo that satisfaction. She gazed
back out again through her window as Cicada jolted on through the tent
field, too quickly to catch its lullabies and laments. The sky was a deep
indigo blue and everything was glinting in the moonlight. Gradually
there was more open ground between the dwellings, even the occasional
stunted bush. The air was fresh, the road smoother as the crossings dimin-
ished. They passed a squat tower of stacked container shelters, then a
circle of tents and a sheep pen. A fleecy cloud of slave animals huddled in
a rock-wall enclosure and two camels were tethered to the gate. Then
there were no human shelters any more, just scrubland and sheep prisons,
and beneath the stars, a low black wave of hills on the horizon. Rudo
picked up speed and to the tinkle of gravel hitting the chassis they entered
the hills. The road climbed gently until they reached the crest of the slope.
Astra could see in the distance a road spotlit at intervals with pools of
white light, and behind it, just visible, the broad silver Mikku with its flo-
tilla of countless small moon-boats.

At last the scrub road met the tarmacadamed River Road. There was
no other vehicle in sight, but Rudo stopped and checked in both
directions.

'We could be in luck. Looks like N-LA ain't road-checking tonight.'
He turned south, the river gleaming at Astra's shoulder, until they reached
a side road on the right that went delving down between more scrub.

Gritty and potholed, with no ramps or wheelchair crossings, this road looked nearly abandoned, but shortly they reached a parking lot: rows of battered vehicles, bicycles, scooters and carts, harnessed donkeys standing patiently between their shafts.

'Hey, hey.' Rudo pulled over and cut the engine. The music stopped. 'We be here.'

'So be the media,' Sandrine commented. Astra peered out. At the end of the first row was a black jeep, parked at an angle to one of the carts.

'Are IMBOD here too?' she asked, suddenly afraid.

'Oh no,' Sandrine replied. 'IMBOD don't get invites to River Ravens.'

Photon opened the glove compartment. 'Okay, guys. Gear-up time.'

Rudo groaned. 'No—Phot, really?'

'Sorry, Rudo.' Photon passed around what looked like frisbees but were in fact circlets of white cable. 'It is important for people to see our faces. And when we get lost, we need to be able to find each other in the dark. Test please.'

Copying the others, Astra tugged the cable around her head. It had an adjustable clip and a flat round disc that went at the front. Sandrine showed her how to twist on the power. One after another the circlets emitted four planes of pale blue light, filling the cabin with an eerie underwater glow.

'Hay-lo, Hay-lo.' From beneath his flat blue brim, Rudo flashed Astra a grin. 'What's a nice Saint like you doing in a hell-hole like this?'

Sandrine cut him off. 'She's not looking for Lucifer, Rudo. There's a torch function, too, Astra.' She twisted her own front disc again and a bright white beam shot out from her forehead like the horn of a mythical beast.

'Careful,' Rudo complained, 'this devil wouldn't mind using his eyes tonight.'

Sandrine turned her torch off. 'The devil can keep his hush-puppy eyes to *himself* out there. We're working tonight, let's remember. Briefing, Phot?'

'Sandrine's right.' His pale face as blue and crackled as the ancient glaze on the compound walls, Photon addressed them all. 'We are honoured guests tonight. We must observe the YAC ritual only, and rebuild trust. Please be using formal registers, and never call anyone Nonners.' Rudo raised his palms – *who, me?* – and Photon went on: 'Practicalities: the driver is drinking water or pop. Everyone else, one beer maximum, and plenty of water. In no circumstances must you turn off your headband or remove your CONC uniform.'

'You mean no *swimming*?' Rudo grinned. 'Hell, these Ravens used to be mega-fling-dings. I'm gonna have to have a word with the Major, I tell ya. *And* whoever designed these cosmic light-rings.' His voice rose in annoyance. 'It don't do us any kinda good prancing in to hostile environs looking like we think we're some kinda angels.'

'It's not a hostile environment,' Photon contradicted patiently. 'We're *guests*.'

'They're just party costumes,' Sandrine joined in. 'Don't you guys ever dress up in Mount Reality?'

'You can be lodging your formal complaints at a future date, Rudo,' Photon added, 'over coffee and crumpets. Tonight, stick to Sandrine. Okay: final security protocol. Never to lose sight of your buddy. Astra, that is meaning me. If separated, use your watch to contact your buddy and then return to the place you last saw each other. If that is not possible, or if you are waiting longer than for ten minutes, contact the team and return to the vehicle. Got it?'

'Got it.' Astra and Sandrine spoke as one.

'Yo.' Rudo unclipped his belt. 'The Angel Army is ready to party hearty.'

They were walking between low sandy dunes, down a stepped wooden ramp that sloped at a gentle incline with flat sections at regular intervals. Spotlit in Astra's torch beam, scraggy wind-bent plants swooned to the pale soil as if in thrall to the deep bass beats rolling up from the river valley. Ahead, Sandrine and Rudo's halos floated through the night like hazy rings of neon midges. Dwarfing the blue lights, splayed over the near shore of the river as if drawn on the earth in giant purple glitter lipstick, was a huge, irregular, darkly dazzling star, the moon hanging in the sky above it like a white cheek awaiting a kiss.

The star was the dance floor, Astra realised, rimmed with purple stage lights. Extending over the river, the top point cast violet sparks out over the moon-dazed water; lavender, magenta and plum sequins flickered in the interior. Twisted right across the centre was a moving infinity symbol: two purple teardrops joined with a silver flare, with two more silver lights rising from the centre of each oval. Silver bonfires? Astra strained to see, but it was still too soon to say.

The music was coming into focus, the booming drum beats now embroidered with intricate fingertip rhythms over which an untrammelled chorus wailed an ecstatic lament. Astra shivered. This was like no music she'd ever heard before. It wasn't neat and orderly like Klor's classical favourites, nor plangent and painful like the Major's Shostakovich, nor chaotic and kaleidoscopic like Rudo's songstream in Cicada. Cascading and swelling, pulsing and beckoning, continuously morphing into new textures and dimensions, this music sang of water and sand, wind and stone, the dead of night and the dawn. *This is Gaia's songstream*, she thought, with a sharp heart-burst of need.

The ramp was veering to the right. Surely it would be faster to cut down through the foothills? She stepped off the platform and sank ankle-deep in the dunes' embrace. Laughter trickled down from the slopes above her and she looked up and caught three bleached soles in her head-lamp: a couple entwined in the dunes. For a moment she thought she might cry.

Pssst. Photon gave a sharp whistle. Rudo and Sandrine had stopped and were shining their headlamps at her. Skewered in the beams, she abandoned her impulse and climbed back up on the ramp. If she wasn't careful, they'd make her sit in Ciccy all night.

'What did I just say?' Photon chided over the music. 'You must not to wander off on your own.'

'Sorry, I thought it was a shortcut.'

'Not if you want that promised beer, babes.' Rudo nodded at a row of lavender fairy-lit shacks lining the ramp as it curved to meet the star platform.

'No beer for you, driver.' Sandrine poked him in the ribs.

'I know, I know.' He threw up his hands. 'Just keepin' the youth on the straight and narrow, that's all.'

They walked on, the ramp widening as it neared the dance floor. Inside the star, the three silver lights Astra had thought were bonfires were in fact people. Crowned in tall silver headdresses, faces obscure, they stood, one in the centre of each teardrop, one at the intersection of the infinity symbol, head and shoulders above the dancers – who were mesmerising. Garlanded with purple necklaces, bracelets and anklets, glo-sticks and water squirters, their crutches and wheelchairs also studded with lights, the dancers were spinning and whirling, swooping and looping, flinging themselves into handstands and dramatic wheel spins. And somehow they were chanting too, searing the air with whatever breath they had left.

The music seemed to be coming from the star tips. In the nearest, a cluster of robed figures hunched over *tablas* and *jambes* while across the platform Astra could make out the silhouettes of a massive drum and gong. This close to the stage she could detect another aspect to the music as well: a faint, eerie, persistent whine. Like the sound mosquitoes made, or a malfunctioning light-strip, or a kind of inhuman singing, it permeated the complex patterns of the percussion, and once she'd noticed it, she couldn't *not* hear it. Almost inaudibly, it stained every other noise in the night.

She wanted to ask Photon what it was but they were nearing the beer shacks now, and entering a crowd of Non-Landers – people milling on the ramp, lounging in the dunes, queuing for drinks at the shacks. Very few were in robes. The men were in trousers, shorts and shirts, the women in long-sleeved shirts or dresses, trousers or overskirts, some in headscarves, some not. Most were flashing star medallions. Her heart fluttering, Astra surreptitiously scrutinised each one they passed. Lil or her father could be standing right beside her.

No, she realised, probably not Zizi; these were all youths: older teens, twenty-somethings. The women were mostly around her height, the men not much taller. They were slight like her too. Beside them, Rudo and Sandrine looked pumped up, overfed, and Photon towered like a pampas grass stalk in their midst. Astra realised with a slow-burning shock that the dancers were sizing up not the internationals, but *her*. Gleaming in the weird purple light of their headbands and necklaces, Non-Lander eyes checked her out – but that wasn't the only thing making her heart beat faster.

Everyone here had her colouring, she could tell that even in the purple light: her olive skin, dark brows and black hair. It was unnerving. In Or, in the CONC compound, people were all different Code-blends of shape and shade. She had never before been surrounded by people who, in fundamental ways, all resembled her. The sudden multiplication of her identity was frightening, as if the Non-Lander youths would suddenly reach out and grab her, pull her into their bony clutches, dissolve her in their damp violet embrace.

But no one touched her. The youths melted away as she passed. She cast sly glances in all directions. The dancers were all different, of course:

this boy had round eyes and a soft, flat face; that one's eyes were deepset, his cheeks hollow. This girl had a long nose; that one a square jaw. But everyone's hair was thick and black, their eyebrows strong, and they were all clocking *her*.

Registering her sameness? Planning to claim her? Her stomach turned. *When?*

No, she was being ridiculous. No one could possibly know she was half Non-Lander. Lots of people from all over the world had similar features to her. She could be from anywhere.

But she wasn't. She was from here. She was half-Coded from these people. For a moment she lost her nerve, ached to go back to Ciccy, back to the compound – back to the laundry, to not thinking about anything except how to avoid pain.

Photon pressed a warm bottle into her hand. He was holding a beer too, and shifting his shoulders in time with the music, his movements making alarming sense of his angles. Despite herself, she nearly smiled. Who would have thought gawky Photon could dance? She took a glug of malty effervescence. It was stronger than the courtyard brew, good beer. She was here, and she was going to drink it.

Photon recorked his bottle and slipped it in his pocket and she did the same. Sandrine was pointing out the re-use crates stacked at the side of the shack and Rudo was leading the way up towards the platform. As they approached its black network of struts, an enormous figure stepped out of the shadows, blocking their path and, as he straightened, the light from the stage.

Rudo halted. Astra bumped into Sandrine and hovered, part hidden, behind her. The man was the giant Non-Lander from the Diplomeet. Taller than Photon, broader than Rudo, he looked as if he could reach out and grab the two men by the throats if he wanted, lift them off the ground and shake them like rattles. But with his massive hand he made only the universal sign for 'stop'. They raised their palms in return and Photon held out his Tablette for inspection.

Still in his purple T-shirt and silver star, the YAC member was now also wearing a band of purple spikes around his head and violet light claws streaked his square face. 'Welcome,' he said in Somarian, his voice booming with the music. One by one he scanned their faces. Was it her imagination, or did his gaze linger over her?

'Thank you,' Photon shouted. She didn't understand the man's reply, but followed his finger back towards the beer shacks. There was a rickety platform beside them, a wooden structure decked out with benches. Oh.

'Sorry, guys.' Photon turned. 'He says we have to—'

But beside him Rudo was stepping forward, talking rapidly, opening his jacket.

'Wha—?' Sandrine put her hand on Rudo's arm, but Rudo was already reaching into his breast pocket, pulling out a strip of . . .

What? Oh, right.

. . . condoms. At least a dozen of the small square packets were dangling from his hand in a long shiny tail.

'Oh jeez, Photon!' Sandrine was getting agitated.

The Non-Lander's face remained set, calculating.

'They're mine, Sandrine,' Rudo shouted over the music. Then, to the man, 'Donation. For the youth!'

'Stop him, Photon,' Sandrine demanded.

'Rudo—' Photon attempted, but Rudo shushed him. The Non-Lander had stepped back, was speaking into his own Tablette. The conversation seemed to go on forever, while Sandrine continued sputtering at Photon, with Rudo hissing them both to be quiet, but at last the party guard stuck the device back in his pocket. Returning to the group, he delicately lifted the strip of condoms from Rudo's hand.

'No blue,' he rumbled in Inglish, indicating their heads. 'Star Party purple.'

'Bingo Bongo.' Rudo stripped off his headband as the man stooped back into the shadows. 'Two miracles in one.'

Sandrine flung her hands in his face.

'What the hell do you think you're doing? Since when do we go out *bribing* people?'

'They were *mine*, Sandrine,' Rudo repeated stubbornly, 'and I can give them to who I like. You and Photon go sit in the bleachers if you want. It's Astra's first River Raven and she should get a boogie in.'

Whatever you do, don't listen to Rudo. The reception officer's voice came floating back to her. She wanted to dance, to venture into the Star – but she didn't want to side with Rudo over Sandrine. 'Photon's my buddy,' she stated loudly. 'I'll go wherever he goes.'

It was down to Photon. He rubbed his forehead. 'The bouncer has called his superior,' he said slowly. 'It looks like we have the YAC permission, Sandrine.'

Sandrine was not happy, but finally she agreed, on condition they all wore their headbands unlit, ready to switch on immediately should anyone get lost. Rudo grumbled, but put his back on his head. Halo light off, Photon behind her, YAC's weird, unearthly music droning in her ears, Astra moved up the ramp into the River Raven.

PEAT

Peat stretched. That blessed hour was upon them again: the start of Gaia playtime. Sex in high school had always taken place in the afternoon; here in training they slept during siesta and poured out into the woodlands after dinner. In Atourne these had been short evening sessions, but here they played deep into the night; since the booster shot no one needed more than three or four hours' sleep. The sessions were incredible: erotic marathons, sexual adventure parks, carnal war games. Whether it was the shot, the daily martial arts training or just part of becoming an adult, Non-Land Barracks sex pushed every physical, emotional and imaginative boundary. There were shackles bolted to the trees, jungle gyms with padded benches and handcuffs, treasure chests brimful with toys: sateen ropes, artisan chains, nipple clamps, and gadgets Peat still didn't know what to do with. People had laughed at first, but now even the quietest Sec Gens were into biting, spanking and bondage games.

No matter how wild things got, though, there were never any ill effects. Peat's Gaia plough and Gaia tunnel never felt sore in the morning, and though Jade had bitten his shoulder the other night until he cried out – she had latched on, dug down to the bone – the mark had healed in a day. He looked over at her bunk now, admiring the tawny curve of her buttocks as she lay reading her Tablette. She lifted a leg, revealing tufts of dark hair and two fat lips.

The sight aroused him. 'Ready soon, Jade?'

'Umm hmm.' She scratched her bottom, lifting her cheek to fully expose her damp garden. He wanted to go over to her bunk, take her right now, but that was not allowed in the dorm. *Discipline.* Self-relief was permitted in the showers, that was all.

He rolled over. 'Laam?'

'Sorry, guys. I'm going to skip tonight.'

'Skip it? Why?' Robin laughed. 'Did Peat wear you out last night with his donkey dong?'

They all giggled and Laam grinned and put his hand on his abs. 'No. I've got a stomach ache. I don't want to get sick and spoil it for the rest of you.'

'Aw. I'm sorry, Laam.' Jade sat up. 'Do you want some camomile pills?'

'I've taken some, thanks.'

'Maybe it was the kim chi?' Robin asked. 'How are you with spicy food normally?'

'Usually fine. I dunno what it is. I'm sure I'll be okay tomorrow.'

The others accepted it and started getting ready – taking off rings and necklaces, going off to wash – but Peat lingered. You weren't allowed to pester people, but Laam wanted to Gaia-play; he just thought he shouldn't, that was all. He went and lay on his friend's bed, curled up around him, nuzzled Laam's shoulder with his chin.

'Just come for a bit,' he urged quietly. 'An hour. I'll take care of you if you get sick.'

Laam paused. 'Nah, Peat. I'm going to stay in. Just for one night.'

Then he wriggled round, pressed his long, sensitive, bone-hard Gaia plough, with its wondrously wet tip, into Peat's groin. 'That's my promise for tomorrow,' he whispered before flipping onto his stomach.

'Shower's free, Peat,' Robin called.

Against Laam's flank, Peat's own erection was heavy as packed wet earth. Could the cameras see? He took a breath. As much as he could, he detumesced.

He stood up. 'Coming.'

'Save some for us,' Robin grinned.

ASTRA

Eyes closed, heads rolling in ecstatic circles, the *tabla* and *jambe* players bent over their drums, their hands dizzying blurs. The dancers in the star tip were trembling and swaying, arms raised to the heavens, rapture streaming from their throats. As if the drummers' fingers were pilfering her will, Astra turned towards the source of the tempest shaking the wooden platform. A kinbattery attached to this stage would light Kadingir for a week.

Photon reached out and steered her back behind Rudo, who was weaving ahead through randomly scattered dancers. She followed into the star's vortex of violet tracers and swirling shadows. All around her the gong and bass drum, the chants and wails, and the strange ringing drone were merging into one thick rich tapestry of sound. Rudo was right: far better to be here than sitting on the bleachers – and to be anonymous, not shining like baby-blue frisbees in a night-purple inferno.

They weren't the only non-Non-Landers in the star. Ahead, camera on shoulder, the female journalist from the Diplomeet was crouching in their path. Rudo led the team around her up to the crotch of the star. Down at the tip of the next point the gong was a black moon slowly moaning its secrets to the night, the bass drum a giant womb, reverberating to the passionate strokes of a robed figure wielding a massive pommelled beater. Between them another percussionist was shaking an urgent cascade of sound from a tall sheet of metal. The dancers in this star point were barely moving. They simply stood, heads thrown back, letting the thunderous waterfall crash through them. Was Lil among them? None looked like her. That white hair was familiar, though: it was the pale journalist, filming the metal sheet, silhouetted in its frame like a menhir or a scaffold against the sparkling drift of stars.

Rudo was dancing now, his shoulders twitching as he moved towards the left teardrop of the infinity symbol. Close up, these dancers were almost frightening, a dangerous crush of leaping, clapping bodies, swerving wheelchairs and flailing crutches, throats emitting a high, unearthly keening. Edging between the frenzy and the purple spotlights lining the platform, the team slipped into the dark third star point. Ahead was the river, light scattered like amethysts across the moonlit sheen of the water. The droning sound, Astra was vaguely aware, was slightly fainter here. To her left, for the first time in the star, she sensed silence.

She gazed into the tip of the third point. Most of the purple lights here adorned wheelchairs and their users. Some of the people were obscured, others dimly profiled – a lolling head, a pair of legs stretched out on a cushioned rest. There were people not in wheelchairs too. Someone, Astra could see, was holding a straw to a person's lips. Close by, someone else was giving a woman an injection. A man was kneeling: giving a massage? No. He stretched an arm out over the edge of the star and upturned a bottle.

It was a caring station for emptying catheters, refreshing thirst, providing food and medical aid. Was Lil there? She might be looking after the man she had pushed up the ramp at the Diplomeet. But the carers were crouching, their faces only barely lit; it was impossible to say. And though no one had said so, Astra knew this star point was off-limits. She would just have to keep an eye on it, see who came and went. For now, she looked away. Rudo and Sandrine were assessing the infinity dance. Photon's expression was solemn, distant, respectful. She'd seen that expression before, on the faces of international visitors to Or, when they'd happened to see a new mothers' breastfeeding circle in the orchard, or had been shown the seeds of the plant that, given a few more years' investment, would one day cure the disease they suffered from.

'We go in,' Rudo shouted, making a figure eight in the air with his forefinger. 'Watch the ceremony. Meet back here.' Like an asteroid drawn into orbit, she let herself get sucked into the dazzling purple spin of bodies, crutches and wheels.

The stream of dancers was five or six people thick, some plunging ahead, others whirling into eddies you had to carefully squeeze past. The musk of sweat and incense smouldered in her nostrils and for a moment she felt immensely free. Here, though water squirters sprayed her cheeks, singers yodelled in her ears, stray elbows jabbed her in the back, and a wheelchair nearly crushed her toe, no one was looking at her. The dancers were lost in their own exultation and Rudo and Sandrine were soon too far ahead to see. She was melting into the crowd, into the music – except Photon, behind her, was placing his hand on her shoulder, steering her to the inner rim of the teardrop where she could, at last, clearly see the figure blazing inside it.

It was Asar. Dressed in long robes and a tall silvery crown, the Singular was standing on a cloth-covered dais between three violet footlights. His arms were outstretched, his face raised to the moon, his broad mouth glistening open. Saliva hung in curtains from his lower lip, dangling into a large silver bowl held by a plump robed woman lounging at his feet. Like the dancers in the gong star point, he was trembling. It didn't matter, Astra realised, if he couldn't see or hear. His chest was vibrating, scalp tingling, throat thrumming, every cell of his body awakened to the tre-mendous power of the dance. As she watched, Asar raised his arms and wailed, his long fingers fluttering up to the luminous moon.

Around her, dancers whooped and ululated; from the star points, the drummers converged, bass, *tablas* and *jambes* together cresting a new wave of elation. She was past Asar now, being steadily pulled to an infin-ite intersection, the point at which the two teardrops met. Here the dancers bunched and slowed, jigging and twirling in place as the two streams milled through each other – and around, she saw now, the Singu-lar singer with two voices. She too was on a dais, and taller than Photon. Sucked into a purple jam of Non-Landers, all reaching out to touch the singer's floaty lavender robe as they passed, Astra could only see one of the Singular's faces, glowing beneath her silver crown. Her eyes were glazed and her thin-lipped mouths were silver flutes, blessing the conflu-ence of dancers with the ecstatic serenity of her song.

Then she was herself touching the hem of her garment and dancing on. Photon's hand was no longer on her shoulder. She turned, but he wasn't there. Her stomach leapt. But he must be near by. She strained on tiptoe, her view blocked by the crowd, but at last she caught a glimpse of a white shock of hair and Photon's anxious face, peering straight over her. He was just a few feet behind her but he might as well have been a decade away for all she could call to him over the noise. She tried to raise her arm to wave, but the people around her were crushing her, shoving her on.

'Hey!' she cried out, but the crowd snatched her cry and flicked it away like a beer cork. She was well past Simiya now, pouring into the second teardrop, the dancers pressing faster and harder around her. Hard-bodied, their faces unlit, they were gripping her arms, shoving at the backs of her knees.

These weren't dancers, she realised with a cold stab of panic. This was a *posse*: a unit intent on jostling her to the outer rim of the dance. She had to think fast: Photon *had* to see her. She wrenched her elbow away, desperate to turn on her headtorch, but one of the women grabbed the circlet, tore it off and stuffed it into her pocket.

'Give that back,' she shouted, but she was helpless to stop them. Now openly manhandling her, the posse bustled her out to the edge of the dance. She went limp, forcing the youths to shoulder her entire weight, but they just lifted her off her feet and carried her into the black maw of the top star point, out over the river. There were no dancers or drummers here, just a few prone figures, lying on the platform looking up at the stars, the waves slapping against the platform rigging beneath them. Standing in their midst was Lil.

'Lil!' she yelled, struggling with fury. 'Tell them to let me *go*.'

Barefoot and bare-armed, Lil was garbed in a short-sleeved dress and leggings, her thick hair loose around her shoulders, her tin star glinting on the bicycle chain round her neck, a headband of violet stars shedding purple petals down her cheeks. She placed her finger on her lips. In the dark light, her naked forearms looked like sword scabbards: scales of bronze skin riveted with blisters.

Lil made a gesture and the posse relaxed their grips, but there was no escape; she was enclosed in a semicircle of hostile Non-Landers. Heart pounding, she wrested her arms free and placed her fists on her hips. Lil might have snatched the upper hand, but she wasn't going to let her keep it.

'I came here to find you, Lil,' she announced in Gaian. 'You didn't have to *kidnap* me.'

Lil tilted her head and stepped forward, holding out both her hands. 'I'm sorry for the greeting committee, Astra.' Her Asfarian was high and lilting. 'I was going to meet you at the observer stand. But YAC appreciated your friend's gift, so plans changed.'

Astra stood quivering. Was she supposed to hug Lil, after *that*?

'Come. We need to talk.' Lil turned and started walking to the top tip of the star, where the platform jutted over the river. Glancing back, lifting the same finger she'd just *shhh'd* Astra with, she beckoned her to follow.

The posse loosened around her. The woman who'd snatched her head-band, a stocky girl with short hair, held it out. Another man bowed, his toe pointed, and made a courtly gesture back towards the infinity symbol. *Do you want to return to the dance?*

Frig them. She grabbed her headband and followed Lil, past an extra-large wheelchair that turned out to be a kissing couple, towards the edge of the platform. At the very tip, her bare feet glowing in the border lights, Lil stopped.

The eerie drone was loud here, floating over from the next star point, but nearer still was the hush and shush of the river, the slap of waves against the platform pillars. There was a breeze, and the sweetish whiff of something rotten: not an animal but compost, decaying fruit or vegetables. She hesitated.

Lil laughed. She stepped back from the edge and flung her arms around Astra. 'I knew you'd come,' she crooned in Gaian. 'I knew it.'

Her bones light as a bird's, Lil's arms rested gently on Astra's shoulders. Somehow, impossibly, her hair smelled of the forest still, of pine sap and Owleon and sun-baked earth. Astra desperately inhaled the last wispy gasps of Wise House.

'*How* did you know?' She was stung by a sudden suspicion. 'Did Hokma tell you my dad was a—'

'I'm sorry about Hokma,' Lil pulled her closer, her unbound breasts and soft hips cushioning Astra's. 'I'm sorry.'

This was *Lil*. She pulled away from the embrace. 'Did Hokma tell you I was half Non-Lander?' she insisted.

'No. *No.*' Her voice husky and low, her face strewn with purple light petals, her hands stroking Astra's arms, Lil was a hypnotic night flower. 'She didn't know *I* was until IMBOD sent the message about my dad. Do you remember? When we were having your Blood & Seed picnic.'

Suspiciously, she nodded.

'I knew she knew' – Lil twitched, that old one-shoulder shrug – 'just by the way she acted that night. So I decided it was time to go. She told your dad I was coming and he sent people to look for me. We knew you would come one day too.'

We. Her heart leapt. She wanted to shake Lil. 'Where's Zizi? Can you take me to him?'

But Lil was immune to urgency. 'He's waiting to meet you. We're all waiting to meet you.' She unclasped her headband of violet stars and hooked it around Astra's neck. 'This is for you.'

The stars were spiky on her collarbone. She didn't want the gift. She wanted her father. And she had to hurry – if she didn't get back to Photon soon, the whole team would come looking for her. Above the sore crust of Lil's cheek, she met the girl's unreadable gaze.

'You have to tell me where Zizi is,' she demanded. 'I've come all this way. I've left everything behind. Hokma *died*.' Her voice cracked.

In reply, Lil cupped Astra's face in her hands. She should have wrested her head away, but weak, disarmed, on the verge of tears, she hesitated a fatal second. She allowed Lil's lips to gently brush hers.

The kiss was a whole other world, a universe away from rules, plans, party costumes. *This . . . I remember this . . .* Like the silent heat of a predatory beast, a dangerous longing stole over her. Half-closing her eyes, she parted her lips, placed her hands on Lil's damp dress. For an electric second, their tongues met – then Lil pulled away.

'Do you have an ion glove?'

She was breathless, angry, confused. 'No – I mean, yes: I can use one at CONC. But I don't want to—'

'Good. I'll make a date with you. Next week. We can talk more about Zizi, and then you can come and see me in Pithar. There's people there you need to meet.'

She was boiling up. This was the Lil she remembered, seducing her, taking control, ordering her about. 'I want to meet Zizi, not people in *Pithar*, wherever that is,' she flared. 'And it's stupid to use the glove. It's on the internet – CONC might record us.'

'No they won't,' Lil scoffed. That was her all over, switching in a flash from seduction to contempt. 'Ion gloves are data-destroyers. Didn't your CONC boyfriend tell you?'

'He's not my boyfriend,' she retorted.

Lil laughed and moved in again. Her lips at Astra's ear, her breasts squashed against Astra's arm, she whispered, 'If he asks, tell him someone's calling you from home.'

She was furious, but the beast was still prowling, its hot paw prints trespassing the border between her flesh and Lil's. 'We don't have ion gloves in Is-Land,' she managed.

Lil's fingers were in Astra's hair, her radiant body was illuminating Astra's cells. 'Tell him I'm on holiday,' she crooned. 'Say I'm calling you from the morning star.'

She wanted to cry. Why was Lil *like* this? Why couldn't they *talk*, instead of arguing and kissing? That's all they ever did. Argue and kiss. She wrenched away. 'It's not a good idea, Lil. Just tell me where Zizi is. I'll meet you there—'

Lil hugged her, hard, her bike chain indenting Astra's chest. 'I'm so glad you're here. I'll email, okay?' Then, quick, beautiful, and treacherous as mercury, Lil slithered out of her grasp. Robed in darkness, the girl darted to the star tip and in a smooth black arc dived into the river. Soundlessly, her body hit the water, the slimmest of splashes barely disturbing the amethyst and silver shavings scattered on its surface.

The emptiness was stunning. Though she waited for what felt like minutes, Lil did not reappear. The heat of arousal drained from her and the faint stench of the water crept back up her nose. If it wasn't for the necklace of stars biting into her flesh, the whole encounter could have been a dream, a disturbing, chaotic, arousing dream with no resolution.

But this was impossible. Where the frig was Lil? Beyond the platform a row of trees cast deep shadows back onto the shore. She strained to see, but nothing stirred in the blackness spread like a cape behind the trees. Then she registered the marvel: *trees*. Three or four tall, broad ones, oaks she thought, their roots drinking of the Mikku River. Were they survivors of the Dark Time? A scrap remnant of the forests that once, Klor had told her, stretched south of Bracelet Valley and all the way to Dragon's Gorge? As she gazed at their dark spreading branches, an indignant squawking shadow shot out from the canopy and over the water.

The *crows*. Longing welling up in her again, she watched the bird flap back down to its perch. From the foliage of the oaks arose a cacophony of kaahs and groarks and throaty snarls. There were *lots* of birds here. And that meant . . .

Not crows. *Rooks*. She'd seen rookeries on the steppes on family picnics. *Oh*. Her heart caught in her throat. It was like discovering a Tablette full of messages from Or. Rooks were Klor's favourite birds. As a

young man at Code college, he had been part of the project that introduced them to Is-Land.

The quarrel in the treetops intensified. If the birds weren't launching
an aggravated complaint about the music, they were competing with it,
holding their own rave. Another black shape flew up across the water, and
with it a memory. 'Don't look at rooks,' Klor had always said, one of his
treasured Inglish phrases. He had been serious. The birds, she realised,
were complaining about *her*. Protecting their young. If she kept staring at
them, they might desert their nests. As she turned hastily away, her watch
vibrated on her wrist.

Photon. How long had she been gone? What was the rescue plan
again? *Frigging frack*. Had the team contacted the compound because of
her? Stabbing randomly at her watch buttons, she dashed back to the
dance. Thank Gaia, there he was, hovering just near the intersection of
the infinity loops. Tugging her circlet back down over her forehead, she
rushed over to join him.

'I'm here. I'm okay!' She was suddenly exultant. She had done it: she
had found Lil. And Zizi would be next.

'Astra!' Photon grasped her shoulder – and noticed her necklace. For a
moment the relief on his face was struck off by a frown of confusion.

Even if she had prepared a defence, it was impossible to explain. The
music was loud, fast, urgent, and around them the dancers were shifting,
shuffling, pushing her backwards. It was a change in the dance, she realised: the infinity symbol opening up into one giant circle. Photon held
his ground, ensuring Astra had a front-row spot and a clear view of the
three Singulars at the centre: Asar, rubbing is chest as his devotee kissed
his feet; Simiya on what turned out to be a three-legged stool; and, also
on a dais, the third silver flame: Tiamet. Dressed in a purple robe and tall
silver crown, garlands of white flowers tumbling down around her neck,
the multi-limbed Singular was clubbing and clanging a large tin basin,
holding it aloft with one set of arms. With her other hands she was beating the sides with what looked like *bone*s.

Had Lil returned for the ceremony? Astra scanned the circle but it was
hard to make out faces in the crowd and the only other people she recognised were the journalists. In front of the caring station, the older reporter
was filming a long arc of wheelchair users. Near by, the younger man was
slowly panning around the whole circle, and opposite, the woman was

crouching again, tilting her camera to film the Singulars framed against the sky.

Astra shrank back into the crowd. The journalists were like Ahn, filming everything, all the time, recording her and the Or-kids for IMBOD's archives, his own private pleasure. Did the journalists have Kezcams? She searched the sky but if there were any aerial cameras patrolling the scene, she couldn't see them. Beside her Photon was tapping a message into his watch. She moved slightly behind him, out of shot.

The music was softer now; the drummers pattering lightly, the bass vibrations a dim echo of their former mountainous grandeur. Against their distant rumble, Tiamet burst into a solo on her basin, a strident tumble of clashes and clangs. As the metal sheet gave one last shimmer, she crashed all her sticks at once against the bowl. Simiya raised her arms and emitted a jarring cry, two long high steely notes sawing against each other, threatening to snap. In reply, a thousand throats roared up into the night.

As one, the voices cut out, but not into silence, not into the river's slap and hush – into the weird, oscillating, ever-louder drone. The crowd parted from the direction of the sound.

The drone-makers processed slowly, six robed figures bearing a rising succession of gleaming metal bowls. A small gold teacup, held on a boy's fingertips. A rice bowl, balanced in the circle of a girl's forefinger and thumb. A soup bowl and a serving dish, held by a man and a woman on the flats of their palms. And lastly a tureen, carried by two men between them. The boy and girl were stroking the rims of their bowls with their fingers; the next two players were striking theirs softly with small mallets; and a woman bringing up the rear was playing the tureen with a fat wooden wand. Chiming and ringing, the bowls were like upturned bells, neither in nor out of tune but on a completely different scale.

The gap in the circle closed and the players carefully lowered themselves to sit cross-legged between the Singulars. The crowd was intent on the sound, Astra realised; people were closing their eyes and swaying in place. But as the chiming gradually increased volume, a peculiar feeling grew in her stomach. *Resistance.*

She didn't like this sound. It wasn't unpleasant in an ordinary way, like the Major's unpredictable violin, or arousing like the rough complaints of the rooks. The long, sharp tones were more *cellular* than that. Like stiletto daggers, so thin they were nearly invisible, yet made of metal so dense a single needle would outweigh a standing stone, the strange notes slid into her, reaching places she had never before been aware of, summoning parts of her she hadn't even known she had lost. The sounds found the roots of her teeth, the follicle pits of her cheek hairs, the nerve-endings of her tendons, the marrow of her bones. The cumulative effect was almost unbearable. If this sound continued she was going to liquefy, release some awful fluid from every pore.

She was on the verge of panic. But just as she was about to bolt – to where, she didn't care – from outside the circle, deep in a star tip, the enormous drum began again to boom. A deep, comforting sound, that muffled the whine of the bowls, gave her a big soft space to breathe in. Like the heartbeat of a blue whale or a bull elephant, with solemn authority, the drum led the ceremony into its next dimension.

Beside the older journalist, a wheelchair dancer rolled into the circle: a youth with a fierce nose and hooded eyes. Enki Arakkia.

From the crowd, people beamed white torchlights over the YAC rapper, bleaching the royal purple glow of the lights stitched into his T-shirt neck and sleeves. Biceps gleaming, star medallion glinting on his massive chest, he swung past Astra and Photon towards Tiamet. The hungry beast Lil had awakened prowled after him. Frig Rudo. She'd get a thrill from Arakkia's arms if she wanted to. They were massive, heavy, his forearms as thick as some men's biceps. They were arms you wanted to run your hands over all night, not quite able to believe they were made of flesh, not warm marble. A pulse throbbed between her legs, and her chest panged. Why was she—?

Around her, the dancers began to clap and she forced herself to pay attention to the sharp smacks of palms, the persistent drone, Simiya's spectral wails . . . And then Enki's voice, in time with the claps, and with him the crowd, chanting in Inglish, the words exploding round the circle:

'Pain is the path. Pain is the path. Pain is the path.'

Arakkia approached Tiamet. The Singular held out her shining metal basin. Arakkia braked, reached into his chair-pocket and held up – *what?* Astra squinted – something thin and bright and glinting. Whatever it was, he hurled it into the bowl, where it clattered astonishingly loudly. But Enki Arakkia wasn't finished yet.

'Pain is the path. *Pain is the path.*' The chant rocketed up to the stars. Enki brandished a bottle. Raised it high, shook it. Someone behind Astra

hissed as Arakkia slammed the bottle into the basin. It clashed against
the sides and with a wild grin Tiamet raised the vessel like a chalice. As
she bashed again at the metal with her scimitar, trident and bone, Arakkia made the YAC sign, fingers flared like a star. Simiya erupted in a
screeching duet, Asar released a diamond chain of spit and a long roar
rang around the circle. Beside Astra, Photon exhaled: a long, soft
note . . . *Ohhhh*.

Pain is the path. With the chant still pounding around the crowd,
Arakkia peeled away from Tiamet and circled the Singulars before drawing up in front of Asar. The Seer shuddered, spread his arms. The
grey-robed devotee at his feet dipped her hand in the sacred liquid, Arakkia
leaned forward and with a swift motion she dabbed his forehead with
Asar's holy fluid. Anointed, Arakkia raised both arms, made a double
YAC star flare, then spun back round to join the the arc of wheelchair
dancers crossing the entrance to the third star point.

The next celebrant was already rolling out towards Tiamet. It was the
tiny woman from the Diplomeet, operating her electric chair. She was
not chanting; something was clenched between her teeth. A chill tingle
swept over Astra's skin. It was a hypodermic needle, like the one filled
with Security Serum that Dr Blesserson had given Hokma to keep in her
freezer. The one Lil had shown Ahn. But here, needles weren't used to
turn inquisitive children into placid, happy Sec Gens. Needles here were
full of morpheus, opiates that blew the smoke of useless dreams into
wounded minds.

She understood now: YAC members were refusing to take their medicine. This ceremony would show the world they were rejecting CONC's
painkillers, their mindfoggers, narcotic comforts. They were going to
take on IMBOD with just *the powers of the mind*.

Pain is the path. Pain is the path. With the chant building again, Tiamet lowered the bowl and the small woman spat the needle into the
basin. It tinkled, metal on metal, the amplified sound meshing with
another of Simiya's shrill cries and the crowd's howl of celebration. As the
woman powered on towards Asar, another wheelchair dancer entered the
circle – the limbless man, pushed by a carer.

Astra tensed, but the girl wasn't Lil – it was another young woman,
powerfully built, with short hair. A familiar figure: one of her kidnappers.
She glowered at the girl as the pair approached. The man in the chair was
unseeing: not blind, but intent on keeping the needle gripped between

his teeth, his eyes focused far ahead on some distant ideal, some invisible goal. The girl, though, was alert. When her gaze lit on Astra, she held out her hand.

What? The girl had stopped. She couldn't push the wheelchair with one hand without going in a circle, so she'd *stopped*. Right in front of Astra.

Serenely, the girl gestured again. *Join us.* And now the man was looking at her too. The crowd was clapping and chanting. Everyone was staring at her, waiting for her to obey.

It was horrible. *Worse* than horrible. Her face flushed: what kind of game was Lil playing? Did she really think Astra was going to leave CONC and join her parade of Singular worshippers, YAC warriors, insane renegades bent on self-destruction? Pain was *their* path, not hers. She was *done* with pain. She wanted to shrink further back into the crowd, but she couldn't. There was a wall of bodies behind her, and beside her . . .

Photon took a step into the circle.

Then it was all blotted out: the drone, the ceremony, the very stars above them. Agonising screams filled the air, piercing her eardrums like hot skewers, and the platform shook as if an earthquake had started. She clutched her hands to her ears, but Photon pulled at her arms. Why? The screams were like sirens tearing through her head, stretching her skull bones, making her eyes bulge, her nose stream. Photon stuffed his hands in her cargo pockets, and thrust something in front of her face. She blinked through blurred vision: the earplugs. Gasping against the pain, she fumbled the case open and screwed the plastic plugs into her ears.

The noise torture abated just enough for her to draw breath, to think the only thing possible to think: *get out.* Photon grabbed her arm and heaved her to her feet. His face blue, he fumbled at her headband, turned it on and pointed across the platform. A column of officers in dark uniforms, padded vests and boots, ears encased in solid protectors, wielding dish-muzzle guns, were flooding up the entrance ramp and pouring onto the stage.

She knew that uniform. Not IMBOD. *N-LA* was attacking YAC – and brutally. All around her people were bent double, writhing on the platform planks, some vomiting or clutching their faces, blood streaming through their fingers from their noses. Others had come prepared, with earplugs or, like the limbless man, earmuffs. As he screamed a battle cry, his teeth gnashing, his face a mask of fury, the stocky girl was pulling two iron spikes out of the arms of his wheelchair. Other Non-Landers had formed a dense circle around the Singulars, who were still towering on their daises, arms impaling the sky. Asar's face was shining; Simiya's wide open mouths emitted her own clarion war call; Tiamet, still banging the metal bowl with her bones, was brandishing the sacrificial needles like darts in her upper hands. At the feet of the Singulars' circle of protectors, the bowl musicians, hunched over their instruments, played on, though their disturbing music must be inaudible to everyone now. As Astra watched, an N-LA officer leapt on a player, hurled his bowl across the platform and began raining truncheon blows down on his back.

She gasped, but there was no time to help. They were running past the Singulars now, Photon dragging her on, zigzagging through the battle. The stocky girl had pushed the wheelchair warrior straight into an officer, stabbing him in the thighs – the officer was down bleeding – and when his buddies swamped the girl and tipped the wheelchair, the small man rolled like a cannonball into the back of a female officer's knees. Astra looked back as she ran to see the Non-Lander man biting the N-LA woman's nose. Ahead, another officer was fighting off four boys, their thin frames hanging from his back, hands grabbing at his ear-guards, while nearby the tiny woman was clutching at a hand wrapped around her neck – Astra saw her snap a finger back and the officer's mouth open in a scream. Just beyond, another YAC member was being dragged from his chair.

Dragged and tipped from his wheelchair. It was unbelievable – *barbaric.* Were they all going to be beaten like this? Looking around wildly, she realised there must be a ramp down from the caring station. A row of wheelchair dancers were defending that star point with sticks and behind them she glimpsed purple-lit figures slipping away off the stage.

Photon was yanking her arm nearly out of its socket. They were barging ahead through the oncoming force, the red-shirted N-LA officers allowing their blue halos a free passage through the mêlée. They were nearly at the ramp now, and right there, at the crotch of the star, a bulky pair of ear-guards clamped on his head, two spikes shooting out from his wheelchair arms, Enki Arakkia was charging an N-LA officer. His face split open in a roar of defiance, he propelled himself forward. His chair speared an N-LA officer in the thigh and the man fell to the ground, clutching his leg. Then there were three officers rushing at Enki, huge men stuffing their sonic guns in their belts and raising their sticks. Astra stumbled as Photon tugged her past, unable to tear her eyes away from the sight of Enki fending off his attackers, protecting his head from their truncheons even as his shoulders absorbed the blows. Then a truncheon knocked Enki's chin, and another officer lunged at his chair-arm. Her last sight of Enki was of a massive arm wrenching free of the brawl, neck-locking the officer who was rocking his wheelchair, yanking the man down to the platform with him, as the chair went shooting off over the stage.

Photon pulled her on, swerving round a hunched figure, a girl crouched with hands over her ears like Astra had just been. Feet slipping, she scrabbled after him towards the ramp. Down in the darkness, near the beer shacks, two blue halos wavered in her vision – Rudo and Sandrine. Her earplugs working free, her skull bones fracturing, her brand-wound painful between her legs, she poured herself into her run. Ahead, an N-LA officer was marching the white-haired journalist down the ramp. The journalist was struggling – not trying to get away, but angrily confronting the officer and attempting to dig into a trouser pocket. Photon and Astra hurtled past them down the ramp. Running up towards them was the giant Non-Lander, his ears shielded by massive muffs, his arms like windmill timbers, smashing through rows of attackers, his face cracked open in a roar that would surely shake the moon down from the sky. Ducking and swerving, they evaded his fury and tumbled down the ramp, until Sandrine was running straight at Astra to grab her hand and pull her along up through the dunes.

ASAR

'WARRRRRR!   WARRRRR!   WARRRRRRRRR!'

SEPSU GONE no Sepsu   no Sepsu hand hold no Sepsu fingerword
no Sepsu no soul cloth no big finger kiss NO SEPSU nonono bad feeling
BAD feeling SOUL EMPTY FEELING SOUL BROKEN BOWL
    no wind no sun no earth no ramp no river no tent walls walls walls
hard walls hard floor Asar fall fall down fall on people legs arms heads
NO SEPSU no woman breasts no woman belly no mothersoft people
all manhard people man legs man chest man arms pull Asar
HURT Asar

    'WARRRRR! WARRRRRR! WARRRRRR!'

    NO pull Asar NO
    Asar big finger wet robe wet floor wet
    ASAR WET HOT WET
big man solar post big beer barrel big man hold Asar hold Asar down
sit down hard wall hard floor

    Asar HIT man
    HIT

            HIT

                HIT

Sepsu say NO HIT   Sepsu GONE   SOUL BROKEN
big man hold Asar
hold Asar tight
man two hold Asar hand
~ Hello Asar   Enki here   Enki here ~
Enki?   nose knife Enki?   wheelchair Enki?   PARTY ENKI?

SOUL HURT PARTY   SOUL BREAK PARTY
'WARR! WARR! WARRRRRR!'
big arms hold Asar   stroke Asar head   hold Asar tight
~ before now later, Asar   Sepsu here before   Enki here now
Sepsu here later   Asar sleep now   Asar sleep ~
no before no later NOW HURT NOW HURT no sleep NO SLEEP
    Asar cry
    Asar *cry*
    head hurt cry
    heart hurt cry
    belly hurt cry
    river soul cry
    rain soul cry

    Asar mouth soul wet   robe soul wet
    Enki cloth dry Asar mouth
    Asar head rest Enki chest
    O
    Enki no legs
    Enki no shirt   skin hot sticky   chest big   arms big
    big man let go Asar
    Enki arms hold Asar
    ~ Sepsu here later   sleep Asar sleep ~

floor hard stone
Enki chest warm wet earth
Asar soul small seed
world big hole
             big
                  Y
                    A
                      W
                        N

ASTRA

Indiday was the official compound rest day. Astra slept through most of the morning and woke groggy and dazed. Had all that really happened? But there was her dirty uniform. There was the purple star necklace, hanging over the frame of her bed. There, floating like a ghost in the room, was Lil, teasing her with promises of Zizi, inviting her to an ion-glove session, inviting her to Pithar, wherever that was.

She couldn't think about Lil right now. She had to eat. The dining hall was half empty when she arrived, and strangely quiet. All attention, she realised as she set down her tray of bean dip and flatbread a few seats along from Christophe and Honovi, was on the wallscreen. Tuned as usual to CONC Comchan – which normally provided fascinating updates on personnel changes in Amazigia and dispensed sound advice on saving toothpaste – today the wallscreen was broadcasting reports from various international media outlets on the situation in Non-Land. She watched, stunned. After a violent struggle, N-LA had arrested Enki Arakkia and more than thirty YAC members, including the three Singulars. Arresting divinities was unprecedented, and Non-Landers were demonstrating outside N-LA HQ. There had been no word from the prisoners, but YAC had released a media statement, officially announcing a morpheus strike. Its members were going to refuse all opiates until their demands were met: an open border with Is-Land, and the honouring of pre-Collapse land claims.

'Refuse painkillers,' Christophe scoffed. 'What kind of stupidity is that?'

'It's different, for sure.' Honovi reached for a carrot stick. 'Maybe like a hunger strike? Hey, Astra, how are you? Heard things got pretty hairy last night.'

She tore at her flatbread. 'I'm okay.' Christophe was annoying her already. On screen, the female journalist was interviewing a young woman in a Treatment Ward bed.

Her face was drawn, agonised, the words squeezed out. 'We have been robbed,' she gasped, 'robbed and then drugged. Drugged into submission, into a false dream of powerlessness. We want the world to know we have the courage to feel the pain of our loss. The loss of wholeness, of oneness. This is the world's pain. We ask the world to feel it with us too.'

'See?' If it was possible to crunch a celery stick smugly, Christophe could give a masterclass. 'This YAC is bunch of lunatic drug addicts. Is no wonder their own people want to lock them up.'

It was all Astra could do not to throw a jug of ice water over him. 'Didn't Photon and Rudo tell you? N-LA was *beating* them,' she interjected. 'People in wheelchairs. *Hitting* them with sticks.'

'Wheelchairs?' Christophe turned his snarky guns on her. 'I saw that report. More like tanks. And all this biting, breaking fingers. Not so peaceful sound to me.'

'They were defending themselves. *I* was there. I *saw* it—'

'Shh,' Honovi interrupted, 'there's Rudo and Sandrine.'

The report had returned to the Star Party. On screen, her team mates, sweaty and goggle-eyed, were running for their lives down the ramp. 'CONC officers were present, but unable to defuse the situation,' the white-haired journalist intoned. 'Increasingly, questions are being asked about CONC's effectiveness and indeed, their legitimacy in the region.'

Now Honovi had to shush the whole room. A head shot of Major Thames appeared on the wall. 'Our officers were invited as observers to a religious ceremony,' heesh snapped at the camera. 'It is not our job to enforce the law in Kadingir, nor to negotiate in the field.'

'No. Our job is to bring food and water and medicine to superstitious, violent, drug-addicted ingrates,' Christophe announced to the room.

YAC were trying to get *off* drugs. But there was no point in arguing with Christophe. And her bean dip tasted burnt. She'd had enough. She got up and went to the Reading Room. After last night there were quite a few things she needed to look up. She was curled in an armchair staring at her Tablette when Photon appeared. His face was a shade of ash-white she'd not considered humanly possible. 'Astra,' he whispered as other readers glanced disapprovingly over. 'Did not you get my email? We are due to see the Major right away.'

Sandrine and Rudo were waiting out in the hall. They headed to the Major's office, Sandrine making the occasional *tsking* sound, invariably followed by a short huff.

'You're making me nervous, girl,' Rudo complained.

'You should be nervous,' Sandrine replied. She wasn't joking.

At the end of the carpet, Photon stopped. The Major's lobby was filled with the ion curtain, but the ghostly model of CONC HQ wasn't empty today. Two slender boot soles were floating in the centre of the light spiral, a darkly clothed body stretched out behind them. As Astra waited for Photon to show her what to do, a hand pointed a small baton towards the dial on the wall. The ion curtain disappeared and in a single fluid motion the figure dropped, cat-like, to the floor. Without a word, Major Thames glared at them all, swivelled on hir heel and strode to the hammered metal doors.

The command was clear. They marched single file into the office and lined up on the carpet. The Major was pacing already.

'Here you are: my prize team, fresh from your midnight adventure. Forgive me if I do not offer you all a tumbler of the finest single malt. For you see, I am confused. And currently, I do not have time to be confused. The imposition makes me feel, I am afraid, *rather less than generous*. So, please, officers, de-confuse me.'

Photon cleared his throat, but the Major swept on, 'It was my understanding that you were to *observe* the ceremony. From THE OBSERVERS' STAND. And yet I see you – indeed, the *entire world* sees you – stumbling like addled sheep across a field of charging bulls. In addition to this perplexing, and dare I say *humiliating*, scenario, your watch logs indicate that Astra Ordott went missing shortly before the mass arrests began. Officer Moses, tell me, pray, what *in hell's name* were you all doing on the stage in the first place?'

Sandrine cleared her throat. 'We were given permission at the site, sirm.'

'Is that so? I was sent a list of specific restrictions, to which I signed my personal agreement. Why were they lifted?'

Silence. Sandrine swallowed. 'We made a donation, sirm.'

'A donation? Of wildflowers? Of home-baked cookies? Of spare *buttons*?'

'No, sirm.' She paused. 'Condoms. Officer Acadie's private supply, sirm.'

'Sirm.' Rudo threw out his chest. 'Permission to speak, sirm?'

'Permission DENIED.' The spit flying through the air was not in anyone's book a blessing. 'Officer Acadie, it is as I suspected: indulging in schoolboy fantasies of *opening sesame* and winning the *admiration* of fair ladies, you have taken prophylactics into Kadingir to use as a *bribe*. This practice might have been common under my predecessor, but I have made it *Waterford-crystal* clear that it is *not tolerated* under my regime. But as the three veteran staff members present do not appear to have read any of my announcements on the subject, and for the benefit of the new driver, I am forced to repeat myself.'

The bow was standing with the violin on the side table, but the Major's forefinger made a more than adequate replacement. 'Non-Landers' – heesh jabbed as heesh paced – 'are provided with free CONC-issue prophylactics, diaphragms, femidoms, coils and dental dams. Any shortages are dealt with at a diplomatic level. Why is that, you may wonder, Astra Ordott? Why do CONC officers not graciously sacrifice our own personal supplies of sperm catchers in exchange for little favours from the locals?'

Astra didn't like being personally addressed, even for rhetorical effect. She focused on the opposite end of the room. The afternoon sun cast a honeyed light over the conch trumpet and water jug, but nothing could sweet-coat the Major's bitter diatribe.

'Well, Astra Ordott' – the Compound Director was glaring, thank Gaia, not at her, but at Rudo – 'I will tell you why. In the past, unscrupulous officers *pilfered* supplies, turning a private profit on birth control intended for free distribution. Encouraged by this success, other officers smuggled in crates of out-of-date or sun-ruined latex which they sold at wildly inflated prices. An epidemic of leakages and breakages ensued, causing widespread anger at CONC. It took me *two years* to rebuild trust with community leaders, and I will not allow this fragile bridge to be kicked over by reckless, selfish *infants*. Officers Augenblick and Moses, you are accomplices to Officer Acadie's grave misdemeanour. All of you will be docked pay. In addition, Officer Acadie will have to buy his condoms from the medical clinic at retail cost until the end of his contract. He will also forfeit his next three ion-glove sessions. Officer Augenblick will lose the stars he earned earlier this month. Officer Moses will go back through the records and account for all the condoms dispensed to the Treatment Wards under your watch.'

The three officers absorbed the blow in silence. Astra waited, her left calf muscle cramping. Surely the Major would ask now about her time apart from the others. In Ciccy on the way home, the team had admired the necklace of violet roses – she'd said she'd found it on the platform when she'd got caught up with a chaotic group of dancers and then been distracted by the rooks, but by his silence, she knew Photon knew she was lying.

'Officer Augenblick.' It was Photon's turn first. 'I made you responsible for the safety of Astra Ordott. I trusted you to take her to a night gathering. Why did you allow her to become separated from the team?'

That wasn't fair. 'Sirm,' Astra offered, echoing Rudo, 'permission to sp—'

'Permission denied!'

Her stomach tightened. Now was Photon's chance to get rid of his troublesome baggage and offload her on some other poor equerry.

But Photon didn't mention the necklace. In a toneless voice he told the Major that he and Astra had been parted in the chaos of the dance, but had followed emergency protocol and been reunited in eleven minutes.

'She was pushed out of the dance. And then she saw the crows' nests, sirm. As a Gaian, she was drawn to them. She says, sirm, that they are rooks.'

'Rooks? Indeed?' The Major spun to face her. 'And how did you tell *that* in the middle of the night?'

'Yes, sirm. I mean, they were noisy, sirm. There were too many to be crows. My Shelter father taught me the difference.' She was gabbling and her voice was cracked with fear. She wet her lips and repeated what she'd told the others in Ciccy: her only phrase of old Inglish dialect. '*Where tha's a rook, tha's a crow. Where tha's crows, tha's rooks.*'

The Major inhaled, hummed a shivery hum. One of hir triumphant smiles glittered over the room. '*The Broads.* My mother met my father in the Broads. On the occasion of the greatest concert of her career.' Lost in reverie, as if heesh hirself recalled the night, the Major strode across the room and picked up the photograph of the woman at the piano.

'Franz Liszt. *Years of Pilgrimage*,' heesh murmured, examining hir mother at arm's length. '"What do I want? Who am I? What do I ask of nature?"'

Again, it didn't feel like a reply was expected. The Major replaced the photograph, angling it neatly to face the picture of hir father. 'The answer to those fundamental questions,' heesh declaimed, 'Liszt found in Byron: "I live not in myself, but I become – Portion of that around me".'

The words hung in the air. Back from the Broads now, wherever they were, the Major bore down upon the team. 'DO YOU UNDER-STAND ME, OFFICER ACADIE? *"PORTION OF THAT AROUND ME."* PART OF THE *COLLECTIVE*. OBEYING THE RULES SET BY THOSE RESPONSIBLE FOR SETTING RULES. RULES SET FOR THE GREATER GOOD. RULES THAT ARE NOT TO BE BROKEN OR BENT FOR THE SAKE OF *EINE KLEINE NACHTMUSIK*.'

'Yes, sirm,' Rudo barked. 'Understood. Loud and clear. Apologies, sirm.' But that was only the beginning. In the end, Astra was the only member of the team to escape the meeting unquestioned and unscathed. The Major finished hir diatribe by upbraiding the others for setting her a bad example and potentially endangering her safety. Finally, heesh paused, scanned the line of wilting officers.

'You are all back here alive, in one piece. I remain grateful for infini-tesimal mercies. *Dismissed*.'

Rudo waited until they'd passed back through the ion-curtain lobby. His eyes were flashing.

'Why'd you have to fracking spill about the condoms, Sandrine? Jean-ette's gonna go ape-shit when I tell her I lost three months' worth of glove sessions.'

Sandrine faced him, fists on hips. 'Because my superior asked me a dir-ect question, Rudo. Bend the rules if you like but don't expect me to lie for you to anyone, let alone my commanding officer.'

'Oh c'mon. I woulda fudged for *you*. A little team loyalty, how about? Or don't you do brother-and-sisterhood any more down in South New Zonia?'

'*Oh.*' She narrowed her volatile eyes. 'Don't you dare bring *race* into this, Rudo. The *team* here is CONC – which has its HQ in Nuafrica, in case you forgot.'

Sandrine was walking again now, fast, down the hall. Astra and Pho-ton hurried behind as Rudo dogged her steps. 'I ain't forgettin' nothing, Sandrine. CONC built their big schmanzy seashell in balmy Amazigia because it's a great place to kick back and look like they care that Central Nuafrica is still a raging war zone. They recruit grunts like you and me from the New Zonian hinterlands to do their dirty work while Neuropasian silver spooners prance about playing violin on the fracking rooftops. New Continents, my black ass. Nothing's changed in three thousand years and you know it. You and me are still at the bottom of the human antheap and the only way we'll ever crawl out is by helping *each other*.'

Sandrine's hand was on her office doorknob. 'Major Thames has earned hir stripes,' she said coldly. 'Just like you and I have the chance to – *if we do our jobs right*. Speaking of which, Rudo, thanks to you, *I've* got an afternoon of report writing ahead of me.' With that she stepped inside her office and slammed the door shut behind her.

What had just happened? Dazed, Astra waited for Photon to say something, anything, to make this all better. But Photon's counselling certificate didn't appear to have covered this situation. He stood in the hall, as knock-kneed and tongue-tied as she was.

'What the frack are you two looking at?' Rudo muttered.

'Rudo, I am sorry about Jeanette,' Photon managed, 'I am sure she will under—'

But Rudo was already stomping ahead to the staircase.

Photon sighed. 'Would you like to fancy a trip to the roof?'

She wanted to go back to the Reading Room, but she owed Photon big time. She followed him along the halls and up a spiral staircase to the roof of the new wing.

ENKI

Reaching, endlessly reaching and stretching for a metal shelf that was always too high above him, yearning for a glass, a cup, a bright bauble that rose, floated ever further away. Reaching and straining, lunging and grabbing, at a shelf that came toppling down around him in a crash of tin pans, a smashing of dishes and glass, knocking him sideways, sending him spinning down a bottomless well. Spinning, dizzy, slamming from the walls, her laughter echoing after him, bouncing off him like spiteful little stones. Her and her brothers. Their laughter. Her laughter. Her beautiful teeth. The sharp curves of her lips. All stuck like gravel in his throat, as his rage burned a hole in his chest. It was the bad dream. He knew it was the bad dream but he couldn't awaken, couldn't end it. He was falling, falling forever. Hot and hurting. Crying and whimpering. Rocking back and forth. Because he was a *baby*. A *baby* again. The rage of it detonating in his chest as he rocked against the hard walls, the black walls, closing in on him, trapping him in the long, endless echoing well of her laughter. She was laughing at him because he was a *baby*. A big baby. He was bawling like a baby. His eyes wet. His nappy wet. His nappy—

He woke, shuddering, piss welling up in his cock, a wet patch in his foam guard, that moment of alarm when he wasn't quite sure . . . no, his bladder was hurting, still full, loosening, ready to gush . . .

He was awake, bladder clenched tight.

'Enki. Brother. You okay?'

Bartol. Whispering, leaning in between him and the dream. Bartol, shielding him from echoes and shadows, the ghosts fleeing through the high barred window, the slit in the cell wall none of them, even Bartol, could see out of. He must have cried out, to wake Bartol up. His friend was reaching across Asar's sleeping body, clasping his shoulder. He gripped Bartol's hand. *Yeah, bro.*

Bartol withdrew and Enki lay there, breathing hard. It was dark: a darkness torn by snores, reeking with the stench of stale sweat, piss and shit. How long had he slept? A couple of hours? His whole body ached, but he couldn't stretch, do sit-ups, isometrics. Couldn't even shuffle over to the foul toilet hole in the corner. Asar was curled on the floor beside him and the longer the Seer slept off his panic, the better. He rested against the wall, with each exhalation attempting to expel the dream. But the dream was stronger than the stink in his nostrils, than the sharp throbs in his muscles. It clung to his skin, penetrated his chest, his belly, his mind, with its deep, sour poison.

He hated the dream. Like a lifelong enemy it forced itself upon him, returning after every triumph, dragging him under, crushing his lungs, destroying his dignity. Why? It was the dream of his childhood; that much he understood. It sprang from the days his mother had let him find out for himself what was safe. She had never stopped him, never carried him, harangued him if he cried. These were the days of the skateboard he propelled over the ramps, his hands in flip-flops, Bartol towering above him as the girl from the next tent raced on ahead up the slopes, her long hair streaming, giggling to her brothers. But those days were long over. When he'd started school his mother had asked a neighbour to build him a set of portable steps, planks that slotted together. He had strapped them to the skateboard, constructed the steps in the classroom and climbed up to sit at his desk, the same as anyone.

A year later his mother had queued overnight to put his name on a list for a CONC wheelchair: an adult chair, one he would never grow out of. After two months propelling it, his arm muscles had nearly burst from the skin. Later, he had started going to the gym tent, met Abgal Izruk, and the orphans. He'd started rhyming, and learned how to remake the world.

But then the girl in the next tent, that mindless girl with her Asfarian soap operas and sudden new, beautiful breasts, had got engaged. She had invited him to the party: invited him to watch her dancing with that scrawny roadsweeper with the blotchy moustache, her pathetic excuse for a groom. That night the bad dream had debuted. His piss had soaked the sheets. His mother was incensed – she said he'd drunk too much beer, but he hadn't. It was the dream. Just as he was getting stronger, his rhymes catching fire, the dream had driven its nails of failure into his guts, his bladder, his head. Gradually, he'd learned to recognise it, wake up in time to push it aside and get on with his day. Then Abgal Izruk had died and the gym tent fell apart. Soon the dream came every other night and there was no day to get on with. His mother had started harping on about marriage, a job – to whom? doing what? He was a *rhymer*. He'd started hanging out on the riverbank, with Ug and the drifters. Ug applauded him, tempted him, reached up and toppled him over . . . And when he fell, he discovered that morpheus transformed the dream. In the morpheus dream, he was running: running in mid-air, flying over the firesands and up into the velvet blue darkness that fit like a glove. Up to meet her, her breasts, her belly, her hair, her softness flowing over him, endlessly, with no need of deliverance, no need to spill seed, no need to need.

He had not been permitted to remain in that primordial bliss. Ug had died and Bartol and his mother had hauled him back to the sordid earth, from which he had risen to astounding heights. A pinnacle of achievement. He had floored four N-LA officers last night, broken their wrists, slammed their heads against the platform, all while scoring a major international media victory. But still the bad dream was not vanquished. *A baby. Just a baby.* It hit him again, like ten N-LA officers at once, and for a moment he craved morpheus all over again, like a starving man craved bread, a drowning man air.

No.

He stared up at the small pale grey square of the window. He had been through this over and over again. Just as he had to let go of the bad dream, he also had to relinquish the good dream. He shifted his arse, flexed his core muscles and focused on the pain shooting through his body, each cramp, every bruise. Pain was the problem, but pain was also the answer, not bliss. *Pain is the path*, he chanted. And meditation, as Chozai said, was the royal unrolling carpet. The singing bowls were inner spacecraft. They transported you wherever you needed to go to heal. Whenever Enki had tried, lying on a mat in the bowl tent, he'd gone nowhere, just felt a strange wash of tingles, pins and needles and tension in his temples, as if before he took off he needed to be scoured clean of rust, repaired, every joint oiled, a job that would take years. But other people, he knew, awoke from their voyages amazed, restored, whole. He was a YAC core member. He would learn how to lead the inner quest too.

The light was changing, a vague grey dust floating over the dim shapes of his warriors, their lattice of bruised limbs and blood-crusted torsos. Men stirred and groaned. His warriors: none had fled. The carers, as agreed, had taken anyone unable to fight for long down the back ramp to the escape carts and vans; everyone else had resisted to the bitter end. It had taken six N-LA officers to arrest Bartol – two to climb on his back to rip off his earmuffs and tear out the earplugs beneath them, four to kick and grapple him to the ground. Their giant trophy captured, the police had abandoned the fight, content to take two van loads of warriors and the three Singulars away. The women were in another cell. This one was wall-to-wall bodies – except for the sewage-hole corner.

'Fuck, this place stinks,' Malku announced.

Khshayarshat farted, a short toot. 'That better?'

The men were all laughing, sitting up. Malku shifted back against the wall. There were no benches in the cell, and N-LA had taken their wheelchairs – or left them scattered in pieces over the Star platform, who knew. Careful not to disturb Asar, Enki pushed himself up too, the basalt bricks rough against his bare back. He'd taken his shirt off last night and used it to clean Asar. He found a dry corner of it and gently dabbed away the string of drool hanging from the Seer's mouth. He'd been terrified last night that Asar would drown in his sleep. Getting him out of this cell was a top priority. The Singular needed his carer. N-LA must know that.

The dream was just a nagging pulse in Enki's stomach now; the day ahead was his pressing challenge. As soon as those sheep turds of guards came back to give them some bread, Enki would demand the men's right to a Tablette call each. First up: Malku's uncle. The man was a Nagu Three magistrate; he didn't like YAC and his speciality was camel-trading disputes, but he had always helped out his sister and Malku thought he might represent them for the promise of some kind of trade. Enki cursed under his breath. The uncle was a known frequenter of sex tents – a strip of CONC condoms would have gone a long way to persuade him but those maggot guards had gone through their pockets and confiscated Bartol's new stash last night.

'I mean it. I'd give my right lung for a breath of fresh air,' said Malku, looking up at the window. 'Give us a lift, Bartol.'

Malku could shuffle with the best of them: he could bowl himself at high velocity – he did it for fun down the slopes of the riverbanks. He could propel himself on skateboards too, on the flat, with sticks strapped to his shoulders. But a man with no limbs sometimes needed to be lifted, and Malku made no bones about that.

Bartol stood. 'Come on then. You can tell us where we are.'

They'd been unloaded in the dark. Some had thought they were in the Nagu Four jail, on the edge of the scrublands, but most had argued not. Even at three in the morning it was too quiet for that. Bartol lifted Malku by the ribcage, his head just reaching the window. There was no glass, just bars in the centre of a half-metre-thick wall, the basalt bricks coated with an almost silvery patina now.

'Ahhh,' Malku breathed. 'The sweet smell of burning uranium.'

'Firesands.'

'Told you.'

The men grunted. As suspected, N-LA had locked them up in IMBOD's old jail, transferred as part of Dayyani's new policing agreement. What better symbol could there be of N-LA's betrayal of the dreams of a people?

'Really, Malku?' Khshayarshat asked. 'Is there a detonation?'

'Two. On the horizon. Like big black trees made of smoke. I can see the shadow of the tower too. Reckon we're twenty storeys up, lads.'

'Any sand foxes?' Khshayarshat asked. '*Mergallá-lá*?'

'No foxes. No *mergallá-lá*. Plenty of sand. All colours.' Malku contemplated the scene. 'It's pretty. Like one of them wall-hanging weavings my grandmother used to do to use up her threads.'

'Oo-oh!' the men teased. 'Watch out, Enki, he'll be rhyming next.'

'Come on, Malku, don't hog the view.' Khshayarshat stood up. 'Give us a foot up, Bartol.'

Khshayarshat wasn't alt-bodied but an orphan with severe eczema he never complained about; he was one of YAC's top warriors. A bantam boxer, he sparred and wrestled with Bartol on the mats, sometimes climbing over the man mountain for aerial leap practice. With Malku settled back against the wall, Khshayarshat hopped up on Bartol's joined hands, grabbed the bars and peered over the sill.

'Urgh,' he groaned. 'Reckon I'm getting a whiff of your bad breath, Malku.'

'What'dya expect? I've been breathing your rancid gut air all night!'

The men chuckled as Khshayarshat hoisted himself up higher and pressed his face to the bars.

'It's magic out there,' he said, his voice dreamy. 'I never saw the dawn without the sun before.'

'Anyone else,' Bartol asked, 'while I'm having my morning gym session?'

The firesands. Enki had never been out on them – how could he, when N-LA allowed only date-plantation workers over the footbridge? He'd seen the sunrise stealing over the dunes a few times, after being out all night by the river, the sands glowing pink and gold between the scarlet brushstroke of poppies and the deep turquoise wash of the sky. But to say you'd seen the firesands from the old IMBOD jail, with two munitions explosions on the horizon? That would be something to rhyme about.

His stomach pulsed again. Apart from his mother, years ago, no one lifted Enki Arakkia. He had climbed the steps at school, then practised at home until he could hoist himself backwards from the floor into his chair. From his first day at the gym he had worked on his arms, building them up to their maximum strength. He might need to queue up for a sack of CONC grains once a month, but in every other way, Enki Arakkia supported his own weight.

And he was broad-chested, solid, heavy. Probably the only man who *could* lift him was Bartol. But even as a child it had been Bartol asking Enki for help – with his school sums, his Asfarian lessons, his money-making schemes that never added up because as soon as Bartol had money he gave it away. He stared at his friend's huge back as he patiently supported Khshayarshat, as he had Malku and would any man in this cell who wanted to gaze out the window of the old IMBOD jail. From the first days in the gym tent, Abgal Izruk had given Bartol the role of support worker, and not just because of his size. Abgal Izruk had understood who you were inside. As the cell slowly brightened, the old man's words floated back to Enki: 'Weakness will lead you to strength – if you listen closely to its whispers.'

When he had fallen, Bartol had come to his tent every day. He had brought dumb-bells Enki had refused to lift. He had looked sorrowfully upon his wasted arms and jutting ribs. Then, when news of Ug's death broke, Bartol had taken Enki's wheelchair away to his container, returned with a sack of grain and just stayed in the tent with Am Arakkia. When he wasn't delirious, Enki had been furious. He didn't need wheels, he'd croaked, lifting himself up on his elbow. He'd shuffle to the riverbank if he wanted. Bartol could have picked him up like a used tissue and dumped him back on the bedmat, but he never did. He just squatted in the tent flap, blocking the way, as Enki's mother flew at him, screaming and hitting and hair pulling, beating him back to the bed. There he had collapsed, writhing in withdrawal. And from there he had risen.

During his first days of clarity, Bartol had stubbornly repeated Abgal Izruk's words. His friend said they meant listening to your body: understanding that it wanted exercise, food, rest, a girl – not morpheus. That was all true. But here in this grey cell, Enki realised for the first time that listening to your weakness meant listening to your soul weakness too.

For despite all he'd done for YAC, he was still weak. The bad dream was still in his system. For now, the dream had escaped through the window, but its seeds were still in his gut, ready to sprout again, ready to undermine him, humiliate him, just when YAC needed him most. He didn't want to think about the bad dream any more but he had to. He had to listen to its whispers.

He closed his eyes. What was the dream whispering? That he was a baby.

He swallowed. No, the dream was shouting that he was a baby. It was *whispering* that he was afraid of *being seen* as a baby.

His eyes half open, his gaze rested on Malku.

Malku needed to be lifted. He needed help wiping his arse. But no one thought of Malku as a baby.

Asar had wet himself. But no one thought of the Seer as a baby.

No one in YAC thought of anyone else as helpless.

He was the only one who thought of himself that way, and that secret shame was keeping him apart from the others, locking him away in a jail only he had the key to.

Across the cell Bartol was setting Khshayarshat down. He couldn't let Bartol lift him by the ribs – even if Bartol could manage his weight, he couldn't allow it.

His mouth was dry, but his words were strong. 'If you need a real workout, my friend,' he announced, 'I'll take a back lift.'

If the others were surprised, they didn't show it. Bartol crouched in front of Enki, his thick forearms interlocked behind his back. Enki gripped his friend round the neck and shifted his soft, boneless feet into the crooks of Bartol's elbows. Beneath his shorts his foam guard pressed against Bartol's wrists. Bartol's back was firm as a weights bench, his shoulders two warm damp walls.

'Ready?' Bartol asked.

'Ready.'

When the giant man stood, the cell fell away. The height was dizzying. This was what it was like being Bartol, looking down on everyone – yet Bartol looked up to people. He looked up to Enki. In two strides, the humble giant stepped across the cell and stood beneath the window.

Tall as he now was, Enki was still only a head higher than Bartol. One hand pushing against Bartol's shoulder, with the other he reached for the ledge. Bartol grunted and shifted his locked arms higher up his back. Enki's fingertips brushed a bar. As he strained for a hold, Bartol swung round, put his back to the wall and pushed up, his palms beneath Enki's feet, his head to the side of his hips.

Then Enki was there.

Gripping the bars, inhaling dust from the stone ledge and the dry air of the firesands, he bathed his eyes in the shell-pink glow of the desert, a flat expanse gently shading into the gold and violet curves of the dunes. This mesmerising vision was split by the shadow of the jail, which stretched like a long black well out towards the horizon, where a billowing inferno and a spindly spiral of smoke unfurled like huge grey flowers into the weird, pale sky.

The utterance came from his gut, spurting out of him, an Arakkia free flow:

> *Boom.* A dawn without a sun
> *Boom.* Youth without a gun
> *Boom.* Golden dreams serenely spun
> *Boom.* Jailers on the run
> *Boom.* A wrongful world undone
> *Boom.* Grandmothers having fun
> *Boom.* The people's passion sung
> *Boom.* A bloody battle *won*

The men boomed with him. And there – barely audible, but there – were the women, booming too from the next cell, their voices joining their brothers', a flock of birds, a *consensus*, bursting through the bars of their captivity, fluttering out across the firesands, making a legend of this day. The shadow of the jail tower could stretch around the world; Enki Arakkia would never spin helpless, alone, down into that black well again. YAC would always pull him out, into the ever-mutating shapes of resistance. He was one with the others now: not simply their Speaker, their Rhymer but one with their souls. The men and the women in the cells, the rest, unarrested, back in their tents: all the dancers, warriors, trainers, the Singulars. He was rising up with them all, bruised, bloodied, unafraid. There on the horizon, the grey toxic shadows of the mockers and jeerers, stone-throwers and tempters, were burning away. His body might be caged, beaten, broken, but his spirit was boundless, uplifted on the warm shoulders of friendship, buoyed by the booming laughter of warriors, flying on a magic carpet of indigo and pink, turquoise and gold, the majestic shades of an infinite dawn spreading like the promise of freedom over the world – a promise he was destined to fulfil ... or, he understood, accepted, owned in his soul – die trying.

ASTRA

The roof of the new wing was a recreation area. Cushions and crates were scattered across the flagstones and piled beneath marquee tents and around small low tables with chessboard surfaces inlaid with mother-of-pearl and ebony. Photon pulled two crates over to the low parapet and they sat looking out over the city. His face was bathed in the rays of the setting sun, his white hair tinted apricot in the light. The moon was up, full with a shaved edge. The silence lengthened.

'I'm sorry,' she said at last. 'It's all my fault. I should have said I didn't want to dance.'

'Oh that. It is not your fault. I wanted to go dancing too. Rudo will cool down.' Photon winced, and his voice softened with disappointment. 'Astra? Who gave to you the necklace?'

She examined a spot of dried bean dip on her trousers, scratched her elbow. The lowering sun was gilding their skins. Perhaps it would turn them both into gold statues, for the Major to plant outside hir office as a warning to everyone not to give condoms to men with crowns of phosphorescent thorns.

'Astra,' Photon quietly pressed, 'I am not only your equerry any more. I am your buddy now. You need to trust me, but I also need to trust you.'

It was excruciating. She wanted to stand up, kick the crate off the roof. But Photon was as mild as hemp milk. And apart from needlessly saving her life, he had done nothing so far but help her.

'You'll tell Rudo,' she blurted. 'And the Major. Like Sandrine did.'

'I didn't say about the necklace to the Major, did I? Okay, if you break a rule, then yes, I have to tell. But if you think you might be in the possibility to break a rule, you should tell me so I can be helping to stop you.'

She scraped at the patch of bean dip with her thumbnail. It was true, he hadn't mentioned the necklace. And the thing was, she was reluctantly coming to the conclusion that she needed to tell Photon about Lil. When she'd searched 'Pithar' on Archivia today she had discovered it was a Nagu in Zabaria, near the rare-earths mine, and not just any Nagu but a district full of 'brothels' – not soup shacks, but sex-worker tents where, astonishingly, CONC, IMBOD and IREMCO officers had been arrested for buying sex with Non-Lander women and boys. She'd stopped after the first paragraph, not believing her eyes – the Major would never let CONC officers buy sex, and surely Gaians only played with each other? – but Photon had taught her how to identify a genuine media outlet, and the article was definitely authentic: the page displayed the logo from the young male journalist's T-shirt. Looking more closely, she'd realised that the story was six years old. Reading on she'd learned that not only was prostitution illegal in Non-Land, but CONC officers were duty-bound not to sexually exploit the people they were supposed to be assisting. The fact that more than two dozen of them, including the then Head of Staff, were spending their wages in Pithar had become an international scandal. Even though she'd known nothing about it, the Compound Director, a Neuropean woman, had resigned. Major Thames' jumpy control-freakery and gender prejudice was now completely understandable.

IMBOD and IREMCO, the article had said, were going to refer their officers to an 'internal investigation'. A whole station-full of Zabaria N-LA police had been arrested on suspicion of taking bribes, but there was nothing about what was going to happen to the sex workers. She'd web-searched but the trail had run dry. Still, Lil, annoyingly, was right: if IREMCO was still breaking the law in Pithar, she did need to go there. Preferably before Lil booked an ion-glove session with her; she still didn't trust the CONC communication box. The problem was, Zabaria was miles away and there was no way she'd get there on her own.

'I didn't run off,' she said, more aggressively than she'd intended. 'A gang pushed me out of the dance.' She paused, but she'd started now and she had to continue. 'They took me to meet someone – someone I knew when I was younger. She's called' – she hesitated again – 'she's called Lil. She stayed with us for a summer after her dad died. It turned out he was a Non-Lander, so IMBOD wanted to send her to a special school. She ran away. I thought she might be here. Then I saw her at the Diplomeet. She's part of YAC. I don't want to get into trouble, Photon, but I need to talk to her again. She says she knows where my dad is.'

Photon was silent. 'So Lil gave you the necklace?' he asked at last.

'Yeah. And she said I should come to somewhere called "Pithar". Then she disappeared. I looked it up and I think maybe she works there. Can we go and find out?'

He grimaced. 'I don't think you want to go to Pithar, Astra. That's where—'

'I *know* what happened in Pithar. But I have to find her,' she insisted. 'I have to find my dad. The Major said it was my *right*.'

'Maybe you should tell the Major about Lil, then?'

'*No* . . . Lil ran away from IMBOD. I'm not letting her get arrested. If you tell anyone about her, Photon, I'll . . .' She faltered. She didn't know what she would do. She could hardly kill Photon, or crush his balls like she'd crushed Ahn's. Gaia knew where she'd be sent then. And besides, it would be like torturing a kitten. 'I'll never talk to you again,' she finished haughtily.

There was another long silence. The sun was balanced on the rim of the world now, burning the clouds around it to cinders. She braced herself. *Trust*. What did *Photon* know about trust?

Finally, he spoke. 'The Major said I was to show you around. There is a Treatment Ward in Pithar. Eduardo and Msandi service it. I could ask to make a swap, tell to them I want to show you the whole story here. When you are finish your training, we can go.'

She scrutinised his face, but his expression was as open and patient as ever. 'With Rudo?'

'*Ja*.' He shrugged. *Why not?* But Rudo was unpredictable.

'Why can't we just take Ciccy out there by ourselves?'

'I cannot just sign Ciccy out whenever I feel like it. There has to be a reason. Rudo does not have to know about Lil.'

She glowered at the sun as it absented itself from the argument. She would have to wait for ages. Rudo would be there. Sandrine would know. Everyone would know. But apart from tying a knotted-sheet rope down these walls and walking for kilometres on her own, it was the only way she could get to Pithar.

'Okay.' Across the parapet, stones were merging into shadow. 'Thank you,' she muttered.

'You are welcome, buddy.'

There was warmth in Photon's voice again. She glanced at him. He was stretching his long pale arms, shaking out his gangly legs. He had – what was the idiom? – *gone out on a limb* for her, 'fudged' his report to the Major. For no reason that she could see, the Alplander was treating her like a best friend. That should make her feel warm towards him too, but it didn't – not quite. Photon could be trying to win her trust for all sorts of reasons.

But at the same time, something had changed between them. He had asked her a straight question and she had answered it fully. That gave her the right, surely, to ask *him* one. Something she had been wondering about since she first got to know him.

'Photon?'

'*Ja.*'

'Why are you the way you are?'

'The way I am?'

'Yeah. You know. Psychometrically nice. Not like the other guys.'

'Oh, I think I am not so nice, really.' He giggled. 'I am just hiding my not-niceness very nicely.'

'No, you are,' she insisted. She wasn't sure why she wanted to know, but she did. If he could explain it, then maybe, just maybe, she would trust it one day. 'You never get angry or upset. Is it because of your Tai Chi? Or is it an Alplander trait?'

He laughed again. 'No, not that. Alplanders are very not so known for being nice.' He paused. 'Okay. You told to me a secret, so if you like, I will tell you one too.'

A secret. She wasn't sure she needed another one of those. But she had asked a question and would have to take the answer how it came. 'Okay,' she muttered.

He tugged at a forelock. 'You see my hair?'

She had wondered about his hair too. 'Yeah.'

'It was not born white. It turned white one day, when I was a boy. The doctors say it cannot happen, but it did to me. The reason was that I came home early from school one day and I saw my father beat my mother.'

'What?' She didn't think she'd heard him right.

'Yes.' Photon's tone was calm. 'Like last night. Very bad. With fists. And a strap. He was hitting her in body, so no one would see the bruises. I ran at him, I tried to pull him away and he punched me too, in the face.

Then I made to lie down on top of my mother and even though my father kicked me, I would not get up. At last he left the house. When he was gone my mother told me that this was his habit. That he did this for years. She even lost a baby from it.'

Kadingir fell away. She was lost inside the incredible words. 'But . . . that's *terrible*. How could he *do* that?' She was filling up with fury again, as if from a gushing pipe, just thinking about it.

'To me it was end of world. My father was very religious man. He taught us so many rules to be good. I could not understand it. I hated him so much. I was very angry with my mother too, for not telling me. I could have protected her, I thought. I yelled at her, and threw things at the wall. When I woke up, my hair was white. And for this, my mother gained the courage. That day, she took us all to her sister's farm, and even though my father followed us and banged on the door, they would not let him in. That night, something I decided. I would never be like my father, angry like him. I took a different name too, not his: Photon, for light. Augen-blick for being in the moment.'

He was happy, she realised: happy telling this story. She wasn't. She was tense; her fury was shrinking and twisting into something smaller but even more uncomfortable: a knot of fear.

Photon giggled. 'And then for some time I thought I was an angel. I helped my mother and her sister milk the cows, I looked after my little brother and sister and I studied hard.' He paused, then continued sol-emnly, 'I learned about what Rudo just said. The problem of whiteness. And so I wanted even more not to be like the white men of the Old World, always looking to profit, to conquer other people. Okay, no coun-try conquers another any more, and we are equal as human being, but this looking for profit, this drive to control a circumstance, to win a game, is still very strong with the Alpish culture. The people say it is like a life force, important for regeneration. In this way, this single-mindedness, really, they are much like the Gaians, it is said. Many Alpish people move to Is-Land, in fact. But me, I wanted to work for CONC.'

Klor. She was terrified that Photon would ask her if she knew any Alpish Gaians. She reached for CONC like a rock in a tempest. 'But Rudo said CONC is still like the Old World. Racist.'

Photon grimaced. 'Yes and no. The continents are equal in votes, but the Servers also have votes, and normally the Servers are from Nuasia, New Zonia and Neuropa. So yes, Nuafrica is still with less representation.

And more problems. With the heat, and old wars, and many places CONC is still afraid to go. But I think this can change. Like Sandrine says. With more Nuafricans and people of Nuafrican descent working high in CONC. It is happening.'

They were back into politics. The danger had passed. But she couldn't muster an argument. She had no idea where the truth lay. 'In Is-Land no one cares about skin colour,' she muttered. 'It doesn't matter. Most people are brown. A few are as dark as Sandrine, or pale like you. But they don't get treated any different.'

'No.' Photon leaned forward, his tone earnest. 'But that is because you are all Gaians. In other countries, skin colour is closely related to culture and history. People value their difference. The Gaian model feels to them like erasing their identity.'

The sun had set now and the evening star spiked the darkening sky. Kadingir looked eerie, lines and forms blurring together, merging into amorphous fantastical shapes. Her mind was blurred too. The gathering dusk seemed to be drawing a curtain on the conversation.

'Thank you for telling me about your hair, Photon,' she said. 'I won't tell anyone else.'

'No.' He giggled again. 'I think the white saviour is not a good look.' He stood up. 'I do not know about you, but I am needing to stretch. Do you fancy to do some Tai Chi?'

She fingered the rough brick of the parapet. She wanted to go back to the Reading Room but it felt wrong to stalk off after Photon had told her his story. In any case, the last couple of days had been tense; she could do with some relaxing exercise.

'Yeah, okay,' she agreed.

After Tai Chi, it was impossible not to fall into step with Photon's evening. An hour later, she was sitting at a dining table with him, Christophe and Sandrine, watching Comchan. YAC were demanding the release of all Star Party prisoners without charge, and the return of their singing bowls, gongs and drums. At the same time, they seemed to have plenty of bowls. Players, alone or in duos or trios, had appeared in the streets outside the Treatment Wards, and passing Non-Landers had started dumping hypodermic needles and bottles of pills at their feet. The young male journalist was on the scene, interviewing a player, a tall robed youth with a shaved head.

'So, Chozai: I'm standing here with you and your singing bowls. They certainly make an unusual sound. What can you tell our viewers about them?'

Astra toyed with her dessert, a greyish gluten-free cake drizzled with hemp custard. The bowl ringing had unnerved her last night; she wasn't sure she wanted to hear it again.

'The singing bowls,' Chozai replied, his Farashan subtitled in Inglish across the bottom of the screen, 'are YAC's greatest treasure. They were a gift from the Himalaya, from monks and nuns who heard our call for solidarity in their dreams.'

'Fascinating. And did the bowls dream their way here then?'

Chozai indulged him with a wry eyebrow. 'The bowls left the Himalaya in a yak convoy. When the heat of lower altitudes became too much for the mountain animals, camels continued the journey to Kadingir.'

'Amazing! What a trek! And tell us, what exactly is so special about these bowls?'

The camera zoomed in on Chozai's hands, his scaly fingers resting lightly on the rim of his largest bowl. 'Traditionally, the singing bowls are made of seven metals: gold, silver, mercury, copper, tin, antimony and meteorite iron. Meteors that fall in the Himalaya pass though only a thin layer of oxygen, so their extra-terrestrial iron content is very high. This gives the bowls extraordinary powers. They resonate at a frequency that cures pain, heals chronic health conditions, and even enables astral travel, so the monks and nuns say.'

'That's an incredible story. What is your own experience? Have you found all that to be true?'

The camera rose again to Chozai's face. 'We are indebted to the Himalaya for providing healing for so many,' he said evenly.

'But many of your best bowls have been confiscated. So what is YAC to do now, short of hire a few more yaks?'

'Do not worry, my friend. We have many bowls. In addition, we are learning how to forge new ones from scrap metals. For a long time our knowledge of the bowls was a secret, but YAC is ready to speak out. YAC is ready to end our culture of dependency.' The singing-bowl player turned to the camera. 'Our message to the world is that N-LA can arrest our leaders, and IMBOD can poison our children, but no one can chain our inner power. We are all avatars. We all have the power to transcend our imprisonment, to free ourselves from mental pain.'

'But what about physical pain? Can the bowls really help with that?'

Chozai smiled. 'Much of physical pain is in the mind also. Morpheus dulls both.'

Astra pushed her pudding away. She would néver join YAC. She needed her anaesthetic spray and headache pills. Life without them was unthinkable.

'*Imbécile!*' Christophe exclaimed as the report ended. Sandrine shushed him, but he barged on. 'Bunch of religious lunatics. Try to make their own people feel guilty for get medical treatment. Arrest the lot of them.'

'You can't arrest people for playing music,' Astra countered.

'On the street, without a licence?' Photon considered it. 'I think you probably can.'

'N-LA should reclassify these things as sonic weapons,' Christophe persisted.

'Weapons?' Sandrine said. 'They're ancient meditation tools.'

'When someone throw one at your head, you change your tune,' Christophe scoffed.

'Yo, folks,' Rudo intervened. He was dressed in a tracksuit, standing opposite Sandrine with his tray. Astra had seen him on her way to the dining hall, whirling storm-faced round the hoopball court. Probably he courted official reprimands as a kick-start to athletic super-stardom. 'Room for a repentant sinner at the table?'

Sandrine shrugged.

He set his tray on the table and stuck out his fist. 'Sorry about losing my cool earlier, Sandrine. I shoulda played it by the book out there, kept us all squeaky-clean. I'll make it up to you and Photon. Beer's on me this week. Astra, you too.'

Sandrine was still for a moment. Then she knocked his knuckles with hers. 'No problem, Rudo. And there's nothing to make up. The stress gets to all of us sometimes.'

'Especially to Christophe,' Photon remarked.

The others laughed. Astra braced herself. But across the table, Christophe stretched, his sallow face crumpling up in a gappy grin.

'Hey, some love and understanding at last. This place is a stress factory. Makes *le Bastille* look like *un* garden party. I'll have Sandrine's beer this week, Rudo, if she does not want it.'

Then even she was laughing, and for a moment YAC and Lil and Zizi and the Major all seemed very far away.

UNA DAYYANI

Journalists? Make them wait. Odinson? Ditto. Her husband? All right, she would reply, but the Lioness was in no mood to placate him. I don't know, Beloved, just set a dish for me, and if I can I will be home to beg the Bull to fill it . . . xxx. She sent the text and turned her personal device to silent. She had been awake all night and working all day, giving interviews, liaising with the police and the jail staff, running her team. She didn't need pressure to entertain her boorish son-in-law, she needed caffeine. Not that dreadful CONC dirtwater, but a tarry brew of Asfarian beans flavoured with cardamom, freshly ground from the hessian sack donated this week by the Mujaddid.

'More coffee, Marti?' she suggested. 'A tray to go round?'

Marti complied, like the angel she was. It had been an interminable night. But Una's brain was still buzzing and she would work until midnight if she had to. For now, she riveted her attention back on her screendesk.

One day Kadingir would have its own media station, but since the arrival of the Major, CONC Comchan had been doing an assiduous job of broadcasting local news. Today's reports had focused on the demonstration still being held on the Beehive forecourt. Una had been out many times, reassuring the crowd, enduring the tooth-drilling sound of those bowls, assessing the nature of the chants and placards. All thus far was legitimate: a peaceful protest. Staff members had been assigned to alert her to any alarming developments, but it was still necessary to watch the evening news herself. This was CONC's global report, a summary of highlights from compounds all over the world: how they spun today's demonstration was crucial. And there he was, the rumpled white-haired journalist, the one who'd stuck his mic under her nose this afternoon.

The journalist was prowling around the protesters. There was that piti-ful-looking one – a pretty young woman on crutches, arms grazed, head bandaged. 'We were holding a peaceful ritual,' she insisted. 'Our cere-mony expressed our spiritual commitment to the ideals of the Youth Action Collective. N-LA had no right to brutally disrupt it, or to arrest our members.'

Peaceful ritual. Spiritual commitment. Una snorted softly to herself. The Star Party had been an illegal incitement to open rebellion. Arakkia knew that. Why else had his people been armed and trained like warri-ors? Her officers had suffered broken fingers, toes, collarbones, noses. But these youths would present themselves as delicate victims. Her media team was preparing a counter-strategy; for now she had to keep abreast of the coverage, wet her finger for the winds of world sympathy.

N-LA supporters had gathered on the ramp court too, counter-pro-testers she had greeted at length. The journalist homed in on a dignified elderly man in worn robes. 'Young people have always held dances by the river,' he commented. 'For spiritual cleansing. But this gathering last night was a political meeting. This is not right. It is important that we respect our leaders and stand together. A split flock is quick prey for wolves.'

People around him nodded and murmured. Good. Anyone sane, sens-ible, mature, was with her still. The only wolves in Non-Land were IMBOD: surely even a child in New Zonia understood that.

A cup of coffee appeared on her desk. The small, quiet hands of Marti, always assisting, never interrupting. Dayyani sipped the thick brew. She must be up next, surely. Yes, there she was, standing at the top of the fore-court, her crimson robes and black bob framed by the Beehive behind her. After a quick discussion with Marti she had forgone the turban in favour of large gold earrings. World audiences were accustomed to seeing her in headdress at Amazigia; they should be reminded that she was free to look how she pleased. The camera zoomed in on her face. Her hair had held up well but her eyes looked tired. Men didn't have to worry about these things, but since her fortieth birthday all those years ago she had imported make-up, skin creams, shampoo and conditioner from Asfar, paid for from her ministerial budget, or even occasionally sent as gifts from the Mujaddid. Worth every penny when you considered that at any moment the international media might swoop down on your struggle. The average woman in Non-Land might not wear mascara, but oh, they all did in New Zonia.

'YAC is fully aware of the regulations governing political gatherings,' she watched herself announcing. That wasn't right. She frowned, caught Marti's eye. She had said a lot more on the steps, a full emollient prelude regretting the recent turn of events, assuring the world that the last thing N-LA wanted to do was fill its jails with its own youth. But the journalist had framed her at her sternest. 'Political gatherings must be held in authorised spaces, with full agendas publicly circulated a week in advance,' she was barking. 'These regulations were agreed by consensus. They ensure the people of Non-Land remain united, despite our differences.'

The journalist had clipped the end of her speech as well, her expression of hope for cooperation from the youth. But at least he had given her the last word – as befitted the N-LA Lead Convenor, daughter of a long line of distinguished judges, and the ultimate authority on the complex laws governing the Southern Belt.

But now what? *Unbelievable.* The report had returned to the young woman. 'The consensus on political gatherings was agreed before most YAC members were old enough to vote,' the sly, pathetic creature complained, the camera lingering on her bloodstained bandage. 'We demand a referendum, a new consensus.'

Outrageous! Consensus decisions were reviewed every seven years. N-LA couldn't stage a referendum just because a bunch of teenagers' hormones were exploding. The journalist should have come back to her on that, but he was summing up now, standing in front of that man playing those unbearable bowls, the Beehive obscured by placards and protesters. 'Once again, following yesterday's contentious Emergency Diplomeet, there have been more than thirty arrests of young alt-bodied activists in Non-Land,' the journalist intoned. 'On the eve of the arrival of IMBOD's mysterious "Security Generation", and in the midst of growing concern over the Hem, we see internal dissent, factional strife and questions raised about the leadership of Una Dayyani. Is there a new force for unity rising in Non-Land? Is the region on the verge of violence? Yonatan Prague for Neuropean World News.'

Una cut the sound. *Factional strife.* YAC was a bunch of outcast kids. But the reporter had given them the last word. As for the Diplomeet, the coverage had been abysmal. Her rousing speech and the unprecedented

N-LA walk-out had barely featured at all. All yesterday's reports had slavered over the wheeling-dealing YAC and its hlappy-cappy Singulars. And now the world was being treated to footage of its new icons being violently arrested. Completely out of context! Of course it looked appalling, seeing someone being dragged from a wheelchair, but if alt-bodied people wanted to break the law, they had to take the consequences just like anyone else. She had trusted the international public to understand that. Did she have to send Artakhshathra out to tell them in so many words?

She channelled her temper and shot off emails to people at screendesks two metres away, and to Asfar too. Now that she had definitively rejected Odinson's terms, the Mujaddid would need to be informed of every development. Those terms, she and her cabinet had agreed, had been utterly devious. IMBOD, Odinson had claimed, was prepared to allow N-LA's Statehood bid to proceed uncontested in Amazigia. Is-Land would stand aside, abstain, not rouse its powerful allies, he had said; effectively permitting Non-Land independent nation status. He had even magnaminiously offered to 'tolerate the use of slave beasts on Is-Land's borders'. In return Odinson had demanded N-LA shelve its alliance with Asfar; ensure IMBOD engineers were allowed to complete the cladding operation in peace, and permit IREMCO to maintain its ownership of the Zabaria mine. In other words, Is-Land wanted the guaranteed right to build its mysterious war wall in safety, all the while continuing to exploit and poison Non-Land's people, plunder its natural resources and prevent its powerful neighbour from opposing whatever stealthy ambitions the Gaians had up their invisible sleeves. In return, Una Dayyani was supposed to accept a massive risk of failure: without aid from CONC or Asfar, or the income from the mine, Non-Land nationhood could collapse like a mud pie in a storm, leaving Odinson and his Sec Gens to wash the dirt from their doorstep.

Still, the Mujaddid had pointed out that offering to abstain was a remarkable concession, one that suggested a sinister long-range game. According to his spies in Amazigia, Is-Land had been making advances to Alpland—

'Una?' Marti returned from the prayer dome and sat down at her desk. 'Did you want to have a check-in about the Prophecy?'

'The Prophecy is just a children's story,' she snapped. 'It can wait for bedtime.'

Artakhshathra and Marti exchanged glances. 'Our people in the gym tent say that YAC seem to believe it,' Artakhshathra said. 'They're trying to contact the girl. I think we have to start taking her seriously.'

That was the problem with a core team. You chose them because they had enough backbone to answer back to you sometimes.

'All right.' She sighed. 'Did you get a full translation in the end?'

Artakhshathra had, of course; several. He sent them each the file and the team read over the Somarian version: phrases they recollected from childhood, forgotten or never learned:

> She is placeless . . . She will appear in the night, enchained by the light of a day that is dead. A child amongst the mighty, knowing among the innocent, with her first kiss, she will appoint her vizier, the Black-haired Helpmeet of Harpies. Charging her chains with the anger of ages, she will drive her chariot through star fire and arrive resplendent at the tent of Abundant Women. The Seer shall bless her, and she shall heal his warriors. Attended by the Prince of Shepherds, she will move like a mergallá over the windsands. She will greet her father, drink his beer, steal his . . . and her lustre will illume his alliance. Alone, she will fly to the ashlands and bury herself in the earth. When she arises the placeless ones shall be in all places, and all places shall sing glad hymns of welcome and . . .

'It says nothing! It could mean anything!'

'But it does fit the girl,' Marti mused. 'She's in exile, so she's placeless. She appeared at the Star Party. Her father is probably drunk, wherever he is. And that eight-armed Singular, the drummer, she's from Pithar, it turns out. All the women there have—' Marti searched for the diplomatic phrase, 'extra attributes.'

Oh, this was all nonsense. 'We don't need to worry about the girl. I thought we were sending her to school in Neuropa.'

'We emailed an offer to the Major,' Artakhshathra said, 'but we haven't heard back yet. And the girl may prefer to be elevated to godhead than packed off to study verb tables in Andalus.'

Marti smothered a giggle.

'All right.' Una accepted it. 'The Prophecy is a problem. A minor one. So solve it, people. Fast.'

Marti frowned at her screen. Artakhshathra rubbed his wheelchair armrests with the heels of his palms. He grimaced, stared up at the dome, bit his lip, squeezed his eyes shut – and snapped them open. 'Got it!'

'What? Indigestion?'

'No! A solution! You're right, Una – the Prophecy could mean anyone. So why not you?'

Annoyance flowered into sheer disbelief. How had she done it – picked a boy with a brain like a mouldy grape for her core team? She and Marti had a little joke about Una being Istar, but that was precisely what it was: a joke.

'No. No. NO. Artakhshathra, I am a *secular* leader. From an esteemed family of judges who founded a regional government capable of moderating disputes without linguistic, religious or cultural bias. The first sign that I'm on my way to becoming a theocratic despot and my opponents will roast me alive, whizz me up in a blender and serve me with spelt flatbread for breakfast.'

He wasn't fazed. 'You deny it, of course – vehemently. But as long as enough people believe it, YAC won't be able to exploit this girl the way they might hope to. Think about it, Una: they stole our thunder at the Diplomeet. Now we steal their starlight and reflect it onto *us*.'

Artakhshathra was trying to think politically, she would give him that. But he was naïve: a smart boy from an Oasis town, unsteeped in the issues at stake. 'I'm sorry, Artakhshathra, but I cannot allow it. My father would die of shame if he knew I was dabbling in deification.'

'Your father started the Alliance,' Artakhshathra countered. 'See – that's in the Prophecy.'

'My *grand*father—'

'Lots of bits fit,' Marti said eagerly. 'You're placeless—'

'We're Non-Landers. We're all placeless!'

'Yes, but if you get us nationhood, we'll have passports.' Artakhshathra completed Marti's thought, the two of them galloping ahead without her. 'Then we can go everywhere. So your vision is compatible with the Prophecy.'

'Except, as you might recall, we won't be going to Is-Land any time soon. I'm not rewriting my mission statement to fit some broken old stones.'

'Eventually, we will get to Is-Land,' Marti said confidently. 'Everyone believes that.'

'"A child amongst the mighty",' Artakhshathra recited. 'That was you,

growing up, inevitably more politically experienced than other children.
You appointed Marti the day you were elected. She has black hair, I
assume—'

'Unless she's been tortured in a beauty salon, or is the victim of a bleach
attack, every woman in Non-Land has black hair!' she exploded. 'And
Marti is hardly the Helpmeet of Harpies. Unless *that* means me too!'

Artakhshathra and Marti giggled. It was open mutiny. She would have
to replace them. But with who?

'Is Harpies the only translation?' Marti asked Artakhshathra, as if Una
were just background noise! 'I used to work with female prisoners. Some
were violent offenders.'

He swiped at his screendesk like a boy playing a River Road Tablette
game. 'The Karkish version calls them Wild Wind Women!'

'Were your prisoners flatulent, Marti? I am telling you both *now*' – she
slapped her palm on the screendesk – 'for once and for all: Una Dayyani
is *not* going to start a rumour that she is some kind of figure of mythical
legend. People call me the Lioness: *that's* my symbol of strength, and if
you two pugcubs would stop lunging for my throat, I might just manage
to keep living up to it.'

The pair had the decency to look sheepish. For a moment.

'Una,' Marti pleaded, 'it can work. I know it can. Look, Odinson is
afraid of the Prophecy so we should use it against him. You have to deny
being Istar, definitely. But you can say that we *all* embody the Prophecy:
Istar is the indomitable spirit of Non-Land. The star we all wish on, the
woman who never abandoned her home, who fought to return there.
That way, even if people do follow the Ordott girl, you won't alienate
them.'

Artakhshathra was impressed. 'Nice thinking, Marti. That way we can
even work with the girl if we want.'

'If she's anointed as Istar, we can offer her a scholarship to study *mer-gallá*-dancing in Asfar,' Una shot back. 'That might get her out of our
black hair for a while.'

But they were grinding her down. The problem was, Artakhshathra
was right. And so, she begrudgingly had to admit, was Odinson. Her
people were mystics and the risk that huge swathes of Non-Landers
would suddenly adopt this girl as their leader was in fact real. And Marti's
plan was sophisticated. Inclusive. Respectful of people with faith, but

appealing to the literary types, all those poets with their endless beer-tent recitations. It might just work.

She pinched the bridge of her nose. 'And who is going to start spreading this devious jam?'

'The usual candidates: beer-hall talkers, tea-sellers.'

'All right.' She threw up her hands. 'Get the rumourmongers in place. But they don't breathe a word unless the girl becomes an issue. Right now I have to deal with an odious journalist attempting to sabotage my life's work. Marti, be a good Redeemed Harpy – go see if there are any more nut clusters floating around the Beehive.'

ASTRA

On Redday, everything seemed to go on hold. Over breakfast, Comchan reported that as a gesture of goodwill, N-LA had freed the three Singulars, but otherwise just reran yesterday's reports. Astra had turned her Tablette to high-vibrate, but had had no word from Lil or the Major about Zizi. Still, it was her first training day with Sandrine. Soon she would be back out in Kadingir.

Sandrine's office was sunny, compact and organised. There was a screendesk and a wallscreen, a table she'd cleared a space at for Astra to use with her Tablette, and a tall set of shelves sparsely furnished with a kettle, mugs, colourful tins and framed photos. The room was also fertile. The variegated leaf clusters of a grandmother spider plant plummeted down from the top of the shelfcase like green-and-white fireworks; a wall of its offspring exploded along the edge of Sandrine's screendesk and a row of cuttings propagated in jars on the windowsill, their root buds sending tuberous white shoots down into the water. 'My babies, getting ready to crawl out into the world,' Sandrine cooed, tickling a leaf tip. It was the most greenery Astra had seen anywhere in Kadingir. The sight triggered a lingering flash of the Earthship greenhouse corridor, its tangle of banana and mango leaves sparring with the light, and for a moment she couldn't speak.

Fortunately, they didn't stay in the office long. As well as managing the drivers, Sandrine's main duty was monitoring supplies; a new morpheus shipment had just come in and she wanted Astra to help her count it. She took her down to the storeroom, a high vaulted room in the cellars, filled with wooden shelves and teetering columns of boxes.

'Behold the Femidom mountain.' Sandrine pointed at a chaotic stack of pink boxes that miraculously stretched all the way to the arched ceiling. 'None of the women here want them. They have enough tents already, they say.'

Contraceptives were obviously very important here. It was all so backwards. Her implant stopped her period so, thankfully, she didn't even need tampons and pads – not even being the Gaia Girl had made bleeding every month fun. She peered closer at a shelf. 'These hormone sticks are out of date.'

'I know.' Sandrine sighed. 'The Non-Landers don't trust them. Or IUDs. They think IMBOD's tampered with them. Understandable, but it puts a strain on our condom supplies.'

'I thought men didn't like using condoms,' she ventured. 'Isn't it like kissing with a bioplastic bag on your tongue?'

Sandrine laughed. 'Quite a few of them say so. But there was an outbreak of MAIDS a few years ago that put the frighteners on. A sex worker infected nearly fifty men before she was traced.'

Dr Tapputu had warned her about MAIDS. Like 'sex workers', AIDS, Mutated or otherwise, was unheard of in Is-Land. She wanted to ask Sandrine if the woman had worked in Pithar, but it was probably best not to reveal that she was interested in the place. Anyway, Sandrine was already moving ahead, down another row of shelves. 'New linens – well, new to us. They're secondhand, donated by New Zonian hospitals. They may be a little thin, but if they rip the volunteers sew the good halves together.'

Astra trailed behind, learning that supplies were replenished at supposedly regular intervals: medicines and linens came from Asfar by the River Road, hospital equipment and birth control from New Zonia and Neuropa, flown by Zeppelin to Atourne and then transported by CONC vans through the Boundary Gate, though it was not unknown for the Asfarian drivers to sell supplies to Non-Landers en route, then claim they had been stolen. As for the deliveries from Is-Land, IMBOD could hold up cargo for weeks at the Barracks. Because you never knew when you might run short, it was vital to eke out supplies carefully, and as fairly as possible, to the Treatment Wards.

'YAC could help us, in a way.' Sandrine flicked down a stack of boxes with her fingernail. 'The more people who renounce morpheus, the more there'll be for those who want it. It's awful if a Ward runs out just before a new delivery is due.'

She set Astra to work counting cartons, an opportunity she used to mentally rehearse her numbers in Somarian. The totals didn't add up, so she and Sandrine recounted, proving conclusively that two cartons – twenty boxes – of morpheus syringes were missing.

'Time for a morale booster.' Leaving Astra to stockcheck linens, Sandrine went back up to the office and brought down a tray of peppermint tea and one of her tins. It was filled with translucent toffee-coloured triangles.

'Mom's peanut brittle! Keeps fresh for months out here.'

Sitting cross-legged on the floor, Astra took a bite of the long hard shard. Crunchy, caramelly and bubbling with nuts, it was the best thing she'd eaten in months.

'It's good,' she mumbled.

'Dee-lish,' Sandrine agreed. 'I need a treat after that. I suppose I should be grateful it wasn't the condoms that went missing. The Major would have worn a groove right through hir floor.'

She was still thinking about Pithar. She finished her mouthful and asked, cautiously, 'Are lots of people here sex workers? I mean, is it part of the Non-Land religion?'

'Ho no. Prostitution's illegal, and very frowned upon. The religions vary, but the attitude to sex here is generally pretty conservative. You're not supposed to be gay, or sleep with anyone before you're married, and then you're supposed to have a ton of kids. Most of those dancers we saw at the Raven will be married off by the time they're twenty.'

That was a strange phrase. 'What do you mean, married off?'

'You know. Arranged marriages.'

'Arranged? By who? N-LA?'

'No, no. The families. There's usually a degree of choice, though you still do see some young girls getting married off to older widowers.' Sandrine contemplated her peanut brittle. 'Personally, I think it's more of a political strategy than religious piety. Keeping the population up, ensuring order in a crowded space, making sure that everyone is taken care of by a family. Once they're hitched and have popped a few kids, loads of people end up fooling around. They keep it secret, but I heard some of the religions even allow for spouse-swapping.'

Astra put her last corner of brittle down on her plate. A nasty feeling was percolating in her stomach. 'What do you mean, "young girls"? Child marriage is illegal – that's in the CONC Regeneration Manifesto.'

'Sorry, it's just an expression. The legal age for marriage is sixteen. But in Kadingir they usually wait until eighteen, when people finish school.'

She was getting increasingly agitated. 'In Is-Land we'd *never* make anyone get married. Especially not when they're young. What if a girl doesn't want to?'

Sandrine took a sip of tea. 'Depends on the family. Some might accept her as an aunt, or allow her to go to a celibate commune in the windsands. Others would cast her out or beat her until she gives in. If a girl runs to us, we'll shelter her, give her a cleaning or cooking job. We've got programmes to help sex workers too. It's definitely possible for a woman to live independently. But family ties are really important here, and most people want to get married.'

She couldn't believe Sandrine could accept this outrageous system. 'It's Abrahamism, isn't it? Men owning women. Like in the Old World. That's *slavery*. That's supposed to be *over* now.'

'Oh, it's not that bad. It's not like the men have harems. Marriage is a cornerstone of Non-Land society, that's all. Wives and mothers have high social status, and Dayyani's pretty hot on enforcing the divorce and domestic-violence laws. I mean, whoah, in New Zonia we've got some real scary Abrahamic cults. The leaders have sex with all the women, even their own children. They castrate the smaller boys to use as guards, and train the others as warriors.'

She set her cup down and folded her arms. 'Why is that allowed?'

'It's not.' Sandrine brushed a flake of brittle off her trouser leg. 'But it's very difficult to arrest these men. They live in strongholds, and there aren't enough police to rout them out. Mainly they're tolerated as long as they don't steal crops or kidnap women from neighbouring farms.' She checked her watch. 'But we should be counting the surgical dressings.'

Astra was glad to stop talking. She had tried, but she didn't seem to be able to have a normal conversation here. Apart from with Photon, she just ended up getting furious. She counted boxes and tidied the shelves in near silence for another two hours and then went for lunch, where Sandrine complained about the morpheus needle discrepancy to anyone who'd listen.

'Just when the Major's double-checking all the report forms.'

'N-LA should punish the drivers,' Christophe contributed. 'Then they'd get the message.'

'The drivers blame thieves.' Sandrine stirred her muck-coloured soup dolefully. 'Or *mergallá-lá*. The last guy said that desert ghosts stole the key to the truck while he was sleeping, and stuck a sharpened stick in the sand to cast a dawn shadow over his throat as a warning.'

'I'm sure the Major won't blame you, Sandrine,' Tisha said sympathetic-ally. 'It's just bad timing, that's all.'

Astra let them talk. She couldn't get the morning's revelations out of her mind. Why was she trying to find Lil and Zizi? Lil would probably want her to work in Pithar, selling sex to IMBOD officers, and Zizi would probably want to marry her off to one of his friends. She pushed her bowl away. Around her the CONC officers chattered and laughed. It was all right for *them*. They had homes to go back to.

After lunch Sandrine gave Astra a slideshow on the office wallscreen. Perched on the end of her desk, behind its wall of spider plants, she zoomed in and out of a chaotic map of Kadingir, pointing out the horse and camel market, the CONC food tents, the proposed site of the second hospital – currently grazing land for camels – the six Nagu Treatment Wards and the areas of the highest 'social problems': alcoholism, domestic violence, sexually transmitted diseases, the rejection of alt-bodied children.

'It's a challenging job,' she said, 'although the biggest problem for us is the disappearing roads. When IMBOD policed Kadingir, people would shift their tents and ramps to confuse them. The habit stuck, and now people move around to avoid a local sewage flood, or to thwart N-LA raids on morpheus dealers, so you'll be rushing a patient to hospital and the road won't be where it was the day before.'

A map that went out of date as you used it: that was her whole life. She glared at Sandrine, solidly planted behind her barricade of greenery, the curved blades sharp as scimitars. Why did Sandrine always seem so *safe*?

'What about where you grew up?' she asked abruptly. 'Are there social problems there too?'

'My hometown? Sugarberry, South New Zonia?' The name pranced off Sandrine's tongue. 'Some, sure. But nothing like before. I mean, Rudo's right of course, black people have a hard history in New Zonia. Defin-itely we were enslaved there, don't let anyone tell you that was a myth. But in the South, any how, the Dark Time changed things.' She rubbed a spider-plant leaf as if polishing the tip. 'In Sugarberry, we say it was called the Dark Time because it was black folks' turn to lead the way, with love, not fear.'

This was puzzling, this question of racism. 'But black people aren't nicer than other people, are they?'

Sandrine smiled. 'Not too many people are nicer than Photon, if that's what you mean.'

'*No.*' Why did everyone think Photon was her boyfriend all of a sudden?

'Hey. I'm just teasing. He looks after you like a momma dog with an adopted kitten. And sure, folks are folks. But in South New Zonia, more black folks were poor. Rich people hoarded food and were afraid to leave their homes, so when the tins ran out, they died: starved or committed suicide, or got shot defending their empty cupboards. Poor people, though, had access to food charity networks. A lot of good souls had been organising for years to keep hungry folk alive, and they kept right on doing that. So the poor communities shared food, and when it ran out they went hunting together. They caught wild cats and dogs, mice and rats and possums, and when those ran out they ate snakes, and bugs too.'

Sandrine's accent and diction had changed. She was settling into story-telling mode.

But Astra knew this story too. 'People ate their own *pets*,' she muttered.

'Yeah. They did. My grandpa said his momma told him it was very sad eating feral cats and dogs, but the animals were hungry too and in a way it was putting them out of their misery. And it was important to get out-side, find other survivors. Grandpa said that if your party met someone else with a gun, you all held yours up in the air and invited them to join you. They usually didn't shoot. People were lonesome. They wanted to talk.'

'In New Zonia,' Astra challenged, 'the survivors hunted *people*. A lot of Gaians got *eaten*. That's one of the reasons CONC gave us Is-Land.'

'Yes, I know,' Sandrine said gently. 'But that wasn't around Sugarberry, Astra. I know some survivors did eat human flesh, but they only did that if the person had said they could. My town looked after our Gaians. They're still there, helping us live right.'

She stared at Sandrine. 'What do you mean, live right?'

'It's a small town with lots of land, and we work it together so we all have a nicer diet. We've got wind farms and solar-power stations, so we're self-sufficient energy-wise too. A few folks still like to own stuff – property and businesses, refurb cars – but no one gets too big for their britches. There's a community shindig once a month, and we all drink just enough beer to forgive each other all our run-of-the-mill sins.' Sandrine chuckled. 'Apart from adultery and boozing, the biggest social problem is boredom. Some young people head off to the city. I joined CONC. My mom gets worried about me, but we Face-chat every week and I tell her it's really boring here too. That usually calms her down.'

Astra scowled down at her lap. Why had she started this conversation? She didn't want to hear about hunting, or Sandrine's mother, or shindigs, whatever they were. And it wasn't boring here. There was an end-of-Hudna *war* brewing.

'But howdy howdy hey.' Sandrine slid off the desk. 'Stuck at work we stay. Let's finish up the delivery report, then I can give you an online tour of Sugarberry if you like.'

Astra didn't like, but the problem with rarely smiling was that people couldn't tell when you really *were* uninterested. Sandrine pulled an extra chair up to her screendesk and after she'd made Astra watch her fill in the requisite forms with the requisite polite requests and confirmations and email them to all the requisite offices, she logged on to ShareWorld. Astra had visited the site once and never returned. ShareWorld was cluttered with photos of cats and plates of food, unfunny cartoons, and links to random news articles and stupid music videos. Underneath these meaningless entries, people exchanged 'comments', many of which were entirely composed of exclamation marks. The global internet, Klor had said, would stuff your mind with nonsense quicker than Nimma could stuff a lavender pincushion, and having seen ShareWorld, Astra understood exactly what he meant.

'Astra, meet Sugarberry!' Sandrine said proudly, clicking through to a page filled with pictures of cornfields, red wooden barns, people raising beer glasses, and, right at the top, a black pig wearing a huge red rosette. 'Whay *hey*.' Her eyes lit up. 'Johnny Fudmucker's pig won first prize at the Fair. The Mayor will be *steaming*!' Typing rapidly, she added a comment: 'Way to go the whole hog, Johnny!!!!'

'Johnny's the town clown,' she chuckled, clicking open a photo of a grey-skinned, weather-gouged man. His chin was grizzled and his nose looked like a red spider had been splatted over it. 'His family's land was swamped in the tornado floods. When people took new names after the Dark Time, his grandpa said that if history had taught him anything, it was that nothing ever changes and the poor always end up mud-fucked.

He turned his hand to making corn whiskey, and now Johnny runs a honky-tonk jug-time bar. The Mayor's been trying for years to change the by-laws to get the music to stop at midnight, but so far he always loses the vote.'

Astra didn't see what was so funny. 'Will the pig get a bonus?' she asked.

'Sorry?' Sandrine was smiling at a photo of a group of musicians playing what looked like kitchen cutlery.

'A bonus payment. In its retirement account.'

Sandrine laughed. 'In New Zonia pigs don't get retired, they get roasted!'

Astra was silent.

Sandrine winced. 'Sorry, Astra, I forgot. Animal rights are important to lots of folk back home, but you've got to remember that in most places there was virtually no agriculture during the Dark Time. It's like I said, people had to hunt to survive. They can't yet see animals as workers with the same rights as human beings.'

Astra's throat was too tight to reply. There had been hundreds of international visitors to Or over the years but they had been apologetic, bashful about their shameful history. They had never, in her hearing, laughed about the death of an animal.

'We eat mainly veg, and we treat our animals real good.' Sandrine was scrolling through photos of people brandishing enormous vegetables or patting the flanks of slave cows. They were smiling, but they didn't look healthy. They were fat – fatter than anyone she'd ever seen. No one in Sugarberry over the age of thirty would be able to jog a lap on a Kinbat track without running the risk of a coronary arrest. And the town's Birth House must be enormous.

'Where are the people buried?' she asked shortly.

'You want to see the graveyard? Some folks might find that a whisker depressing!'

Sandrine was making fun of her, but she keyed 'cemetery' into a search box and brought up a photo of a white box being lowered into a hole in the ground. People, all shades, all dressed in black, were standing around the hole, some throwing flowers into the earth after the casket. Behind the mourners, to the right, were rows of white crosses and statues.

'Oh. Millie Pageturner's funeral.' Sandrine's tone was reverential.

Astra was remembering what a cemetery was. Not like a nurturing

Birth House, where people were entombed with their community, but a big open place where people were lined up, labelled, slotted into the earth like books on a shelf. Was everyone in a cemetery buried in a box, she wondered? She understood the flowers, but the casket seemed very wrong. When you were alive you needed shelter from the elements, but when you returned to Gaia She enrobed you in her dark embrace. Why would anyone want to put a box between their body and Gaia?

'Millie was one hundred and twenty-one.' Sandrine was lingering on the photo. She didn't seem *depressed*, Astra thought. Almost lovestruck, in fact. 'Practically the whole town came to the service. She was a librarian and during the Dark Time she kept as many books as she could safe in her house. They're on display now, in the Town Hall. Millie always said that the good Lord was writing an epic, and you couldn't stop turning the pages just because He decided to throw a little fire and brimstone your way.'

She kept silent. Sandrine was still lost in the photo. 'Yeah, so that's the Sugarberry cemetery. The church was one of the only places in town to survive the Dark Time. They say people used to watch over the graves, waiting for the resurrection – you know.' She raised her arms chest height. 'For rotting bodies to rise and walk again among us. But then one day a cherry tree – one that had been hit by forked lightning – budded again, and the pastor said that by God's grace, innocence had been reborn. That's kind of the town's motto now.'

How you could roast pigs and enslave cattle and consider yourself innocent, Astra didn't know. And if people were really waiting for bodies to arise from those caskets, they needed brain transplants. Gaia consumed your body and returned your spirit to the elements, where everyone could commune with it. At least the pastor seemed to have recognised that Gaia was sending that ignorant town a message.

Sandrine shut down the photo. 'Does your hometown have a Share-World page?'

'We don't have ShareWorld in Is-Land,' Astra said stiffly.

'Really?' Sandrine sounded baffled. 'But there's plenty of Is-Land pages. There's one for Atourne, and a ton of individual IMBOD officer profiles.'

'That's an IMBOD thing then. No one else has ShareWorld at home.'

Sandrine was incredulous. 'But ShareWorld is for *everyone*. Only

Abrahamic cults don't let people use it. You must at least have restricted access.'

'No. We have *Is-Land* internet and *Is-Land* e-journals. We exchange knowledge, peer-reviewed information that everyone needs to know. Not *gossip.*'

'Nah, Astra, it must be something to do with your school, or your family. Maybe you grew up with kid-blockers, but Is-Land is pretty much CONC's pet project: adults must have access to the global web. Or hey' – Sandrine swivelled back to the screendesk – 'Is-Landers abroad might be sharing. What's your town's name? We can check it out.'

Astra pushed back from the desk. 'It won't be there,' she said coldly. 'No one would be allowed to put up photos of where I'm from. We work on top-secret Code projects. Visitors have to get special passes and all their photos are monitored and share-proofed. They can show them to friends or in work presentations, but if the pictures ever get posted online IMBOD will sue them.' She stopped. She had said far too much. On the verge of panic, she stood up. 'Can't the Major tell that we've been looking at your home photos?' she snapped. 'Won't we get in trouble?'

'Hey, don't worry, Astra.' Sandrine reached out a hand, bewilderment and concern mingling in her voice. 'Social networking is a professional skill. And ShareWorld is CONC's main interface with the global community. Participating is fine, as long as it doesn't get out of control.'

Astra stuck a finger in the soil of a spider plant. 'Your plant needs watering.'

Sandrine lowered her hand; studied Astra's face. 'Astra,' she said quietly, 'I really am sorry if I offended you. All of the IMBOD officers eat alt-meat, and I've seen that Odinson nibble a bit of cheese sometimes, so it's easy to forget you guys are vegan. And I know Gaianism isn't a cult. I just didn't know your internet security protocols cut so deep.'

Astra rubbed the lip of the plant pot. 'You didn't offend me. I learned a lot today. Would you like me to water the plants now?'

Sandrine said nothing. Then she pointed to a green metal can on the shelf beneath the kettle. 'The tap's in the toilet down the hall. Thanks, Astra.'

Astra stalked off to fill the can. She had to get a stepladder from a storage cupboard too, and by the time she'd done all that, Sandrine was back in form-filling mode, her fingers galloping over her screendesk. With a bright smile, she assigned Astra a load of protocol documents to read and summarise to show comprehension. At the end of the day she checked over Astra's work and emailed it back with 'Excellent!!' and 'Well done!!' typed at the bottom. Then she let Astra study Somarian for an hour, for her Level One Test on Vioday. 'Thanks for a great first day, Astra,' she said before they locked up. 'I learned a lot too.'

Arranged marriages. Roasted pigs. Sandrine treating her like a child. It had been a *horrible* day. She avoided the courtyard and ate dinner early, by herself. She was in the Reading Room when the email came. The sender was a generic CONC medicare address, the subject header just her name. She thought it was a reminder about renewing her prescriptions. But it wasn't.

> Astra Ordott:
> You have an Ion-Glove Date Request from:
> stargazer@morning.nl
> Due to a cancellation, a booking is available:
> Oranday 22:00 – 00:00.
> Otherwise, there is a waiting list of one month.
> Please confirm your attendance by noon tomorrow.
> Please note:
> This message is automatically generated.
> No emails are archived.
> No Ion-Glove Date recordings are possible.

She hunched down in her chair. She didn't want to have an ion-glove date with Lil. So why was the pit of her stomach throbbing?

What should she do? Searching 'Ion Glove' brought up endless blogs and articles and photo streams of people in Tantric zero-gravity embraces. There was more to the technology than ions, of course: magnets, wireless data grids, holograms and thermal sensors were involved as well. But it was clear that the glove used data as a kind of fuel, and that CONC destroyed any residual traces of each session.

Yet again, Lil was right. They could meet in the compound, under the Major's nose, and no one would know a thing about it. Not only that, Lil had somehow jumped the queue and got her a date tomorrow.

No, she realised, that wasn't Lil's doing. It was Rudo's. They would be taking one of his and Jeanette's slots.

She emailed back, confirming the appointment.

And instantly regretted it.

Then she got up and went to her room. There on the bed, her mind lost in images of moon and rook feathers, indigo starlight and watery kisses, for the first time since the neurohospice she played with herself until she peaked.

PEAT

'Sec Gens!' The entire cohort was out on the lecture lawn, being treated to an enormous silvery shot of Odinson's mouth, the Chief Super's lips, teeth and bristles filling the Boundary lecture screen, his deep, rich voice slithering down Peat's spine. He stood straight, glowing – *radiating*. Something was happening, he could feel it. He was getting larger, yes, but not just physically. His *awareness* was growing: his connection not just to Laam, Robin, Jade, his division, the cohort, but to the glorious nature of their mission here. This was what he'd been missing, what Astra had sucked out of him, the sweet, rich, shining syrup of confidence, no, more than confidence – *joy*.

'I hear you've been having some fun!' Odinson's massive mouth was flanked by two images of his body: his gleaming teeth bared, their leader clenched his fists, pumped his hips. 'Rough *tough* kinda fun.'

Yes, that kind of fun! A field of Sec Gens jumped and roared, hugged each other, grabbed, shook and squeezed. This was a murmuration field-meet, straight lines forbidden – spontaneous reactions, milling and cavorting, skins touching, heartbeats merging were the responses required. Their uniforms were hanging in their closets. Today was a sky-clad day. Shared passion built stamina, their Division Officer had said. They were to enjoy the meet! Enjoy it!

'Biting, I hear! Throat gripping!' Odison's hands loomed, two hairy-knuckled cages bracketing his gnashing teeth. 'Pinching and twisting and FIST FUCKING!'

Yes, YES, they roared. All that and more! Spanking and throttling, scratching and whipping, harder and harder, for longer and longer each night. Everywhere cocks were springing to attention, nipples twanging assent. Robin was humping Jade, Laam sliding his hand down the cleft of Peat's buttocks, grabbing and squeezing his balls. Laam was full of energy these days, doing much better on the training field. He had been right: he did need more sleep, but that didn't have to stop the fun. Last night Laam had come to the woodlands, played for an hour, then curled up under a tree. 'Wank over my face when I'm sleeping,' he'd whispered to the others. 'Pretend you found me there, passed out after being gang-banged by the officers.' Peat had done so, first alone, then with Robin, the thought of his friend unconscious, Odinson's cum dribbling out of his arsehole, intolerably exciting.

'Sec Gens!'

The tumult subsided. Arousal levels must be contained, sustained, for powerful release tonight in the woodlands. On the Boundary screen, Odinson cocked his head. Placed his finger on his cheek. 'And have there been any boo-boos?' he cooed, puckering that marvellous masculine mouth into a succulent orifice, a shining whirlpool Peat wanted to dive head first into.

HA HA HA. Around him, an acre of Sec Gens burst into laughter. No! No boo-boos. No injuries, no wounds. Just love bites and bruises that faded overnight, scratches that disappeared, cuts that healed before you even noticed they were there.

'No! All is well. Sec Gens, DO YOU LOVE IMBOD?'

'*YES!*' Peat roared with his cohort. 'YES.'

'Say it then, for all the world to hear: WE LOVE IMBOD.'

'*WE LOVE IMBOD. WE LOVE IMBOD. WE LOVE IMBOD.*' Three thousand voices, united in a barrage of adulation, exploding up from the Barracks, over the trees and the walls, to shake the sky, the clouds, the very ground the enemy walked upon. Peat's heart soared. Let them hear us. Let them know. We LOVE it. We LOVE being Sec Gens.

'IMBOD loves you too,' Odinson declaimed. 'So let me reassure you, Sec Gens, about recent developments.'

The Sec Gens shifted into listening mode. Peat wrapped his arms around Laam and Jade. Yes, he wanted to know about the news reports. A sob caught in his throat. He was a knowledge-seeker. Gaia help him, that was his special role in Her plans.

'You have seen on your Tablettes the depravity of the Non-Landers.' Odinson was sober now. The screen was displaying his whole face, his sharp eyes, concerned brow. 'First they train their children to attack CONC, the very people who are helping them torment us. Now they attack *each other*. What greater gift, Sec Gens, can I give you, than a full-length preview of the tactics they plan to use against you? Yes, we have acquired footage of a battle between factions in the Belt, footage your Division Officers will talk you through this afternoon. Right now, I must say again, you are *not to fear* your upcoming encounter with these barbarians.'

Cocks were soft, nipples detumesced, minds alert. What was happening in Kadingir was a constant topic of discussion in Peat's core group. Was an internal uprising brewing? Had the Non-Landers acquired weapons? Laam wondered, would CONC be sending their own police back in, troops from Amazigia? Or would the Sec Gens be all alone out there on the Hem?

'As you know,' Odinson continued, 'IMBOD has been working hand in hand with CONC to de-escalate global violence. Rest assured, the Non-Landers will carry no firearms. Swords, spears or bows and arrows are all illegal. Sticks and stones, darts and nails, kitchen knives: these are the most they can muster.'

Now Odinson was getting down to it. Brass tacks. And rusty thumbnails, the Atourne Chief Superintendent had assured them, were all that the Non-Landers could muster for weapons these days. The Southern Belt was virtually treeless; Kadingir was an impoverished encampment. There were no factories, and the few smithies were carefully monitored, every last drop of scrap metal accounted for. Still, now that the day of battle was getting closer, it was hard not to worry. A home-made spear would not be hard to construct: a rusty tin can and a broom handle would do it. Scrapyard daggers, junk projectiles, all could be dangerous. Peat shouldn't feel fear – he had just been told not to – but for a second he did, and others did too: a *frisson*, a tiny chill ran through the field, visible as head twitches, audible as small intakes of breath.

Framed by the glass gleam of the Barracks, Odinson leaned forward on his podium. He had seen, heard, understood. Even for Sec Gens, it was not always easy not to fear. 'Why then, you may ask,' he asked kindly, 'do we not train you with sticks? Why do we not give you pocketfuls of rocks? I will tell you why, Sec Gens.' He straightened, his eyes blazing black from the screen. 'It is because IMBOD stands for *moral self-defence*. CONC knows, the whole world knows, that Is-Land uses only the force that is necessary to police our borders. And you, Sec Gens, are *a force unto yourselves*. You are taller, stronger, fitter than your opponents can ever dream of being. You know from your night-time adventures here that bites, whips, paddles, even knives, CANNOT HURT YOU. In addition to your natural assets, your uniforms are the lightest, most comfortable and effective body armour ever created. Should the Non-Landers break the new policing agreement, should they dare to invade the Hem, attempt to halt the cladding operation, rest assured, Sec Gens: fighting Non-Landers will be FUN!'

FUN! Peat cheered again, hugged his Sec siblings. Beneath his arms Jade was jumping, Laam trembling with excitement. Why had he worried, even for a nanosecond? IMBOD was in charge. IMBOD loved them. IMBOD would never let them come to harm.

'But not just fun, Sec Gens.' Odinson was serious again. 'This is a noble, pioneering endeavour. Never forget, you are Is-Land's greatest ambassadors. Out on the Hem you will show the world that Gaian policing is disciplined, cooperative, self-defensive, a vital model for a new non-violent world. You are to go now and join your Division Officers, but before you do, Sec Gens' – Odinson was calm now, calm and gracious – 'I want to thank you for your outstanding response to my last field lecture. I have received dozens of emails proposing missions, investigations, highly original initiatives. I am reading every single one, and I will respond to you all in good time.'

The Sec Gens' fear had vanished, droplets of chill soaked up by a warm soothing cloth. The entire field was serene, satiated, spritzed with promise. Peat drew his Gaia mates to him, shivered with a delicate ecstacy. Odinson was reading their emails – dozens of them. Surely he would note the name of Peat Orson, to whom the Chief Super had already personally written?

No, he chastised himself, that was an egotistical thought. His was a group proposal, and must be judged on the same terms as all the other hopeful groups. Ideally, all would be approved. All would have the chance to shine for their magnificent leader. He stood, chin in the air, earpiece switched to a Gaia hymn as Odinson faded from the screen, the Chief Super's mouth, fists and thighs replaced by a panoramic loop of time-lapse lilies, their white trumpet flowers bursting into bloom, again and again, spraying their pollen all over the Sec Gens' clear, sweet, lifted faces.

ASTRA

The next day Sandrine was as cheerful as ever and Astra was polite and cooperative. She followed instructions, didn't ask questions unless they related to invoices and maps, and ate peanut brittle when it was given to her. After lunch, she even started a ShareWorld page. Using the name 'NuDriver' – yes, she'd go skinny-dipping in the Mikku if she wanted, Christophe – and a stock photo of Ciccy, she set up a profile, friending anyone with an interest in the Southern Belt, Is-Land or YAC. All over the world, people were posting stories about the singing bowls, the living conditions in Kadingir, the mine, even the history of the conflict. But many of the comment threads were almost gloating, predicting a back-lash of carnage; it was strange that people out in towns like Sugarberry thought they knew what was going on in the Belt.

The person who knew everything there was to know about the Belt was, of course, Lil. As the day wore on Astra grew more and more anx-ious. She hadn't told anyone about the date. Thank Gaia it was late at night. At last work was done. After dinner she rushed up to her room, stripped off her uniform and lay down on the bed. This was important. She had to mentally prepare.

Lil, she considered, might think they were having a *real* date. Usually people met in an ion glove in order to Gaia-play. But she couldn't let Lil's kisses distract her. She had to talk to her about Zizi, the tunnels out of Is-Land, other dissidents – anyone who might help her get revenge on Ahn and Blesserson. After telling Ahn about Astra's shot, helping her was the least Lil could do. She would remind her of that if she had to.

What should she wear? If she went in a CONC uniform it would be clear she meant business. But Lil had scoffed at CONC. Lil might call her a CONC mule, as she used to say about school students. Astra took her robe down from its hanger. She wore it sometimes to the shower room and back. It was soft and flowing, and if it wasn't wet with sweat it could be comfortable – in comparision with the uniform, almost as comfortable as going sky-clad. And it would surprise Lil, show her she couldn't take Astra for granted.

People would wonder why she was wearing the robe outside the women's sleeping wing, though. She hesitated, then put it on. She wasn't going downstairs, and anyway, other officers sometimes wore tracksuits when they were off-duty so why shouldn't she wear a robe? She sat on the edge of the bed. She felt empty-handed. Should she take the poem? Her Belonging Box?

Her hipbeads were in the box, and Silver's feather, but it hurt her stomach to think about sharing those things with Lil. What if Lil laughed at them? Thought she was childish for bringing them here? No, the Belonging Box would stay put.

The star necklace was still hanging on the foot of her bed. It was prickly, but it would look good with the robe. And Lil might be friendlier if she wore her gift. She put it on. Then she took it off. She didn't want anyone in the compound to think she had dressed up for a date. She'd carry the necklace in her hand and put it on in the ion glove.

At last she was heading down the red carpet. As she reached the end of the corridor, the Major swung out of hir lobby towards her.

'Astra Ordott. How are you?'

She bunched the necklace tighter in her hand. 'Fine, thank you sirm.'

'You look much better, I must say. Did all go well with Dr Tapputu?'

'Yes sirm.' She squirmed inside. Should she say nothing? But it was obvious where she was going. 'He said I should try the ion glove for my headaches, sirm.'

That wasn't a fudge, was it? Maybe a shard of peanut brittle.

'The doctor is a wise man. I find a solo session a marvellous lift myself.' The Major appraised her. 'Still no word about your father, I'm afraid. But the temperature is rising in the Belt and that should get his atoms moving.'

'I hope so, sirm.'

The Major snapped hir fingers. 'Ah yes. I knew there was something I needed to tell you. In recognition of your unique Code status, N-LA has offered you a scholarship to take an undergraduate degree of your choosing in Asfar or Neuropa. I have told them that you must first earn a CONC passport. Still, it's something to work towards, is it not?'

She frowned. 'I didn't know N-LA knew about my father, sirm.'

'They don't – not his name, at any rate. The approval of your application was a matter of public record, that is all. I will keep the offer on file. Enjoy your session. Don't forget: I'm on the roof in the mornings if you'd like to talk.'

'Thank you, sirm,' she managed.

The Major marched on. She brushed off the strange non-news, of a scholarship she didn't want and wasn't allowed to accept and turned into the side hall. It was empty. The confirmation email had informed her that the ion glove took fifteen minutes to auto-clean between sessions, ensuring privacy at the point of entry and exit. Beside the carved wooden doors there was a lock panel. As instructed in the confirmation email, she took off her flip-flops, input the key code and entered the ion glove.

The plain, square stone chamber was walled with pale screens emitting a diffuse, yellowish light. To her right an armchair and small sofa were arranged either side of a low round screentable; to her left was a padded platform, the material not fabric but some kind of faux leather. In the corner was a stand with a jug of water and a glass, and a tealight burner and selection of essential oils. The air hinted of lemons, whether from the previous user or the auto-clean she didn't know.

She needed to log in on the screentable. She padded over the cool floor and sat down in the armchair. The necklace was digging into her palm now so she put it on, wiped her sweaty palms on her robe and swiped her password on the screen.

The voice came from behind the sofa. 'I told you it was safe.'

Then she was there, sitting right opposite: Lil, or rather, her ghost: a pale, translucent form, as if Lil was invisible but had been dipped in luminous white dust. Astra had evidently chosen the right apparel, yet come as a dowdy inferior; Lil was dressed in a sleeveless robe with a plunging neckline, like a marble statue of an ancient goddess. The ion form smoothed out detail so Lil's long, brushed-out hair fell round her face like soft curtains and her skin condition was visible only as concentrated streaks of light. Her outlines, though, were breathtaking. Astra could see the curve of Lil's lip, the folds of her clothing, the cleft between her breasts as she leaned over the screentable. When the form moved it blurred slightly, leaving traces in the air like veils.

'The standard setting is Invisible Ink. But we can adjust it.' Lil swept a finger over the screen – there must be an identical set-up in her glove. 'Do you want me skintone or red-light district?'

As she spoke, her form changed hue. The skintone option made her shine like a bronze sculpture; the red made her look like moulded jelly.

'Skintone,' Astra said.

'Me too. You can change yours here.' She tapped the screen.

Astra adjusted her own controls. She didn't look any different to herself but presumably she would to Lil, though Lil didn't appear to notice. She was still playing with the controls.

'What about the glove? Forest? Seashore? Mirror Hall? Vault?'

As she whizzed through the options, the wallscreens changed. First glowing green leaves sent dappled shadows floating over the furniture and floor; next a band of azure water lapped against bright golden sand. Then the walls became mirrors, reflecting her and Lil into a dizzying infinite distance, and finally they were sitting in semi-darkness, the walls illuminated only by rows of candle flames. As if to compensate for the dimness, Lil's form gleamed a little brighter. Then the room was back to normal, softly lit up again.

She didn't like the forest. She didn't want to start remembering Or and neither did she want to pretend she was outdoors, in Gaia, when she wasn't. That was one of the things Old World people had done. Even though she hated rooms without windows, darkness was comforting, and in its way as spacious as the beach scene.

'Vault,' she said.

'Yeah, me too. Mirror Hall is so overrated.'

Lil adjusted the setting. The room darkened again, and the candle flames flickered like cat's eyes watching them from a deep black cavern.

'Do you want to feel me?'

Lil laid her arm across the screendesk, hand facing up. Her palm had no lines. 'People look younger in here,' she said. 'New Zonians like that.'

Astra hesitated. 'Will I hurt you? Your skin, I mean?'

'You'll heal me. You're an ion bath.'

She placed her palm on Lil's – or rather, *in* it. The ion form offered no resistance. Once, as a child, she had stroked an angora rabbit, a worker animal on a local wool farm. Lil's hand was as downy and warm as that cloud of fur had been. Her hand passed right through it and rested on the table, obscured within the glowing bronze form. She felt her skin begin to heat, a gentle tingle spreading up her wrist.

'Ion bodies don't get wet,' Lil whispered, 'but some people think they're sexier than flesh.'

She withdrew her hand and looked Lil in the face. In monochrome the cut on Lil's cheek looked less painful, more like furrowed soil. The form's eyes didn't shine but they were clearly intent on hers.

'Where are you?' she asked.

'Right here. Stargazing.'

She ignored the flirt. 'No, really. Are you in Pithar? Is there a CONC compound there too?'

Lil shrugged, raising one shoulder. The remembered movement sent a dart through Astra's heart. 'Pithar, yes. CONC, no. I'll show you when you come.' She leaned back in the sofa, flexed her hand. 'Thanks for the ion dip. It really helps.'

Why was Lil ill? Her mother was an Is-Lander. 'Aren't you Coded for radiation?'

'Yeah, sure. But they don't give Non-Lander mine-workers top-ups. It's okay, though. I got out in time. My rash is mild compared to most people's.'

Lil had worked in the mine? There was so much she needed to know. 'How did you get here?' she blurted. 'Did you find your family? Your dad's family, I mean?'

Lil replied in a singsong voice, like a child, 'I walked through the tunnel into the barren mountains. I wasn't looking for anyone. My dad stayed in Is-Land because his parents died. But he told me that everyone in Non-Land is your family, and that's true. Everyone helped me – mountain hunters, nomads. Himalayan pilgrims. I flew with the singing bowls. I learned the ancient prophecies. Then Zizi found me.'

'How?'

'Like I said: Hokma told him to look out for me. She sent Helium to Cora Pollen with a message, and Cora Pollen sent a Rookowleon over the Boundary. His people said a girl had been found in the mountains, and he told the pilgrims to bring me to Kadingir. I told him all about you and he helped me. I didn't like Kadingir. He helped me move to Zabaria. Then he . . .' She trailed off. 'Well, anyway, he helped me. Like I'm helping you.'

Astra was breathing heavily. It was a plausible story, but could you ever trust Lil? *Did you set the fire in the dining hall? Did you kill Torrent and Stream?* she wanted to shout. But she didn't; shouting at Lil could end everything. Lil could just vanish, snuff herself out like a candle.

'I've never heard of a Rookowleon,' she said. *That* she could challenge.

'Zizi's people Coded them using the information Hokma sent. They're like Owleons but they have pure black feathers so the Boundary guards don't see them at night.' Lil smiled. 'Rooks on their own wouldn't be good messengers: they all fly together and they can't keep secrets.'

She assessed the information. Hokma *had* sent Owleon Code to Cora Pollen, and for that Cora Pollen was in jail. She would ask about her later; the most important thing was Zizi.

'Where's Zizi now?'

'He's safe.'

'So are we. So tell me.'

'I can't.'

'Why not?'

'It's not my right to tell you.'

'What do you mean, "it's not your right"?'

'You'll know when you get here – to Pithar – and meet the people I want you to meet. They'll tell you where he is. Then you'll understand.'

It was too much. She folded her arms and glared at Lil. 'Don't *play with me*, Lil. I've come a long way too, you know. I see you at the River Raven and you just disappear. Now you're pretending you know where Zizi is. Why should I trust you?'

Lil frowned. 'I'm not pretending. And I had to jump in the water. My arms were hurting – because I hugged you, actually.'

Oh so it was *her* fault Lil had frigged off without even saying goodbye? She was speechless.

'Look' – Lil rolled her eyes – 'I'm sorry I can't tell you, but I'm not *playing* with you. We won't have much time in Pithar. You'll be with CONC, probably, and it will be hard to get away. I wanted to talk to you properly beforehand, in private. I thought that's what you'd want too.'

Lil was sulking now – or was *she* sulking? She didn't know. But she only had two hours a month in the glove and she couldn't afford to fight.

'Of course I want to talk. Okay, so you can't tell me where Zizi is – but you must be able to tell me something about him. What's he like?'

'Zizi?' Lil thought about it. 'He likes his beer. And he can be a bit bossy sometimes. I mean, it's not like I'm his kid. I had to make that clear.'

She didn't like the sound of that. She was going to ask if Zizi had tried to get Lil to marry anyone, but Lil was back in charge now.

'Look, Astra, the main thing about Zizi is that he and his people are Non-Gaians. The Non-Gaians aren't in YAC, yet, but some of us think they ought to be. That's partly why my people in Pithar want to talk to you.'

She gasped. 'You can tell *your people* that I'm not their data-courier. They can send Zizi a Rookowleon if they have a message for him.'

'Tell them yourself if you like. You don't have to do what they say. I just promised I'd introduce you, that's all. You do want to meet people here, don't you?'

Lil hadn't changed one ion. She was still insufferable.

She'd just have to pump as much information out of her as possible. 'What's a Non-Gaian?' she asked.

'You know. I told you already – that time on the cliff. They're Non-Landers who worship Gaia.'

Had Lil said there were Gaians in Non-Land? She didn't remember. And no one here had mentioned such a thing. 'I don't think that's right. The religions here are all Abrahamic.'

Lil snorted. 'Abrahamic shamanic, you mean. It's not like they taught you at school, Astra, a bunch of monotheistic sects all fighting each other. Okay, some people bang on about God and obey stupid rules, but in general religion here is a mishmash of old and new traditions, cult prophets and nature worship.'

'*Nature* worship?' Okay, the Star Party music had sounded like a Gaia song to her, but otherwise she hadn't seen a shred of evidence for eco-spirituality at the dance – drinking beer and having sex in the dunes didn't count.

'Aren't these mics working? Yes, *nature worship*. The Farashani revived their ancient sun-worshipping traditions, some of the Somarians are animists, and even the strictest Karkish sects teach that we're here to look after the planet. Basically, except for marriage, meat-eating and clothes, most Non-Landers think exactly the same as Is-Landers: that the Old Worlders got punished for trying to be bigger than God, and we need to be humble now and take care of His or Her or Whoever's creation. That's pretty much Gaianism, isn't it?'

No, it wasn't, but Lil was barrelling on, 'Non-Gaianism started about twenty years ago: a group of vegans in Kadingir started spouse-sharing and living naked in their tents. About ten years ago they made a formal application for Is-Land citizenship. They said they should be treated like Gaians from anywhere in the world. CONC supported them – it's all on Archivia; you can look it up. But IMBOD rejected them, of course, on the grounds that some of the applicants had been arrested as children. After that, other Non-Landers turned against them, so they left Kadingir. Now they live in the desert. Zizi joined them when he was evicted, but he drinks too much for them, so he comes back to Kadingir and hangs out sometimes.'

She ignored the dig. She'd check the history later herself, on Archivia. 'So are you a Non-Gaian?'

Lil gave a dramatic sigh. 'Sure I love Gaia, but the Non-Gaians are just *lifestylers*, Astra. They lost their political moment a decade ago. They need to join YAC to regain any credibility at all.'

And here they were, back at Lil's agenda again. All she could do was refuse to play along.

Lil stretched. 'Look, I know it's a lot to take in, especially after being brainwashed by IMBOD.'

'I was not *brainwashed*.'

'You grew up in Is-Land. You had MPT in a neurohospice. What would *you* call it?'

She was silent. IMBOD had tried to erase Lil, but she didn't want to tell her that. 'It was just a short course,' she said tightly. 'I got all my memories back. I can think for myself, thank you. And how did you know about the neurohospice?'

'Zizi told me. It was in the Is-Land news, and Cora Pollen's people sent him a Rookowleon. I said, Astra, we've been waiting for you.' In a sudden blurred series of outlines, Lil leapt up and slid over the screentable until there she was, perched on the edge, her ion face close to Astra's, ion hands drifting down into Astra's shoulders, a tickle of heat spreading through her robe.

'I'm sorry. I didn't want to fight. You're here! I can't believe you're here. We're the only two, do you know that? The only two outside Is-Land. We have to stick together, Astra. I'm going to help you. Don't worry about YAC. Don't worry about anything.'

The form had no smell but somehow it had breath; it caused a movement of atoms over her cheeks. And beyond that it emitted some kind of aura, a diffuse warmth penetrating Astra's chest. She pulled away, but she was trapped in the armchair.

'I don't want to fight either,' she said stiffly. 'I just want to find my dad.'

Lil stroked her hand. 'Come to Pithar. Talk to my friends. Then I'll help you find Zizi. It will all be great. He'll be so happy to see you.'

'I'm coming to Pithar,' she muttered. 'With CONC. It's all arranged.' She pushed the chair back, stood up, went over to the little table and poured herself some water. She drank it as Lil's form leaned back on its elbows on the screentable, watching her.

She set the glass down. 'Who are Cora Pollen's people?' she demanded. 'Did they tell you that Hokma was *murdered*?'

Lil sat up. 'I don't know their names. They don't communicate with YAC. But of course I know Hokma was killed. When YAC forces CONC to open the Boundary, we're going to find out who did it.'

It was her turn to snort. Lil could be waiting a long time for the Boundary to open. 'I can tell you who did it. It was Ahn and Samrod Blesserson. They ordered it – because they were going to have to testify in court. They didn't want their reputations to suffer. Ahn told IMBOD he knew about my shot and he did a deal with them to protect himself.'

She didn't have to spell it out; the recrimination seeped from her voice.

Lil would never flinch, but she drew herself up to a regal height and was silent for a moment. 'I'm sorry I told Ahn about you,' she said at last. 'I was a stupid kid. I was mad at you. I understand things better now. But they would have found out when you started IMBOD Service – there's no way you could have kept up with the Sec Gens. I'm sorry about the neurohospice too, but you're better off here, finding Zizi, honestly.'

This was the crux of it: Lil's betrayal. It would be so easy to blame Lil for everything – but that wasn't fair. 'I'm not angry about being found out,' she said slowly. 'I'm angry about Hokma being killed. But it's not your fault she was arrested. She could have stopped sending Owleons after you told Ahn. She knew the risks and she still took them.' Her voice trembled and the tears welled up, a muddy flood. '*She didn't stop sending the Owleons.*'

She was sobbing and Lil was looming up in the glove and floating over to hug her, the form engulfing her in its eerie bronze glow. 'That's right, Astra,' she whispered, 'Hokma couldn't stop – none of us can stop.

You'll see. We all love Hokma because she couldn't stop sending the Owleons – like she sent you. Look, you think Cora Pollen's in prison, right? But what's Is-Land if not a big green leafy prison? People's minds are locked up. They think what IMBOD tells them to think and their bodies do what their Code tells them to do: eat and work and Gaia-play – be happy like animals. Sure, great, be an animal, but not if you give up being human. You'll see, Astra, it's better here. We're free to make things happen – *big* things. And we're going to set Is-Land free too. You and me.'

No. No she wasn't.

'I can't, Lil. I'm so tired. I'm so sad. I'm crying – maybe you can't feel it, but I am.'

'I know you are.' Lil ran her fingers over her face. 'Look. I'm wiping them away.' There was warmth on her cheeks, ion breath, but not enough to dry her tears. She rubbed her face, her hands mingling with Lil's. Lil was trying to be nice, she understood that, but no one could help her. *No one*: not Lil and not Zizi – her father was just another projection, a ghost in her mind. She had to meet him, she couldn't not, but when she did, Zizi, like everyone here, would try and suck her into his own agenda.

Everything was hopeless. All she wanted was to learn how to survive on her own. She would get that CONC passport, take up the N-LA scholarship and get out of here, forever.

'Thank you, Lil. I'll come to Pithar, I promise. But I have to go now. I can't keep *talking*. Everyone's always *talking* at me.'

'I know – I'm sorry. You're tired. Come, lie down. Let the glove hold us. It's nice, you'll see.'

Words: more meaningless words. Lil's form was embracing her, but it couldn't hold her. And she couldn't lie down with Lil. 'I can't kiss you, Lil. We're not in Or any more.'

'We don't have to kiss. I'll wash you, that's all. It's like a big bubble bath, I promise. It will help you feel better. We've still got half a session – you don't want to waste it, do you?'

Her sobbing fit was over and the urge to push Lil away had passed too. Though everything was still impossible, she felt calmer, somehow, her body as light and hollow as Lil's form. She had come to the glove, she realised, not only to extract information from Lil, but to share the past: to take it out, look at it, remind herself it was real. For now, she had shared as much as she could bear. She was empty and she needed to be recharged.

Maybe Lil was right; the doctor *had* said the technology would help her head. And she wouldn't get another booking for a month. She should try it now, even if she didn't really feel like it.

She let Lil cajole her over to the platform bed where they lay down, the screen candles flickering behind the long flame of Lil's form, a phalanx of cats' eyes.

'The necklace hurts,' she complained.

'Take it off,' Lil whispered, her voice seeming to come up through the bed. 'Just rest. Lie still. Let me give you a massage.'

As Astra undid the clasp, Lil pressed a button on the side of the platform. She placed the necklace beside her pillow and let Lil wrap her ion arms around her, pressing up close, closer still, until they were occupying the same coordinates on the data grid and all she could see of Lil's form was a bronze glow emanating from her own body.

'You're here,' Lil whispered, 'with me.' And then slow rhythmic pulses were spongeing her spine and words were only echoes of far distant events, faint ripples soon lost in the warm burnished waves flowing through her, soothing and dissolving all her doubt and confusion in a vast amber ocean of light. Perhaps, she would think afterwards, Lil had lied. Perhaps they had had sex. But where sex ignited your nerve endings, sent hungry flames jetting through your veins, this pleasure began as coils deep in her cells and grew like sea anemones, their soft tentacles quietly undulating in the immense glowing honey of complete reassurance, an ocean of light so all-encompassing she didn't even question the moment of levitation, her gentle rise into the air, the absence of pressure anywhere on her body, her robe fluttering around her and the bed somewhere beneath her, unnecessary now as she floated in the constant, calm, slow, washing bronze tide of Lil's arms.

That moment could have lasted an hour or an age.

When at last it faded, she was lying on the bed again, Lil facing her, holding her face in her hands.

'I'm part of you,' Lil whispered fiercely, her voice reverberating from all corners of the room. 'I'm always here for you.'

And then she disappeared.

MUZI

One moment he was aloft in a dream of warm winds, fast cars, white sandy roads; the next, he was back in the watch-hut. He blinked, flicked the sleep from his eyes and sat up, admiring his new domain again. The hut was small, but highly accommodating. The roof was low, but he could stand up straight if he needed to. A third of the space was occupied by his wool mattress on a raised wooden platform; beneath it he'd stored some dishes, a wash basin and his shoes. On the wall were two new hooks for his clothes, on the freshly swept floor some cushions and a rug his grandmother had insisted he have from the house. In the corner opposite the door hung the cord from the solar roof panel that powered his Tablette, his camp stove and a reconditioned wafter. The fan he had found and fixed up stood in the corner. He'd used it once, but the whirring blades and shaking cage made a noise like a dying ewe and he couldn't sleep with it on. Still, the fan looked good: like a flower propellor. One day he would attach it to the front of the hut and take off up into the clouds.

Taking off: that was what Kishar had kept saying at the Star Party. YAC were taking off now, were going to fly like the river rooks over the Jailwall. Muzi didn't know about that. He liked YAC. The rain had said they were a powerful, cleansing force for the good, and the rain would not lie. But perhaps, he wondered now, YAC's purpose was simply to cleanse the adults. Or themselves.

Yes, the political situation was complicated, and the sky-god had not yet given any indication that He wanted Muzi to understand it any further. That was fine with him; he had already benefited from YAC's defiance. Like everyone, he'd seen the Comchan reports of the Emergency

Diplomeet, heard the Rhymer's chants and the Singulars' clapping and singing, and when his uncle had called Enki Arakkia a good-for-nothing bigmouth sponging off CONC and a legless layabout pissing on the sacrifices of his elders and betters, Muzi had decided that he would go to the Star Party. He was a man now; he had done his day's work, and as long as he got up and did it again the next day his uncle couldn't stop him going where he liked.

The family had complained; they'd said he would wake them when he returned, so he'd said he would sleep in the watch-hut – and here he had remained. In these hot months the family slept on the roof beneath the stars, but his father snored and his uncle kicked in his sleep and Muzi had been thinking for a while that he'd rather just take his mattress to the hut. Lambing season was over and he didn't have to be close to the sheep pen. If there was an emergency, his father could call his Tablette.

He had won that battle, but the Star Party had ended in another one. He'd been on the way home by then – he'd left just before the ceremony, which Kashir had said would be dull, with no dancing, just those strange meditation bowls and a speech. But he'd heard all about it the next day at breakfast: his uncle ranting about the arrests and the waste of N-LA resources, and the arrogance of this half-man Arakkia, splitting the people just when they needed to hold strong.

'Gibil,' his grandmother had flared, glancing at Muzi.

'He's a half-man in his *head*,' his uncle had yelled, jabbing at his temple. 'He's an *idiot kid*, drunk on old stories – stories of *us*. We're the ones who fought in the streets – fought *Gaians*, not our own people.'

'The boy might be wrong-headed,' Muzi's mother had said, chipping in from her dough bowl, 'but he's a bigger man than some who spend all day in the beer tents. He's been looking after all those orphans, hasn't he?'

'Looking after them.' Gibil snorted. 'Training them to wreck ten years of their elders' hard work, you mean. Maybe a spell in the firesands will drum some sense into his hot head.'

His grandmother had chuckled then. 'Like the firesands calmed your hot head,' she commented fondly.

His uncle had *harrumphed* and left the house to see to the horse, but Muzi's father agreed with him, and so did all the men who'd come round for tea the next evening.

So yes, the political situation was unsettled; what was more important to think about right now was the girl.

The morning of the argument Muzi had been watching the Tablette news while his aunt tidied up the breakfast dishes. Suddenly, his grandmother had gasped, leaned over and started tapping the screen.

'Astra! Muzi! That's Astra!'

She meant the little CONC officer – the young one. He had noticed her at the Party, arriving just before he and Kashir left, but thought nothing of it. But now here she was, running across the screen into his house. His grandmother had grabbed the Tablette from his hand, swiped replay, passed it over to his mother and aunt. They had rolled their eyes, indulged his grandmother. 'Looks like she's holding another man's hand,' his aunt had said with a laugh.

'Oh him? He's an Alplander. Look how tall he is. Why would she want to marry him?'

His grandmother had been pestering him ever since: did he like the Gaian girl? Should she invite her here for lunch? Would he be charming, her own sweet Muzi? And she had worn down his parents' resistance too, so the lunch invitation was now, it appeared, up to him.

He hadn't replied yet. He understood why marrying this Astra girl was a crazy idea, bound to make his uncle as angry as a ram with a thorn through his tongue. But the thing was, the girl didn't look like he'd imagined her: she was no Gaian brood ewe with a swollen rump. She was cute. Her hair was short and curly, soft like a lamb's, she looked fit, a fast runner, and her face was nice. She even looked a little like a Non-Lander.

He got up, poured some rainwater into his kettle, turned on the camp stove and sat gazing out over the southern hills. It was cosy up here in the watch-hut, and private. Maybe he could bring a wife here. The Gaian girl was the right size: not too tall.

ASTRA

She awoke feeling calm, and whether it was the effect of the ion glove or the relief of talking about Hokma, the feeling endured throughout the day. The compound bustled on around her but she was encased in a secret bubble of knowledge. Lil, for all her aggravating games, was going to help her find Zizi. He was out there, safe, waiting for her. Compared to that, the other things Lil had said about Zizi didn't feel so important. Lil thought he was bossy, but that was because Lil had to be in charge of every situation. And Zizi liked to drink beer. Well, so did she.

Or perhaps her calmness was just a symptom of admin. End-of-Hudna or no, by the end of the week Astra realised working in a CONC office *was* boring. She spent her days filling in forms, tidying the storage room, counting out boxes for drivers and following the progress of Sandrine's email campaign to get a full investigation into the missing supplies. On Vioday, when Astra swung back into the office after acing her Level One Somarian test, Sandrine was Face-talking a woman at her screendesk.

'I *know* that twenty boxes falls short of the minimum required for a windsands investigation,' she said as Astra slipped behind her own screendesk. Keeping half an ear on the conversation, she opened a file of old driver reports Sandrine had assigned her to cross-index, then the Archivia page on Non-Gaianism, the CONC communications channel and her ShareWorld page.

ShareWorld, she had secretly admitted to herself, could be funny. Compound officers submitted scathing reviews of the food and when Rudo described one vile, off-green spaghetti alt-bolognaise as 'a bootlace cowpat' the comment thread had spawned an impromptu compound country music band. Last night at dinner the band members had burst into song and Astra had found herself laughing along with everyone else. Nothing extreme – not until her eyes watered or her sides ached – but a stifled giggle that gradually erupted in a snort and lingered on as a chuckle she couldn't quite shut off. Rudo had pointed a finger at her – *gotcha!* – Photon had winked, and during the tumultuous applause for the kitchen staff, she'd felt a strange warm glow in her chest. It wasn't Gaia Power but something softer, like a good memory, like of the circle at Birth House, listening to a witty storyteller. *Human harmony*. Recalling Hokma's name for the feeling, she'd felt a small stab in her heart, but the glow had lingered.

Then as the clapping had died down, Christophe made a sarcastic remark to Tisha about 'the productive use of ShareWorld privileges' and Astra had decided then and there that however pathetic most posts were, she was on the side of the social networkers. If all CONC jobs were as dull as Sandrine's, people had to do something to keep their minds alive.

'It's always twenty boxes that go missing,' Sandrine was saying, 'and that makes eighty this year so far. If there's a gang operating, we should be trying to find them.'

In the end, just to get Sandrine to shut up, the N-LA officer promised to kick the issue up to her superior. Astra could tell she was lying. Photon had told her that N-LA had not one grain of interest in policing the desert. If they picked up the missing syringes or morpheus in a Kadingir raid they would prosecute, but they weren't going to send valuable officers out into the sandstorms, not for a handful of painkillers.

As Sandrine hung up, Astra shut down the Archivia page. She hadn't mentioned Non-Gaianism to anyone else yet – it might be dangerous to Zizi if the information got out.

'Argh.' Sandrine leaned back and stuck her fingers in her dreads. 'What a waste of Diplomeet training. I just hope that morpheus is going straight to people who need it and not into the hands of profiteers.'

It was odd how Sandrine could defend YAC every mealtime, and then come straight back to the office to dispense morpheus and mercilessly track down its thieves. But that, Astra was learning, was called working with CONC: doing your job, no matter how much it propped up the status quo. She was about to return to the driver reports when an interesting headline crossed Comchan. 'There should be more morpheus to go around,' she commented. 'N-LA's done a swap. They've released all the prisoners – all except Enki Arakkia.' She clicked, and scanned the story. 'In response YAC's issued a statement saying refusers don't have to destroy their vials any more. They can just return them to the Treatment Wards.'

'*That's* a concession.' Sandrine pounced on the news. 'Sounds like they want to win over N-LA.'

Before she could speculate, Astra's Tablette vibrated in her pocket. *Oh Gaia.* But Sandrine was absorbed in the article so she quickly opened her inbox on her screendesk – but no, the email wasn't from Lil but Dr Tapputu. She was supposed to go back and see him. With a ping of guilt in her gut, she opened the mail:

Astra Ordott, Salutations!
The Major tells me you are flourishing – active and curious and none the worse for your night adventures in Kadingir. Tremendous! If you need to adjust your medication, I am here. Meanbetimes, an update on your swabs. The hospital detected no known bacterial or viral infection, so I am sending your samples to the lab at CONQ HQ in Amazigia for further tests. A Zeppelin departs on Monday from Atourne and results should be emailed by the end of next week.

Yours in Pursuit of Truth!
Dr Tapputu

'You okay, Astra?'

She was gawping at the screen, she realised. Her perineum swab was going to be sent back to Is-Land and then on to Amazigia? She was supposed to learn how to laugh – so okay, she would. Somehow the notion of her Gaia-garden tissue sailing to CONC HQ right under IMBOD's noses made her feel like a *distinguished personage.*

'Yeah, fine.' She flicked back to ShareWorld. A Neuropean band called Hope and the Singulars had released a pop song to support the political prisoners, and she wanted to read more reviews of the singing bowls. Was she the only person they made feel ill?

'*Hey!*' It sounded like Sandrine had just spotted something ultra-exciting on ShareWorld – but no, she was addressing Astra. 'So how did it *go?*'

'Huh?'

'Your Level One test! You passed, right?'

Oh that. She tried to sound modest. 'One hundred per cent.'

'No way.' Sandrine's voice was a bassoon. 'That is *soooo* excellent.' To Astra's alarm, she rose from her seat and strode across the room with her arms outspread. 'Congratulations, Astra.'

Did Sandrine want to *hug* her? To forestall that dreadful possibility she did something she'd seen Rudo do on the hoopball court: she raised her hand for a high five. She fumbled the smack, but Sandrine seemed more than satisfied by the contact.

'I *knew* you'd pass. Now I can confirm you on the driver schedule.' She opened up a file. 'I need you guys to check out a proposed site for the new Nagu Two algae-scrubber. And the Major wants you to get out and chat a bit, test the mood of the residents. It's a great job for your first day.' She rubbed her hands together. 'This calls for a cookie! Even if you are going to leave me on my ownsome again. It's been really nice having company, Astra.'

Sandrine brewed a pot of tea and opened a tin. Her mom had sent another care package, this time with a batch of chocolate chunk cookies. They had survived the Zeppelin journey remarkably well, but needed to be eaten *right away*, Sandrine had said, rubbing her hands. She arranged four cookies on a plate; Astra broke one in half and dunked a piece in her tea. The melting chocolate must have coated her throat with some kind of confessional lubricant because as she dipped the cookie again she found herself saying, 'My Shelter mother used to make really good berry biscuits.'

'Oh yeah?' Sandrine licked a splodge of chocolate off her finger. 'Do you have the recipe?'

Why had she mentioned Nimma? 'You need forest berries,' she replied, whipping the cookie out of the tea far too soon – it would still be hard, but she needed that mouthful *right now*.

'Not too many forests around here,' Sandrine agreed, 'but the kitchen staff might have dried berries.'

'They're local berries,' she mumbled through her mouthful. 'We don't export them.'

Sandrine put her own half-eaten cookie down on the tray. 'Hey, would you like a spider plant?' Without waiting for an answer she brushed the crumbs off her lap and jumped to her feet. She returned with a thriving new plant from the sill.

'When it has babies, you have to bring them back to meet Grandma.'

Astra wiped her fingers and took the pot. It was like getting an electric shock or dunking her face into a bowl of ice water. The light from the window caught the leaf clusters and the perky little plant was a green-and-white starburst of pure energy in her hand. Sharp as scimitars, the leaves hissed their vision: *Wake up. You're here now. On your way. Out into Kadingir. Out into your own world.*

LAAM

It was noon and the sun was an interrogation lamp. Beneath his white uniform his body was swimming in sweat. The clothes were a damp, wrinkled skin he wanted to tear off, but following Peat, he trooped after the Division Officer across the Barracks lawn towards the row of trees that bordered the training field – not the Gaia-play woodland but a restricted area reserved for advanced training.

The shade was a fleeting relief. Through the trees was a clearing and at the centre of that was a blinding dazzle. He lined up shoulder to shoulder with his Sec Gen siblings on the stone lip of an ancient pond. His head was boiling. He imagined diving in, but there was no room for him in the water: the pond was swarming with flesh – gold, copper and bronze, the fish were like living pipework, gleaming, perpetually interweaving conduits of hunger and speed.

On the far side of the pond, the Division Officer spread her arms. 'Sec Gens,' she exulted in his earpiece, 'feast your eyes on the heart of the Barracks: the most sacred site in all of Is-Land, for the possession of which oceans of our Pioneers' blood was spilled. Thousands of years ago, right here on this ground, the Old World prophet Abraham was thrown into a furnace. He was saved, it is said, when his god turned the fire to water and the burning coals to fish. A pretty story?'

The officer had been learning from Odinson's lectures, for she had started sprinkling her own lectures with rhetorical appeals. Either side of him, Peat and Robin shook their heads, murmuring *No*.

No, Laam echoed under his breath.

'No,' the officer bellowed, 'It is a foul account of human arrogance and greed. In honour of Abraham, for centuries the pond was kept over-stocked with golden carp – can you imagine it: Gaia's precious sun drops imprisoned in filthy water, stressed and infected, livers bloated by a diet of *breadcrumbs*, while all around them Abraham's people gutted and fil-leted Gaia down to the last spiny bone. At last came the Dark Time, when the pond stood empty, the bottom littered with the dried sediment of Gaia's great sacrifice. When IMBOD finally fought for and established the Barracks we cleaned the pond and filled it with crystal-clear fresh water. Now, in honour of you, the Sec Gens, we have stocked it thick with a thriving new beast: Carpira eels, as fierce as the sun, as graceful as water. Creatures Coded, like you, to revel in each other's company, to move as one, to tranform the world from an Abrahamic *cesspit* to a Gaian *cauldron*.'

The officer was saluting, fist from chest: a clear signal, and the division followed suit. Framed by his and Peat's arms, the fish twisted and seethed. The eels resembled his Shelter mother's glossy red hair, the tresses he'd loved to coil round his fingers. His own hair was black, like his Code-Shelter father's: cropped now, but when left to grow, a soft fleece his three parents adored.

'Wild and free,' they had whispered whenever he'd shouted and stormed. 'We wanted your mind to be free. That's why we gave you the antidote.' *Did they want him to* die? he had screamed. *Did they want him to cause the deaths of his friends?*

He lowered his arm. Across the pond, the Division Officer opened her pac, and like electricity through water, a shiver shot down the line of Sec Gens. Their reflexes were connected like Tablette circuits; his were off-grid. He had to be constantly alert for the visible, audible aftershocks – the gasps, sighs, slow blinks of that instinctive muscular current – so he would never let himself be the broken link in the chainmail. He twitched alone sometimes, at night in his bed: a spasm rooted in terror. The Sec Gens were taller than he was, and stronger and faster, even the girls. They could drink less water, eat less food, sleep fewer hours, spend longer in the sun. But though their thick skin was not easily punctured and their wounds healed rapidly, they were not invincible: Sec Gens could be shot in the heart, stabbed to death, kidnapped, humiliated, raped and blown up by nanobombs, just like anyone, and so they could feel fear. But while his fear made him weak, theirs made them more powerful: more acutely con-nected, more determined to attack the source of that fear. Right now, they seemed to be gathering themselves for a collective reaction he could not even guess at and he trembled, not simply in echo.

Beside him, Peat stiffened: across the pond, the officer had plunged her hand into the pac; as if aiming for the sun itself, she raised a dripping red fist above her head.

'Let this bleeding alt-goat represent the rotten hearts of the meat-eaters,' she hissed in his ear. 'Let the meat-eaters meet their own fate.' In one smooth movement, she hurled the chunk of alt-meat into the centre of the pond, an arc of red juice scattering in its wake. When it hit the shimmering surface, the water frothed like his head.

'*Let the meat-eaters meet their own fate!*' the Sec Gens roared.

Unmistakeably, the officer's head turned towards him and his bladder nearly loosened. He had missed the cue completely. Sweating, he drew himself up and stared into the shifting shade of the trees behind the officer. Her hand still dripping with alt-blood, she threw chunk after chunk of alt-meat into the pond. The fish leapt, the water churned and foamed. The Sec Gens were breathing hard. In a minute they would be rubbing and hugging each other. When the officer turned, they would turn with her and run berserker back out on to the training lawn.

He, though, was back on his bunk, reading and rereading the email that had arrived this morning: the summons for the medical test to 'assess the effects of the booster shot'. His head was blistering inside. It *wasn't fair*. He had been trying so hard – had been *succeeding*. In Atourne, where that other girl had been so stupid and been discovered, he had danced on his wits, cultivated his alliance with Peat, sweet Peat . . . who had helped him on the training field, had even, unknowingly, helped him survive the horror of the woodland nights. But it had been too good to be true. The lack of sleep, the exhaustion, the bruises and bites, the rough sex that had shredded his anus and made running agony: they had all caught up with him and his deficiencies had at last been noticed and tracked. No doubt his sleep scheme in the woodlands had been videoed and analysed.

So now what? When his Code test confirmed the officers' suspicions would his parents be arrested, tried for treason? Would he be exiled like Peat's sister and cast out into enemy territory?

The officer was assessing him again. In the pond, the Carpira eels were thrashing and glistening, their snapping jaws revealing raw red gullets and razor-sharp rings of flashing white teeth.

'Some say Abraham was a man of peace,' his Code father had once told him. 'That he was the first prophet of mercy and one-ness; that his was a path to reconciliation between nations.'

Abraham, though, had been willing to sacrifice his son. And for that willingness, his son was saved.

'Gaia forever,' the officer roared.

'Gaia forever,' he mouthed. Sweat was pouring down his forehead now, drenching his clothes. At the lip of the pond, the eels were lashing water over his boots. As Peat and Robin reached to clasp his shoulders, he grasped the neck of his uniform and lifted his face to the sun. Ripping his shirt open, Laam stepped into the blazing field of fish.

ASTRA

'Handbrake off?'

It was half past nine in the morning and the sky was a soft pearly blue. Cicada was stuffed to the gills with bags of clean laundry and barrels of drinking water, and the team had two important jobs on their agenda: the reconnaissance visit to Nagu Two, and a regular supply visit to a Treatment Ward in Nagu Six, down by the river. Nagu Two, Sandrine had told them in the briefing, was a potential hotspot for two reasons: it bordered the Hem, and it was home to Enki Arakkia, who lived there with his mother. YAC had a strong following in the Nagu, and even its N-LA supporters had been on edge lately. Some of them suspected the proposed algae-scrubber of being a bribe, to get them to accept the cladding operation without fuss. The team's job was to take the temperature of local attitudes, and attempt to reassure the residents of CONC's good will. It was going to be an interesting day. First, though, she had to endure the humiliating ritual of a driving lesson.

'Handbrake off,' she confirmed. On her test drive around the compound on Indiday, Ciccy's engine had dragged for ten minutes before Photon had realised what was wrong. She did have a driving licence, she'd explained, but Or only owned three vehicles and she hadn't driven much after she'd passed her test. Today, embarrassingly, Photon was subjecting her to a tick list of instructions before she was even allowed to start the engine.

'Mirrors checked?'

'Checked.'

'In neutral?'

'Yup.'

'Turn her on!'

Rudo whooped behind her; knees spread, he was straddling the back seat like a driver between two carthorses.

She turned the key and Ciccy rumbled into life. She shifted into reverse, released the clutch and pulled out of the parking spot. Her hands were high on the steering wheel and Eya's bracelet – Zizi might be in Kadingir, out looking for her too – winked in the sunlight pouring in through the windscreen.

The gate guard waved her onto the circular road around the compound. The morning crowd was on the move: a river of people, carts and cars moving to market, to beer tents, to CONC aid queues, to the concrete row of public showers behind the fortress. A kid skipped past on the walkway, delirious with joy, followed by a robed woman carrying a red football. Behind her trailed a small child, crouching and hopping as if pretending to be a frog – or, no, Astra realised as the mother turned to scold him, the child's bones were knitted that way.

She concentrated on the road. Taking the wheelchair crossings slowly, she turned onto the wide dirt road dividing Nagu One from Nagu Two. It didn't take long to learn that driving in Kadingir was frustrating: she was constantly jerking to a halt to avoid hitting people. She had to bump over the crossings, veer around potholes and be on the alert for stubborn cart beasts who might suddenly bray or spit and refuse to keep going. Embarrassingly, she stalled twice and had to restart the engine while gaggles of small children laughed at her and cart drivers banged Ciccy's side with their sticks. But it was good to be out, soaking up Kadingir. Close-up in daylight, she could see many of the habitations were ingenious, even appealing.

Many of the tents were embroidered and tasselled, the painted hexayurts were equipped with solar panels, and some of the containers hosted roof gardens: jumbles of potted plants and the occasional trellis. The people were interesting too. Ahead, a gaggle of boys and girls in colourful skull caps were following a man wearing a gold-embroidered black robe, a black hat, ringlets and a long beard. As she pulled past them, he led the children into a tent bearing a symbol the same design as their caps: a yin/yang, half blue and white, half red, white and green.

'Is that a CONC school?' she asked.

'Nah, one of the old Karkish sects,' Rudo told her.

'They are forerunners in restorative justice techniques,' Photon added, 'one of the founders of N-LA, though normally they do not like to take leadership roles.'

It looked like an opening: time for her big question. 'Didn't the Non-Gaians live in Nagu One?' she asked casually. There hadn't been much about the movement on Archivia, but Lil had been correct: it had originated in Kadingir, with vegans who lived in 'Gaian-style' buildings. She wanted to see them – maybe Zizi had lived in one for a while.

'Non-Gaians?' Photon considered it. 'Oh yes, that faction. But that was some time in the past. They are living in the windsands now, I believe.'

'I know – I just wanted to see the houses.'

'Them freaky-creaky nest things, you mean?' Rudo asked. 'Worth a look, deffo.'

Photon checked his watch. 'I think we do not have the time today.'

She couldn't really argue; it was her first day and she shouldn't be interfering with the work schedule.

But unexpectedly, Rudo came to her aid. 'Oh c'mon, Phot,' he objected. 'It's right on the way.'

Photon caved in and a few minutes later he directed her into a rutted Nagu One street. She entered carefully, slowing to avoid a woman chasing a flock of chickens across the road. It was a market, the stalls with their sparse offerings of garlic, limp lettuces, sun-bleached flip-flops and the occasional stuffed toy set back from the road by wooden boardwalks. The vendors were sitting in the shade of tattered awnings: a haggard man whose entire stock appeared to consist of three grey lengths of timber and a cartwheel with broken spokes; a fat merchant with a black eyepatch minding a rack of dusty hydropacs; a robed woman at a rickety table, shuffling a deck of cards as a girl poked through her tray of black and white crystals.

Ahead, a ramp blocked her way. There was no one wheeling over it, but she braked; this wasn't like the cement crossings and she was afraid she'd splinter the wood if she drove across.

'Now what?'

'*Phweet!*' Photon whistled, and a couple of small boys ran up to his window. He gave them a coin and they pulled the ramp to the side. She drove on, Photon and Rudo quibbling over which was the next turning, and finally she was driving up towards a cluster of what looked at first like half-finished buildings: gappy frameworks of sticks and boards, draped inside with builders' sheets. She inched Cicada past, craning her neck at the chaotic assortment of weathered planks, poles, chair spindles, cupboard doors and lengths of mismatched timber, scrapyard materials lashed together with lengths of coloured rope, the buildings knitted into a tunnelling latticework of walls, ceilings and floors. The rooms were shielded by opaque white bioplastic sheeting. Around the edges of these interior tents, the sky flashed through the wood-webs like broken bits of blue china.

'Told you they were wild,' Rudo said.

Astra was silent. She had been expecting a living roof, perhaps, maybe even an Earthship, but these were Pure Gaian buildings: nail-free and roofless. Pure Gaians believed that to drive metal through wood was a violent act, and to shelter from the elements was akin to turning your back on Gaia. Proper Pure Gaian buildings had no protective inner veils: the inhabitants worked, ate and slept exposed to the weather, even during cyclone season. They didn't eat alt-meat or employ worker animals, not even bees or worms. Theirs was a noble and consistent stance, most Is-Landers agreed, but it isolated people from the world. Pure Gaians objected to Tablettes and Code-births, and home-schooled their children – or had done, until IMBOD had forbidden home-schooling. Once their children were exposed to the rest of Is-Land society and started to want the things everyone else had, Pure Gaian communities had begun to fall apart and they were now increasingly rare in Is-Land. But there was still one near Cedaria, a group of older people living in branch-and-string houses built on stilts between the trees. She'd visited once, on a school field trip, and she'd been enthralled by the buildings: they had been elegant and intricate, made of branches and wool – not scrapyard junk, and not stuffed with this ugly tenting.

'It's not typical Gaian biotecture,' she muttered, 'but I've seen it before.'

A robed woman came out of one of the houses and stood on the ramp, staring at her from a few metres away. She had severe eyebrows; she was holding a child by the hand. Astra looked back up at the buildings. She was finding it hard to fit them into her picture of Zizi. Were Non-Gaians more Gaian than the Gaians? She hadn't been prepared for that. Pure Gaianism was a very strict doctrine. Maybe that was what Lil had meant about Zizi's bossiness.

'They look a little draughty to me,' Rudo joked.

'No more than a tent is,' Photon contradicted.

Astra cut into the bickering. 'The tenting isn't Gaian,' she said tensely. 'The new people must have added that.'

'Exhibitionist houses?' Rudo mused. 'Makes sense, I guess, if you consider the Gaian dress sense.'

She wished she hadn't come here now. 'They're not normal houses,' she muttered. 'They're more like artworks. Or shrines. They're supposed to remind us that we don't need shelter from Gaia; she *is* our shelter.'

She'd said far too much. She clammed up.

'Hear that, Rudo?' Photon chided. 'They are not porno-theatres: they are concept houses, to illustrate the *idea* of shelter.'

'Yeah, well. How's about next time you're hungry I draw you the *idea* of dinner?'

Photon smiled. 'It would probably go down better than the CONC kitchen cowpat.'

'No *sheet*!' Rudo mimicked Christophe and the men laughed, but Astra was trapped in a splintery cage of memories. Yoki had returned from the Pure Gaian school trip determined never to eat honey again. Astra had chatted incessantly about the buildings, until Nimma had taught her how to macramé twigs into a hanging doll's house basket, a project that had occupied her for weeks. Where was that basket now? *The idea of shelter*: that said it all; it summed up her whole life.

The woman on the ramp took a step towards them, holding out one hand and beckoning with the other.

'Better head on, Astra,' Rudo told her. 'She'll be wanting a palmful of CONC cash to show us around.'

'Maybe Astra wants to talk to her?' Photon suggested.

He got it now: he understood she was looking for Zizi. But this was a dead end. The Non-Gaians, pure or not, were long gone.

She was going to have to perform a complicated manoeuvre now, and in front of this woman. She jammed the gear stick into reverse and began the turn. The woman folded her arms and stood watching impassively. For some unaccountable reason, Astra felt guilty. Why? Couldn't you stop and look at a building in Kadingir? A building she knew far more about than the *Abrahamites*, or whoever they were, currently dwelling inside it.

She drove in silence back through the market, waiting again at the ramp crossing for the boys to take their toll. At the main road, she stopped and looked both ways. A red van was rattling towards them from the north.

'Wait,' Photon said quietly. 'Let them pass.' The van was driving at a good speed, relying on the crowd to scatter in front of it. As it approached, two red-shirted officers in the front seat raised their hands in greeting. N-LA. Photon gestured in return. The N-LA sigil, a red palm tree in a white circle, glared from the side panel; the back windows flashed beneath two metal grilles, and then the van was gone, trailing a cloud of brown dust.

N-LA. Keeping order in a chaotic, volatile place. She had to put thoughts of Zizi aside and keep her mind on the task ahead. She turned left and drove on until Photon ordered her to turn right into a tented zone: Nagu Two, Enki Arakkia's neighbourhood.

She inched Cicada into a narrow lane, aware of people watching her, their shifting shapes half visible behind the tent flaps. The smell from an open sewage gutter snaking between the road and the boardwalk was gut-curling. Photon rolled his window up; she did the same.

'Now,' Photon said, pulling out his Tablette, 'the playground is—' He surveyed the dwellings as she bumped slowly on, noting the offshoot lanes and footpaths and rechecking his screen. 'Hmm. I think to say some remapping has taken place. Try this lane, Astra, and see where it goes.'

Jagging right and left, criss-crossed with ramps and cart-ruts, in places pockmarked with holes, the lane was a fiendish obstacle course.

'Yes: a big move has taken place. These are tent-peg marks,' Photon told her, 'from the previous habitation configuration. Rudo, can you email Sandrine and let her know?'

Rudo got his Tablette out. 'Don't know why we're doing N-LA's job,' he complained. 'If Dayyani thinks this place is about to go up in flames she should send her own people in. Why should we risk our skins so they can take potshots at kids in wheelchairs?'

'We are not working for N-LA,' Photon replied as she stopped to let a bulky young man on crutches swing across the lane. 'And YAC has called off the attacks. Our skins are in no danger.'

'Are you kidding? When does N-LA *ever* do any mapping? They're supposed to be governing the place.'

As the young man passed in front of Cicada, he suddenly raised his arm and banged his fist on the bonnet.

'*Tabernacle!*' Rudo swore and Astra jumped. Photon's hand flew to the door lock and Rudo lunged forward, gripping the back of her seat. The youth gave a snaggle-toothed grin and a jerky thumbs-up. *Up your Gaia tunnel*, the friendly gesture said. Then he moved on, his boulder-like back disappearing between two faded tents.

Rudo exhaled. 'Frackin' joker.'

'CONC does all the mapping now in Kadingir, Astra,' Photon said, 'because N-LA is not wanting to make a document that might be used to help IMBOD. We will be fine. Just drive slow.'

So she continued, stopping at the crossings, avoiding the cart-ruts, sometimes taking Ciccy dangerously close to the tents. Once she nearly crushed a tent peg anchoring a guy rope festooned with dishcloths and children's clothes. Finally the lane ended at the entrance to a beer tent, by the look of the tables outside.

He likes his beer.

She scanned the crowd, her stomach sinking. Zizi couldn't be one of these paunchy-faced men, drunk before noon, could he?

'Time for some diplomatic refreshment?' Rudo enquired. 'Major's orders, after all: get out and talk to the locals, heesh said.'

'Morning drinkers,' Photon mused. 'I am so not sure we would get a genuine response.' He gestured at a gap between two tents on the left and she nosed Cicada into it. In the side mirror, a tableful of men lifted their glasses and cheered.

Back at the fork in the road, Photon directed her to take the third lane.

'You know what,' Rudo announced as she navigated the ruts, 'this mapping is a farce. If N-LA wants to round up YAC, they'll just pile-drive through the place.'

'N-LA is not allowed to do that,' Photon said mildly.

'IMBOD weren't allowed to do that twenty years ago, either.'

'That was different. Major Thames wasn't in charge then.'

'Yeah, well. I ain't so sure Major Thames is as "in charge" as heesh-or-sheesh seems to think heesh-or-sheesh is. Ten shells says IMBOD's gonna widen the Hem, even if the whole of Amazigia Zeppelins here for a Diplomeet on the Barracks lawns. Astra, wanna bet that Odinson hulk sends a tank full of salivatin' Sec Gens through Kadingir first chance he gets?'

'*Rudo.*' Photon sounded shocked. 'Astra's siblings are Sec Gens.'

'Then she knows what I'm talking about. The Sec Gens are a tank unto themselves, ain't that right, Astra?'

She was beyond getting offended by Rudo. 'Quiet in the back,' she ordered as she braked for another wheelchair ramp, 'or I'll show you a tank girl.'

'Promises, promises,' Rudo sighed.

Ahead was a clearing.

'Oh very good,' Photon said. 'Pull up here, Astra.'

At the end of the road stood a large battered metal sign bearing the CONC emblem and the words *ALGAE-SCRUBBER PROPOSED SITE* in the four regional languages and Inglish for good measure. Someone, she saw as she approached, had spray-painted a purple star over the conch shell. Behind the sign was a makeshift playground. Tyre swings hung from scabby metal fence posts, a couple of kids kicked a ball around a dusty pitch marked out with stones, and three robed women on a bench watched over toddlers in a sandpit. The ground was on a slight rise; beyond, tents sloped down towards the Boundary, halting in a crowded line before a barren strip of land.

It was the Hem.

There wasn't a fence. CONC wouldn't allow anything that resembled a permanent attempt to extend Is-Land's border. And there didn't need to be one, not when snipers patrolled the Boundary, protecting the Hem from invasion, standing all day and night over the IMBOD road and its flow of vans to Zabaria. Behind the traffic, as she'd seen from the Major's balcony, images were moving on the long grey screen. From here she could see what they were: looped shots of an eagle landing, its beak open, claws extended, the footage interspersed with flashing IMBOD Shields.

She parked between the sign and a red-tasselled tent. As the engine shuddered off, a frowning, big-bellied man, beer in hand, emerged. Photon rolled down his window.

'Good morning, sir,' he said in Somarian. The man replied in Farashan or Karkish, Astra wasn't sure which, and Photon switched, sounding as though he was trying not to sneeze. That would be Farashan, then. The man yelled back into the tent, a woman stuck her head out, examined Cicada, made an extended contribution to the discussion and withdrew into the shade. The man proffered his hand. Photon shook it, and the man ducked back inside his home.

'We're giving him a barrel of water and we can stay until his brother comes back with his cart this afternoon. Plenty of time.'

'So they don't mind that we're aiding and abetting the imminent IMBOD demolition of Nagu Two?' Rudo drawled.

'They don't *mind*, Rudo, that we have come to make a reassurance that CONC is still hoping to give them an algae-scrubber.' Photon located the clearing on the Tablette map, erased an old spiral-like road and fingered in a rough estimate of the new one. 'They have not tented over the proposed site or removed our sign. That is good sign!'

The women at the bench had gathered their children between their legs. One stuck her fingers in her mouth and blew a piercing whistle. The boys with the ball stopped playing and ran over to join them.

'They ain't exactly flapping out the welcome flag either,' Rudo commented.

Photon took a floppy cloth hat off the dashboard, put it on and opened his door. 'Rudo, can you please to give the man his water and mind Cicada? I want to chat with these women. Astra, do you like to come?'

She opened the door and dropped to the ground.

Rudo exited behind her. He yawned and stretched, sliding a hand up his arm to his shoulder.

'Don't go joining the resistance, Phot,' he warned. 'Not unless you got a tankette on your side.'

Ignoring him, Astra followed Photon over to the sandpit. The three women had gathered all the children to them now, three toddlers between their legs and the two older boys draped from their shoulders.

'Good morning.' Photon greeted the group in Farashan. She couldn't understand it, but it was better being here than stuck fending off Rudo's non-jokes. The woman who had whistled shaded her eyes and examined them both.

'Good morning,' the woman replied in Somarian. None of them were smiling. Like the children, they had facial rashes; the older boys' exposed arms were mottled as well, one of the little girls was cross-eyed and the small boy's low forehead was angled back sharply from his brows. He was gazing up at Photon, his expression wavering between fascination and fear.

'We are here to map the new roads and inspect the algae-scrubber site.' Photon shone a smile down at the boy, who stuck his thumb in his mouth and nestled closer to his mother.

'We are here to make sure *we* still exist,' the first woman replied evenly. The vocabulary was basic, Level One Somarian. Astra could follow every word but had no idea how to reply. Neither, it appeared, did Photon. After a moment he managed a quiet 'umm'.

The boy's mother pinched the first woman's shoulder and twisted.

'*Ai!*' she shouted. It was a clowning moment. The women laughed and chivvied their startled children into laughter too. Photon chuckled and for a moment Astra relaxed. But the women weren't smiling. The one at the end of the bench, a slight woman with a long nose, was scrutinising her. The woman's eyes lingered on her wrist, then flicked up to her face.

'Enki Arakkia says pain is our path.' The slight woman spoke quietly. 'Only pain will lead us to freedom.'

The woman was looking at her bracelet. Astra wanted to tuck it back up inside her sleeve, but she was afraid that would be construed as an insult. Suddenly her stomach hurt. She wanted to leave, to go back to Ciccy, to that vain, maddening idiot Rudo, but Photon wasn't moving.

'How are the children?' he asked.

The clowning woman put her hand on the boy's shoulder. 'He has stars in his head. At night: white flowers.'

Photon knelt. 'Hello,' he said to the children.

'Hello,' the boy whispered, clinging to his mother's knee.

'Hello.' The little girls giggled, then hid their faces in their hands.

Photon addressed the mother. 'I can drive him to the Treatment Ward if you like. Or if he's in pain now, I can give him a shot of morpheus. We have some in the unit.'

The women's silence was a wall, as distant, guarded and unbreachable as the Boundary.

'We don't need your treatments,' the slight woman said at last.

'His stars light our path,' the mother replied.

That's crazy, Astra wanted to shout. *He's just a little boy. Fine if you don't want to take morpheus, but why should he have to suffer?*

But Photon didn't argue. He stood up and brushed the dust from his knees. 'We have water too – a barrel. We can deliver it to a tent if you like.'

The women exchanged glances. There was veiled interest in their eyes now, and then clear agreement.

'We can roll a barrel,' the clown woman said. 'Leave it by the sign.'

She made a dismissive hand gesture: the interview was over. But Astra had another question. This one she was determined to ask.

'Where do Enki Arakkia lives?' she blurted. The Somarian words were fuzzy in her mouth; the grammar, she instantly realised, was entirely wrong.

At the end of the bench the slight woman stiffened like a cobra. 'Enki

Arakkia lives in your jail.' The venom in her voice was sprayed right at Astra.

'Enki Arakkia!' one of the older boys yelled, fisting his hands and making a circular motion with his arms.

'Enki Arakkia!' His playmate echoed the gesture, like a dance movement.

Astra tensed. 'He's not in *my* jail. CONC doesn't—'

The woman pointed her finger at Astra's wrist, then, swinging her arm in a wide arc over the sandpit and back towards the Boundary, hissed, 'You stole the Lake Chain. All the jails are yours.'

She followed the woman's finger. At the sight of the children's playpit, her mouth dried. Jutting out of the sand, a wall of broken Tablettes had been arranged into a shape she knew as well as her own navel: Is-Land. Inside the miniature Boundary, two blue ropes had been pressed into the sand for the rivers, rocks placed accurately for the cities. Mounds formed the steppes, white stones the white desert, charred paper the ash fields, twigs, bits of wood and cardboard the dry forest. And there, on the far left of the children's sculpture, were five long shards of broken glass.

She looked up at the Boundary. The eagle was landing, again and again. From here, the effect of the strobe was at the same time mesmerising and disturbing – and if you were prone to headaches, she realised, sick-making. No wonder the bench faced away from the wall. The Non-Landers weren't supposed to sit and dream about what lay behind those grey flashing lights, but they knew, of course: arable land, sheltering forests, strange and beautiful crystals, magnificent lava fields, grand cities and, to the west, the five sacred lakes of Bracelet Valley. Though she had never seen them, they glistened in her mind, each long body of water thronging with Yangtze dolphins, Gulf manatees, Beluga sturgeon, Azraq killifish and giant orange carp. Pride in this sanctuary, the birthplace of her mother, swam in her Code.

But that didn't mean *she* had built any *jails*.

Beside her, Photon sucked in a breath. 'This is my driver, Astra Ordott. She is a Gaian political refugee. She is not with IMBOD. She's—'

Her heart pumping, Astra cut him off. 'I'm a *Non-Gaian*. I want to see Enki Arakkia's mother. I want to give her water.'

The woman held out her hand. 'Give it to me.'

She stuck her arm behind her back. 'It's from my *mother*.'

The woman replaced her hand in her lap. *Your mother is a thief too*, her sardonic eyebrows replied.

'Enki Arakkia lives in our hearts,' the little boy's mother announced into the silence. 'Enki Arakkia lives in our children's future.'

'Leave two barrels,' the clown woman ordered. 'We will give Am Arakkia her water.'

Concentrating on the side mirrors, she reversed Cicada and made the turn, then drove back down the lane in silence. In the back seat, Rudo was reporting on his conversation with the couple in the tent: the man and his wife had said that everyone in Nagu Two still wanted the algae-scrubber but didn't believe they would get it without being forced to make a serious compromise in the anticipated upcoming battle with the Sec Gens. 'CONC will delay and delay. You will strongly suggest that we let our neighbours in Nagu One fend for themselves.' Rudo imitated the man, in an exaggerated Farashan accent. 'If we do, the scrubber will be our reward. But we've lived on beer and mother's milk for decades. You never know, my friend, we might decide we can last a little longer without clean water to dip our toothsticks in.'

'I do not think the Major will make such an offer,' Photon's hat was back on the dashboard, and there was a bright red line across his forehead. Somehow he just wasn't very convincing today. 'CONC aid is no strings.'

'So we say,' Rudo commented dryly. 'What about your lot? Never seen three Nonners less excited about two barrels of water in all my days in Kadingir.'

'They were YAC supporters,' Photon replied. He paused. 'They are refusing morpheus for the kids. I offered to take the boy to the clinic, then something went strange. Astra, what was the problem for your bracelet?'

'It's from Bracelet Valley,' Astra muttered.

'Sloping into YAC HQ wearing Is-Land bling,' Rudo drawled. 'Looks like we might have to add another no-no to the driving training, Phot.'

'I've never even been there,' she snapped. 'How was I supposed to know the bracelet was such a big deal?'

'Rudo,' Photon chided, 'if we did not know, how was Astra supposed to? Maybe just to wear it in the compound from now on?'

She didn't reply. *No one* here understood her. It wasn't her fault where she was born. She was trying to help people, bring them water and medicine. And her Code was Non-Gaian; she should have told that woman her father was a returnee, a rebel; *that* would have shut her up. She needed to carry the bracelet in Kadingir in case she met Zizi. But she would put it in a pocket – an inside pocket, so none of these *Nonners* could steal it.

They were back at the road between Nagu One and Two. She stopped and looked both ways.

'What you say we take the River Road, Phot?' Rudo drawled. 'Get Astra back up to *sp-e-e-e-d*?'

'It is out of our way,' Photon objected.

But Rudo wouldn't have it. 'C'mon, we can have lunch at that hut, the spicy one. With the hot waitress.'

So, stop-starting through yet more rickety dwellings and empty shop stalls, leaving many happy ramp-boys in their wake, she drove through Nagu One, down a meandering dirt track to the first paved road she'd seen in Kadingir.

'This is the Barracks road,' Photon told her as she pulled up at the intersection. 'A direct route to the CONC compound. Previously IMBOD was using it many times a day, but now only with CONC permission, for Diplomeets and orienteering.'

Her chest tightened. 'I thought IMBOD weren't allowed to send troops into Kadingir?'

'They're only troops if they're fighting,' Rudo said. 'They got rights to check the place out. Lay o' the land, fear in the hearts, that type o' thing.'

The road was filled with carts and cars; the pedestrians and wheelchair-users kept to the paved verges. She waited for what felt an age to cross, but traffic was heavy on both sides and the gaps never coincided. Then from the direction of the Barracks came the uncoiling sound of a siren: a white van was approaching, a green light flashing from its cabin roof. The carts and cars pulled over, lining up in front of Ciccy: a barrier against what Astra could now see was an oncoming cavalcade.

The lead van was far bigger and slicker than Ciccy, its white bonnet emblazoned with the red, green and gold IMBOD Shield. As it passed, the officer beside the driver raised his hand in greeting and Photon gestured in return. Astra gripped the steering wheel. The officer was Odinson.

He was gone in a flash. Behind the van came a fleet of white open-topped jeeps crowded with IMBOD officers. Standing proud in bright white shirts and padded golden vests, they surveyed Kadingir like a conquering army.

Rudo whistled. 'Meet the Sec Gens.'

She ignored him. Her heart was pounding. *Peat.* She scoured the faces as the jeeps rolled past. These were Sec Gens, yes, absolutely; their expressions serene and confident; even taller and broader in physique than she remembered. These youths were strong, invincible – *merry.* They would be able to stand for hours in those baking jeeps, laughing, sucking peppermints, sipping water, and when they got back to the Barracks they would still be up for a berserker murmuration or ten laps round the Kinbat track. For a moment a miserable swill of anger and grief washed through her, but whether the dirty dishwater remains of IMBOD's grey wave or her own self-pity she didn't know. *She* could have been a Sec Gen: powerful, protected, shining in the sun, and here in Non-Land for a year and then home.

But she wasn't a Sec Gen. She was a CONC driver. And this might be her only chance to see Peat ever again.

On the jeeps, the Sec Gens noticed Ciccy. Some of them waved and pointed, took out Tablettes, snapped photos. She shrank down behind the wheel but she couldn't look away.

And then there he was, Peat, on the very last jeep.

But he wasn't the Peat she knew. Peat was amiable, keen, sometimes even goofy. This boy was rigid and glaring, his chin high, his face taut, unsmiling. His cheekbones were jutting, the puppy fat vanished from his happy round face; his hair was cropped short, and his muscles were so pumped up she hardly recognised him.

But it was him: her Shelter brother: sweet, sweet Peat.

Why wasn't he like the others, cheerful, loose-limbed? A girl resting her arm lightly on Peat's shoulder looked solemn too. The boy on his other side was stern, laughing at a joke, but in a hard, cruel way. Around them their jeep-mates were taking photos. She didn't know if she should wave? Try and reach him?

But it was already too late. As she sat frozen at the wheel the jeep rumbled past and the cart-driver in front of Ciccy lashed his beast to get it moving again.

'Anyone you know, Astra?' Rudo asked.

'No,' she replied.

'Just nudge out,' Photon suggested. 'We'll never get across otherwise.'

The crowd was milling back onto the road. Trembling, she stepped on the pedal and stalled, restarted the engine and nosed out into the stream of traffic. As she silently crossed the road, the ghost of Peat's rigid face was plastered over the windscreen, the procession of Sec Gens still driving through her head.

PEAT

He stumbled off the jeep and was first down the ramp. His division siblings let him pass. He wanted to retch, but he'd done the whole tour. He couldn't have made it without Jade and Robin, supporting him, urging him, 'Do it for Laam. Do it for Laam.' And the syrup, too, of course, the dose of healing serum the doctor had given everyone in his division, even those at the back who hadn't known what had happened until later, when the official email went out.

But he had been standing right beside Laam when he had had his accident – at least that's what he and Jade and Robin had assumed it was. None of them had seen exactly what happened. They'd been entering murmuration mode, conscious of *everyone*, not specific individuals. In those first blurred, distraught moments Laam must have tripped, Peat had thought. He must have been jumping with excitement and slipped, misjudged, fallen . . . into a cloudy crimson wash of blood and flame, screams and splashes, wet boots and trousers, all the while the Division Officer shrieking commands in their ears. It was still impossible to believe: Laam was there one moment, and the next had utterly vanished. It had been so *quick*. For that, Odinson had told them, they should be grateful.

Gratitude, though, was still a distant goal. All yesterday he had been afflicted by an appalling nausea, a desolate sense of grief and confusion. The first couple of hours had been the worst, after the initial shock had subsided and before the syrup had started taking effect. While sitting waiting to be debriefed he had felt split, sawn in two by a terrible, traitorous thought: why had IMBOD allowed them so close to the edge?

At the first sight of Odinson, the Chief Super's eyes brimming with fatherly concern, this disloyal thought had vanished. 'It's all my fault,' he had sobbed. 'I must have jostled him – made him slip.'

Then Robin was crying too. 'I let him down – I should have grabbed him.'

'Me too,' Jade wept. 'I should have seen him lose his balance.'

'If—.' Peat had choked, then stopped.

'What, Peat?' His Division Officer sounded kind, not frenzied and sharp as a butcher's knife, like when she'd screamed FREEZE in his earpiece.

'I wouldn't have disobeyed an order, of course,' Peat had continued slowly, his eyes on the table, 'but if I'd been quicker . . . If I'd jumped in after him before the order came, I mean, I could have pushed him to the side so the others could pull him out.'

'Sec Gens, Sec Gens,' Odinson had rumbled soothingly, 'your loyalty is commendable. But Laam's death was not your fault. Your Division Officer saw everything. You were his special friends, so we want to tell you now, before the official email goes out: Laam walked into the pond.'

'But—?' Peat looked at Jade and Robin for support. His Gaia mates were equally bewildered. Why would Laam do that?

The Division Officer spoke next. *Did they know*, she asked, *that Laam had been summoned to a performance review?*

No, Laam hadn't told them.

'As we suspected,' Odinson said. 'He felt ashamed of letting you down.'

'He never let us down!'

Peat went rigid: Jade, wild in her grief, had *contradicted* the Chief Superintendent. 'He sacrificed himself for us.' She gasped. 'He wouldn't even come to Woodland Siesta if he thought he might be sick.'

The officers exchanged a glance.

But his Sec Gen sister was not to be punished.

'Jade,' their Division Officer said gently, 'did you know that Laam consistently scored at the lower range of Sec Gen abilities?'

'Yes – but it wasn't that low! We did the calculations!'

'His scores were the lowest of the whole cohort.' The officer addressed them all. 'We had decided to reassign him to non-combat Hemline duties. These would have formed an essential part of the defence operation, but Laam clearly decided they were a demotion. Tragically, misguidedly, entirely unpredictably, he chose to end his life rather than despoil the battle honour of his division.'

Odinson shook his magnificent head. 'Normally Sec Gen obedience to authority is marginally stronger than group loyalty, but in Laam's case that ratio was slightly askew. That is a tribute to you all.'

'It was a noble instinct,' the Division Officer intoned. 'His action proves that on the battlefield Laam would have eagerly sacrificed himself to save any of you. And in his death, he has demonstrated that your own instincts are sound. Though, like Peat, no doubt you felt the urge to jump in after him, you all obeyed my order to freeze.'

'Your officer gave the correct order,' Odinson concluded. 'Even with a rope or a life belt, against a pool of Carpira eels there was nothing anyone could have done. Please be assured that Laam returned to Gaia as swiftly as a raindrop returns to a lake, an autumn leaf curls to smoke on a bonfire. None of you could have saved him, and now you must carry on with him in your hearts. Do your duty for Is-Land, in honour of your friend.'

The beautiful words, the reassurances had meant nothing at the time. Laam was gone, and a gaping hole had been ripped in his soul. But gradually the syrup had calmed his raw nerves. The doctors had said the Booster shot would be helping too – the Sec Gens' increased emotional stability levels enabled them to recover much faster than usual from such a sudden loss. Today he still felt tense, ill, but no longer so desperately disoriented. As he looked up at the Boundary, its looped image of a white petal slowly falling, falling, falling against a background of ascending white feathers, Odinson's words came back to him: Laam had fallen so that the rest of his division might rise. He must carry on.

He sat with Jade and Robin in the meadow. The sun was gracing the grass and the scent of dry earth was curing the memory of the human stench of Kadingir. How could people live like that, wallowing in their own filth?

Jade was flicking through photo streams of the tour. 'He would have been so upset about the camels,' she said.

'And the dogs,' Peat agreed, leaning over. 'I couldn't believe it. Those *ribs*.'

The next photo was of a CONC van. He vaguely remembered passing it: a crude, peculiar design, and one of the only other motor vehicles on the streets. Mostly the Non-Landers relied on slave beasts to haul their selfish carcases around.

'Hey, Peat . . .' Jade's tone was wondering, tentative. 'Didn't your Shelter father say . . . I mean, is that . . . *her*?'

She enlarged the image of the driver. Peat took the Tablette. Her hair was short, but yes: it was . . .

His chest tightened. Why was she intruding on today?

Laam would have known what to say. Robin and Jade were silent.

'At least she hasn't joined the slavers yet,' he said, swiping the stream to the next photo.

Jade took the Tablette from him and set it aside. 'We're so lucky,' she said, reaching out to stroke his leg. 'We have each other.'

He took a deep breath and gazed up at the Boundary. It was screening a field of lambs now – gentle, innocent, happy lambs, bred only for their wool, paid properly, given long and happy retirements with full medical and dental care.

'Yeah,' he replied, 'we have everything anyone could ever need.'

They lay for a while, skin touching, Peat on his back, staring up at the sky. Their Tablettes buzzed. Jade and Robin were sleeping, but he reached for his.

'Whoah,' he breathed. 'No way.'

Dear Constable Peat Orson,

Further to our meeting yesterday, I wish to send you an official record of my personal condolences on the tragic loss of your Sec Gen brother and Gaia mate, Laam Vistason. Especially following your difficult family circumstances earlier this year, I am sure this loss must have felt a terrible blow. As I have assured your parents, let me stress that you are receiving the best possible care. As your progress report suggested, I am confident you will honour your fallen comrade with great achievements in his memory.

I am writing also to inform you that I have approved your team proposal for a Special Initiative. You, Robin Steppeson and Jade Sundott will meet with your Division Officer tomorrow to discuss the details. Congratulations on a striking and articulate proposal. Its successful completion will be a suitable tribute to Constable Vistason.

Chief Superintendent Clay Odinson

He poked Jade and Robin and made them wake up, read their own Tablettes. Apart from the reference to family circumstances, they had received the same message. They all read it over and over.

Congratulations. Striking. Articulate.

'That was you, Peat.'

'No, you changed that comma, Jade.'

'And Laam. The uniforms were Laam's idea.'

Peat drew his Sec Gen siblings, his closest companions, into a head huddle.

'For Laam.'

'For Laam.'

They straightened. Overhead, the Boundary lambs gambolled and nuzzled. The sun dazzled Peat's eyes and shouts from the murmuration field rang in his ears. Odinson had called on *him* to make Laam's ultimate sacrifice worthwhile.

ASTRA

'Big frackers,' Rudo remarked.

Yes, they were, much bigger than she remembered. But she had to leave the Sec Gens behind. Bumping over cement crossings, ignoring Rudo's chat, she followed Photon's directions through Nagu Six, at last turning south onto the broad paved road running alongside the Mikku River, the orderly rows of grains and vegetables growing in the CONC fields on the opposite shore, and behind them a bright, high scarlet bank of poppies.

'Yo baby! Step on the pedal,' Rudo urged.

The speed limit on the River Road was sixty. Her gauge needle was on forty, the top limit in Is-Land. She unrolled her window to let in the fresh river air. 'No.'

'Whaddya mean, no?'

'There could be animals,' she retorted. From the corner of her eye she could see Rudo's forearm, stretched over the front seat. 'And don't block the driver's view.'

'This is Kadingir, babe,' he scoffed, moving the offending arm a centimetre away. 'There's not a wild creature squeaking, not even a field mouse.'

'It's true, Astra,' Photon told her. 'All worker beasts are penned or harnessed and there are not any rodents here – some across the river in the farm fields and some at the scrap heaps, that is all. You can go the speed limit and there will not be any road kill, I promise.'

She could smell Rudo again. His musky vanilla smell reminded her of Nimma; like Lil's hair, one minute it made her want to close her eyes and cry, the next to cut off her nose and never smell anything again, because she wasn't in Is-Land any more. She was in another world now, not a place she had chosen: a place that had summoned her into its maze of dead ends, shifting roads and chaotic battle lines, and was keeping her trapped here. She had no control over any of these paths or how they changed beneath her feet; other people – in the Barracks and the CONC compound, in the N-LA Beehive and the tents of Nagu One, in Amazigia and the Wheel Meet in Atourne – made all the decisions here. She was nothing, nobody, not even a field mouse, just a collection of atoms spinning along for the ride, an agonising stop-start lunch towards a destination that receded even as she approached it.

It was the thought of Odinson that did it: Odinson, in the front seat of the IMBOD van, triumphantly touring Kadingir. Perhaps if she sped down the River Road, she would get away from him at last. Get to Pithar a fraction faster, find Zizi a crucial moment sooner, arrive at last in a place she had a chance of understanding.

She stepped down hard on the accelerator and drove faster than she had ever done before. With the wind on her face, the river glistering beside her, the fields green, brown and red blurs, she devoured the road. Rudo whooped and banged the seat with his fist; Photon reached into his bag, peeled a tangerine and passed around the segments. The thin crescents burst in her mouth like tiny gold explosions of sunshine. She spat the pips out of the window, let them skip along in the dirt behind Cicada – maybe they would root in the verge and she would return here one day to find shelter in a leafy orange grove.

The riverside snack hut was just a few buckled boards haphazardly knocked together on the brink of the water. Shaded by palm-leaf parasols, the tables each boasted a small red chili pepper plant in a terracotta pot. The customers were drinking beer and playing backgammon as the broad green river flowed lazily past. Would Zizi come to a place like this? She tried to inspect the men, but apart from the superficial details of colouring, none looked remotely like her. Photon chose a table near the bank and she sat gazing out over the river. The poppy fields covered the opposite shore: scarlet carpets flung out for the sun to dance upon. The river in between was clogged with garbage, the bobbing glass bottles, soggy fabrics and broken sticks of furniture all rapidly floating downstream.

'Why don't they clean up the rubbish?' she demanded.

'The city midden is upstream,' Photon explained. 'Lately it has been spilling into the river.'

'Why don't they string up a net? Or fish the junk out? I thought they were all post-Abrahamic *nature worshippers* out here.'

'It is a new situation. Normally there will be a committee forming.'

'It doesn't take a committee to clean up a river! It just takes a few volunteers.'

'That current is fast,' Rudo chipped in. 'Not too many people fancy volunteering to drown, I guess.'

Lil had swum in the river, but she'd couldn't tell Rudo that. She gave up. This place was *hopeless*. Even CONC's poppy fields were a terrible problem, feeding the region's morpheus addiction. She stared out beyond the scarlet field to the firesands, those pale, toxic dunes no amount of rain could re-green. Suddenly a fierce orange flame shot up on the horizon, followed by plumes of black smoke and a loud crack.

'Phwoar!' A roar went up from the customers. People stood up, laughing, and money changed hands.

'A *mergallá*,' Rudo chuckled. 'Comin' to get you for speeding, Astra.' She glared at him.

'That is why they are called the firesands,' Photon explained. 'Sometimes the winds expose old munitions, and if people or animals step or drive on them, or the timers are sun-sensitive, explosions occur.'

The waitress, a young curly-haired woman about Astra's age, arrived. There was only one item on the menu, as far as Astra could make out. Photon ordered in Farashan as the waitress openly inspected her.

'*Duvit paranam,*' she greeted Astra. Then *something something something*, shushing and clacking and creaking like doves fighting to get out of a broken wooden box.

'*Duvit paranam,*' Astra mumbled. That was the extent of her Farashan. At least she had taken off Eya's bracelet and put it in her cargo pocket.

'This is Azarmidokht,' Photon said. 'Azarmidokht. Astra.'

'Farashan very difficult,' Azarmidokht said in Asfarian. She sounded pleased with the fact.

'It does not take much to make people happy, yes?' Photon remarked as the woman departed. 'Some beer, a view, a small bet to make things interesting. Occasionally a – what do you call it, Rudo? – *little roll in the hay*. Do you ever wonder why we did not realise this some millennia ago?'

'I believe we did, Professor Augenblick,' Rudo replied. 'It's just I think you'll find that some people's idea of a good game and a hay roll is *un petit peu* more violent than others'. Take those Sec Gens. They're bursting their gold buttons for a fight, eh, Astra?'

She tensed. 'The Sec Gens aren't violent,' she muttered. 'They're Coded to defend Is-Land, that's all.'

Even as she said it, she stopped believing it. Why had Peat looked so miserable? Had he, like her, discovered the truth about IMBOD? It was a strangely painful thought: Peat, with his eager legal brain, learning that all the codes of behaviour he'd been taught were false fronts for torturing children with Gaia's toxic waste. How crushed, how disappointed he would be.

'Thought you said IMBOD were liars,' Rudo said lightly.

'Rudo,' Photon warned.

'IMBOD is,' she snapped. 'But the Sec Gens aren't psychokillers, okay? They're good fighters and they're loyal to each other, that's all. They only get aggressive if they're attacked first. And Non-Landers kill people too, you know. Have you ever heard of a suicide nanobomber, Rudo?' She was sputtering, and her voice was getting louder. The men at the next table were looking at her.

Photon looked uneasy. 'Can we talk about this in Cicada, please?'

Rudo, though, had to have the last word. He raised his water flask. 'Peace.'

'Peace,' Photon echoed.

'Peace,' she muttered as the waitress returned, her tray bearing three small bowls of soup and a long brown loaf cut into chunks.

'Food here's a damn sight better than that CONC muck.' Rudo dunked a heel of bread into the neon-orange gruel. 'Not that that's hard!'

He was right. The food was the best she'd eaten in Non-Land. The squash gruel was thin but spicy and the bread was flecked with caraway seeds. Astra eyed the cool beers on the other tables, but she was driving and they were on duty, so they stuck to the water in their flasks.

Her bowl was empty far too soon. 'Can I order another one, please?' she asked.

Photon glanced at a nearby table, where a woman was feeding two children from one bowl, the spoon dipping into first one waiting mouth, then the other. 'Normally we do not like to order two at one shack,' he whispered. 'If you are still hungry we can visit another place a little further along.'

Oh. She set her own spoon down in her bowl. The utensil and dish shone as if Uttu had just washed them.

Rudo patted his stomach. 'Good to travel light.'

Azarmidokht returned. Photon paid her in coin and as she picked up Astra's bowl she laughed and said something friendly-sounding, as if the doves in her throat had escaped their confinement and were preening in the sun.

'She says you liked the soup.'

The Farashan word for 'delicious' eluded her. She said it in Asfarian instead.

'Thank you.' The waitress smiled. 'I will tell my mother.'

'Nagu Six is *famoso* for red peppers,' Rudo said. 'They grow 'em on the rooftops.' He added the Farashan word Astra had been searching for and kissed his lips with his fingertips.

Azarmidokht spoke again in her own tongue.

'It is a Farashan proverb: "When the stomach growls, throw the tongue a bone",' Photon translated.

A bone? Was there *meat* in the soup?

Photon caught her alarm. 'Do not worry,' he reassured her. 'It is only a saying. I would not order you a meat broth. They are made on only special occasions anyway.'

Someone brushed her arm. The young parents were leading their children down to the water's edge. The kids were carrying what looked like fishing nets, loosely woven pouches at the end of long bamboo poles.

'Do they kill the fish on the tables?' she muttered as the team stood up.

'There are no fish in the Mikku,' Photon quietly replied. He was watching as the children dipped their nets into the water. The little boy scored first, scooping out a green bottle while his sister struggled to keep her grip on the pole against the fast-flowing current. The father cheered his son, then grasped his daughter's hands to help her, and the mother popped the boy's bottle in her bag.

'Entrepreneur,' Photon commented. 'CONC gives a refund for recycled bottles.'

'Happy now, Gaian Inspectress?' Rudo grinned.

She ignored him. They shouldn't be cleaning up the river for *money*, she thought. But as the boy's skinny arm reached out across the current, she wondered how many returned bottles it would take to buy a bowl of soup.

* * *

Photon drove now, Rudo beside him, and Astra sat in the back. As they made their way along an interior artery into Nagu Six there was a ping in the cabin. Rudo switched on Comchan.

Sandrine's voice crackled over the speakers: 'I repeat, Sniper fire in Nagu Two has just killed an eleven-year-old boy. Tisha and Dix are attending to the scene. Demonstrations are being reported throughout Kadingir. I repeat: All meet-and-greet operations are suspended. Please finish up quickly at your Treatment Wards and return to the compound ASAP.'

Nagu Two?

'Sandrine,' Photon spoke loudly, 'we're in Nagu Six. Do Tisha and Dix need back-up?'

'We're covered, thanks, Phot.'

Her mind was whirring. The boys playing football in the playground. *Had IMBOD—?*

'Any word on the Sec Gens, Sandrine?' Rudo asked.

'They're back at the Barracks, not scheduled to come out again today. Keep in touch, guys, and get home safe.'

'Will do, Sandrine.' Photon clicked off Comchan.

Astra sat trapped in the back, panic rising in her throat. 'Can't we find out more?' she asked. 'What if it was one of the boys we met? Shouldn't we go and help?'

'They don't need us,' Photon said. Then, softly, 'That playground was not on the Hem. I am sure the boys we met are fine.'

But that wasn't the point, was it? Some other little boy had been shot: shot and killed by an IMBOD sniper. Her skin was burning with shame as surely as if she had pulled the trigger herself. At the same time, a wall of automatic responses was shooting up inside her: the sniper must have felt threatened – maybe he or she had lost a family member, like she and Peat had lost Sheba. Or maybe the sniper had been terrified of letting a Non-Lander get near Is-Land. Maybe he or she had just made a mistake...

She couldn't say any of that. She wanted to disappear, but she was stuck in Ciccy, stuck in Non-Land, stuck behind Photon as he rattled on down the narrow road, bumping to a halt periodically to let ramp boys clear the way.

Rudo twizzled the Comchan knob, but the reports of the shooting were scanty, the circumstances 'unconfirmed'.

At last she could see the end of the road, and a crowd of people gathered outside a clunky arrangement of conjoined containers. They were shouting, angry people. If she'd been driving she would have reversed down the street, all the way back to the Mikku, but though Photon slowed, he kept heading straight for the demo. There were old people, young people, children, some in red N-LA shirts and robes, others in purple. Some were brandishing signs, others yelling. There were people in wheelchairs, people milling around, people standing behind a long table or sitting on a carpet laid out on the ground. Someone was playing singing bowls, she realised as a high whine met her ears. The musician was surrounded by a group of meditators, people silent and serene in the midst of this bedlam. She could barely see the front door of the ward, and with all these people spilling everywhere there was nowhere to park.

Photon stopped in the middle of the street and a small, sturdy man in a burgundy fez and black robes came tumbling out of the crowd. Beaming, Dr Tapputu gestured to a space beside the containers. As Photon edged around the crowd, someone banged their fist along Ciccy's side, sending laughter up from the crowd.

Photon turned the engine off. 'Okay, leave the supplies for now. Just follow the doctor. We are here to help the patients. It is a peaceful protest. Everything will be fine.'

She desperately wanted to stay in the unit, but she'd rather cut off her tongue than say so. As they got out of Cicada the noise of the crowd assaulted her ears. Beneath it, the drone of the singing bowl was uncoiling towards her like an invisible metallic serpent. Was it going to make her sick again? She hung back behind Photon and Rudo. Ahead, the doctor was parting the crowd, clearing a corridor to the door. The protesters were obeying him, shuffling backwards, but still shouting and brandishing placards. Photon and Rudo waded into the demo and she followed, passing a carpet where the singing-bowl player was sliding his finger around the rim of a coppery tureen. Around him, the meditators were swaying, their faces alight with inner sunshine. In front of them was a dish: a collection of vials and needles.

She tensed, bracing herself for that weird nerve pain in her teeth, the unpleasant electricity shooting up her follicles, but instead it was her arm that was gripped.

'Welcome, Astra,' Dr Tapputu exclaimed as he grabbed her elbow. His black robes billowing around him, he drew her into the crowd. 'How fine to see you,' he shouted in her ear, chatting as if they were strolling through a garden. 'I'm just inspecting the ward myself. There are some remarkable things going on here, I must say.'

She couldn't reply. Her fear was compounded by that spooky feeling of being trapped in a Code mirror hall, surrounded by people she recognised though she'd never seen any of them before. And here, in the heart of the crowd, Dr Tapputu was drowned out by the chants. She understood the Somarian and Karkish, and she could guess at the Farashan: 'Non-Land. Non-Land,' the N-LA supporters were yelling. 'One Land. One Land,' the purple-shirted protesters shouted back. And something else too: 'One World. One World.' The words were booming from the body of someone she *had* seen before, the giant man from the Diplomeet and the River Raven, looming ahead of her as if guarding the door; she barely came up to his waist. Then she was climbing the steps to the ward, looking into his enormous – very clean – ear, and, Dr Tapputu behind her, stepping at last inside.

The clinic reception was sparsely furnished and the container walls were grey, but the room was bright, thanks to a row of windows cut into the back wall. A faint scent of vinegar hung in the air. Photon and Rudo were loitering beside a row of sacks filled with dirty laundry. She wanted Dr Tapputu to close the door, shut out the noise and the anger, but he didn't. 'Sit, sit,' he urged, gesturing at a long table. They pulled up chairs and he picked up a box – no, not a box but a small set of wooden steps with a handle cut into the side – and went behind a counter in front of the windows. He set the steps down, climbed up on them and turned on a tap.

'The mood was peaceful all day,' he said, the sound of the water gushing over the shouts of the crowd, 'until the news of the shooting arrived.'

As he began clearing the mugs from the countertop into the sink she realised Dr Tapputu looked dressed for a party. The black fez fringe dangled over his forehead and there was an orange badge on his chest – no, not a badge; it was the head of his toy, the rubber yogi doll. What was that thing's name?

'Have you heard any more about it?' Photon asked.

'The usual story: a boy chasing a ball. Witnesses claim he stopped at the Hemline, but his body was blasted backwards, and the sniper says he crossed over.'

Rudo exhaled. 'Frackin' IMBOD.'

'Indeed.'

With his warm tone, his amber glance, Dr Tapputu bathed her in sympathy. She didn't want it. She felt agitated, not quite here, not able to breathe properly. There was a chain around her throat: a chain of murder, of killings, violent deaths. This boy in Nagu Two had been shot. Sheba had been blown up. The Non-Land boy who had shot Hokma's eye had been tortured to death by Hokma's fellow officers. And in between, many many more people had died, one killing linked to the next, a hurting iron circle cinched tight around her neck like a leash – a double leash, one end stretching back, endlessly back into the past, and the other endlessly forward into the future. How was *she* supposed to break the chain? She wasn't in IMBOD – none of it was her fault. Peat's face stamped back into her mind, hard as a steel-capped boot. Peat was in IMBOD. He was part of the chain now, pulling it tighter, so tight her eyes bulged, her lungs burned . . .

Photon spoke. 'Will they let us deliver the supplies?'

Breathing hard, she jerked herself out of her trance. She glanced up at Dr Tapputu. He didn't appear to have noticed her departure from the room.

'Oh, I should think so. No one's stopping anyone enter, and we've established a good rapport with both sides.' The doctor lifted a teapot lid and inspected the contents. 'The volunteers have been serving refreshments and we've had some excellent conversations. I must say I find some of YAC's ideas most interesting.' The doctor plunged his hand into the pot and retrieved a fistful of sodden yellow leaves. He held the mulch to his nose. 'Camomile and lemonwort: an excellent blend for peace talks.'

Peace talks. She'd only seen people yelling and arguing and walking out of a Diplomeet, beating each other, getting arrested, shouting in a crowd – talking wasn't solving anything here. Not that Rudo cared. 'So you won't be wanting our morpheus, Doc?' He grinned. 'It's all smells and bells from now on in Ward Six?'

Dr Tapputu dumped the herbs in a bin beneath the counter, rinsed out the teapot and set it back on the counter. He smiled his wolfish smile. 'I am in the wards today checking on that very question myself, Rudo. There is still a high demand for morpheus here. But a handful of the patients have refused it, and apart from withdrawal symptoms, they seem to be doing well.'

'Morpheus withdrawal. Ouch.' Rudo winced.

Astra looked away from the teapot. Something about its glistening wet potbelly made her want to cry.

The doctor rinsed his hands and turned off the tap. '*Pain is the path*, they say. And sometimes a little pain *is* necessary to catalyse a greater healing.'

She swallowed. *Pain tells you that there's something wrong, Astra. Everyone needs a little bit of pain in life, even emotional pain.* Hokma had told her that once, a long time ago, on the meadow roof of Wise House, when she was convincing her not to have her Security shot. For a moment everything was still. With the tap off, she could hear the drone of the singing bowl again. It was amazing how the sound cut through the shouts of the crowd, slid stealthily into the container. But whether it was because she was safe inside, or the fact there was only one bowl at the demo, this drone wasn't irritating her nerves. It was just there, like the light in the room was there, falling over the counter, draping Dr Tapputu's shoulders, lending his robe a feathery grey aura and the teapot a fresh glazed sheen; like the scent of lemonwort was there in the air, and the Wise House wildflowers were floating in her mind, her past mingling with the present, Hokma's voice echoing Dr Tapputu's, or was it the other way round? Perhaps it was the ordinariness of just watching the doctor do the dishes, but from being desolate, hopeless, suddenly everything seemed incredibly calm. More than calm – harmonious.

But that was wrong: it wasn't harmonious here. It couldn't be, ever. A boy had just been killed. People were shouting outside. In the compound Kovan and Sulu and Tamanina were running around with their skin rashes. The little boy in the park had stars in his head.

'Are YAC supporters bringing their children in for painkillers?' she demanded.

The doctor's golden eyes glittered at her. 'You have a fully operational heart, Astra. I was concerned about these reports, but from my investigations this week I believe they have been wildly exaggerated. All the children with terminal illnesses are on morpheus. The rest are being offered alternative pain relief. I myself have been prescribing some of these remedies for years.' He dried his hands on a thin grey towel. 'Turmeric is a wonderful anti-inflammatory, as are chilies. And the singing bowls are a fascinating discovery. The player outside today told me that when combined with the use of controlled breathing techniques, they help Himalayan yogis and monks perform feats of great physical endurance.' He wiped down the counter with the cloth. 'There's more than one way to cure a ham, as Rudo once memorably told me.'

Rudo and Photon chuckled. But meat jokes weren't funny. She looked at the tufty head of Dr Tapputu's doll sticking out of his pocket. Sri something . . . yes, Auroville, that was its name. She knew about yogis: she'd researched them when she was trying to convince Nimma to let her wear dreadlocks. Some yogis tied their Gaia ploughs in knots around a stick, others stood on one leg for months or even years. Further north in Himalaya, monks and nuns sat in the snow for hours wearing only thin robes, or underwent operations without anaesthetic. Vishnu had told her that these achievements were the result of a lifetime's dedication to spiritual practice. Outside, the protesters were chanting in unison now: *One Land. One Land. One World. One World.* Could YAC really tear down the Boundary by *meditating*?

'So this ward currently has a surplus of morpheus?' Photon asked.

Laughing, Dr Tapputu hopped down from his steps and, box in hand, came out from behind the counter. 'Oh no, this is Kadingir! But there is sufficient here to treat the terminally ill.' He pulled out a chair, and climbed up on to it. 'Maybe that's also part of YAC's plan. If their sacrifices enable pain-free deaths for those in need, they'll win tacit support from patients and relatives.'

'Best take some more anyway,' Rudo said. 'You might need it soon. We saw the Sec Gens on recce today.'

The doctor fingered his goatee. 'Ah, yes, I heard IMBOD was on parade. And how did they look?'

'Mega frackers.' Rudo answered. 'Tall as Photon, wide as the compound gate – even the girls. Not salivating at the mouth yet, but hey, you gotta have something to look forward to.'

'Rudo,' Photon started, 'we said we would not discuss this—'

She could fight her own battles. 'I told you, Rudo,' she interrupted, 'the Sec Gens are defensive warriors. N-LA respects the Hem and YAC is non-violent. So the Sec Gens won't be killing anyone.'

Dr Tapputu regarded her curiously. 'Astra,' he said, 'is this your first time out on the wards?'

She nodded. Rudo was smirking; he'd got a rise out of her.

'Then I must give you a tour. Gentlemen, why don't you bring in the supplies and I'll show Astra around.'

She didn't know if she wanted to see terminally ill people – she was just a driver, not a medic – but she couldn't very well refuse. Photon and Rudo took the dirty-laundry sacks out to Ciccy and she let Dr Tapputu lead her through a door into a long container lined with beds. It smelled different in here: the vinegar had a nasty chemical edge. There were windows along the back wall, but their yellow curtains were drawn. Beneath them, a nurse was taking a patient's temperature. Dr Tapputu closed the door and the sound of the crowd outside disappeared.

'This is the men's ward,' he whispered. 'We've put the YAC patients together at the far end.' Clumping over the metal floors, the doctor led her down the aisle. The patients were mostly sleeping or listlessly staring into space. Not everyone was zoned out though. An old man sat up as they passed his bed and called out in Somarian, 'She! Who is *she*?'

Astra started. Hollow-cheeked with skin like parched earth, the man was surely far too old to be her father?

'This is Astra Ordott. The new CONC driver,' Dr Tapputu told him. 'Astra, meet Kuma.'

The man scrutinised her with watery eyes. She forced a brief smile.

He raised an arthritic finger. 'Somarian,' he announced with an air of satisfaction.

The doctor took it as a question. 'She's a CONC officer, Kuma. But she does look a bit Somarian, doesn't she?'

She couldn't manage 'Non-Gaian' again today. But did the man know her father? She faced the bed. If Kuma said she looked just like someone he knew, then she would have to ask Dr Tapputu to help her talk to him.

'Somarian,' Kuma repeated, tapping his chest and sinking back against his pillow.

Oh . . . had he just wanted to tell her what *he* was? She lingered at the bedside as Dr Tapputu took Kuma's pulse. She was allowed to talk to Dr Tapputu about her father, but if she mentioned Zizi in front of Kuma, was that breaking the rules?

She kept silent. Kuma waved his tendon-thin arm for the nurse and the doctor steered her on towards the end of the container. The patients in the last four beds were sitting up. The doctor stopped, stayed her arm. The men were young, all very thin, their eyes closed, chests gently rising and falling. They were meditating, she realised. Their expressions were not serene like the meditators outside: their faces looked tight, pinched, as if they were working extremely hard. One was grinding his jaw, another was clutching his stomach. Their breathing was heavy: like snores. Nevertheless, watching them, she experienced that shroud of stillness once more. *A matter of time*, the doctor had just said. Today time felt enormous, large enough to hold everything in the world.

The doctor tugged at her sleeve. She bent and he whispered into her ear: 'One of the protesters has been giving them lessons. The singing-bowl player wanted to come in too, but I thought it would disturb the other patients. If the crowd leaves, perhaps the patients can sit outside.'

In Dr Tapputu's pocket, Sri Auroville was stretching, the toy's orange rubber arms rising over his head, palms meeting in tree pose.

'He wants to help them,' she whispered back.

The doctor patted his pocket and twinkled up at her. 'Yes, he does.'

Beckoning, he took her past the YAC patients and opened another door. They stood at the threshold of a ward filled with women and children, a group of meditators again at the far end of the aisle. A nurse looked up from a little boy's bed and greeted Dr Tapputu with a wave.

'Gud,' he said softly. 'Let's see how he is.'

They went over to the bed. The little boy's head was small on his pillow. He had the saddest face Astra had ever seen. Dr Tapputu sorted out his steps and climbed up. He took Sri Auroville out of his pocket and placed him on the blanket beside the boy's chest.

'Hello, Gud,' he said in Somarian. 'This is Astra. And this is Sri. They've come to say hello.'

'Say hello, Gud,' the nurse gently urged.

The boy moved his eyes only, over Sri, over Astra, out towards the door. She felt she might fall into his gaze and drown.

The doctor walked Sri down the bed to Gud's hand. The doll's arms came down, its palms pressed together at its chest in a *namaste*. 'Shall we see if Sri can do a headstand today?' Dr Tapputu turned the doll upside down in the air beside the boy's curled hand. Sri's arms extended and his toes pointed to the ceiling.

Slowly and lightly, like sea anemone tentacles, the boy's fingers closed around the doll.

'Ah. You like him. He likes you too. Oh? What's that, Sri?' The doctor let go of the doll and leaned over the bed, hand cupped at his ear. 'You want to stay here with Gud? Yes, of course you can. Gud means strong, doesn't it? Strong like a bull. Gud will look after you very well, won't you, Gud?'

The boy did not reply. He was still staring at the door. But he was gripping Sri tightly now.

The doctor climbed down from his steps. 'We should be getting back, Astra. But I'm glad you met Gud.'

'Goodbye, Gud,' she managed. 'Goodbye, Sri.'

They walked back through the wards to the reception. As she followed the small, black-robed man, Astra found herself wishing very hard that, when she finally met him, Zizi would be just a little bit like Dr Tapputu.

Photon and Rudo were leaning on the counter, the clean-linen bags behind them, the new supplies of morpheus and condoms stacked on the table.

'So?' Photon asked. 'Anyone we need to take to the hospital?'

'Not today, thank you,' the doctor replied briskly. 'All under control. Self-medicating with meditation, aren't they, Astra?'

'Yeah. It's working. I think.'

Photon got his Tablette out. 'Good. So we just need your signature here, Doctor.'

Rudo jerked a thumb at the remaining bag of dirty laundry. 'C'mon, Astra. Time to earn your soup.'

She picked up the bag. 'Goodbye, Dr Tapputu,' she said.

He raised his hand. 'Goodbye, Astra. Wonderful to see you looking so well. And we'll be in touch, won't we?'

The swab test. She nodded, and Rudo led her out past the huge man and down the steps. The protesters were taking a break, chatting among themselves now, resting their arms on their Tablette placards instead of raising them high. She wanted to say something to the YAC supporters, something encouraging, but she didn't know if that was allowed, and she worried that if she did the N-LA people might yell at her. So she followed Rudo as he headed back to Cicada. The singing-bowl tone was almost appealing now, she realised as she passed the player, like a warm, plangent sunbeam easing her path through the crowd.

UNA DAYYANI

Tahazu Rabu was made of Dragon's Gorge sandstone; though his majestic features had been carved and battered over the ages by the weather, his convictions would never crumble. Una had known him since they were children, their families sharing meals in the Beehive before her father donated it to the people. Some had thought her father should have matched them, but handsome as he was, she had never longed for Tahazu. Despite all the arguments of the early years, she knew her father had chosen well for her: her husband was a man with fire in his nostrils and butter in his heart. She had never seen Tahazu roar with rage, never heard him laugh as if he could not stop, or speak about a lavish meal he had made. Even as a boy, he was impassive, methodical, his vision set – not on change, like hers, but on maintaining control. Over the last decade, she realised, he had controlled himself as well as her people, for now, for the first time in her reign, she saw her Chief of Police's hand shaking as it pointed down at the dust.

'He did not touch the line.'

The boy's body had been blasted backwards. Witnesses swore he had not crossed into the Hem. His friends, the adults on the street, they all said he had run full tilt after his ball – then stopped, arms spread, laughter bubbling from his lungs . . . lungs blown apart a moment later by the bullet that ripped through his chest. And here, inside the yellow ropes of the police cordon, was the proof. Deep scuff marks in the dirt. A dead boy's heels still digging into Non-Land, a good twenty centimetres from the Hemline. If IMBOD wanted to claim further footsteps had been brushed away by the boy's friends, Odinson would have to provide video proof. The heel marks and the black stains of blood spoiling the sand a metre away were enough for Tahazu Rabu.

'For years, we protect them,' he growled. 'We rid the entire Belt of guns, of bombs. We fill their jail cells with our people. And for what, Una? So they can shoot our children like mangy dogs?'

Tahazu had not liked the disarmament agreement but he had been persuaded. And he must stay persuaded.

'So that we can have a nation, Tahazu. We're nearly there. One more step.'

He shook his head. 'Our nation is splitting in two, Una. I can keep beating and jailing limbless kids if you like, but they will keep fighting back and the world will keep cheering them on. And in the meantime, Odinson will clad that Boundary. Then what? Will he flip a switch to send poison gas seeping from the wall? Will he turn on a magnetic force-field to give us all migraines, motion sickness, brain tumours?'

She was silent.

'The boy did not cross the line, Una. IMBOD have broken the agreement. All promises are off. YAC will storm the Hem. I say we join them.'

'No,' she snapped. 'If we do that, we lose all leverage with CONC.'

'CONC are Odinson's hamsters,' Rabu scoffed. As a child, Una had had a pair of the animals as pets. He had never liked them. 'They nip his fingers, and he brushes their fur and refills their water bottles. When he's tired of them, he will wring their necks. We need better helpers. When is the Mujaddid going to keep all his promises?'

'Soon, Tahazu,' she snapped. 'But Amazigia has to vote him into place, remember? In the meantime, we have to maintain the moral high ground: the Rabus and the Dayyanis, the battle-chiefs and the judges, the noble leaders of our people. We must think quickly, act *slowly*.'

He spat into the Hem. High on the Boundary, a gun flashed.

'This noble chief says it's time for battle, Judge.'

She faced the Boundary, that loathsome grey screen, spooling new footage of the Sec Gens, pumped-up youths in white uniforms, drilling in rows beneath the saw-crest of sniper turrets. The Sec Gens were Code monsters, everyone knew that. Their ears would be tuned to all frequencies, their bodies resistant to injury, their minds immune to any normal human sense of mortality. What possible indent would N-LA's sonic weapons make against their remorseless onslaught?

But Tahazu was right. All bets were off.

'Yes,' she sighed, 'all right, Tahazu. But we do it my way.'

She stepped up to the Hemline. The crimson hem of her robe trailed the white line in the dust.

'Don't do it,' he said, 'unless you want a Dayyani to fall first in this war.'

ASTRA

It was Rudo's turn to drive. She buckled up in the back and waited for Photon. And waited.

'What's taking him?' she grumbled.

'Oh, you know, yakking. The old-fashioned kind.' Rudo yawned. 'Tapputu speaks Alpish, or thinks he does. They hold some Neuropean philosophy seminar every time we catch him on his rounds.' Though he sounded unbothered by the delay, a second later he hit the horn, making Astra jump.

'C'mon, Phot!' Rudo groaned. 'There's beer and hoopball waiting back at the fort. Hey' – he turned – 'you gonna play tonight, Astra?'

'Against you guys? You're all giants. Why don't you ask that guy at the door?'

He snorted. 'Him? He's just a YAC terrorist. You're a Gaian. Sec Gen or no, you never say die.'

He had provoked enough reactions from her today. 'Maybe. I'll see how I feel.'

Then Rudo started asking her about sport, and soon she was talking, reluctantly at first, but then with animation, about cricket and archery and marathon-running, all of which he followed in the Neolympics, though his passion was lacrosse, which he called *bagataway*. He'd even tried out for the Mount Reality *bagataway* team but he'd flunked it because he earned too many minutes in the sinbin.

'The sinbin?'

'You know. Ye olde penalty box.' He folded his arms over the back of his seat, and rested his chin on his wrist. 'The way I sees it, Astra, you gotta take a risk or two if you want your balls to score.'

Rudo's breath was scented with aniseed. His big brown eyes were doing a half-melty, half-mocking, all-round-appealing thing. She held his gaze. 'I like to fire when I'm certain of the target,' she replied evenly. 'Then I shoot hard.'

'I reckon you do.' He turned and looked out the windscreen. 'And speak o' the devil.'

Photon had emerged onto the steps of the ward and his shock of white hair was bobbing down through the crowd. She stiffened. *Speak of the devil?* Was Rudo implying—? But Dr Tapputu was standing on the step now, waving a final goodbye. She reached over and waved back as Photon clambered into the front seat.

'*Alles gut*,' he said as Rudo started the engine.

She kept quiet on the way back, watching the roads over Photon's shoulder, clocking milestones and orientation points. All around Cicada the faded, peeling sea of tents and containers slumped and glinted in the afternoon sun. People were hidden inside their meagre dwellings, sheltering from the heat. Some were sleeping or drinking beer, others were meditating, chanting, playing singing bowls, composing YAC manifestos. Astra leaned her head against Cicada's inner panel. She felt exhausted. The day's events were wildly confusing, impossible to hang together in any kind of recognisable shape. In Nagu Two, accused of being a thief from Bracelet Valley, she had said she was a Non-Gaian. Crossing into Nagu One she had, secretly, just for a moment, wished to be a Sec Gen. Then she had seen Peat, changed into a stranger. Later in Nagu Six an old man had recognised her as Somarian. So who was she? Who would she support if a war broke out here? And who would trust her?

They jolted over a crossing. She needed to find Zizi, she realised, not to help her get back to Is-Land, but simply to give her a better idea of where she might conceivably stand in this world of shifting paths underfoot and firestorms on the horizon. She needed to know if her Code father was *on her side*. If Zizi considered her to be a young brood mare for Non-Land, an asset to marry off to one of his ageing friends; if he sat around all day in beer tents, stumbling home to beat his wife, she would stay with CONC. But if her father, after all his time in Is-Land, was like Klor and wanted his daughter to be happy, to be free and strong, a powerful person in this dangerous world; if he was like Dr Tapputu, clever and kind and interested in plants, then maybe, just maybe she could live with him. Yes: maybe she could go and live with her father and the Non-Gaians, far away from disease and arguments and IMBOD.

Photon turned on Comchan. The CONC announcer's voice filled the cabin, though Astra, lost in dreams of building an Earthship in the windsands, paid scant attention. 'In breaking news,' the voice crackled on the periphery of her consciousness, 'thanks to intense diplomatic efforts on the part of Major Thames, Enki Arakkia has been released from N-LA custody. YAC's lawyer is preparing defences for all those arrested that night. Please stay tuned for a statement from Enki Arakkia.'

Astra, wide awake now, sat up. Enki Arakkia was *free*. Where was he? Back at home with his mother, drinking the water she had insisted Photon leave for the woman?

'Possibly he will be speaking in Somarian, Astra,' Photon instructed. 'Normally there is a translation on your Tablette screen.'

'*I* bet he ain't going to be too happy,' Rudo remarked.

She pulled out her Tablette. 'Coming to you live from the Nagu Two Treatment Ward, we bring you Enki Arakkia,' the Comchan announcer reported. Cheers went up in the background. A metallic rattle shook and chattered. Singing bowls transmitted their sinuous sounds. She imagined the YAC rhymer, surrounded by protesters, splitting the air with his star-sign hand gesture. The women in the park would be there, their little boys hopping with excitement in the presence of their hero.

Then Enki was chanting in Inglish, his voice harsh and unwavering, rocking the cabin:

> Here I am, back with YAC
> But I never left ya.
> No prison cell can keep me
> from the heartbeat of my people.
> A heart that's deeply grieving
> for the youth we lost today.
> Yet another boy-child
> shot down in his play-time
> by yet another sniper
> intent on causing mayhem.
> Coz mayhem's what you'll get
> when you mess with YAC.

She put her Tablette aside. Rudo was drumming his fingers along the steering wheel; Photon was nodding his head. But this wasn't a disco; it was a war dance.

> Brace yourselves for thunder:
> the storm-clap of a people
> free of fevered dreams,
> united in a vision
> of One Land beneath the sun.
> Yeah, YAC has been preparing,
> Meditating, sharing,
> And if IMBOD tries to stop us,
> If N-LA acts to block us,
> If CONC wants to 'good cop' us,
> They're in for a surprise.
> We don't respect no wall
> between liberty and justice,
> and we don't accept the *murder*
> of our *children* and our *future*.

Enki's voice rose, became more insistent, angrier. She could almost feel his spit on her cheeks.

> Yeah, we walked your endless talk,
> we dipped your Diplomeeting,
> we showed the whole wide world
> we are a proud and peaceful people.
> But N-LA locked us up.
> CONC looked the other way.
> IMBOD shot a child
> who had not crossed the line –
> and now the time has come
> to meet the Sec Gens at the Hem,
> to show them what we're made of:
> heart and soul and sinew,
> meteorites and muscle.
> Yeah, this is Enki speaking,
> speaking for his people

who say to you: time's up:
the time has come to
YAC ATTACK

'*YAC ATTACK. YAC ATTACK*,' Enki's people shouted with him.
Then the noise of the crowd was cut off.

'That was Enki Arakkia with a new campaign statement from YAC.
Stay tuned for analysis, after the break.'

'Did I win that bet?' Rudo mused.

Photon hushed him. 'I want to hear discussion.'

The weird thrill of the war rhyme was over. Astra sank back in her seat,
her stomach a nest of anxiety. She didn't know if Rudo was right. Maybe
Enki was happy declaring a Hem battle. Maybe, as one of the analysts was
now suggesting, that had been YAC's plan all along. All *she* knew was
that the temperature in Kadingir had shot up today to near boiling point.

'Amma's home! Amma's home!' Tiamet was twirling round the Welcome Tent, holding Ebebu aloft, her lower arms clapping and tingling her bells. She had bells on her anklets now too, a gift, she said, from the Kadingir Singular Simiya mother. She and Lilutu had stayed with Simiya for nearly a week after her release from jail, resting and attending YAC meetings. Now, at last, Lilutu had driven her back to Zabaria.

'Better kiss him quick,' Neperdu advised. 'You've got a backlog of ion clients to attend to, my girl.'

'Yes, madame. Just let me nuzzle my little one.'

Tiamet rubbed her nose in Ebebu's belly. His face wrinkled as if he'd eaten a mouldy grape. 'Oh my little man. He looks like a puglion!' Tiamet cooed. 'Doesn't he, Anunit?'

'He's up so high,' she complained. 'He's not used to it.'

A *puglion*. Tiamet thought she was a Prophecy scholar now. In Kadingir she had visited the CONC compound and snapped a ton of Tablette photos to show off to everyone in Pithar. All the noble creatures parading across Istar's Gate were the honour guard of the Star Girl, she said, the half-Gaian refugee she had seen with her own eyes. The Star Girl was an *Is-Lander*? No one had mentioned that before. And frankly, you could see photos of the compound on Archivia if you wanted. Anunit would have preferred Tiamet to get back home a little earlier.

The last week had been awful: Tiamet arrested and driven away from the Star Party in an N-LA van, right there on the news. All that worry, watching report after report, until at last, on the morning of the second day, she had been released along with Simiya and Asar, the other Kadingir

Singulars. That morning the frozen breast milk Tiamet had left had run out and when Ebebu had woken screaming, Anunit had had to go out to the Zabaria stores, dodging spits and stares, to find a box of CONC baby-milk powder. She had never dreamed of doing such a thing, but there it was. The powder was out of date, grainy, the colour of sick – and utterly horrid. Ebebu had refused it, but she'd added honey and tried again, and at last he had fed, sucking the bottle nipple so hard she'd thought he'd pull it out of her hand. His traumatised eyes had stared up past hers in sheer despair.

But at least Tiamet was free, and surely she would be coming straight back – but no, when the car drove up two hours later, only Lilutu had got out. She'd waltzed into the Welcome Tent, as if Neperdu's rules on visitors meant nothing – as if she was now an honorary sister. And Neperdu *allowed* it. But how could she not, when the YAC girl was triumphant, full of news and gifts and lordly vindication. She had a carved wooden lamb for Ebebu to chew on and an engraved copper ring for Anunit, both sent from Tiamet, along with a big tin of goats'-milk formula, the best on the market, she said. But more than that, she was bearing a grand tale for the women; all the sisters had to hear it. Lilutu had driven straight here to tell it, before the first flesh clients arrived and they all began work.

Work. *What did Lilutu know about work?* Anunit thought bitterly. The girl had hauled rare earths down the mine for a year or two, but now she just floated around, living on CONC rations and children's fantasies. Anunit's work began at noon each day and finished at midnight – and yes, she had long breaks, and she mainly did glove sessions, but that did not make her life easy. Some of the workers thought glove sessions were fun, like pleasuring yourself or acting in a movie, but not Anunit. The things the men said and did and made you say and do were the same as with flesh clients. The way she shut off inside, counted coins in her head, dull copper discs falling through the darkness, slow and heavy as womb blood, was the same. The way the memories lined her skull, thin and rubbery like boiled milk skin, building up month after month, year after year, until there was no room to dream any more, was the same. In an ion glove the men couldn't make you pregnant or ill, that was all.

She just wanted to know when Tiamet would be back. But the others all clamoured to hear Lilutu's story. Ever since the sisters had seen that Tiamet had followers, a palpable excitement had been building in the Welcome Tent. As the report came on the news, the crowd of orphans

gathered outside the Beehive waiting for the Singular's release, Neperdu
had tilted her screendesk up to face the tent. Taletha and Roshanak had
sat in the front row hugging each other. Anunit had been sure the followers were waiting for Simiya. Simiya was a real cult Singular: her parents
had worshipped her since the day she was born and when it turned out
she could sing, her entire Nagu had claimed her – never mind she apparently never deigned to actually speak to anyone with either of her two
perfect mouths. But Simiya and Tiamet had emerged together, holding
hands, a conjoined star-fist to the heavens, and the orphans had swept
around both of them, stroking their robes, ululating and weeping. In the
Welcome Tent, there had been a stunned silence. Taletha's face was radiant, painted mouth agape, kohled eyes shining. Roshanak was shaking.
All around the tent, workers had strained to see, bottoms lifting off cushions, hands clapping to mouths.

'It's true, Neperdu!' Taletha cried. 'She's got a *following*!'

Anunit had expected Neperdu to snap back with a cutting comment
to put Tiamet in her place, but she didn't. 'So she has, Taletha,' was all the
concierge said, her eyes on the screen. 'So she has.'

Tiamet and Simiya, Anunit noticed, hadn't fondled their followers
long before moving quickly to a familiar car. *Lilutu* hadn't been arrested,
had she? She was free as a bird, driving to Zabaria a few days later with her
story of summoning the Star Girl.

'Istar is here,' Lilutu had announced, standing in front of Neperdu as
the sisters lounged on their pillows. 'She was at the Diplomeet. You've
seen her on the news. She was the small CONC officer.'

Anunit recollected her: a short-haired girl being dragged across the
stage by a tall Neuropean. She hadn't looked as though she could save
herself, let alone Non-Land. But the others were interested. This girl
existed. They could picture her. That was something new to chew over.

Neperdu, at least, wasn't so easily hooked. 'CONC is part of the
Prophecy now?' she'd drawled from behind the screendesk.

Lil had held up her hands. 'She's biding her time, establishing alliances.
We didn't want to break her cover. We invited four CONC officers to
the Star Party. If she came, it was a sign she understood we needed her.
She did. I spoke with her, but it was too noisy to have a proper conversa-
tion. We arranged to speak longer in an ion-glove session. Tiamet agrees.
Sisters—'

'Lilutu!' Neperdu barked, 'back up a second. Who exactly is this girl?'

Lilutu drew herself up. 'Istar's earthly name is Astra Ordott. She comes to us from over the Boundary, in the guise of a Non-Gaian CONC officer.'

'You're talking gobbledegook, my girl. The Non-Gaians live in the windsands. They don't work for CONC. And Ordott is an Is-Lander name.'

An Is-Lander. There was a slump in the air, as if a silver ring had been bitten and found to be tin. But nothing fazed Lilutu. She had launched into a twisting, twining story of her childhood in Is-Land, her miraculous escape from an IMBOD jail, the half-Non-Lander girl she'd left behind. There were tunnels and camel cavalcades, and networks of dissidents: the girl's mother had been arrested as a traitor, murdered in jail; her Code father was a returnee, now living with Non-Gaians and High Healers in Shiimti. It was an extraordinary story, and by the end of it Lilutu had recaptured the sisters' attention.

'The Star Girl is not an Is-Lander. She's an *outcast*,' Lilutu declared. 'A refugee under CONC protection, looking for her father. In her heart' – the girl smacked her hand to her chest – 'she's a Singular like you. I could just tell her where her father is, but I want her to meet you – to help you get respect, like I've helped Tiamet. My sisters! Do you want to be part of the One Land revolution? To be free? Or do you want always to be hidden away, excluded, despised by your own people?'

That was nasty, Anunit thought. They didn't come to work to be insulted. There was enough of that outside.

'We're workers,' Roshanak had said stiffly. 'We make good money.'

'Why shouldn't you get respect too?' Lilutu pressed. 'Non-Gaians don't look down on sex workers. If they join YAC, they will help us all get our rights.' Lilutu grasped her YAC amulet and thrust it forward on its long loop of bicycle chain. 'We need unity! Between all the points of the star: YAC, Pithar, Shiimti, N-LA and CONC too. We can do it. Together, we can force IMBOD to open the Boundary.'

Open the Boundary. That would never happen. Anunit had reached for Ebebu, stroked his plush forehead. She had her first glove session at noon. Neperdu would have to look after him then.

She waited for Neperdu to kick this fantasist out where she belonged, in the windsands with the *mergallá-lá*. But Neperdu had assessed Lilutu, her eyes narrowed. 'Why would this girl want to lead us? She just wants to find her father.'

Lilutu shook the star. 'Istar is not a *leader*. She's a *link* between the star points: a catalyst to spark the chain reactions of the revolution. But your energy has to be part of the process. Look what happened to Anunit! Anunit – if you can tell your story to the world, how long do you think CONC will keep supporting IMBOD and IREMCO?'

That was evil of Lilutu. As if she *wanted* to keep quiet! It made no difference who you told, she wanted to shout; the whole world could know what had happened – and they wouldn't care. Look what happened last time the international media had come. Was anything better now? They had just lost their CONC clients, that was all, and without the CONC clients, far worse things had happened in Pithar.

'Leave Anunit out of it,' Neperdu had ordered.

Lilutu had lifted her chin. 'Anunit can decide for herself. You can all decide for yourselves. I need a glove session to speak with Istar.'

Istar. The girl's name was *Astra*.

'Glove time's expensive,' Neperdu said.

Yes, it was: very expensive. Nearly half Anunit's wages went on rental. So was Lilutu planning to pay for her session?

The YAC girl took a battered tin bowl out of her bag. She set it on the rug at her feet, reached into her pocket and brought out a fat, gold-embroidered pouch.

'This is the coin Tiamet's followers pressed into her hands. She is donating it to the glove session.' Lilutu opened the pouch and a cascade of coppers clattered into the bowl. She lifted it above her head. 'If you want to be part of the unfolding of the Prophecy, please contribute also. If there is enough coin in the bowl to pay for the session, I will invite Istar to visit Pithar to meet you. Any coin left over I will give to YAC, to help feed their orphans. If there's not enough for a session, Tiamet will pay Neperdu the remainder from her account, and I will just tell Istar where her father is and she will leave you all alone.'

Anunit wanted to point out that an ion glove would be out of commission for two hours, meaning one of them would lose a session's work. And she didn't see Lilutu putting her hand in her own purse.

'Who's first?' Lilutu offered the bowl to the Compartment.

Taletha stood.

Of course. Taletha had started wearing her hair up and using finger-cymbals with clients. She'd been talking about going to Kadingir to help Tiamet. She made a great show of emptying her purse into the bowl.

Roshanak followed, contributing a fistful of coin. Then Duranki, then everyone. Some sisters gave just one coin, but no one wanted to be left out; even Neperdu contributed – plink, plink, plink; one, two, three coins. When the bowl reached Anunit, she had no choice. She'd reached under her cushion, taken out her purse, and counted out three coins as well . . . No, two: she'd had to pay for the milk powder, hadn't she?

There had been enough for two sessions. Lil had made the appointment, come back to the Welcome Tent to meet with this Is-Lander girl and emerged from Glove Four beaming. Her arms looked better too. *That was convenient, wasn't it?* Anunit had thought meanly, but she'd not said it.

For it was pointless trying to enlist her sisters' support. This Astra had been invited to Pithar and now Tiamet was back and everyone was bubbling with anticipation – well, everyone except Neperdu, who couldn't bubble if her life depended on it. And Anunit. Her back turned to her sisters, she lounged on her cushions and stroked her finger over the little hole in the tent canvas. She could poke her finger right through it and rip an escape hatch . . .

Tiamet plumped herself down behind her, her flank pressed against Anunit's hips. 'There, there, Amma's milk. That's tasty, isn't it?' she cooed.

Anunit withdrew her hand and rested her head on her arm as Ebebu suckled.

'All done. Time for baby's cradle.' With a great show of hushing and clucking, Tiamet tucked Ebebu in. Then she lay down, snuggled closer and rested her chin on Anunit's shoulder. 'Thank you so much, Sister Aunty.'

Tiamet's hair smelled of coconut: some shampoo she'd bought in Kadingir and was sharing with Taletha. Despite herself, Anunit felt something give in her chest. Tiamet was young; soon she would be ground down, bitter as coffee dregs, like her and Neperdu. How could she begrudge the girl this short season of happiness, resent the brief flurry of excitement and hope she was scattering like wind-blown pollen into their lives?

'You're welcome,' she muttered. 'But he missed your milk.'

Tiamet draped three arms around her. 'I want you to meet Istar when she comes,' she whispered. 'I want you to tell her your story. I want you to get justice, Anunit.'

Anunit stared at the hole. Through it she could see light, and more canvas, the neighbouring tent where the young boys plied their trade. 'Have you heard from his father?' she asked.

'He was posted back to Atourne last month,' Tiamet whispered, gripping Anunit's shoulder, waist and hip. 'Ebebu is safe, Anunit. I am telling you, he's safe.'

Tiamet's chin was digging into her shoulder, her breasts pillowed against her back. She tugged at her robe, pulling it tighter around her. Tiamet thought safety was a place, somewhere real and warmly lit, like a tent that sheltered you from storms. But safety was not that. Safety was empty and still and dark like a night desert without wind. Safety was not knowing or caring where you were going, or who was coming with you.

ASTRA

When the call came she was playing hoopball, tearing up and down the court with a bunch of agronomists and water techies, battling it out against Rudo's crew, panting, sweating and laughing until she got a stitch when the ball came bouncing back in to a player's face. The courtyard paving stones made the game more of a challenge, Rudo said. Though he still needled her sometimes, she was glad she'd taken up his invitation to play. Since YAC's statement ten days ago the mood in the compound had become strained. The Major had raised the Alert Level again and recreational visits into Kadingir were banned. Tempers flared, and people had formed little cliques in the dining hall, watching the news with those who agreed with their own analysis. Though so far the Sec Gens had stayed within the Barracks, most people seemed to think YAC were provoking IMBOD to further violence, should step back and let N-LA deal with the sniper incident. There were demonstrations all over Kadingir, and the cladding operation would surely begin any day. It was good to be able to release the tension on the court.

She was covering Rudo as he ducked and swivelled between her and a tall water specialist. His back foot planted squarely on a paving stone, Rudo's lithe frame twisted in and out of reach, until somehow his arms shot out from his chest to send the ball flying over to Honovi.

Honovi, big surprise, scored: a long, perfect arc from centre court, the ball plummeting straight into the basket.

'Three pointeroonies!' Rudo whooped.

'Dream team!' The blonde giantess smacked his palm, her ponytail swinging like a victory pennant.

Hands on hips, breathing hard, Astra checked the game clock. Twenty seconds to go and it read 'Spanners 106 – Wingnuts 108'. If only she were better at hoopball. She could score from a free throw seven times out of ten – not bad – but Rudo had been humouring her in Cicada: she was too short to be a star player. Still, her team liked her. Feeling fitter every day, she zipped up and down the court, making herself a nuisance, blocking the odd pass with a killer vertical leap or, more often, darting under elbows to steal a low ball. She had fans too: cheers would rise up from the beer tables at her better moves, and the other day people had whooped at her new haircut – Rudo had insisted on treating her to a visit to his barber, a tattooed water techie with an impressive set of razors and scissors, and though she'd refused a patterned temple, her curls had shape now, trimmed at the sides but still covering her scar at the nape. Ignoring the applause, she'd dribble as far as she could, head up, clenching her arm bar, until someone grabbed the ball off her or she managed a pass. There was always a forest of bodies in the way.

Play started again. The ball was flying between her teammates, a full frontal assault. Running to check Rudo she caught sight of Photon at the edge of the court. He waved, a cartoon grin animating his face, and sat down at a table on his own. With his height he should be playing, on *her* team, but he'd just laughed when she'd urged him to join them.

'Hoopball is making me dizzy. All that spinning and leaping. And Rudo throwing a big hard pumpkin at my teeth. No, I will stick to Tai Chi, thanks, Astra.'

Dix, her team captain, had the ball. He was jumping from behind the three-point arc. The ball left his hands. He was still in the air.

Wheeeeeeeet. The game clock whistled. Dix hit the floor. The ball was flying towards the net. It would count. *It would count.* Astra held her breath. The silence in the courtyard was a wave rushing over her ears.

The ball smacked against the backboard and shot back into the court.

'Yessss!' Rudo leapt into Honovi's arms, who staggered backward, then burst into laughter as he dropped back to the flagstones and the rest of the Wingnuts swarmed their star players.

At least the Spanners had learned that Astra wasn't into group hugs. Dix patted her shoulder and grinned ruefully. 'Well played. We'll get 'em next time.' Then her team high-fived the Wingnuts and dispersed, some heading for the showers before dinner, some straight to the bar for a beer.

She slapped Rudo's palm.

'Mighty mosquito!' he teased.

'Ha ha.' She searched in vain for a comeback.

Behind him, Honovi was steadily bouncing the ball. 'Hey, Astra? Wanna warm down with a dribble drill?' she called.

She'd never get better if she didn't practise, but over Rudo's shoulder Photon was craning at her, jerking his head.

'Next time, thanks, Honovi,' she called, heading off court. 'Hi, Phot. What's up?'

Her equerry was still cracking an enormous grin. 'Good news is up. I have exchanged our Bluday shift with Msandi and Eduardo. We are going to Pithar! With a visit to Uttu too, on the way.'

Bluday? Bluday was – *perfect*. And Uttu would be so pleased: Astra had visited the laundry room the other day and the elderwoman had repeated her invitation to meet her grandson, not prepared to accept the new Alert Level as an excuse.

'Hey, that's great.' She sat down. Over Photon's shoulder, Rudo was dribbling the ball through his legs, back and forth in a figure of eight, Honovi laughing as she lunged to get it off him, missing each time.

'Rudo too?' she asked, frowning.

'*Ja*. But do not worry.' Photon lowered his voice. 'He will not know about Lil.'

That wasn't good enough. 'When we find her, you have to make sure Rudo doesn't hear me talk to her? Okay?'

'I will do my best. But, Astra,' Photon's grin twisted into a warning. 'We do not know that we will find her or, if we do, under what circumstances. She might not have too much time.'

'She told me to come.' Astra stood up. She was sticky. She needed to wash. 'Thanks for arranging it, Phot,' she said as Honovi grabbed the low crotch of Rudo's shorts and tugged, only letting go as the waistband slid down towards his hips and Rudo shouted, 'Foul!'

Bluday was prayer day for many of Kadingir's residents, and some CONC shifts started later to accommodate the morning off, so they left the compound near noon. She was driving. Photon sat in the back and Rudo was beside her, his boot up on the dashboard. Kadingir was quiet, the roads nearly empty.

'Why we driving long-haul midday, Phot?' Rudo complained. 'Ciccy will be shake and bake out there.'

'Uttu has invited us for lunch. It is our only visit to this Nagu.'

'Couldn't we have asked to have breakfast instead?' he whined.

'It was an invitation for lunch,' Photon repeated.

The road was badly rutted and Astra changed gear, slowing down for a cement crossing as high as a step.

'If Astra would drive faster than a tortoise on morpheus, we might get a breeze at least.'

What was up with Rudo today? 'We'd drive faster with a lighter load,' she warned. 'I can stop right here if you like.'

'Yeah, yeah.'

'Please relax, Rudo. We'll be back in time for your game.' It was rare for Photon to lose his patience with Rudo. The three of them fell silent as she drove on, carefully. She wanted to get back in time to play hoopball tonight too, but she wasn't going to speed just because Rudo was in a bad mood.

Ahead was the hospital, a squat grey three-storey building with rows of small black windows and a flat roof. She had been there a few times now, bringing patients from the Treatment Wards. There was something magical in the way patients were transported in Ciccy, not strapped onto the stretcher but suspended in the ion glove in the back chamber, protected from the bumps in the road while receiving the healing benefits of the ions. But the spell was broken at the hospital, when gravity reasserted itself and the patient was unloaded at a building that looked like a jail . . . a sick jail. The sheer cement walls of the hospital were tired and crumbling, scarred with age and neglect. She was driving around the back now, a route she hadn't yet taken. This wall was peppered with deep round gouge-marks. 'Are those *bullet holes*?' she asked.

'*Ja*.' Photon was peering out the window too. 'From the last big Kadingir battle.'

That was *decades* ago. 'And no one's filled them in yet?' This place defeated her. How much would a bit of clay and paint cost?

'It is discussed every year, but the doctors would rather CONC budgeted for another hospital. They must fix the holes in the people first.'

'Oh I dunno,' Rudo chipped in. 'The Nonners like their scars. Always good to stand around weeping over a few bullet wounds when the journos show up.'

'You are being rather more irritation than normally, Rudo,' Photon remarked placidly. 'Did Honovi have other plans last night, then?'

'Whoah!' Rudo choked. 'Not in front of the Gaian minor, Phot.'

Astra didn't want to know what designs Rudo had on Honovi, she didn't want to ask why IMBOD had fired at the hospital, and she didn't want to think about the cladding operation. She trundled on down the long road between Nagu Three and Four, heading towards the northeast outskirts of Kadingir. When the road rose, the Boundary was occasionally visible on the left, but she concentrated on the dwellings, mostly tents and shacks, some with gardens and the odd chicken coop. She readied herself to brake in case a bird escaped, but the journey was uneventful. Beside her, Rudo had stuck his elbow out of his open window and was resting his head in his hand, eyes closed. The dwellings on the right side of the road became more and more infrequent until eventually the eastern vista was mainly scrubland. The low, sparsely grassed hills stretched out as far as she could see.

'Nearly there, I think.' Tablette in hand, Photon leaned over the front seat. '*Ja*. Pull up by the tree, Astra.'

Astra parked. In the near distance was a long mud hut with a solar-panel unit and a blue rain barrel on its flat roof. Beside the dwelling there was a sheep pen. She grimaced: did Uttu own slave beasts? She turned her attention back to the tree. Apart from the date palms and the rookery in the oak trees along the river, she hadn't seen many trees in Non-Land. This one was more like a bush: fat and thorny, small dusty leaves and what looked like faded tags adorning its tangle of branches.

Rudo yawned. 'Lunchtime?'

'This is Uttu's place, yes.' Photon was putting on his hat. Well, it was more than three steps to the house. 'She said to meet at the Nagu Three wishing tree. Traditionally, people leaving the city tie a ribbon to a branch and make a wish for their journey. Do you want to wrap a scrap around it, Astra? You could use a bandage from the First-Aid kit.'

The tags were grimy, bedraggled bits of wool or ribbon. The tree itself was grey and cracked. It needed water, not fabric shackles.

'No,' she replied.

Rudo stretched, thrusting one arm out the window and the other nearly in Astra's face. He wiggled his fingers. Then he clasped his hands behind his head and rested his right boot on his left knee. 'I'm always trippin' over these damn bootlaces. And you're right, Phot. I could use a little luck in the old Honovi *departmento*. Chuck us that kit.'

Photon obliged. Rudo retrieved the small bandage scissors, and snipped off a length of his black bootlace. Astra had never seen them come undone, or Rudo trip over anything, but he was right, they were plenty long enough to spare a segment.

'That gaffer tape still in the back?'

Photon got up again and rooted around.

'Catch.'

The roll of black tape dropped neatly into Rudo's hand. Astra watched as he nimbly cut off two slivers of tape and twisted them round the shorn ends of the lace. When he'd re-knotted the lace around the top of his boot, he admired his new wishing string, comparing the improvised tip to the original sheath.

'In Inglish, "aglets",' he announced. 'What you call 'em in Gaian, Astra?'

'"Lace-tips".' She said the word in Gaian, and then translated it. Gaian was full of compound words that made the language easy to learn – Gaians came to Is-Land from all over the world so it was important for them to be able to communicate in a common tongue.

'"Lace-tip". Sexy. Simple. Inglish always gotta be complicated. Who knows what "aglet" frigging means – a small ag? The creative outlet of Aunt Agatha?'

'The word comes from a Dead Tongue; it means "needle",' Photon contributed.

'Who needs a Tablette when you got Phot around?' Rudo was being annoyingly cheerful now. He offered the scissors to Astra. She waved them away.

'Sure? Thought you Gaians were always making wishes on trees. Might help the Spanners get that extra hoop tonight?'

Rudo knew *nothing* about asking Gaia for assistance. People should take care of Gaia's creatures, not demand favours from them. She was about to tell him to go shove his aglet through a rusted wingnut when Photon piped up: 'Hey, there is Uttu.'

He was right. The tiny woman was flying out of the mud dwelling, both arms waving as if powered by an overcharged kinbattery pack. Time to get away from Rudo. Astra opened her door and dropped to the ground. She was glad of her sunglasses. The tree was taller than she was, but it cast little shade. The sun was high in the sky and the air smelled of baked earth and some kind of herb. Mountain mint? She looked around. Yes, the plant was growing wild along the verge, with bits of rubbish – hemp bags, an old shoe – caught in its stems. But there was no time to pick up litter for Uttu was upon her.

'Astra. Astra. You are here. Welcome. Welcome to my home.' Uttu seized her hands and Astra bent to kiss her friend's autumnal cheeks.

'*Gúñarña tuš-ukkin-na*, Uttu.' Her Somarian pronunciation was getting better.

Uttu clapped. 'Very good. Very good.' Her friend was wearing a special robe, made of white gauzy material with silver embroidery, the thread worn in places, but the flowery pattern still complex and detailed. She reached into a pocket and pressed something into Astra's hand. It was a short length of red ribbon, bordered with gold cross-stitches.

'For you,' she declared. 'My guest. For wish tree.'

Beside her, Rudo snickered. There was no way out. Uttu grasped her wrist and stepped with her to the tree. The elderwoman's watery hazel eyes were trained on her, worse than a pair of IMBOD gun barrels. Frig Rudo.

'Thank you, Uttu,' she said.

The elderwoman placed a gnarled finger on a branch. Her yellow nail was as ridged and fissured as the bark.

'Here,' she commanded in Inglish, gripping Astra's wrist so hard it nearly hurt. 'Next my ribbon. My ribbon for YOU.'

There was a new ribbon tied around the branch tip: a gold one, with red stitches.

'You made a wish for me?' Suddenly she really wasn't sure about this.

Uttu released her wrist and patted it, replying joyously in Somarian, too quickly for Astra to catch the meaning.

'She tied it there when we accepted her invitation,' Photon translated. 'It's a wish for you, but she can't tell you what it is. Wishing tree wishes are secret. Don't tell anyone, even if it comes true.'

'Damn.' Rudo twirled his bootlace around a finger. 'I already told you guys mine.'

'Make another one, then,' Astra ordered. 'You've got no chance with Honovi anyway.'

'Oo-ooh.' Rudo flashed her a grin. 'A little spanner in the works, is there?'

The wingnut was doing it again, using an idiom she wasn't quite sure of, but his tone clearly indicated he'd just deftly turned her own attack against her. She was sputtering for a retort when Uttu slapped the driver's hand. '*Shhh*. Astra wish.'

She stroked the ribbon. The fabric was faded, but the edges were neatly hemmed and the cross-stitches evenly patterned. Uttu had put care and attention into the sewing.

'Can we give the tree some water?' she asked Photon.

He was puzzled. 'Is that your wish?'

'No, but it needs water. Not now, in the evening. We can leave some with Uttu, can't we?'

'We've got a barrel for her family anyway.'

'But they'll need that to drink. Can we leave her extra, for the tree?'

Photon looked at Rudo. His driving partner shrugged. 'Sure. Just don't go tying any condoms round the old oak tree, Astra. I ain't answering to the Major if you do.'

'Oh, shut up, Rudo.'

She moved away, round to the other side of the bush. *I'm sorry, tree*, she told it. *I know you're not a work beast. But this is the way they do things here. I wish for you, tree, that you keep growing, stay alive.*

Through the prickly branches, his tongue tip sticking out of his mouth, Rudo was tying his bootlace around a twig, fixing it in a small droopy bow. Chattering loudly, Uttu was pulling a loose silver thread from her robe and giving it to Photon.

She stepped back round to the branch with Uttu's ribbon. *I wish to find my father soon . . .* Then as she tied the red ribbon around the branch the words whistled through her head in a fierce rush . . . *and that he won't want to marry me off to some old man – to anyone. That he will help me find my own way.*

Beside her Uttu cackled, the tiny elderwoman put her arms around Astra and squeezed her hips. 'You wish what I wish,' she whispered. Then she took Astra's hand and tugged her towards the mud dwelling, Photon and Rudo following behind.

Clustered around the doorway was a small group of people: two men, two women, two girls and a boy. The children's skins were smooth, and if they were using prosthetics the limbs were exceptionally well made. The two smallest were wriggling between the women's long skirts; the eldest girl was standing straight, her hand in her father's. The men were wearing

smocks and brown trousers with baggy gussets that hung down nearly to
their knees. The loose clothing couldn't hide the fact that the adults were
as bone-thin as Uttu; but though neither man was tall, their bushy black
moustaches and strong noses made Rudo and Photon look like over-
grown schoolboys. The women were in full finery, their arms laden with
gold bracelets, their gauzy robes, like Uttu's, surely not for everyday work:
one midnight-blue, the other emerald-green, and both intricately patterned with gold-embroidered flowers.

'Astra meet *my* family,' Uttu crowed, still showing off her Inglish. 'My
one son, Kingu, wife Habat. My two son Gibil, wife Nanshe. Children
Geshti, Hadis, Suen.'

She pushed her sunglasses back on her head. 'Hello, I am pleased to
meet you,' she said in Somarian. The adults' sun-beaten faces signalled
pleasure at her effort.

'Astra. I want you meet my *special* grandson.'

She held out her hand to the little boy. Uttu swatted her wrist away.
'No. No Suen. *Damuzi.*'

Kingu and Habat stepped apart and from the dim entrance to the
dwelling Habat pushed forward a youth with thick black hair and start-
ling blue eyes, like sparks of sky dancing in the earthen slopes of his face.
Like his family, the youth was thin, but his features weren't pinched by
hunger: his fine nose and jaw had been elegantly moulded by Gaia Herself, and his embroidered ivory smock exposed a planed chest and a
work-taut right forearm. His left arm was thinner and ended in a flat
wedge at the wrist. Uttu grabbed his other elbow and shook it.

'We call Muzi. Muzi *very happy* to meet you.'

'Hello, Astra.' The youth's eyes were dazzling, laughing at his grandmother, but his smile, like his one word of Inglish, was slow, shy, serene.
His cheeks were smooth, but his upper lip sported a slight black fuzz.

'I'm happy to meet you too, Muzi,' she said in Somarian. The whole
introduction was peculiar: strangely formal and ceremonious. At the
same time, it was like a mirage: there was an impossibility about the boy's
beauty that made her think he would next be springing past her like a
gazelle, leaping over the sheep-pen walls and bounding out into the scrub.

But he didn't. He just scratched his ear with his short arm, tilted his
head and squinted up at the sun, then at Astra, as if to say, *Don't worry. I
don't know what she's so worked up about either*.

Everyone else was laughing, Rudo and Photon too. Habat stepped forward; pulling at Astra's arm, she led her into the dark interior of the dwelling. 'Come, eat. No worry,' Muzi's mother urged. 'You no have marry my son today.'

'She no have to marry him any day!' Kingu boomed as the family closed in behind her. 'Only meet. Okay Astra. Only meet.'

The entrance opened into a long room lined with mats and cushions. The rough walls were washed in lavender paint, light spilled in through a row of high windows, and a Tablette was recharging from a socket in the corner. The family took off their outer footwear and Uttu set a pair of slippers at Astra's feet.

She wanted to run back to Ciccy, far away from this trap, but she couldn't do that. She cast a pleading look at Photon, but he was joking with Kingu, who was scissoring his fingers, threatening to cut the brim off his hat. She took a deep breath. She was with CONC. This was just a lunch break. She wasn't going to have to marry *anyone*. She just had to be nice to her friend Uttu, be polite to an elderwoman for an hour.

She tugged off her boots, stuck her sunglasses in the left one and stepped into the slippers. Uttu thrust out an apron: floor length, gathered at the waist and beautifully embroidered with lemons and limes, it was more like a fancy skirt than anything you would wear to cook in. Beside her, Rudo and Photon were tying on shorter ones, square red panels, each boasting a big red embroidered rooster. Photon giggled.

'Tablette photo. I want!' Rudo told Nanshe, who giggled too as she tied his strings.

'Photo later,' Uttu ordered. 'Now for sit.' Astra let Uttu fix her bow and direct her to a cushion, the elderwoman outdoing Major Thames with finger-jabs as she ordered everyone into place. The men sat crosslegged beneath the windows, the women along the opposite wall. Astra was trapped between Habat and Uttu, with Muzi right across from her, between Kingu and Gibil. To Kingu's right Photon and Rudo were settling back into their cushions, exchanging greetings with the menfolk and waving at the shy little girls. Gibil's wife, Nanshe, unrolled a long white cloth down the centre of the room, and disappeared through a far door. A strong sweetish smell drifted in, rich and garlicky and a little sickening.

'Long cloths.' Uttu tugged at Astra's apron. 'Sit man floor, sit woman floor. Good.'

Oh. Loose clothes: yards of fabric. Male walls and female walls. Such elaborate measures to control Gaia's power. In Is-Land if you had a picnic you sat how you liked, next to whomever you liked. You laid napkins on your laps to catch crumbs and drops of sauce, and while the men might tuck their Gaia ploughs between their legs to protect them from bouncing children, and the women's Gaia bushes hid their private gardens, if you did want to sit crosslegged or a man became erect, no one stared. If you felt aroused you just enjoyed the sensation quietly, knowing everyone else felt good too and sooner or later you would feel even better with someone you liked very much.

Even if they had shared a language, she couldn't explain all that to Uttu. She sat politely as Nanshe re-entered, bearing a tray laden with dishes, cutlery, a jug of water and cups. She set it down on the cloth and began passing out plates. Astra took one. It was made of tin, battered and scratched. The family were not rich, not at all, but the aprons were colourful and skillfully stitched and the children happy and healthy, and apart from Muzi, no one seemed to have been affected by Non-Land's poison. Is that why they wanted an Is-Land bride for him, to better his children's Code chances?

Just as she was thinking this mean thought Muzi picked up a spoon and held it out to her, upright between finger and thumb, like a silver flower.

'Ah!' Uttu and Habat clapped. By the door, Rudo joined in.

'*Gúañarña*,' she growled, taking the spoon.

It wasn't Muzi's fault Uttu had decided to marry her off to him. Still, she was careful not to touch his fingers or give him any other false indication that she was somehow consenting to perform in this outrageous piece of theatre.

'You. Are. Well. Come.' Again, though he pronounced the Inglish as if it were a sly joke, his amused face was fresh as a girl's. Gibil, though, had a face like a dried date. As the other adults applauded Muzi's star turn, Muzi's uncle made some complaint to Nanshe. His wife dropped a fork in his dish and let it clatter as she turned back into the kitchen.

His bright blue eyes still on Astra, Muzi lifted his eyebrows, his mouth on the brink of a smile.

'Well come,' Uttu repeated proudly. 'Astra well *come* to my house. Astra very hard work,' she told the others in Asfarian. 'Very good look girl too.'

'Hair short like Uttu!' Kingu joked. They seemed to have decided on Asfarian as the language of the occasion, which was just as well, as she was running out of Somarian. 'Is why you think good look!'

'Hair grow,' the matriarch countered. 'And Astra *well*! No poison!'

'No poison. No poison,' the adults concurred, apart from Gibil who was reaching for a plate of flatbread. Scowling, he took a wheaten disc in his knuckly hand and tore it in half.

'Muzi not poison,' Uttu announced. 'Muzi accident: baby accident. My family, no Code poison.' She spread her arms wide.

It was true. The family's skins were puckered only by the sun, their backs straight, and apart from Muzi's missing hand, their limbs were intact.

'Strong Code,' Photon said.

Kingu chuckled. 'Code, so-so. No work Zabaria, good.'

'Sheep work,' Gibil grunted, 'scrap work. No money, no good. No poison, very good.'

'Code *very* good!' Uttu exclaimed, defending her contribution to the family fortune. 'Laundry work. Money good.'

'Yes, okay,' Kingu humoured her. 'CONC money good.' They were the joint heads of staff, Astra understood: eldermother and first son. Gibil, hunched over his piece of bread, crumbs in his moustache, was just a bitter shadow of his brother.

'So, Kingu. Do you think that the health problems in the region are caused only by—?' Photon was at least trying to keep the conversation on politics. But Uttu reached into her robe and, pulling out a purse on a neck-string, interrupted him.

'Money for Muzi,' she cackled, the purse clanking in her hand. 'For Muzi wedding Astra.'

Frigging Gaia! Not back to that again. The room was in uproar once more, Rudo holding his side as he laughed along with everyone except her, Photon and Gibil. And Muzi. Her unwanted betrothed picked up the plate of flatbreads and offered it to her across the white cloth.

She was hungry, and the sooner she ate, the sooner she could leave. The breads were stacked like pancakes. She took the top one. It was warm and flecked with shiny seeds, and it smelled of toasted sesame. She set the bread on her plate, tore off a little piece and popped it in her mouth. Sesame, yes. Beneath her lashes, she flicked a look at Muzi.

He was regarding her solemnly. Unsmiling, he slowly crossed his blue eyes.

She nearly spat the bread out onto her plate.

'She *Gaian*,' Gibil roared, so no one except Muzi heard her choke with laughter.

'Yes. She *Gaian*.' Uttu shook her fist at her second son. '*She* Is-Land. *We* Is-Land. *All* Is-Land. Together. One Land. Muzi go live Is-Land. *My* home. Muzi live *my* home.'

'Man no live woman home,' Gibil flared. 'Woman live *man* home. Gaian wife *crazy* plan.'

Then Kingu and Habat piled in, and down the row the little girls started squealing. The adults abandoned Asfarian as they argued, but it was clear that everyone was against Gibil, who was the only one on her side, except for the fact that he hated her. It was unbearable. Rudo was brimming over with silent laughter, Photon was sending her exaggerated sympathy, and Muzi . . . hooking his short arm in the handle, Muzi pulled the jug of water towards him. He picked it up, poured a tin cup full and with a graceful flourish, offered her a drink. His sky-blue eyes were laughing again, but not at her.

She took the cup. Nanshe returned with the tray, bearing a large stew pot and a salad bowl. The steam rising from the tureen carried wafts of that rich, sweetish, brothy aroma.

'Eat time.' Uttu clapped and the room fell quiet.

Treading along the edge of the meal cloth, Nanshe placed the tray in front of Astra. Then she arranged herself next to Habat, smoothing her midnight-blue robe and gesturing to Muzi for the water jug.

Astra's stomach turned.

The stew was greasy and lumpy. It wasn't made of lentils; it had chunks of meat in it – not alt-meat, but *slaughtered animal*. There were bones sticking out of the cooked flesh, cross-sectioned, as if sawed through the joint, and she thought the meat near the bone might be smeared with traces of blood.

Her nerves were crawling, her body an anthill of horror. They had *killed an animal* to celebrate *capturing* her; they were treating her like she was an animal herself, a cow or a dog, with no voice, no rights, no life of her own. The whole thing was revolting. What were they thinking? They were deprived, depraved, unevolved Non-Land peasants and she was a CONC officer. She just had to stand up and leave, trample all over Nanshe's white cloth, stamp on Gibil's plate, kick over Kingu's cup, pick up her boots and stalk out the door, tearing off this smothering apron as she went. Photon and Rudo would follow, they would get back in Ciccy and drive far away and never come back.

But she couldn't do that. She wasn't a slave at auction; she was their special guest. They were trying to impress her. And she couldn't hurt Uttu – but she couldn't eat this stew either.

'I'm not *Gaian*,' she announced, 'I'm *Non*-Gaian. But I don't *eat animals*.'

Gibil grunted softly.

'*No.*' Uttu gripped her knee and shook it. 'No meat Astra. Astra *salad*. Good salad.' The elderwoman jangled her money purse again. 'CONC salad. Chickpea. A-breecot. Pum-*kin* seed. And Muzi salad. Wild salad. Muzi pick Astra.'

Uttu pulled the salad bowl towards them. Habat gestured at Kingu, who moved the stew away. The salad bowl was full of wild greens, seeds and pulses and dried fruit, all glistening in a light dressing. With the bread, it would be a very good meal.

'*Gúañarña.*' Astra let Uttu pile her plate high. But she had to stop this whole charade, now. 'I don't eat meat and I can't marry *anyone*,' she said loudly. 'Photon, tell them: I'm Gaian and I can't bond with anyone until I'm *twenty*. I'm eighteen today, so that's not for two more years.'

'It's your birthday?' Photon was holding out his bowl for Kingu's ladle. 'You did not say.'

'You didn't ask. Please tell them Muzi is very nice but if he's over twenty then I can't even Gaia-play with him. When I'm twenty I can form a Gaia bond, but in Is-Land we don't get married until much later. And tell Uttu that I'm not allowed to go back to Is-Land – even if I did get married to Muzi, I can't take him there.'

Uttu was listening intently.

'Astra birthday?'

Photon translated. The Non-Lander adults murmured and nodded. Gibil took the stew pot and ladled a bowlful for Suen, then he dolloped himself a big helping of meat, clacking the ladle against the rim of the pot.

Habat stroked her knee. 'You no worry Astra. Happy birthday.'

'Astra birthday salad,' Uttu declared.

Muzi stood up. She stared miserably at the shins of his woven trousers. She had offended him now – but it wasn't her fault. She couldn't be expected to roll over and marry someone just because Uttu thought a Gaian passport would be an asset to her family.

Muzi reached along the windowsill, picked up a small wooden box and sat back down. He placed the box on the white cloth. It had been carved by an expert Craft worker, the grooved surfaces alive with intertwining tendrils and trumpet blossoms. Muzi removed the lid. Inside was a clutch of beeswax candles.

'Astra birthday,' he said.

Uttu wagged her finger at her grandson. 'Gaians no honeybee.'

The golden aroma overwhelmed her with longing and brought the tears welling to her eyes, dissolving her indignation.

'No,' she mumbled, 'is okay. Beeswax okay. Just no eat bees.'

The adults laughed. Muzi took out a candle and placed it upright on the empty tray. The golden-brown wax was rolled from a sheet, like a scroll of handmade paper – *Hokma's* handmade paper – and the outer surface was impressed with little hexagons, patterned in homage to the honeycomb cells formed by the hundreds and thousands of worker bees who had secreted this wondrous substance. But at a cost: in order to keep producing the wax cells in which to store their pollen and honey and shelter their babies, worker bees needed to consume most of their own produce, and they also gradually wore out, their mirror glands atrophying a little more each day. In the Old World, bees had been housed in industrial hives, transported in the backs of trucks that disturbed the bees' sense of direction; the honey they made was regularly stolen from them and replaced with sugar syrup, tricking them into working until they were exhausted, then died prematurely. People had *enslaved* bees, just to feed their sweet tooth, and the near extinction of bees in the wild had been one of the major causes of the Dark Time.

But some humans, she knew, had tried to take care of bees. Some people never harvested their hives. Others, like the Or beekeepers, only took honey that the bees didn't need. It was true that the bees didn't volunteer their gifts: the hives were cool-smoked while the beekeeper removed the cells, but the smoke calmed the bees and unless they swarmed, they had a home for life. It was thanks to the bees' industry that the kitchen staff baked honey-cake for the Or-kids on birthdays. And on *special* birthdays – your seventh, thirteenth and eighteenth – a beeswax candle was lit.

Tucked in with the candles was a small blue cardboard envelope. Muzi took it out and flipped it open. Inside was a comb of cardboard matches, their little red heads lined up like Shelter siblings packed into a bed. Gaians normally used tinderboxes but, like beekeeping, under certain circumstances matches could be allowed. It depended if the wood was sourced sustainably. She'd never seen cardboard matches before. With his thumb, Muzi bent one back and deftly flicked the head against the sandpaper strip on the other side of the envelope. The match flared. He lit the candle, blew out the match, tucked the burnt head back next to its virgin bedmates, and put the matchbook back in the box. Then he picked up the candle and tilted it, letting molten wax drip onto the tray. When enough had pooled, he pressed the bottom of the candle into the seal.

Gaia was in the room, Her perfume of warm honey stealing into the air. Astra closed her eyes and silently thanked the bees who had worked so hard to secrete the candlewax being burned for her today. For her birthday.

She opened her eyes. 'Thank you, Muzi.'

He replaced the lid on the carved box. 'Astra eighteen,' he said in a tone of great satisfaction. 'Muzi *nine*teen.'

'Eat.' Uttu clapped. And eat they did, Astra polishing off her salad, then taking a second helping as the rest of the banqueters dipped their bread into the stew. Focusing on the scent of the candle, she tried not to watch them eat, not to listen to Photon and Rudo congratulating the family on the tenderness of the lamb, which they had slaughtered the day before in honour of their guests.

At last the meal was done. As the children chattered and Habat taught Astra the Somarian words for the flowers on her robe, Nanshe tidied up the plates and returned from the kitchen with a wooden tray full of clay cups of camomile tea. The engraved tray remained in the centre of the cloth, the golden candle burning steadily.

'Uttu?' Astra set her teacup back down. 'Where did you live in Is-Land?'

'Me, no,' Uttu said, 'my Amma and Ibu. In Is-Land, no. *Somaristan*.' Uttu drew a circle on the cloth with her finger, then traversed it with a wandering line. 'Shugurra River.' She jabbed the cloth. 'White Desert.' Then again: 'Steppes. Hill city. Kurgal. My city.'

Astra frowned at the tablecloth. 'You mean Hilton?'

'Hilton Is-Land name. My house *Kurgal*.'

Kingu gestured to the girls and the eldest unplugged the Tablette from its recharge socket and passed it over to her father.

'Our house,' he said, his fingers whizzing over the screen. 'Here, my great-grandparents. Here, bank paper.'

Photon and Rudo were leaning over, inspecting the files as Kingu opened them. At last Kingu handed his mother the Tablette and Uttu placed it down in front of the tray so the little girls crowding close could see too.

The photos were colourful. There was a tall white stone house on a green hillside, with a roof terrace and a verandah covered in magenta bougainvillea growing from royal blue pots. In the next frame, standing on the verandah, above a vista of roofs descending down to the steppes, a young man and woman smiled shyly into the camera. The woman was holding a baby snuggled into a creamy yellow cloth.

'My Amma!' Uttu crowed, pointing at the baby. The little girls burst into giggles. Astra remained silent.

'You visit Kurgal?' Habat asked eagerly. 'You know Uttu house?'

She shook her head. She'd never been to Hilton, but she recognised the buildings and the aspect from other photos. Hilton was 'the moonstone in the crown of the steppes'. City Gaians had flocked there and started craft galleries and restaurants and hymn choirs. They'd named the retrofitted town after a famous Old World luxury hotel, because they'd said that all were guests in Gaia's opulence. There were lots of visitor-friendly communities in Hilton, where people went and stayed for short holidays, helping with local activities in the morning, and in the afternoons and evenings wandering through the town's winding lanes and up its steep stone stairways, taking tea in its rooftop cafés and relaxing in its domed thermal baths. Klor had taken Nimma there for her sixtieth birthday.

Kingu was showing her the legal papers. She should ask how and when Uttu's grandparents had left Kurgal, but the back of her skull was beginning to burn. The pills were in her combat pocket, but she didn't want to dig around for them under the apron or take her medication in front of people. She also didn't want to hear the story: it was about something that had happened in the past, that couldn't be changed now. Only the future could be changed and she was on her way to do that. It wouldn't be long now; Rudo was in a hurry and they would soon be back in Ciccy and on the road to meet Lil. She just had to be polite for a little longer.

'I've seen photos of Hilton,' she said. 'I was born here.' She pointed to a breadcrumb. 'In the dry forest.'

'Dry forest no Somaristan,' Uttu told her. 'Farashanland.'

Gibil snorted and reached for his cup. 'Dry forest *Is-Land*,' he reminded his mother.

'Today Is-Land,' Uttu countered. 'Tomorrow One Land.'

Muzi pressed his short arm to his chest. He smiled again at Astra. 'My heart, One Land.'

Gibil drained his cup. His eyes were black sparks. 'Gaians no heart. No One Land,' he retorted.

Anger overtook her. She was sick and tired of people thinking they knew who she was, judging her, patronising her. She was eighteen today. She didn't have to obey the Major's stupid rules any more.

'*IMBOD* has no heart,' she blurted. 'Lots of Gaians have *big* hearts. And anyway, I'm a *Non-Gaian*. My Code father is a Non-Lander. Tell them, Photon: his name is Zizi Kataru. He was an aglab in the steppes and he stayed after the Boundary Gate was closed. Gaians hid him – good Gaians. He got caught and sent back to Non-Land. He's somewhere here still, and I'm going to *find* him.'

Beside Photon, comprehension dawned over Rudo's face. Yes, let him know too – let everyone know. Let the Major kick her out; she would go and live with Zizi – or Lil. Or here, with Uttu. She wasn't a stray dog. She had friends and family here.

Photon looked worried, but he interpreted for their hosts. Uttu interlaced her fingers in Astra's. When he finished, as she'd done in the laundry room, the elderwoman lifted her arm and shook it. This time no one laughed. She and Uttu were flank to flank, interlaced, a united force.

'One Land,' Uttu declared.

'One Land,' Astra echoed.

'One Land.' Muzi thumped his arm against his chest.

'One day. Maybe. We see,' Kingu commented placidly, as Gibil started complaining again at Nanshe. She poured her husband another cup of tea and, raising the pot, offered it to the rest of the room.

Rudo put his hand over the top of his cup. 'We gotta be getting on, sad to say.'

'Too hot drive Zabaria. Siesta. Here,' Uttu objected, patting the floor. But with many politenesses, the CONC officers stood and removed their aprons and said their goodbyes. At the door, Astra hugged the women and children. Gibil was edging towards the sheep pen. He raised a half-salute as she shook Kingu's hand. Muzi was loitering behind his father, leaning against the door frame. She hesitated.

'Goodbye, Muzi,' she offered.

'Astra birthday.' The youth held out the beeswax candle, its wick black, but still with hours left to burn. She took it, pressing her finger and thumb beneath his. He blinked his dazzling blue eyes, smiled and with a gesture like a butterfly opening its wings, let go.

MUZI

She's like the patch-eyed ewe, the sheep with a taste for mountain mint. Dainty and stubborn, she halts, goes her own way, strays from the path, leads me to hilltops with views of the windsands, the city, the river, the future, the past. She's a spitfire, a *mergallá*-dancer. Needs coaxing back to her lamb, stands out in the flock. Fixes me with a look and dares me to chase her, then when I pen her, nudges and bleats, lets me bury my hands in her fleece . . .

. . . her soft fleecy black hair. Drifting into my thoughts as I wake, watch the clouds, hold the ewe that likes being milked, that noses my trousers as I grip her small horns, as my grandmother squeezes her udders and the milk hits the dish like the tinkling of bells. The patch-eyed ewe that head-butts the others, kicks out at the ram. *Women give most of their grief to each other*, my father laughs. *But don't worry, son, they save their best grief for us* . . .

. . . the ewe that comes to the door of the watch-hut, stands there with her lamb, inspecting my dwelling – is it to her liking? Would she spread sweet-smelling straw on the floor, strew flowers on the bed, fling open the window, demand I build steps to the roof? I'll ask her, listen for her answers, wait for her foot to cross over the threshold, her funny little face to examine my fan. The *mergallá*-fan that will lift us, take us up to the stars. The first star of the night, a candle on the roof, the moon shadow of our marriage moving over the land . . .

. . . soon the clouds will gather, drench the dry land. Soon, she will nibble mint from my hand.

ASTRA

Rudo burped, a long indulgent rumble chased by a smug sigh. 'No prizes for guessing Uttu's wish, then.'

'Frig off, Rudo,' she retorted, her eyes on the road.

'He's cute. Got manners. Family's got livestock, land, well outside the Hem. Wouldn't be so quick to turn up my nose if I was you.'

'I'm not *turning up my nose*. But I'm too young to get married and I'm not living in a house where they eat meat.' Why was she even *discussing* this?

'Oh, the family will not be eating meat every day,' Photon corrected. 'Normally, they would kill a lamb three or four times in one year. They have to sell the wool and milk and cheese, not to eat the profits for dinner.'

'Yeah, well. I don't fancy sitting across from Gibil three times a day. If I see Muzi at a River Raven I'll take him out for a roll in the dunes, how about that?'

Photon giggled, but Rudo shot back, 'That's as good as renting the wedding tent hereabouts, chicklet. And you get up the duff, they ain't gonna wait till you're twenty to make the kid legal.'

She was regretting playing along now. 'Aren't you tired, Rudo? I thought meat was supposed to make people sleepy.'

She heard him beat his stomach with his palms, a flat tattoo. 'Meat, Astra, stimulates a man's natural juices.'

'Please, Rudo,' Photon objected, 'we are going to Pithar. Astra, turn right up ahead. This is the Belt Road.'

Of course she'd turn right: they were heading out of Kadingir, weren't they? She stopped at the intersection, waiting for a break in the heavy traffic. Beyond it, in the near distance, stretched the Boundary, a towering grey cliff with vehicles moving at its foot along the IMBOD road. It hadn't taken her long, she realised, to start to accept the Boundary. It was ugly, an outrage, but a fact, as much a part of the landscape as the Mikku River. She almost didn't think beyond it any more. She didn't imagine the steppes, Atourne, everyone she had ever loved, living behind it, moving forward in their lives just as she was pulled along by the currents of hers. It was as though only this place was real now: this place, and the past.

But it wasn't just *her* past, it was Uttu's past too. Behind that grey barrier with its indistinct images of predatory beasts drifted the ghosts of people she'd never before been allowed to imagine.

She couldn't imagine them today though. The Boundary was screening looped alligators, the rare beast thrashing up white water with its tail and opening its jaw until its teeth and throat stretched as tall as the wall.

'Does IMBOD ever screen anything nice?'

'Hey, this *is* nice,' Rudo drawled. 'When the Nonners rush the Hem with pitchforks, IMBOD shows films of burning heaps of Nonner corpses.'

'They do not,' Photon contradicted. 'And Amazigia would not be so happy if they did.'

There was a gap at last, after a cart and before an N-LA van. She bumped up from the gravel road onto the tarmac. The Belt Road might be a highway, but the surface was cracked and a broad pothole gaped ahead.

'So are we gonna try and find Astra's dad in Pithar?' Rudo asked.

Oh, why had she spoken out at lunch?

'No,' she said curtly.

Her voiced chimed with Photon, who replied, 'No, I just wanted to give her a tour of Zabaria.'

'He could be there,' Rudo pressed. 'Worth asking.'

She had to move quickly. 'The Major's put the word out. Heesh thinks Zizi's gone into the desert. I'm waiting to hear back from hir scouts. And can you keep it a secret please, Rudo. I wasn't supposed to tell anyone.'

'Yeah. Sure. It'll cost you though.' She waited for the punchline. But Rudo didn't follow through. 'I dunno, Astra,' he said. 'Sometimes your folks skip off, it's best to let 'em. This Zizi guy wasn't around much when you were growing up, I take it.'

'He didn't *skip off*. He's a Non-Lander. IMBOD arrested him and kicked him out.'

'Okay – but what was he doing making babies with a Gaian lady? I thought you lot had that side of things sewn up tight, so ta speak. He sounds a bit of a chancer to me.'

What the *frig* was he implying?

'Rudo,' Photon chided, 'we don't know anything about Astra's Code father. Or her Birth mother. These things happen, even in Is-Land.'

'Yeah, sure – I know about way too many of these *happenings* back in Mount Reality. And they don't always turn out the way you think they oughta, Astra.'

'I'm sure Astra knows that she doesn't know what will happen, Rudo,' Photon went on, attempting to tie the conversation up in a loose knot.

She unpulled it with a single yank. 'Zizi didn't *rape* my Birth mother, if that's what you're trying to say, Rudo. I never met her, but I know the whole story. It wasn't like that, okay?'

Rudo was silent. 'Okay,' he said at last. 'Sorry if I overstepped. You're a good kid and I don't want you getting hurt, that's all.'

A good kid. Was Rudo volunteering to *Shelter* her? 'I won't get hurt,' she retorted, veering to avoid another craterous pothole. 'I just want to meet him. He's my Code father and I've got the right to find out what diseases he has, at least.'

Rudo grinned. 'I 'spect you might find he has a bad case of big mouth-itis. And quite possibly a short fuse.'

'Ha HA.' She reached for the Comchan dial on the dashboard. 'Do we get reception out here?'

Rudo got out his Tablette. 'For the first ten clicks, then *nada*. But I got a great new download, perfect siesta substitute.'

And that was the way they played it, no talk for an hour, just wailing sax and wild women, all along the hot, bone-rattling road to Zabaria, the scrublands sloping endlessly south, the grey IMBOD patrol road and teeth-snapping Boundary keeping pace to the north. All the long road they saw no one but sheepherders, boys making the sign for water, balling a fist, and pointing thumb towards mouth, but they'd given all the extra water to Uttu, and Astra was driving at sixty clicks and didn't stop.

Up ahead was a long queue of cars and carts. She slowed down. The traffic was waiting to be let through a gate, two squat stone towers either side of the road.

'What's this?' she asked.

'IMBOD checkpoint,' Photon told her.

Her heart thumped. 'IMBOD? But they're not allowed in the Belt.'

'They are allowed in Zabaria, to protect the mine. They use the IMBOD road to get here. But they have the right to police who comes into the town.'

She was at the end of the queue. She braked behind a cart. In the opposite lane, a van was coming towards her; there was traffic backed up on the other side of the barrier too.

'Just drive down the centre, kid,' Rudo yawned from the back.

'Don't call me kid,' she ordered tersely. 'And I think you'll find that's illegal.'

'Ooh! We've passed our driving instructor test now, have we?'

'You can take the verge, Astra.' Photon cut Rudo off. 'CONC has priority.'

Stuffing her panic deep down inside her, she drove carefully past the Non-Landers parked in the baking sun. Some had left their vehicles and were stretching their legs at the side of the road. One group was having a picnic under a floppy green parasol that was missing a spoke.

'Sheesh,' Rudo commented, 'this is one helluva queue. They'll be setting up tents next.'

'Short-staffed?' Photon speculated. 'Maybe they have put extra protection on the Boundary now the cladding is to begin?'

Astra was silent. The picnickers had scowled at her as she passed, whether because she'd had to drive close to their party or because she was jumping the queue, she didn't know. But she hadn't chucked sand in their food, and surely they knew Ciccy was delivering medical supplies? They shouldn't be blaming her or CONC for IMBOD's stupid rules.

They were beside the head of the queue now, waiting for a battered orange two-seater to be let through a red-and-white-striped barrier. There were four IMBOD officers on the road, in white uniform and golden vests, sonic guns in their belts, and the shadowy figures of others were moving in the turrets of the towers. The young woman questioning the driver of the red car raised a hand in greeting. She was pale-skinned, with a high brow and long black hair tied back behind her ears. She was of medium height, and slender; she didn't look Sec Gen.

'Okay, open your window, Astra,' Photon said. 'Tablette ID everyone.'

'I have to show her my ID?' She glared at Photon. Why hadn't he warned her about this?

'Don't worry, it's just a formality.'

'Maybe don't mention you're a Non-Gaian, eh?' Rudo handed Photon his Tablette. 'She'll probably want to do some kind of re-conversion ceremony with you under the—'

'Shut *up*, Rudo,' she hissed. The officer was waving the red car through, striding towards them. She fumbled for her Tablette, her hands trembling. Her name was a dead give-away. And she doubted very much that a Gaian in CONC clothing would pass without comment through the gates to Zabaria.

But the inspection really was only cursory. The officer clocked their faces and glanced over the ID photos, not appearing to look at the names. She handed the Tablettes back and gestured at her colleague in the tower to lift the barrier again.

'They never give us any hassle,' Photon said as Astra picked up speed. 'It is the Non-Landers they shake down.'

The road was veering to the south, lined on the right with a swell of dusty tents, spreading like a choppy brown sea over the scrubland. The dwellings here weren't colourful or various or solid like they sometimes were in Kadingir. They were drab and uniform, and they looked as though a strong wind might blow them away.

'Where's the mine?' she asked.

'Up ahead. There.' Photon pointed to the other side of the road.

The Boundary was a long smudge in the distance. The land between was dominated by a bulging rise in the scrub, a sandy ridge stretching north and east at a right angle. In its lee, parallel to the road, was a line of low brick buildings. Vehicles, small as beetles, were moving along an off-road between them.

'That's it?' She didn't know what she had expected. A big red gash in Gaia's side? A black cave?

'It's an open pit mine,' Photon said. 'Very large and deep, I gather from photos.'

'I went on a tour of it,' Rudo announced. 'It's like a massive fracking Neolympic stadium. Terraces all the way down, relay teams of Nonners bent double under baskets of lanthanum and gidolium deposits struggling up to the top, doing their backs in so we's can play five-card stud on ShareWorld, and speed along in solar vehicles and canoodle with our honeypies in the ion glove. *P'tite vie*, Astra. Outside Is-Land, pretty much, life sucks.'

Astra ignored the poetry. 'What about thorium and uranium? Do they carry them up too?'

'Those are by-products,' Photon said. 'They are not mined directly, or at least not that CONC is aware of.'

'Hey now, let's not get speculative,' Rudo drawled. 'Like your IMBOD man said, ain't no proof—'

'The thorium causes the dermatitis,' Photon cut him off. 'That is proven. Why it is now passed on to the kids, we do not know.'

'Doesn't IMBOD *care?*' she asked hotly. 'I mean, what would it cost to Code the workers against radioactivity, at least?'

'They say they'll Code Zabaria if the whole of Kadingir packs up and goes back to Asfar,' Rudo declared. 'But the people are itching for "justice" – nothing we can do about it except hand out the morpheus to them that still wants it.'

It was the beer courtyard all over again. Rudo was doing his 'I'm just a dumb-luck hick from Mount Reality, don't bug me with politics' routine. Well, let him. They were approaching the off-road now. More vehicles were turning into it – workers, it looked like: Non-Landers in carts and beat-up cars, on foot, on bicycles.

'Do IREMCO people live here too?' she asked.

'The overseers have—' Photon started.

'*Overseers.*' Rudo snorted. 'My ancestors were *slaves*, Phot. Please don't insult them. The Nonners get paid to work here. They can pack up any time. Like I said, Astra, it's the people's choice.'

'I am sorry, Rudo. The *managers,*' Photon corrected himself. 'They live in the IREMCO buildings.'

Rudo's ancestors were slaves? She wanted to ask how he knew that, but the way she was feeling the question would come out wrong and make his bad mood worse. She gazed out the side window. Even at a distance, the buildings were impressive: sandstone ziggurats, backs to the rise of the ridge. Their terraces climbed to living roofs, palm trees and hanging plants cascading over the sides. Gaian biotecture. Designed to reflect the landscape and accentuate its dramatic features: except here the 'feature' was a toxic mine.

'They got swimming pools on the roofs.' Rudo stretched. 'Like schmanzy hotels. Most of the managers live in Is-Land, the guy told me. They come in and out with the transport trucks, and work two weeks on, two weeks off. When they're here they put in twelve-hour days. That kinda shift work ain't easy, you know. And the Nonners are damn lucky there's some kind of economy here, not just CONC aid. There's only so much we can do for them all, Astra.'

He was really getting on her nerves. You'd think with his slave ancestors he would have some sympathy for the Non-Landers. 'Yeah, well, it's not much of a *choice* either, is it? Work in a place that will make you sick and your kids alt-bodied, or live on hand-outs and . . . *red peppers.*'

'The kids aren't alt-bodied because Mommy and Daddy dug up a few minerals! The whole of the Belt was an Old World war zone! If the Nonners want to camp here waiting for Amon or Asar or Postman Abraham to crack open the gates to the promised land, that's up to them!'

He was like a frigging mynah bird, just squawking back Odinson's lies. 'I don't get you, Rudo! You don't trust the Sec Gens so why do you believe what IMBOD says about the mine? You know exactly what they're like, and what they can do if they want.'

'I don't see *shit* in black and white, Astra! Live a little longer and you'll learn that the world's a bit more complicated than that, okay?'

'You do *so* see things in black and—'

'Hey, *guys*!' Photon waved his hand between them. 'Time out. We can't solve the conflict today, so let us not let it infect the team, okay?'

Rudo pushed his partner's arm down. 'I don't like IMBOD's freaky army, Astra. I wouldn't let any kid of mine get pumped up into some kind of hive-mind war-bot, and thank frack you got out. But IMBOD ain't doing nothing illegal. They're running a CONC-authorised business and protecting their big old silver-screen Boundary, that's all. Why do you wanna go on the rampage against IMBOD, anyway? You missed your big genetic zap shot, you've been expelled from Is-Land, your dad's a Nonner – why the hell are you going looking for more punishment?'

'I'm not looking for *punishment*,' she yelled as Photon shook his head. 'I'm looking for my *dad.*'

'In Pithar? *Ostie de calisse de criss!* Is he some kinda pimp? What the frack do you even know about this guy?'

'Rudo, *chill out*,' Photon shouted. 'She has a normal *right* to look to find her father.'

She'd never heard Photon yell before – and maybe Rudo hadn't either. Miraculously, he shut up. Except for the low ragged sigh of a saxophone from the speakers, the cabin was quiet.

They crossed the road to the mine, a broad gravel street running between square grey buildings with dirty white canopies that sagged over the pavements. A few carthorses clopped up and down.

'Old Zabaria,' Photon said calmly. 'The original workers' quarters. The buildings are IREMCO and CONC shops now, and the workers mainly live in the tents. We are just showing Astra the lay of the land, Rudo. She ought to see Zabaria, and Pithar too. It's not pleasant, but we all have to experience the worst of this place.'

'Yeah, okay, whatever.' Rudo was bored now. 'Are we nearly there yet?'

Up ahead was another checkpoint, but there were no queues, just two towers with their candy-stripe barriers, and the Belt Road arcing out in a dark, wet curve away from the Boundary and south into the scrubland. Looking at that road, she wanted to step on the accelerator, smash through that skinny pole and drive along that curve into the warped, ever-receding horizon, on and on until she'd left all the faded tents and scraggy plants and endless arguments far behind her, drive deep into the windsands, into *mergallá* country, down below the Belt Line, not stopping, ever, until a whirlwind came and sucked her up into the sky.

'Turn right here, Astra,' Photon said. The grey buildings were behind them now, and ahead was a narrow lane running between another vast swathe of tents.

She slowed down as ahead, an IMBOD officer emerged from one of the towers and marched across the road in front of the barrier. She had a sonic gun in her belt. At the top of each tower, beneath their pointed, gazebo roofs, were two more officers. They too would have sonic guns, handcuffs, all her details on their Tablettes. *No, Rudo: she wasn't looking for punishment. Punishment was looking for her.* But before it found her, she was going to do as much as she possibly could to deserve it. Maybe she didn't know exactly how her Code father and mother had met; maybe Hokma hadn't told her the whole story. Maybe Zizi had lied to Eya about who he was, or abandoned her before he was deported. But unless Hokma's letter had been a complete pack of lies, she did know that Gaian dissidents had protected her Code father in Is-Land; and according to Lil he had kept contact with them, and with Hokma, somehow. She was going to find him.

'Do they change the roads here too?' she asked as she drew up to the side turning.

'No,' Photon replied, 'people in Zabaria don't resist IMBOD. They work long hours, sleep, save money, leave.'

'It's a mining town, dudes.' Rudo's tone was lazy again. 'They drink and screw a lot.'

Photon laughed. 'Yes, okay, they do.'

Astra was silent. Sandrine had said that all four Treatment Wards here dealt with high rates of alcohol-related conditions and STIs. The first one on their list was somewhere near by. She turned off the Belt Road, into the tent lanes of Eastern Zabaria.

The lanes between the tents did look more permanent than those in Kadingir. The boardwalks were rubber-matted, though hardly anyone was out. On the way to the first Treatment Ward she saw just one woman, pushing a child in a wheelchair. The ward itself was full, but apart from being a tent, it was no different to those she'd seen in Kadingir. They dropped off the supplies, picked up the laundry and exchanged news with the staff. It was the same at the next two wards, the second in the southeast quarter of the township and the third across the main off-road, in the southwest quarter. All three needed as much morpheus as possible.

'YAC isn't catching on here,' she commented as they left the third ward. It was perplexing: why would Lil want to live in such a political dead zone?

'YAC activists might be concentrating in Kadingir, where the media are,' Photon suggested. 'Workers here could be sending money to support them. Astra, turn right.'

They were heading back towards the main drag, towards the flat grey tops of the IREMCO stores. It was approaching evening now and the grey stone buildings were bathed in a golden haze. Images of Old World cities and naked women dancing in windows flashed into her mind.

'Is Pithar an IREMCO *shop*?' she asked.

'Nah. It's a tent district behind,' Rudo replied. 'I told you, it's a mining town. There's been a back-alley sex trade in Zabaria since the first tent peg got banged in.'

They bumped along, slowed by the presence of more people on the streets, both adults and children – as if a shift had changed, or school had let out.

The Treatment Ward came into view, a large round tent like the other three, the CONC flag drooping in the windless sky above the entrance. Astra pulled up and turned off the engine. The tent flap opened and Lil stepped across the threshold.

* * *

Lil's hair was twisted up in an outlandish topknot. She was wearing a long blue garment, halfway between a robe and a dress, with a full skirt gathered at the waist and a close-fitting, long-sleeved top. She didn't come out to greet them, as other nurses had done, but remained at the tent flap, icily observing Cicada, as if the team were hours late.

Astra undid her seatbelt. She couldn't communicate with Photon, couldn't risk even a glance that might alert Rudo that something else was going on here, something beyond a simple laundry pick-up and drug drop.

Rudo groaned. 'Four wards in a shift, a matchmaking lunch *and* meet-the-sex-freaks. That's a lotta Non-time, folks. Can we just do the dirty and get outta here quick, please?'

'They are not freaks,' Photon sighed, 'they are Singulars. And we must take as long as we need. Astra should get a tour of this ward.'

'Singular all right. Singular experiences, for the guy who's tried everything twice. They freak *me* out, okay, Phot? And I mean it. I gotta big date on the court tonight and I don't wanna be late. Neither does Astra – the Spanners need her.'

Singular experiences. She was tense too, she realised, because she was going to meet women who sold themselves for sex – to IREMCO managers and IMBOD officers, the article had said, though she still couldn't really believe that. Sex work was a symptom of a male-dominant society, a culture in which men earned more money than women and women's sexuality was considered their primary asset. No Is-Lander she had ever met would want or need to visit Pithar. Surely the Zabaria mine officials would Gaia-play with each other, in hammocks slung around the swimming pools on the roofs of the ziggurats?

But the news article had not been a fake. At least a few Gaians had visited Pithar before the CONC scandal had erupted, and if mine-managers and Barracks officers were still customers here, she needed to know about it. Such information could hurt Samrod Blesserson one day.

And in any case, she was here to meet Lil. 'Let's stop moaning and get going then.' She opened her door. It was good that Rudo didn't want to be here – maybe he'd just head back to Cicada and wait for them there. She hit the ground and slammed the door shut.

As she walked into the tent behind Photon and Rudo, each lugging a sack of clean linens, Astra tried to catch Lil's eye. But Lil was sweeping ahead of them, chin in the air, as if her head was being dragged backwards by the weight of that enormous bun.

'The doctor is with a patient,' she announced over her shoulder in Inglish. 'The laundry is to be put there.'

She pointed to row of dirty laundry sacks, slumped together against the tent wall. It was an average Treatment Ward reception area: a large round tent furnished with chairs and mats, a long desk, shelves and cupboards.

'We'll grab those now.' Rudo dumped his load and took a sack by the neck. 'Doc can sign for them when he's back.'

Lil shot him a disdainful glance. 'I am the Pithar Singulars' Liaison Officer,' she declaimed. 'I represent the Singular patients in this Treatment Ward. If CONC is interested in their working conditions and healthcare needs, I can take you to meet them. Women only.'

Photon lifted the other two sacks and slung one over his back.

'That is sounding like a good idea, Astra,' he said, his expression blank. 'We can sort out the supplies if you want to take a tour.'

'Yeah. Okay,' she said, also trying to keep her voice neutral.

The men exited; Lil watched them go as if inspecting children attempting to tidy their room.

How did Lil always manage to take charge of a situation? Here she was in this regal garb, crowned by a headdress of her own hair, not even bothering to look at Astra. It was as if their session in the ion glove had never happened. She wanted to hiss in Gaian, 'What the frig is going on?'

But before she could speak, a wiry, middle-aged man entered the tent through one of the interior flaps. He wore a CONC-issue blue doctor's gown. 'Oh good,' he said, clocking the fresh laundry bags. 'Thank you, Lilutu. Hello.' He strode towards Astra and stuck out his hand. 'I'm Dr Nimutu. You're new, I think?'

Lilutu. She shook his hand. 'Astra Ordott. I'm in training.'

'It's her first time in Pithar,' Lil declared. 'I'm going to give her a tour of the ward. The other drivers will be back in a minute to take the morpheus order. You can give them a cup of tea while they wait for us.'

It was incredible: Lil was ordering him about too. But the doctor didn't seem to mind. 'Very good. Take your time. Talk to the patients, Astra. It's important that CONC understands their situation.'

Beckoning as though Astra were a dog, Lil swept towards the interior tent flap.

She had no choice. She followed.

It was a mixed ward, a long rectangular tent with men and women in beds in rows either side. Most of the patients were sleeping, but as Astra passed down the aisle behind Lil, a woman propped herself up on her pillow.

'Where's Msandi?' she asked, panic tingeing her voice. 'Is Msandi coming back?'

'Msandi's coming next time,' Lil replied, marching on. 'This is Astra. She's new.'

'Let her talk to us, then,' the woman demanded. 'I want to talk to Astra.'

'She doesn't have time today.' Lil flung the comment over her shoulder.

'Who are you to tell her who she can talk to?' an old man wheezed. 'She needs to talk to all of us.'

Beside him, another man was assessing Astra through narrowed eyes, as if she were fatally contaminated by Lil's company. She didn't blame him. She didn't like scurrying after the imperious Lil – it was like being back in the woods around Or, following Lil through the pathless trees and knowing she didn't know how to get home.

Lil stopped at a door flap at the opposite end of the tent. Astra caught up.

'Why can't I talk to them?' she hissed.

'These patients,' Lil jerked her head towards the beds, 'are mine-workers. They suffer from exhaustion, dermatitis and cancer. You've seen cases like them in the other wards.'

How did Lil know what she'd seen and not seen? Before she could challenge her, Lil leaned closer. Her breath was mint-fresh, her eyes gleaming.

'This is the Pithar Singulars' ward. You can't meet them anywhere else.'

The doctor had said to talk to everyone. Only Rudo wanted to get on, and he could wait. But Lil pushed through the flap. With an apologetic glance to the mine-workers, Astra followed, an unwilling shadow.

They'd walked into in a small round tent. It was bright but muggy, and a sweetish smell hung in the air, a scent that reminded Astra of alt-yoghurt. The beds were arranged around the edge and their occupants were all sitting up, as if expecting her. She hesitated, but Lil grabbed her hand and pulled her to the centre tent pole, into the middle of the circle. Now she saw where the smell came from: in front of her, a woman was cradling a baby in two of her eight arms, feeding it from one of her many breasts.

It was Tiamet. Astra had last seen the Singular on Comchan, being released from jail. Now here she was in bed, a white sheet artfully rumpled around her waist, a purple robe hanging open from her shoulders. Between the silky curtains of the robe, the Singular's breasts resembled a batch of squashy brown eggs with an infant nestling in their midst. It was a beautiful, completely unexpected sight, exuding contentment and abundance.

But she was staring. Embarrassed by her own naked curiosity, Astra looked Tiamet in the face. It was an exquisite face, framed by tumbling copper curls. The young woman widened her eyes as if mocking Astra's flustered reactions. Her eyes were outlined in brown kohl and decorated with two diamanté sparkles at the temples.

No one spoke. The silence was unnerving. Above the Singular's magnificent body, Tiamet's amused expression challenged her – but to do what, she didn't know. Should she look, or not look?

She glanced over at the next bed to see a small, round woman with hunched shoulders swathed in a shapeless black robe. Her ageing face was puffy and creased, but a muscle was working in her jaw and her eyes were flamethrowers, blackly lit and aimed straight at Astra.

She tensed. She could feel eyes drilling into her back too. These women were staring at *her*. She had been invited on a 'tour' but in a matter of moments *she* had become the exhibit, trapped between the beds like a work beast in a pen being inspected for hire.

'She's here.' Lil gripped Astra's wrist and raised her hand in the air. 'Istar: the Gaia Girl who demanded to live in Non-Land. I've brought her like I said I would. She is here to fulfil the Prophecy.'

'Istar, Istar, Istar,' Tiamet hissed.

Istar? Like the compound gate? What the frig was Lil up to?

'Look, I'm not—' she sputtered, trying to wrench herself free of Lil's grasp, but Lil just lifted her hand higher and wheeled her around, showing her off. All she could do was stare back at the women staring at her. Tiamet was leading the incantation. The small, hunched woman was a dense ball of silence, her lips clamped shut, but next to her a moon-faced young woman with hair swirled up on her head and cheekbones dotted with gold sequins echoed the sibilant chant.

An impossibly tall, rake-thin boy-girl, four hands clasped at hir flat chest, angular face lacquered in silver, was huskily chanting too. On the other side of Tiamet was a large square woman, the bedsheets flat around her, hand-wings drooping from her sleeveless white robe. Beneath her close-cropped hair, this woman's pouchy face was still and stern, as if she were reserving judgement on this madness.

'Istar, Istar, Istar,' the three younger Singulars chanted.

She couldn't bear it any longer. 'My name is *Astra*,' she declared. 'Who are *you*?'

'Shhhh,' Lil yanked her arm. 'The mine-workers will hear you.'

So what? She *wanted* someone to hear her, someone to come and rescue her from Lil's sacrificial altar. But right now, at least the incessant chanting had stopped.

'I am Tiamet,' said the Singular in Asfarian. She lifted her baby. 'This is my child Ebebu. We were separated while I was jailed.' She gestured at the small woman in the next bed. 'Anunit fed him for me.'

The woman rolled her shoulders, but did not break her silence.

'I am Taletha.' Fluttering her lashes, the moon-faced woman laid her hands in her lap. She appeared to have numerous legs; her body fanned out in long arcs beneath the sheet.

'I am Roshanak.' The tall boy-girl rested hir four hands in a prayer position and gently bowed.

'I am Neperdu,' the last woman intoned. 'Welcome to Pithar, Astra.'

'Your name means "star",' Tiamet declaimed. 'In my language, we call you Istar. Your arrival has been long prophesied.'

Her command of Asfarian pleasantries had abandoned her. This was either a very weird and big mistake, or one of Lil's cunning schemes, but either way she had to end it, right now.

She tugged her hand from Lil's grip at last. 'I'm sorry, but you must have me confused with someone else. Lil, tell them: I work for CONC. Honestly, I'd like to help, but—'

But Lil's face was shining like a gold medal. 'Tell her, Tiamet,' she urged.

'She will arise in the night,' Tiamet recited, 'enchained by the light of a day that is dead.'

The last woman – Neperdu? – had called her Astra. She turned to her now and said, imploring, 'I didn't—'

'We saw you,' Taletha trilled, 'at the Star Party. Your forehead was bound in sky-blue light.'

'That was my uniform. The CONC halo—'

But Tiamet was sailing on. 'A child among the mighty, knowing among the innocent, with her first kiss she will appoint her vizier, the raven-haired Helpmeet of Harpies.'

'Lilutu said you kissed her!' Roshanak was in raptures. 'And you agreed to meet us—'

'—us, the outcasts,' Taletha enthused, 'the Code demons, the harpies flying back to our rightful thrones at the heart of our culture!'

She shot Lil an angry glance. '*She* kissed *me*. And I'd like to help you get your rights, if I can, but I said I would come here because Lil said you knew where my father was.'

Taletha's shrill voice cut through her gabble. 'She will greet her father!'

'Her chariot charged with the anger of ages,' Tiamet announced, 'she will wend her own way to the House of Abundant Women.'

'*No.*' She wanted to shake the beds until these silly women's teeth rattled. 'I came in a *van*. And I didn't "wend my own way". I came with CONC – with Rudo and Photon. They gave me directions.'

'She came with her underlings,' Lil said. 'She was driving the chariot.'

'Istar, Istar, Istar.' Taletha and Roshanak were rocking back and forth, murmuring again.

'You came as prophesied,' Tiamet informed her grandly. 'Your vizier came ahead of you from the homeland, to prepare us to greet you.'

She had to dismantle this ridiculous fiction, break it down, piece by piece, burn it to ashes. 'You mean *Lil*? She's not my *vizier*. She was my friend, back in Is-Land. That's all. She said you knew where my dad—'

Lil took her arm, pulled her close. 'Shhhh,' she whispered. 'Don't be afraid. It's true – it's why we're here. It's our destiny, we both know that. Don't you remember? *You're my Star Girl*,' she recited softly, '*You're my fire.*'

It was if she'd been whisked back into the ion glove. Was it the words of the love poem from that long-ago summer, the woodsmoke scent of Lil's hair, or the sensation of her body, warm and lush beneath her robe, that sent a tingling wave rushing over Astra's skin? She didn't know, and she didn't care. For a moment all she wanted was to be alone with Lil, to duck under the side of the tent and fly out into the scrubland. She'd sit Lil down in the shade of a bush and ask her a million questions, because this was Lil, who had always known more than she'd said – said more than Astra ever wanted to hear. She wanted to shout at Lil, to hug her and shake her until the truth came tumbling out of her lips, until they were both empty of words and just bodies in the heat, bodies that had their own way of communicating . . . as they were quietly doing now.

She pushed Lil away. 'What are you doing, Lil?' she demanded. 'What did you tell these people?'

'I'm not doing anything,' Lil softly replied. 'You're doing everything, just by being who you are.'

Neperdu was regarding her keenly. 'Astra, you are Gaian. But your father is a Non-Lander?'

She turned to her eagerly. *This* was why she was here. 'Yes. His name is Zizi Kataru. Do you know—?'

'You are placeless,' Neperdu declared, as if her answer had settled a crucial argument against her. 'She *is* placeless, Anunit.'

Anunit shrugged, her mouth making a hurt twist.

She looked between the older women. They hadn't been chanting. *Surely* they couldn't believe this crazy fantasy.

'Neperdu, Anunit. Everyone. It's really nice of you to welcome me like this, really it is. I'm honoured. But I don't know anything about a prophecy – I just want to find my father. If I can help you at CONC, just tell me what I should put in the report. Do you need more morpheus? Or birth control? We have femidoms, loads, no one's using them and they'll go out of date soon.'

'We don't want femidoms,' Tiamet said. 'Gaians have good Code. Ebebu is alive and well.'

The words took a moment to compute. She stared at the baby. His father was an *Is-Lander*? That made no sense. Even if mine-managers or IMBOD officers did come to Pithar, curious about these 'Singular' experiences, Gaian men knew how not to get a woman pregnant.

'They like to *sow their seeds*.' Anunit spoke for the first time, her voice a low, bitter rasp. She was holding something in her hands: something she was pulling and squeezing. 'They like to *plough Gaia's ripening fields*.'

Astra flinched. That was the Is-Land phrase for penetrative sex with pregnant women. It was a way of worshipping Gaia, though you had to be careful not to induce an early labour. But Code-fathering a child wasn't like scattering apple seeds on a wild sowing day: it was a major responsibility.

'Then what?' She addressed the circle, her voice rising. 'Do they Shelter the children too?'

Against the silence of the tent, Tiamet laughed, a brittle, tinkling sound. 'No, Istar. The mine-managers are not what we call fathers.'

'We are a game to them,' Neperdu said, her voice hard as stone. 'They use us to demonstrate the strength of their Code. They score one hundred points for a live birth, and deduct marks for any Singularities. They see the child once, and then, if we are lucky, they play the game again with another woman.'

The silence curdled.

Anunit's eyes were closed. Whatever was in her hands, she was wringing it until it was dry as an old camel carcase. 'All *right*,' she spat, in that hoarse, evacuated voice. '*Tell her.*'

'If we are unlucky' – Neperdu's small eyes glittered – 'they kill our children. They come in the night to our tent, or our families' tents, with their friends. They wrench the babies from our breasts and smother them in front of us. They say it is Gaia's will – that monstrosities with Is-Lander Code must not be allowed to live. They take our babies' bodies away to be burned.'

'*What?*' Neperdu was speaking Asfarian and she understood – but surely she must be hearing it all wrong? Dizzy with incomprehension, she turned to Lil. 'That can't be true.'

Neperdu raised her voice: 'Anunit lost her daughter.'

As she gaped at Anunit, the woman raised her fist and brandished a dirty white crocheted square. 'This is my daughter's suckling blanket,' she croaked, her puffy face contorted with fury. 'The stains of her spit will identify her father. You want to help us? Then *level the Boundary. Find* him – find *all* the men like him, who come here and take everything – *everything* – away from us. Find them, and make them *pay* for what they've done.'

The woman's anger was forcing Astra backward until her spine scraped against the tent pole. 'I'm sorry,' she spluttered. 'I didn't know—'

'You know now,' Tiamet hissed, her eyes dark jewels.

'You are Istar.' Taletha raised her arms to the heavens. 'You are here to fight for our freedom.'

'I'm not Istar! I'm—'

'*Astra*,' Neperdu intoned, 'you say you want to help us. There is only one thing we want: for IMBOD and IREMCO to be defeated, for the Boundary to fall and this land to belong to all who live here. A great battle is brewing: a battle for justice and freedom, in which no one can stand on the sidelines. You are here. You fit the Prophecy like a ring fits a finger. Will you accept your destiny? Will you assume the mantle of Istar and join our struggle?'

It was all too much. She was in Pithar looking for her father, and maybe some dirt on Blesserson, not tragedies to tear her heart out, or the rings and mantles of some ancient goddess. 'I'm sorry,' she repeated stubbornly, 'I just came to find out where my father is. Lil told me you knew.'

The silence was worse than the barrage of demands; it was hostile, barbed with contempt.

'She doesn't give a sheep's shit about us.' Anunit dabbed at her face with her piece of crochet. 'Tell her where her father is and let her go.'

That stung. Anunit had suffered, that was obvious – but so had she. So had *everyone*.

'I *do* care about you,' she flared, 'and your baby. My Shelter sister was killed. I don't want children to die. I'm a Non-Gaian: I believe in One Land too. But I don't know how to help you. I'm not a prophet. I can't play music like Tiamet. I can't even speak Somarian very well. Look—' She cast about for something, anything she could do to appease these people. 'There are international journalists in Kadingir right now. I can tell them about Anunit. If she wants to speak to them, maybe they can come out here and visit.'

This, it appeared, was not a completely stupid thing to say. Taletha was pouting and Roshanak looked downcast, but the beaks and claws of the silence retracted.

'Journalists have come before,' Neperdu said calmly. 'They expose us, they leave, and we take the punishment. IMBOD must leave. The Boundary must fall. You must accept your destiny. Yes, tell the journalists about us, but only as Istar: only as part of our resistance.'

This was nuts. 'I like YAC,' she declared, 'and I hate IMBOD. I want to help you, but I'm not this Istar person, and even if I wanted to pretend, I don't know how to be her either.'

'Lil is your vizier,' Neperdu said. 'She will help you.'

'You don't have to pretend,' Lil insisted. 'You don't have to do anything different. You *are* Istar. You must simply accept it.'

'When your followers acknowledge you,' Tiamet's voice rang out, 'when they kiss the hem of your robe, press coin into your hand, just smile and thank them for their faith in you. Be humble, and rejoice in our unity.'

'Her name is Istar,' Taletha recited softly. 'She is placeless. She arises in the night, enchained by the light of a day that is dead.'

It was an absurd, bizarre cage of words, a children's story closing in around her. She wanted to turn on her heel and leave . . . But there was Anunit, clutching her crocheted scrap of blanket, tears glazing her face. The small woman was a sculpture of grief.

Astra's throat tightened. Enchained, yes; placeless, no. She was chained to this place now, Pithar's anguish yoked to the cold iron links – Sheba's death, Nimma's pain, Klor's sorrow, Hokma's murder, Peat's hard face, the boy shot on the Boundary – already cinched tight round her neck. And now there was Anunit and her baby. She was trying to break that chain, but the more she tugged, the deeper the links dug into her flesh. She might stalk out of the tent right this minute but that hunched shape – Anunit, who lifted her head and looked Astra straight in the eyes, her red-rimmed gaze a desolate bolt of accusation and despair – would be stamped on her heart wherever she went.

She exhaled.

'Look. I'm on your side, okay? If people want to call me Istar, I won't argue with them – they can believe what they like. But I don't want any followers, and I can't guarantee *anything*.'

'Istar!' Tiamet snapped her fingers, Taletha and Roshanak applauded, Lil hugged her and Neperdu's square face exuded satisfaction. Anunit wiped her cheeks with the fleece and lowered that dreadful gaze.

'Istar, we honour you,' Neperdu purred. 'Zizi Kataru is waiting for you in Shiimti. It is prophesied you will meet him. When you drink his beer, all will follow as foretold.'

'Shiimti.' She pounced on the word like a key. 'Where's that?'

'What. Not where,' Lil said. 'Shiimti is a community, not a place. An open gathering of Non-Landers charged with holding the energy of the resistance.'

'Shiimti moves below the Belt Line,' Tiamet intoned, 'where Is-Landers are afraid to go. Where rootless plants patrol the dunes, and the *mergallá-lá* pour sand down your throat.'

'They shelter there in ancient honeycomb monasteries,' Anunit whispered.

'And caves of tarmacadam and rubble,' Neperdu completed the itinerary.

'They plant seeds in barren soil,' Tiamet declared.

'Oases spring up in their footsteps,' Anunit contributed dully.

'Date palms and water clouds that travel to meet the travellers,' Neperdu triumphantly concluded.

Well, that was all *very* useful information. 'How can I find it then?'

'Currently,' Neperdu said, 'Shiimti is situated 314 kilometres east of Kadingir, 25 kilometres below the Belt Line and 52 kilometres from the Shugurra River.'

She seized the information, repeated it in her mind, then asked, 'How do I get there?'

'You will move there like a *mergallá*,' Neperdu helpfully instructed. She was about to press further when a male voice invaded the room.

'Lilutu?' The doctor was sticking his head around the door flap. 'I'm sorry to interrupt the tour, everyone, but Astra's colleagues are ready to leave. They've a long drive ahead of them. I'm sure Astra can come back soon.'

She couldn't leave now – she still didn't know how to get to Shiimti.

But Lil was batting her eyes at the doctor. 'Perfect timing. We're just finished.' She placed her hand on Astra's back.

'But—'

'You are one of us,' Tiamet declared, 'destined to triumph.'

'Destined to dance in the dunes' Neperdu echoed as Anunit raised her fleece in farewell. Astra stammered her goodbyes, letting Lil steer her out of the tent after the doctor. They were met by a gauntlet of hostile looks from the mine-workers' beds.

'Wait!' called the panicky woman as Lil strode rapidly down the aisle. She sounded angry now. 'Stop and talk to *us*.'

'Why did you take her to see *them*?' a man demanded.

'I'm sorry,' Astra said miserably as she followed Lil back into the clinic reception tent. Photon and Rudo were leaning against the table, a teapot and three cups behind them.

'Great. Here she is.' Rudo straightened up. 'All oriented then?'

She was too dazed to speak, but Lil, of course, was fine. 'Astra Ordott is most appreciative of our efforts here. She is going to write a report requesting a delivery of femidoms for the mine-workers. To thank her, I have offered her a tour of the Black Desert and the Shugurra chott. I can pick her up from the Far Oasis Treatment Ward. Just let the doctor there know when to expect you.'

She had vaguely heard of the Shugurra chott, a dried-up salt lake near the Shugurra River. Lil was making all the decisions again, announcing this trip without even discussing it with her first.

'That is very kind of you,' Photon was saying. 'The chott is not to be missed. Here, let me to give you my Tablette number. I am sure we can arrange to take a shift out to the oases wards.'

'We got a bit more driving to get through today, though, first.' Rudo was making movements to go. But Photon, unbelievably, was exchanging Tablette numbers with Lil. *She* didn't even have Lil's number. When she asked for it, Lil didn't even look up from her thumb-typing; she just said to get it off Photon later. They all shook the doctor's hand, and then, finally, Astra brushed Lil's fingers with hers.

'Thanks for the tour,' she muttered. 'See you soon.'

'I will meet you at the head of the Salt Route, beneath the last palm tree in the Southern Belt,' Lil announced. 'I will wait until the last star falls from the sky.'

AM ARAKKIA

Her boy was back again. When he was young, she had dragged him home from the dream badlands, and though he'd roamed everywhere since, far from the temple tent, far from marriage or a job, still he'd returned every night, from the gym tent, the meditation tent, the scrapheap, the girls on the riverbanks he smelled on his fingers when he thought his mother wasn't looking. Now he was back from the firesands, the IMBOD jail, where she'd warned him he'd end up. Did he listen to her? No, never. But he always came back to the tent, to eat, sleep, play Tablette games with Bartol, practise his rhymes. And today he was back as a hero, like his father, except Enki was a hero in life, not in death.

Her son was a new star rising over the world – even the temple tent priest had said so, leading daily prayers for the safe deliverance of a boy who reminded his elders not to abandon their dreams. And all week the neighbours had given her respect. *He got his sharp tongue from you, Am Arakkia*, the girl had said. That porridge-brained child didn't have a clue what her son's rhymes meant, but she did. And though for so long she had doubted it, now she knew it was true: her boy Enki had become a man. And if he didn't have a wife, or a job, a man needed a vision.

All men needed their brothers. Bartol was such a good boy – always by her son's side. They were sitting quietly now, hammering wood and steel together, cutting up old tent canvas, attaching a seatbelt they'd got at the scrapheap, making their chariot, discussing their battle plans. His father would be proud – and her father too, and all the ancestors coming to witness this moment, their shapes swirling in the smoke from her cigarette, lingering in the high corners of the tent.

The sun was warm and bright through the tent walls. There was still a quarter of a barrel of CONC water in the corner by the shelves. Bartol had brought six tomatoes and half a head of garlic. This was a golden moment to keep in your purse. With it you could buy silk sheets at the market, a she-goat, new unchipped dishes, a vase of cut glass. But she would never spend it, because the boys would be gone soon.

The morning of her son's arrest, five youths had come to her tent flap with food, Tablette reports and a message: Enki had said she must move her tent and let the youths take away the box beneath his bed.

She knew what was in that box; she had argued with him – *begged* him – not to build this coffin box, let alone sleep on it every night, and in *her* tent.

'Everyone is helping,' he'd hissed, that steel-tongued boy of hers. 'We all have to take risks!'

And though she had argued, she knew in her heart that was true. Why was she living here and not in Asfar? Because her grandfather had dreamed of returning to a small house in the steppes. Why should other women's sons die for her grandfather's dream?

The box was heavy: there were many weapons inside. With Bartol's help she had called a halt to Enki's insolence and checked them all, one by one:

A long bag of spears, made of broom handles, railings, car parts.

A fat sack of knuckle-dusters, garrottes and bicycle chains.

A chef's roll of sharpened blades – kitchen knives and a butcher's cleaver.

A crate full of red-pepper spray cans.

And a cardboard box full of needles – empty needles. He had rattled it at her, then sulked while she inspected the box. Later, when she'd pressed him, he'd blown up, insisting that the needles came straight off the back of an Asfarian truck.

'I am back from the poppy fields, Amma,' he'd blazed. 'My dreams are my people's now – my dreams are yours, if you only dared to share them.' And now she did dare to dream. She had moved her tent, given shelter to youths, watched the Tablette reports, gone on demonstrations. She had spoken at the temple tent and prayed to all of the gods. And her boy had returned. There was no box beneath his bed now. His sheets were fresh-washed in the river and he was sitting at her table, as he always had done, hammering with Bartol, playing a game with his brother, as they had always done – marbles in the dirt, IMBOD versus N-LA, rhyme against reason – all things in their season.

And keeping no secrets from a mother who sat warm in the sun.

She got up, knelt by the metal kitchen shelves, took the baskets of cutlery from the middle shelf and lined them up on the canvas behind her.

'Amma,' Enki called, 'leave the cleaning.'

'Relax, Am Arakkia. We'll do that for you later,' Bartol said.

She took a knife, reached to the back of the shelf, inserted the blade and pried open the stiff lid. 'Boys,' she said, getting up, turning, 'it is time.'

It was time to give her son his inheritance: his great-great-grandfather's sword, a curved blade kept polished like a silver trumpet in its velvet casing, inside a metal shelf her father had constructed, saying to her mother, 'We'll keep it with the knives. No one will look for it there.'

ASTRA

They left Zabaria in silence with Rudo driving and Astra in the back seat. Photon wanted to chat about the chott and her tour, but she answered in monosyllables. When they passed the ziggurats, she stared out of the opposite window at the brown sea of tents, glowing in the early evening light. Once past the checkpoint, they headed straight into the lowering sun. The scrubland soaked up the gold wash of the sky; the bushes cast long, grasping shadows through the tangerine sand. It was gorgeous but they were driving in the wrong direction. She'd had the right instincts in Zabaria. She needed to go east. And she would. But she had to be careful. Lil was as dangerously confusing as ever.

She trailed a finger down the window. Why had she agreed to the women's wild scheme? In order to leave that sickly-smelling tent without feeling hated? To keep Lil on her side? To put another bullet in the gun she was training on the pinprick figure of Samrod Blesserson? To appease, somehow, Anunit's terrible gaze? Thinking of Anunit's baby, anger boiled up inside her. If she could prove Blesserson was involved, that he knew about the IREMCO men's psychopathic 'competition', surely that would destroy his career? No matter how much they feared Non-Landers, Gaians wouldn't accept men killing their own children.

She ought to tell Photon and Rudo about the mine-managers, but she didn't. Rudo was being testy today, and he had already defended IREMCO. He wouldn't believe her. And the women had said only to tell CONC or the media if she joined YAC and took on the mantle of Istar. *Istar*. What on earth were Lil's plans for her? She had quoted that childhood poem like the centrepiece of this so-called Prophecy. A peculiar thought occurred to her: had Lil been grooming her for this role way back in Or?

She studied the thought. How on earth would Lil have known she too was half Non-Lander? Had Lil's dad known Zizi? Had he told Lil to come to Or and befriend her? Her thoughts led her on, like a desert path, burning her bare soles: had Lil's dad known Hokma? Had *Hokma* intended her to grow up into this Istar figure?

No, Hokma couldn't have *wanted* her to be cast out of Is-Land – and if she had known Lil's father she would have said so in the letter. It was *Zizi* who had burdened Astra with this prophecy business: Nimma had always said Astra's Code father had chosen her name. But he couldn't honestly have believed his daughter was destined to unite Is-Land and Non-Land – it was like calling a girl Kali or Pythia or any of the names of the goddess, that was all. He had just wanted to inspire her, to make her feel part of Non-Land one day – and, maybe, to work towards the vision of One Land. Because Astra was Coded half Non-Lander, everyone here wanted to claim her for their cause – Uttu thought Astra had been sent to unite Is-Land and Non-Land too, starting with her marriage to Muzi. Well, she was doing what she could so people would have to stop pushing her now.

In front of her, Rudo scratched his neck. 'Was I a real pain in the arse today?'

'Just a bit,' Photon replied. 'My left buttock hurts only.'

'Sorry, folks.' Rudo stretched. 'Been feeling a bit ratty lately. I'm well overdue for some shore leave. Didn't spoil your birthday, did I, Astra?'

'No,' she said tartly, 'I suspected it was just sexual frustration. I'm sure Honovi will oblige if you promise to treat her buttocks nicely.'

'Ooo. Turns eighteen and her mouth runs foul as the Mikku.'

'Are you for sure dating Honovi now?' Photon asked. 'What about Jeanette?'

'Oh, she's got the hump about ye old lack o' humping. And it was never a ring thing, anyways.'

A small blue car squealed past them at a reckless speed.

'See,' Rudo said, 'I ain't the only one gets the heebie-jeebies in Zabaria.'

'Is that the rooks?' Photon asked suddenly, pointing up through the windscreen.

'All the ways out here?' Rudo craned to see.

She sat up and followed Photon's finger. Against the neon orange sky, a vast black river of birds was streaming over the Boundary, heading south: not a billowing flow with the smooth contours of a starling murmuration but a ragged, flickering torrent, swooping and swirling on and on, a mesmerising rush of black stars, alive in the flaming sky. Rooks, yes: *thousands* of them. Photon rolled down his window and the chattering cries of the birds enhanced the spectacle of their flight, a mass of sound arcing over the road, a cacophony of alarm and urgent exultation sweeping across the sun-burnt land.

'It's a consensus,' she said, 'flying to their roost. There must be some tall trees in the scrubland somewhere.' The thought was astonishing. 'But there'd be more food in Is-Land, I expect.'

'Let's hope they're shitting all over the snipers, eh, Astra?'

It was Rudo's peace-feather. She took it. 'Right splat in the face.'

And maybe, she thought, sliding back in her seat as they passed under the birds, *the joke wasn't far wrong: maybe there was a Rookowleon hidden among the counsel, flapping towards her father, bringing messages from Cora Pollen's people, building the Non-Gaian resistance*. Like the huge, wild movement of the rooks, ignoring human laws and borders, the secret thought sent a thrill stirring through her. She sat quietly, everything she'd experienced today, her birthday, bleeding together in her mind like the colours in the sky: from people eating sheep meat to Gaians killing babies. Non-Land was an impoverished, cruel, violent place, but at the same time freedom was in the air – in people's talk, their dreams, their plans for action. The majestic, volatile flight of the rooks was a Gaia vision, she slowly realised. She didn't have to pretend to be a goddess to make things happen here. They happened anyway; she was just a tiny, twisting, turning speck in the pattern. She relaxed, stretched out on the back seat, and the beeswax candle in her pocket pressed against her thigh.

The spark she'd felt when her fingers met Muzi's rekindled in her belly.

Ciccy juddered on as she lay in the darkening cabin, dreaming of holding someone, kissing, sliding her arms down a slick, warm back. *Desire.* IMBOD had tried to suck it out of her through the hole in her head, but Muzi, Enki, Lil – even, she had to admit, Rudo and his maddening smell – had reignited her powerful human need to merge with another body, the mystery of another person. She had an appointment with Dr Tapputu soon. She would find out what was wrong with her Gaia garden and when it was fixed, frig Is-Land age laws, she would find someone to play with – one of the younger CONC officers. A hoopball fan, maybe. She could do it in the dark so the person couldn't see her brand. She had to have a life outside work and Lil and Uttu's schemes.

They passed a milestone glowing white in the headlights. Rudo turned on Comchan.

'—repeat,' Sandrine's voice crackled over the speakers, 'the cladding operation has begun. YAC warriors have stormed the Hem. Fighting has commenced. Casualties *are* expected. All available MMU are to check in on Comchan and divert to Nagu One *immediately*.'

'Oh yay.' Rudo sighed and reached for the mic. 'That's my big date shot.'

She was on the edge of her seat, thoughts of sex banished in an instant. 'MMU Eight checking in, sister,' Rudo drawled. Beside him, Photon was getting his Tablette out.

'MMU Eight: I read you. Where are you?'

'Just inside Comchan lines. Heading straight to Nagu One.'

'Great, thank you, guys.' For a moment, Sandrine sounded her normal self. 'With any luck the others will all be there soon.'

'So where's we heading, exactly?'

'To the Barracks. The Sec Gens marched out about an hour ago, about a thousand of them, along the first hundred metres of the Boundary. YAC warriors were waiting in the tents. They stormed the Hem, and more people are flooding into the Nagu now to help them. We were expecting N-LA to arrest people, but they didn't. Dayyani and Rabu have announced that since IMBOD had broken the Hemline ruling, they won't be respecting it either. They're checking everyone for firearms, but otherwise they're refusing to be held responsible for holding the line. Odinson's screeching foul play, and the Major's kicking down the doors, but Dayyani's got Asfar on side. The Mujaddid is—'

'Whoah, whoah, whoah,' Rudo interrupted Sandrine's info-rattle. 'Stick to the Hem. What we heading into, weapons-wise?'

'The snipers have their rifles. N-LA police are equipped with author- ised firearms. Dayyani's threatened to shoot any Sec Gen who steps into Kadingir. So far as I know, no shots have been fired. N-LA are controlling the roads – they'll direct you as you get closer. I'm here if you need me. Tablette-message me if I'm channelling news.'

'Roger, sister. Over and out.'

Photon had the map up. 'The Barracks are 15.2 kilometres from here,' he announced, 'but the roads in Nagu One are normally difficult.'

Astra felt sick. They were racing well over the speed limit towards the dim lanterns of Kadingir. The Belt Road was running close again to the Boundary, the afternoon's yawning images of alligator throats now replaced by strobing bright-white, punch-black squares, flashing fast enough to cause headaches, seizures, even. Her heart pounding, she trained her vision on the road. At this rate, they would be there in a few minutes. *At the Barracks.*

'MMU Seven is first on the scene,' Sandrine announced. 'MMU Seven is reporting hand-to-hand combat in the Hem. Arms include spears, knives and red-pepper spray. I repeat, severe ground fighting in the Hem. Non-ballistic weapons in play. All MMU personnel are to adopt Emergency Protocol. I repeat. All MMU personnel are to adopt Emergency Protocol, with immediate effect.'

MMU Seven. That was Msandi and Eduardo, doing the route they should have been on today.

'Astra, can you get the flak jackets out of the back, please?' Photon asked. He'd pointed them out on her first day: four bulky vests stashed on the shelves.

'And some energy packs,' Rudo added. 'It's gonna be a long night.'

Her body moved automatically, lifting the middle seat section, finding the kit and clambering back laden with the jackets and packs. They put on the protective gear, Photon helping Rudo as he continued to drive.

'C'mon, Sandrine.' Rudo reached again for the mic. 'What's going on out there?'

'Don't overload her.' Photon intercepted his hand. 'She'll forward reports as soon as she gets them.'

'But we don't even know where we're taking the casualties. The Treatment Wards will be poppin' at the seams.'

'I'll message her.' Photon started typing on his Tablette.

'Ten MMUs.' Rudo sounded disgusted. 'If those snipers start taking Nonners down, we'll be about as useful as ten tin buckets tryin' to bail out the ocean.'

She licked her lips. This was something she thought she knew – something she had figured out on her own. 'IMBOD won't use the snipers,' she said. 'Not many, anyway.'

'Why not? They got infrared sights; it'll be easy pickings.'

She had started, so she had to go on. 'IMBOD's always known they have to fight this battle on the ground. Normally Non-Landers wouldn't charge at the Boundary – they can't get over or through it – but during the cladding operation, a big enough attack force could damage equipment, or even take an engineer hostage. That's why IMBOD created the Sec Gens: they're trained to fight crowds. They can even stop a car. But they fight as a . . .' She faltered, not sure how to explain berserker murmurations. 'They work as a swarm. They don't use shields, and they don't hold a line. They surge and surround. So the snipers can't risk shooting at the battle or they might kill the Sec Gens too.'

'That is interesting,' Photon mused. 'Though if a Non-Lander breaks through the battle, the snipers would of course be authorised to shoot.'

'Stop a car?' Rudo asked. 'How'd they do that?'

She was silent, glad the men couldn't see her flushed face. She had promised herself she would never tell anyone anything about the Sec Gens, but she'd wanted to stop Rudo from complaining, and, more importantly, to help the team prepare. She hadn't said anything that would endanger Peat, had she?

Sandrine's brusque voice saved her from replying. 'Okay, folks, more reports coming in. Exercise *extreme caution* on the roads. Drive slowly in Nagu One. Cooperate fully with N-LA police.' But she must have got Photon's message. 'Nagu One Treatment Ward reports five empty beds, and floor space for twenty-two. Nagu Two Treatment Ward reports six empty beds and floor space for eighteen. Until further notice take all Code One casualties to Treatment Wards One and Two. Take all Code Two casualties to the hospital. I repeat, take all Code Two injuries directly to the hospital.' She paused. 'All Code Three casualties are to be left in the custody of N-LA police at the Hem.'

The sick feeling was swishing around again in her stomach. Code One wounds were non-lethal. Code Two were life-threatening. Code Three meant the person was dead – not just dead but killed by a Sec Gen.

'Eat up, folks,' Rudo ordered. 'Chew nice and slow, Astra.'

Oat and nut bars, chocolate and dried fruit. She wasn't hungry, but she munched and swallowed. The food might as well have been plaster for all she tasted it. They were entering Kadingir now. The road was filled with carts and cars and people, trundling, inching, walking, rolling towards the Barracks. Were they all going to Nagu One to fight?

Ciccy slowed to a crawl. 'Time to get pushy, folks.' Rudo pressed a button on the dashboard. A blue light spilled over the road and a siren began to wail. The traffic parted, cart drivers lashing their animals to get out of the way; now Rudo was stepping on it, picking up speed, driving straight down the middle of the road, jerking over the crossings until Astra feared for Ciccy's tyres. The Boundary was a blinding white strip half a kilometre to the north as they barrelled through Nagu Three and into Nagu Two. To the south somewhere were the women and children from the playground, and Enki Arakkia's mother – unless they too were on the move like the rest of Kadingir.

The road had narrowed and zigzagged; it was packed with even more people. The crowd still made room for Ciccy, but there was far less of it to be had, what with vehicles parked on the sides of the road and the ragged river of people pressing up against the MMU's sides. Rudo turned off the siren and at last the reason for the congestion became clear: two red vans, bonnet to bonnet, were blocking the road and in front of them a row of people in uniform were standing firm against the crowd.

N-LA. 'Controlling the roads'. How effectively, she didn't know. She could see people slipping off the ramps, making their way into Nagu One through the tents.

'Okay. They will let us through when they can,' Photon said as Rudo inched Ciccy forward through the crowd. 'We must make a plan: Astra, when we get to the Hem, you can stay and guard Ciccy. Rudo and I will take the stretcher out, and you can drive us to the ward when we get back.'

She was outraged. 'No. I want to help – I ate my oat bar. I'm getting out if you are.'

'You are not yet trained in emergency protocol.' He sounded worried. 'And we only need two people for the stretcher.'

'*Sacrement!*' Rudo exclaimed. 'She can duck and run, can't she? And carry a first-aid bag. Ain't no better training for an emergency than an emergency, Phot.'

She would have chimed in, but N-LA were letting them through now, guarding Ciccy's back so the crowd couldn't follow, and then they were hurtling down the nearly empty road which, instead of heading straight to the Barracks, swerved south as though being dragged to the river. Sandrine erupted again on the radio.

'MMUs Two, Four, Six and Seven are all reporting the same. Listen up everybody. The fighting is still non-ballistic combat, right on the Hemline. YAC members are dragging their wounded back to the medical tent. Injuries so far include crushed windpipes, broken bones, dislocated limbs and—' for a moment, Sandrine's professionalism broke down into shock and incredulity, '— four ripped-off ears, one bitten-off nose and two cases of eye-gouging. Major Thames has ordered you *not* to enter the Hem. I repeat: you are not, *under any circumstances*, to enter the Hem.'

There was silence in the cabin. Astra's mouth filled with bile and her stomach shrank. She wanted to vomit all over the windscreen.

'We cannot take her, Rudo,' Photon insisted. 'It is far too dangerous.'

'Ya fight,' Rudo said flatly, 'ya get hurt. So far no snipers and the Nonners are collecting the wounded up in a nice pile for us. Good chance for Astra to get her feet wet.'

Wet in blood from chewed-off noses and gouged-out eyeballs? Even more than revolted, she felt humiliated. The berserker murmuration: why had she never guessed? They had practised on the lawn, group-wrestling, learning how to throw each other, how to land. Once, at the start of Year Twelve, they had swarmed a car from the side, skidding it, tipping it and rolling it over. But then she'd been quarantined – so had biting and ripping been taught while she was absent, or just when the Sec Gens started IMBOD Service? She ransacked her memory, but no clue emerged: Peat had never come home looking disturbed or shocked, or the harbourer of a dreadful guilty secret. Though maybe to a Sec Gen, tearing people's faces apart would seem completely normal, even fun. She couldn't stand to think about Peat out there, right now, *enjoying* savaging people with his bare hands and teeth.

She forced herself back into the conversation.

'It's not right we cannot enter the field,' Photon was saying. 'We should be attending to the fallen.'

'We ain't gonna be much use to the fallen with our faces chewed off,' Rudo scoffed. The argument was stopped by another N-LA roadblock: a policewoman on a horse came out of the night to greet them, Rudo rolled the window down and Photon leaned over with his Tablette map.

'Your maps are useless,' the officer shouted through the window as the horse stomped and snorted, showing the whites of its eyes. Shouts were audible in the distance and out of Photon's window, over the tents, the eerie white flash of the Boundary hurt Astra's eyes. 'We've cleared a road for medics,' the N-LA woman continued. 'You'll have to park, then trolley through the tents. So far the system's been working fine, but if fighting breaks through into the road, I can't guarantee your safety. In that case, your Comchan officer will issue new instructions. Got it?'

'Got it,' Rudo affirmed.

Kicking the horse and yanking at its cruel bit and reins, the officer led them a few metres up a side road and pointed them on.

'You must stay in Ciccy, Astra,' Photon fretted. 'You can help us lift the wounded into the chamber when we return.'

'You kidding, Phot?' Rudo exclaimed. 'If we're gonna be stretchering and trolleying bleeding people over ruts and through a sea of tents then I want all hands on deck.'

They were at the end of the road and the shouts drew nearer, keying her up. Rudo parked beside three other MMUs and Photon took two headbands out of the glove compartment.

Astra said, 'I'm eighteen, Photon. I don't need to be protected any more.'

'C'mon, Phot.' Rudo reached for the glove compartment. 'We can't leave her here on her own.'

He gave in. 'Okay. But you must *stick close*. We cannot afford to come looking for you out there.'

Coming from Photon, that hurt – but she knew she deserved it.

'I won't run off,' she muttered. 'I promise.'

He passed her a headband and she tugged it on, lighting up the forehead bulb and the blue halo.

'Nice big blue bullseyes,' Rudo commented cheerfully.

'IMBOD has not shot a CONC medic for more than twenty years,' Photon replied. On the last word, a loud report cracked the air, followed by a split second of silence, then a rising, collective scream.

'Okay, guys,' Rudo said. 'We stay safe out there, squeaky clean. We don't put a toe over the Hemline. Let's go.'

They dropped to the ground and headed to the back to unload the stretcher. It was faster to carry it with the trolley still folded, the men each taking one end and Astra bringing up the rear with the first-aid bag. The heavy bag hung high on her back over the bulk of the flak jacket. As they looked around for the path, another N-LA officer stepped out of the dark and shone a torch down the space between two tents. Astra half-jogged after Rudo and Photon, focused only on the beam of light at her feet, the scuffed trolley tracks in the soil. Then a man ahead called, 'Make way, make way!' and she pulled up short and stood aside, her heart racing, to

let a stretcher-trolley pass. Eduardo was at the front with Msandi pushing, one hand steadying an IV drip.

Beneath his blue halo, Eduardo's face was dripping with sweat. 'The
wounded are in the big tent,' he barked without losing pace.

Msandi's gaze was fixed on the patient. 'It's hell back there,' she shouted
as the trolley rattled past. 'Get in and out quick.'

Rudo and Photon ran faster, Astra scrambling behind them, the first-aid
bag thudding on her back, the screams and shouts of battle pouring through
her ears. Her stomach felt hollow, her chest made of ice, but the adrenalin
in her veins propelled her on. The path widened and another trolley jerked
past, then another, the CONC officers intent on their work, the patients
cocooned in the stretchers. Rudo and Photon veered to the left but didn't
falter. Light as aluminium, as titanium, she leapt after them through the
tents, until there were no more tents, just an open space flanked by a couple
of N-LA officers and, right in front, on the other side of a broken white line
in the dirt, a heaving, roaring, grunting chaos of bodies.

The battle was like no murmuration she had ever been part of. It wasn't
smooth and intuitive, wing-tip to wing-tip, but a monstrous agglomeration of rage. Everywhere she looked legs and arms, heads and torsos,
were lunging and grappling, merging into one hideous self-cannibalising
creature: an endless dark bulk violently engaged in devouring itself, its
writhing mass of human nodules and tentacles seared bright white by the
light strobing from the Boundary. *Peat*, she thought again with an acid
pang, but it was impossible to identify anyone in that churning beast. She
could make out flashes of white uniforms, the glints of what looked like
spear tips, and here and there, as if being excreted from the monster, half-
figures in dark shirts – Non-Landers? – raining down blows with what
looked like clubs and knives and iron bars.

Above and behind the mêlée was the stroboscopic Boundary, its stark
screen a grid of huge bloodshot eyes: whirling black irises caged by a
crackle of veins, framed by heavy black lids and black squares, square after
square, stacked like cubes across the screen. The eyes blinked, disappeared. For a second the screen was blank – but no, not blank; long black
lines remained – ropes and platforms: the cladding engineers. Then more
graphics flashed: huge open mouths, scarlet blood dripping from the corners of pitch-black lips, teeth gnashing and clashing back into the grid of
eyeballs popping open, snapping shut again.

If she squinted with unfocused eyes, she could look into the strobe without pain. In this way, the Boundary was hypnotic. She stood, trans-fixed, part of her mind wondering how on earth the Shelltech engineers could be working in that manic intensity of light. Wearing goggles, probably.

AIIIIEEEEEEEEEE!

An ear-piercing shriek broke the spell and as someone hurtled across the empty stretch of ground into battle she shook herself back into duty mode. She was here to *help* people. She shouldn't be gawking at the Boundary, trying to work out its tech spec like a Year Ten student. Rudo had unfolded the trolley and Photon was talking to an N-LA officer, the woman pointing left down the Hemline towards a golden glow rising up into the sky as if from some vast treasure chest. No, Astra realised: it came from behind the Barracks wall, unlit, low compared to the Boundary, but still undeniably, remorselessly there: ten-metre-high basalt brickwork stretching deep into Kadingir at the far end of the battlefield.

She swallowed. She was going to have to head towards the Barracks – but not all the way. The N-LA officer was indicating a large, marquee-style tent in the middle distance. Before and beyond it, all along this side of the contested ground, the dark shapes of YAC warriors were charging out from between the tents into the fight, as beneath their feet, a countervailing tide, crouching figures were dragging the wounded off the field.

There were spectators too, people standing or sitting on carts and boxes and chairs, and N-LA officers with guns, authorised to shoot Sec Gens if they stepped an inch outside the Hem. Clearly there was no room to push the trolley; that was why Photon and Rudo were detaching the stretcher. With half an eye on the battle, she head-huddled closer for instructions.

'N-LA will guard the trolley,' Photon yelled. 'We head straight to the medical tent. No stopping for injured on the field: that's YAC's job. Astra, let me take the bag now.'

Was she going to be useless, just a frightened tag-along? But she couldn't argue with orders. Rudo carried the stretcher pad under his arm and Photon shadowed him with the bag. She ran hard after them, weav-ing in between the Non-Landers crowding the Hemline, jumping over bodies. She had felt light before; now, without the bag weighing her down, she thought she might lose touch with the ground, lift up and sail into the night sky. Ahead, the battle bulged dangerously close, as if a wedge of Sec Gens were pushing the Non-Landers back to the Hemline. But YAC kept coming. The Sec Gens might be bigger and stronger, but YAC were many, well-armed and unpredictable. There were wheelchair teams on the edge of the battle, steerers pushing alt-bodied warriors, their chairs bristling with spikes aimed at Sec Gen shins, knees, thighs. Everywhere were youths with spears, swords and flailing chains. And in the middle of the battle, like a flag, the giant YAC man was fighting like an elemental force, head and shoulders above the tallest Sec Gen, roaring and thrashing, a club in one hand, a sword in the other. He was even taller than his comrade, a warrior lunging forward on a horse.

Would a Sec Gen blind a horse? It made her want to retch to think about it – but there was no time to throw up: a skinny boy in a vest rushed out in front of her brandishing a torch. She cut to the side as he leapt into the Hem, thrusting his flame into the face of a Sec Gen, a woman who howled and doubled over, her windmilling arms knocking the torch to the ground. The boy leapt onto the Sec Gen's shoulders and clung on, then was lost to sight as Astra rushed past. Everything ahead was a glazed blur: more orange torches streaking into the battle, the sheen of sweat on forearms and faces. There was a glint of silver as a YAC star twisted on a man's chest, the dizzy black-and-white dazzle of the Boundary, with its snapping mouths and blinking eyes, and the golden radiance rising from behind the Barracks wall: a harvest of light, the rounded glass roofs of the Barracks themselves glimmering, the Boundary there not a game board but a vista of black eagles beating their wings.

As when she'd noticed the cladding engineers, the Is-Land half of her mind detached itself and told her things no one else could: the Barracks, Astra realised, her feet flying beneath her, was a Congregation Site: a square kilometre of Is-Land. That meant the Sec Gens were defending Gaia's most sacred soil; they would be *honoured* to die in this fight. As she ran, her heart in the pit of her stomach, a row of figures appeared on the Barracks wall. They spread their arms like wings and then *leapt down* into the battle.

She ducked, narrowly avoiding a big man staggering off the field, blood streaming down from the place where his eyes should be. And then she was at the marquee entrance, a young woman was ushering them inside, and everything was completely different again.

'All clear, squad?' the Division Officer barked.

'All clear!' nine strong young voices affirmed to the night. Nine Sec Gens, charged up and standing tall after an hour of drill and final instructions in the scrubland behind the Zabaria mine. Zabaria! The mission had evolved in ways Peat had never anticipated. It was grander, more ambitious and more dangerous now: a fitting tribute to their fallen comrade Laam, Odinson had said this afternoon in the Barracks. To tell the truth, hearing the new mission goals had planted a seed of fear in Peat's stomach and not even an hour of press-ups and murmuration judo had dislodged it.

'Excellent! Commence the final stage!'

Fear was good though: like hunger, like anger, a small dose of it made you keen and alert. Jogging back to his van, Peat took a harsh breath of dry night air, thrilling again to the severity, the drama and the sheer enormity of this place. The mine rose, a dark plateau streaked with lamp-spill, against a distant grey haze the officer had said was tents – grim, mean Non-Lander dwellings, menacing the horizon, then stopping abruptly, ceding either side to an appalling black emptiness. Incredible to believe that behind him, right on the other side of the Boundary, was the steppes Congregation Site, a vibrant place of celebration. The Non-Land scrubland was nothing like the steppes, not mounded or rich and smelling of fertility. The IREMCO mine was a rampart, a bulwark against a barren vista of ignorance, squalor and evil. Oh, the honour of holding a Gaian outpost firm in an endless plain of hostility! The mine-managers deserved medals.

He climbed back into his van. He was driving! One day he would tell people – Klor, Nimma, his Birth Code parents, Laam's parents – all about his role in this historic operation, but for now the mission was top secret. So secret he had not even known when it would launch. This morning he had hoped against hope he would be fighting on the Hem tonight, defending the Barracks, one of the first divisions of Sec Gens charged with repelling the attack of the treacherous Non-Landers. But Odinson was unimaginably clever: a genius. He had understood that the cladding operation provided the perfect cover for the mission. N-LA, YAC and CONC forces were fully diverted, the Belt roads were empty and the international media lined up at the battlefield. Tonight was the night. And not only for immediate, pragmatic reasons; Odinson also knew that YAC's anticipated assault on the cladding operation required a strategic, long-term response. The new, *heightened* mission plan anticipated the Non-Landers' next moves and put IMBOD firmly in control of the game playing out not only in Kadingir, but also in Amazigia.

Yes, executing the mission successfully was the biggest responsibility of Peat's life. It had started like a fantastic race, the journey out along the IMBOD Boundary road a blur of nerves and exhilaration. With Robin whooping beside him, Peat had driven at top speed, safe in the wake of the Division Officer's van. That was right, of course; even if the mission hadn't expanded from his group's original idea, they would still need guidance, a superior to lead them. They also needed physical help now: behind him were three more vans, their cabins filled with six more Sec Gens, hand-picked for their courage, fitness and exceptional ability to perform as one in this noble feat of daring. Still, they were only *helpers*. Flying along the Boundary, its flashing images of leaping, snarling honey badgers flooding the cabin with white light, bleaching their new red uniforms, Peat had allowed himself one small moment to bask in glory. The N-LA vans and uniforms had been *his* group's idea; they deserved their place at the head of the convoy, he and Robin in charge of a van, Jade sitting with the officer at the very front.

The Zabaria mine road was dark and brooding, its infrequent lamps bathing him and Robin in a murky, yellowish glow. He rounded the corner of the mine, heading south towards the line of tent haze. Above, the sky was a sprawling, magnetic black glitter. If not for the steady compass-needle of the officer's van he might sail into its void. The road turned again and ran along the front of the mine ridge. He passed a long row of buildings, the lights of their windows climbing like steps in the darkness.

'Those are the mine-managers' ziggurats,' Robin said. 'My uncle lived in one when he worked here.'

Peat drove on, his chest swelling with a riot of emotion. The spotlit roofs of the ziggurats, he could see now, were palm glades: green and fruitful oases! Is-Land architects knew how to accentuate the beauty of Gaia, to honour Her majesty in even the most desolate place. The tents were pathetic, a dirty puddle staining the soil. And you would not want to compete here with the sky and the horizon, not build ridiculous tower blocks – but steps of light, gardens in the wilderness, the humility and grandeur of that? *Yes*. He wanted to cry.

The officer's van turned right, down a road that ran like an arrow to the tents. They were far beyond the Hem and now they were leaving the shelter of the mine behind too. It was like standing on a high diving board above a fathomless black ocean. The seed of fear in his stomach was sprouting; he was scared, yes, but not scared to die, afraid only to fail: to somehow let everyone down, disgrace Odinson, Laam, his officer, the squad.

But failure was *not* an option. You couldn't stand on the board, looking down; you had to jump. He and the squad were trained up, pumped up, jack-kniving for glory, and there would be no surfacing until their mission was done.

ASTRA

The tent was lit by high-voltage electric lamps hanging from the poles. Wounded warriors were lying on mats laid out in rows across the ground. Between their long lines moved robed figures, nurses dispensing water and bandages. From everywhere rose the coppery tang of blood and a low chorus of groans, cries and whimpers, a tuneless hymn of distress soldered together by a familiar insistent ringing.

The music of the singing bowls came from the perimeter: the bowl-players sitting at the feet of three figures on three podiums against three walls of the tent. To the far right was Asar, cross-legged on a stool, swaying as his carer dabbed his lips with her ceremonial cloth; to the left Simiya was standing and singing, her mouths stretched open wide. And opposite the entrance, her arms spread wide above her musicians, Tiamet was clashing her finger cymbals and flashing her kohl-lined eyes.

How had Tiamet got here so quickly? Was Lil here too? As Astra scanned the tent, the small splashes of Tiamet's cymbals floated like kisses towards her, while Simiya's beautifully discordant voices penetrated the drone of the bowls like a shining, double-edged blade. This was not like the River Raven music, chaotic and surging; it was monotonous, elevating, profoundly still. She couldn't see Lil, but that didn't matter, she realised. All questions could be answered later. She was here with Photon and Rudo, with their backs to the battle, in a place that offered a slight possibility of doing their job.

Though where to possibly begin? At her feet a woman was rocking back and forth, a gash in her skull, her hair matted with blood, knees pressed to her chest. Beside her a man was shaking from head to toe; from his rigid expression she could see he was trying desperately not to scream. All around, fallen warriors were scrunched up in foetal positions, clutching their stomachs, biting their own wrists. Here and there, whole bodies were covered in white sheets. She swallowed. *The Code Threes*.

Rudo grabbed a nurse, a young boy no more than twelve. 'Kid – where're your Code Twos?'

The boy pointed to the centre of the tent. '*Psssst*,' he hissed, and a small, dark-robed man looked their way.

Dr Tapputu's face lit up when he saw them – was he *smiling*? – and he gestured: *come, come*. She followed Rudo and Photon deeper into the tent.

'Gentlemen. Astra. How glorious to see you.' Dr Tapputu was on the move already, gliding ahead of them between the mats, towards Asar's podium. 'There's someone here I'd very much like you to meet.'

Astra bumped behind, nearly stepping on Photon's heels. The sound of the singing bowls filled her body now, banishing the past, and the future. They gave you concentration and certainty – that was why Dr Tapputu was smiling, she thought.

But there was nothing to smile about. Propped up against the podium was Enki Arakkia. His face drained, his eyes half open, rolling back in his head, the YAC warrior was clutching his shoulder, his hand clamped to a blood-soaked bandage. For a moment Astra thought he'd grown a beard, but the shadow on his face was a smear of dried blood; at his throat it wasn't hair but a massive purple bruise. Tenderly, Asar's carer leaned down from the stage and soothed the wounded man's forehead with the blessing cloth.

Dr Tapputu beckoned them aside. 'He was brought in twenty minutes ago.' He pointed to a pile of bloodstained canvas at the foot of Enki's mat. 'He was fighting from inside a kind of cage strapped to the back of a fellow warrior – his friend Bartol – but the Sec Gens dragged them apart. His man-mount managed to save Enki from their attack; he got him back to the Hemline. I believe he then returned to the frenzy.'

'The man mountain?' Rudo nodded. 'Clocked him wielding a scimitar.'

'I gather that was the Arakkia family sword: he led the charge with it, and he knows Bartol still has it. His pride is intact – but otherwise, he is not in good shape. His arm needs specialised suturing and his larynx has been crushed; I'd like it properly examined.'

'Okay,' Rudo agreed, 'let's get him on the stretcher.'

Photon, though, looked anxious. 'Our orders are strictly Code Two. Are his injuries life-threatening?'

Dr Tapputu spread his hands. 'Call him Code One and Three-Quarters. He's lost a lot of blood and I can't guarantee he won't haemorrhage. But officers: forget Major Thames. The problem we have is that he's clogging the bottleneck. He won't leave his people, but none of them will take his place in the queue.'

Rudo and Photon exchanged glances. 'I think,' Photon began, 'we do not normally ask the wounded if—'

'This is not a normal operation,' the doctor cut in. 'This is YAC. I can't authorise you to lift an alt-bodied warrior without his permission.'

'All right.' Rudo was getting impatient. 'We don't take him. Who's next then?'

'She is.' Dr Tapputu pointed to a big-shouldered woman curled up on a bloody mat next to Enki. 'But I'm telling you, she won't go instead of him.'

'Fine. We won't take her either.' Rudo was getting impatient now. 'Who's after her, then?'

'I've been talking to all the Code Twos for the last ten minutes: none of them will go instead of Arakkia, but he won't listen to me when I tell him that. It's infuriating – for all YAC is a collective organism, he is its international spokesperson and I can't in all conscience allow him to lose his voice, his arm or his life.'

'Oh for frack's sake. Let me talk to him.' Rudo crouched beside Arakkia and Astra leaned in as the team gathered round. 'Enki Arakkia.' Rudo spoke loudly over the drone of the singing bowls. 'I'm a CONC medic, here with a stretcher. Doc says it's time for you to go to the hospital. That good with you?'

Arakkia opened his eyes to a dark slit.

'Not. Dying,' he wheezed.

'Please,' Dr Tapputu said, 'I've told you: You are not to speak. And I can't promise that you aren't dying.'

Arakkia shook his head, a tremor of pain rippling over his features.

Was that it? Astra gulped. *How could he sacrifice himself like this? Wasn't there any way to persuade him?*

Rudo turned to the woman. Her eyes were two creases, her face shuttered up. 'Hear that?' he said. 'Enki's not going. You're next, okay? We got the stretcher right here.'

It hurt her to move, Astra could see, but the woman shook her head too. 'Enki go,' she croaked.

Rudo stood up. 'Look, Tapputu, we ain't got time for this. The next Code Two comes in from the field, we take. No questions, no choices.'

'Yes, yes. I know.' He grimaced. 'I'm sorry. I was just trying to respect their solidarity. The nurses will alert us. We still have a few minutes to persuade him.' He knelt and said, 'Enki, stop being a pig-headed dolt. Your people want you to go to the hospital. We're not going to win this war without you.'

Up on the podium, Asar was swaying. *The Seer*, Astra thought: Enki would listen to Asar. Edging quickly between the wounded warriors, she stepped up to the stage.

'*Astra*,' Photon hissed.

'I'm right *here*,' she shot back over her shoulder. 'I'll just be a minute.'

'Oh let her be, Phot,' Rudo sighed. 'She ain't running off.'

She climbed up between the carer and a singing-bowl player. Her back to the tent, she knelt at Asar's feet. He was sitting on an upholstered stool, his hands resting on his robed knees, his body swaying within the concentric rings of the singing bowls. The carer smiled and raised her blessing cloth. Astra closed her eyes and felt the woman press the warm, damp reassurance to her forehead as she gathered her courage. The carer removed the cloth. Astra opened her eyes. 'Please,' she stammered in Somarian, 'I'm sorry – he's busy – but can I ask Asar a question?'

ASAR

song bowl playing   quiet playing   slow playing
many souls one soul   many bowls one song   souls rising song
souls flying song   night birds flying   goodbye souls goodbye

~ Asar   star girl here   soul question time? ~
~ star girl? ~

small girl
girl head lamb wool
girl head bump hole
soul hole

soul hole hot
star hot
Asar soul
touching
star girl soul

~ question time yes   girl question good ~
girl no fingerword speak   Sepsu ask girl question
~ girl say Enki hurt   Enki want soul fly   people want Enki stay
fly or stay, Asar, fly or stay? ~
Enki song bowl tent   Enki river party   Enki bad hard place
Enki friend   Enki big soul bird   Enki bird broken wing
no fly no fly

Enki soul no flying   Enki soul . . .
'*Arr arr arr!*'

                                    . . . *dancing*   Enki soul dancing

~ fly or stay, Asar? ~
~ dancing answer Sepsu! dancing answer! ~

ASTRA

Asar laughed, soft breathy gusts of delight brushing the strident singing-bowl tones, and a string of his saliva fell onto the carer's hand. As the woman gasped and pressed her hand to her face, wiping the spit on her cheeks, Asar lifted his arms from his knees, and half flapped, half pushed his palms through the air.

It was the sign for Enki – the one the boys in the playground had used. Enki's wheelchair – *Enki's wheelchair*. Of course!

'Dancing.' The carer was signing with the Seer. 'He says the answer is dancing.'

'I understand,' she whispered, 'thank you. Thank you, Asar.' He stretched his foot out, wiggling his toes. On an impulse she took his foot in her hand. The skin was as soft as a baby's. She pressed the sole against her cheek, kissed it, and he laughed softly again, *arrr arrr arrr*, his breath melding with the ecstatic drone of the bowls. Beside him the carer was crying, her face wet with joy. Astra touched the woman's knee – thank you – then slid off the stage and back to the team.

'Asar says to take Enki in his wheelchair,' she told them. 'Then Photon and Rudo can take the woman in the stretcher. Ask them if they'll agree to that.'

Photon ran his hand through his hair. 'You asked Asar what to do?' *Thank you, Photon*: he sounded not sceptical or angry but wondering.

'The carer signed the question. She knows what he said. Tell everyone.'

'I dunno, Astra,' Rudo objected. 'It's heavy going out there. Ground's getting pretty dug up, and then there's all those tent pegs.'

'It's dry – I can do it. I can pull the pegs out and put them back in.'

Rudo looked at Photon. 'And where we going to put them both in Ciccy? We ain't allowed to put two in the chamber.'

'His condition looks stable to me,' Photon said. 'We can put the woman in the ion glove and Enki in the back seat. If we lower it, we can strap him in, and Astra can sit at his head.'

'Yes, yes. She's absolutely right.' Dr Tapputu slapped his forehead. 'Why didn't I think of it myself?' He knelt again beside Enki. 'Arakkia, listen to me. We have a solution. The Seer has spoken: the team can take both you and Dorkas. It's a special team. There are three medics here: it's a sign that you are both to go to the hospital. Arakkia, are you listening? We can take both of you.'

Arakkia's eyes fluttered open. For the first time he attempted to focus on the officers, but whether taut with pain or suspicion, his expression did not waver.

'The carer,' Astra urged. 'Tell the Seer's carer to tell him. *Wheelchair*. Asar said to take him in the wheelchair.' Enki's gaze wavered over her and his mouth twitched.

Dr Tapputu bundled up to the stage and spoke to the carer. The woman leaned down and traced a wet finger over Arakkia's brow. Then she whispered in his ear.

He sank back, his body relaxed, his eyes closed.

'Asar has spoken!' the doctor cried out so all the tent could hear. 'Enki and Dorkas are going to the hospital together – do you hear that, Dorkas?' He marched over to the Code Two woman. 'Enki agrees: the three medics will take you both.'

'Clever work, Astra.' Rudo had laid the stretcher on the ground and was unclipping the straps. 'So where's his chair, Doc?'

Dr Tapputu pulled the young nurse towards him. 'Boy – run like a *mergallá* to the warrior armoury and fetch Arakkia's chair. Bring it to the front of the tent.'

The boy sped off. Expertly, Rudo and Photon slid the stretcher between Arakkia and Dorkas and eased him onto it. Astra followed as the men lifted the fallen YAC warrior and carried him across the tent. It was a victory procession, with the singing bowls intensifying, Simiya's voices soaring, Tiamet's cymbals cascading, and all who could chanting, 'Enki, Enki, Enki.' Eyes half closed, his limbs strapped into the stretcher, Enki raised a blood-smeared hand, his fingertips saluting his warriors.

They stopped inside the door. Outside, the battle was still raging, but the massive wrestle of bodies looked closer to the tents now, as if the Sec Gens were winning, forcing the Non-Lander warriors back. Out of the darkness the boy came racing towards them, thrusting a wheelchair in front of him. Photon and Rudo set the stretcher down.

'We want to lift you now, Enki,' Photon asked in Somarian. 'Don't speak: just blink once for yes, twice for no.'

Enki blinked. Holding him at the waist and good shoulder, supporting his head, careful not to disturb his wound, the two men lifted him into his chair.

'Is there a seatbelt in it?' Rudo asked.

Photon slid his hands down the sides. 'No.' He took off the first-aid bag, rummaged inside and brought out a white roll of bandage. 'We're going to bandage you in, Enki,' he shouted over the music. 'If it's too tight, blink twice, okay?'

Enki grimaced as the medics improvised a seatbelt, wrapping the bandage around his torso and the back of the chair.

'Great,' Rudo encouraged, as Photon cut another length of gauze. 'I need you to keep holding that shoulder tight for me, Enki,' he said, 'just like you've been doing. I am going to put your arm in a sling, to help you keep your hand up there. If you need to use the arm, you can just slip it out of the sling, okay?'

Arakkia grunted assent, Rudo and Photon fixed the sling, then stepped back, satisfied.

'Good,' Photon said. 'We'll get Dorkas now. Wait here, Astra. *Right* here.'

The men stepped quickly back through the mats. Astra took one last look around the tent. Behind Dr Tapputu, Asar was waving his arms to the roof. Simiya's serenade was setting the tent walls aquiver; Tiamet's finger cymbals were sending gasps of passion flying everywhere. And there, smack dab in the centre of the tent, was Lil.

Astra wanted to run to her, ask what she was doing here, what was happening in Zabaria – if Neperdu and Anunit and the others were here, if they were okay. But she couldn't leave Enki; she was charged with delivering him to the hospital and she couldn't fail, not at her first task in that journey. The whole tent was aware of her guarding their warrior. She gripped the wheelchair handles, stood up straight.

Lil raised her arm and spread her hand open in the YAC star symbol. Behind her, raised on her podium, Tiamet shook her tumbling hair and smiled a broad, open-throated smile. The Singular clashed all her cymbals together at once, a bright resounding tremble. To the wounded, it was a salute to Enki Arakkia, but Astra knew it was far more than that.

'Istar!' Lil cried.

'Istar!' Tiamet echoed.

'Istar, Istar, Istar.'

The cry went around the tent and Astra cringed. *No.*

But she had said she would pretend. She stood rooted to the spot, the chants and drones circling through her like a gathering cyclone. In the wheelchair, Enki raised his head, listening as Simiya sang to her too, *Isssssstaaaaaarrrrrrr.*

And then, for a long moment, she wasn't pretending: she was merging, recharging, her body humming, her heart flaring with understanding: she might be a Non-Gaian in CONC clothing, but somehow she belonged to everyone here – and not just as a speck in the pattern. Right now the pattern needed a pivot, a fulcrum. For random reasons accruing the force of law, she had been chosen to hold the tent's spinning energy constant and focused, gathering the momentum it needed to whirl them all up over the battlefield, up and over the Boundary and into a whole new world.

UNA DAYYANI

Istar, Istar, Istar.

She pressed pause, then play, and listened again.

'It's a tent full of wounded people! Are you sure they're not just wheezing?'

'Positive,' Artakhshathra declared. 'They're definitely chanting "Istar".'

'Definitely,' Marti agreed.

She closed the file, passed the Tablette back to Artakhshathra and pressed her fingertips to her forehead. 'And the Ordott girl was there?'

'That's what the boy said: she asked the Seer a question and the answer convinced Arakkia to go to hospital. The boy himself fetched the wheelchair. He says everyone believes Istar has arrived now, and as long as YAC keeps fighting the Boundary will fall.'

She shut her eyes and massaged her temples. It had been another exceptionally long day. Refusing to police the Hemline for IMBOD while continuing to honour CONC's firearms de-escalation policy had been a bold move, as Tahazu Rabu had agreed, but also a major gamble. Had Odinson sent his human pitbulls charging out into Kadingir, the corpses of N-LA police would now be carpeting the hospital wards. Fortunately, Is-Land too wanted to impress Amazigia, so IMBOD had shown restraint. For now. The forty-four dead and nearly three hundred seriously injured youth were all YAC members – but their leader was still alive, and people were rallying to his cause, and not just in Kadingir. Once again, the international media reports were adulating YAC. From his hospital bed a blinded warrior had calmly stated that the Sec Gens could gouge his eyes out and chew his limbs off, one by one, but he would never let them take his dignity or his rights. The clip was going viral. Even her own people had been affected. In the street protest outside the hospital, an old woman in a red robe had declared that all good sane people condemned the monstrous beings IMBOD had created, and she hoped it was only a matter of time before N-LA police joined YAC in the Hem.

If Rabu had his way today at the Cabinet meeting, perhaps N-LA would. But the last thing she needed right now was her staff pushing her to make key policy decisions on the basis of the reports of a twelve-year-old boy.

At the same time she had to accept it was true: the Prophecy had been invoked. It was being quoted on Tablette placards today, and now this bothersome recording had emerged.

'All right.' She sighed. 'Put the rumourmongers on the meeting agenda.'

'Good.' Marti was already typing. 'Shall I make you an appointment with the Seer, too?'

'Why?' she snapped.

'It would be good if he blessed you now,' Artakhshathra replied. Her staff had become a beer-hall act, a double-headed cloth donkey speaking with the same straw mind. 'You could visit the hospital afterwards, to heal his warriors. That would work with the Pro—'

'Oh for—' She rose and scooped up her handbag. Rabu was due any minute. She had to freshen up, slather on some of that new Asfarian moisturiser, prepare to meet her Chief of Police and Co-Convenors beneath the conference dome. 'Yes, all right – but I want that rebuttal statement written and ready to go, Marti. Now!'

Marti beamed. 'It's in your inbox.'

'And what about my thank-you note to Mujaddid? We can't keep him waiting!'

As Marti bent her head to the task of crafting the necessary pleasantries, Una swished across the Beehive to the washroom. Despite the exhausting nature of battle, its little hitches and frustrations, she was feeling supremely confident. ShareWorld might be more interested in sensationalist newsclips, but she had made her mark on the *real* news today. Out on the Beehive forecourt at dawn she had roundly denounced IMBOD's *militarisation of human Code* – a fantastic phrase; one Artakhshathra had coined. Let Amazigia chew on *that* for a while. She had also praised her officers for enforcing the prohibition on firearms: no fewer than twelve guns had been confiscated at the checkpoints and their owners arrested, proving that N-LA was the only political body in the region determined to keep the peace. Ignoring their own sniper's murderous violation of the Hemline agreement just a few days ago, IMBOD was squawking 'breakdown of trust', while CONC was still squatting on the fence, wringing their hands over the unnecessary cladding operation and the lamentable outbreak of violence. The Mujaddid, however, had followed up her media appearance with his own dignified endorsement of her handling of the crisis. Yes, all with eyes to see in Amazigia would clearly understand that N-LA had firmly staked its claim to the moral high ground in this conflict.

The best way to keep command of that lofty plateau was to remain serene, well-groomed and fragrant. She closed the door and unzipped her bag. That new moisturiser was heavenly: infused with essential oils, bergamot, sandalwood, myrrh and something rare and precious, the Mujaddid had written: a few drops of sacred frankincense, harvested from his own private grove, a scent to centre and ground her, open her heart and crown chakras, release her highest wisdom. *It had certainly*, she thought as she smiled into the mirror, *released her husband's sacred cream*.

But she digressed ... Wisdom, yes: the wisdom to know that peace was a weapon, a strategic advantage to be wielded like any other. Only a fool would believe last night's battle was simply a 'skirmish', one to be defused by diplomatic reshufflings of CONC agreements. She'd burned her bridges with IMBOD now, and Odinson was doubtless planning retaliation, most likely to be announced when he finally released his casualty figures. And while on the face of it YAC had been thoroughly trounced, the hospital had reported that seven of their dead had been killed by sniper fire; though the doctors had ordered Enki Arakkia not to speak, writing on a Tablette he had issued a victory statement, declaring that his shot comrades had broken the Sec Gen line:

> IMBOD's 'monsters' are only human.
> Who can stop them? We all can!
> YAC will bite back, again and again
> And Non-Land will rise, or this rhyme don't scan!

Yes, the lines were shifting, Una knew. Even out in the Beehive forecourt, some of her supporters were calling for N-LA to join YAC in the Hem. She smoothed the moisturiser into her cheeks, inhaling the woody, balsamic aroma. Frankincense was also anti-ageing, and balanced female hormones; Marti had looked it up on Archivia. She rubbed some of the lotion into her forehead too. Some cooling eye gel would be nice. All these sleepless nights were giving her the wrong sort of puffy pillows. Dropping a hint in an email might be too obvious, but if the Mujaddid called, she might mention it when they next spoke. The whole world was watching her now. She owed it to her people to maintain not only her composure, but her regal appearance.

Still, shadows were signs she had been working hard for the people. Despite the fatigue, she had not felt this alive since she was a teenager, accompanying her father on his beer-tent rounds, learning how to hold her own in the hurly-burly of male argument. After years of urging hot-headed men to tread the path of patience and cooperation, to finally openly embrace the conflict was invigorating. YAC, those young cubs, had done that for her. Leaning into the mirror, she smoothed a stray speck of moisturiser into her nose. Marti and Artakhshathra were right, though: under no circumstances must Arakkia and his confused scrap of a Gaian girl be allowed to usurp the noble lineage, the sacred vision, of the Lioness Una Dayyani. The Lioness had been born to lead this war – even if it meant flirting with the notion of the divine right of Queens.

She closed her eyes and took one last sniff of the moisturiser. The scent filled her with a sense of her own potency. When she opened her eyes, her next move was clear. The Mujaddid's position rested on ancient founda-tions, did it not? Forget the eye gel; what she needed to ask of him was how he balanced his divine right to rule with the democratic aspirations of his people and the ambitions of his under-governors. She would arrange another diplomatic mission to Asfar – such a fascinating place. She would bring her husband, take him on a boat trip to see the reintro-duced manatees: that would stop him moaning about all those ruined dinners.

She closed the jar and slipped it back into her bag. They could grow frankincense trees here in Non-Land, she was sure. Though it would be better to start with another rare plant, not to rival the Mujaddid. *Myrrh trees.* She clicked her fingers. Now *that* would be evocative. The more ancient myths in the pot the better. This was Non-Land after all.

Skin, moral qualms and war diary attended to, she ran her fingers through her hair. It was a little gritty and lacklustre; there had been no time to wash and condition it properly. The solution to that was obvious. She set her purse on the ledge, pulled out her gold headscarf and began to wrap it into a turban.

Marti and Artakhshathra were right about something else. She might not be a goddess, but she was no longer simply a political leader either: she was a figurehead now, a symbol of her people's aspirations and defiance. Henceforth, from Cabinet meetings to street demonstrations, all Una Dayyani's appearances were formal occasions.

ASTRA

She woke at noon, every muscle in her body groaning. She had worked until four in the morning, returning again and again to the Hem, long after the fighting had stopped, until all the wounded had been attended to. Around midnight, when the Sec Gens had pushed YAC back to within a foot of the Hemline, a call had gone out to withdraw – she'd seen it happen: the fighting cease, the Non-Land warriors stepping or limping or rolling back to safe ground, the Sec Gens refusing the bait, lining up on the Hemline roaring and growling, fists and faces oozing blood. Frantically, she'd searched for Peat, but she'd not seen him. And then her work had really begun. As Non-Lander cart-drivers had started arriving in the MMU car park, queuing up to ferry the wounded to the hospital, she'd run back and forth with the trolley, more wheelchairs, helping move everyone who could be moved.

The most severely wounded had gone in the MMUs, the rules against more than one patient per back chamber soon broken, with one warrior suspended in the ion glove and another laid out in the stretcher on the floor. It might be dangerous – but unless there was a rare fault in the circuitry, an ion glove would only fail and drop its occupant on the floor if the MMU battery ran low, a risk easily averted by keeping a close eye on the gauge. The back seats had been used as well, and Rudo had even found some singing-bowl tracks on ShareWorld to channel through the speakers.

Lil had worked too, passing Astra often on the route between the tent and the parking lot, but there was no time to talk, just to run and fetch the wounded and drive, until two-thirds of the mats in the medical tent were empty and the rest were filled with white shrouds.

In the light of her room, it all felt like a warped dream. Her eighteenth birthday had begun with the scent of a beeswax candle and ended with wave after wave of bloodstained and dead bodies.

She lay and stared up at the ceiling. Above her head, the spider plant on the windowsill was putting out a new baby. It had three now, little green-and-white starbursts that had been giving her small tickles of happiness when she woke up. But what was one tiny new plant next to a hospital full of gravely wounded people and a huge tent filled with corpses? The Gaia visions she'd been having were all about patterns, wholeness, hope; but death, like IMBOD's alligators and grizzly bears, mangled and devoured all that. A person's eyes closed forever, and the loss ripped an irreparable tear in the whole.

The light caught the new baby leaf bud: a twinkle in the room. She had thought this place was a prison, a cell, but in fact it was a palace. She was one of the lucky ones. She had survived the night. She forced herself to consider her position, the possible futures randomly sprouting for her: joining YAC, playing a part in the Istar story; working for CONC during a war in Kadingir; going to Shiimti; staying with Uttu, getting to know Muzi . . . There were long-term options too: a CONC passport, a scholarship, even.

Somehow all these possibilities stemmed from her, were rooted in the same soil, but it was hard to see how they could all keep growing together.

Her Tablette buzzed. If only to stop feeling dizzy, she supposed she ought to see who it was.

Officer Ordott! Felicitations!

Congratulations again on your sterling performance last night. Would that we both could rest. But your test results have arrived from Amazigia, and I need to see you urgently. I will be in the compound clinic all afternoon. Please come in the moment you arise.

Yours faithfully,
Dr Tapputu

She let the Tablette drop in the sheets. After last night, a botched brand-wound hardly felt urgent.

But lying in bed forever was one option she didn't have.

'Astra. My apologies for no doubt interrupting your sleep.'

Dr Tapputu's skin was cracked grey bark and his robe was rumpled. She felt a twinge of guilt. The last she'd seen of him, he was attending to patients at the hospital, crouching over the warriors lining the corridor floors. He should be sleeping himself, not looking after her.

'That's okay. How are Enki and Dorkas?' she asked.

'Both stable – but it was a good thing we got Enki in. His shoulder needed immediate attention. He won't be able to use it for some time, but he should regain full function eventually.'

'And his throat?'

The doctor ghosted a smile. 'I believe we have managed to convince him that his voice needs a short rest.' The smile disappeared. 'But Astra, it's you I'm concerned about right now.'

Dr Tapputu was so nice, but he shouldn't be worried about her. 'I feel fine. The medication you gave me is working well.'

'I'm glad to hear that.' He grimaced, stroked his goatee. 'But the test results indicate that you don't have a medical problem.'

Was it her brain, or his, not working properly today? 'So what's the big deal?'

'Unfortunately, I am not authorised to tell you on my own. Major Thames has to be here. Do I have your permission to invite hir in?'

This was weird. 'What if I say no?'

'Then Major Thames will summon us both to hir office. I thought you might prefer a less formal approach.'

So she didn't have a choice. She folded her arms. 'Okay. *Summon* Major Thames, then.'

The doctor sent the Tablette message and they waited in silence. On the doctor's picture frame, Sri Auroville was sitting in lotus position, eyes closed and palms pressed together in a *namaste*.

'How's the little boy?' she asked.

'I'm sorry?'

'The boy in the Treatment Ward, who was looking after Sri Auroville.'

'Gud.' Dr Tapputu paused. 'Gud has, I believe you would say, returned to Gaia.'

'Oh.' She pushed her chair away, stared at the wall and tried to ignore the pain in her chest.

'Aren't my medical reports *confidential*?' she blurted.

'It's not a medical problem, Astra. I really can't say any more until the Major gets—'

The door swung open. 'Doctor Tapputu. Astra.'

'Ah, Major Thames.' Dr Tapputu rose to his feet and Astra reluctantly followed suit.

'No, no, don't stand.' Major Thames pulled up a chair and sat bolt upright beside the doctor. 'Astra Ordott.' Hir eyes bore into her. 'It is my job to moderate the longstanding conflict between Is-Land and Non-Land. On current showing it may be said that I have *singularly failed* in this duty.'

Was she supposed to answer? She glanced at Dr Tapputu, but he was rubbing his ring, avoiding her gaze.

'Let there be no mistake,' the Major went on, 'a war has broken out on my watch. My primary responsibility now is to protect my personnel. Astra, I am afraid to say that I am no longer sure if you qualify for that protection.'

A cold panic prickled through her veins, and with it a familiar, stiff resolve. She was on trial again. All right, she would defend herself – but first she had to discover what exactly the Major was holding against her.

'Major Thames,' Dr Tapputu broke the silence, 'may I say that Astra performed with exceptional courage and stamina last night. It was her quick thinking that ensured Enki Arakkia received prompt medical attention—'

It wasn't her 'quick thinking' that had saved Enki's life; it was Asar's vision, but now was not the time to correct the doctor.

'Dr Tapputu!' the Major barked, 'Astra's performance last night is irrelevant to my concerns. Astra, Officer Augenblick informs me that the Sec Gens' – shall we say, *unique* – combat skills came as much as a surprise to you as to everyone else. Frankly, I find that hard to believe.'

The Major had been quizzing Photon? Her stomach heaved, but she was determined not to show her fear. This was a stupid suspicion, easily cleared. 'It's true,' she declared. 'All I ever practised with the Sec Gens was martial arts skills and berserker murmurations.'

'*Berserker murmurations?*' The Major's plucked eyebrows shot up. 'Tell me more.'

'It was like . . . swarm-fighting. The—' She paused, wincing, then carried on, 'the *biting* must have come later in the training.'

'You were not aware,' the Major snapped, 'that berserkers were ancient Norse warriors who fought naked and counted no battle victorious until they had tasted the blood of their foe?'

'No! Going berserk means going into a group trance . . . at least, that's what the teachers told us.'

'If I may, Major,' Dr Tapputu murmured, 'it is entirely possible that the animalistic behaviour is triggered later in the Sec Gens' development. Possibly only during their IMBOD Service. One would certainly not wish to risk unleashing such atavistic violence upon members of one's own society, after all.'

The Major sat back, scrutinising Astra. 'Perhaps, Doctor. Perhaps.'

This silence felt like a momentary reprieve, perhaps even a space in which to regain the Major's sympathy. 'I didn't know, honestly,' she repeated. 'My older brother never bit anyone. I'm worried about *him*, actually – Major Thames, do you have any meetings with IMBOD? Can you find out if Peat Orson was fighting yesterday?'

'I am sorry, Astra.' The Major was booming as if to fill the Gold Theatre. 'I am sorry that a member of your immediate family is involved in this entirely sordid and treacherous development in the evolution of our species. I am afraid, however, that I do not have access to IMBOD's battle rota – and even if I did, I have far more pressing concerns today.' Heesh glared at the doctor. 'Dr Tapputu has received the final report on your brand-wound. You do not have any kind of virus or bacterial infection, but, Astra, alarmingly, foreign matter – nanocircuitry to be exact – has been detected in your perineal tissue. Are you aware of this, and why that might be the case?'

Dr Tapputu was regarding her with an anxious expression; the Major was tense and glittering, like a cat ready to pounce.

Nanocircuitry in her brand? Suddenly she badly wanted to pee. She clenched her bladder. 'No.'

The Major pursed hir lips. 'And what if I told you that the engineers at Amazigia believe it is probably some kind of tracking device?'

Her pelvis spasmed. She wanted to rip off her trousers and her underpants and scratch out whatever it was IMBOD had sewn into her, but she couldn't move; she was paralytic with fear, stuck to the chair as securely as if her brand were an ice-cold metal lock.

'IMBOD put a *tracker* in me?' she quavered. 'But . . . but that's not *allowed*, is it?'

'It most certainly is not.' The Major's voice was as harsh as a steel blade drawn against rock. 'Unless, of course, the recipient gives her permission. Astra Ordott, tell me the *truth*: are you here on an IMBOD mission? Is your mission to track down your Code father, to infiltrate YAC and record the movements of my staff? Are you reporting to Chief Superintendent Odinson? Should I just send you back to the Barracks right now?'

The double horror of it, the accusation and the threat, nearly choked her. 'No,' she said, her voice shaking, then, '*No!*' and she was shouting this time, rising from her seat and looking wildly between the Major and the doctor, 'I *hate* IMBOD!' How could she make them understand? 'They said my Shelter mother was a *traitor* – they *killed* her! They were going to send me to a special school, give me more MPT – I *had* to come here. Tell hir, Dr Tapputu, *tell hir—*'

She looked desperately at Dr Tapputu for support. His amber eyes sorrowed for her but, sheep-faced, he made no effort to interrupt the Major's attack.

'I am warning you, Astra,' the Major thundered, 'do not take me for a *fool*. You have not responded to my generous offers to meet with you. You did not want to see the doctor when you arrived. Were you afraid he would discover the tracking device?'

Panic flooding her now, she gripped her chair arms and screamed, 'I *hate* doctors! They *tortured* me, all right? In the Barracks, they hurt me so much.' Babbling now, and breaking down in sobs, she implored Dr Tapputu to understand. 'I was all right when I left the neurohospice – I felt fine, but Odinson jammed something up in my *skull-hole*, he showed me pictures of people and it hurt when I looked at them, and then later, when I got here, if I thought about those people, it hurt so much I wanted to *die*. I didn't want to see you because I didn't know who you were or what you'd do to me – I didn't know you were so *nice*. I'm sorry – I'm *sorry—*'

'Shhhhh . . . it's all right, Astra,' Dr Tapputu said soothingly, reaching over for her hand, 'it's all right. You're here now. No one's going to hurt you.'

The doctor was being kind at last, but the Major was still staring at her, hir face expressionless, unmoved.

'Everything *hurt*,' Astra pleaded. 'My brand-wound was burning right through me. I could hardly sit down – that day that I met you? Photon was right: I *was* going to jump off the ramparts. Okay, you were right: I was going to kill myself. But I'm not now – I'm better now. Please, don't send me back there,' she begged. 'You can't send me back – I just want to find my Code father, and—' she caught a sob and stumbled on, '—be good, and help people, and maybe be allowed to visit Is-Land again one day. Dr Tapputu believes me.' She clutched at his robe. 'Don't you, Dr Tapputu?'

Again, the doctor spoke up for her. 'A short course of MPT creates highly disorienting and unpredictable effects, Major. In my professional opinion, it's extremely unlikely that IMBOD would trust Astra with a mission of the sort you are describing. Also, she did request treatment for her brand-wound herself.'

'I did. I *did*,' she sobbed, 'I told him I needed some spray.'

'It's all in my notes, Major.' Dr Tapputu's hand was still on her arm. 'And there is enough in her file to suggest that IMBOD has good reason to want to keep an eye on her whereabouts.'

There was another long silence, torn only by her sniffles. 'All right, Astra,' the Major said at last, 'I believe you. It is clear that IMBOD will stop at nothing to ensure the security of the Boundary. But you *must* tell me: why exactly might Odinson want to know where you are going in Non-Land? Does he want to find your Code father? Or is there anything else I should know about, anything not on your file?'

Dr Tapputu patted her arm and released her. She was out of immediate danger, but the interrogation was not over, and even as she was trying not to retch with relief, she had to keep thinking what to say. *Why* would IMBOD want to follow her – to find Zizi? Lil? To stop her becoming part of the Prophecy? She couldn't tell the Major about Lil, or Istar, or Shiimti. She *couldn't*. The Major might lock her up – or decide to give her back to IMBOD after all.

'No. I don't know,' she stalled.

'Officer Augenblick tells me that you've had an invitation to visit the Black Desert – so why is that? Are you trying to contact the Non-Gaians?'

She was aghast, furious, completely thrown. Photon had *told* on her? Why? She scrambled to think what exactly he might have said? She hadn't told him she was going to Shiimti – did he and the Major even know it existed?

'The guide, at Pithar,' she stammered. 'She wanted to take me – to thank me for listening to the Singulars . . .' Slowly it dawned on her that she wasn't the only one in danger. 'What does IMBOD know?' she demanded. 'Can they hear me? Are they *recording me*?'

'Apparently not,' the doctor answered. 'The engineers said no audio device embedded between the legs would be able to detect spoken words.'

'It's a location sensor,' the Major confirmed, though hir steely expression suggested heesh wasn't entirely content with her response to hir question, 'most likely tracked by the IMBOD Tablette towers embedded in the Boundary. It is possible to implant more sophisticated recording devices in Tablettes themselves, but ours are all triple-checked before we distribute them.'

She'd been in a *neurohospice*: *anything* could have been done to her, anything at all. 'What about my head-wound? Could they leave a recorder in there?'

'No, brain activity can't yet be read by wireless technology,' the doctor said, trying to reassure her. 'You would need to be plugged in again for them to access any thoughts. The engineers are one hundred per cent sure that IMBOD simply wants to know where you have been going.'

It didn't matter if Odinson had heard Anunit's story or not. He knew she had been to Pithar. 'Then we have to go back to Zabaria,' she said. 'We have to make sure the Pithar Singulars are okay.'

'We'll message all the wards you've visited.' Now it came, the Major's pounce. 'Where else have you been, Astra? Anywhere not accounted for on your MMU reports?'

'I visited a friend.' Tears sprang afresh to her eyes. If IMBOD had hurt Uttu, she didn't know what she would do. 'Yesterday, for lunch – I visited Uttu, from the laundry. I met her family. Can I go to the laundry, please, now? I want to make sure Uttu's okay.'

'We will go together,' the Major stood, 'as soon as Dr Tapputu has deactivated your tracker. Agreed?'

Yes: get this thing ripped out of her. Still battling the tears, she climbed up on the gurney.

The doctor drew the curtains and showed her a device that looked like a dentist's mirror. 'It is not in fact medical equipment. I got it from the IT team. But I've tried it out on my mouth. It won't hurt you.'

As he brought it close to her brand she heard a rapid squeaking sound and felt a sudden hot itch . . . then nothing.

The circuitry was still threaded through her flesh, but it was burnt out now: like her heart, like her trust in Photon, the doctor, the Major, *everyone*. Lil had told the Singulars she was a divinity, sent to save them, but she was no goddess, she was just a stupid little pawn in a game played according to rules she couldn't begin to understand and had never even dreamed possible. As much as the cladding engineers, hanging down the Boundary with their backs to a field of bestial carnage, she was a puppet jerking around on IMBOD's long strings. Sitting there miserably, with her legs open and her brand still faintly burning, she had no desire at all to follow those strings back to her would-be masters; she just wanted to find a hole where she could curl up and die, to join the mass grave on the outskirts of Kadingir and wrap her arms around little Gud so she could protect his small body for all time.

'Deactivated.' The doctor rolled away on his wheelie chair. She could hear the Major pacing. She clapped her legs together and pulled up her trousers. It didn't matter about her. She'd been dead since the day she was born. She had to find Uttu, make sure she and her family were safe.

'You said we could go to the laundry,' she demanded, pulling open the curtain.

'Chop chop.' The Major was opening the door.

She dropped to the floor. 'Thank you, Dr Tapputu,' she called over her shoulder as she followed the Major's quick-step march out of the clinic and down the hall. The Major took the shortcut Photon had shown her, the small back spiral staircase. When they hit the workers' courtyard she ran ahead, through the hot sun, the shade of the colonnade, straight into the steam of the laundry.

'Uttu,' she cried, 'is Uttu here?'

Hamta and Azarakhsh turned from the pool. Neither mustered a smile.

'Astra.' Hamta managed the bare minimum of greeting. 'Uttu not here.'

'Where is she? Is she safe?' she implored. 'Is Muzi safe? Did Muzi fight last night?'

Hamta shrugged her massive shoulders. 'Many people fighting. Many fall.'

'Uttu has a Tablette,' she pressed. 'We can message her.'

'Tablettes no work,' Azarakhsh said.

'That is correct, Astra.' The Major was at the door. 'IMBOD has scrambled the signal. They say they haven't, but we know they have; it will take a little time to sort out.'

The washers nodded at their employer, but no one saluted. Hamta began prodding the washing again.

Astra reeled back to the Major. 'Then we have to go to Uttu's house,' she demanded.

The Major was inspecting the laundry room. 'Hamta is right, Astra: there was a battle last night. Uttu is probably at home tending to the wounded.'

'Uttu's family are N-LA supporters – they wouldn't be fighting.'

'Uttu never miss work,' Hamta announced. 'Only no work for funeral.'

'You *see*? Something bad has happened – she's my *friend*. I want to see her.'

'Thank you, Hamta.' The Major stepped outside into the colonnade. Astra followed, nearly tripping on the edge of a paving stone.

'Please let me—'

'Astra, it is not safe outside. No one is leaving the compound today except on medical visits.'

'It *is* a medical visit – Uttu might be hurt. Or her family.'

'IMBOD is not authorised to send troops into Kadingir—'

'IMBOD doesn't need authorisation! Look what they did to my brand!'

'You are accusing IMBOD of an unprovoked incursion—'

She was challenging the Major's authority again, but who cared? If she couldn't go and find Uttu she might as well be locked up in a dungeon. 'They'll say I'm a traitor and that *I* provoked them! I have to make sure Uttu is okay; I don't need your permission – I'm eighteen now. I can leave the compound. I can go and live with Uttu.'

'You don't know what you're talking about,' the Major barked. 'A war is breaking out, and you, Astra Ordott, if not IMBOD Enemy Number One, are ranked pretty high on their list!'

'I *know*. But it won't take long,' she pleaded. 'I'll go with Photon – or Rudo. It's not far. We'll come right back. The hospital is on the way. We can take someone there, or—'

'*Stop*,' the Major roared.

She shut up. The Major took a pace towards her. 'Astra, what aren't you telling me?'

What, this again? Hopelessness overwhelmed her. 'I'm not an IMBOD spy. How can you believe that?'

'I don't: but you're hiding something. I can *smell* it. Why does IMBOD want to track your movements so badly? Do you have contacts in the resistance here? If you answer me that, I might let you go under CONC protection. Otherwise you leave here alone and the door will be closed when you return.'

It was so tempting to storm off, to leave this bullying Shelter forever. But what if something had happened to Uttu and her family? Where would she stay? She'd have to get Lil's number from Photon, but could she even trust him any more? She stood, quaking, uncertain, her head spinning. Should she tell the Major about Lil? No, never – but what about Anunit? That would help YAC, wouldn't it? Even if the Major only cared about CONC's reputation, surely heesh ought to know that IREMCO managers were killing babies in Pithar?

But the Singulars had said she should only speak for them in Istar's name. Lil was supposed to help her with all that. *Why was she having to think about all this right now?* Lil could tell the journalists about Pithar; she just wanted to find Uttu.

'I didn't come here to join the resistance,' she said slowly. That wasn't a lie. 'But it's like you said: people here are interested in me. Some of them think I can help them. Uttu thinks if I marry her grandson, I can take him to Is-Land one day. Maybe IMBOD is afraid I might do something like that. Become, I don't know . . . like a symbol of One Land.'

The Major arched a brow. 'I see: a local attachment has formed. You do recall that if you marry a Non-Lander you will relinquish your CONC political refugee status?'

'I don't *want* to marry him! *I only just met him!*' But her stomach was turning. She did like Muzi, and not just Muzi: she liked the house, the land, the wishing tree, the children, the women and their toe rings, and Uttu, laughing, so proud of her banquet. She hadn't had time to think about it properly, but as she spoke, she realised exactly how the lunch had made her feel. 'I like them all, though, a lot. They're a *family* – not like here. I mean, Photon, and Rudo and Sandrine, all the CONC officers, they're nice to me, but they'll all be going home one day. Non-Land is my home now – I want to be part of the people here. I could work for CONC, but live with them, couldn't I? Uttu would help me, I know.'

The Major stepped away. Paced. Halted. Swivelled on hir heels.

Snapped hir fingers. 'All right, Astra. You're eighteen and I am not responsible for your safety any longer. Find Photon and go to Uttu's house – don't tell him about the device for now. That information stays between you, me and Dr Tapputu. Just say we have reason to believe that IMBOD is spying on you. If anyone is hurt, bring them to the hospital. If everything is fine, *or* if the situation looks in the slightest way suspicious, you are to come straight back here.'

'Really?' she gasped. 'Thank you, Major. *Thank you.*'

'Do you comprehend me, Astra? You are now off IMBOD's radar. Their signal has gone dead, so they may use other means to find you. I am allowing you to venture forth, but I want you back here in the compound as soon as possible. If you desire my cooperation in your life-plans, you will remain here until this outbreak of violence is contained and I have brought up the matter of your embedded circuitry through the proper channels. To start with, I want you to make an official statement about your appalling treatment at the Barracks.'

'I understand. I'll be right back. Honestly – I just want to make sure she's okay.' She turned to go, hesitated, then swung back to face the Major. 'I'm sorry I didn't come and see you on the roof. You helped me fit in here, and I liked your violin playing, I just . . .' She faltered, how could she tell the Major she'd been afraid heesh was just like IMBOD? 'I've had bad experiences with people in uniforms before.'

The Major placed hir right foot in front of the left, heel to arch. 'Frail or sturdy, stooped or straight, the human body is our noblest garment, Astra. Wear yours with pride and fellow feeling, and no uniform can define you.'

'Thank you, sirm. I will, sirm, I promise.' Raising her fingers to her temple, she spun back to the courtyard exit. Yes, she needed to talk to Photon. What the hell was he thinking, telling the Major about Lil's offer?

'Astra Ordott, I salute *you*,' the Major cried after her, so loudly a row of rooks along the ramparts flung themselves up into the air. 'A young woman made of stardust, honey and fire!'

ANUNIT

She woke with her mouth in the dirt, the sun searing her eyelids, sweat prickling the creases and folds of her body beneath her black robes.

'Pah.' She spat, rubbing the grit from her lips with her sleeve. Beside her, Ebebu whimpered.

Ebebu. She seized him, kissed his lambskin forehead, clasped him to her chest. How had she slept, even for a moment? A moment ago it had been dark, eternally cold: she had cowered under the stars, afraid to go further into the scrublands, afraid to go back to the Welcome Tent. Now the sun had risen and the oven of the day was firing up. On the road in the distance traffic was streaming from two short queues forming either side of the checkpoints.

Ebebu began crying. She would have to go back: the tin of goat's milk was in the tent.

No. She remained where she was, in the shelter of a bush on a low slope. She couldn't ever go back to the Welcome Tent, not after last night.

It had been late, near the end of the shift. The tent was fuller than usual because the last batch of flesh clients had not shown up. The workers had gathered, complaining to Neperdu that she should increase the deposit. Ebebu had been fretting at the chatter, so she had taken him into the wash tent with the milk blanket, hoping the quiet would help him drop off. But just as he'd fallen asleep, she'd heard shouting – men's voices. With her heart thumping, she'd shrunk up against the tent flap, pulled her robe around Ebebu and peeked down the passageway.

At the far end, shadowy figures crossed her view: six or more men. They were not here for flesh sessions.

'Where are they?' a tall one had demanded loudly into the silence. 'The YAC whore, the one with the bitch tits. and the brat.'

He meant Tiamet and Ebebu. But Tiamet had left in the car with Lil and gone back to Kadingir. Trembling, she'd drawn Ebebu deeper into her robes.

'Tiamet is not working tonight,' Neperdu had said, dry as a *mergallá*'s cough. 'May I help you select an alternative experience? Several of my workers have multiple bosoms.'

The men had been furious: they had stormed down the corridor, flinging open the glove doors, dragging women out by the hair. In half a minute, they would be tearing into the wash tent.

Thank you, Neperdu, for choosing a wash tent with no groundsheet. Her heart in her mouth, Ebebu waking in her arms, Anunit had squeezed under the canvas and out into the night.

But where could she go? She couldn't leave her sisters.

Music was blaring from the neighbouring tent: those boy workers were a party team, entertaining their flesh clients around a jacuzzi pool. She looked around, but there was no one else out there. She placed Ebebu at the edge of the music tent – he would cry, but no one would hear him. Then she crept between the tents, catching her ankles on guy ropes in the dark, making her way towards the pale patch of light on the canvas ahead. At the hole behind her cushion, she knelt and peered in.

'She's not here,' a man was panting.

'There's no baby either,' another one reported. They were mine-managers – IREMCO. She recognised them; usually they came as flesh clients.

'Off in *Kadingir*, is she?' The tall man, the leader, put his boot through Neperdu's screendesk. 'Prancing about at Diplomeets? On the *news*?' He turned, grabbed Taletha's hair, forced the girl's terrified face close to his. 'Those ion clients: you talk to them about us, do you?'

'No – no, we don't talk to anyone,' Taletha had sobbed, her hands fluttering over his fist. 'We just do what they want. Same as for you.'

'Same as for us,' he'd jeered, shaking her head like a ragdoll's. 'You telling me some meat-eating New Zonian slaver knows how to make a woman come?'

'No, no,' the girl whimpered. 'You're the best, the Gaians are the best clients – we all say so, don't we?'

They'd all nodded, agreed: Roshanak, Duranki, everyone. Everyone except Neperdu. Beside her shattered screendesk, Neperdu had flicked a glance down the passageway. Only Anunit had seen her.

'Tell you what.' The man flung Taletha aside. 'We're your *only* clients. This ion-glove shit, it's over. You' – he looked at Neperdu – 'Madam Two Cunt, do you hear me? Your globe-rolling whore days are *done.*'

'If IREMCO wishes to secure our exclusive services, I suggest we discuss the terms in the morning,' Neperdu had replied coldly.

The man stood over her. 'You sure ain't the beauty around here, are you? Think you're the brains then, do you? Got an extra set of grey cells stuffed up that extra cock-hole of yours?'

'I have had enough sense to build up this business with the full cooperation of *your boss.*' Neperdu's voice had remained steady. 'And I don't believe he's going to be pleased to hear you've been coming in here terrorising my staff.'

'I've had frigging enough of your lip. Take her,' the leader ordered one of his men. '*My boss* will send you a new manager in the morning, girls. This little business is going to be run *our way* from now on.'

A man had jammed his arms around Neperdu's chest and hauled her outside. The others had taken iron bars out of their boots. Two had stayed in the Welcome Tent, threatening the sisters, the bars held at the ready, while the others had gone down the corridor and smashed the ion gloves, all that technology the workers had contributed so much of their wages to purchase. Tearing herself away from the crying and pleading and crashing, Anunit had dashed back to Ebebu, gathered him up and stolen away into the night.

Ebebu was screaming. She pulled the milk blanket out of her robe and offered it to him, but he pushed her hand away, kicking at the air.

'Shhh, shhh.' She tucked the blanket back down her front, picked him up and walked in a circle around the bush, thinking hard. The Welcome Tent was finished – but why? Just because Tiamet had been on the news?

Or was it her fault too, for talking to that girl, the one Lilutu said was Istar? She was not; she was just a girl, a young frightened girl hoping CONC would save her, the way Tiamet was just a silly, pretty, excitable girl, hoping YAC would make her into an international celebrity; and Simiya was undoubtedly just another vain girl, spoiled by her whole Nagu since she was a child; and Asar the Seer was a sensitive boy who needed his carer. Anunit had known all this, but she had gone along with Lil's schemes and told this Astra her story, and Astra had probably told some-one in CONC, who had in turn told IMBOD. Or maybe this half-Gaian Astra had told IMBOD herself – how did Lilutu know she could be trusted?

Ebebu was still crying. She couldn't just keep walking around this bush – but where could she go? To the Treatment Ward or the orphan-age? No, if the men really wanted to find Tiamet, they would surely look in those places for her too.

She would have to go to her parents. It was a trek to their tent on the other side of Zabaria, and her mother would not be pleased to see her, but year in, year out, she had paid her wages into their account, keeping her father in medicine and her brother in school, and at least they owed her a night in her old bed.

The thought was barely formed, wordless, just a cloud of dust on the horizon: an evil, whirling *mergallá*, drawing closer, taking shape—

If they saw Ebebu, his perfect, strong little body... If she said he was...

It was a wrong thought; she must not think it. As best she could, she brushed the dirt off her robe. She stank like a goat. Her mother would rail at her, accuse her of bringing disrepute on her house, but her father would let her in. She walked south, skirting the town. She would wait until dusk, when the neighbours were eating, and slip into the tent when no one was looking. She would withdraw all her savings, give the coin to her parents, make her mother buy tinned milk. Ebebu would be hungry all day, but then he would be safe, and that was all she wanted: for Ebebu to be safe.

ASTRA

'You told the Major about the Black Desert,' she accused.

Photon was driving. He kept his eyes on the road. '*Ja.* Heesh said your security was in danger. Heesh asked if you had visited or planned to visit any sensitive areas.' He slowed, stopped to let a man cross the road. 'The Black Desert is not dangerous, I think. But it is a political zone. The Non-Gaians live out there, I believe.'

From the ramp, a boy offered her a cup of tea from the tray around his neck. She waved him away. Photon drove on.

'And you took Lil's number,' she accused.

'*Ja*: she gave it to me. If you are going to travel in the desert together, I need to be able to contact you both. Maybe you are getting separated – is only good idea, Astra.'

She was silent.

'Did Lil make an offer to take you to Shiimti?' he asked.

'Yes,' she snapped. 'She says Zizi's living there – I was going to tell you. But now I don't know what I should tell anyone! Photon, did you tell the Major about Lil?'

'No. I did not. I told you on the roof: I would only say something if I thought you were in danger to break the law.'

She wasn't satisfied. 'Why not?'

'Why not what?'

'Why didn't you tell the Major about Lil? You know she's with YAC – they break the law all the time. Didn't you think you should tell the Major about her now, in case you got in trouble later?'

Photon scratched his neck. He still wasn't looking at her. 'I am your buddy, Astra. I told you I would keep your secret. I am glad you know where Zizi is now. That is excellent news.'

They bumped over a crossing.

'Thanks, Photon,' she muttered. 'And sorry I growled at you. It's just weird thinking someone's been following us – it makes me jumpy.'

'Oh, this place is doing that, for sure,' he agreed. They passed another demonstration, a crowd of people in red and purple, waving Tablette placards. The whole of Kadingir was protesting; she'd seen it on the news while she'd been waiting for Photon to finish eating lunch: people were marching and shouting and demanding justice everywhere. It was hard to tell if this lot were still arguing with each other, or united in outrage at the Sec Gens' atrocities. She peered at a Tablette placard and tried to decipher the Somarian.

The screen was brandished by a woman in red; it displayed a photo of Una Dayyani. Across the image was printed . . . oh Gaia . . . was that word *Istar*? She craned her neck, scanned the crowd. Yes: *Istar, Istar, The Prophecy*, screaming from the placards. Then she saw it and froze: the people in purple, the YAC supporters – their Tablette screens were displaying photos of *her*, blurry, cropped and blown up from the River Raven footage, but definitely her. *The Placeless One*. One of the YAC protesters caught sight of her and in a second, his face transformed from fury to rapture, his eyes liquid with wonder, his mouth a perfect O.

Heart thumping, she shrank back in her seat. She hadn't told Lil she could use her photo! What would the Major say now?

'Will you still go to Shiimti?' Photon asked.

He hadn't seen and now the demonstration was behind them. She had to talk to Lil – but she didn't even have her Tablette phone number.

'I don't know.' Her mind was a million miles away. The only way to escape this Istar cult was to get to Shiimti – but from what she'd been told, Shiimti was full of stargazers. What if Zizi was the worst of the lot? What if her Code father had built some massive reputation around her supposed destiny? And anyway, this war changed everything.

'Lil's busy here now,' she said, gaining control. 'And for all I know Zizi might come back to Kadingir to fight.'

They drove on. 'Are you worried about what Rudo said?' he asked after a bit.

'About what?'

'About Zizi.'

'No – and it's none of Rudo's business. He shouldn't try and tell me what to do.'

Photon didn't take the hint. 'I understand Rudo had a bad parental experience himself,' he mused. 'When I first started to work with him, I had some difficulties to understand his communication style. I was speaking to Honovi about it, and she said to me that he told her once that his mother left the family home when he was small. Maybe he tried to find her one day, and it did not work out. I think he was just trying to warn you not to inflate your expectations too high.'

Oh. New Zonians didn't have Shelter parents, not official ones, anyway. Under those circumstances, being abandoned by your Birth-Code mother didn't sound good. But still, none of them, not Rudo, Photon or the Major, understood what looking for Zizi was like.

'My Code father didn't abandon me,' she said. 'He was *evicted*. And my expectations are as flat as old tyres, Photon.'

As the high blue walls of the hospital came into view up ahead, Photon said brightly, 'I doubt Shiimti will send fighters. It is more of a strategic gathering, I think, and mainly for older people. If Lil cannot take you, when this all has died down I will get you out to the Oasis Ward as soon as I can.'

Things dying down soon didn't look likely. More protesters were surrounding the hospital, waving placards and shaking their fists, the crowd spilling over into the road. She tensed, but Photon, thank Gaia, turned right. 'We should get an update,' he said, reaching for Comchan.

Powerless to stop him, she leaned her head against the window, bracing herself to hear her deification announced to the world. *You're hiding something*, the Major had said. She would be facing another frigging interrogation soon.

'IMBOD has released its casualty figures for last night's battle in the Hem,' the presenter's voice crackled. 'According to Chief Superintendent Odinson, thirteen Sec Gens were killed and six wounded. We bring you IMBOD's full statement in response.'

'Six wounded?' Photon sounded puzzled. 'I saw many bloody spear tips last night.'

She didn't reply. Nothing would surprise her about the Sec Gens any more.

'Is-Land mourns its fallen.' Odinson's voice was deep as a grave. 'Thirteen brave young men and women who faced armed invaders with only their bare hands, who showed the world that Is-Land is a nation of peace – a nation that respects not only the letter, but the *spirit* of CONC's de-escalation and national defence policies – who, though boundlessly provoked, attacked by hordes of illegal invaders wielding illegal weapons, staunchly upheld the international principle of defensive policing, defending themselves with only tooth and nail, these noble young constables were brutally murdered, barbaric killings the manner of which I can barely bring myself to speak about.

He cleared his throat, a sound that was almost a growl, then continued, 'As the honorary Shelter father to our Sec Gen defenders, I cannot allow them to face such danger again. IMBOD hereby announces that from henceforth the Sec Gens will be equipped with non-ballistic weapons and backed up with jeep units. In addition, N-LA having demonstrated its complete lack of integrity, the Hemline agreement is to be considered dissolved. Any further incursion will be treated as an invitation to redraw the line. Any use of firearms against my forces will result in the immediate use of the same in response.'

'Jeep units.' Photon exhaled. 'Sounds like he is going to flatten tents with people inside them.'

'And now for the official statement from Una Dayyani,' the presenter announced.

'For the last ten years,' the N-LA Lead Convenor declared, 'the Non-Land Alliance has attempted to walk the path of peace and reconciliation, to dance the high tightrope between the impossible past and a possible future. But when our enemies cut that rope out beneath our feet, our agility, flexibility and noble restraint all stand for naught. At such a time, we must fall or fly. My people – my mystical, faithful, ever-resourceful people – are calling on me to fly. Take up the wings of Istar, they say: be for us the placeless one who opens all places to all people. My people, I say to you, *we are all Istar*. We are all destined to dance with the *mergallá-lá*, all destined to rise from our suffering and soar over the walls of injustice. Call me Istar if you wish, but do not refuse your own feather of her flight.'

Let Una Dayyani claim Istar's wings. Good. She reached to turn off Comchan, but Photon's hand was there first, turning up the volume.

'No, wait, I want to hear this.'

'To the world, I say now,' Dayyani's voice rose, 'that my Cabinet, my Chief of Police, my allies in Asfar and I are united in agreement: any attempt on IMBOD's part to extend the Hem will be met with a full battle response from N-LA forces, up to and including the use of fire-arms. If Amazigia does not support us one hundred per cent in this decision, we will unilaterally reject CONC's authority in the region and call on the Mujaddid of Asfar to send reinforcements to our lines. My people, I speak again to you: N-LA is currently recruiting new police officers, so all Non-Landers who wish to effectively defend their rights should apply at the Beehive. YAC members, the brave, unruly youth of Non-Land, I call on you to join the legitimate force of this region. Asfar is with N-LA, and united we will prevail.'

'Ho boy,' Photon sighed. 'So not a Diplomeet call.'

No, the Major was right: it was war. A war of words, a war of bodies, and both raging on and on. Next YAC would come on and announce that *she* was their new leader. She turned off Comchan at last.

'Istar.' Photon sounded puzzled. 'That was a YAC chant too, last night in the tent, yes?'

She shrugged and lolled her head against the door frame. She would have to tell Photon at some point, but right now all she wanted was to make sure Uttu had survived the night. They were heading up the outskirts road through the hot, hazy day. Animals were clustered in the shade of bushes or covered pens. The low scrubby hills stretched out to the east. Was it really only yesterday they'd been on their way to lunch? It felt as though a hundred years had passed since then. She kept her eyes trained on the side of the road for the wishing tree. Was *that* it?

'Photon!' she gasped.

He'd seen it too. He pulled over sharply, crying, 'Astra, don't get out.'

But she was already dropping from the cabin and dashing over to the tree – what used to be the tree. It had been pulled up by its roots and dragged out of the soil. Ribbons had been scattered, branches broken – *destroyed*. Uttu's wish tree had been murdered by *Gaians*.

A door slammed, and then Photon was beside her, wearing his ridiculous hat against the sun against which there could be no protection, the sun that beat down on her head like a hammer, was already bleaching the bones of the tree she had given water to, had ribbon-wished would stay alive.

'We have to go back. The Major said if anything looked suspicious—' He clutched at her arm, but she wrested it away.

'We have to find out what happened! Uttu! Muzi! We're here!'

She was haring up to the house, yelling out their names, but no one was running out to meet them. The place was silent: a silence without echoes, a silence that deadened her voice and hardened her mind.

'Come back, Astra. It's not safe.' Photon was on her heels, grasping at her shirt, but she'd had a head start, and she was at the door now: the kicked-in door of an unrecognisable place. A long room buzzing with flies and stinking of shit. Slashed pillows had been tossed everywhere; bootmarks were imprinted on the fabric and feathers settled in drifts over smashed Tablettes and broken crockery. The aprons she and Photon and Rudo had worn had been ripped into shreds, Muzi's little wooden box had been broken open, the beeswax candles trodden on, crushed. She covered her nose. There, in the middle of the floor, the flies were circling great piles of human turds.

'So terrible.' Photon was hovering behind her. 'You were right, Astra. Come. We have to go back and make a report.'

Make a report. *Make a report.* That was all anyone ever did at CONC: add words to the word *war*: meaningless words with no power to stop anything at all.

'No, we have to look. The children – maybe they're hiding. Hadis,' she called out, stumbling into the room, down to the kitchen, 'Suen – it's Astra. Come out.'

He gave in then and helped her, watching out the front while she checked every room – but every room was the same: carnage. Pots and pans, knives and forks, jars of pulses and grains, plants, clothes, bedmats, soap, toothbrushes – all the little things that nestled together under a roof to make a home, all pulverised, scattered, despoiled with the foul stench of excrement.

'They are not here, Astra. They have been taken.'

'They killed them,' she sobbed.

'No – no, I'm sure they would not kill anyone, not outside the Hem. They have taken them to the Barracks for some reason, that is all, and we will find them. The Major will bargain with them. We'll get them back.'

'They'll want *me*. Odinson wants *me*. I'll have to go to the Barracks, Phot. I can not let them keep Uttu.'

'No, the Major won't let that happen. *I* won't let that happen. We will get them back, I promise. But we can't do anything to help them here. Come on, please.' He was tugging her and they were halfway back to Ciccy, when—

'*Psssst.*'

She spun. There, behind the sheep pen, was a head of hair: Muzi.

He wouldn't come out. She ran to him, Photon keeping pace behind. He was crouching behind the empty pen, in a narrow band of shade. He was cradling Uttu's head on his lap.

'Uttu.' She fell to her knees in the dirt, reached for her friend's hand.

But Uttu wasn't moving. Uttu's eyes were closed. Her robe, torn almost in half, was gathered up to disguise its rent state.

'No, Astra.' Muzi's red eyes were still wet. 'Uttu gone.'

Her breath was being ripped out of her lungs; her eyes were swelling up, burning like stars in her head. She threw herself on Uttu, clasped her tight, shook her shoulders, but Uttu's body was stiff.

'Photon,' she cried, 'can we put her in the ion chamber? Can we take her to Ciccy?'

Photon was holding Uttu's wrist. He shook his head. 'It's too late, Astra,' he said in Asfarian, the language Muzi had used. 'She's gone. For some hours now, isn't that right, Muzi?'

'IMBOD come in night.' Muzi's voice was dull. 'Family sleep roof. I sleep watch-hut. I hear vans. I watch. On hill. N-LA vans. Big people. Too big. One van take sheep.' His voice broke. After a moment he continued, 'All sheep in one van. Kingu Tablette-message me. Say hide, run, get help.' He shook his head. 'No time get help. Kingu, Gibil, come down stairs. Big people go up roof. Lights on. I see. No N-LA. IMBOD.'

'Are you sure, Muzi,' Photon asked gently, 'that they weren't N-LA?'

The boy pinched his arm, rubbed his head. 'Skin different. Too big. Gaians. No Non-Landers. Sec Gens, I know. No can fight Sec Gens. I hide, watch. Sec Gen girl take Kingu. *Girl!* Take Kingu to van, everyone in van, but Uttu no. Uttu bite – I see it, Uttu bite boy hand. Uttu only small, boy big. But he—'

He crooked his arms, and made a quick jerking motion. Then he burst into tears.

'My Uttu – my Anamma. My Anamma,' he cried, stroking her face, bending to kiss her forehead.

Then Astra was bent double, the knife of grief scoring through her. It was her fault. Surely Muzi knew that – *it was all her fault.*

'It's b-b-because of me.' She was choking, could barely get the words out. 'Be-be-cause I c-c-c-ame for lunch – they were p-p-punishing you all because of m-m-me.' It was *unbearable*, and speaking the words just made them more true. *She* had killed Uttu, just like she had killed Hokma. Not with her own hands – she didn't even have to lift a finger; no, she had killed them just by being alive. She was a curse on everyone she loved: first her mothers, now Muzi, his whole family. *It had to stop.*

She wiped the dust from her knees, stood up. 'I'm going to the Barracks, Photon. They can have me, if they just give Kingu and everyone back.'

'*No.*' Muzi grabbed her arm, pulled her back down. '*IMBOD* kill Uttu. Uttu love Astra. I look after Astra now.'

'Astra.' Photon put his hand on her back. 'It is *not* your fault. You must to come back to the CONC compound. You too, Muzi; we will give you diplomatic protection. And we can bring Uttu to the hospital, with all the fallen.'

'No hospital.' Muzi gestured to the nearest hill. 'No CONC. I stay here. Bury Uttu. Today I dig hole. I wash Uttu. I take Uttu now.'

Photon exhaled. 'We don't know if they'll come back, Muzi. It's not safe here.'

She wiped her eyes. She felt ashamed. She was leaking her own self-loathing all over Uttu's dead body. She *would* hand herself over, but right now Muzi had seen his grandmother killed and he wanted – he *needed* – to bury her.

'We can't just leave her in the hospital, Photon,' she declared. 'What are they going to do with her? We have to help Muzi – it won't take long. If we take her in Ciccy, no one can see us from the road.'

Photon gave in – he had to. He couldn't drag Uttu away from them both even if he tried. And he knew it was true: the hospital corridors were lined with bodies, too many for the morgue. The doctors were all desperate for people to identify their loved ones and take them away before they began to rot in the heat. They had to be buried in the pits being dug on the outskirts. Therre was no way he would let that happen to Uttu.

She stayed with Muzi while Photon went back for Ciccy, but they didn't speak. She smoothed Uttu's gown, caressed the hands and feet Muzi had washed, while Muzi murmured to his grandmother in Somarian – a lullaby, maybe, or a mourning song. *I'm here with you, Uttu. I'm saying goodbye*, she thought, and began weeping afresh. *Saying goodbye*. At least she was saying goodbye – what kind of a world was it when you felt lucky to be able to stroke a murdered woman's hands?

Uttu's wedding ring on its slender copper chain was resting in the wrinkled hollow of her collarbone. Muzi reached behind her neck and slid the clasp round to the front. At first Astra thought he would ask her to undo it, but he didn't need her help: it was a simple shepherd's hook and he undid it deftly. His short arm pressing the chain to Uttu's chest, his nimble fingers eased the flat beaten hook from the eye. Leaving the gold weaver's charm on the chain, he slipped off the ring and showed it to Astra on the flat of his palm.

Her heart stopped. She'd already told him – she was too young to get married. Tense as a bow-string, she met his gaze.

His dark lashes swept over his dazzling eyes. 'I take Kurgal,' he vowed. 'One day I bury Uttu ring in Kurgal. In her house garden.'

Her heart began beating again. 'I will help you,' she promised. How, she didn't know, but she would.

He re-hooked the chain and put the ring into the breast pocket of his shirt. Ciccy pulled up beside the pen and Photon got out. He picked up a clean, folded sheet from the seat. 'From CONC,' he said, 'with our sorrow.'

He and Muzi spread the sheet out on the ground and lifted Uttu onto it. Photon took the long edge to fold over her, but Muzi stayed his hand.

'No: Astra help. Astra take robe away – IMBOD robe, no good bury. Astra wrap sheet. We not look.'

He was right: Uttu's robe had been ripped and dirtied in her struggle with the Sec Gen. She should be buried in clean linen. And here in Non-Land, a grandson could not undress his grandmother, not if there was a woman present to perform the duty.

Photon understood and didn't argue, but he was worried, she could tell. 'Quick as you can, Astra,' he said, and the two men walked to the other side of Ciccy, leaving her to do the only thing she could do to repay Uttu for all her kindness: ensure she would return to Gaia cleansed of the violent traces of her death.

She took off her boots and wiped her feet clean with her socks before crouching on the sheet beside Uttu. It was good to be barefoot, to feel the clean sheet Uttu had probably washed herself, and the gritty soil through it. She was Gaia's servant now as well as Uttu's. At first she tried tugging the robe up over Uttu's head, but her body was too stiff and she was afraid she wouldn't be able to free the arms. She sat back on her heels and thought for a moment, then she got up, slipped her socks back on and collected Ciccy's replenished first-aid kit.

Barefoot again on the sheet, her hands trembling, she cut Uttu's robe until she had enough cloth to grasp with each hand, then she ripped the fabric apart. The sound scored her heart, as if the very weave of the world were being torn in two, but she had to continue. She cut and ripped off the sleeves next, at the shoulders. Then she tugged the shorn robe gently out from beneath Uttu's dainty body and bundled it beside Muzi's backpack at the base of the stone wall of the sheep pen. She cut away Uttu's underwear too. It was ridiculous to bury her in undergarments; she should return to Gaia as naked as the moment she was born.

There before her was Uttu – or the form that Uttu had been given and had inhabited all her life, had shared with others and created others with. Her body was drinking in the sun; her skin, with its thousand tender creases, was waiting to enter the parched soil.

Beneath Ciccy she could see Photon's boots and Muzi's sandals. There was one more thing she needed to do. She cut off a long strip of bandage, soaked it with water from her pack and quickly washed Uttu's body: her armpits, her arms, her flattened breasts, her stomach. Lifting her up, she gave a rapid rub down her spine, then used more water for her legs. Finally, quickly, she drenched the cloth and squeezed it over her friend's Gaia garden.

Uttu had been touched all over by sun and water. She was clean.

Astra folded the sheet over her.

'She's ready,' she called.

The sheet didn't look right: it was limp and floppy, not neat and tight like the shrouds in the hospital. Photon bent to pick up Uttu at the feet, but Muzi remained standing.

'We need tie sheet,' he said. 'I get from house.'

But he didn't move. Astra looked back at the house: all the sheets and clothes there had been destroyed – worse, desecrated. They couldn't bury Uttu tied up with one single thread of cloth that IMBOD had touched.

'No,' she said, 'the bandage.' She retrieved the wet strip of material and cut it into three strips. They tied the sheet at the top and bottom, and around Uttu's waist. Muzi took her robe and pushed it into his backpack.

'I burn,' he said firmly, as if making a battle vow.

The men lifted Uttu into Ciccy, placing her wrapped form on the stretcher on the folded-down trolley – but that was wrong: Uttu wasn't injured any more, no longer vulnerable. She was safe in her cocoon now, her chrysalis, beginning her body's final transformation, her majestic and mysterious voyage home to Gaia.

'Can't we take her in the ion chamber?' she asked Photon. 'She would have liked that.'

'*Ja.* Nice thinking.' Photon climbed through into the driving seat. He started the engine and turned on the ion chamber. The cylindrical cloud of light filled the back of the unit, making Muzi look up, startled.

'It's okay, Muzi. Better than stretcher.'

He didn't understand, but he obeyed her commands. With him at Uttu's head and Astra at her feet, they lifted the white cocoon. When she dropped her hands and Uttu's legs remained level in the air, Muzi's eyes widened. He released Uttu's shoulders and her shrouded body hung between them, suspended between earth and sky, this world and the next.

'Anamma spirit fly,' Muzi whispered. 'Always. Everywhere. Now body fly too.'

ENKI

'Where's Bartol?' His throat was on fire, but he forced the question out through the flames.

'Don't talk!' Ninti ordered.

'Bartol is sleeping, my boy,' his mother announced tartly from the other side of the bed. 'Slaying monsters takes a little more energy than chasing girls down at the riverbank.'

He sank back against the pillow and drew a burning breath of relief. At first he'd suspected they were lying: that Bartol had fallen, or was gravely injured, but no one would risk telling him until his own life was out of danger. But though falling in and out of consciousness – for how long he didn't know – he had been lucid enough at one point to co-write the media statement, and each time he woke his mother's tongue was sharper. Surely if Bartol were dead, she would have said so by now.

He fingered his bandage. The shoulder was swollen to the size of a small watermelon: a planet of pain. But Chozai and other singing-bowl players were keeping vigil in the ward, and travelling on the sonic grooves the bowl-tones were carving, his mind had transcended, if not the pain, then at least the desperate urge to beg for morpheus. The agony had also subsided a fraction. After the wound-cleaning and stitches last night, this throbbing globe was almost a reward. He wondered what the stitches looked like. Would it be a big scar?

'Don't do that, either.' His mother slapped his hand, hard. 'Did those brutes suck the brains from your head, son?'

He was back. What time was it? What day? What was *happening*? He shifted himself up and as the shoulder jarred the movement triggered an eye-watering pain near the top of his back, as if someone had reached into his spine and twisted a vertebrae three hundred and sixty degrees.

He was a pain warrior. His body might test him, but it would never defeat him. He patted the bedclothes and Ninti passed him his Tablette from the bed table.

Ibu's sword? he typed one-handed. His mother arched an eyebrow, but it was not her words that filled the ward.

'*Where is he*? We have to *see him*!'

The cry speared the room. Patients moaned, nurses bustled down the aisle, but Lil was unstoppable, elbowing past trolleys and doctors in an angular flurry of self-importance. Behind her floated the tall, spidery figure of Tiamet – but not the Tiamet he knew. The Singular's hair, normally elegantly spun, was an abandoned rooks' nest, her skin dull, her eyes, he saw as the women reached the foot of his bed, bloodshot and bruised with smeared kohl.

'Enki.' Lil gripped the iron frame at the foot of his bed. She was wearing a sleeveless robe with a plunging neckline. Only Lil would dress up to come to a hospital.

'He's resting, Lilutu,' Ninti said tightly. His mother shifted her gaze from Tiamet and cast a shrewd look at the little woman and her son.

'We have news' – Lil jutted out her chin – '*terrible* news from Pithar.'

'This is the *hospital*, Lilutu,' Ninti flared. 'We're holding Conclave in two hours at the gym tent. Can't it wait?'

'N-n-n-no.' Tiamet flung her arms into the air and burst into tears.

Women crying. Women fighting. *Oh Gods Who Have Abandoned Us, please send me back to the Sec Gens.*

'No, it can't wait, Ninti.' Lil retorted over Tiamet's sobs. 'This is BIG. Enki needs to know what's going on.'

Big, urgent news or not, the quickest way to end this scene was to allow Lil to vent.

Let them speak, he typed.

Ninti pursed her petal-pink lips. 'All right, Lilutu, but make it quick.'

Lil pressed her belly against the bed bars. Her drama might be unwelcome, but her cleavage was a life-affirming sight. 'IREMCO have raided the Pithar Welcome Tent,' she hissed. 'IREMCO and IMBOD, of course – they've kidnapped two of Tiamet's sisters and *stolen her baby*.'

His mother shot out a hand to Tiamet's. With a watery blink the

Singular accepted the touch as she burst into a fresh round of weeping. Ninti's expression softened. 'Oh – I'm so sorry, Tiamet,' she offered.

'We don't know about my baby.' Tears glazing her face, the Singular wrung four of her hands. 'Taletha thinks Anunit might have saved him, but Anunit's d-d-d-disappeared – and there were *so many* men.'

'YAC has to do something,' Lilutu announced. 'IREMCO kidnapped the concierge and sent a mine-worker stooge to run the tent. Tiamet's sisters are being kept like slaves. Taletha hasn't sent a message for six hours.'

Ninti's little face was furrowed in that heart-rendingly cute expression of complete concentration. 'Those are all criminal violations of jurisdiction: shouldn't N-LA investigate?'

'Oh come on, Ninti.' Lilutu tossed her head. 'The Zabaria police are in IREMCO's pocket, everyone knows that.'

Ninti bristled, invisible needles bursting from every pore.

'*I want my baby*,' Tiamet wailed. His mother squeezed her hand.

'We'll find him, my girl,' she promised. 'Just wait until my son is out of this bed. He and Bartol will turn Zabaria upside down in search of your son.'

'*Amma*,' he rasped. He and Bartol were needed in Kadingir. And since when did *his mother* decide YAC strategy?

'Don't *TALK*,' she and Ninti barked, a two-headed dog at the gates of the underworld.

Enough. Information was needed: hard facts with which to build a bulwark against all this chaotic emotion.

Where's the Gaian girl? He passed the Tablette to Lilutu, who peered down her nose at it.

'You mean Istar? She's safe at the compound. But I have to get her to Shiimti,' she said airily. 'I can't have her running around on a battlefield snapping at Sec Gens before she's fully trained.'

Get Lilutu out of here. Ninti's eyes were trained on him now. But he needed to think. The Gaian girl was hiding in the CONC fortress. Well, that was one less thing to worry about. *Put Pithar on the Conclave agenda*, he typed. *We need to build YAC in Zabaria – good way in.*

Lil peered over at the screen. '"Good way in"?' She glared at him. 'That's not very sensitive, Enki! Tiamet's lost her baby!'

'You know what he means, Lilutu. We'll *deal* with it, okay?' Ninti was still livid. But Lil's response was lost in the wave of exultation suddenly flooding the ward: people were clapping and whistling and the musicians rapidly striking the singing bowls, for a giant was among them, stooping and shambling down the aisle in dusty clothes, his bashful head scraping the ceiling.

'My brother! As always, surrounded by women!' That deep rumble travelled to Enki's heart, balm even for the excruciating wince in his spine. Tiamet wiped her eyes and batted her lashes as Bartol stood sentinel beside her at the foot of the bed. Addressing the ward, the Sec Gen Slayer raised his hand. 'I come to re-arm Enki Arakkia with his ancestor's blade!'

The scimitar flashed for all to see; the curved blade that had sliced through a churning forest of white shirts, hacking at thick wrists and forearms trained to counter his blows, until – his grandfather's blade would not be denied – at last it had found flesh.

YES! The battle memory, submerged until now in the miasma of pain, surfaced: the electric shock in the Sec Gen's wide eyes as the sword severed the boy's jugular, sending a jet of blood spurting into Enki's mouth – his tongue curled as he recalled the cloying sweet taste with its iron after-tang. He had lost the sword as the enemy swarmed over him, ripping his chariot apart and dragging him to the ground where, in a black haze of unknown duration, he'd ducked and rolled away from the ripping, tearing teeth, his arm plastered over his eyes. With superhuman strength Bartol had saved him: had wrested the blade back, hauling the pack of mad dogs off their prey, beheading first one, then another and flinging their heads like discuses over the battle. The other Sec Gens had screamed, forgetting for a crucial moment their half-eaten prize, and Bartol, wielding the sword against all comers, had carried his brother back through the battle to the medical tent. The sword had returned to the Hem, to slay ten more Sec Gens, before Malku on the Hemline sounded the call to withdraw.

Now Enki's man-mount, his brother, his greatest friend, laid Enki's weapon in his hand.

'Pain is the path,' Bartol boomed. 'Enki's weapon is the way.'

Gripping the handle, he croaked, 'I name you Is-Land's Pain.'

'ENKI!' Ninti and his mother shouted in unison.

He shut his mouth, half grimacing, half grinning. Ignoring the inferno of pain raging in his muscles, he brandished his ancestor's scimitar.

Lilutu turned to the ward, raised her arms. 'He names his weapon Is-Land's Pain.'

'*Is-Land's Pain!*' YAC erupted.

His spine was screaming, his throat a furnace, his clenched fist steady as Bartol's broad grin.

ASTRA

The shovel was stuck upright in the soil beside a large bush, a mound of dry earth and a ladder. She wondered for a moment how Muzi had managed to use the shovel with his short arm, but he obviously had, and well, because the grave was deep. They took Uttu out and laid her beside it.

'Fire,' Muzi said. 'Burn robe.'

'I don't know – what about the smoke?' Photon glanced up at the sky.

She wasn't sure either. 'We don't want to leave a firepit by the grave, do we Muzi?'

'There.' He pointed a distance away. 'We light after. Then go.'

Photon was in a hurry, but Muzi was not. They were deep in his time, Astra realised. He had been here all day, digging, washing Uttu. Grieving. And though she understood Photon's concern, it didn't seem likely that IMBOD would send a squad in broad daylight. Even if N-LA came, they were hidden from the road and the house, and could hear any vehicles approaching.

'It won't take long,' she said. They gathered sticks and built the fire a little distance from the bush. Muzi opened his pack and placed the robes on top. Returning to the grave, they lowered Uttu into the earth and stood in silence at the edge. Bitter tears rose again in Astra's throat. Beside her, Photon was emanating unease, but she shut him out of her mind. This was her goodbye to Uttu.

'My Anamma. Good woman,' Muzi said at last. 'Good life. Good death. Fight for freedom death. Please we all have such good life, good death.'

It hadn't occurred to her to consider being killed by a Sec Gen as a good death, but Muzi was right: Uttu was a warrior; like Enki Arakkia she had had no fear of death. She, Astra, did. In moments of despair, she longed for death, but now she actually faced returning to the Barracks, she was terrified. But that didn't matter. To free Uttu's family, she would turn herself in. She would suffer, be locked up like Hokma or like Cora Pollen; she might even die as well – but if it meant she saved a whole family, then what happened to her wasn't important. That was Hokma's gift to her: to show her that some things were worth suffering for. Maybe that was her destiny; maybe that was what being Istar meant.

'Thank you, Uttu,' she whispered to the small bundle in the earth. *Thank you, Hokma*, her mind ghosted. 'Please Gaia, help me be as brave as you.'

Photon waited a moment, then asked, 'Can I help cover her, Muzi? I have a shovel on the roof.'

'Yes, earth now.'

Photon strode back to Ciccy. Muzi knelt and opened his pack. He took out a rubber sleeve: a suction sock, like the one Klor used for his mechatronic leg. *The YAC masks.* She realised now what they were. Muzi rolled the sock over the end of his short arm and dug again in the pack, producing a prosthetic hand. The artificial extremity was nothing like Klor's shiny, intricate leg; it was more like a solid, scuffed rubber glove. Muzi inserted his socked arm into the hollow wrist before standing and picking up the shovel. He squeezed the prosthetic fingers into a loose grip around the handle, then he began to fling the soil into the grave.

Photon joined him and the two men started working fast. Astra, feeling useless, watched the grave fill. There should be a marker, not just the bush. At Birth House there were always stones. She marched away, searched the ground and returned with two large egg-shaped stones, one red, one white. As Photon and Muzi smoothed the soil, she placed them together at the foot of the grave. To anyone who didn't know, they would look ordinary, resting together by chance: Gaia's whimsical will.

'One Land,' she said.

'One Land,' Muzi echoed.

'One Land,' Photon repeated. Then, 'Okay. Uttu is safe. We can light the fire. Then I must take you to the compound.'

Muzi stepped back from the grave and turned to Photon. 'My brother. Thank you.' He thumped his chest. 'My heart thank you. You help bury my grandmother. You live in my heart always. When your grandmother

die, you call me. I come. I come to New Zonia. I come to Neuropa. I
come to Himalaya. But I not go compound.'

Photon exhaled. 'Muzi—'

But Muzi wasn't finished. 'CONC okay,' he conceded. 'CONC good
work. Uttu like CONC. Me no. Astra no. CONC talk IMBOD.
IMBOD want hurt Astra. Astra come with me. I hide Astra. I keep Astra
safe.'

What?

'No, Muzi,' she said. 'What about your family? I can trade myself in,
give myself to the Barracks, get them back.'

He shook his head. 'Uttu love you, Astra, like granddaughter. You my
family too. I no let IMBOD get you.'

He was speaking with utter certainty, but he couldn't possibly mean it.

'IMBOD won't—' Photon began.

She overrode him. 'What about Kingu? And Gibil?' she demanded.
'And Nanshe and Habat and the children?'

'Kingu, Gibil strong men. Strong here.' He tapped his head. 'Gibil in
jail before, two years, no problem. Nanshe and Habat strong too: strong
women. Look after children. Many Non-Landers go jail. We strong
people, Astra.'

'But they shouldn't go to jail for *me*.' She was getting angry now.
'You've only met me once, Muzi – well, twice now. What about your
brother, and your little sisters? They should be in school—'

'*You* my sister, Astra.' He faced Photon again, waved his arm in a gesture of disavowal. 'Photon, you no worry for Astra. No marry. Not wife.
Astra my *sister*. I protect my sister. We hide. We go Kargul. For Uttu.'

She understood: he was as stubborn as she was, and he had made up
his mind. She saw it in his spread-leg stance, in his fierce blue eyes. It
would murder his pride and stain his honour forever to give her up to the
Barracks. If she defied him, turned herself in despite his wishes, he would
feel that he had failed – not her, but Uttu.

'Please, Muzi,' Photon said, 'let us talk about this back at the compound. You will both be safe there—'

Muzi wanted to protect her, but she could protect him. She swung
round. 'Muzi, can you take me to Shiimti? My father is there. He can
help us.'

'Shiimti.' He frowned. 'Shiimti moving places. No one find.'

'I have directions. I know where it is.'

She reeled off the coordinates and Muzi nodded. 'Okay. Far, but okay. We go.'

Exhilaration filled her. '*Gúañarña,* Muzi. *Gúañarña.*'

Photon clapped his hands to his hat, rubbing his exasperation back into himself. 'I do not think you understand, Astra: there is a war breaking out. You cannot drive to Shiimti. There are IMBOD checkpoints at Zabaria.'

'No roads.' Muzi addressed Photon. 'Horse and cart, over hills. Oasis town, then camel trade, Salt Route.'

'Astra, I *cannot* allow this. You are under the Major's protection—'

'Photon,' she cried, 'I'm *eighteen*. I don't have to go back to the compound. The Major knows IMBOD is hunting me down; heesh will understand. Tell hirm thank you for everything – I'll come back when I can but right now I have to go. I'll be safe with Muzi.'

Photon shook his head. 'I do not like this plan, Astra. You will be in the windsands. There is not normally even any Tablette signal. How will I know how you are?'

'I'll be okay, Photon. I was going to go to Shiimti with Lil, wasn't I?'

'Yes, but that was from the Oasis Ward, on a tour. This is off-road, with a person who does not know the way – and with a war on.'

'We'll be travelling away from the war. And we can tell Lil I'm going. Maybe she can meet us in the oasis.'

'But—'

'I'm going, Photon. It's the only way. Come on. We have to light the fire.'

She strode over to the firepit, followed by the men. Muzi knelt, took a matchbook from his bag; the twigs crackled, the smell of smoke filling her nostrils. They stood watching the branches catch and the flames licking the air.

'If you are really going,' Photon said quietly, 'I must to tell you some things.'

The edges of Uttu's robe were embroidered with a searing orange-and-black fringe. She frowned. 'What things?'

'Please to believe me: Dr Tapputu is your friend.'

The robe caught the flames. 'He's a good doctor, you mean?' she asked.

'Not only this.' Photon paused. 'He is a secret leader in the resistance. He has approached other medics in CONC – well, me and some researchers in Alpland – we are interested in the Sec Gens: how to make a cure for their condition. Dr Tapputu is thinking that YAC is not yet ready for this action. He is wanting to contact the Non-Gaians. He was very interested to hear you are going to the Black Desert. Please, if you can, ask Shiimti to contact him in some safe way.'

She was furious. '*You've been telling Dr Tapputu about me?* Why didn't you tell *me* about *him*?'

His tone was apologetic, but as in Ciccy, he could not meet her eyes. 'You had the MPT. Your siblings are Sec Gens. We did not want to trouble you with such a proposal.'

We didn't trust you, he meant. 'Did the Major tell you I was working for IMBOD?' Her voice squeaked with hurt. 'Did you *believe* hir?'

'No – *no*, Astra, heesh asked my opinion on your political beliefs, that was all. I said I did not think you were political. You do not like IMBOD of course, but . . . it is just that, well' – he faltered – 'in a war situation involving the Sec Gens, the doctor did not know which way you would jump.'

She turned back to the fire. Muzi was poking the robe with a stick, pushing it deep into the fire: the robe that had been dirtied and ripped by a cowardly Sec Gen as he kidnapped and killed an innocent old woman. Images fought in her mind: YAC warriors with bleeding eye sockets; Enki Arakkia's gnawed shoulder; the shit-smeared wreckage of Muzi's house; Peat's impossible chest and shoulders and stone-hard face. Then another circle of light arose from the firepit: Birth House at story-time, and Peat, a plump boy glugging water, his laughing eyes reflecting the shining flames of the fountain. For all she knew, Peat had been killed by YAC last night. But even if her brother had survived the battle, the boy she had grown up with was dead.

'The Sec Gens aren't my siblings,' she said, slowly. 'IMBOD stole my brothers and sister and friends a long time ago.' She faced Photon squarely. 'If Dr Tapputu wants to try to bring them back, then I'm his friend too. But you have to tell me *everything*. Who else knows about this plan? Rudo? The Major?'

'It is not yet a plan, only an idea. We need to gather much more information about the Sec Gens before we can act. Also, YAC or N-LA must approve Tapputu's initiative. Maybe if this is happening, we will tell Rudo and Sandrine, but the Major . . . I think not. The Major does not like Odinson, but heesh answers to Amazigia. Also, many people in Alpland are allies for Is-Land, so I must protect my contacts there. It is very complicated, Astra.'

He didn't know the half of it. When he returned to the compound, Photon would discover just how entangled she was in the knots of this war. When it came to Istar, though, she hadn't jumped: she had been sucked in against her better judgement.

'Photon,' she said, slowly, 'I'm a One-Lander, but Lil thinks I'm more than that. She thinks I'm part of this Istar story. I can't stop her believing it, and I need her help – but you have to remember, whatever people say about me, I'm just *Astra*. I'm looking for my Code father, and I want to help people here return to Is-Land one day. That's all. You can trust me on that.'

'I know, and I am here for you. If your CONC email is disabled, you can call me or message me on ShareWorld. But you must go now, for honest.'

He glanced at the fire. The robe had been nearly consumed by the flames and behind it, Muzi's body was wavering in the heat rising from the fire. Nearly everything she'd ever been told about Is-Land and Non-Land, she understood now, was distorted, warped, a *mirage*. The Sec Gens *weren't* noble defenders of Gaia; they were ruthless killers, sacrificial Code monsters. Is-Land wasn't the sparkling emerald in CONC's crown: it was a rogue nation, an out-of-control experiment the world was increasingly regretting. Non-Landers weren't hate-filled terrorists – the people she had met here were poor and proud, and they were fighting for a reason. And some didn't fight at all. There was Muzi, shimmering with grief and determination. He looked like a spirit, her spiritual brother, and looking at him, something inside her shimmered too. Muzi had gathered wild herbs and leaves for her. He cried over his sheep as well as his grandmother. Maybe one day he would stop killing animals . . .

She reached out, wrapped her arms around Photon's skinny waist and pressed her cheek against his ribs. 'I'll miss you, Photon. Thank you for being my buddy.'

The tall Alplander embraced her shoulders and rested his cheek on her head. 'We say *auf wiedersehn*: until we meet again.'

She pulled away. Muzi removed his prosthetic; for a moment she thought he was going to toss it on the fire, but he knelt to put it back in his bag. Behind him, the low hills stretched away, east, south and westwards, towards her Code father, the Himalaya, Asfar . . . the world.

PEAT

He woke shaking from a restless sleep, echoes of the night racing through his head trampling all of his dreams into dust. His IMBOD career was over. He would be sent home in disgrace today and the mission report would be forever stained by his failure. The squad had freed the sheep and taken the slavers hostage; the poor creatures were even now grazing in the meadow, and the wretched family were somewhere deep in the Barracks, learning what it meant to be deprived of your freedom. Elevating their mission to the highest possible level of accomplishment, the squad had also, entirely unexpectedly, punished and eliminated a vicious Non-Land terrorist, so he should be waking full of joy. But *he* had ruined the triumph, all in a moment.

He relived that moment over and over again: his hand clamped over the mouth of that tiny old woman, sealing it, he'd thought, but somehow she'd bitten his little finger – her teeth were sharp – and he'd reacted without thinking, whipping her chin to the side. He'd used no strength at all – Jade would have laughed, shoved her bottom in his groin – but the old woman's neck had cracked and then there she was, dead in his arms.

Why hadn't he just shaken her a little? The squad wasn't supposed to kill anyone: hostages were no use dead. He had panicked, blocked the steps and confused his Sec Gen siblings, until the Division Officer stepped in.

'Drop her,' the officer had ordered. 'She fell down the steps, that's all.'

Those few minutes were running in his head like a video. After that, it had been a relief to trash the house: smashing plates, ripping pillows, stamping on the Tablette. He'd left that foul dwelling flying high as a sea-eagle. But the elation was temporary. At the road the squad had tried to rescue the Non-Landers' tree from its bondage as well, but its roots resisted their strength and instead they'd ended up breaking its dry branches, snapping its trunk. 'Never mind,' hissed the Officer. 'Better to die than live as a slave to meat-eaters.' But the failure had sapped his nerve, and back in the van, hands shaking, he had fumbled with the key. Stalled the engine.

'You want me to drive, Peat?' Robin had asked.

'No.' This time the engine caught and he'd pulled out, following the Division Officer. But his mind wasn't on the road. He was safe, driving on an empty road, but the seed of fear that had sprouted earlier in his stomach had returned and was shooting its chill tendrils through his veins until his teeth were chattering.

'Relax, Peat,' Robin laughed. 'Tell you what's wrong with you: you need a shit!'

It was true: he'd been so tense he hadn't been able to empty his bowels on the wreckage like Robin had done.

'Yeah! I need a shit, a big shit!' he'd yelled, and Robin had whooped and together they'd cackled like hyenas as they sped through the night.

At Zabaria, the Division Officer ordered them to park at the back of the mine and wait to move on until they'd had word that the Hem battle had ended. He had tried then, out in the dark, flat scrubland, but he still hadn't been able to take a dump, however much he'd strained. Still, at least there was something to do: the sheep had been terrified after their rescue, so the squad had sedated the poor beasts. Scrambling in the back of the van, lunging for the creatures' soft fleeces, holding them steady, took his mind off his fear. Carrying the sleeping beasts out to lie on the earth, Peat almost relaxed. But then, behind him, in the dark, came a growl: another van arriving.

It was an IMBOD van, so clearly nothing to be frightened of. The Division Officer ordered the squad over to a streetlamp and lined them up in a semicircle around its pool of yellow light. He was hot, his hands greasy with lanolin from the fleeces, his left shin still stinging slightly from the sharp kicks of the sheep. Around him his Sec Gen siblings' familiar faces were coated with a ghoulish sheen, masks hovering on the edge of that sulphurous glow.

Three men emerged from the van. Two were carrying a bundle.

'Sec Gens,' the Division Officer commanded, 'salute IREMCO, completing their own mission of the night.'

The men were mine-managers: Gaian workers here in the barren land. With the others he thrust his fist from his chest. The first man pointed, and his colleagues dumped the bundle onto the soil.

The dumpy figure, swathed in fabric, was bundled up in a ball.

'YAC *scum*.' The lead mine-manager kicked the body. Then he reached down and tore off the robe.

A jittery ripple of confusion travelled through the squad. The head was still hooded but the obese body was both limbless and female – although whether it was human or not was another question. Its breasts and belly were bulging rolls of flab, its missing arms and legs not stumps, but floppy flaps. It could have been Coded part penguin, but there was nothing comical or sweet about this brown flesh lump writhing on the ground at their feet. This thing was *sinister*. Instinctively the Sec Gens tensed and shifted closer together. Someone snarled.

'Don't be *fooled*,' the mine leader bellowed. '*This* is what we're up against here. It doesn't look like it could wipe its own arse, but believe me, this thing is your worst enemy. This is a *YAC trainer*. It's been nurturing fighters, sending them out to the Hem – but it won't be doing *that* any more.'

He kicked it again, and the mass wobbled like jelly. Then he turned to the Division Officer. 'How many Sec Gens have fallen tonight in the Hem?'

She brandished her Tablette. 'Three,' she declared. 'Three of your siblings lost so far, to fighters this *lump of shit* has trained and armed and financed.'

Sec Gens *killed*? Hatred burned in his chest like the sun, a battery charged by the squad, their teeth bared, fists clenched, throats rumbling like engines. This thing was responsible for Sec Gen deaths? It must *suffer*.

'All together!' the mine leader roared, and he and his men started kicking all at once, heaving the thing-body over on its gelatinous front. Peat flinched: the wet gash between the thing's leg-flippers was *enormous* – and was it even possible? Did the thing really have *two* woman holes?

'Frigging Gaia but I'm *hot*.' The mine-manager ripped off his shirt, pulled off his trousers. 'C'mon, Sec Gens, don't be shy. Why should *it* be the only one sky-clad?'

They hung back, hesitant. Peat's breath was harsh in his ears, his eyes fixed on the abomination glistening in the pool of orange streetlight.

'You heard him!' the Division Officer yelled. 'Stand before Gaia as you were born!'

Heart racing, Peat stripped off the N-LA uniform and cast it aside, standing with the night air on his skin, his eyes on the mine-manager, who scoffed, 'Look at those damp worms! Am I the only one here who gets fired up when I'm angry?'

'Honey badgers,' the Division Officer roared, her nipples hard as iron spikes, 'bear cubs, black mambas: you have *exceeded* yourselves tonight. This is your *reward*.'

'Sec Gens,' the mine man commanded, 'your nature is *wild*. Take what you *want*!'

With that, the cage-door broke open and the Sec Gens lunged forward, the Division Officer urging them on.

The fear of it – doing what he wanted, breaking all the laws he'd ever been taught – loosened Peat's bladder, but that was good; following the mine-men's lead, everyone was pissing over the body, first taking turns and then piling in, straddling and spraying the obscene mounds of flesh, golden arcs glittering in the sulphurous street light.

An arm plunged into the joyous fountain – the mine-man – and ripped off the hood. For a moment Peat froze, for the thing was rearing its head, its face bloody and squashed, its mouth gagged, dark eyes blazing – but not with fear, with unmistakeable hatred. The mine-manager punched the eyes shut and suddenly Peat was lost in a crush of flesh. Someone jumped on his back, knocking him down against the thing's shoulder, and his head was right up against its disgusting mash of sounds – no, not sounds but *words*. The thing was screaming in Gaian – and he couldn't not listen.

'Dogs,' the thing gargled, 'mangy dogs ... on your Masters' chain.'

How dare it insult them? Insult dogs? It was insulting Gaia! The shock moved something deep inside him ... then his nostrils filled with a sweet earthy stench and the whole squad was laughing, *howling*, playfully gnawing him, until everything was a sticky blur of bodies, bodies brawling and squatting, humping and pummelling not just the doughy breasts, the swollen face, the twin Gaia\gardens, but each other, no one left out. Who bit the thing first? He didn't know, but someone squeezed its tit, clamped a mouth round the rocketing nipple, tore back, mouth black with blood, and spat a gobbet of fat at the feet of the Division Officer.

'YES,' their superiors roared, 'YES, SEC GENS, *YES*.'

The taste of blood was fresh and tangy: hot cherry juice, sweet and rich, warming every cranny of his guts. Like all special treats, the feast felt like it lasted a lifetime, but was over all too soon. The thing was gone, nothing but a few scraps strewn all over the soil, leaving the Sec Gens to pound each other into the dirt: bear cubs brawling, mambas entwining, honey badgers sinking their teeth into each other's hides, mouths dripping with the taste of shit and viscera and ripe red fruit, until at last Peat's seed was erupting, his fear flying out of him, all over Jade, and he lay, dazed in the soil with his squad, a whimpering litter of newborn puppies slick with their mother's juices: creatures of clay moulded together into a sobbing, tender tangle of sated lust and grief and rage.

Afterwards, they climbed the lip of the mine, showered in the wash-huts near the entrance, where they were given toothbrushes and floss, moisturiser, combs. When they were clean, the Division Officer lined them up again, congratulated them on a job well done, and reminded them that all mission details were classified information. Then they lay down again and huddled with the sheep, the creatures' pacified heartbeats soothing Peat until the call came to drive back along the Boundary road and home to the Barracks.

Where he'd barely slept. He lay in the morning light, trying desperately to recover last night's astonishing feeling of power, awe, sublime togetherness – but the orgy at the mine was a fleeting trifle compared to the moment in Kadingir. He stared at the beautiful curve of Jade's back, that sick moment crunching over and over again in his mind. *She fell down the steps*, the officer had shouted. But she hadn't: he'd *killed* her. He was unpredictable, unstable – how could he have let Jade and Robin, the squad, *everyone*, down like this? He had been twitchy, on edge, because of Laam and Astra, that was why. *He* was the weak link, the runt of the litter. The thing's words were stuck like shit to the inside of his skull: he *was* the dog that had failed its master and he deserved to be castigated, demoted, dishonourably discharged.

He closed his eyes, swallowed, and accepted the metallic taste of defeat. His Non-Land service was over. Tail between his legs, he would be going home.

He entered the debriefing room. Between his Division Officer and Odinson was another sky-clad officer who was somehow familiar; was it the shape of his face?

He saluted, fist from heart.

'Constable Orson,' his Division officer said. 'Please welcome Superintendent Samrod Blesserson to the Non-Land Barracks.'

Of course: Hokma's Code brother. He had come once to Or to give an Inspection Report. The resemblance was clear now as the man stood and extended his hand.

'Peat Orson,' he said warmly. 'I remember you well. Please, just call me Dr Blesserson. IMBOD has honoured me with advancement, but at heart I remain simply a medical researcher.'

The Superintendent was a scientist; his body was softer than Odinson's, his chest was sagging, but his grip was firm, his handshake vigorous.

He sat with his back straight. If Blesserson had been summoned to escort him home, he would go with dignity.

'Constable Peat Orson,' Odinson addressed him formally. 'Congratulations on your stellar performance last night. I trust you enjoyed your reward at the mine.'

At the best of times he lost his voice in Odinson's presence, but what had happened at the mine was already a dream. He nodded dumbly and looked at his Division Officer out of the corner of his eye. Had she not said?

'Your Division Officer tells us you reacted promptly to being bitten.' Dr Blesserson's voice was quiet, his eyes behind his glasses curious, and *kind*.

He wiped his hands on his thighs. Opened his mouth. Closed it.

They waited, all of them regarding him kindly.

'I couldn't help it,' he whispered.

'Peat,' his Division Officer said, 'Dr Blesserson is here to monitor the performance of the cohort. We've invited him to the debriefing to reassure you.'

'Of course you reacted as you did.' Blesserson leaned forward. 'You are Coded and trained to respond instantaneously to threat. In a world that has severely limited the use of weapons to defend our borders, IMBOD requires warriors who can unleash all their natural instincts when attacked. Like your berserker swarm at the mine, what you did in Kadingir was entirely understandable.'

'Fear sharpens the nerves, Constable Orson,' Odinson said, 'but it doesn't have to whittle us away. Relax now, and prepare for your next challenge.'

'B-but—' he stammered, trying to take it all in, sort it through in his mind. 'I'm sorry. I don't understand. In Zabaria, we were given an order. M-m-my action in Kadingir—' He glanced again at the Division Officer. 'It wasn't in the mission statement.'

'The death of a hostage was not intended,' Odinson agreed, 'but last night, many things occurred that were beyond our power to control. Thirteen Sec Gens fell in battle and a war on Is-Land was launched. On such a night if Gaia decrees the death of a stray Non-Lander, we do not argue with Her! Indeed, Constable Orson, we thank you for serving as Her channel.'

He lowered his eyes. The names of the fallen had echoed through the breakfast hall. He had assumed his own name would forever taint the glory of their sacrifice, but now, unbelievably, it appeared that was not to be the case. Rather, he was being *praised* – and praise from superiors was craved even more deeply than the skinship of Sec siblings. He sat quietly, soaking up its healing touch.

'All we are concerned about, Peat, is your emotional stability.' Blesserson was very like Hokma, in fact: she with her shaved head in later years, he with his erudite temples and quiet authority. 'I know only too well what it is like to carry the burden of a traitorous sibling. We share that burden, don't we?'

It hit him then, how selfish he was. After Astra's betrayal he had wallowed in misery, but what must it be like, being the Code brother of Hokma Blesser? What suspicions had the Superintendent suffered? This man, who worked like no other for the nation, for the Sec Gens, for *him*. He couldn't meet Blesserson's gaze. He was not worthy. And yet, to hear *sympathy*, from someone who *knew*—

His eyes welled up. 'I've been trying so hard—' Oh Gaia, he was blubbing now.

'Exceptionally hard,' Odinson declaimed. 'Your achievements last night will ring down the ages, Constable Orson. Perhaps you think that the old woman was harmless – but like the creature you disposed of in Zabaria, she was far from innocent. She and her family stand at the centre of a plot that could threaten the very foundations of the long alliance between IMBOD and CONC. You have rid us of a great scourge, believe me.'

He mustered control of himself and allowed the praise to flow deep into his aching heart.

'All we want is for you to feel calm, Peat,' Blesserson reassured him. 'You are to keep taking your soother syrup – all the Hem warriors will be getting the treatment too. We have tasked your generation with Is-Land's fiercest battle, and we owe you the best possible aftercare.'

'As ever, Peat, Superintendent Blesserson is being modest.' His Division Officer smiled. 'Thanks to his trailblazing research, post-traumatic stress syndrome will soon be a thing of the past. You and your siblings will return home as a flourishing young people, leaving any unpleasantness here in Non-Land where it belongs.'

Was he allowed to ask a question? He looked between the officers.

'Sirs?' he ventured. 'Ma'am?'

'Yes, Peat?' Odinson encouraged.

'What happened in Zabaria . . .' He faltered. 'I know it's confidential, but is it the way we'll be fighting in the Hem, if . . . if things get worse?'

Odinson licked his lips, but it was Blesserson who replied, 'Your squad has done us an exceptional favour, Peat. We know a great deal more about the berserker gene today than we did yesterday. We don't expect to unleash its full potential in the Hem, but you're right, the way things are going it could get very nasty out there, and it is reassuring to know that the Sec Gens have that extra ounce of zest in reserve.'

'All right, Peat?' the Division Officer said kindly. 'There's nothing to worry about, is there?'

His mouth watered and the tang of hot cherries flooded his tongue. 'No.' He shook his head. 'Everything's fine.'

'Good.' Odinson smiled. 'Then I will see you at the ceremony. We want to celebrate your famous victory: the first, I know, of many!'

And so here he was: not discharged but elevated. He and the mission squad were standing in the front row, ahead of the entire cohort, gazing up at Dr Blesserson at the podium, with Chief Superintendent Odinson poised at the lip of the stage, the engineers and officers arranged behind, and above them all, the Boundary alive with rook flight: vast black skeins of birds twisting and hurling themselves out above the Barracks and far over the walls into the Hem. It was exhilarating watching the screen, thrilling beyond the dim memory he had of rooks in the steppes. This fluttering, swirling, electric black congregation was flying in perfect harmony with IMBOD, parting like curtains to reveal the giant figures of his masters on stage. His *masters*, yes: disciplined, powerful men and

women who surmounted all challenges, exhibited perfect self control and
had been trusted to lead their entire country to victory over *scum*, savage
scum.

'Sec Gens! You have battled – and who has come to congratulate you?'
Odinson thrust his arm towards the scientist. 'The man who knows more
about you than anyone on earth – your chief Code designer, Superintendent Samrod Blesserson!'

Blesserson saluted. The man's modesty was genuine, Peat understood
that, but so was his pride in serving them all.

'So, Sec Gens' – Odinson was prowling the stage, glossy and tense as a
panther – 'tell him: are you *wounded*?'

'*NO.*' The black curtains of rooks shivered, the leaves on the trees
trembled, the clouds in the sky quivered; the very Barracks shook with
the loud, crashing miracle of Sec Gen health. All who had fought and
survived were healed; their wounds had closed, bruises faded, all their
stiff arms and legs were limber once more.

'Tell him: are you *frightened*?'

'NO!' No, he realised, he wasn't, not any more – and never again.
Eagerness would sharpen his battle senses now, eagerness and exultation
and the secret, slick red taste of triumph!

'Are you ready for more Hemline *action*?' Fists pumping, hips thrusting, teeth gnashing and clashing, now Odinson was rude as a billy-goat, a
wild, horny joy to behold.

'YES!'

'Are you ready,' Odinson growled, 'to *avenge your dead*?'

'YES!' Peat roared, tears springing to his eyes as above the Barracks
the Boundary screen flashed images of the thirteen fallen Sec Gens, faces
he knew from months of training, their tragic deaths confirmed now, not
just to their grieving parents but to a whole nation. His siblings were lost
forever, executed in their prime. Yes, *please* let him fight now: let him battle
that killer giant, the beast who had *beheaded* twelve of the fallen – a Non-
Lander taller and broader than even the largest of the cohort, his legs like
oak trunks, his hands big as bronze platters. Photostreams had circulated
the man's moronic face; it was emblazoned on everyone's minds. Even if
this Non-Land ogre, this YAC oaf, knelt, crawled, slithered on his belly
or hopped like a frog, he could not hide from them now. From tonight
the Sec Gens would be armed with daggers and spears, so those monstrous fingers would be sliced off, one by one, before they got anywhere

near another Gaian throat. And if Peat's squad got the giant, alone, away from the journalists . . . the crimson thrill of their secret sluiced again down his throat.

'Sec Gens,' Odinson bellowed, 'are you ready to HALLOW YOUR HEROES?'

'YEEEEESSSSSS!'

He moved as if in a dream. His cue had come: not to shout and rave but to humbly *lead the way*. With Jade and Robin, then the entire squad, behind him, he mounted the steps to the stage. Lining up at the front, the squad turned and faced the cohort. The field of white shirts dazzled his eyes.

'Today is a historic day,' Odinson boomed. 'Today we celebrate the glorious success of IMBOD's first ever *slave rescue* mission: a mission proposed by you, the Sec Gens!'

His knees were shaking. The cohort was blurring into one wild white sheet rippling out before him, out to the meadow and the trees, a square of white inside a green frame, itself bordered by the severe black lines of the Barracks walls, walls he could for the first time see over. Beyond them floated the dirty grey haze of a world without compassion, beauty or a shred of moral decency. Behind him, the sound of Odinson's bootsteps anchored him to his place.

'Last night,' Odinson declared, 'this brave mission squad ventured deep into enemy territory and freed eighteen slaves: eighteen gentle beasts, ewes and lambs, who will soon be living out their natural lives on the rich pastures of Is-Land!'

A cheer went up: a cheer for the sheep and the lambs, woolly and content in the meadow, no longer in danger of being slaughtered and eaten, but also a cheer for him, Jade and Robin – and for Laam. He swallowed. He would never forget Laam. He should have been there last night, sharing in the adventure, the bounty, the taste of rage . . .

The bootsteps stopped. 'Your courageous brothers and sisters have also captured *seven slavers*.'

'*BOOO. BOOOO. BOOOOO.*' The cries were so loud the slavers in their dungeons could surely hear them!

'Seven sordid beast-abusers are held here now as collateral against the barbaric and treacherous designs of our foe. Fear not death, Sec Gens, for tonight we will disable the ogre. Fear not wounds, nor pain, for you are Coded to heal. And *fear not capture by the barbarians*, for we hold the slavers ready to bargain for you. We are Is-Landers and we give each other security! What do we give each other, Sec Gens?'

It was the greatest moment of his life. Peat gripped Jade and Robin's fists, interlocked their fingers with his, and in concert with their squadmates, they raised their arms in white arches, a homage to the Barracks towering behind them. The IMBOD photographer was snapping away, the sun was bouncing off the shoulders of his cohort. Over the trees, over the Barracks walls, the dirty, squalid Non-Landers were listening *to him.*

'SECURITY,' Peat bellowed with his Gaia mates, his squad, his generation. 'SECURITY. SECURITY. SECURITY.'

ASTRA

They drove Ciccy to Muzi's watch-hut. She got out and helped him collect things for the journey: a bedmat and bedding, a stove, kitchenware. She thought he was done, but he went back for a relic he'd nailed to the front of the hut: a rusty old electric fan with some rook feathers hanging from the grille. It looked like a dreamcatcher she had made once with Nimma, based on an Old World design. She tried to tell Muzi, but he didn't understand. She would explain later, using the Somarian dictionary on her Tablette.

The tidy, wood-scented watch-hut was cute; it had been nice to peek inside. But then they were back in Ciccy and driving down the hill to find the horse and hitch it to the cart.

'IMBOD want take her. She say no.' Muzi patted the horse. 'Big kick no.'

She didn't like seeing him force the bit between those sensitive gums, but even in Is-Land some people harnessed horses. As long as this one had fair working conditions and a good retirement, she reckoned it would be okay to let it pull the cart. She'd just have to make sure the horse came to Shiimti with them and not be sold or traded to a cruel camel-driver.

'Why do you think they took the sheep, Astra?' Photon asked.

'I don't know.' She looked back at the pen. 'Maybe to set them free?'

Muzi was dumping stuff off the cart – scrap metal, wooden planks, farming tools, small electronics. He piled the things up inside a lean-to, leaving a solar panel, some poles and a cloudy bioplastic tarpaulin.

'Rain. Sun. No problem.' He pointed out slots in the cart frame for the poles. 'Water?' he asked Photon.

'*Ja*.' Photon hauled a barrel from Ciccy. 'Will that be enough?'

'Water in hills. Streams okay for horse.' He pointed at the solar panel. 'Tablette recharge.'

'Astra, do you know how to access your CONC bank account?'

The horse would be drinking toxic water. It would not live to retire unless she got it to Shiimti. But there would be time later to fret about the horse.

'Yes – and I've had my first wages.' It wasn't a lot of money, but enough to buy food and water in an Oasis town, surely.

'If you need more money, let me know and I will make a transfer,' Photon said.

'Oh.' She'd almost forgotten. 'Lil's number?' As Photon gave it to her, Muzi checked the pile he'd discarded. He picked up a trowel and a hoe head and tossed them back in the cart. 'Maybe for trade.' He rubbed his hands clean. 'Okay, house now.'

They went back into the house together, picking their way through the carnage, and gathered up whatever they thought they could use. Muzi slung two slashed bedmats over his shoulder and she hunted for a sewing kit. In the kitchen Photon knelt on the floor and poured handfuls of spilled grain back into a couple of unsmashed jars. She found the sewing box and a whole beeswax candle.

The horse whinnied; it was time to go. But there was one more thing to make sure of. 'Photon, under my bed, there's a box. Can you keep it safe for me?' she asked.

'*Ja*. Forever.'

She gave him one last hug, told him to say goodbye to Rudo and Sandrine, and hopped up beside Muzi. He had fixed the old fan to the front of the cart and one of the feathers dangled down by her legs. There was a path between the hills, heading due east. He flicked the reins and she twisted in her seat to wave at Photon and Ciccy. As the horse trotted off she faced forward. The rook feathers danced in the air.

ZIZI

A black speck in the brightening sky – an expected speck, though he never waited for it. He felt it coming: a tickle in the corner of his eye as he sat cracking jokes and playing mancala in what passed for a beer tent in Shiimti – more people drank camel-milk lassi than beer, even in the evenings, and you had to work two full shifts to afford to get squiffy, but never mind that; this was Shiimti and the real highs were free. He always got the itch in his eye when the Rookowleon approached . . . who said beer smeared the inner vision?

'Pardon me, my friend.' He pushed back from the table and creaked to his feet. Where had this enormous belly come from? He must find its rightful owner one day and return it. The man's gizzards must be awfully cold.

'You concede defeat yet again, oh Holy Kataru?' Salamu reached for his glass. Salamu was a good man, no stranger to the notion of beer for breakfast. He was, however, as bony as a camel's knee. Where he put all those bubbles was a question science and faith had yet to answer.

'Not at all, my friend. My mancala awaits the heavenly clatter of your polished pebbles. Lubricate your cogitations; I must greet an arrival.'

The speck became larger and lower, homing in on his Tablette signal – the bird's ability to find him was no mystical bond and nor did it possess particularly elegant landing skills, as the white slashes on Zizi's forearm attested. In Kadingir beer tents, when women asked about them, he always said they were a souvenir of the IMBOD Barracks. In Shiimti, everyone knew they were the love scratches of this hag-footed bird.

He glanced at the bar. Borandukht was serving the Zardusht,

sprinkling cinnamon over the High Healer's lassi. Zizi quickly grabbed
the cushion from his seat, wrapped it round his wrist and stepped out
from under the canopy.

'Eh, Kataru,' Salamu chuckled, 'you like sewing up cushion shreds?'

'I shall be buying a new pillow with my morning winnings, my friend.
Just you keep drinking.'

Here it came, barrelling down, wings slashing, claws flexing in bird
panic. If he ducked to avoid it, the thing would go for his head. If he
placed his Tablette on the ground and stood back, an expensive device
would end up shattered. There was only one way for it: averting his head
and gripping the cushion, he stuck out his arm and staggered back
as – *whoomph!* – the bird hit home, beating its wings and clutching at the
improvised landing pad. Perched at last, it ruffled its feathers and looked
past him with that look of lawyerly disdain. The Zardusht could learn a
thing or two from a Rookowleon.

'Cinders,' he greeted the bird. 'Pleased to see me, as usual, are you?'

The bird was iridescent black with a ridged crater face, a cinder
snatched from the furnace of war, a wedge of charcoal to mark the bone
tablet of history. Around its ankle was the memory clip.

'Spirit willing,' Salamu said quietly, 'it brings good news of your
daughter.'

Yes, Salamu was a good man: a meditator, mosaic-maker, widower,
father of two daughters and three sons – all married now, save the young-
est son. Salamu deserved his morning beer.

'If she is still alive, that is all a father can ask.'

His words were at peace with all outcomes, but his heart was beating
faster in his chest. His daughter's friend, that haughty girl, had promised
to send his little Istar to Shiimti, and whatever Lilutu wanted, it appeared
that she got it. He really should feed the bird first, but he couldn't wait.
He lowered his arm and offered Cinders the back of his chair. The bird
considered it, then stepped over, bringing the cushion with it – a talon
was stuck in the weave. Zizi tugged it free.

'Hai!' Borandukht shrieked from the bar. 'Kataru! My *cushion*. HAI!'

There was a small tear, barely noticeable, nothing at all to worry about.
'Oh Empress of the Golden Ambrosia.' He waved the wounded cushion
for all to see. 'We fly the flag of Shiimti here and all are welcomed by it.'

She was pulling a pint but she'd be over soon to inspect the damage, to
flirt, to ask about his daughter. He sat down and fiddled with the bird's

ankle, his hands trembling as he retrieved his Tablette from his pocket and inserted the memory clip. Salamu was quiet, watching as he waited for the files to open. Behind him, the bird nipped at his hair, what was left of it. How had that happened too? Those pesky Kadingir women, that was how, each wanting a black curl for their pillow-box. Well, Cinders could have what was left. His Kadingir beer tent days were behind him: here in Shiimti the women admired the look of a monk's gleaming temples.

The file sprang to life and he swiped the screen, his palm damp. 'So. Some not-so-good news, my friend.'

'Oh?' Salamu's eyes were compassion itself.

'No, as we expected: war in Kadingir, so many files to distribute.'

It was foretold. Salamu did not flinch. 'But your daughter? What word of her?'

His eyes were wet and he didn't care who saw it – not only beer blurs the vision. 'She is coming, my friend, over the scrublands and windsands. She has a guide, she has water and she knows the way.'

'*Yes!*' Salamu stood up. 'Boranduhkt,' he called, so all could hear, 'another beer for this man – my great friend. His daughter is coming – she will mend your cushions; she will marry my son. She will bring peace to this man's broken heart. Yes, Kataru? Is that not so!'

He stood too, raised his glass to the tent. 'Yes, it is so: my little Istar is coming to steal my thunder and drink my beer, to bring peace to my heart and grandsons and granddaughters to my friend. To share stories of the homeland and bestow hope on us all.'

A light smattering of applause pleased his ears. Pious though so many of them were, Shiimti people knew how to honour a dream.

Scraww, Cinders croaked. *Scrrraawwww.*

'I hope she brings a scrubbing brush, Kataru,' Boranduhkt shouted. 'Your bird is shitting all over my floor!'

'Fear not, Empress of Morning Delight,' he cried, beer sloshing and foaming over his hand. 'My daughter will bring brushes made of Harpy feathers and claws! She will bring brushes to scrub the world clean!'

Acknowledgements

I thank Peter Owen Ltd, London, for their kind permission to quote from *Prisoner of Dunes* by Isabelle Eberhardt, translated by Sharon Bangert, and also Invocations Press for permission to reproduce *The Prophecy*, an anonymous ancient Mesopotamian text, translated by Hortense Penelope Thursby Curtis (1889–1921) and published in *An Antique Land*, collected and edited by John Shire.

A previous version of Laam's chapter was written for *Litro Magazine* and published as *The Sacred Pond* at www.litro.co.uk/tag/sciencefiction.

The Royal Literary Fund generously provided financial assistance that enabled me to concentrate on completing this book.

My understanding of disability politics was hugely informed by Hannah Thompson's blog *Blind Spot*, Mik Scarlet's personal blog and column for the *Huffington Post*, and conversations with both writers. Paul Richards, Kate Ogden, Jesse Cutts and the Storm and Thunder Team – Luc Eisenbath, Daniel Randall-Nason, Michael White and Bernie Wood – of the Brighton-based 'gig buddies' charity Stay Up Late, all gave me a warm welcome into the world of campaigning for the rights of people with learning disabilities. Jens Streck encouraged my woolly ideas about gravity-free ions; Patricia Grinham and Iain McLeish pointed me in the direction of Mik Scarlet, and Mark Cocker gave freely of his ornithological expertise, greatly enhancing my understanding of rook behaviour.

While Non-Land is its own place, my active interest in the Middle East has inevitably fed its creation. As acknowledged in *Astra*, *The Gaia Chronicles* owe a founding debt to my travels in Turkish Kurdistan. *Rook*

Song draws also on my subsequent visit to Israel-Palestine, where the staff and students of the Freedom Theatre, Jenin; Munther Fahmi, the then 'Bookseller of Jerusalem'; Omar Barghouti and Falastine Dwikat of the Palestine Academic and Cultural Boycott of Israel; and Israeli peace activists Tamar Freed and Ofer Neiman all took good care of me during my trip. Back home, Tony Greenstein, Judith Kazantzis, Irving Weinman, Lee Whitaker and other members of the Brighton and Hove Palestine Solidarity Campaign constantly invigorated my thought; while in London Andy Simons of 'Library Express' fed me books, articles, music and, in his role as programmer of the 2014 Tottenham Palestine Literature Festival, the opportunity to discuss Middle Eastern travel and SFF with Sarah Irving, Ruqayyah Kareem, Yasmin Khan and Dervla Murphy.

Of my various research sources the online journal *Pulse Media* deserves special mention for educating me about the truly heroic popular Syrian revolution; while Shereen El Feki's *Sex and the Citadel* enlightened me about sexual mores and marital practices across the Arab world. Many Somarian Non-Lander names are taken from John A. Halloran's Sumerian Lexicon Version 3.0, available online; others from are the Ancient Sumerian dictionary that was once accessible at www.ping.de. Old Persian, Aramaic and other names came from various sites.

As research turned into revision, Amina Yaqin, James Burt, Mark Cocker, Hugh Dunkerley, Jose Garcia, Rob Hamberger, Joanna Lowrey, Aidy Norton, Paul Richards and Mik Scarlet all gave invaluable feedback. Hannah Thompson and Sarah Hymas stupendously read the entire manuscript, while to John Luke Chapman, who did so three times, must go the honorary title of the Alpha and Omega of Readers.

Finally, heartfelt thanks once again to Jo Fletcher, Nicola Budd, Andrew Turner, John Berlyne and John Richard Parker for professional support and personal kindnesses, while the very last nod goes to the internet, for allowing me to conduct rapid research into topics ranging from Québecois curses to duct-tape surfing; depleted uranium to rook flightpaths. All errors are my own, and part of the pattern now . . .

photo © John Luke Chapman

Naomi Foyle was born in London, grew up in Hong Kong, Liverpool and Canada, and currently lives in Brighton. She spent three years in Korea, teaching English, writing travel journalism and acting in Korean educational television. She is a highly regarded poet and performer. Her debut novel, *Seoul Survivors,* and the first in The Gaia Chronicles, *Astra,* are also published by Jo Fletcher Books.

You can visit her at www.naomifoyle.com, or tweet her @naomifoyle.

COMING SOON

THE BLOOD OF THE HOOPOE
Naomi Foyle

War is breaking out in Kadingir. Still struggling to accept her role as a long prophesied icon of unification between Is-Land and Non-Land, Astra Ordott is on a journey across the wind sands to join her father and his people – the mystics of Shiimti, who claim to hold the secret of truly healing the damaged relationship between human beings and the Earth.

Astra's desperate to get there quickly, but when her guide and companion, the shepherd Muzi, leads her off course into the path of a vicious sandstorm, she is forced to confront what the gods of their devastated world might be telling her: that there will be no refuge from her destiny.

Jo Fletcher
BOOKS

www.jofletcherbooks.com

ASTRA
Naomi Foyle

Like every child in Is-Land, all Astra Ordott wants is to have her Security Shot, do her National Service and defend her Gaian homeland from Non-Lander 'infiltrators'. But when one of her Shelter mothers, the formidable Dr Hokma Blesser, tells her the shot will limit her chances of becoming a scientist and offers her an alternative, Astra agrees to her plan.

When the orphaned Lil arrives to share Astra's home, Astra is torn between jealousy and fascination. Lil's father taught her some alarming ideas about Is-Land and the world, but when she pushes Astra too far, the heartache that results goes far beyond the loss of a friend.

If she is to survive, Astra must learn to deal with devastating truths about Is-Land, Non-Land and the secret web of adult relationships that surrounds her.

Jo Fletcher
BOOKS

www.jofletcherbooks.com

SEOUL SURVIVORS
Naomi Foyle

A meteor known as Lucifer's Hammer is about to wreak destruction on the earth, and with the end of the world imminent, there is only one safe place to be.

In the mountains above Seoul, American-Korean bio-engineer Dr Kim Da Mi thinks she has found the perfect solution to save the human race. But her methods are strange and her business partner, Johnny Sandman, is not the type of person anyone would want to mix with.

Drawn in by their smiles and pretty promises, Sydney – a Canadian model trying to escape an unhappy past – is an integral part of their scheme, until she realises that the quest for perfection comes at an impossible price.

Jo Fletcher
BOOKS

www.jofletcherbooks.com